RED RABBIT

Also by Tom Clancy

The Hunt for Red October
Red Storm Rising
Patriot Games
The Cardinal of the Kremlin
Clear and Present Danger
The Sum of All Fears
Without Remorse
Debt of Honor
Executive Orders
Rainbow Six
The Bear and the Dragon

RED RABBIT

Tom Clancy

MICHAEL JOSEPH
an imprint of
PENGUIN BOOKS

MICHAEL JOSEPH

Published by the Penguin Group
Penguin Books Ltd, 80 Strand, London WC2R ORL, England
Penguin Putnam Inc., 375 Hudson Street, New York, New York 10014, USA
Penguin Books Australia Ltd, 250 Camberwell Road,
Camberwell, Victoria 3124, Australia
Penguin Books Canada Ltd, 10 Alcorn Avenue, Toronto, Ontario, Canada M4V 3B2
Penguin Books India (P) Ltd, 11 Community Centre,
Panchsheel Park, New Delhi - 110 017, India
Penguin Books (NZ) Ltd, Cnr Rosedale and Airborne Roads,
Albany, Auckland, New Zealand
Penguin Books (South Africa) (Pty) Ltd, 24 Sturdee Avenue,
Rosebank 2196, South Africa

Penguin Books Ltd, Registered Offices: 80 Strand, London WC2R ORL, England

www.penguin.com

First published in the United States of America by Penguin Putnam Inc. 2002
First published in Great Britain by Michael Joseph 2002
1

This is a work of fiction. Names, characters, places and incidents either are the product of the author's imagination or are used fictitiously, and any resemblance to actual persons, living or dead, business establishments, events or locales is entirely coincidental.

Printed in Great Britain by Clays Ltd, St Ives plc

A CIP catalogue record for this book is available from the British Library

UK ISBN 0-718-14501-1
AIRSIDE ISBN 0-718-14607-7

To Danny O and the men of Engine 52 and Ladder 52

Heroes are often the most ordinary of men.

HENRY DAVID THOREAU

ACKNOWLEDGMENTS

Leanart, Joni, and Andy, for holding my hand behind the Old Curtain, and the crash-course in smuggling.

Alex, of course, for holding the other one at all times.

Tom and the lads at Her Majesty's Royal Palace and Fortress. So fine a body of men is difficult to find, and a rare pleasure to discover.

The FSOs at the United States Embassy, Budapest, for so graciously handling an unannounced walk-in.

And to Michael, Melissa, Gilbert, and CDR Marsha, in anticipation of your superior professionalism.

The most momentous thing in human life is the art of winning the soul to good or to evil.

PYTHAGORAS

Without recognizing the ordinances of Heaven, it is impossible to be a superior man.

CONFUCIUS

PROLOGUE

THE BACK GARDEN

THE SCARY PART, Jack decided, was going to be driving. He'd already bought a Jaguar—pronounced *jag-you-ah* over here, he'd have to remember—but both times he'd walked to it at the dealership, he'd gone to the left-front door instead of the right. The dealer hadn't laughed at him, but Ryan was sure he'd wanted to. At least he hadn't climbed into the passenger seat by mistake and really made an ass of himself. He'd have to remember all that: The "right" side of the road was the *left.* A right turn crossed oncoming traffic, not a left turn. The left lane was the slow lane on the interstates—*motorways,* he corrected himself. The plugs in the wall were all cockeyed. The house didn't have central heating, despite the princely price he'd paid for it. There was no air-conditioning, though that probably wasn't necessary here. It wasn't the hottest of climates: The locals started dropping dead in the street when the mercury topped 75. Jack wondered what the D.C. climate would do to them. Evidently, the "mad dogs and Englishmen" ditty was a thing of the past.

But it could have been worse. He did have a pass to shop for food at the Army–Air Force Exchange Service—otherwise known as the PX at nearby Greenham Commons Air Base—so at least they'd have proper hot dogs, and brands that resembled the ones he bought at the Giant at home in Maryland.

So many other discordant notes. British television was different, of course, not that he really expected much chance to vegetate in front of the phosphor screen anymore, but little Sally needed her ration of cartoons. Besides, even when you were reading something important, the background chatter of some mindless show was comforting in its own way. The TV news wasn't too bad, though, and the newspapers were particularly good—better than those he normally read at home, on the whole, but he'd miss the morning *Far Side.* Maybe the *International Tribune* had it, Ryan hoped. He could buy it at the train station kiosk. He had to keep track of baseball anyway.

The movers—*re*movers, he reminded himself—were beavering away under Cathy's direction. It wasn't a bad house, though smaller than their place at Peregrine Cliff, now rented to a Marine colonel teaching the earnest young boys and girls at the Naval Academy. The master bedroom overlooked what seemed to be about a quarter-acre of garden. The realtor had been particularly enthused about that. And the previous owners had spent a lot of time there: It was wall-to-wall roses, mainly red and white, to honor the houses of Lancaster and York, it would seem. There were pink ones in between to show that they'd joined together to form the Tudors, though that house had died out with Elizabeth I—and ultimately made way for the new set of Royals, whom Ryan had ample reason to like.

And the weather wasn't bad at all. They'd been in country three days and it hadn't rained at all. The sun rose very early and set late, and in the winter, he'd heard, it never came up and immediately went back down again. Some of the new friends he'd made at the State Department had told him that the long nights could be hard on the little kids. At four years and six months, Sally still qualified for that. Five-month-old Jack probably didn't notice such things, and fortunately, he slept just fine—he was doing so right now, in fact, in the custody of his nanny, Margaret van der Beek, a young redhead and daughter of a Methodist minister in South Africa. She'd come highly recommended . . . and then had been cleared by a background check performed by the Metropolitan Police. Cathy was a little concerned about the whole idea of a nanny. The idea of somebody else raising her infant grated on her like fingernails on a chalkboard, but it was an honored local custom, and it had worked out pretty well for one Winston Spencer Churchill. Miss Margaret had been vetted through Sir Basil's agency—her own agency, in fact, was officially sanctioned by Her Majesty's government. Which meant precisely nothing, Jack reminded himself. He'd been thoroughly briefed in the weeks before coming over. The "opposition"—a British term also used at Langley—had penetrated the British intelligence community more than once. CIA believed they hadn't done so at Langley yet, but Jack had to wonder about that. KGB was pretty damned good, and people were greedy all over the world. The Russians didn't pay very well, but some people sold their souls and their freedom for peanuts. They also didn't carry a flashing sign on their clothing that said I AM A TRAITOR.

Of all his briefings, the security ones had been the most tiresome. Jack's dad had been the cop in the family, and Ryan himself had never quite mastered that mode of thinking. It was one thing to look for hard data amid the cascade of crap that worked its way up the intelligence system, quite another to look with suspicion at everyone in the office and yet expect to work cordially with them. He wondered if any of the others regarded him that way . . . *probably not,* he decided. He'd paid his dues the hard way, after all, and had the pale scars on his shoulder to prove it, not to mention the nightmares of that night on Chesapeake Bay, the dreams in which his weapon never fired despite his efforts, Cathy's frantic cries of terror and alarm ringing in his ears. He'd won that battle, hadn't he? Why did the dreams think otherwise? Something to talk to a pshrink about, perhaps, but as the old wives' tale went, you had to be crazy to go to a pshrink. . . .

Sally was running about in circles, looking at her new bedroom, admiring the new bed being assembled by the removers. Jack kept out of the way. Cathy had told him he was unfitted even to supervise this sort of thing, despite his tool kit, without which no American male feels very manly, which had been among the first things unpacked. The removers had their own tools, of course—and they, too, had been vetted by SIS, lest some KGB-controlled agent plant a bug in the house. It just wouldn't do, old boy.

"Where's the tourist?" an American voice asked. Ryan went to the foyer to see who it—

"Dan! How the hell are you?"

"It was a boring day at the office, so Liz and I came out to see how things are going for you." And sure enough, just behind the Legal Attaché was his beauty-queen wife, the long-suffering St. Liz of the FBI Wives. Mrs. Murray went over to Cathy for a sisterly hug and kiss, then the two of them went immediately off to the garden. Cathy loved the roses, of course, which was fine with Jack. His dad had carried all the gardening genes in the Ryan family, and passed on none to his son. Murray gazed at his friend. "You look like hell."

"Long flight, boring book," Jack explained.

"Didn't you sleep on the way across?" Murray asked in surprise.

"On an airplane?" Ryan responded.

"It bothers you that much?"

"Dan, on a ship, you can see what's holding you up. Not in an airplane."

That gave Murray a chuckle. "Better get used to it, bud. You're gonna be building up a lot of frequent-flyer miles hopping back and forth to Dulles."

"I suppose." Strangely, Jack hadn't really considered that when he'd accepted the posting. *Dumb,* he'd realized too late. He'd be going back and forth to Langley at least once a month—not the greatest thing for a reluctant flyer.

"The moving going okay? You can trust this bunch, you know. Bas has used them for twenty-plus years, my friends at the Yard like them, too. Half of these guys are ex-cops." And cops, he didn't have to say, were more reliable than spooks.

"No bugs in the bathroom? Great," Ryan observed. During his very short experience of it so far, Ryan had learned that life in the intelligence service was a little different from teaching history at the Naval Academy. There probably *were* bugs—but wired to Basil's office . . .

"I know. Me, too. Good news, though: You'll be seeing a lot of me—if you don't mind."

Ryan nodded tiredly, trying to manage a grin. "Well, at least I'll have somebody to have a beer with."

"That's the national sport. More business gets done in pubs than at the office. Their version of the country club."

"The beer's not too bad."

"Better than the piss we have at home. I'm fully converted on that score."

"They told me at Langley that you do a lot of intel work for Emil Jacobs."

"Some." Murray nodded. "Fact of the matter is, we're better at it than a lot of you Agency types. The Operations people haven't recovered from seventy-seven yet, and I'm not sure that'll happen for a while."

Ryan had to agree. "Admiral Greer thinks so, too. Bob Ritter is pretty smart—maybe a little too smart, if you know what I mean—but he doesn't have enough friends in Congress to get his empire expanded the way that he wants."

Greer was the CIA's chief analyst, Ritter the Ops director. The two were often at odds.

"They don't trust Ritter like they do the DDI. Carryover from the Church Committee mess ten years ago. You know, the Senate never seems to remember who ran those operations. They canonize the boss and crucify the troops who tried to follow his orders—though badly. Damn, was that a—" Murray searched for the word. "The Germans call it a *schweinerei.* No translation, exactly, but, you know, it just sounds like what it is."

Jack grunted with amusement. "Yeah, better than fuckup."

The CIA's effort to assassinate Fidel Castro, which had been run out of the office of the Attorney General during the time of Camelot, had been right out of Woody Woodpecker, with a sprinkling of the Three Stooges: politicians trying to imitate James Bond, a character made up by a *failed* Brit spook. The movies just weren't the real world, as Ryan had learned the hard way, first in London, and then in his own living room.

"So, Dan, how good are they really?"

"The Brits?" Murray led Ryan out onto the front lawn. The removers *were* vetted by SIS—but Murray was FBI. "Basil is world-class. That's why he's lasted so long. He was a brilliant field spook, and he was the first guy to get a bad vibe about Philby—and remember, Basil was just a rookie then. He's good at administration, one of the most agile thinkers I've ever come across. The local politicians on both sides of the aisle like him and trust him. That isn't easy. Kinda like Hoover was for us once, but without the cult-of-personality thing. I like him. Good dude to work with. And Bas likes you a lot, Jack."

"Why?" Ryan asked. "I haven't done much of anything."

"Bas has an eye for talent. He thinks you have the right stuff. He flat loved that thing you dreamed up last year to catch security leaks—the Canary Trap—and rescuing their next king didn't exactly hurt, y'know? You're going to be a popular boy down at Century House. If you live up to your billing, you might just have a future in the spook business."

"Great." Ryan still wasn't entirely sure that was what he wanted to do, though. "Dan, I'm a stockbroker who turned into a history teacher, remember?"

"Jack, that's behind you now. Look forward, will ya? You were pretty good picking stocks at Merrill Lynch, right?"

"I made a few bucks," Ryan admitted. Actually, it was a lot of bucks, and his portfolio was still growing. People were getting fat on The Street back home.

"So, apply your brains to something really important," Dan suggested. "I hate to tell you, Jack, but there aren't that many smart people in the intelligence community. I know. I work there. A lot of drones, a lot of moderately smart people, but damned few stars, pal. You have the stuff to be a star. Jim Greer thinks so. So does Basil. You think outside the box. I do, too. That's why I'm not chasing bank robbers in Riverside, Philadelphia, anymore. But I never made any million bucks playing the market."

"Getting lucky doesn't make you a great guy, Dan. Hell, Cathy's dad, Joe, has made a lot more 'n I ever will, and he's an opinionated, overbearing son of a bitch."

"Well, you made his daughter the wife of an honorary knight, didn't you?"

Jack smiled sheepishly. "Yeah, I suppose I did."

"That'll open a lot of doors over here, Jack. The Brits do like their titles." He paused. "Now—how about I drag you guys out for a pint? There's a nice pub up the hill, The Gypsy Moth. This moving stuff'll drive you crazy. It's almost as bad as building a house."

HIS OFFICE WAS in the first basement level of The Centre, a security measure that had never been explained to him, but it turned out there was an exact counterpart room in the headquarters of the Main Enemy. There, it was called MERCURY, messenger of the gods—very apt, if his nation acknowledged the concept of a god. The messages passed through the code and cipher clerks, came to his desk, and he examined them for content and code words, before routing them to the proper offices and officers for action; then, when the messages came back down, he routed things the other way. The traffic broke into a regular routine; mornings were usually inbound traffic and afternoons usually outbound. The tedious part was the encrypting, of course, since so many of the people out in the field used one-time pads unique to themselves—the single copies of those pads were located in the set of rooms to his right. The clerks in there transmitted and kept secrets ranging from the sex lives of Italian parliamentarians to the precise targeting hierarchy of American nuclear-strike plans.

Strangely, none of them talked about what they did or what they encrypted, inbound or outbound. The clerks were pretty mindless. Perhaps they were recruited with those psychological factors in mind—it would not have surprised him. This was an agency designed by geniuses for operation by robots. If someone could actually build such robots, he was sure they'd have them here, because you could trust machines not to diverge too greatly from their intended path.

Machines couldn't think, however, and for his own job, thinking and remembering were useful things, if the agency was to function—and function it must. It was the shield and the sword of a state which needed both. And he was the postmaster of sorts; he had to remember what went where. He didn't know everything that went on here, but he knew a lot more than most people in this building: operation names and locations, and, often enough, operational missions and taskings. He generally did not know the proper names and faces of field officers, but he knew their targets, knew the code names of their recruited agents, and, for the most part, knew what those agents were providing.

He'd been here, in this department, for nine and a half years. He'd started in 1973, just after graduating from Moscow State University with a degree in mathematics, and his highly disciplined mind had gotten him spotted early on by a KGB talent scout. He played a particularly fine game of chess, and that, he supposed, was where his trained memory came from, all that study of the games of the old grandmasters, so that in a given situation he'd know the next move. He'd actually thought of making chess his career, but though he'd studied hard, it wasn't quite hard enough, it seemed. Boris Spassky, just a young player himself then, had annihilated him six games to none, with two desperate draws, and so ended his hopes of fame and fortune . . . and travel. He sighed at his desk. Travel. He'd studied his geography books, too, and in closing his eyes could see the images—mainly black-and-white: Venice's Grand Canal, London's Regent Street, Rio de Janeiro's magnificent Copacabana beach, the face of Mt. Everest, which Hillary had climbed when he himself had just been learning to walk . . . all those places he would never get to see. Not him. Not a person with his access and his security clearances. No, KGB was very careful with such people. It trusted no one, a lesson that had been learned the hard way. What was it about his country that so many tried to escape from it? And yet so many millions had died fighting for the *rodina*. . . . He'd been spared military service because of his mathematics and his chess potential, and then, he supposed, because of his recruitment to #2 Dzerzhinskiy Square. Along with it came a nice flat, fully seventy-five square meters, in a recently finished building. Military rank, too—he'd become a senior captain within weeks of his majority, which, on the whole, wasn't too bad. Even better, he'd just started getting paid now in certificate rubles, and so was able to shop in the "closed" stores for Western consumer goods—and, best of all, with shorter lines. His wife appreciated that. He'd soon be in the entry level of the *nomenklatura*, like a minor czarist prince, looking up the ladder and wondering how far he might climb. But unlike the czars, he was here not by blood but by merit—a fact that appealed to his manhood, Captain Zaitzev thought.

Yes, he'd earned his way here, and that was important. That's why he was trusted with secrets, this one for example: an agent code-named CASSIUS, an American living in Washington; it seemed he had access to valuable political intelligence that was treasured by people on the fifth floor, and which was often seconded to experts in the U.S.–Canada Institute, which studied the tea leaves in America. Canada wasn't very important to the KGB, except for its participation in the American air-defense systems, and because some of its senior politicians didn't like their powerful southern neighbor, or so the *rezident* in Ottawa regularly told his superiors upstairs. Zaitzev wondered about that. The Poles might not love their eastern neighbor either, but the Poles mostly did what they were told—the Warsaw *rezident* had reported with unconcealed pleasure in his dispatch the previous month—as that union hothead had found out to his discomfort. "Counterrevolutionary scum" had been the term used by Colonel Igor Alekseyevich Tomachevskiy. The Colonel was thought to be a rising star, due for a posting to the West. That's where the really good ones went.

TWO AND A half miles across town, Ed Foley was first in the door, with his wife, Mary Patricia, just behind him, leading Eddie by the hand. Eddie's young blue eyes were wide with a child's curiosity, but even now the four-and-a-half-year-old was learning that Moscow wasn't Disney World. The culture shock was about to fall like Thor's own hammer, but it would expand his horizons a bit, his parents thought. As it would theirs.

"Uh-huh," Ed Foley said on his first look. An embassy consular officer had lived here before, and he'd at least made an effort to clean the place up, no doubt helped by a Russian domestic—the Soviet government provided them, and diligent they were . . . for both their bosses. Ed and Mary Pat had been thoroughly briefed for weeks—nay, months—before taking the long Pan Am flight out of JFK for Moscow.

"So, this is home, eh?" Ed observed in a studiously neutral voice.

"Welcome to Moscow," Mike Barnes told the newbies. He was another consular officer, a career FSO on the way up, and had this week's duty as the embassy greeter. "The last occupant was Charlie Wooster. Good guy, back at Foggy Bottom now, catching the summer heat."

"How are the summers here?" Mary Pat asked.

"Kinda like Minneapolis," Barnes answered. "Not real hot, and the humidity's not too bad, and the winters are actually not as severe—I grew up in Minneapolis," he explained. "Of course, the German army might not agree, or Napoleon, but, well, nobody ever said Moscow was supposed to be like Paris, right?"

"Yeah, they told me about the nightlife," Ed chuckled. It was all right with him. They didn't need a stealthy Station Chief in Paris, and this was the biggest, ripest plum assignment he'd never expected to get. Bulgaria, maybe, but not the very belly of the beast. Bob Ritter must have been really impressed by his time in Tehran. Thank God Mary Pat had delivered Eddie when she had. They'd missed the takeover in Iran by, what, three weeks? It had been a troublesome pregnancy, and Mary Pat's doc had insisted on their coming back to New York for the delivery. Kids were a gift from God, all right. . . . Besides, that had made Eddie a New Yorker, too, and Ed had damned well wanted his son to be a Yankees and Rangers fan from birth. The best news of this assignment, aside from the professional stuff, was that he'd see the best ice hockey in the world right here in Moscow. Screw the ballet and the symphony. These fuckers knew how to skate. Pity the Russkies didn't understand baseball. Probably too sophisticated for the muzhiks. All those pitches to choose from . . .

"It's not real big," Mary Pat observed, looking at one cracked window. They were on the sixth floor. At least the traffic noise wouldn't be too bad. The foreigners' compound—ghetto—was walled and guarded. This was for their protection, the Russians insisted, but street crime against foreigners wasn't a problem in Moscow. The average Russian citizen was forbidden by law to have foreign currency in his possession, and there was no convenient way to spend it in any case. So there was little profit in mugging an American or Frenchman on the streets, and there was no mistaking them—their clothing marked them about as clearly as peacocks among crows.

"Hello!" It was an English accent. The florid face appeared a moment later. "We're your neighbors. Nigel and Penny Haydock," the face's owner said. He was about forty-five, tall and skinny, with prematurely gray and thinning hair. His wife, younger and prettier than he probably deserved, appeared an instant later with a tray of sandwiches and some welcoming white wine.

"You must be Eddie," the flaxen-haired Mrs. Haydock observed. That's when Ed Foley noticed the maternity dress. She was about six months gone, by the look of her. So the briefings had been right in every detail. Foley trusted CIA, but he'd learned the hard way to verify everything, from the names of people living on the same floor to whether the toilet flushed reliably. *Especially in Moscow,* he thought, heading for the bathroom. Nigel followed.

"The plumbing works reliably here, but it is noisy. No one complains," Haydock explained.

Ed Foley flipped the handle and, sure enough, it was noisy.

"Fixed that myself. Bit of a handyman, you see," he said. Then, more quietly, "Be careful where you speak in this place, Ed. Bloody bugs everywhere. Especially the bedrooms. The bloody Russians like to count our orgasms, so it seems. Penny and I try not to disappoint." A sly grin. Well, to some cities you brought your own nightlife.

"Two years here?" The toilet seemed to run forever. Foley was tempted to lift the tank cover to see if Haydock had replaced the plumbing hardware inside with something special. He decided he didn't have to look to check that.

"Twenty-nine months. Seven to go. It's a lively place to work. I'm sure they told you, everywhere you go, you'll have a 'friend' handy. Don't underestimate them, either. The Second Directorate chaps are thoroughly trained. . . ." The toilet ran its course, and Haydock changed his voice. "The shower—the hot water is pretty reliable, but the spray pipe, it rattles, just like the one in our flat. . . ." He turned the faucet to demonstrate. Sure enough, it rattled. *Had someone worked on the wall to loosen it?* Ed wondered. Probably. Probably this very handyman with him.

"Perfect."

"Yes, you will get a lot of work done in here. Shower with a friend and save water—isn't that what they say in California?"

Foley managed his first laugh in Moscow. "Yeah, that's what they say, all right." He gave his visitor a look. He was surprised that Haydock had introduced himself so early, but maybe it was just reverse-English tradecraft to be so obvious. The business of espionage had all manner of rules, and the Russians were rule-followers. So, Bob Ritter had told him, toss away *part* of the rulebook. Stick to your cover and be a dumbass unpredictable American every chance you get. He'd also told the Foleys that Nigel Haydock was one guy they could trust. He was the son of another intelligence officer—a man betrayed by Kim Philby himself, one of the poor bastards who'd parachuted into Albania into the waiting arms of the KGB reception committee. Nigel had been five years old then, just old enough always to remember what it was like to lose your father to the enemy. Nigel's motivation was probably as good as Mary Pat's, and that was pretty damned good. Better even than his own, Ed Foley might admit after a few drinks. Mary Pat hated the bastards as the Lord God Himself hated sin. Haydock wasn't the Station Chief here, but he was the head bird-dog for the SIS's operation in Moscow, and that made him pretty good. The CIA's Director, Judge Moore, trusted the Brits: after Philby, he'd seen them go through SIS with a flamethrower hotter than even James Jesus Angleton's fly rod and cauterize every possible leak. In turn, Foley trusted Judge Moore, and so did the President. That was the craziest part of the intelligence business: You couldn't trust *anybody*—but you had to trust *somebody.*

Well, Foley thought, checking the hot water with his hand, *nobody ever said the business made much sense.* Like classical metaphysics. It just was.

"When's the furniture get here?"

"The container ought to be on a truck in Leningrad right now. Will they tamper with it?"

Haydock shrugged. "Check everything," he warned, then softened. "You can never know how thorough they are, Edward. The KGB is a great bloody bureaucracy—you don't know the meaning of the word until you see it in operation here. For example, the bugs in your flat—how many of them actually work? They're not British Telecom, nor are they AT&T. It's the curse of this country, really, and it works for us, but that, too, is unreliable. When you're followed, you can't know if it's an experienced expert or some bloody nimrod who can't find his way to the loo. They look alike and dress alike. Just like our people, when you get down to it, but their bureaucracy is so large that there's a greater likelihood it will protect the incompetent—or maybe not. God knows, at Century House we have our share of drones."

Foley nodded. "At Langley, we call it the Intelligence Directorate."

"Quite. We call ours the Palace of Westminster," Haydock observed, with his own favorite prejudice. "I think we've tested the plumbing enough."

Foley turned off the faucet and the two men returned to the living room, where Penny and Mary Pat were getting acquainted.

"Well, we have enough hot water anyway, honey."

"Glad to hear it," Mary Pat responded. She turned back to her guest. "Where do you shop around here?"

Penny Haydock smiled: "I can take you there. For special items, we can order from an agency in Helsinki, excellent quality: English, French, German—even American, for things like juices and preserved foods. The perishables are Finnish in origin, and they're generally very good, especially the lamb. Don't they have the finest lamb, Nigel?"

"Indeed it is—as good as New Zealand," her husband agreed.

"The steaks leave something to be desired," Mike Barnes told them, "but every week we get steaks flown in from Omaha. Tons of them—we distribute them to all our friends."

"That is the truth," Nigel confirmed. "Your corn-fed beef is superb. I'm afraid we're all quite addicted to it."

"Thank God for the U.S. Air Force," Barnes went on. "They fly the beef into all their NATO bases, and we're on the distribution list. They come in frozen, not quite as good as fresh at Delmonico's, but close enough to remind you of home. I hope you guys brought a grill. We tend to take them up on the roof to cook out. We import charcoal, too. Ivan just doesn't seem to understand about that." The apartment had no balcony, perhaps to protect them from the diesel smell that pervaded the city.

"What about going to work?" Foley asked.

"Better to take the metro. It really is great," Barnes told him.

"Leaving me with the car?" Mary Pat asked, with a hopeful smile. This was going exactly to plan. That was expected, but anything that went well in this business came as something of a surprise, like the right presents under the Christmas tree. You always hoped Santa got the letter, but you could never be sure.

"You might as well learn how to drive in this city," Barnes said. "At least you have a nice car." The previous resident in this apartment had left behind a white Mercedes 280 for them, which was indeed a nice car. Actually, a little too nice at only four years old. Not that there were all that many cars in Moscow, and the license plates surely marked it as belonging to an American diplomat, and thus easy to spot by any traffic cop, and by the KGB vehicle that would follow it most places it went. Again, it was reverse-English. Mary Pat would have to learn to drive like an Indianapolis resident on her first trip to New York. "The streets are nice and wide," Barnes told her, "and the gas station is only three blocks that way." He pointed. "It's a huge one. The Russians like to build them that way."

"Great," she observed for Barnes's benefit, already dropping into her cover as a pretty, ditsy blonde. Around the world, the pretty ones were supposed to be the dumb ones, and blondes most of all. It was a hell of a lot easier to play dumb than to be smart, after all, Hollywood actors notwithstanding.

"What about servicing the car?" Ed asked.

"It's a Mercedes. They don't break much," Barnes assured them. "The German embassy has a guy who can fix anything that goes bad. We're cordial with our NATO allies. You guys soccer fans?"

"Girls' game," Ed Foley responded immediately.

"That's rather coarse of you," Nigel Haydock observed.

"Give me American football any time," Foley countered.

"Bloody foolish, uncivilized game, full of violence and committee meetings," the Brit sniffed.

Foley grinned. "Let's eat."

They sat down. The interim furniture was adequate, something like you'd find in a no-tell motel in Alabama. You could sleep on the bed, and the bug spray had probably done for all the crawly things. Probably.

The sandwiches were okay. Mary Pat went to get glasses and turned on the taps—

"Recommend against that one, Mrs. Foley," Nigel warned. "Some people come down with stomach complaints from the tap water. . . ."

"Oh?" She paused. "And my name's Mary Pat, Nigel."

Now they were properly introduced. "Yes, Mary Pat. We prefer bottled water for drinking. The tap water is good enough for bathing, and you can boil it in a pinch for coffee and tea."

"It's even worse in Leningrad," Nigel warned. "The natives are more or less immunized, they tell me, but we foreigners can get some serious GI problems there."

"What about schools?" Mary Pat had been worried about that.

"The American-British school looks after the children well," Penny Haydock promised. "I work there myself part-time. And the academic program there is top-drawer."

"Eddie's starting to read already, isn't he, honey?" the proud father announced.

"Just *Peter Rabbit* and that sort of thing, but not bad for four," an equally pleased mother confirmed for the rest. For his part, Eddie had found the sandwich plate and was gnawing through something. It wasn't his treasured bologna, but a hungry kid is not always discriminating. There were also four large jars of Skippy's Super Chunk peanut butter packed away in a safe place. His parents figured they could get grape jelly anywhere, but probably not Skippy. The local bread, everyone said, was decent, if not exactly the Wonder Bread that American children had been raised on. And Mary Pat had a bread-maker in their cargo container, now on a truck or train between Moscow and Leningrad. A good cook, she was a positive artist at baking bread, and expected that to be her entrée into the embassy social set.

NOT ALL THAT far away from where they sat, a letter changed hands. The deliverer was from Warsaw, and had been dispatched by his government—actually, by an agency of his government to an agency of the recipient government. The messenger was not all that pleased by his mission. He was a communist—he had to be in order to be entrusted with such a task—but he was nonetheless a Pole, as was the subject of the message and the mission. And that was the rub.

The message was in fact a photocopy of the original, which had arrived by hand to an office—an important one—in Warsaw only three days before.

The messenger, a full colonel in his country's intelligence service, was personally known to the recipient, by sight if not especially by affection.

The Russians used their western neighbors for many tasks. The Poles had a real talent for intelligence operations, for the same reason the Israelis did: They were surrounded by enemies. To their west was Germany, and to their east was the Soviet Union. The unhappy circumstances involved in both had resulted in Poland's putting many of its best and brightest into the intelligence business.

The recipient knew all that. In fact, he already knew word for word the content of the message. He'd learned it the previous day. He was not surprised at the delay, though. The Polish government had taken that day to consider the contents and its import before forwarding it, and the recipient took no umbrage. Every government in the world took at least one day to go over such things. It was just the nature of men in positions of authority to diddle and waver, even though they had to know that delay was a waste of time and air. Even Marxism-Leninism couldn't alter human nature. Sad, but true. The New Soviet Man, like the New Polish Man, was, in the end, still a man.

The ballet being played out now was as stylized as any performed by the Kirov troupe in Leningrad. The recipient even imagined he could hear the music playing. He actually preferred Western jazz to classical, but in any case the music at the ballet was just the garnish, the system that told the dancers when to leap together like pretty, trained dogs. The ballerinas were far too slender for Russian tastes, of course, but real women were far too heavy for those little fairies they called men to toss about.

Why was his mind wandering? He resumed his seat, falling back slowly into his leather chair as he unfolded the letter. It was written in Polish, and he didn't speak or read Polish, but affixed to it was a translation in literate Russian. Of course, he'd have his own translators go over it, plus two or three psychiatrists to consider the mental state of the drafter and to compose their own multipage analysis, which he'd have to read, time waster though that would be. Then he'd have to report on it, to provide his political superiors—no, his political *peers*—with all of these additional insights so that they could waste *their* time going over the message and its import before considering what to do about it.

The Chairman wondered if this Polish colonel realized how easy his own political bosses had had it. In the end, all they'd had to do was forward it to their own political masters for action, bucking the decision up the tree of responsibility as government functionaries all do, regardless of place or philosophy. Vassals were vassals the world over.

The Chairman looked up at him. "Comrade Colonel, thank you for bringing this to my attention. Please extend my greetings and my respects to your commander. Dismissed."

The Pole snapped to attention, saluted in the curious Polish way, did his best parade-ground about face, then headed off to the door.

Yuriy Andropov watched the door close before turning his attention back to the message and its appended translation.

"So, Karol, you threaten us, eh?" He clucked his tongue and shook his head before going on as quietly as before. "You are brave, but your judgment needs adjustment, my cleric comrade."

He looked up again, pondering. The office had the usual artwork covering the walls, and for the same reason as in any other office—to avoid blankness. Two were oil paintings by Renaissance masters, borrowed from the collection of some long-dead czar or nobleman. A third portrait, rather a good one, actually, was of Lenin, the pale complexion and domed forehead known to millions all around the world. A nicely framed color photograph of Leonid Brezhnev, the current General Secretary of the Communist Party of the Soviet Union, hung near it. The photo was a lie, a picture of a young and vigorous man, not the senile old goat who now sat at the head of the Politburo table. Well, all men grew old, but in most places, such men left their jobs for honorable retirement. But not in his country, Andropov realized . . . and looked down at the letter. And not this man, either. This job, too, was for life.

But he is threatening to change that part of the equation, the Chairman of the Committee for State Security thought. And in that was the danger.

Danger?

The consequences were unknown, and that was danger enough. His Politburo colleagues would see it the same way, old, cautious, and frightened men that they were.

And so he had not merely to report the danger. He must also present a means of dealing with it effectively.

The portraits that ought to have been on his wall right now were of two men who were semiforgotten. One would have been Iron Feliks—Dzerzhinskiy himself, the founder of the Cheka, the antecedent of the KGB.

The other ought to have been Josef Vissarionovich Stalin. The leader had once posed a question that was relevant to the very situation that faced Andropov now. Then, it had been 1944. Now—now maybe it was even more relevant.

Well, that remained to be seen. And he'd be the man to make that determination, Andropov told himself. All men could be made to disappear. The thought should have surprised him when it leapt into his head, but it didn't. This building, built eighty years earlier to be the palatial home office of the Rossiya Insurance Company, had seen a lot of that, and its inhabitants had issued orders to cause many, many more deaths. They used to have executions in the basement. That had ended only a few years before, as KGB expanded to include all the space in even this massive structure—and another on the inner ring road around the city—but the cleanup crew occasionally whispered about the ghosts to be seen on quiet nights, sometimes startling the old washerwomen with their buckets and brushes and witch-like hair. The government of this country didn't believe in such things as spirits and ghosts any more than it believed in a man's immortal soul, but doing away with the superstitions of the simple peasants was a more difficult task than getting the intelligentsia to buy into the voluminous writings of Vladimir Ilyich Lenin, Karl Marx, or Friedrich Engels, not to mention the turgid prose attributed to Stalin (but actually done by a committee formed of frightened men, and all the worse because of it), which was, blessedly, no longer much in demand except to the most masochistic of scholars.

No, Yuriy Vladimirovich told himself, *getting people to believe in Marxism wasn't all that hard.* First, they hammered it into their heads in grammar schools, and the Young Pioneers, and high schools, and the Komsomolets, the Young Communist League, and then the really smart ones became full Party members, keeping their Party cards "next to their hearts," in the cigarette pockets of their shirts.

But by then, they knew better. The politically aware members professed their belief at Party meetings because they had to do that to get ahead. In the same way, the smart courtiers in pharaonic Egypt kneeled and shielded their eyes from the bright-light-emanating face, lest they be blinded—they held up their hands because, in Pharaoh, in the person of their Living God, was personal power and prosperity, and so they knelt their obeisance and denied their senses and their sensibility and got ahead. So it was here. Five thousand years, was it? He could check a history book. The Soviet Union turned out some of the world's foremost medieval historians, and doubtless some competent antiquarians as well, because that was one area of scholarship where politics didn't matter much. The facts of ancient Egypt were too distant from contemporary reality to matter to the philosophical speculation of Marx or the endless ramblings of Lenin. And so some fine scholars went into that field. More went into the pure sciences, because pure science was pure science and a hydrogen atom had no politics.

But agriculture did. Manufacturing did. And so the best and brightest stayed away from those areas, opting instead for political studies. Because there success was to be found. You didn't have to believe it any more than you believed that Ramses II was the living son of the sun god, or whatever the hell god he was supposed to have issued from. Instead, Yuriy Vladimirovich figured, the courtiers saw that Ramses had numerous wives and even more numerous progeny, and that, on the whole, wasn't a bad life for a man to have. The classical equivalent of a dacha in the Lenin Hills and summers on the beach at Sochi. So, did the world ever really change?

Probably not, the Chairman of the Committee for State Security decided. And his job was largely to protect against change.

And this letter threatened change, didn't it? It was a threat, and he might have to do something about the threat. That meant doing something about the man behind it.

It had happened before. It could happen again, he decided.

Andropov would not live long enough to learn that in considering this action, he would set in motion the demise of his own country.

CHAPTER 1

RUMBLINGS AND DREAMS

"WHEN DO YOU START, JACK?" Cathy asked in the quiet of their bed.

And her husband was glad it was their bed. Comfortable as the New York hotel had been, it is never the same, and besides, he'd had quite enough of his father-in-law, with his Park Avenue duplex and immense sense of self-importance. Okay, Joe Muller had a good ninety million in the bank and his diversified portfolio, and it was growing nicely with the new presidency, but enough was enough.

"Day after tomorrow," her husband answered. "I suppose I might go in after lunch, just to look around."

"You ought to be asleep by now," she said.

There were drawbacks to marrying a physician, Jack occasionally told himself. You couldn't hide much from them. A gentle, loving touch could convey your body temperature, heart rate, and Christ knew what else, and docs hid their feelings about what they found with the skill of a professional poker player. Well, some of the time.

"Yeah, long day." It was short of five in the evening in New York, but his "day" had lasted longer than the normal twenty-four. He really had to learn to sleep on airplanes. It wasn't as though his seat had been uncomfortable. He'd upgraded the government-issue tickets to first class on his own American Express card, and soon the frequent-flyer miles would build up so much that such upgrades would be automatic. *Yeah, great,* Jack thought. They'd know him by sight at Heathrow and Dulles. Well, at least he had his new black diplomatic passport and didn't have to be troubled with inspections and such. Ryan was technically assigned to the U.S. Embassy at London's Grosvenor Square, just across the street from the building that had housed Eisenhower's WW2 office, and with that assignment came the diplomatic status that made him a super-person, untrammeled by such inconveniences as civil law. He could smuggle a couple pounds of heroin into England, and no one could so much as touch his bags without permission—which he could summarily withhold, claiming diplomatic privilege and urgent business. It was an open secret that diplomats didn't trouble themselves with customs duties for such things as perfumes for their wives (or significant others) and/or booze for themselves, but to Ryan's Catholic measure of personal conduct, these were venial sins, not mortal.

The usual muddle of thoughts in a fatigued brain, he recognized. Cathy would never allow herself to operate in this mental state. Sure, as an intern they'd kept her on duty for endless hours—the idea being to get her accustomed to making good decisions under miserable circumstances—but part of her husband wondered how many patients were sacrificed on the altar of medical boot camp. If trial lawyers ever managed to figure out how to make money off of that . . .

Cathy—Dr. Caroline Ryan, M.D., FACS, her white lab coat and plastic name tag announced—had struggled through that phase of her training, and more than once her husband had worried about her drive home in her little Porsche sports car, after thirty-six straight hours on duty in obstetrics, or pediatrics, or general surgery, fields she wasn't interested in herself, but about which she had to know a little in order to be a proper Johns Hopkins doc. Well, she'd known enough to patch up his shoulder that afternoon in front of Buckingham Palace. He hadn't bled to death in front of his wife and daughter, which would have been pretty ignominious for everyone involved, especially the Brits. *Would my knighthood have been awarded posthumously?* Jack wondered with a stifled chuckle. Then, finally, his eyes closed for the first time in thirty-nine hours.

"I HOPE HE likes it over there," Judge Moore said, at his end-of-the-day senior staff get-together.

"Arthur, our cousins know their hospitality," James Greer pointed out. "Basil ought to be a good teacher."

Ritter didn't say anything. This Ryan amateur had gotten himself a lot of—way the hell too much—publicity for any employee of the CIA, even more so since he was a DI guy. As far as Ritter was concerned, the Directorate of Intelligence was the tail wagging the Operations Directorate dog. Sure, Jim Greer was a fine spook and a good man to work with, but he wasn't a *field* spook, and—Congress to the contrary—that's what the Agency needed. At least Arthur Moore understood that. But on The Hill, if you said "field intelligence officer" to the representatives who controlled appropriations, they recoiled like Dracula from a golden crucifix and collectively went *ewwwwww.* Then it was time to speak.

"What do you suppose they'll let him in on?" the DDO wondered aloud.

"Basil will regard him as my personal representative," Judge Moore said, after a moment's consideration. "So, everything they share with us, they will share with him."

"They're going to co-opt him, Arthur," Ritter warned. "He's into things they don't know about. They will try to squeeze things out of Ryan. He doesn't know how to defend against that."

"Bob, I briefed him on that myself," Greer announced. The DDO knew that already, of course, but Ritter had a real talent for acting grumpy when he didn't get his way. Greer wondered what it had been like to be Bob's mother. "Don't underestimate this kid, Bob. He's smart. I'll wager you a steak dinner that he gets more things out of the Brits than they get out of him."

"Sucker bet," the Deputy Director (Operations) snorted.

"At Snyder's," the Deputy Director (Intelligence) goaded further. It was the favorite steak house for both executives, located just across the Key Bridge in Georgetown.

Judge Arthur Moore, the Director of Central Intelligence, or DCI, watched the exchange with amusement. Greer knew how to twist Ritter's tail, and somehow Bob never quite figured out how to defend against it. Maybe it was Greer's down-east accent. Texans like Bob Ritter (and Arthur Moore himself) deemed themselves superior to anyone who talked through his nose, certainly over a deck of playing cards or around a bottle of bourbon whiskey. The Judge figured he was above such things, though they were fun to watch.

"Okay, dinner at Snyder's." Ritter extended his hand. And it was time for the DCI to resume control of the meeting.

"Now that we've settled that one, gentlemen, the President wants me to tell him what's going to happen in Poland."

Ritter didn't leap at that. He had a good Station Chief in Warsaw, but the guy only had three proper field officers in his department, and one of them was a rookie. They did, however, have one very good source agent-in-place inside the Warsaw government's political hierarchy, and several good ones in their military.

"Arthur, *they* don't know. They're dancing around this Solidarity thing on a day-to-day basis," the DDO told the others. "And the music keeps changing on them."

"It's going to come down to what Moscow tells them to do, Arthur," Greer agreed. "And Moscow doesn't know either."

Moore took off his reading glasses and rubbed his eyes. "Yeah. They don't know what to do when someone openly defies them. Joe Stalin would have shot everyone in sight, but the current bunch doesn't have the gumption to do that, thank the Good Lord for that."

"Collegial rule brings out the coward in everyone, and Brezhnev just doesn't have the ability to lead. From what I hear, they have to walk him to the men's room." It was a slight exaggeration, but it appealed to Ritter that Soviet leadership was softening.

"What's CARDINAL telling us?" Moore referred to the Agency's premiere agent-in-place in the Kremlin, the personal assistant to Defense Minister Dmitriy Fedorovich Ustinov. His name was Mikhail Semyonovich Filitov, but to all but a bare handful of active CIA personnel, he was simply CARDINAL.

"He says that Ustinov despairs of anything useful coming out of the Politburo until they do have a leader who can actually lead. Leonid is slowing down. Everybody knows it, even the man on the street. You can't camouflage a TV picture, can you?"

"How long do you suppose he has left?"

A collection of shrugs, then Greer took the question: "The doctors I've talked to say he could drop over tomorrow, or he could dote along for another couple of years. They say they see mild Alzheimer's, but only mild. His general condition is progressive cardiovascular myopathy, they think, probably exacerbated by incipient alcoholism."

"They *all* have that problem," Ritter observed. "CARDINAL confirms the heart problem, by the way, along with the vodka."

"And the liver is important, and his is probably suboptimum," Greer went on, with a gross understatement. Then Moore finished the thought.

"But you can't tell a Russian to stop drinking any more than you can tell a grizzly bear not to shit in the woods. You know, if anything ever brings these guys down, it will be their inability to handle the orderly transition of power."

"Well, gee, Your Honor." Bob Ritter looked up with a wicked grin. "I guess they just don't have enough lawyers. Maybe we could ship them a hundred thousand of ours."

"They're not that stupid. Better we shoot a few Poseidon missiles at them. Less net damage to their society," the DDI said.

"Why do people disparage my honorable profession?" Moore asked the ceiling. "If anybody saves their system, it will have to be a lawyer, gentlemen."

"You think so, Arthur?" Greer asked.

"You can't have a rational society without the rule of law, and you can't have the rule of law without lawyers to administer it." Moore was the former Chief Judge of the Texas State Court of Appeals. "They don't have those rules yet, not when the Politburo can reach out and execute anyone they don't like without a semblance of an appeals process. It must be like living in hell. You can't depend on anything. It's like Rome under Caligula—if he got a notion, that notion had the force of law. Hell, though, even Rome had *some* laws the emperors had to abide by. Not our Russian friends." The others couldn't really appreciate how horrid a concept that was to their Director. He'd once been the finest trial lawyer in a state noted for the quality of its legal community, and then a learned judge on a bench replete with thoughtful, fair men. Most Americans were as accustomed to the rule of law as to the ninety feet between bases on a baseball diamond. For Ritter and Greer, it was more important that, before his legal career, Arthur Moore had been a superior field spook. "So, what the hell do I tell the President?"

"The truth, Arthur," Greer suggested. "We don't know because *they* don't know."

That was the only truthful and rational thing he could say, of course, but: "Damn it, Jim, they *pay* us to know!"

"It comes down to how threatened the Russians feel. Poland is just a cat's paw for them, a vassal state that jumps when they say 'jump,' " Greer said. "The Russians can control what their own people see on TV and in *Pravda*—"

"But they can't control the rumors that come across the border," said Ritter. "And the stories their soldiers tell when they come home from service there—*and* in Germany, *and* in Czechoslovakia, *and* in Hungary, and what they hear on Voice of America and Radio Free Europe." CIA controlled the first of those outlets directly, and, while the other was theoretically almost independent, that was a fiction nobody believed. Ritter himself had a great deal of input on both propaganda arms of the American government. The Russians understood and respected good agitprop.

"How squeezed do you suppose they feel?" Moore wondered aloud.

"Just two or three years ago, they thought they were on the crest of the wave," Greer announced. "Our economy was in the toilet with inflation and we had gas lines, the Iran mess. They'd just got Nicaragua to drop into their lap. Our national morale was bad, and . . ."

"Well, that's changing, thank God," Moore went on for him. "Full reversal?" he asked. It was too much to hope for, but at heart Arthur Moore was an optimist—otherwise, how could he be DCI?

"We're heading that way, Arthur," Ritter said. "They're slow to catch on. They are not the most agile of thinkers. That's their greatest weakness. The top dogs are wedded to their ideology to the point that they can't see around it. You know, we can hurt these bastards—hurt 'em bad—if we can analyze their weaknesses thoroughly and come up with a way to exploit them."

"You really think so, Bob?" the DDI asked.

"I don't think it—I damned well know it!" the DDO shot back. "They are *vulnerable,* and best of all, they don't yet know that they are vulnerable. It's time to do something. We've got a President now who'll back our play if we can come up with something good enough for him to invest his political capital. Congress is so afraid of him, they won't stand in the way."

"Robert," the DCI said, "it sounds to me like you've got something rattling up your sleeve."

Ritter thought for a few seconds before going on. "Yes, Arthur, I do. I've been thinking about this since they brought me in from the field eleven years ago. I haven't written a single word of it down." He didn't have to explain why. Congress could subpoena any piece of paper in the building—well, almost any piece—but not something carried only in a man's mind. But perhaps this was the time to set it down. "What is the Soviets' fondest wish?"

"To bring us down," Moore answered. That didn't exactly require a Nobel-class intellect.

"Okay, what is our fondest wish?"

Greer took that one. "We aren't allowed to think in those terms. We want to find a modus vivendi with them." That was what *The New York Times* said, anyway, and wasn't that the voice of the nation? "Okay, Bob. Spit it out."

"How do we attack them?" Ritter asked. "And by that I mean nail the bastards right where they live, hurt them—"

"Bring them down?" Moore asked.

"Why the hell not?" Ritter demanded.

"Is it possible?" the DCI asked, interested that Ritter was thinking along such lines.

"Well, Arthur, if they can aim that big a gun at us, why can't we do it to them?" Ritter had the bit in his teeth now. "They send money into political groups in our country to try and make it hard on our political process. They have antinuclear demonstrations all across Europe, calling to eliminate our Theater Nuclear Weapons while they rebuild theirs. We can't even leak what we know about that to the media—"

"And if we did, the media wouldn't print it," Moore observed. After all, the media didn't like nuclear weapons either, though it was willing to tolerate Soviet weapons because they, for one reason or another, were not destabilizing. What Ritter really wanted to do, he feared, was to see if the Soviets had influence on the American mass media. But even if it did, such an investigation would bear only poisoned fruit. The media held on to their vision of its integrity and balance as a miser held his hoard. But they knew without having the evidence that KGB *did* have some power over the American media, because it was so easy to establish and exercise. Flatter them, let them in on supposed secrets, and then become a trusted source. But did the Soviets know how dangerous a game that could be? The American news media did have a few core beliefs, and tampering with them was like tinkering with a live bomb. One wrong move could be expensive. No one in this Seventh-Floor office was under much illusion about the genius of the Russian intelligence service. It had skilled people, certainly, and trained them thoroughly and well, but KGB also had its weaknesses. Like the society it served, KGB applied a political template to reality, and largely ignored the information that didn't match up with the holes. And so, after months, even years, of painstaking planning and preparation, they often had operations go bad because one of their officers had decided that life in the land of the enemy wasn't quite so bad as it was portrayed. The cure for a lie was always the truth. It just had a way of smacking you in the face, and the smarter you were, the worse it hurt.

"That's not important," Ritter said, surprising both his colleagues.

"Okay, keep going," Moore ordered.

"What we need to do is examine their vulnerabilities and attack them—with the objective of destabilizing their entire country."

"That's a very tall order, Robert," Moore observed.

"You take an ambition pill, Bob?" Greer asked, intrigued even so. "Our political masters will blanch at that large an objective."

"Oh, I know." Ritter held up his hands. "Oh, no, we mustn't hurt them. They might nuke us. Come on, they're a hell of a lot less likely to lash out than we are. People, they are *afraid* of us, a lot more than we are of them.

They are afraid of *Poland,* for Christ's sake. Why? Because there's a disease in Poland that their own people might catch. It's called rising expectations. And rising expectations are the one thing they can't satisfy. Their economy is as stagnant as stump water. If we give them a little push . . ."

" 'All we have to do is kick in the door, and the whole rotten structure will collapse,' " Moore quoted. "That's been said before, but Adolf had himself a nasty little surprise when the snow started falling."

"He was an idiot who didn't read his Machiavelli," Ritter retorted. "First, you conquer 'em, then you murder 'em. Why give them warning?"

"Whereas our current adversaries could have taught old Niccolò a lesson or two," Greer agreed. "Okay, Bob, exactly what do you propose?"

"A systematic examination of Soviet weaknesses with an eye to exploitation. In simplest terms, we investigate the possible shape of a plan to cause great discomfort to our enemy."

"Hell, we ought to be doing that all the time anyway," Moore said, agreeing at once with the concept. "James?"

"I have no problem with it. I can get a team together in my shop to toss some ideas together."

"Not the usual suspects," the DDO urged. "We'll never get anything useful from the regular crew. It's time to think way the hell outside the usual box."

Greer thought about that for a moment, then nodded agreement. "Okay, I'll do the picking. Special project. Pick a name for it?"

"How about INFECTION?" Ritter asked.

"And if it turns into an operation, call it PLAGUE?" the DDI asked with a laugh.

Moore shared in the chuckle. "No, I've got it. MASQUE OF THE RED DEATH. Something from Poe sounds about right to me."

"This is really about having the DO take over the DI, isn't it?" Greer thought aloud.

It wasn't a serious undertaking yet, just an interesting academic exercise, the same way a corporate trader might look into the fundamental strengths and weaknesses of a company he might want to take over . . . and then, if the circumstances justified, break it up for parts. No, the Union of Soviet Socialist Republics was the center of their professional world, the Bobby

Lee to their Army of the Potomac, the New York Yankees to their Boston Red Sox. Defeating them, however attractive a dream it might be, was little more than that, a dream.

Even so, Judge Arthur Moore approved of that sort of thinking. If man's reach didn't exceed his grasp, then what the hell was heaven for?

APPROACHING TWENTY-THREE hours in Moscow, Andropov was enjoying a cigarette—an American Marlboro, in fact—and sipping at his vodka, the premium Starka brand, which was brown like American bourbon. On the record player was another American product, an LP of Louis Armstrong on the trumpet, blowing some superb New Orleans jazz. Like many Russians, the Chairman of the KGB regarded blacks as little more than monkey cannibals, but the ones in America had invented their own fine art form. He knew that he ought to have been a devotee of Borodin or one of the other classical Russian composers, but there was just something about the vitality of American jazz that rang some sort of bell in his mind.

But the music was merely an aid for thinking. Yuriy Vladimirovich Andropov had heavy brows over his brown eyes and a lantern jaw suggestive of another ethnic origin, but his mind was entirely Russian, which meant part Byzantine, part Tartar, part Mongol, and all focused on achieving his own goals. Of these he had many, but above all: He wanted to be the leader of his country. Someone had to save it, and he knew exactly how much it needed saving. One of the advantages of being Chairman of the Committee for State Security was that few things were secret from him, and this in a society that was replete with lies, where lies were indeed the highest of art forms. This was especially true of the Soviet economy. The command-driven structure of that flaccid colossus meant that every factory—and every factory manager—had a production goal that both it and he had to meet. The goals might or might not be realistic. That didn't matter. What did matter was that their enforcement was draconian. Not as draconian as they'd once been, of course. In the 1930s and '40s, failure to meet the goal set forth in The Plan could mean death right here in this very building, because those who failed to meet The Plan were "wreckers," saboteurs, enemies of the state, *traitors* in a nation where state treason was a crime worse than any other, and so demanded a penalty worse than any other, usually a .44-caliber bullet from one of the old Smith & Wesson revolvers the czars had purchased from America.

As a result, factory managers had learned that if they couldn't meet The Plan's expectations in fact, they'd do so on paper, thus prolonging both their lives and the perks of their office. The facts of their failure were usually lost in the elephantine bureaucracy that had been inherited from the czars and then nurtured to further growth under Marxism-Leninism. His own agency had a lot of that same tendency, Andropov knew. He could say something, even thunder out the words, but that didn't mean that any real result had to happen. Sometimes it did—indeed, fairly often of late, because Yuriy Vladimirovich kept his own personal notes and would follow up a week or so later. And, gradually, his agency was learning to change.

But there was no changing the fact that obfuscation was the foil of even his brand of ruthlessness. Even Stalin reborn could not change that—and *nobody* wanted Stalin reborn. Institutional obfuscation had reached all the way to the summit of the Party hierarchy. The Politburo was no more decisive than the management staff of State Farm "Sunrise." No one had learned efficiency, he'd observed on his climb to the top of the heap, and as a result a great deal happened with a wink and a nod, with an understanding that it really wasn't all that important.

And because so little progress actually happened, it devolved on him and KGB to make right all the things that went wrong. If the organs of the State could not come up with what the State needed, then KGB had to go steal it from those who did have it. Andropov's spy agency, and its sister service, the military's GRU, stole all manner of weapons designs from the West. *They were so efficient,* he thought with a grunt, *that Soviet pilots occasionally died from the same design defects that had killed American pilots years before.*

And that was the rub. However efficient KGB was, its most stirring successes merely guaranteed that his country's military was five years behind the West *at best.* And the one thing he and his field officers couldn't steal from the West was the quality control in their industries that made advanced weapons possible. *How many times,* he wondered, *had his people secured designs from America and elsewhere only to learn that his country simply could not replicate them?*

And that was what he had to fix. The mythical tasks of Hercules seemed trivial in comparison, Andropov told himself, stubbing out his cigarette. Transform his nation? In Red Square, they kept the mummy of Lenin as some sort of Communistic god, the relic of the man who had transformed Russia from a backward monarchic state into . . . a backward socialist state. The Moscow government expressed contempt for any countries that tried to combine socialism with capitalism—except for one little thing: KGB tried to steal from them, too. The West rarely shed blood and treasure to find out about Soviet weapons—except to find out what was wrong with them. The Western intelligence services did their best to frighten their parent governments, proclaiming every new Soviet weapon to be Satan's own tool of destruction, but then they later found out that the Soviet tiger wore lead boots, and couldn't catch the deer, however frightening the tiger's teeth might appear. Whatever original ideas Russian scientists did come up with—and there were many of them—were duly stolen and converted by the West into instruments that actually worked.

The design bureaus made their promises to the military and to the Politburo. They told them how their new systems would improve, with just a little more funding . . . *Hah!* And all the time, this new American president was doing what his predecessors hadn't: He was feeding *his* tiger. The American industrial monster was eating raw red meat, and actually manufacturing in numbers the weapons they'd developed over the preceding decade. His field officers and their agents reported that morale in the American military was rising for the first time in a generation. Their Army in particular was training on increased tempos, and their new weapons . . .

. . . Not that the Politburo believed him when he told them. Its members were too insular, they were unexposed to the real world beyond the Soviet frontiers. They assumed that all the world was more or less like it was here, in accord with the political theories of Lenin—written sixty years ago! As if the world hadn't changed at all since then! Yuriy Vladimirovich raged silently. He expended enormous funds to find out what was happening in the world, had the data run through exquisitely trained and qualified experts, presented superbly organized reports to the old men who sat around that oaken table—and *still* they didn't listen!

And then there was the current problem.

This is how it will start, Andropov told himself, with another long sip of his Starka. It takes only one person, if it's the right person. Being the right person meant that people listened, paid attention to his words and deeds. And some people just got that sort of attention.

And those were the ones you had to be afraid of . . .

Karol, Karol, why must you make such trouble?

And trouble it would be if he took the action he threatened. The letter he'd sent to Warsaw hadn't been just for those lackeys in Warsaw—he had to have known where it would end up. He was no fool. In fact, he was as shrewd as any political figure Yuriy had ever known. You couldn't be a Catholic clergyman in a communist country and rise to the very pinnacle of the world's largest church, to be *their* General Secretary, even, without knowing how to operate the levers of power. But his post went back nearly two thousand years, if you happened to believe all that nonsense—well, maybe so. The age of the Roman church was an objective fact, wasn't it? Historical facts were historical facts, but that didn't make the belief structure underneath it any more valid than Marx said it was—or *wasn't,* to be more precise. Yuriy Vladimirovich had never considered belief in God to make any more sense than belief in Marx and Engels. But he knew that everyone had to believe in something, not because it was true, but because it in itself was a source of power. Lesser people, the ones who needed to be told what to do, had to believe in something larger than themselves. Primitives living in the remaining jungles of the world still heard in the thunder, not just the clash of hot air and cold, but the voice of some living thing. Why? Because they knew they were weaklings in a strong world, and they thought they could influence whatever deity controlled them with slaughtered pigs or even slaughtered children, and those who controlled that *influence* then acquired the power to shape their society. Power was its own currency. Some Great Men used it to gain comfort, or women—one of his own predecessors here at KGB had used it to get women, actually young girls, but Yuriy Vladimirovich did not share that particular vice. No, power was enough in and of itself. A man could bask in it as a cat warmed itself by a fire, with the simple enjoyment that came from having it close by, knowing that he enjoyed the ability to rule others, to bring death or comfort to those who served him, who pleased him with their obeisance and their fawning acknowledgment that he was greater than they.

There was more to it, of course. You had to *do* something with that power. You had to leave footprints in the sands of time. Good or bad, it didn't matter, just so they were large enough to command notice. In his case, a whole country needed his direction because, of all the men on the Politburo, only he could see what needed to be done. Only he could chart the course his nation needed to follow. And if he did it right, then he would be remembered. He knew that someday his life would end. In Andropov's case, it was a liver ailment. He ought not to drink his vodka, but with power also came the absolute right to choose his own path. No other man could tell him what to do. His latent intelligence knew that this was not always the wise thing to do, but Great Men did not listen to lesser men, and he considered himself the foremost of the former. Was not his force of will strong enough to define the world in which he lived? Of course it was, and so he had the occasional drink or two, or sometimes three, in the evening. Even more at official dinners. His country had long since passed beyond the point of rule by a single man—that had ended thirty years before with the passing of "Koba," Josef Vissarionovich Stalin, who'd ruled with a ruthlessness to make Ivan the Terrible quake in his boots. No, that sort of power was too dangerous to ruler and ruled. Stalin had made as many errors as good judgments, and as useful as the latter had been, the former had very nearly doomed the Soviet Union to perpetual backwardness—and, in fact, by creating the world's most formidable bureaucracy, he'd largely foresworn progress for his nation.

But one man, the right man, could lead and direct his political associates on the Politburo in the correct direction, and then by helping to select the new members, could accomplish the needed goals by influence rather than by terror. Just maybe, then, he could get his country moving again, keeping the single control that all nations needed, but adding the flexibility that they needed just as much for new things to happen—to achieve the True Communism—to see the Radiant Future that the writings of Lenin proclaimed awaited the Faithful.

Andropov did not quite see the contradiction in his own mind. Like so many Great Men, he was blind to those things that conflicted with his own capacious ego.

And, in any case, it all came back to Karol and the danger he posed.

He made a mental note for the morning staff meeting. He had to see what the possibilities were. The Politburo would wonder aloud how to deal with the problem announced by the Warsaw Letter, and eyes would turn to his chair, and he'd need something to say. The trick would be in finding something that would not frighten his colleagues out of their conservative wits. They were so fearful, these supposedly powerful men.

He read so many reports from his field officers, the talented spies of the First Chief Directorate, always probing into the thoughts of their counterparts. It was so strange, how much fear there was in the world, and the most fearful of all were so often those who held the power in their hands.

No, Andropov drained his glass and decided against another nightcap. The reason for their fear was that they worried they did not have the power. They were not strong. They were henpecked by their wives, just like factory workers and peasant farmers. They dreaded losing what they so greedily held, and so they used their power in ignoble enterprises directed at crushing those who would seize what they held. Even Stalin, that mightiest of despots, had used his power mainly to eliminate those who might sit in his elevated chair. And so the great Koba had spent his energy not looking forward, not looking outward, but looking down. He was like a woman in her kitchen who feared mice under her skirt, instead of a man with the power and the will to slay an onrushing tiger.

But could he do otherwise? Yes! Yes, he could look forward and see the future and chart a path to it. Yes, he could communicate his vision to the lesser men who sat around the table in the Kremlin, and lead them with the force of his will. Yes, he could find and refocus the vision of Lenin and all the thinkers of the governing philosophy of his country. Yes, he could alter the course of his nation and be forever remembered as a Great Man. . . .

But first, here and now, he'd need to deal with Karol and his annoying threat to the Soviet Union.

CHAPTER 2

VISIONS AND HORIZONS

CATHY ALMOST PANICKED at the thought of driving him to the train station. Seeing him walk to the left side of the car, she'd assumed, as any American would, that he'd be driving, and so she was visibly surprised when he tossed her the keys.

The pedals, she discovered, were the same as in an American car, because people all around the world were right-footed, even if those in England drove left-handed. The gear shift was in the center console, and so she had to use her left hand to shift. Backing out of the brick driveway was not terribly different from normal. Both instantly wondered if it was as hard for Brits to transform their driving to the right—in more ways than one—side of the road when they came to America, or hopped the ferry to France. Jack decided he'd ask somebody over a beer someday.

"Just remember, left is right, and right is left, and you drive on the wrong side of the road."

"Okay," she replied with annoyance. She knew she'd have to learn, and the rational part of her brain knew that this was as good a time as ever, even though *now* had a nasty way of appearing out of the ground like a guerrilla out of a spider hole. The way out of the mini-development took them past a one-story building that looked like it housed a doctor's office, past the park with the swing set that had sold Jack on this particular house. Sally liked swings, and she'd surely meet and make new friends here. And Little Jack would get some sun there, too. In the summer, anyway.

"Turn left, babe. It's a right turn here when you go left, you don't cross traffic."

"I know," Dr. Caroline Ryan said, wondering why Jack hadn't called for a cab. She still had a ton of work to do with the house, and didn't need a driving lesson. Well, at least it seemed to be a nimble car, she found, giving it a kick that was answered by rapid acceleration. Not her old Porsche, though.

"Bottom of the hill, turn right."

"Uh-huh." Good, this would be simple. She'd have to find her way home, and she hated asking for directions. It came from being a surgeon, as in command of her world as a fighter pilot in his cockpit. . . . And, being a surgeon, she wasn't allowed to panic, was she?

"Right here," Jack told her. "Remember oncoming traffic." There was none at the moment, but that would change, probably as soon as he got out of the car. He didn't envy her attempt to learn local navigation solo, but the surest way to learn to swim was to jump in—assuming you didn't drown. But the Brits were hospitable people, and if necessary some kind local driver would probably lead her all the way home.

The train station was about as impressive as a Bronx elevated platform, a smallish stone building with stairs and/or escalators that led down to the tracks. Ryan bought his ticket with cash, but noted a sign that offered books of commuter tickets for daily use. He picked up a copy of *The Daily Telegraph.* That would mark him to the locals as a conservative sort of person. Those of a more liberal bent chose *The Guardian.* He decided to pass on the tabloids that had naked women on the inside. Hell of a thing to see right after breakfast.

He had to wait about ten minutes for the train, which arrived with little noise, being a cross between an American electric intercity train and a subway. His ticket was first class, which placed him in a small compartment. The windows went up and down if you pulled on a leather strap, and the compartment door hinged outward to let him exit directly instead of walking down the corridor. With that set of discoveries made, Ryan sat down and scanned the paper's front page. As in America, local politics covered about half of the sheet, and Ryan looked at two of the articles, figuring he might as well learn the local customs and beefs. The schedule said about forty minutes to Victoria Station. Not too bad, and much better than driving it, Dan Murray had told him. In addition, parking a car in London was even worse than it was in New York, wrong side of the street and all.

The ride on the train was agreeably smooth. The trains were evidently a government-run monopoly, and somebody spent money on the roadbeds. A conductor took his ticket with a smile—doubtless marking Jack as a Yank instantly—and moved on, leaving Ryan to his paper. The passing scenery soon overtook his interest. The countryside was green and lush. The Brits did love their lawns. The row houses here were smaller than those in his childhood neighborhood in Baltimore, with what looked like slate roofs, and Jesus, the streets were narrow here. You'd really have to pay attention while driving, lest you end up in someone's living room. That probably wouldn't sit well, even to Englishmen accustomed to dealing with the shortcomings of visiting Yanks.

It was a clear day, some white fluffy clouds aloft, and the sky a delightful blue. He'd never experienced rain over here. Yet they had to have it. Every third man on the street carried a furled umbrella. And a lot of them wore hats. Ryan hadn't done that since his time in the Marine Corps. England was just different enough from America to be dangerous, he decided. There were a lot of similarities, but the differences rose up and bit you on the ass when you least expected them. He'd have to be very careful with Sally crossing the street. At four and a half, she was just imprinted enough to look the wrong way at the wrong time. He'd seen his little girl in the hospital once, and that was, by God, enough for a lifetime.

He was rumbling through a city now, a thick one. The right-of-way was elevated. He looked around for recognizable landmarks. Was that St. Paul's Cathedral off to the right? If so, he'd be at Victoria soon. He folded his paper. Then the train slowed, and—yeah. Victoria Station. He opened the compartment door like a native and stepped out on the platform. The station was a series of steel arches with embedded glass panes, long since blackened by the stack gasses of steam trains long departed. . . . But nobody had ever cleaned the glass. Or was it just air pollution that did it?

There was no telling. Jack followed the rest of the people to the brick wall that seemed to mark the station's waiting/arrival area. Sure enough, there were the usual collection of magazine stands and small stores. He could see the way out and found himself in the open air, fumbling in his pocket for his Chichester map of London. Westminster Bridge Road. It was too far to walk, so he hailed a cab.

From the cab, Ryan looked around, his head swiveling, just like the tourist he wasn't quite anymore. And there it was.

Century House, so named because it was 100 Westminster Bridge Road, was what Jack took to be a typical interwar structure of fair height and a stone façade that was . . . peeling off? The edifice was covered with an orange plastic netting that was manifestly intended to keep the façade from falling onto pedestrians. Oops. Maybe somebody was ripping through the building, looking for Russian bugs? Nobody had warned him about that at Langley. Just up the road was Westminster Bridge, and across that were the Houses of Parliament. Well, it was in a nice neighborhood, anyway. Jack trotted up the stone steps to the double door and made his way inside for all of ten feet, where he found an entry-control desk manned by someone in a sort of cop uniform.

"Can I help you, sir?" the guard asked. The Brits always said such things as though they really wanted to help you. Jack wondered if there might be a pistol just out of view. If not there, then not too far away. There had to be security here.

"Hi, I'm Jack Ryan. I'm starting work here."

Instant smile and recognition: "Ah, Sir John. Welcome to Century House. Please let me call upstairs." Which he did. "Someone's on his way down, sir. Please have a seat."

Jack barely had a chance to feel the seat when someone familiar came through the revolving door.

"Jack!" he called out.

"Sir Basil." Ryan rose to take his extended hand.

"Didn't expect you until tomorrow."

"I'm letting Cathy get everything unpacked. She doesn't trust me to do it anyway."

"Yes, we men do have our limitations, don't we?" Sir Basil Charleston was pushing fifty, tall and imperially thin, as the poet had once called it, with brown hair not yet going gray. His eyes were hazel and bright-looking, and he wore a suit that wasn't cheap, gray wool with a broad white pinstripe, looking to all the world like a very prosperous London merchant banker. In fact, his family had been in that line of work, but he'd found it confining, and opted instead to use his Cambridge education in the service of his country, first as a field intelligence officer, and later as an administrator. Jack knew that James Greer liked and respected him, as did Judge Moore. He'd met Charleston himself a year earlier, soon after being shot, then he'd learned that Sir Basil admired his invention of the Canary Trap, which had been his path to high-level notice at Langley. Basil had evidently used it to plug a few annoying leaks. "Come along, Jack. We need to get you properly outfitted." He didn't mean Jack's suit, which was Savile Row and as expensive as his own. No, this meant a trip to personnel.

The presence of C, as the job title went, made it painless. They already had a set of Ryan's fingerprints from Langley, and it was mainly a matter of getting his picture taken and inserted in his pass-card, which would allow him through all the electronic gates, just like the ones at the CIA. They checked it through a dummy gate and saw that it worked. Then it was up in the executive elevator to Sir Basil's capacious corner office.

It was better than the long, narrow room that Judge Moore made do with. A decent view of the river and the Palace of Westminster. The DG waved Jack into a leather chair.

"So, any first impressions?" Charleston asked.

"Pretty painless so far. Cathy hasn't been to the hospital yet, but Bernie—her boss at Hopkins—says that the boss-doc there is a good guy."

"Yes, Hammersmith has a good reputation, and Dr. Byrd is regarded as the best eye surgeon in Britain. Never met him, but I'm told he's a fine chap. Fisherman, loves to take salmon out of the rivers in Scotland, married, three sons, eldest is a *lef*tenant in the Coldstream Guards."

"You had him checked out?" Jack asked incredulously.

"One cannot be too careful, Jack. Some of your distant cousins across the Irish Sea are not overly fond of you, you know."

"Is that a problem?"

Charleston shook his head. "Most unlikely. When you helped to bring down the ULA, you probably saved a few lives in the PIRA. That's still sorting itself out, but that is mainly a job for the Security Service. We don't really have much business with them—at least nothing that will concern you directly." Which led to Jack's next question.

"Yes, Sir Basil—what exactly is my job to be here?"

"Didn't James tell you?" Charleston asked.

"Not exactly. He likes his surprises, I've learned."

"Well, the Joint Working Group mainly focuses on our Soviet friends. We have some good sources. So do your chaps. The idea is to share information in order to improve our overall picture."

"Information. Not sources," Ryan observed.

Charleston smiled understandingly. "One must protect those, as you know."

Jack did know about that. In fact, he was allowed to know damned little about CIA's sources. Those were the most closely guarded secrets in the Agency, and doubtless here as well. Sources were real people, and a slip of the tongue would get them killed. Intelligence services valued sources more for their information than for their lives—the intelligence business was a business, after all—but sooner or later you started worrying about them and their families and their personal characteristics. *Mainly booze,* Ryan thought. Especially for the Russians. The ordinary Soviet citizen drank enough to qualify him as an alcoholic in America.

"No problem there, sir. I do not know the name or identity of one CIA source over there. Not one," Ryan emphasized. It wasn't quite true. He hadn't been told, but you could guess a lot from the character of the information transmitted and the way he/she quoted people—they were usually "he," but Ryan wondered about a few of the sources. It was an intriguing game that all analysts played, invariably in the confines of their own minds, though Ryan had speculated a few times with his personal boss, Admiral Jim Greer. Usually, the DDO had warned him not to speculate too loudly, but the way he'd blinked twice had told Ryan more than he'd wanted to convey. Well, they'd hired him for his analytical ability, Ryan knew. They didn't really want him to turn it off. When the information transmitted got a little kinky, it told you that something had happened to the source, like being caught, or going nuts. "The admiral is interested in one thing, though. . . ."

"What's that?" the DG asked.

"Poland. It looks to us as though it's coming a little unglued, and we're wondering how far, how fast, and what it'll do—the effects, I mean."

"So are we, Jack." A thoughtful nod. People—especially reporters in their Fleet Street pubs—were speculating a lot about that. And reporters also had good sources, in some areas as good as his own. "What does James think?"

"It reminds both of us of something that happened in the 1930s." Ryan leaned back in the chair and relaxed. "The United Auto Workers. When they organized Ford, there was trouble. Big time. Ford even hired thugs to work the union organizers over. I remember seeing photos of—who was it?" Jack paused for a moment's thought. "Walter Reuther? Something like that. It was in *Life* magazine back then. The thugs were talking to him and a few of his guys—the first few pictures show them smiling at each other like men do right before the gloves come off—and then a brawl started. You have to wonder about Ford's management—letting something like that happen in front of reporters is bad enough, but reporters with *cameras?* Damn, that's big-league dumb."

"The Court of Public Opinion. Yes," Charleston agreed. "It is quite real, and modern technology has made it even more so, and, yes, that is troubling to our friends across the wire. You know, this CNN news network that just started up on your side of the ocean. It just might change the world. Information has its own way of circulating. Rumors are bad enough. You cannot stop them, and they have a way of acquiring a life of their own—"

"But a picture really is worth a thousand words, isn't it?"

"I wonder who first said that. Whoever he was, he was no one's fool. It's even more true for a moving picture."

"I presume we're using that . . ."

"Your chaps are reticent about doing so. I am less so. It's easy enough to have an embassy functionary have a pint with some reporter and maybe drop the odd hint in the course of a conversation. One thing about reporters, they are not ungracious if you give them the odd decent story."

"At Langley, they hate the press, Sir Basil. And I do mean *hate*."

"Rather backward of them. But, then, we can exercise more control over the press here than you can in America, I suppose. Still and all, it's not that hard to outsmart them, is it?"

"I've never tried. Admiral Greer says that talking to a reporter is like dancing with a rottweiler. You can't be sure if he's going to lick your face or rip your throat out."

"They're not bad dogs at all, you know. You just need to train them properly."

Brits and their dogs, Ryan reflected. *They like their pets more than their kids.* He didn't care for big dogs all that much. A Labrador like Ernie was different. Labs had a soft mouth. Sally really missed him.

"So, what's your take on Poland, Jack?"

"I think the pot's going to simmer until the lid slides off, and then when it boils over, there's going to be a hell of a mess. The Poles haven't really bought into communism all that well. Their army has *chaplains,* for Christ's sake. A lot of their farmers operate on a free-agent basis, selling hams and stuff. The most popular TV show over there is *Kojak,* they even show it on Sunday morning to draw people away from going to church. That shows two things. The people there like American culture, and the government is still afraid of the Catholic Church. The Polish government is unstable, and they know they're unstable. Allowing a little wiggle room is probably smart, at least in the short term, but the fundamental problem is that they operate a fundamentally unjust regime. Unjust countries are not stable, sir. However strong they appear, they're rotten underneath."

Charleston nodded thoughtfully. "I briefed the PM just three days ago out at Chequers, and told her much the same thing." The Director General paused for a moment, then decided. He lifted a file folder from the pile on his desk and handed it across.

The cover read MOST SECRET. *So,* Jack thought, *now it starts.* He wondered if Basil had learned to swim by falling into the Thames, and thought everyone should learn the same way.

Flipping the cover open, he saw that this information came from a source called WREN. He was clearly Polish, and by the look of the report, well placed, and what he said—

"Damn," Ryan observed. "This is reliable?"

"Very much so. It's a five-five, Jack." By that he meant that the source was rated 5 on a scale of 5 for reliability, and the importance of the information reported was graded the same way. "You're Catholic, I think." He knew, of course. It was just the English way of talking.

"Jesuits at high school, Boston College, and Georgetown, plus the nuns at Saint Matthew's. I'd better be."

"What do you think of your new Pope?"

"First non-Italian in four centuries, maybe more: That's saying something right there. When I heard the new one was Polish, I expected it to be Cardinal Wiszynski from Warsaw—guy's got the brains of a genius and the cunning of a fox. This guy, I didn't know beans about, but from what I've read since, he's a very solid citizen. Good parish priest, good administrator, politically very astute . . ." Ryan paused. He was discussing the head of his church as though he were a political candidate, and he was damned sure there was more substance to him than that. This had to be a man of deep faith, with the sort of core convictions that an earthquake couldn't budge or crack. He'd been chosen by other such men to be the leader and spokesman for the world's largest church, which, by the way, also happened to be Ryan's church. He'd be a man who didn't fear much of anything, a man for whom a bullet was his get-out-of-jail-free card, a key to God's own presence. And he'd be a man who felt God's presence in everything he did. He was not someone you could scare, not someone you could turn away from what he deemed the right thing.

"If he wrote this letter, Sir Basil, it's not a bluff. When was it delivered?"

"Less than four days ago. Our chap broke a rule getting it to us so quickly, but its importance is patently clear, is it not?"

Welcome to London, Jack, Ryan thought. He'd just fallen into the soup. A big pot, like they used to boil missionaries in the cartoons.

"Okay, it's been forwarded to Moscow, right?"

"So our chap tells us. So, Sir John, what will Ivan have to say about this?" And with that question, Sir Basil Charleston lit the fire under Jack's personal cauldron.

"That's a multifaceted question," Ryan said, dodging as artfully as the situation allowed.

It wasn't very far: "He will say something," Charleston observed, leveling his hazel eyes at Ryan.

"Okay, they won't like it. They will see it as a threat. The questions are how seriously they will take it and how much credence they will attach to it. Stalin might have laughed it off . . . or maybe not. Stalin defined paranoia, didn't he?" Ryan paused and looked out the windows. Was that a rain cloud blowing in? "No, Stalin would have acted somehow."

"Think so?" Charleston was evaluating him, Jack knew. This was like the orals for his doctorate at Georgetown. Father Tim Riley's rapier wit and needlepoint questions. Sir Basil was more civilized than the acerbic priest, but this exam was not going to be an easy one.

"Leon Trotsky was no threat to him. That assassination came from a combination of paranoia and pure meanness. It was a personal thing. Stalin made enemies, and he never forgot them. But the current Soviet leadership doesn't have the guts to do the stuff he did."

Charleston pointed out the plate glass window toward Westminster Bridge. "My lad, the Russians had the intestinal fortitude to kill a man right on that bridge, less than five years ago—"

"And got blamed for it," Ryan reminded his host. It had been a combination of good luck and a very smart British doctor, and it hadn't been worth a damn in saving the poor bastard's life. They had identified the cause of death, though, and it hadn't resulted from a street hood.

"Think they lost any sleep over that incident? I do not," C assured him.

"Looks bad. They don't do much of this anymore, not that I've heard about."

"Only at home, I grant you that. But Poland is 'home' for them, well within their sphere of influence."

"But the Pope lives in Rome, and that *isn't.* It comes down to how scared they are, sir. Father Tim Riley at Georgetown, back when I got my doctorate, he said never to forget that wars are begun by frightened men. They fear war, but more than that, they fear what will happen if they don't start one—or take equivalent action, I suppose. So, the real questions are, as I said, how seriously they will take the threat and how serious it will appear to them. On the former, yes, I don't think this is a bluff. The Pope's character, background, and personal courage—those are not things to be doubted. So the threat is a real one. The larger question is how to evaluate the magnitude of the threat to them. . . ."

"Go on," the Director General ordered gently.

"If they're smart enough to recognize it—yes, sir, in their position, I'd be concerned about it . . . maybe even a little frightened. As much as the Soviets think they're a superpower—America's equal and all that—deep down they know that their state is not really legitimate. Kissinger gave a lecture to us at Georgetown. . . ." Jack leaned back and closed his eyes for a moment to recapture the performance. "It was something he said near the end, talking about the character of the Russian leaders. Brezhnev was showing him around some official building or other in the Kremlin, where Nixon was going to come for his last summit meeting. He was lifting cloth covers off the statuary, showing how they'd taken the time to clean everything up in preparation for the visit. Why do that, I wondered at the time. I mean, sure, they have maids and maintenance people. Why make a point of showing it to Henry? It has to be a sense of inferiority, fundamental insecurity. We keep hearing that they're ten feet tall, but I don't think so, and the more I learn about them, the less formidable I think they are. The Admiral and I have argued this one back and forth for the last couple of months. They have a large military. Their intelligence services are first-rate. They are *big*. Big ugly bear, like Muhammad Ali used to say, but you know, Ali beat the bear twice, didn't he?

"That's a roundabout way of saying that, yes, sir, I think this letter will scare them. Question is, scare them enough to do something?" Ryan shook his head. "Possibly yes, but we have insufficient data at this time. If they decide to push that particular button, will we know beforehand?"

Charleston had been waiting for Ryan to turn the tables on him. "One can hope so, but it's impossible to be sure."

"In the year I've been at Langley, the impression I get is that our knowledge of the target is deep but narrow in some areas, shallow and broad in others. I've yet to meet somebody who feels comfortable analyzing them—well, that's not exactly true. Some are comfortable, but their analyses are often—to me at least—unreliable. Like the stuff we get on their economy—"

"James lets you into that?" Basil was surprised.

"The Admiral sent me all around the barn the first couple of months. My first degree was economics from Boston College. I passed my CPA exam before I went away with the Marine Corps—certified public accountant. You call it something different over here. Then, after I left the Corps, I did okay in the stock-and-bond business before I finished up my doctorate and went into teaching."

"Exactly how much did you make on Wall Street?"

"While I was at Merrill Lynch? Oh, between six and seven million. A lot of that was the Chicago and North Western Railroad. My uncle Mario—my mom's brother—told me that the employees were going to buy out the stock and try to get the railroad profitable again. I took a look at it and liked what I saw. It paid off a net of twenty-three to one on my investment. I ought to have dropped more into it, but they taught me to be conservative at Merrill Lynch. Never worked in New York, by the way. I was in the Baltimore office. Anyway, the money's still in stocks, and the market looks pretty healthy at the moment. I still dabble in it. You never know when you're going to stumble across a winner, and it's still an interesting hobby."

"Indeed. If you see anything promising, do let me know."

"No fees—but no guarantees, either," Ryan joked.

"I'm not accustomed to those, Jack, not in this bloody business. I'm going to assign you to our Russian working group with Simon Harding. Oxford graduate, doctorate in Russian literature. You'll see just about everything he sees—everything but source information—" Ryan stopped him with two raised hands.

"Sir Basil, I do not want to know that stuff. I don't need it, and knowing it would keep me awake at night. Just so I see the raw. I prefer to do my own analysis. This Harding guy is smart?" Ryan asked with deliberate artlessness.

"Very much so. You've probably seen his product before. He did the personal evaluation on Yuriy Andropov we turned out two years ago."

"I did read that. Yeah, that was good work. I figured he was a pshrink."

"He's read psychology, but not quite enough for a degree. Simon's a clever lad. Wife is an artist, painter, lovely lady."

"Right now?"

"Why not? I must get back to my work. Come, I'll walk you down."

It wasn't far. Ryan immediately learned that he'd be sharing an office right here on the top floor. This came as a surprise. Getting to the Seventh Floor at Langley took years, and often meant climbing over bloody bodies. Somebody, Jack speculated, must have thought he was smart.

Simon Harding's office was not overly impressive. The two windows overlooked the upriver side of the building, mainly two- and three-story brick structures of indeterminate occupancy. Harding himself was crowding forty, pale and fair-haired with china-blue eyes. He wore an unbuttoned vest—waistcoat locally—and a drab tie. His desk was covered with folders trimmed in striped tape, the universal coding for secret material.

"You must be Sir John," Harding said, setting down his briar pipe.

"The name's Jack," Ryan corrected him. "I'm really not allowed to pretend I'm a knight. Besides, I don't own a horse or a steel shirt." Jack shook hands with his workmate. Harding had small, bony hands, but those blue eyes looked smart.

"Take good care of him, Simon." Sir Basil immediately took his leave.

There was already a swivel chair in place at a suspiciously clean desk. Jack tried it out. The room was going to be a little crowded, but not too badly so. His desk phone had a scrambler under it for making secure calls, Ryan wondered if it worked as well as the STU he'd had at Langley. GCHQ out at Cheltenham worked closely with NSA, and maybe it was the same innards with a different plastic case. He'd have to keep reminding himself that he was in a foreign country. That ought not to be too hard, Ryan hoped. People did talk funny here: gr*ah*ss, r*ah*sberry and c*ah*stle, for example, though the effect of American movies and global television was perverting the English language to the American version slowly but surely.

"Did Bas talk to you about the Pope?" Simon asked.

"Yeah. That letter could be a bombshell. He's wondering how Ivan's going to react to it."

"We all are, Jack. You have any ideas?"

"I just told your boss, if Stalin was sitting there, he might want to shorten the Pope's life, but that would be a hell of a big gamble."

"The problem, I think, is that although they are rather collegial in their decision-making, Andropov is in the ascendancy, and he might be less reticent than the rest of them."

Jack settled back in to his chair. "You know, my wife's friends at Hopkins flew over there a couple of years ago. Mikhail Suslov had diabetic retinopathy of the eyes—he was also a high myope, very nearsighted—and they went over to fix it, and to teach some Russian docs how to do the procedure. Cathy was just a resident then. But Bernie Katz was on the fly team. He's the director at Wilmer. Super eye surgeon, hell of a good guy. The Agency interviewed him and the others after they came back. Ever see that document?"

There was interest in his eyes now: "No. Is it any good?"

"One of the things I've learned being married to a doc is that I listen to what she says about people. I'd damned sure listen to Bernie. It's worth reading. There's a universal tendency for people to talk straight to surgeons and, like I said, docs are good for seeing things that most of us miss. They said Suslov was smart, courteous, businesslike, but underneath he was the sort of guy you wouldn't trust with a gun in his hand—or more likely a knife. He really didn't like the fact that he needed Americans to save his sight for him. It didn't tickle his fancy that no Russians were able to do what he needed done. On the other hand, they said that the hospitality was Olympic-class once they did the job. So they're not complete barbarians, which Bernie halfway expected—he's Jewish, family from Poland, back when it belonged to the czar, I think. Want me to have the Agency send that one over?"

Harding waved a match over his pipe. "Yes, I would like to see that. The Russians—they're a rum lot, you know. In some ways, wonderfully cultured. Russia is the last place in the world where a man can make a decent living as a poet. They revere their poets, and I rather admire that about them, but at the same time . . . you know, Stalin himself was reticent about going after artists—the writing sort, that is. I remember one chap who lived years longer than one would have expected. . . . Even so, he eventually died in the Gulag. So, their civilization has its limits."

"You speak the language? I never learned it."

The Brit analyst nodded. "It can be a wonderful language for literature, rather like Attic Greek. It lends itself to poetry, but it masks a capacity for barbarism that makes the blood run cold. They are a fairly predictable people in many ways, especially their political decisions, within limits. Their unpredictability lies in playing off their inherent conservatism against their dogmatic political outlook. Our friend Suslov is seriously ill, heart problems—from the diabetes, I suppose—but the chap behind him is Mikhail Yevgeniyevich Alexandrov, equal parts Russian and Marxist, with the morals of Lavrenti Beria. He bloody hates the West. I expect he counseled Suslov—they are old, old friends—to accept blindness rather than submit to American physicians. And if this Katz chap is Jewish, you said? That would not have helped, either. Not an attractive chap at all. When Suslov departs—a few months, we think—he'll be the new ideologue on the Politburo. He will back Yuriy Vladimirovich on anything he wishes to do, even if it means a physical attack on His Holiness."

"You really think it could go that far?" Jack asked.

"Could it? Possibly, yes."

"Okay, has this letter been sent to Langley?"

Harding nodded. "Your local Station Chief came over to collect it today. I would expect your chaps have their own sources, but there's no sense taking chances."

"Agreed. You know, if Ivan does anything that extreme, there's going to be hell to pay."

"Perhaps so, but they do not see things in the same way we do, Jack."

"I know. Hard to make the full leap of imagination, however."

"It does take time," Simon agreed.

"Does reading their poetry help?" Ryan wondered. He'd only seen a little of it, and only in translation, which was not how one read poetry.

Harding shook his head. "Not really. That's how some of them protest. The protests have to be sufficiently roundabout that the more obtuse of their readers can just enjoy the lyrical tribute to a particular girl's figure without noticing the cry for freedom of expression. There must be a whole section of KGB that analyzes the poems for the hidden political content, to which no one pays particular attention until the Politburo members notice that the sexual content is a little too explicit. They are a bunch of prudes, you know. . . . How very odd of them to have that sort of morality and no other."

"Well, one can hardly knock them for disapproving *Debbie Does Dallas,*" Ryan suggested.

Harding nearly choked on his pipe smoke. "Quite so. Not exactly *King Lear,* is it? They did produce Tolstoy, Chekhov, and Pasternak."

Jack hadn't read any of them, but this didn't seem the time to admit to it.

"HE SAID *WHAT*?" Alexandrov asked.

The outrage was predictable, but remarkably muted, Andropov thought. Perhaps he only raised his voice for a fuller audience, or more likely his subordinates over at the Party Secretariat building.

"Here is the letter, and the translation," the KGB Chairman said, handing over the documents.

The chief-ideologue-in-waiting took the message forms and read them over slowly. He didn't want his rage to miss a single nuance. Andropov waited, lighting a Marlboro as he did so. His guest didn't touch the vodka that he'd poured, the Chairman noted.

"This holy man grows ambitious," he said finally, setting the papers down on the coffee table.

"I would agree with that," Yuriy observed.

Amazement in his voice: "Does he feel invulnerable? Does he not know that there are consequences for such threats?"

"My experts feel that his words are genuine, and, no, they believe he does not fear the possible consequences."

"If martyrdom is what he wishes, perhaps we should accommodate him. . . ." The way his voice trailed off caused a chill even in Andropov's cold blood. It was time for a warning. The problem with ideologues was that their theories did not always take reality into proper account, a fact to which they were mostly blind.

"Mikhail Yevgeniyevich, such actions are not to be undertaken lightly. There could be political consequences."

"No, not great ones, Yuriy. Not great ones," Alexandrov repeated himself. "But, yes, I agree, what we do in reply must be considered fully before we take the necessary action."

"What does Comrade Suslov think? Have you consulted him?"

"Misha is very ill," Alexandrov replied, without any great show of regret. That surprised Andropov. His guest owed much to his ailing senior, but these ideologues lived in their own little circumscribed world. "I fear his life is coming to its end."

That part was not a surprise. You only had to look at him at the Politburo meetings. Suslov had the desperate look you saw on the face of a man who knew that his time was running out. He wanted to make the world right before he departed from it, but he also knew that such an act was beyond his capacity, a fact that had come to him as an unwelcome surprise. Did he finally grasp the reality that Marxism-Leninism was a false path? Andropov had come to that conclusion about five years before. But that wasn't the sort of thing one talked about in the Kremlin, was it? And not with Alexandrov, either.

"He has been a good comrade these many years. If what you say is true, he will be sorely missed," the KGB Chairman noted soberly, genuflecting to the altar of Marxist theory and its dying priest.

"That is so," Alexandrov agreed, playing his role as his host did—as all Politburo members did, because it was expected . . . because it was necessary. Not because it was true, or even approximately so.

Like his guest, Yuriy Vladimirovich believed not because he believed, but because what he *purported* to believe was the source of the real thing: power. What, the Chairman wondered, would this man say next? Andropov needed him, and Alexandrov needed *him* as well, perhaps even more. Mikhail Yevgeniyevich did not have the personal power needed to become General Secretary of the Communist Party of the Soviet Union. He was respected for his theoretical knowledge, his devotion to the state religion that Marxism-Leninism had become, but no one who sat around the table thought him a proper candidate for leadership. But his support would be vital to whoever did have that ambition. As in medieval times, when the eldest son became the lord of the manor, and the second son became the bishop of the attendant diocese, so Alexandrov, like Suslov in his time, had to provide the spiritual—was that the proper word?—justification for his ascension to power. The system of checks and balances remained, just more perversely than before.

"You will, of course, take his place when the time comes," Andropov offered as the promise of an alliance.

Alexandrov demurred, of course . . . or pretended to: "There are many good men in the Party Secretariat."

The Chairman of the Committee for State Security waved his hand dismissively. "You are the most senior and the most trusted."

Which Alexandrov well knew. "You are kind to say so, Yuriy. So, what will we do about this foolish Pole?"

And that, so baldly stated, would be the cost of the alliance. To get Alexandrov's support for the General Secretaryship, Andropov would have to make the ideologue's blanket a little thicker by . . . well, by doing something he was already thinking about anyway. That was painless, wasn't it?

The KGB Chairman adopted a clinical, businesslike tone of voice: "Misha, to undertake an operation of this sort is not a trivial or a simple exercise. It must be planned very carefully, prepared with the greatest caution and thoroughness, and then the Politburo must approve it with open eyes."

"You must have something in mind. . . ."

"I have many things in mind, *but* a daydream is not a plan. To move forward requires some in-depth thinking and planning merely to see if such a thing is possible. One cautious step at a time," Andropov warned. "Even then, there are no guarantees or promises to be made. This is not something for a movie production. The real world, Misha, is complex." It was as close as he could come to telling Alexandrov not to stray too far from his sandbox of theories and toys and into the real world of blood and consequences.

"Well, you are a good Party man. You know what the stakes in this game are." With those words, Alexandrov told his host what was expected by the Secretariat. For Mikhail Yevgeniyevich, the Party and its beliefs were the State—and the KGB was the Sword and Shield of the Party.

Oddly, Andropov realized, this Polish Pope surely felt the same about his beliefs and his view of the world. But those beliefs weren't, strictly speaking, an ideology, were they? *Well, for these purposes, they might as well be,* Yuriy Vladimirovich told himself.

"My people will look at this carefully. We cannot do the impossible, Misha, but—"

"But what is impossible for this agency of the Soviet state?" A rhetorical question with a bloody answer. And a dangerous one, more dangerous than this academician realized.

How alike they were, the KGB Chairman realized. This one, comfortably sipping his brown Starka, believed absolutely in an ideology that could not be proven. And he desired the death of a man who also believed things that could not be proved. What a curious state of affairs. A battle of ideas, both sets of which feared the other. Feared? What did Karol fear? Not death, certainly. His letter to Warsaw proclaimed that without words. Indeed, he cried aloud for death. He *sought* martyrship. *Why would a man seek that?* the Chairman wondered briefly. To use his life or death as a weapon against his enemy. Surely he regarded both Russia and communism as enemies, one for nationalistic reasons, the other for reasons of his religious conviction. . . . But did he *fear* that enemy?

No, probably not, Yuriy Vladimirovich admitted to himself. That made his task harder. His was an agency that needed fear to get its way. Fear was its source of power, and a man lacking fear was a man he could not manipulate. . . .

But those whom he could not manipulate could always be killed. Who, after all, remembered much about Leon Trotsky?

"Few things are truly impossible. Merely difficult," the Chairman belatedly agreed.

"So, you will look into the possibilities?"

He nodded cautiously. "Yes, starting in the morning." And so the processes began.

CHAPTER 3

EXPLORATIONS

WELL, JACK'S GOT HIS DESK in London," Greer told his colleagues on the Seventh Floor.

"Glad to hear it," Bob Ritter observed. "Think he knows what to do with it?"

"Bob, what is it with you and Ryan?" the DDI asked.

"Your fair-haired boy is moving up the ladder too fast. He's going to fall off someday and it's going to be a mess."

"You want me to turn him into just one more ordinary desk-weenie?" James Greer had often enough fended off Ritter's beefs about the size and consequent power of the Intelligence Directorate. "You have some burgeoning stars in your shop, too. This kid's got possibilities, and I'm going to let him run until he hits the wall."

"Yeah, I can hear the *splat* now," the DDO grumbled. "Okay, which one of the crown jewels does he want to hand over to our British cousins?"

"Nothing much. The appraisal of Mikhail Suslov that the doctors up at Johns Hopkins did when they flew over to fix his eyes."

"They don't have that already?" Judge Moore asked. It wasn't as though it were a super-sensitive document.

"I guess they never asked. Hell, Suslov won't be around much longer anyway, from what we've been seeing."

The CIA had many ways to determine the health of senior Soviet officials. The most commonly used was photographs or, better yet, motion-picture coverage of the people in question. The Agency employed physicians—most often full professors at major medical schools—to look at the photos and diagnose their ills without getting within four thousand miles of them. It wasn't good medicine, but it was better than nothing. Also, the American Ambassador, every time he went into the Kremlin, came back to the embassy and dictated his impressions of everything he saw, however small and insignificant it might seem. Often enough, people had lobbied for putting a physician in the post of ambassador, but it had never happened. More often, direct DO operations had been aimed at collecting urine samples of important foreign statesmen, since urine was a good diagnostic source of information. It made for some unusual plumbing arrangements at Blair House, across the street from the White House, where foreign dignitaries were often quartered, plus the odd attempt to break into doctors' offices all over the world. And gossip, there was always gossip, especially over there. All of this came from the fact that a man's health played a role in his thinking and decision-making. All three men in this office had joked about hiring a gypsy or two and observed, rightly, that it would have produced results no less accurate than they got from well-paid professional intelligence officers. At Fort Meade, Maryland, was yet another operation, code-named STARGATE, where the Agency employed people who were well to the left of gypsies; it had been started mainly because the Soviets also employed such people.

"How sick is he?" Moore asked.

"From what I saw three days ago, he won't make Christmas. Acute coronary insufficiency, they say. We have a shot of him popping what looks like a nitroglycerine pill, not a good sign for Red Mike," James Greer concluded with Suslov's in-house nickname.

"And Alexandrov replaces him? Some bargain," Ritter observed tersely. "I think the gypsies switched them at birth—another True Believer in the Great God Marx."

"We can't all be Baptists, Robert," Arthur Moore pointed out.

"This came in two hours ago on the secure fax from London," Greer said, passing the sheets around. He'd saved the best for last. "Might be important," the DDI added.

Bob Ritter was a multilingual speed-reader: "Jesus!"

Judge Moore took his time. *As a judge should,* he thought. About twenty seconds later than the DDO: "My goodness." A pause. "Nothing about this from our sources?"

Ritter shifted in his chair. "Takes time, Arthur, and the Foleys are still settling in."

"I presume we'll hear about this from CARDINAL." They didn't often invoke *that* agent's code name. In the pantheon of CIA crown jewels, he was the Cullinan Diamond.

"We should, if Ustinov talks about it, as I expect he will. If they do something about it—"

"Will they, gentlemen?" the DCI asked.

"They'll sure as hell think about it," Ritter opined at once.

"It's a big step to take," Greer thought more soberly. "You suppose His Holiness is courting it? Not too many men walk up to the tiger, open the cage door, and then make faces at him."

"I'll have to show this to the President tomorrow." Moore paused for a moment's thought. His weekly meeting at the White House was set for 10:00 the following morning. "The Papal Nuncio is out of town, isn't he?" It turned out that the others didn't know. He'd have to have that one checked out.

"What would you say to him, anyway?" This was Ritter. "You have to figure that the other guys in Rome tried to talk him out of this."

"James?"

"Kinda takes us back to Nero, doesn't it? It's almost as though he's threatening the Russians with his own death. . . . Damn, do people really think that way?"

"Forty years ago, you put your life on the line, James." Greer had served his time on fleet boats in the Second World War, and often wore a miniature of his gold dolphins on the lapel of his suit coat.

"Arthur, I took my chances, along with everybody else on the boat. I did *not* tell Tojo where I was in a personal letter."

"The man has some serious *cojones,* guys," Ritter breathed. "We have seen this sort of thing before. Dr. King never took a step back in his life, did he?"

"And I suppose the KKK was as dangerous to him as the KGB is to the Pope," Moore completed the thought. "Men of the cloth have a different way of looking at the world. It's called 'virtue,' I think." He sat forward. "Okay, when the President asks me about this—and for damned sure he will—what the hell do I tell him?"

"Our Russian friends might just decide that His Holiness has lived long enough," Ritter answered.

"That's a hell of a big and dangerous step to take," Greer objected. "Not the sort of thing a committee does."

"This committee might," the DDO told the DDI.

"There would be hell to pay, Bob. They know that. These men are chess players, not gamblers."

"This letter backs them into a corner." Ritter turned. "Judge, I think the Pope's life might be in danger."

"It's much too early to say that," Greer objected.

"Not when you remember who's running KGB. Andropov is a Party man. What loyalty he has is to that institution, damned sure not to anything we would recognize as a principle. If this frightens, or merely worries them, they will think about it. The Pope has hurled down his gauntlet at their feet, gentlemen," the Deputy Director (Operations) told the others. "They just might pick it up."

"Has any Pope ever done this?" Moore asked.

"Resign his post? Not that I can remember," Greer admitted. "I don't even know if there's a mechanism for this. I grant you it's one hell of a gesture. We have to assume he means it. I don't see this as a bluff."

"No," Judge Moore agreed. "It can't be that."

"He's loyal to his people. He has to be. He was a parish priest once upon a time. He's christened babies, officiated at weddings. He *knows* these people. Not as an amorphous mass—he's been there to baptize and bury them. They are *his* people. He probably thinks of all Poland as his own parish. Will he be loyal to them, even at the peril of his life? How can he not be?" Ritter leaned forward. "It's not just a question of personal courage. If he doesn't do it, the Catholic Church loses face. No, guys, he's serious as hell, and he isn't bluffing. Question is, what the hell can we do about it?"

"Warn the Russians off?" Moore wondered aloud.

"No chance," Ritter shot back. "You know better than that, Arthur. If they set up an operation, it'll have more cutouts than anything the Mafia's ever done. How good do you suppose security is around him?"

"Not a clue," the DCI admitted. "I know the Swiss Guards exist, with their pretty uniforms and pikes. . . . Didn't they fight once?"

"I think so," Greer observed. "Somebody tried to kill him, and they fought a rear-guard action while he skipped town. Most of them got killed, I think."

"Now they mostly pose for pictures and tell people where the bathroom is, probably," Ritter thought out loud. "But there has to be something to what they do. The Pope is too prominent a figure not to attract the odd nutcase. The Vatican is technically a sovereign state. It has to have some of the mechanisms of a country. I suppose we could warn them—"

"Only when we have something to warn them about. Which we don't have, do we?" Greer pointed out. "He knew when he sent this off that he'd be rattling a few cages. What protection he does have must be alerted already."

"This will get the President's attention, too. He's going to want to know more, and he's going to want options. Jesus, people, ever since he made that Evil Empire speech, there's been trouble across the river. If they really do something, even if we can't pin it on them, he's going to erupt like Mount Saint Helens. There's damned near a hundred million Catholics right here in America, and a lot of them voted for him."

For his part, James Greer wondered how far out of control this might spin. "Gentlemen, all we have to this point is a fax of a photocopy of a letter delivered to the government in Warsaw. We do not know for certain that it's gone to Moscow yet. We have no sign of any reaction to this from Moscow. Now, we can't tell the Russians we know about it. So we can't warn them off. We can't tip our hand in any way. We can't tell the Pope that we're concerned, for the same reason. If Ivan's going to react, hopefully one of Bob's people will get us the word, and the Vatican has its own intelligence service, and we know that's pretty good. So, for the moment, all we have is an interesting bit of information that is probably true, but even that is not yet confirmed."

"So, for the moment, you think we just sit on this and think it through?" Moore asked.

"There's nothing else we can do, Arthur. Ivan won't act very fast. He never does—not on something with this degree of political import. Bob?"

"Yeah, you're probably right," the DDI agreed. "Still, the President needs to hear about it."

"It's a little thin for that," Greer cautioned. "But, yes, I suppose so." Mainly he knew that *not* telling the President, and then having something dire happen, would cause all of them to seek new employment. "If it goes further in Moscow, we ought to hear about it before anything drastic happens."

"Fine, I can tell him that," Judge Moore agreed. *Mr. President, we're taking a very close look at this.* That sort of thing usually worked. Moore rang his secretary and asked for some coffee to be sent in. Tomorrow at ten, they'd brief the President in the Oval Office, and then after lunch would be his weekly sit-down with the chiefs of the other services, DIA and NSA, to see what interesting things they had happening. The order should have been reversed, but that's just how things were usually scheduled.

HIS FIRST DAY at work had lingered quite a bit longer than expected before he'd been able to leave. Ed Foley was impressed by the Moscow Metro. The decorator must have been the same madman who'd designed Moscow State University's wedding-cake stonework—evidently beloved of Joe Stalin, whose personal aesthetic had run the gamut from Y to Z. It was strangely reminiscent of the czarist palaces, as interpreted by a terminal alcoholic. That said, the metro was superbly engineered, if somewhat clunky. More to the point, the crush of people was very agreeable to the spook. Making a brush-pass or other sort of pickup from an agent would not be overly trying, so long as he kept to his training, and that was something Edward Francis Foley was good at. Mary Pat would love it here, he was sure now. The milieu for her would be like Disney World was for

Eddie. The crush of people, all speaking Russian. His Russian was pretty good. Hers was literary, having learned it at her grandfather's knee, though she'd have to de-tune it, lest she be made out as someone whose language skills were a little too good to be merely those of the wife of a minor embassy official.

The subway worked well for him. With one station only a couple of blocks from the embassy, and the other practically at their apartment house's doorstep, even the most paranoid Directorate Two shadow would not find his use of it terribly suspicious, despite the well-known American love for cars. He didn't look around any more than a tourist would, and thought that maybe he'd made one tail. There'd probably be more than that for the moment. He was a new embassy employee, and the Russians would want to see if he wiggled like a CIA spook. He decided to act like an innocent American abroad, which might or might not be the same thing to them. It depended on how experienced his current shadow was, and there was no telling that. For certain, he'd have a tail for a couple weeks. That was an expected annoyance. So would Mary Pat. So, probably, would Eddie. The Soviets were a paranoid bunch, but then, he could hardly complain about that, could he? Not hardly. It was his job to crack into the deepest secrets of their country. He was the new Chief of Station, but he was supposed to be a stealthy one. This was one of Bob Ritter's new and more creative ideas. Typically, the identity of the boss spook in an embassy wasn't expected to be a secret. Sooner or later, everyone got burned one way or another, either ID'd by a false-flag operation or through an operational error, and that was like losing one's virginity. Once gone, it never came back. But the Agency only rarely used a husband-wife team in the field, and he'd spent years building his cover. A graduate of New York's Fordham University, Ed Foley had been recruited fairly young, vetted by an FBI background check, and then gone to work for *The New York Times* as a reporter on a general beat. He'd turned in a few interesting stories, but not too many, and had eventually been told that, while the *Times* wasn't going to fire him, it might be better for him to seek employment with a smaller newspaper where he might blossom better on his own. He'd taken the hint and gotten a job with the State Department as a Press Attaché, a job that paid a decent bureaucratic wage, though without a supergrade's destiny. His official job at the embassy would be to schmooze the elite foreign corespondents of the great American papers and TV networks, granting them access to the ambassador and other embassy officials, and then keeping out of the way while they filed their important stories.

His most important job was to appear competent, but little more. Already the local *Times* correspondent was telling his colleagues that Foley hadn't had the right stuff to make it big as a journalist at America's Foremost Newspaper, and since he wasn't old enough to teach yet—the other resting place for incompetent reporters—he was doing the next worst thing, being a government puke. It was his job to foster that arrogance, knowing that the KGB would have its people ping on the American press corps for their evaluation of the embassy personnel. The best cover of all for a spook was to be regarded as dull and dim, because the dull and the dim weren't smart enough to be spies. For that, he thanked Ian Fleming and the movies he'd inspired. James Bond was a clever boy. Not Ed Foley. No, Ed Foley was a functionary. The crazy part was that the Soviets, whose entire country was governed by dull functionaries, more often than not fell for this story just as readily as if they were someone fresh off the pig farm in Iowa.

There is nothing predictable about the espionage business . . . except here, the Station Chief told himself. The one thing you could depend on with the Russians was predictability. Everything was written down in some huge book, and everybody here played the game by the book.

Foley got aboard the subway car, looking around at his fellow passengers, seeing how they looked at him. His clothing marked him as a foreigner as clearly as a glowing halo marked a saint in a Renaissance painting.

"Who are you?" a neutral voice asked, rather to Foley's surprise.

"Excuse me?" Foley replied in badly accented Russian.

"Ah, you are American."

"*Da,* that is so. I work at American embassy. My first day. I am new in Moscow." Shadow or not, he knew that the only sensible thing was to play this straight.

"How do you like it here?" the inquisitor asked. He looked like a bureaucrat, maybe a KGB counterespionage spook or a stringer. Or maybe just some officer-sitter for some government-run business who suffered from curiosity. There were some of those. Would an ordinary citizen approach him? Probably not, Foley judged. The atmosphere tended to limit curiosity to the space between a person's ears . . . except that Russians were curious as hell about Americans of every stripe. Told to disdain or even to hate Americans, the Russians frequently regarded them as Eve had regarded the apple.

"The metro is very impressive," Foley answered, looking around as artlessly as he could.

"Where in America do you come from?" was the next question.

"New York City."

"You play ice hockey in America?"

"Oh, yes! I've been a fan of the New York Rangers since I was a child. I want to see the hockey here." Which was entirely truthful. The Russian skate-and-pass game was the closest thing to Mozart in the world of sports. "The embassy has good tickets, they told me today. Central Army," he added.

"Bah!" the Muscovite snorted. "I am Wings fan."

The guy might just be genuine, Foley thought with surprise. The Russians were as picky about their hockey clubs as American baseball fans were with their home teams. But the Second Chief Directorate probably had hockey fans working there, too. "Too careful" was a concept he did not admit to, especially here.

"Central Army is the champion team, isn't it?"

"Too prissy. Look what happened to them in America."

"In America we play a more physical—is that the right word?—game. To you they must seem like hooligans, yes?" Foley had taken the train to Philadelphia to see that game. The Flyers—more widely known as the Broad Street Bullies—had beaten the snot out of the somewhat arrogant Russian visitors, rather to his amusement. The Philadelphia team had even wheeled out its secret weapon, the aging Kate Smith, singing "God Bless America," which for that team was like breakfasting on nails and human infants. Damn, what a game that one had been!

"They play roughly, yes, but they are not fairies. Central Army thinks they are the Bolshoi, the way they skate and pass. It's good to see them humbled sometimes."

"Well, I remember the '80 Olympics, but honestly that was a miracle for us to defeat your fine team."

"Miracle! *Bah!* Our coach was asleep. Our heroes were asleep. Your children played a spirited game, and they won honestly. The coach needed to be shot." Yeah, this guy talked like a fan.

"Well, I want my son to learn hockey over here."

"How old is he?" Genuine interest in the man's eyes.

"Four and a half," Foley answered.

"A good age to learn to skate. There are many opportunities for children to skate in Moscow, aren't there, Vanya?" he observed to the man next to him, who'd watched the exchange with a mixture of curiosity and unease.

"Make sure he gets good skates," the other man said. "Bad ones can injure the ankles." A typical Russian response. In this often harsh country, solicitude for children was endearingly genuine. The Russian bear had a soft heart for kids, but one of icy granite for adults.

"Thank you. I will be sure to do that."

"You live in the foreigners' compound?"

"Correct," Foley confirmed.

"Next stop is yours."

"Oh, *spasiba,* and good day to you." He made his way to the door, turning to nod a friendly good-bye to his newfound Russian friends. *KGB?* he wondered. Perhaps, but not certainly. He'd determine that by whether or not he saw them on the train a month or so from now.

What Ed Foley didn't know was that the entire exchange had been observed by a man a mere two meters away, holding a copy of today's *Sovietskiy Sport.* His name was Oleg Zaitzev, and Oleg Ivanovich *was* KGB.

The Station Chief left the subway car and followed the crush to the escalator. At one time, it would have led him to a full-standing portrait of Stalin, but that was gone now, and not replaced. The outside air was acquiring the early autumn chill, just enough to feel good after the stuffiness of the metro. Around him, ten or more men lit up their foul-smelling cigarettes and walked their separate ways. It was only half a block to the walled compound of apartment blocks, with its guard shack and the uniformed attendant, who looked Foley over and decided he was an American by the quality of his overcoat, without acknowledging his passage by even a nod, and certainly not a smile. The Russians didn't smile much. It was something that struck all American visitors to the country; the outwardly dour nature of the Russian people seemed almost inexplicable to foreigners.

TWO STOPS FARTHER DOWN, Oleg Zaitzev wondered if he should write up a contact report. KGB officers were encouraged to do so, partly as a sign of loyalty, partly to show their eternal vigilance against citizens of the Main Enemy, as America was known within his professional community. It was mostly to show their institutional paranoia, a characteristic openly fostered by KGB. But by profession Zaitzev was a paper-pusher and he didn't feel the need to generate more meaningless paper. It would just be looked at, read in a cursory way at most, and tossed into some file box by some other bureaucrat from his upstairs office, never to be read again. His time was too precious for that sort of nonsense. Besides, he hadn't even talked to the foreigner, had he? He left the train at the proper stop, rode up the moving stairs into the crisp evening air, lighting his Trud cigarette as he got outside. It was a vile thing. He had access to the "closed" stores and could have bought French, British, or even American smokes, but they were too costly, and his funds were not as unlimited as his choices. So, he smoked the well-known "Labor" brand, like untold millions of his countrymen. The quality of his clothing was a tiny bit better than that worn by most of his comrades, but not overly so. Not so much that he stood out from the others. It was two blocks to his apartment building. His flat was #3 on the first—the Americans would have called it the second—floor instead of higher up, and that was fine with him, because it meant that he didn't risk a heart attack if the elevator didn't work, which happened about once a month. Today it worked. The elderly woman who occupied the janitor/superintendent's flat on the ground floor had her door closed today, instead of open to denote some mechanical problem she'd have to warn him about. So nothing in the building was broken today. Not quite cause for celebration, just one of the small things in life for which to be grateful to God or whoever determined the vagaries of fate. The cigarette died as he walked through the main door. Zaitzev flicked the butt into the ashtray and walked to the elevator, which, remarkably, was waiting for him with the door open.

"Good evening, Comrade Zaitzev," the operator said in greeting.

"Good evening, Comrade Glenko." The man was a disabled veteran of the Great Patriotic War, with the medals to prove it. Artilleryman, so he said. Probably the building informer, the man who reported unusual occurrences to some other KGB stringer, in return for which he got a niggardly stipend to supplement whatever pension the Red Army paid him. That was the extent of their exchange. Glenko turned the handle and brought the elevator car smoothly to his floor and opened the door. From there, it was a mere five meters to his home.

Opening his apartment door, he was greeted by the smell of boiling cabbage—so cabbage soup for dinner. Not unusual. It was a staple of the Russian diet, along with rich black bread.

"Papa!" Oleg Ivanovich bent down to scoop up his little Svetlana. She was the light of Zaitzev's life, with her cherubic face and welcoming smile.

"How is my little *zaichik* today?" He scooped her up in his arms and accepted her darling little kiss.

Svetlana attended a day-care center crowded with other children her age—not quite a preschool, not quite a nursery. Her clothing comprised about the only colorful things to be had in his country, in this case a green pullover shirt and gray pants over little red leather shoes. If his access to the "closed" shops had one advantage, it was in what he could get his little girl. The Soviet Union didn't even have cloth diapers for its infants—mothers usually made them out of old bedsheets—much less the disposable kind favored in the West. As a result, there was a premium on getting the little ones toilet-trained, which little Svetlana had managed some time ago, much to her mother's relief. Oleg followed the smell of cabbage to his wife in the kitchen.

"Hello, darling," Irina Bogdanova said from the stove. Cabbage, potatoes, and what he hoped was some ham cooking. Tea and bread. No vodka yet. The Zaitzevs drank, but not to excess. They usually waited until Svetlana went down to bed. Irina worked as an accountant at the GUM department store. The possessor of a degree from Moscow State

University, she was liberated in the Western sense, but not emancipated. Hanging by the kitchen table was the string bag she carried in her purse everywhere she went, eyes always on the lookout for something she might buy to eat or brighten their drab flat. It meant standing in line, which was the task of women in the Soviet Union, along with cooking dinner for her man, regardless of his professional status in life or hers. She knew that he worked for State Security, but did not know his job there, just that it paid a fairly comfortable salary, and came with a uniform that he rarely wore, and a rank soon to take a jump upward. So, whatever he did, he did it well enough, she judged, and that was sufficient. The daughter of an infantryman in the great Patriotic War, she'd gone to state schools and gotten above-average marks, but never quite achieved what she'd wished. She'd shown some talent at the piano, but not enough to go onward to a state conservatory. She'd also tried her hand at writing, but there, too, she'd fallen short of the necessary talent to get published. Not an unattractive woman, she was thin by Russian standards. Her mouse-brown hair fell to her shoulders and was usually well brushed-out. She read a good deal, whichever books she could get that were worth her time, and enjoyed listening to classical music. She and her husband occasionally attended concerts at the Tchaikovsky. Oleg preferred the ballet, and so they went there as well, helped, Irina assumed, by his job at #2 Dzerzhinskiy Square. He was not yet so senior as to allow them to hobnob with senior State Security officials at comradely parties. Perhaps when he got his colonelcy, she hoped. For the moment they lived the middle-class life of state-employed bureaucrats, scratching by on their combined salaries. The good news was that they had occasional access to the "closed" KGB stores where at least they could buy nice things for her and Svetlana. And, who knew, maybe they could afford to have another child in due course. They were both young enough, and a little boy would brighten their home.

"Anything interesting today?" she asked. It was almost their daily joke.

"There is never anything interesting at the office," he joked in reply. No, just the usual messages to and from field officers, which he forwarded to the appropriate pigeonholes for in-house couriers to hand-carry upstairs to the offices of the control officers who really ran things at KGB. A very senior colonel had come down to see the operation the previous week, which he'd done without a smile, a friendly word, or a question for twenty minutes, before disappearing off to the elevator banks. Oleg knew the man's seniority only from the identity of his escort: the colonel who ran his own operation. Whatever words had been exchanged had been too distant for him to overhear—people tended to talk in whispers, if at all, in his department—and he was trained not to show much interest.

But training could only go so far. Captain Oleg Ivanovich Zaitzev was too bright to turn his mind all the way off. Indeed, his job required something approaching judgment for its proper execution, but that was something to be exercised as gingerly as a mouse's stroll through a roomful of cats. He always went to his immediate superior and always started off with the most humble of questions before getting approval. In fact, his judgmental questions were always approved. Oleg was gifted in that, and he was beginning to get recognized as such. His majority wasn't all that far off. More money, more access to the closed stores, and, gradually, more independence—no, that wasn't quite right. A little less circumscription on what he would be able to do. Someday he might even ask if a message going out made good sense. *Do we* really *want to do* this, *comrade?* he'd wanted to ask every so often. Operational decisions were not his to make, of course, but he could—or would be able to in the future—question the wording of a directive in the most oblique terms. Every so often he'd see something going out to Officer 457 in Rome, for example, and wonder if his country really wanted to risk the consequences of having the mission order go bad. And sometimes they did go bad. Just two months before, he'd seen a dispatch from Bonn warning that something had gone wrong with the West German counterintelligence service, and the field officer had urgently requested instructions—and the instructions had been to continue his mission without questioning the intelligence of his superiors. And *that* field officer had disappeared right off the network. *Arrested and shot?* Oleg wondered. He knew some of the field officers' names, virtually all of the operations' names, and a lot of the operational targets and objectives. Most of all, he knew the code names of hundreds of foreign nationals who were agents of the KGB. At its best, it could be like reading a spy novel. Some of the field officers had a literary streak. Their dispatches were not the terse communiqués of military officers. No, they liked to communicate the state of mind of their agents, the *feel* of the information and the mission assigned. They could be like travelogue writers describing things for a paying audience. Zaitzev wasn't really supposed to digest such information, but he was a man with a mind, and besides, there were telltale codes built into every dispatch. The third word misspelled, for example, could be a warning that the officer had been compromised. Every officer had a different such key system, and Zaitzev had a list of them all. Only twice had he caught such irregularities, and on one of those occasions his supervisors had told him to ignore it as a clerical error—a fact that still astounded him. But the mistake had never been repeated, and so, maybe it really had just been an enciphering error by the officer in question. After all, his superior had told him, men trained at The Centre didn't often get caught in the field. They were the best in the world, and the Western enemies were not *that* clever, were they? Then Captain Zaitzev had nodded submission to the moment, written down his warning notation, and made sure it was in the permanent files, covering his ass like any good bureaucrat.

What if his immediate superior were under the control of some Western spy agency, he'd wondered at the time and later on, usually after a few drinks in front of his TV set. Such a compromise would be perfection itself. Nowhere in KGB was there a single written list of their officers and agents. No, "compartmentalization" was a concept invented here back in the 1920s, or perhaps earlier still. Even Chairman Andropov was not allowed to have such a thing within his reach, lest *he* defect to the West and take it with him. KGB trusted no one, least of all its own Chairman. And so, oddly, only people in his own department had access to such broad information, but they were not operations personnel. They were just communicators.

But wasn't the one person KGB *always* tried to compromise the cipher clerk in a foreign embassy? Because he or she was the one functionary, the one not bright enough to be entrusted with anything of importance—wasn't *she* the one person who *was* so entrusted? It was so often a woman, after all, and KGB officers were trained to seduce them. He'd seen dispatches along those lines, some of them describing the seduction in graphic detail, perhaps to impress the men upstairs with their manly prowess and the extent of their devotion to the State. Being paid to fuck women didn't strike Zaitzev as conspicuously heroic, but then, perhaps the women were surpassingly ugly, and performing a man's duty under such circumstances might have been difficult.

What it came down to, Oleg Ivanovich reflected, was that functionaries were so often entrusted with cosmic secrets, and he was one of them, and wasn't that amusing? More amusing than his cabbage soup, certainly, nutritious though it might be. So even the Soviet state trusted some people, despite the fact that "trust" was a concept as divorced from its way of collective thinking as a man is from Mars. And he was such a man. Well, one result of that irony was the cute green shirt his little daughter wore. He set a few books on the kitchen chair and hoisted Svetlana there so that she could eat her dinner. Svetlana's hands were a little small for the zinc-aluminum tableware, but at least it wasn't too heavy for her to use. He still had to butter her bread for her. It was good to be able to afford real butter.

"I saw something nice at the special store on the way home," Irina observed as women do over dinner, to catch their husbands in a good mood. The cabbage was especially good today, and the ham was Polish. So she'd shopped today at the "closed" store, all right. She'd gotten into the habit only nine months before, and now she wondered aloud how she'd ever lived without it.

"What's that?" Oleg asked, sipping his Georgian tea.

"Brassieres, Swedish ones."

Oleg smiled. Those of Soviet manufacture always seemed to be designed for peasant girls who suckled calves instead of children—far too big for a woman of his wife's more human proportions. "How much?" he asked without looking up.

"Only seventeen rubles each."

Seventeen certificate *rubles,* he didn't correct her. A certificate ruble had actual value. You could, theoretically, even exchange it for a foreign "hard" currency, as opposed to the valueless paper that they used to pay the average factory worker, whose value was entirely theoretical . . . like everything else in his country, when you got down to it.

"What color?"

"White." Perhaps the special store had black or red ones, but it was a rare Soviet woman who would wear such things. People were very conservative in their habits here.

With dinner finished, Oleg left the kitchen to his wife and took his little girl into the living room and the TV set. The TV news announced that the harvest was under way, as it was every year, with the heroic laborers on the collective farms bringing in the first crop of summer wheat in the northern areas, where they had to grow and harvest it quickly. A fine crop, the TV said. *Good,* Oleg thought, *no bread shortages this winter . . . probably.* You could never really be sure about what was said on the TV. Next, some complaining coverage of the American nuclear weapons being deployed in the NATO countries, despite the reasonable Soviet requests that the West forgo such unnecessary, destabilizing, and provocative actions. Zaitzev knew that the Soviet SS-20s were going into place elsewhere, and they, of course, were in no way destabilizing. The big show on TV tonight was *We Serve the Soviet Union,* about military operations, fine young Soviet men serving their country. Today would be rare coverage of men doing their "international duty" in Afghanistan. The Soviet media didn't often cover that, and Oleg was curious as to what they'd show. There were occasional discussions over lunch at work about the war in Afghanistan. He tended to listen rather than talk, because he'd been excused from military service, something he didn't regret one little bit. He'd heard too many stories about the casual brutality in the infantry units, and besides, the uniforms were not attractive to wear. His rarely worn KGB uniform was bad enough. Still, pictures told stories that mere words did not, and he had the keen eye for detail that his job required.

"YOU KNOW, every year they harvest wheat in Kansas, and it never makes the *NBC Nightly News,"* Ed Foley said to his wife.

"I suppose feeding themselves is a major accomplishment," Mary Pat observed. "How's the office?"

"Small." Then he waved his hands in such a way as to say that nothing interesting had happened.

Soon she'd have to drive their car around to check for alert signals. They were working Agent CARDINAL here in Moscow, and he was their most important assignment. The colonel knew that he'd have new handlers here. Setting that arrangement up would be touchy, but Mary Pat was accustomed to handling the touchy ones.

CHAPTER 4

INTRODUCTIONS

IT WAS FIVE IN THE EVENING in London, and noon in Langley, when Ryan lit up his secure phone to call home. He'd have to get used to the time zones. Like a lot of people, he found that his creative times of day tended to divide themselves into two parts. Mornings were best for digesting information, but later afternoons were better for contemplation. Admiral Greer tended to be the same way, and so Jack would find himself disconnected from his boss's work routine, which wasn't good. He also had to get used to the mechanics of handling documents. He'd been in government service long enough to know that it would never be as easy as he expected, nor as simple as it ought to be.

"Greer," a voice said, after the secure link was established.

"Ryan here, sir."

"How's England, Jack?"

"Haven't seen it rain yet. Cathy starts her new job tomorrow morning."

"How's Basil?"

"I can't complain about the hospitality, sir."

"Where are you now?"

"Century House. They gave me an office on the top floor with a guy in their Russian section."

"I bet you want an STU for your home."

"Good call, sir." The old bastard was pretty good at reading minds.

"What else?"

"Nothing comes immediately to mind, Admiral."

"Anything interesting yet?"

"Just settling in, sir. Their Russian section looks smart. The guy I'm working with, Simon Harding, reads the tea leaves pretty well," Ryan said, glad that Simon was off at the moment. Of course, maybe the phone was bugged . . . nah . . . not for a Knight Commander of the Victorian Order . . . or would they?

"Kids okay?"

"Yes, sir. Sally's trying to figure out the local TV."

"Kids adapt pretty well."

Better than adults do. "I'll let you know, Admiral."

"The Hopkins document ought to be on your desk tomorrow."

"Thanks. I think they'll like it. Bernie said some interesting things. This other thing with the Pope . . ."

"What are our cousins saying?"

"They're concerned. So am I. I think His Holiness has rattled their cage pretty hard, and I think Ivan's going to notice."

"What's Basil saying?"

"Not much. I do not know what assets they have on site. I imagine they're waiting to see what they can find out." Jack paused. "Anything from our end?"

"Not yet" was the terse reply. It was a step up from *nothing I can talk to you about. Does Admiral Greer really trust me now?* Jack wondered. Sure, Greer liked him, but did he really trust him to be a good analyst? Perhaps this London sojourn was, if not boot camp, then maybe a second trip through the Basic School. That was where the Marine Corps made sure that young men with lieutenant's bars really had the right stuff to lead Marines in the field. It was reputed to be the hardest school in the Corps. It hadn't been especially easy for Ryan, but he had graduated at the top of his class. Maybe he'd just been lucky . . . ? He hadn't served long enough to find out, courtesy of a broken CH-46 over the island of Crete, an event that still visited him in the occasional nightmare.

Fortunately, his gunnery sergeant and a navy corpsman had stabilized him, but Jack still got a chill even thinking about helicopters. "Tell me what you think, Jack."

"If my job were to keep the Pope alive, I'd be a little nervous. The Russians can play rough when they want to. What I cannot evaluate is how the Politburo might react—I mean, how much starch they might have in their backbone. When I talked to Basil, I said it comes down to how scared they are by his threat, if you call it a threat."

"What would you call it, Jack?" the DDI asked from 3,400 miles away.

"Yes, sir, you have me there. I suppose it is a threat of sorts to their way of thinking."

"Of sorts? How does it look to them?" Jim Greer would have been one tough son of a bitch teaching graduate-level history or political science. Right up there with Father Tim at Georgetown.

"Noted, Admiral. It's a threat. And they will see it as such. I am not sure, however, how serious a threat they will take it to be. It's not as though they believe in God. To them, 'God' is politics, and politics is just a process, not a belief system as we understand the term."

"Jack, you need to learn to see reality through the eyes of your adversary. Your analytical ability is first-rate, but you have to work on perception. This isn't stocks and bonds, where you dealt with hard numbers, not perceptions of numbers. They say El Greco had a stigmatism in his eyes that gave everything a visual slant. They see reality through a different lens, too. If you can replicate that, you'll be one of the best around, but you have to make that leap of imagination. Harding's pretty good at that. Learn from him to see the inside of their heads."

"You know Simon?" Jack asked.

"I've been reading his analyses for years."

None of this is an accident, Jack, he told himself, with more surprise than there ought to have been. His second important lesson of the day. "Understood, sir."

"Don't sound too surprised, my boy."

"Aye-aye, sir," Ryan responded like a Marine shavetail. *I won't make that mistake again, Admiral.* And in that moment, John Patrick Ryan became a real intelligence analyst.

"I'll have the embassy deliver the STU to you. You know about keeping it secure," the DDI added as a cautionary note.

"Yes, sir. I can do that."

"Good. Lunchtime here."

"Yes, sir. Talk to you tomorrow." Ryan replaced the receiver in the cradle and then extracted the plastic key from the slot in the phone set. That went into his pocket. He checked his watch. Time to close up shop. He'd already cleared his desk of classified folders. A woman came around about 4:30 with a shopping cart to take them back to central-records storage. Right on cue, Simon came back in.

"What time's your train?"

"Six-ten."

"Time for a beer, Jack. Interested?"

"Works for me, Simon." He rose and followed his roommate out the door.

It was only a four-minute walk to the Fox and Cock, a very traditional pub a block from Century House. A little too traditional: It looked like a relic from Shakespeare's time, with massive wooden timbers and plaster walls. It had to be for architectural effect; no real building could have survived that long, could it? Inside was a cloud of tobacco smoke and a lot of people wearing jackets and ties. Clearly an upscale pub, a lot of the patrons were probably from Century House. Harding confirmed it.

"It's our watering hole. The publican used to be one of us, probably makes more here than he ever did at the shop." Without being bidden, Harding ordered two pints of Tetley's bitter, which arrived quickly. Then he ushered Jack to a corner booth.

"So, Sir John, how do you like it here?"

"No complaints so far." He took a sip. "Admiral Greer thinks you're pretty smart."

"And Basil thinks he's rather bright as well. Good chap to work for?" Harding asked.

"Yeah, big-time. He listens and helps you think. Doesn't stomp on you when you goof. He'd rather teach than embarrass you—that's my experience, anyway. Some of the more senior analysts have had him tear a stripe off their ass. I guess I'm not senior enough for that yet." Ryan paused. "You supposed to be my training officer over here, Simon?"

The directness of the question surprised his host. "I wouldn't say that exactly. I'm a Soviet specialist. You're more a generalist, I take it?"

"Try 'apprentice,' " Ryan suggested.

"Very well. What do you want to know?"

"How to think like a Russian."

Harding laughed into his beer. "That's something we all learn every day. The key is to remember that to them everything is politics, and politics, remember, is all about nebulous ideas, aesthetics. Especially in Russia, Jack. They can't deliver real products like automobiles and television sets, so they have to concentrate on everything fitting into their political theory, the sayings of Marx and Lenin. And, of course, Lenin and Marx knew sod-all about doing real things in the real world. It's like a religion gone mad, but instead of thunderbolts or biblical plagues, they kill their apostates with firing squads. In their world outlook, everything that goes wrong is the result of political apostasy. Their political theory ignores human nature, and since their political theory is Holy Writ, and therefore is never wrong, it must be human nature that's wrong. It's not logically consistent, you see. Ever study metaphysics?"

"Boston College, second year. The Jesuits make you spend a semester on it," Ryan confirmed, taking a long sip. "Whether you want to or not."

"Well, communism is metaphysics applied ruthlessly to the real world, and when things don't fit, it's the fault of the square sods who don't fit into their round bloody holes. That can be rather hard on the poor sods, you see. And so, Joe Stalin murdered roughly twenty million of them, partly because of political theory, partly because of his own mental illness and bloody-mindedness. That insane bugger defined paranoia. One pays a price for being ruled by a madman with a twisted book of rules, you see."

"But how faithful is the current political leadership to Marxist theory?"

A thoughtful nod. "That's the question, Jack. The answer is, we don't bloody know. They all claim to be true believers, but are they?" Harding paused for a contemplative sip of his own. "Only when it suits them, I think. But that depends on who one is talking about. Suslov, for example, believes totally—but the rest of them? To some greater or lesser extent, they do and they don't. I suppose you can characterize them as people who used to go to church every Sunday, then fell away from the habit. Part of them still believes, but some greater or lesser part does not. What they *do* believe in is the fact that the state religion is the source of their power and status. And so, for all the common folk out there, they must *appear* to believe, because believing is the only thing that gives them that power and status."

"Intellectual inertia?" Ryan wondered aloud.

"Exactly, Jack. Newton's first law of motion."

Part of Ryan wanted to object to the discourse. The world had to make more sense than that. But did it? What rule said that it had to? he asked himself. And who enforced such rules? And was it expressed that simply? What Harding had just explained in less than two hundred words purported to justify hundreds of billions of dollars in expenditures, strategic weapons of incomprehensible power, and millions of people whose uniforms denoted enmity that demanded aggression and death in time of war or near-war.

But the world was about ideas, good and bad, and the conflict between this one and Ryan's own defined the reality in which Ryan worked, defined the belief system of the people who'd tried to kill him and his family. And that was as real as it had to be, wasn't it? No, there was no rule that compelled the world to make sense. People decided on their own what made sense and what did not. So, was everything about the world a matter of perception? Was it all a thing of the mind? What was reality?

But *that* was the question behind all of metaphysics. When Ryan had studied it at Boston College, it had been so purely theoretical that it seemed to have no attachment at all to reality. It had been a lot for Ryan to absorb at age nineteen, and, he realized, just as much to absorb at age thirty-two. But here the marks were often recorded in human blood, not on a report card.

"Christ, Simon. You know, it would be a lot easier if they did believe in God."

"Then, Jack, it would be just another religious war, and those are bloody affairs, too, you may recall. Think of it as the crusades, one version of God against another. Those wars were quite nasty enough. The true believers in Moscow think that they are riding the wave of history, that they are bringing perfection to the human condition. It must drive them mad when they see that their country can scarcely feed itself, and so they try to ignore it—but it is difficult to ignore an empty belly, isn't it? So they blame it all on us and on 'wreckers'—traitors and saboteurs—in their own country. Those are the people they imprison or kill." Harding shrugged. "Personally, I regard them as infidels, believers in a false god. It's just easier that way. I've studied their political theology, but that has limited value because, as I said, so many of them do not really believe in the substance of their system. Sometimes they think like tribal Russians, whose outlook on the world has always been skewed by our standards. Russian history is such a muddle that studying it has its own limits in terms of Western logic. They're xenophobes of a very high order, always have been—but for fairly reasonable historical causes. They've always had threats from both east and west. The Mongols, for example, have been as far west as the Baltic, and the Germans and French have hammered on the gates of Moscow. As we say, they're a rum lot. One thing I do know is that no sane man wants them as masters. A pity, really. They have so many marvelous poets and composers."

"Flowers in a junkyard," Ryan suggested.

"Exactly, Jack. Very good." Harding fished for his pipe and lit it with a kitchen match. "So, how do you like the beer?"

"Excellent, much better than at home."

"I don't know how you Americans can stomach it. But your beef is better than ours."

"Corn-fed. Turns out better meat than grass does," Ryan sighed. "I'm still getting used to life over here. Every time I start feeling comfortable, something hits me like a snake in high grass."

"Well, you've had less than a week to get used to us."

"My kids will be talking funny."

"Civilized, Jack, civilized," Harding observed with a good laugh. "You Yanks do ravage our language, you know."

"Yeah, right." Pretty soon he'd refer to baseball as "rounders," which was a girls' game over here. They didn't know dick about a good fastball.

FOR HIS PART, Ed Foley found himself suddenly outraged by the bugs that he knew had to be in his apartment. Every time he made love to his wife, some KGB desk weenie was listening in. Probably a nice perverse diversion for their counterespionage spooks, but it was, by God, the Foleys' love life, and was nothing sacred? He and Mary Pat had been briefed in on what to expect, and his wife had actually joked about it, on the flight over—you couldn't bug airplanes. She'd called it a way of showing those barbarians how real people lived, and he'd laughed, but here and now it wasn't so goddamned funny. It was like being an animal in the goddamned zoo, with people watching and laughing and pointing. Would KGB keep a log of how often he and his wife got it on? *They might,* he thought, looking for marital difficulties as a pretext for recruiting him or Mary Pat. Everyone did it. So, they'd have to make love regularly just to discourage that possibility, though playing a reverse false-flag did have interesting theoretical possibilities of its own. . . . No, the Station Chief decided, it'd be an unnecessary complication for their stay in Moscow, and being Chief of Station was already complex enough.

Only the ambassador, the defense attaché, and his own officers were allowed to know who he was. Ron Fielding was the overt COS, and his job was to wiggle like a good worm on the hook. When parking his car, he'd occasionally leave his sun visor down or rotated ninety degrees; sometimes he'd wear a flower in his buttonhole and take it out halfway down a block as though signalling someone or, best of all, he'd bump into people, simulating a brush-pass. That sort of thing could make the Second Chief Directorate counterspooks go nuts—race after innocent Muscovites, perhaps snatch a few up for interrogations, or put a squad of officers on the poor random bastard to watch everything he did. If nothing else, it forced KGB to waste assets on fool's errands, chasing after phantom geese. Best of all, it persuaded them that Fielding was a clumsy Station Chief. It always made the other side feel good, and *that* was always a smart move for CIA. The game he played made other power moves look like a game of Chutes and Ladders.

But the fact that there were probably bugs in his bedroom pissed him off. And he couldn't do the usual things to contravene them, like playing the radio and talking under it. No, he couldn't act like a trained spook. He had to be dumb, and playing dumb required brains and discipline and the utmost thoroughness. Not a single mistake was allowed. That one mistake could get people killed, and Ed Foley had a conscience. It was a dangerous thing for a field spook to have, but it was impossible not to have. You had to care about your agents, those foreign nationals who worked for you and fed you information. All—well, nearly all—had problems. The big one here was alcoholism. He expected every agent he ran into to be a boozer. Some were quite mad. Most were people who wanted to get even—with their bosses, with the system, with the country, with communism, with their spouses, with the whole perverse world. Some, a very few, might be genuinely attractive people. But Foley would not pick them. They would pick him. And he'd have to play the cards he was dealt. The rules of this game were hard and damned harsh. His life was safe. Oh, sure, he might get a little roughed up—or Mary Pat—but they both had diplomatic passports, and to seriously mess with him meant that somewhere in America some Soviet diplomat of fairly high rank might get a rough time at the hands of some street thugs—who might or might not be trained law-enforcement personnel. Diplomats didn't like such things, and so it was avoided; in fact, the Russians played by the rules more faithfully than the Americans did. So he and his wife were safe, but their agents, if and when blown, would get less mercy than a mouse would get from a particularly sadistic cat. There was still torture here, still interrogations that lasted into long hours. Due process of law was whatever the government at the time felt like it was. And the appeals process was limited to whether or not the shooter's pistol was loaded. So he had to treat his agents, whether drunks, whores, or felons, like his own children, changing their diapers, getting them a bedtime glass of water, and wiping their noses.

All in all, Ed Foley thought, it was one hell of a game. And it kept him awake at night. Could the Russians tell that? Were there cameras in the walls? Wouldn't *that* be perverse? But American technology wasn't that advanced, so he was damned sure the Russians' wasn't. Probably. Foley reminded himself that there were smart people here, and a lot of them worked for KGB.

What amazed him was that his wife slept the sleep of the just, lying there next to him. She really was a better field spook than he was. She took to it like a seal to ocean water, chasing after her fish. But what about the sharks? He supposed it was normal for a man to worry about his wife, however capable she might be as a spook. That was just how men were programmed, as she was programmed to be a mother. Mary Pat looked like an angel to him in the dim light, the cute little sleep-smile she had, and the way her baby-fine blond hair always got messed up the instant she lay down on the pillow. To the Russians, she was a potential spy, but to Edward Foley she was his beloved wife, workmate, and mother of his child. It was so strange that people could be so many different things, depending on who looked at them, and yet all were true. With that philosophical thought—Christ, he *did* need sleep!—Ed Foley closed his eyes.

"SO, WHAT DID HE SAY?" Bob Ritter asked.

"He's not terribly pleased," Judge Moore replied, to nobody's surprise. "But he understands that there's not a hell of a lot we can do about it. He'll probably make a speech next week about the nobility of the workingman, especially the unionized sort."

"Good," Ritter grunted. "Let him tell the air-traffic controllers." The DDO was the master of the cheap shot, though he had the good sense not to say such things in the wrong company.

"Where's the speech?" the DDI asked.

"Chicago, next week. There's a large ethnic Polish population there," Moore explained. "He'll talk about the shipyard workers, of course, and point out that he once headed his own union. I haven't seen the speech yet, but I expect it will be mainly vanilla, with a few chocolate chips tossed in."

"And the papers will say that he's courting the blue-collar vote," Jim Greer observed. Sophisticated as they purported to be, the newspapers didn't catch on to much until you presented it to them with french fries and ketchup. They were masters of political discourse, but they didn't know shit about how the real game was played until they were briefed-in, preferably with single-syllable words. "Will our Russian friends notice?"

"Perhaps. They have good people reading the tea leaves at the U.S.–Canada Institute. Maybe someone will drop a word en passant in a casual conversation over at Foggy Bottom that we look upon the Polish situation with some small degree of concern, since we have so many

American citizens of Polish ancestry. Can't take it much further than that at the moment," Moore explained.

"So, we're concerned about Poland, but not the Pope right now," Ritter clarified the situation.

"We don't know about that yet, do we?" the DCI asked rhetorically.

"Won't they wonder why the Pope didn't let us in on his threat . . . ?"

"Probably not. The wording of the letter suggests a private communication."

"Not so private that Warsaw didn't forward it to Moscow," Ritter objected.

"As my wife likes to say, that's different," Moore pointed out.

"You know, Arthur, sometimes this wheels-inside-of-other-wheels stuff gives me a headache," Greer observed.

"The game has rules, James."

"So does boxing, but those are a lot more straightforward."

" 'Protect yourself at all times,' " Ritter pointed out. "That's Rule Number One here, too. Well, we don't have any specific warnings yet, do we?" Heads shook wordlessly. No, they didn't. "What else did he say, Arthur?"

"He wants us to find out if there's any danger to His Holiness. If anything happens to him, our President is going to be seriously pissed."

"Along with a billion or so Catholics," Greer agreed.

"You suppose the Russians might contract the Northern Irish Protestants to do the hit?" Ritter asked, with a nasty smile. "They don't like him either, remember. Something for Basil to look into."

"Robert, that's a little too far off the wall, I think," Greer analyzed. "They hate communism almost as much as Catholicism, anyway."

"Andropov doesn't think that far outside the box," Moore decided. "Nobody over there does. If he decides to take the Pope out, he'll use his own assets and try to be clever about it. That's how we'll know if, God forbid, it goes that far. And if it looks as if he's leaning that way, we'll have to dissuade him from that notion."

"It won't get that far. The Politburo is too circumspect," said the DDI. "And it's too unsubtle for them. It's not the sort of thing a chess player does, and chess is still their national game."

"Tell that to Leon Trotsky," Ritter said sharply.

"That was personal. Stalin wanted to eat his liver with onions and gravy," Greer replied. "That was pure personal hatred, and it achieved nothing on the political level."

"Not the way Uncle Joe looked at it. He was genuinely afraid of Trotsky—"

"No, he wasn't. Okay, you can say he was a paranoid bastard, but even he knew the difference between paranoia and genuine fear." Greer knew that statement was a mistake the moment the words escaped his lips. He covered his tracks: "And even if he was afraid of the old goat, the current crop isn't like that. They lack Stalin's paranoia but, more to the point, they lack his decisiveness."

"Jim, you're wrong. The Warsaw Letter is a potentially dangerous threat to their political stability, and they *will* take that seriously."

"Robert, I didn't know you were that religious," Moore joked.

"I'm not, and neither are they, but they will be worried about this. I think they will be worried a lot. Enough to take direct action? That I'm not sure of, but they will damned well think about it."

"That remains to be seen," Moore countered.

"Arthur, that is my assessment," the DDO shot back, and with the A-word, it became serious, at least within the cloisters of the Central Intelligence Agency.

"What changed your mind so quickly, Bob?" the Judge asked.

"The more I think about it, from their point of view, the more serious it starts to look."

"You planning anything?"

That made Ritter a little uneasy. "It's a little early to hit the Foleys with a major tasking, but I am going to send them a heads-up, at least to get them thinking about it."

This was an operational question, on which the others typically deferred to Bob Ritter and his field-spook instincts. Taking information from an agent was often simpler and more routine than getting instructions *to* an agent. Since it was assumed that every employee of the Moscow embassy was followed on a regular or irregular basis, it was dangerous to make them do something that looked spookish. This was especially true for the Foleys—they were so new that they would be tightly covered. Ritter didn't want them blown, for the usual reasons and for one other: His selection of this husband/wife team had been a daring play, and if it didn't work, it would come back at him. A high-stakes poker player, Ritter didn't like losing his chips any more than the next man. He had very high hopes for the Foleys. He didn't want their potential blown two weeks into their assignment in Moscow.

The other two didn't comment, which allowed Ritter to proceed, running his shop as he saw fit.

"You know," Moore observed, with a lean-back into his chair, "here we are, the best and brightest, the best-informed members of this presidential administration, and we don't know beans about a subject that may turn out to be of great importance."

"True, Arthur," Greer agreed. "But we don't know with considerable authority. That's more than anybody else can say, isn't it?"

"Just what I needed to hear, James." It meant that those outside this building were free to pontificate, but that these three men were not. No, they had to be cautious in everything they said, because people tended to view their opinions as facts—which, you learned up here on the Seventh Floor, they most certainly were not. If they were that good, they'd be doing something more profitable with their lives, like picking stocks.

RYAN SETTLED BACK into his easy chair with a copy of the *Financial Times.* Most people preferred to read it in the morning, but not Jack. Mornings were for general news, to prepare him for the workday at Century House—back home, he'd listened to news radio during the hour-or-so drive, since the intelligence business so often tracked the news. Here and now, he could relax with the financial stuff. This British paper wasn't quite the same as *The Wall Street Journal,* but the different twist it put on things was interesting—it gave him a new slant on abstract problems, to which he could then apply his American-trained expertise. Besides, it helped to keep current. There were bound to be financial opportunities out here, waiting for people to harvest them. Finding a few would make this whole European adventure worth the time. He still regarded his CIA sojourn as a side trip in life, whose ultimate destination was too far off in the haze. He'd play his cards one at a time.

"Dad called today," Cathy said, perusing her medical journal. This was *The New England Journal of Medicine,* one of the six she subscribed to.

"What did Joe want?"

"Just asked how we were doing, how the kids are, that sort of thing," Cathy responded.

Didn't waste any words about me, did he? Ryan didn't bother asking. Joe Muller, senior VP of Merrill Lynch, didn't approve of the way his son-in-law had left the trading business, after having had the bad grace to run off with his own daughter, first to teach, and then to play fox-and-hounds with spies and other government employees. Joe didn't much care for the government and its minions—he deemed them unproductive takers of what he and others made. Jack was sympathetic, but someone had to deal with the tigers of the world, and one of those somebodies was John Patrick Ryan. Ryan liked money as much as the next guy, but to him it was a tool, not an end in itself. It was like a good car—it could take you to nice places but, once there, you didn't sleep in the car. Joe didn't see things that way and didn't even try to understand those who thought otherwise. On the other hand, he did love his daughter, and he had never hassled her about becoming a surgeon. Perhaps he figured taking care of sick people was okay for girls, but making money was man's work.

"That's nice, honey," Ryan said from behind the *FT.* The Japanese economy was starting to look shaky to Ryan, though not to the paper's editorial board. Well, they'd been wrong before.

IT WAS A sleepless night in Moscow. Yuriy Andropov had smoked more than his usual complement of Marlboros, but had held himself to only one vodka after he'd gotten home from a diplomatic reception for the ambassador from Spain—a total waste of his time. Spain had joined NATO, and its counterintelligence service was depressingly effective at identifying his attempts to get a penetration agent into their government. He'd probably be better advised to try the king's court. Courtiers were notoriously talkative, after all, and the elected government would probably keep the newly restored monarch informed, for no other reason than their desire to suck up to him. So he had drunk the wine, nibbled on the finger food, and chattered on with the usual small talk. *Yes, it has been a fine summer, hasn't it?* Sometimes he wondered if his elevation to the Politburo was worth the demands on his time. He hardly ever had time to read anymore—just his work and his diplomatic/political duties, which were endless. Now he knew what it must be like to be a woman, Andropov thought. No wonder they all nagged and groused so much at their men.

But the thought that never left his mind was the Warsaw Letter. *If the government of Warsaw persists in its unreasonable repression of the people, I will be compelled to resign the papacy and return to be with my people in their time of trouble.* That bastard! Threatening the peace of the world. Had the Americans put him up to it? None of his field officers had turned up anything like that, but one could never be sure. The American President was clearly no friend to his country, he was always looking for ways to sting Moscow—the nerve of that intellectual nonentity, saying that the Soviet Union was the center of evil in the world! That fucking *actor* saying such things! Even the howls of protest from the American news media and academia hadn't lessened the sting. Europeans had picked up on it—worst of all, the *Eastern* European intelligentsia had seized on it, which had caused all manner of problems for his subordinate counterintelligence throughout the Warsaw Pact. As if they weren't busy enough already, Yuriy Vladimirovich grumbled, as he pulled another cigarette out of the red-and-white box and lit it with a match. He didn't even listen to the music that was playing, as his brain turned the information over and over in his head.

Warsaw *had to* clamp down on those counterrevolutionary troublemakers in Danzig—strangely, Andropov always thought of that port city by the old German name—lest its government come completely unglued. Moscow had told them to sort things out in the most direct terms, and the Poles knew how to follow orders. The presence of Soviet Army tanks on their soil would help them understand what was necessary and what was not. If this Polish "Solidarity" rubbish went much further, the infection would begin to spread—west to Germany, south to Czechoslovakia . . . and east to the Soviet Union? They couldn't allow that.

On the other hand, if the Polish government could suppress it, then things would quiet down again. *Until the next time?* Andropov wondered.

Had his outlook been just a little broader, he might have grasped the fundamental problem. As a Politburo member, he was insulated from the more unpleasant aspects of life in his country. He lacked for nothing. Good food was no farther away than his telephone. His lavish apartment was well furnished, outfitted with German appliances. The furniture was comfortable. The elevator in his building was *never* out of service. He had a driver to take him to and from the office. He had a protective detail to make sure that he was never troubled by street hooligans. He was as protected as Nikolay II had been and, like all men, he assumed that his living conditions were normal, even though intellectually he knew that they were anything but. The people outside his windows had food to eat, TV and films to watch, sports teams to cheer for, and the chance to own an automobile, didn't they? In return for giving them all those things, he enjoyed a somewhat better lifestyle. That was entirely reasonable, wasn't it? Didn't he work harder than they all did? What the hell *else* did those people want?

And now this Polish priest was trying to upset the entire thing.

And he just might do it, too, Andropov thought. Stalin had once famously asked how many divisions the Pope had at his command, but even he must have known that not all the power in the world grew out of the barrel of a gun.

If Karol *did* resign the papacy, then what? He'd try to come back to Poland. Might the Poles keep him out—revoke his citizenship, for example? No, somehow he'd manage to get back into Poland. Andropov and the Poles had their agents inside the church, of course, but such things only went so far. To what extent did the church have his agencies infiltrated? There was no telling. So no, any attempt to keep him out of Poland was probably doomed to failure, and, once attempted, if the Pope did get into Poland, *that* would be an epic disaster.

They could try diplomatic contacts. The right Foreign Ministry official could fly to Rome and meet clandestinely with Karol and try to dissuade him from following through on his threat. But what cards would he be able to play? An overt threat on his life . . . that would not work. That sort of challenge would be an invitation to martyrdom and sainthood, which likely would only encourage him to make the trip. For a believer, it would be an invitation to Heaven, one sent by the devil himself, and he'd pick up that gauntlet with alacrity. No, you could not threaten such a man with death. Even threatening his people with harsher measures would only encourage him further—he'd want to come home to protect them all the sooner, so as to appear more heroic to the world.

The sophistication of the threat he had sent to Warsaw was something that only appreciated with contemplation, Andropov admitted to himself. But there was one certain answer to it: Karol would have to find out for himself if there really was a god.

Is there a god? Andropov wondered. A question for the ages, answered by many people in many ways until Karl Marx and Vladimir Lenin had settled the matter—at least so far as the Soviet Union was concerned. *No,* Yuriy Vladimirovich told himself, it was too late for him to reconsider his own answer to that question. *No, there is no God.* Life was here and now, and when it ended, it ended, and so what you did was the best you could, living your life as fully as possible, taking the fruit you could reach and building a ladder to seize those you could not.

But Karol was trying to change that equation. He was trying to shake the ladder—or perhaps the tree? That question was a little too deep.

Andropov turned in his chair and poured some vodka out of the decanter, then took a contemplative sip. Karol was trying to enforce his false beliefs on his own, trying to shake the very foundations of the Soviet Union and its far-flung alliances, trying to tell people that there was something better to believe in. In that, he was trying to upset the work of generations, and he and his country could not permit it. But he could not forestall Karol's effort. He could not persuade him to turn away. No, Karol would have to be stopped in a manner that would forestall him fully and finally.

It would not be easy, and it would not be entirely safe. But doing nothing was even less safe, for him, for his colleagues, and for his country.

And so, Karol had to die. First, Andropov would have to come up with a plan. Then he'd have to take it to the Politburo. Before he proposed action, he'd have to have the action fully plotted out, with a guarantee of success. Well, that was what he had KGB for, wasn't it?

CHAPTER 5

GETTING CLOSE

AN EARLY RISER, Yuriy Vladimirovich was showered, shaved, dressed, and eating his breakfast before seven in the morning. For him it was bacon, three scrambled eggs, and thickly cut Russian bread with Danish butter. The coffee was German in origin, just like the kitchen appliances his apartment boasted. He had the morning *Pravda,* plus selected cuttings from Western newspapers, translated by KGB linguists, and some briefing material prepared in the early hours of the morning at The Centre and hand-delivered to his flat every morning at six. There was nothing really important today, he saw, lighting his third cigarette and drinking his second cup of coffee. All routine. The American President hadn't rattled his sabre the night before, which was an agreeable surprise. Perhaps he'd dozed off in front of the TV, as Brezhnev often did.

How much longer would Leonid continue to head the Politburo? Andropov wondered. Clearly the man would not retire. If he did, his children would suffer, and they enjoyed being the royal family of the Soviet Union too much to let their father do that. Corruption was never a pretty thing. Andropov did not suffer from it himself—indeed, that was one of his core beliefs. That was why the current situation was so frustrating. He would—he *had to*—save his country from the chaos into which it was falling. *If I live long enough, and Brezhnev dies soon enough, that is.* Leonid Ilyich was clearly in failing health. He'd managed to stop smoking—at the age of seventy-six, which, Yuriy Vladimirovich admitted to himself, was fairly impressive—but the man was in his dotage. His mind wandered. He had trouble remembering things. He occasionally dozed off at important meetings, to the dismay of his associates. But his grasp of power was a death-grip. He'd engineered the downfall of Nikita Sergeyevich Khrushchev through a masterful series of political maneuvers, and *nobody* in Moscow forgot that tidbit of political history—a trick like that was unlikely to work on someone who'd engineered it himself. No one had even suggested to Leonid that he might wish to slow down—if not actually step slightly aside, then at least let others undertake some of his more administrative duties and allow him to concentrate his abilities on the really major questions. The American President was not all that much younger than Brezhnev, but he had lived a healthier life, or perhaps came from hardier peasant stock.

In his reflective moments, it struck Andropov as strange that he objected to this sort of corruption. He saw it precisely as such, but only rarely asked himself *why* he saw it so. In those moments, he actually did fall back on his Marxist beliefs, the very ones he'd discarded years ago, because even he had to fall back on some sort of ethos, and that was all he had. Stranger still, it was an area in which Marx and Christianity actually overlapped in their beliefs. Must have been an accident. After all, Karl Marx had been a Jew, not a Christian, and whatever religion he rejected or embraced ought to have been his own, not one foreign to him and his heritage. The KGB Chairman dismissed the entire line of thought with an annoyed shake of the head. He had enough on his professional plate, even as he finished what lay before him. There was a discreet knock on the door.

"Come," Andropov called, knowing who it was by the sound.

"Your car is ready, Comrade Chairman," the head of the security detail announced.

"Thank you, Vladimir Stepanovich." He rose from the table, lifted his suit jacket, and shrugged into it for the trip to work.

This was a routine fourteen-minute drive through central Moscow. His ZIL automobile was entirely handmade, actually similar in appearance to the American Checker taxicab. It ran straight down the center of the expansive avenues, in a broad lane kept clear by officers of the Moscow Militia exclusively for senior political officials. They stood out there all day in the heat of summer and the punishing cold of winter, one cop every three blocks or so, making sure no one obstructed the way for longer than it took to make a crossing turn. It made the drive to work as convenient as taking a helicopter, and far easier on the nerves.

Moscow Centre, as KGB was known throughout the world of intelligence, was located in the former home office of the Rossiya Insurance Company, and a mighty company it must have been to build such an edifice. Andropov's car pulled through the gate into the inner courtyard, right up to the bronze doors, where his car door was yanked open, and he alit to the official salutes from uniformed Eighth Directorate men. Inside, he walked to the elevator, which was held for him, of course, and then rode to the top floor. His detail examined his face to ascertain his mood—as such men did all over the world—and, as usual, saw nothing: He guarded his feelings as closely as a professional cardplayer. On the top floor was a walk of perhaps fifteen meters to his secretary's door. That was because Andropov's office had no door of its own. Instead, there was a clothes dresser in the anteroom, and the entrance to his office lay within that. This chicanery dated back to Lavrenti Beria, Stalin's own chief of clandestine services, who'd had a large and hardly unreasonable fear of assassination and had come up with this security measure, lest a commando team reach all the way into NKVD headquarters. Andropov found it theatrical, but it was something of a KGB tradition and, in its way, roundly entertaining for visitors—it had been around too long to be a secret from anyone able to get this far, in any case.

His schedule gave him fifteen free minutes at the beginning of the day to review the papers on his desk before the daily briefings began, followed by meetings that were scheduled days or even weeks in advance. Today it was almost all internal-security matters, though someone from the Party Secretariat was scheduled before lunch to discuss strictly political business. *Oh, yes, that thing in Kiev*, he remembered. Soon after becoming KGB Chairman, he'd found that Party affairs paled in importance next to the agreeably broad canvas he had here at #2 Dzerzhinskiy Square. The charter of KGB, insofar as it had such a limitation, was to be the "Sword and Shield" of the Party. Hence its primary mission, theoretically, was to keep an eye on Soviet citizens who might not be as enthusiastic as they ought toward their own country's government. Those Helsinki Watch people were becoming a major annoyance. The USSR had made an agreement in the Finnish capital seven years before, regarding the monitoring of human rights, and they evidently took it seriously. Worse, they had attracted the on-and-off attention of the Western news media. Reporters could be a huge nuisance, and you couldn't rough them up the way you used to—not all of them, anyway. The capitalist world treated them like demigods, and expected everyone else to do the same, when everyone knew they were all spies of some kind. It was amusing to see how the American government overtly forbade its intelligence services from adopting journalistic covers. Every other spy service in the world did it. As if the Americans would follow their own lily-white laws, which had been passed only to make other countries feel good about having *The New York Times* snooping around their countries. It wasn't even worth a dismissive snort. Preposterous. *All* foreign visitors in the Soviet Union were spies. Everyone knew it, and that was why his Second Chief Directorate, whose job was counterespionage, was so large a part of the KGB.

Well, the problem that had cost him an hour of sleep the night before wasn't all that different, was it? Not when you got down to it. Yuriy Vladimirovich punched a button on his intercom.

"Yes, Comrade Chairman," his secretary—a man, of course—answered immediately.

"Send Aleksey Nikolay'ch in to see me."

"At once, comrade." It took four minutes by Andropov's desk clock.

"Yes, Comrade Chairman." Aleksey Nikolayevich Rozhdestvenskiy was a senior colonel in the First Chief—"Foreign"—Directorate, a very experienced field officer who'd served extensively in Western Europe, though never in the Western Hemisphere. A gifted field officer and runner-of-agents, he'd been bumped up to The Centre for his street-smart expertise and to act more or less as an in-house expert for Andropov to consult when he needed information on field operations. Not tall, not especially handsome, he was the sort of man who could turn invisible on any city street in the world, which partly explained his success in the field.

"Aleksey, I have a theoretical problem. You've worked in Italy, as I recall."

"For three years in Station Rome, Comrade Chairman, yes, under Colonel Goderenko. He's still there, as *rezident*."

"A good man?" Andropov asked.

He gave an emphatic nod of the head. "A fine senior officer, yes, Comrade Chairman. He runs a good station. I learned much from him."

"How well does he know the Vatican?"

That made Rozhdestvenskiy blink. "There is not much to be learned there. We do have some contacts, yes, but it has never been a matter of great emphasis. The Catholic Church is a difficult target to infiltrate, for the obvious reasons."

"What about through the Orthodox Church?" Andropov asked.

"There are some contacts there, yes, and we have had some feedback, but rarely anything of value. More along the line of gossip and, even then, nothing we cannot get through other channels."

"How good is security around the Pope?"

"Physical security?" Rozhdestvenskiy asked, wondering where this was going.

"Precisely," the Chairman confirmed.

Rozhdestvenskiy felt his blood temperature drop a few degrees. "Comrade Chairman, the Pope does have some protection about him, mainly of the passive sort. His bodyguards are Swiss, in plainclothes—that comic-opera group that parades around in striped jumpsuits is mostly for show. They occasionally have to grab a believer overcome by his proximity to the head priest, that sort of thing. I am not even sure if they carry weapons, though I must assume that they do."

"Very well. I want to know how difficult it might be to get physically close to the Pope. Do you have any ideas?"

Ah, Rozhdestvenskiy thought. "Personal knowledge? No, comrade. I visited Vatican City several times when I was in Rome. The art collection there, as you may imagine, is impressive, and my wife is interested in such things. I took her there perhaps half a dozen times. The area crawls with priests and nuns. I confess I never looked about for security provisions, but nothing was readily apparent, aside from what you'd expect—measures against thefts and vandalism, that sort of thing. There are the usual museum guards, whose main function seems to be to tell people where the lavatories are.

"The Pope lives in the Papal Apartments, which adjoin the church of St. Peter's. I have never been there. It is not the sort of place in which I had any professional interest. I know our ambassador is there occasionally for diplomatic functions, but I was not invited—my posting was that of Assistant Commercial Attaché, you see, Comrade Chairman, and I was too junior," Rozhdestvenskiy went on. "You say you wish to know about getting close to the Pope. I presume by that you mean . . . ?"

"Five meters, closer if possible, but certainly five meters."

Pistol range, Rozhdestvenskiy grasped at once. "I don't know enough myself. That would be a job for Colonel Goderenko and his people. The Pope gives audiences for the faithful. How you get into those, I do not know. He also appears in public for various purposes. I do not know how such things are scheduled."

"Let's find out," Andropov suggested lightly. "Report directly to me. Do not discuss this with anyone else."

"Yes, Comrade Chairman," the colonel said, coming to attention with the receipt of the order. "The priority?"

"Immediate," Andropov replied, in the most casual of voices.

"I shall see to it myself, Comrade Chairman," Colonel Rozhdestvenskiy promised. His face revealed nothing of his feelings. Indeed, he had few of those. KGB officers were not trained to have much in the way of scruples, at least outside politics, in which they were supposed to have a great deal of faith. Orders from above carried the force of Divine Will. Aleksey Nikolay'ch's only concerns at the moment were centered on the potential political fallout to be had from dropping this particular nuclear device. Rome was more than a thousand kilometers from Moscow, but that would probably not be far enough. However, political questions were not his to ask, and he scrubbed the matter from his mind—for the moment, anyway. While he did so, the intercom box on the Chairman's desk buzzed. Andropov flipped the top-right switch.

"Yes?"

"Your first appointment is here, Comrade Chairman." His secretary announced.

"How long will this take, Aleksey, do you suppose?"

"Several days, probably. You want an immediate assessment, I assume, followed by what sort of specific data?"

"Correct. For the moment, just a general assessment," Yuriy Vladimirovich said. "We're not planning any sort of operation just yet."

"By your order, Comrade Chairman. I'll go down to the communications center directly."

"Excellent. Thank you, Aleksey."

"I serve the Soviet Union" was the automatic reply. Colonel Rozhdestvenskiy came to attention again, then left-faced for the door. He had to duck his head going out into the secretary's room, as most men did, and from there he turned right and out into the corridor.

So, how does *one get close to the Pope, this Polish priest?* Rozhdestvenskiy wondered. It was, at least, an interesting theoretical question. KGB abounded with theoreticians and academics who examined everything, from how to assassinate chiefs of foreign governments—useful in the event that a major war was about to be undertaken—to the best way to steal and interpret medical records from hospitals. The broad scope of KGB field operations knew few limitations.

One could not have guessed much from the colonel's face as he walked to the elevator bank. He pushed the button and waited for forty seconds until the doors opened.

"Basement," he told the operator. The elevators all had operators. Elevators were too good a potential dead-drop location to leave unattended. Even then, the operators were trained to look for brush-passes. Nobody was trusted in this building. There were too many secrets to be had. If there were one single place in the Soviet Union in which an enemy would want to place a penetration agent, this building was it, and so everyone looked at everyone else in some sort of black game, always watching, measuring every conversation for an inner meaning. Men made friends here as they did in every walk of life. They chatted about their wives and children, about sports and weather, about whether to buy a car or not, about getting a dacha in the country for the lucky ones with seniority. But rarely did men chat about work, except with their immediate workmates, and then only in conference rooms where such things were supposed to be discussed. It never occurred to Rozhdestvenskiy that these institutional restrictions reduced productivity and might actually hinder the efficiency of his agency. That circumscription was just part of the institutional religion of the Committee for State Security.

He had to pass a security checkpoint to enter the communications room. The watch NCO checked his photo pass and waved him through without much in the way of acknowledgment.

Rozhdestvenskiy had been here before, of course, often enough that he was known by face and name to the senior operators, and he knew them. The desks were arranged with a lot of space between them, and the background noise of the teleprinters prevented ordinary conversation from being overheard at a distance of more than three or four meters, even by the most sensitive ears. This, and nearly everything else about the arrangement of the room, had evolved over the years until the security provisions were as close to perfect as anyone could imagine, though that didn't keep the efficiency experts on the third floor from wandering about with their scowls, always looking for something wrong. He walked to the desk of the senior communications watch officer.

"Oleg Ivanovich," he said in greeting.

Zaitzev looked up to see his fifth visitor of the young day, the fifth visitor and the fifth *interruption.* It was often a curse being the senior watch officer here, especially on the morning shift. The overnight watch was boring, but at least you could work in a straight line.

"Yes, Colonel, what can I do for you this morning?" he asked pleasantly, junior officer to senior.

"A special message to Station Rome, personal to the *rezident.* I think a one-time pad for this one. I'd prefer that you handle it yourself." *Instead of having a cipher clerk do the encryption,* he didn't say. This was somewhat unusual, and it pricked Zaitzev's interest. He would have to see it anyway. Eliminating the cipher clerk just halved the number of people that would see this particular message.

"Very well." Captain Zaitzev took up a pad and pencil. "Go on."

"Most Secret. IMMEDIATE AND URGENT. FROM MOSCOW CENTRE, OFFICE OF CHAIRMAN. TO COLONEL RUSLAN BORISSOVICH GODERENKO, *REZIDENT,* ROME. MESSAGE FOLLOWS: ASCERTAIN AND REPORT MEANS OF GETTING PHYSICALLY CLOSE TO THE POPE. ENDS."

"That's all?" Zaitzev asked, surprised. "And if he asks what that means? It's not very clear in its intent."

"Ruslan Borissovich will understand what it means," Rozhdestvenskiy assured him. He knew that Zaitzev wasn't asking anything he shouldn't. One-time cipher pads were a nuisance to use, and so messages sent that way were supposed to be explicit in all details, lest the back-and-forth clarification messages compromise the communications links. As it was, this message would be telexed, and so was certain to be intercepted, and equally certain to be recognized by its formatting as a one-time-pad encipherment, hence a message of some importance. American and British codebreakers would probably attack it, and everyone was wary of them and their clever tricks. The West's damned intelligence agencies worked so closely together.

"If you say so, Comrade Colonel. I'll send it out within the hour." Zaitzev checked the wall clock to make sure he could do that. "It should be on his desk when he gets into his office."

It will take twenty minutes for Ruslan to decrypt it, Rozhdestvenskiy estimated. *Then will he query us about it, as Zaitzev suggests? Probably. Goderenko is a careful, thorough man—and politically astute. Even with Andropov's name at the top, Ruslan Borissovich will be curious enough to ask for a clarification.*

"If there is a reply, call me as soon as you have the clear text."

"You are the point of contact for this line?" Zaitzev asked, just to make sure he routed things correctly. After all, the message header, as this colonel had dictated it to him, said "Office of the Chairman."

"That is correct, Captain."

Zaitzev nodded, then handed the message blank to Colonel Rozhdestvenskiy for his signature/confirmation. Everything in KGB had to have a paper trail. Zaitzev looked down at the checklist. Message, originator, recipient, encryption method, point of contact . . . yes, he had everything, and all spaces were properly signed. He looked up. "Colonel, it will go out shortly. I will call you to confirm transmission time." He would also send a paper record upstairs for the permanent operations files. He made a final written notation and handed off the carbon copy.

"Here's the dispatch number. It will also be the operation-reference number until such time as you change it."

"Thank you, Captain." The colonel took his leave.

Oleg Ivanovich looked again at the wall clock. Rome was three hours behind Moscow time. Ten or fifteen minutes for the *rezident* to clear-text the message—the field people were so clumsy at such things, he knew—and then to think about it, and then . . . ? Zaitzev made a small wager with himself. The Rome *rezident* would send back a request for clarification. Sure as hell. The captain had been sending out messages and getting them back from this man for some years. Goderenko was a careful man who liked things clear. So he'd leave the Rome pad in his desk drawer in readiness for the return message. He counted: 209 characters, including blank spaces and punctuation. A pity they couldn't do this on one of those new American computers they were playing with upstairs. But there was no sense wishing for the moon. Zaitzev pulled out the cipher-pad book from his desk drawer and unnecessarily wrote down its number before walking to the west side of the capacious room. He knew nearly all of them by number, a product of his chess background, Zaitzev imagined.

"Pad one-one-five-eight-nine-zero," he told the clerk behind the metal screen, handing off the paper slip. The clerk, a man of fifty-seven long years, most of them here, walked a few meters to fetch the proper cipher book. It was a loose-leaf binder, about ten centimeters across by twenty-five high, filled with punched paper pages, probably five hundred or more. The current page was marked with a plastic tag.

The pages looked like those in a telephone book, until you looked closely and saw that the letters didn't form names in any known language, except by random accident. There were on average two or three such occurrences per page. Outside Moscow, on the Outer Ring Road, was the headquarters of Zaitzev's own directorate, the Eighth, the part of KGB tasked with making and breaking codes and ciphers. On the roof of the building was a highly sensitive antenna which led to a teletype machine. The receiver that lay between the antenna and the teletype listened in on random atmospheric noise, and the teletype interpreted these "signals" as dot-dash letters, which the adjacent teletype machine duly printed up. In fact, several such machines were cross-connected in such a way that the randomness of the atmospheric noise was re-randomized into totally unpredictable gibberish. From that gibberish were made the one-time pads, which were supposed to be totally random transpositions that no mathematical formula could predict or, therefore, decrypt. The one-time-pad cipher was universally regarded as the most secure of encryption systems. That was important, since the Americans were the world leaders at cracking ciphers. Their "Venona" project had even compromised Soviet ciphers of the late 1940s and '50s, much to the discomfort of Zaitzev's parent agency. The most secure one-time pads were also the most cumbersome and inconvenient, even for experienced hands like Captain Zaitzev. But that couldn't be helped. And Andropov himself wanted to know how to get physically close to the Pope.

That's when it hit Zaitzev: *Physically close to the Pope.* But why would anyone want that? Surely Yuriy Vladimirovich didn't want anyone to hear his confession.

What was he being asked to transmit?

The Rome *rezident,* Goderenko, was a highly experienced field officer whose *rezidentura* operated many Italian and other nationals as agents for the KGB. He forwarded all manner of information, some overtly important, some merely amusing, though potentially useful in compromising otherwise important people with embarrassing foibles. Was it that only the important had such weaknesses, or did their positions merely allow them to entertain themselves in manners which all men dreamt about but few could indulge in? Whatever the answer, Rome would have to be a good city for it. *City of the Caesars,* Zaitzev thought, *it ought to be.* He thought of the travel and history books he'd read on the city and the era—classical history in the Soviet Union had some political commentary, but not all that much. The political spin applied to every single aspect of life was the most tiring intellectual feature of life in his country, often enough to drive a man to drink—which, in the USSR, wasn't all that distant a drive, of course. Time to go back to work. He took a cipher wheel from his top drawer. It was like a phone dial—you set the letter to be transposed at the top of one dial, then rotated the other to the letter indicated on the page of the transposition pad. In this case, he was working from the beginning of the twelfth line of page 284. That reference would be included in the first line of the transmission so that the recipient would know how to get clear text from the transmitted gibberish.

It was laborious despite the use of the cipher wheel. He had to set the clear-text letter he'd written in the message form, then dial to the transposition letter on the printed page of the cipher-pad book, and write down each individual result. Each operation required him to set his pencil down, dial, pick up the pencil again, recheck his results—twice in his case—and begin again. (The cipher clerks, who did nothing else, worked two-handed, a skill Zaitzev had not acquired.) It was beyond tedious, hardly the sort of work designed for someone educated in mathematics. Like checking spelling tests in a primary school, Zaitzev grumbled to himself. It took more than six minutes to get it right. It would have taken less time had he been allowed to have a helper in the process, but that would have violated the rules, and here the rules were adamantine.

Then, with the task done, he had to repeat everything to make sure he hadn't transmitted any garbles, because garbles screwed everything up on both ends of the system, and this way, if they happened, he could blame them on the teletype operators—which everyone did anyway. Another four and a half minutes confirmed that he hadn't made any errors. Good.

Zaitzev rose and walked to the other side of the room, through the door into the transmission room. The noise there was enough to drive a man mad. The teletypes were of an old design—actually, one had been stolen from Germany in the 1930s—and sounded like machine guns, though without the banging noise of exploding cartridges. In front of each machine was a uniformed typist—they were all men, each sitting erect like a statue, his hands seemingly affixed to the keyboard in front of him. They all had ear protection, lest the noise in the room land them in a psychiatric hospital. Zaitzev walked his message form to the room supervisor, who took the sheet without a word—he wore ear-protectors, too—and walked it to the leftmost typist in the back row. There, the supervisor clipped it to a vertical board over the keyboard. At the top of the form was the identifier for the destination. The typist dialed the proper number, then waited for the warbling sound of the teleprinter at the other end—it had been designed to get past the ear plugs, and it also lit up a yellow light on the teletype machine. He then typed in the gibberish.

How they did that without going mad, Zaitzev did not understand. The human mind craved patterns and good sense, but typing TKALNNETPTN required robotic attention to detail and a total denial of humanity. Some said that the typists were all expert pianists, but that couldn't be true, Zaitzev was sure. Even the most discordant piano piece had *some* unifying harmony to it. But not a one-time-pad cipher.

The typist looked up after just a few seconds: "Transmission complete, comrade." Zaitzev nodded and walked back to the supervisor's desk.

"If anything comes in with this operation-reference number, bring it to me immediately."

"Yes, Comrade Captain," the supervisor acknowledged, making a notation on his set of "hot" numbers.

With that done, Zaitzev headed back for his desk, where the work pile was already quite high enough, and only marginally less mind-numbing than that of the robots in the next room. Perhaps that was why something started whispering at the back of his head: *physically close to the Pope . . . why?*

THE ALARM WENT OFF at a quarter of six. That was an uncivilized hour. At home, Ryan told himself, it was quarter of *one,* but that thought did not bear reflection. He flipped the covers clear off the bed and rose, staggering to the bathroom. There was still a lot to get used to here. The toilets flushed pretty much the same, but the sink . . . *Why the hell,* Ryan wondered, *did you need two spouts to put water in the sink, one for hot and one for cold?* At home you just held your hand under the damned spout, but here the water had to mix up in the sink first, and that slowed you down. The first morning look in the mirror was difficult. *Do I really look like that?* he always wondered on the way back into the bedroom to pat his wife on the rump.

"It's time, honey."

An oddly feminine grumble. "Yeah. I know."

"Want me to get Little Jack?"

"Let him sleep," Cathy advised. The little guy hadn't felt like sleeping the previous evening. So now, of course, he wouldn't feel like waking up.

" 'Kay." Jack headed to the kitchen. The coffee machine only needed its button punched, and Ryan was able to handle that task. Just before flying over, he'd seen a new American company IPO. It sold premium coffee, and since Jack had always been something of a coffee snob, he'd invested $100,000 and gotten himself some of their product—as fine a country as England might be, it was not a place you visited for the coffee. At least he could get Maxwell House from the Air Force, and perhaps he'd get this new Starbucks outfit to ship him some of their brew. One more mental note to make. Next he wondered what Cathy might make for breakfast. Surgeon or not, she regarded the kitchen as her domain. Her husband was allowed to make sandwiches and fix drinks, but that was about it. That suited Jack, for whom a stove was terra incognita. The stove here was gas, like his mom had used, but with a different trademark. He stumbled to the front door, hoping to find a newspaper.

It was there. Ryan had signed up for the *Times,* to go with the *International Herald Tribune* he picked up at the train station in London. Finally, he switched on the TV. Remarkably, there was a start-up version of cable TV in this subdivision, and, mirabile dictu, it had the new American CNN news service—just in time for baseball scores. So England was civilized after all. The Orioles had knocked off Cleveland the previous night, 5–4, in eleven innings. The ballplayers were doubtless in bed right now, sleeping off the postgame beers they'd quaffed at their hotel bar. What a pleasant thought that was. They had a good eight hours of sack time ahead of them. At the turn of the hour, the CNN night crew in Atlanta summarized the previous day's events. Nothing overly remarkable. The economy was still a little fluky. The Dow Jones had snapped back nicely, but the unemployment rate always lagged behind, and so did working-class voters. Well, that was democracy for you. Ryan had to remind himself that his view of the economy was probably different from that of the guys who made the steel and assembled the Chevys. His dad had been a union member, albeit a police lieutenant and part of management rather than labor, and his dad had voted Democrat most of the time. Ryan hadn't registered in either party, opting instead to be an independent. It limited the junk mail you got, and who cared about primaries, anyway?

"Morning, Jack," Cathy said, entering the kitchen in her pink housecoat.

It was shabby, which was surprising, since his wife was always a fastidious dresser. He hadn't asked, but supposed it had sentimental significance.

"Hey, babe." Jack rose to give his wife the first kiss of the day, accompanied by a rather limp hug. "Paper?"

"No. I'll save it for the train." She pulled open the refrigerator door and pulled some things out. Jack didn't look.

"Having coffee this morning?"

"Sure. I don't have any procedures scheduled." If she had a surgery scheduled, Cathy kept off the coffee, lest the caffeine give her hands a minor tremor. You couldn't have that when you were screwing an eyeball back together. No, today was get-acquainted day with Professor Byrd. Bernie Katz knew him and called him a friend, which boded well, and besides, Cathy was about as good as eye surgeons got, and there was no reason for her to be the least bit concerned about a new hospital and a new boss. Still, such concerns were human, though Cathy was too macho to let it show. "How does bacon and eggs grab you?" she asked.

"I'm allowed to have some cholesterol?" her husband asked in surprise.

"Once a week," Mrs. Dr. Ryan replied, imperiously. Tomorrow she'd serve him oatmeal.

"Sounds good to me, babe," Ryan said, with some pleasure.

"I know you'll get something bad for you at the office anyway."

"Moi?"

"Yeah, croissant and butter, probably. They're made entirely out of butter anyway, you know."

"Bread without butter is like a shower without soap."

"Tell me that when you get your first heart attack."

"My last physical, my cholesterol was . . . what?"

"One fifty-two," Cathy answered, with an annoyed yawn.

"And that's pretty good?" her husband persisted.

"It's acceptable," she admitted. But hers had been one forty-six.

"Thank you, honey," Ryan acknowledged, turning to the op-ed page of the *Times.* The letters to the editor here were a positive hoot, and the quality of the writing throughout the papers was superior to anything he found in the American print media. Well, they had invented the language over here, Ryan figured, and fair was fair. The turn of phrase here was often as elegant as poetry, and occasionally too subtle for his American eye to appreciate. He'd pick it up, he figured.

The familiar sound and pleasant smell of frying bacon soon permeated the room. The coffee—tempered with milk instead of cream—was agreeable, and the news wasn't of the sort to ruin breakfast. Except for the ungodly time, things were not all that bad, and besides, the worst part of waking up was already behind him.

"Cathy?"

"Yeah, Jack?"

"Have I told you yet that I love you?"

She ostentatiously checked her watch. "You're a little late, but I'll write that off to the early hour."

"What's your day look like, honey?"

"Oh, meet the people, look around at how things are laid out. Meet my nurses especially. I hope I get good ones."

"Is that important?"

"Nothing screws surgery up worse that a clumsy scrub nurse. But the people at Hammersmith are supposed to be pretty good, and Bernie says that Professor Byrd is about the best guy they have over here. He teaches at Hammersmith and Moorefields. He and Bernie go back about twenty years. He's been to Hopkins a lot, but somehow I've never bumped into him. Over easy?" she asked.

"Please."

Then came the sound of cracking eggs. Like Jack, Cathy believed in a proper cast-iron skillet. Harder to clean, perhaps, but the eggs tasted a lot better that way. Finally came the sound of the toaster lever being depressed.

The sports page—it was called "sport" (singular) over here—told Jack everything he'd ever need to know about soccer, which wasn't much.

"How'd the Yankees do last night?" Cathy asked.

"Who cares?" her husband countered. He'd grown up with Brooks Robinson and Milt Pappas and the Orioles. His wife was a Yankees fan. It was hard on the marriage. Sure, Mickey Mantle had been a good ballplayer—probably loved his mother, too—but he'd played in pinstripes. And that was that. Ryan rose and fixed the coffee for his wife, handing it to her with a kiss.

"Thanks, honey." Cathy handed Jack his breakfast.

The eggs looked a little different, as though the chickens had eaten orange corn to makes the yellows come out so bright. But they tasted just fine. Five satisfying minutes after that, Ryan headed for the shower to make room for his wife.

Ten minutes later, he was picking out a shirt—white cotton, button-down—striped tie, and his Marine Corps tie pin. At 6:40, there was a knock at the door.

"Good morning." It was Margaret van der Beek, the nanny/governess. She lived just a mile away and drove herself. Recommended from an agency vetted by the SIS, she was a South Africa native, the daughter of a minister, thin, pretty, and seemingly very nice. She carried a huge purse. Her hair was napalm-red, which hinted at Irish ancestry, but it was apparently strictly South African–Dutch. Her accent was different from those of most locals, but nonetheless pleasant to Jack's ear.

"Good morning, Miss Margaret." Ryan waved her into the house. "The kids are still asleep, but I expect them up at any moment."

"Little Jack sleeps well for five months."

"Maybe it's the jet lag," Ryan thought out loud, though Cathy had said that infants didn't suffer from it. Jack had trouble swallowing that. In any case, the little bastard—Cathy snarled at Jack whenever he said that—hadn't gone to sleep until half past ten the previous night. That was harder on Cathy than on Jack. He could sleep through the noise. She couldn't.

"Almost time, honey," Jack called.

"I know, Jack," came the retort. The she appeared, carrying their son, with Sally following in her yellow bunny-rabbit sleeper.

"Hey, little girl." Ryan went over to lift his daughter for a hug and kiss.

Sally smiled back and rewarded her daddy with a ferocious hug. How children could wake up in such a good humor was a perverse mystery to him. Maybe it was some important bonding instinct, to make sure their parents looked after them, like when they smiled at mommy and daddy practically from their first moment. Clever little critters, babies.

"Jack, put a bottle on," Cathy said, heading with the little guy to the changing table.

"Roger that, doc," the intelligence analyst responded dutifully, doubling back into the kitchen for a bottle of the junk he'd mixed up the previous night—that *was* man's work, Cathy had made clear to him during Sally's infancy. Like moving furniture and taking out the garbage, the household tasks for which men were genetically prepared.

It was like cleaning a rifle to a soldier: unscrew the top, reverse the nipple, place bottle in pot with four to five inches of water, turn on stove, and wait a few minutes.

That would be Miss Margaret's task, however. Jack saw the taxi outside the window, just pulling onto the parking pad.

"Car's here, babe."

"Okay," was the resigned response. Cathy didn't like leaving her kids for work. Well, probably no mother did. Jack watched her head into the half-bath to wash her hands, then emerge to put on the suit coat that went with her gray outfit—even gray cloth-covered flat shoes. She wanted to make a good first impression. A kiss for Sally, and one for the little guy, and she headed for the door, which Jack held open for her.

The taxi was an ordinary Land Rover saloon car—only London required the classic English taxi for public livery, though some of the older ones found their way into the hinterland. Ryan had arranged the morning pickup the previous day. The driver was one Edward Beaverton, and he seemed awfully chipper for a man who had to work before 7:00 A.M.

"Howdy," Jack said. "Ed, this is my wife. She's the good-looking Dr. Ryan."

"Good morning, mum," the driver said. "You're a surgeon, I understand."

"That's right, ophthalmic—"

Her husband cut her off: "She cuts up eyeballs and sews them back together. You should watch, Eddie, it's fascinating to see how she does it."

The driver shuddered. "Thank you, sir, but, no, thank you."

"Jack just says that to make people throw up," Cathy told the driver. "Besides, he's too much of a wuss to come watch any real surgery."

"And properly so, mum. Much better to cause surgery than to attend it."

"Excuse me?"

"You're a former Marine?"

"That's right. And you?"

"I was in the Parachute Regiment. That's what they taught us: Better to inflict harm on the other bloke than to suffer it yourself."

"Most Marines would agree with that one, pal," Ryan agreed with a chuckle.

"That's not what they taught us at Hopkins," Cathy sniffed.

IT WAS AN hour later in Rome. Colonel Goderenko, titularly the Second Secretary at the Soviet Embassy, had about two hours per day of diplomatic duties, but most of his time was taken up by his job as *rezident,* or Chief of Station for the KGB. It was a busy posting. Rome was a major information nexus for NATO, a city in which one could obtain all manner of political and military intelligence, and that was his main professional concern. He and his six full- and part-time officers ran a total of twenty-three agents—Italian (and one German) nationals who fed information to the Soviet Union for political or pecuniary reasons. It would have been better for him if their motivation was mainly ideological, but that was rapidly becoming a thing of the past. The *rezidentura* in Bonn had a better atmosphere in which to work. Germans were Germans, and many of them could be persuaded that helping out their co-linguists in the DDR was preferable to working with the Americans, British, and French who called themselves allies of the Fatherland. For Goderenko and his fellow Russians, Germans would never be allies, whatever politics whey might claim to have, though the fig leaf of Marxism-Leninism could sometimes be a useful disguise.

In Italy, things were different. The lingering memory of Benito Mussolini was pretty well faded now, and the local true-believer communists were more interested in wine and pasta than revolutionary Marxism, except for the bandits of the Red Brigade—and they were dangerous hooligans rather than politically reliable operatives. Vicious dilettantes more than anything else, though not without their uses. He occasionally saw to their trips to Russia, where they studied political theory and, more to the point, learned proper fieldcraft skills that at least had some tactical use.

On his desk was a pile of overnight dispatches, topmost of which was a message flimsy from Moscow Centre. The header told him it was important, and the cipher book: 115890. This was in his office safe, in the credenza behind his desk. He had to turn in his swivel chair and half-kneel to dial in the combination to open the door, after first deactivating the electronic alarm that was wired to the dial. That took a few seconds. Atop the book was his cipher wheel. Goderenko cordially hated using one-time pads, but they were as much a part of his life as using the toilet. Distasteful, but necessary. Decryption of the dispatch took him ten minutes. Only when it was done did he grasp the actual message. *From the Chairman himself?* he thought. As with any mid-level government official across the world, it was like being called to the principal's office.

The Pope? Why the hell does Yuriy Vladimirovich care a rat's ass about getting close to the Pope? Then he thought for a second. *Oh, of course. It's not about the head of the Catholic Church. It's about Poland. You can take the Polack out of Poland, but you can't take Poland out of the Polack. It's political.* That made it important.

But it did not please Goderenko.

"ASCERTAIN AND REPORT MEANS OF GETTING PHYSICALLY CLOSE TO THE POPE," he read again. In the professional language of the KGB, that could only mean one thing.

Kill the Pope? Goderenko thought. That would be a political disaster. As Catholic as Italy was, the Italians were not a conspicuously religious people. *La dolce vita*, the sweet life—that was the religion of this country. The Italians were the most profoundly disorganized people in the world. How they had ever been allies to the Hitlerites boggled the imagination. For the Germans, everything was supposed to be *in Ordnung*, properly arranged, clean and ready for use at all times. About the only things the Italians kept in proper order were their kitchens and perhaps their wine cellars. Aside from that, everything was so casual here. To a Russian, coming to Rome was a culture shock, akin to being bayoneted in the chest. The Italians had no sense of discipline. You only had to observe their traffic to see that, and driving in it was what flying a fighter plane must be like.

But the Italians were all born with a sense of style and propriety. There were some things one could not do here. Italians had a collective sense of beauty that was difficult for any man to fault, and to violate that code could have the most serious of consequences. For one thing, it could compromise his intelligence sources. Mercenaries or not . . . Even mercenaries would not work against their very religion, would they? Every man had some scruples, even—no, he corrected himself, *especially*—here. So the political consequences of something like this potential mission could adversely affect the productivity of his *rezidentura* and would seriously impact recruitment.

So, what in hell do I do now? he asked himself. A senior colonel in the KGB's First Chief Directorate and a highly successful *rezident,* he had a certain degree of flexibility in his actions. He was also a member of a huge bureaucracy, and the easiest thing for him to do was what all bureaucrats did. He would delay, obfuscate, and obstruct.

There was some degree of skill required for this, but Ruslan Borissovich Goderenko knew all he needed to know about that.

CHAPTER 6

BUT NOT TOO CLOSE

NEW THINGS ARE ALWAYS INTERESTING, and that was true for surgeons, too. While Ryan read his paper, Cathy looked out the train window. It was another bright day, with a sky as blue as his wife's pretty eyes. For his part, Jack had the route pretty well memorized, and boredom invariably made him sleepy. He slumped in the corner of the seat and found his eyelids getting heavy.

"Jack, are you going to sleep? What if you miss the stop?"

"It's a terminal," her husband explained. "The train doesn't just stop there; it *ends* there. Besides, never stand up when you can sit down, and never sit down when you can lie down."

"Who ever told you that?"

"My gunny," Jack said, from behind closed eyes.

"Who?"

"Gunnery Sergeant Phillip Tate, United States Marine Corps. He ran my platoon for me until I got killed in that chopper crash—ran it after I left, too, I suppose." Ryan still sent him Christmas cards. Had Tate screwed up, that "killed" might not have been the limp joke he pretended it was. Tate and a Navy Hospital Corpsman Second Class named Michael Burns had stabilized Ryan's back, at the very least preventing a permanent crippling injury. Burns got a Christmas card, too.

About ten minutes to Victoria, Ryan rubbed his eyes and sat up straight.

"Welcome back," Cathy observed dryly.

"You'll be doing it by the middle of next week."

She snorted. "For an ex-Marine, you sure are lazy."

"Honey, if there's nothing to do, you might as well use the time productively."

"I do." She held up her copy of *The Lancet.*

"What have you been reading up on?"

"You wouldn't understand," she replied. It was true. Ryan's knowledge of biology was limited to the frog he'd disassembled in high school. Cathy had done that, too, but she'd probably put it together again and watched it hop back to its lily pad. She could also deal cards like a Vegas cardsharp, a talent that flat amazed her husband every time she demonstrated it. But she wasn't worth a damn with a pistol. Most physicians probably weren't, and here guns were regarded as unclean objects, even by the cops, some of whom were allowed to carry them. Funny country.

"How do I get to the hospital?" Cathy asked, as the train slowed for its last stop.

"Take a cab the first time. You can take the tube, too," Jack suggested. "It's a new city. Takes time to learn your way around."

"How's the neighborhood?" she asked. It came from growing up in New York and working in Baltimore's inner city, where you did well to keep your eyes open.

"Damned sight better than the one around Hopkins. You won't be seeing too much gunshot trauma in the ER. And the people are as nice as they can be. When they figure out that you're an American, they practically give you the joint."

"Well, they were nice to us in the grocery store yesterday," Cathy allowed. "But, you know, they don't have grape juice here."

"My God, no civilization at all!" Jack exclaimed. "So get Sally some of the local bitter."

"You moron!" she laughed. "Sally likes her grape juice, remember, and Hi-C cherry. All they have here is black-currant juice. I was afraid to buy it."

"Yeah, and she's going to learn to spell funny, too." Jack didn't worry about his little Sally. Kids were the most adaptable of creatures. Maybe she'd even learn the rules for cricket. If so, she could explain the incomprehensible game to her daddy.

"My God, *everybody* smokes here," Cathy observed as they pulled into Victoria Station.

"Honey, think of it as a future income source for all the docs."

"It's an awful and a *dumb* way to die."

"Yes, dear." Whenever Jack smoked a cigarette, there was hell to pay in the Ryan house. One more cost of being married to a doc. She was right, of course, and Jack knew it, but everyone was entitled to at least one vice. Except Cathy. If she had one, she concealed it with great skill. The train slowed to a halt, allowing them to stand and open the compartment door.

They stepped out into the arriving rush of office workers. *Just like Grand Central Terminal in New York*, Jack thought, *but not quite as crowded.* London had a lot of stations, laid out like the legs of an octopus. The platform was agreeably wide, and the rush of people politer than New York would ever be. Rush hour was rush hour everywhere, but the English city had a patina of gentility that was hard not to like. Even Cathy would soon be admiring it. Ryan led his wife to the outside, where a rank of cabs waited. He walked her to the first one in line.

"Hammersmith Hospital," he told the driver. Then he kissed his wife good-bye.

"See you tonight, Jack." She always had a smile for him.

"Have a good one, babe." And Ryan made his way to the other side of the building. Part of him hated the fact that Cathy had to work. His mom never had. His father, like all men of his generation, had figured that it was the man's job to put food on the table. Emmet Ryan had liked the fact that his son had married a physician, but his chauvinistic attitude about a woman's place had somehow or other carried over to his son despite the fact that Cathy made a lot more than Jack did, probably because ophthalmologists were more valuable to society than intelligence analysts. Or the marketplace thought so, anyway. Well, she couldn't do what he did, and he couldn't do what she did, and that was that.

At Century House, the uniformed security guard recognized him with a wave and a smile.

"Good morning, Sir John."

"Hey, Bert." Ryan slid his card into the slot. The light blinked green, and Jack transited the security gate. From there, it was just a few steps to the elevator.

Simon Harding was just arriving, too. The usual greeting: "Morning, Jack."

"Hey," Jack grunted in reply on the way to his desk. There was a manila envelope waiting for him. The cover tag said it had been messengered over from the U.S. Embassy in Grosvenor Square. He ripped the top open to see that it was the report from Hopkins on Mikhail Suslov. Jack flipped through the pages and saw something he'd forgotten. Bernie Katz, ever the thorough doc, had evaluated Suslov's diabetes as dangerously advanced, and predicted that his longevity was going to be limited.

"Here, Simon. Says here the head commie's sicker than he looks."

"Pity," Harding observed, taking it as he fumbled with his pipe. "He's not a very nice chap, you know."

"So I've heard."

Next in Ryan's pile were the morning briefing papers. They were labeled SECRET, which meant that the contents might not be in the newspapers for a day or two. It was interesting even so, because this document occasionally gave sources, and that sometimes told you if the information was good or not. Remarkably, not all the data received by the intelligence services was very reliable. A lot of it could be classified as gossip, because even important people inside the world's government loops indulged in it. They were jealous and backbiting sons-of-bitches, like anyone else. Especially in Washington. Perhaps even more so in Moscow? He asked Harding.

"Oh, yes, very much so. Their society depends so much on status, and the backstabbing can be—well, Jack, you could say that it's their national sport. I mean, we have it here as well, of course, but over there it can be remarkably vicious. Rather like it must have been in a medieval court, I imagine—people jockeying for position every bloody day. The infighting inside their major bureaucracies must be horrific."

"And how does that affect this sort of information?"

"I often think I should have read psychology at Oxford. We have a number of psychiatrists on staff here—as I'm sure you do at Langley."

"Oh, yeah. I know a few of the pshrinks. Mainly in my directorate, but some in S and T, too. We're not as good at that as we ought to be."

"How so, Jack?"

Ryan stretched in his chair. "A couple of months ago, I was talking to one of Cathy's pals at Hopkins, his name's Solomon, neuropsychiatrist. You'd have to understand Sol. He's real smart—department chairman and all that. He doesn't believe much in putting his patients on the couch and talking to them. He thinks most mental illness comes from chemical imbalances in the brain. They nearly chopped him out of the profession for that but, twenty years later, they all realized that he was right. Anyway, Sol told me that most politicians are like movie stars. They surround themselves with sycophants and yes-men and people to whisper nice shit into their ears—and a lot of them start believing it, because they *want* to believe it. It's all a great big game to them, but a game where everything is process and damned little of it is product. They're not like real people. They don't do any real work, but they appear to. There's a line in *Advise and Consent:* Washington is a town where you deal with people not as they are, but as they are reputed to be. If that's true in Washington, then how much more must it be in Moscow? There, *everything* is politics. It's all symbols, right? So the infighting and backstabbing must really be wild there. I figure that has to affect us in two ways. First, it means that a lot of the data we get is skewed, because the sources of the data either don't know reality even when it jumps up and bites them on the ass, or they twist the data for their own ends as they process it and pass it on—whether consciously or unconsciously. Second, it means that even the people on the other side who need the data don't know good from bad, so even if we can figure it out, we can't predict what it means because they can't decide for themselves what the hell to do with it—*even if* they know what the hell it is in the first place. We here have to analyze faulty information that will probably be incorrectly implemented by the people to whom it's supposed to go. So, how the hell do we predict what they will do when they themselves don't know the right thing to do?"

That was worth a grin around the pipe stem. "Very good, Jack. You're starting to catch on. Very little they do makes any bloody sense, objectively speaking. However, it isn't all that hard to predict their behavior. You decide for yourself what the intelligent action is, and then reverse it. Works every time," Harding laughed.

"But the other thing Sol said that worries me is that people like that who have power in their hands can be dangerous sons-of-bitches. They don't know when to stop, and they don't know how to use their power intelligently. I guess that's how Afghanistan got started."

"Correct." Simon nodded seriously. "They are captured by their own ideological illusions, and they can't see their way clear of it. And the real problem is, they *do* control a bloody great lot of power."

"I'm missing something in the equation," Ryan said.

"We all are, Jack. That's part of the job."

It was time to change subjects: "Anything new on the Pope?"

"Nothing yet today. If Basil has anything, I ought to hear about it before lunch. Worried about that?"

Jack nodded soberly. "Yeah. The problem is, if we do see a real threat, what the hell can we do about it? It's not like we can put a company of Marines around him, is it? Exposed as he is—I mean, he's in public so much that you can't protect him."

"And people like him don't shrink from danger, do they?"

"I remember when Martin Luther King got whacked. Hell, he knew—he *must* have known—there were guns out there with his name on them. But he never backed away. It just wasn't part of his ethos to run and hide. Won't be any different in Rome, buddy, and every other place he goes."

"Moving targets are supposed to be harder to hit," Simon observed halfheartedly.

"Not when you know where he's moving to a month or two in advance. If KGB decides to put a hit on the guy, damn, I don't see much we can do about it."

"Except perhaps to warn him."

"Great. So he can laugh about it. He probably would, you know. He's been through Nazis and communists for the past forty years. What the hell is left to scare the guy with?" Ryan paused. "If they decide to do it, who pushes the button?"

"I should think it would have to be voted on by the Politburo itself in plenary session. The political implications are too severe for any one member, however senior, to try something like this on his own authority, and remember how collegial they are—no one moves anywhere by himself, even Andropov, who's the most independent-minded of the lot."

"Okay, that's—what? Fifteen guys have to vote up or down on it. Fifteen mouths, plus staffs and family members to talk to about it. How good are our sources? Will we hear about it?"

"Sensitive question, Jack. I cannot answer that one, I'm afraid."

"Can't-can't or can't-I'm-not-allowed-to?" Jack asked more pointedly.

"Jack, yes, we have sources of which I am aware, but which I cannot discuss with you." Harding actually seemed embarrassed to say it.

"Hey, I understand, Simon." Jack had some of those himself. For instance, he couldn't even speak the words TALENT KEYHOLE here, for which he was cleared, but which was NOFORN, no talking about this one to a foreigner—even though Simon and certainly Sir Basil knew quite a bit about it. It was so perverse, because it mainly denied information to people who might have made good use of it. If Wall Street acted this way, all of America would be under the poverty line, Jack groused. Either people were trustworthy or they were not. But the game had its rules, and Ryan played by those rules. That was the cost of admittance into this particular club.

"This is bloody good stuff," Harding said, flipping to page three of Bernie Katz's debriefing.

"Bernie's smart," Ryan confirmed. "That's why Cathy likes working for him."

"But he's an eye doctor, not a psychiatrist, correct?"

"Simon, at that level of medicine, everybody is a little bit of everything. I asked Cathy: The diabetic retinopathy Suslov had is indicative of a major health problem. The diabetes messes up the little blood vessels in the back of the eye, and you can see it when you do an examination. Bernie and his team fixed it partway—you can't fix it all the way—and gave him back about, oh, seventy-five to eighty percent of his sight, good enough to drive a car in daylight, anyway, but the underlying health problem is a mother. It isn't just the small blood vessels in the eye, right? He's got that problem all over his body. Figure Red Mike will croak from kidney failure or heart disease in the next two years at the outside."

"Our chaps think he's got five years or so," Harding offered.

"Well, I'm not a doc. You can have some people talk to Bernie about it if you want, but everything is right there. Cathy says you can tell a lot about diabetes from looking at the eyeball."

"Does Suslov know that?"

Ryan shrugged. "That is a good question, Simon. Docs don't always tell their patients, probably less so over there. Figure Suslov's being treated by a politically reliable doctor of professorial rank. Here, that would mean a top-drawer guy who really knows his stuff. Over there . . . ?"

Harding nodded. "Correct. He may know his Lenin more than his Pasteur. Did you ever hear about Sergey Korolev, their chief rocket designer? That was a particularly ugly incident. The poor bugger was essentially murdered on the table because two senior surgeons didn't like each other, and one wouldn't bail the other out when the boat began to leak badly. It was probably good for the West, but he was a fine engineer, and he was killed by medical incompetence."

"Anybody pay up for that one?" Ryan asked.

"Oh, no. They were both too politically important, lots of patrons in high places. They're safe, until they kill one of their friends, and that won't happen. I'm sure they both have competent young people under them to cover their backsides."

"You know what they need in Russia? Lawyers. I don't like ambulance-chasers, but I guess they do keep people on their toes."

"In any case, no, Suslov probably does not know the gravity of his condition. At least that's what our medical consultants think. He still drinks his vodka according to HUMINT reports, and that is definitely contraindicated." Harding grimaced. "And his replacement will be Alexandrov, every bit as unpleasant a chap as his mentor. I'll have to see about updating his dossier." He made a note.

As for Ryan, he turned back to his morning briefing pages before starting on his official project. Greer wanted Ryan to work on a study of management practices in the Soviet armament industry, to see how—and if—that segment of the Soviet economy worked. Ryan and Harding would be cooperating on the study, which would use both British and American data. It was something that suited Ryan's academic background. It might even get him noticed high up.

THE RETURN MESSAGE came in at 11:32 hours. *Fast work in Rome*, Zaitzev thought, as he began the decryption. He'd call Colonel Rozhdestvenskiy as soon as he got through it, but it was going to take a while. The captain checked the wall clock. It would delay his lunch, too, but the priority condemned him to some stomach growls. About the only good news was that Colonel Goderenko had started his encipherment sequence at the top of page 285.

Most Secret
Immediate and Urgent
From: Rezident Rome
To: Office of Chairman, Moscow Centre
Reference: Your Op Dispatch 15-8-82-666
Getting close to the priest is not difficult without fixed time constraints. Guidance will be needed for a full evaluation of your request. Priest engages in predictable public audiences and appearances which are known well in advance. To make use of this opportunity will not rpt not be easy due to large crowds attending functions. Security arrangements for him difficult to assess without further guidance. Recommend against physical action to be taken against priest due to expected adverse political consequences. Difficult to hide origin of an operation against priest.
Ends.

Well, Zaitzev thought, *the* rezident *didn't like this idea very much*. Would Yuriy Vladimirovich listen to this bit of advice from the field? That, Zaitzev knew, was far above his pay grade. He lifted his phone and dialed.

"Colonel Rozhdestvenskiy," the brusque voice answered.

"Captain Zaitzev in Communications Central. I have a reply to your six-six-six, Comrade Colonel."

"On my way," Rozhdestvenskiy responded.

The colonel was as good as his word, passing through the control point three minutes later. By that time, Zaitzev had returned the cipher book to central storage and slipped the message form, plus the translation, into a brown envelope, which he handed to the colonel.

Has anyone seen this?" Rozhdestvenskiy asked.

"Certainly not, comrade," Zaitzev replied.

"Very well." Colonel Rozhdestvenskiy walked away without another word. For his part, Zaitzev left his work desk and headed off to the cafeteria for lunch. The food was the best reason to work at The Centre.

What he could not leave behind as he stopped at the lavatory to wash his hands was the message sequence. Yuriy Andropov wanted to kill the Pope, and the *rezident* in Rome didn't like the idea. Zaitzev wasn't supposed to have any opinions. He was just part of the communications system. It rarely occurred to the hierarchy of the Committee for State Security that its people actually had minds . . .

. . . and even consciences . . .

Zaitzev took his place in line and got the metal tray and utensils. He decided on the beef stew and four thick slices of bread, with a large glass of tea. The cashier charged him fifty-five kopecks. His usual luncheon mates had already been and gone, so he ended up picking an end seat at a table filled with people he didn't know. They were talking about football, and he didn't join in, alone with his thoughts. The stew was quite good, as was the bread, fresh from the ovens. About the only thing they didn't have here was proper silverware, as they did in the private dining rooms on the upper floors. Instead they used the same feather-light zinc-aluminum as all the other Soviet citizens. It worked well enough, but because it was so light, it felt awkward in his hands.

So, he thought, *I was right. The Chairman is thinking about murdering the Pope.*

Zaitzev was not a religious man. He had not been to a church in his entire life—except those large buildings converted to museums since the Revolution. All he knew about religion was the propaganda dispensed as a matter of course in Soviet public education. And yet some of the children he'd known in school had talked about believing in God, and he hadn't reported them, because informing just wasn't his way. The Great Questions of Life were things he didn't much think about. For the most part, life in the Soviet Union was limited to yesterday, today, and tomorrow. The economic facts of life really didn't allow a person to make long-term plans. There were no country houses to buy, no luxury cars to desire, no elaborate vacations to save for. In committing what it called socialism on the people, the government of his country allowed—forced—everyone to aspire to much the same things, regardless of individual tastes, which meant getting on an endless list and being notified when one's name came up—and being unknowingly bumped by those with greater Party seniority—or not, because some people had access to better places. His life, like everyone else's, was like that of a steer on a feed lot. He was cared for moderately well and fed the same bland food at the same time on endlessly identical days. There was a grayness, an overarching boredom, to every aspect of life—alleviated in his case only by the content of the messages which he processed and forwarded. He wasn't supposed to think about the messages, much less remember them, but without anybody to talk to, all he could do was dwell on them in the privacy of his own mind. Today his mind had just one occupant, and it would not silence itself. It raced around like a hamster in an exercise wheel, going round and round but always returning to the same place.

Andropov wants to kill the Pope.

He'd processed assassination messages before. Not many. KGB was gradually drifting away from it. Too many things went wrong. Despite the professional skill and cleverness of the field officers, policemen in other countries were endlessly clever and had the mindless patience of a spider in its web, and until KGB could just wish a person dead and have it come to pass, there would be witnesses and evidence, because a cloak of invisibility was something found only in tales for children.

More often he processed messages about defectors or suspected would-be defectors—or, just as deadly, suspicion of officers and agents who'd "doubled," gone over to serve the enemy. He'd even seen such evidence passed along in message form, calling an officer home for "consultations" from which they'd rarely returned back to their *rezidenturas.* Exactly what happened to them—that was just the subject of gossip, all of it unpleasant. One officer who'd gone bad, the story went, had been loaded alive into a crematorium, the way the German SS was supposed to have done. He'd heard there was a film of it, and he'd talked to people who knew people who knew people who'd seen it. But he had never actually seen it himself, nor met anyone who had. Some things, Oleg Ivanovich thought, were too beyond the pale even for the KGB. No, most of the stories talked of firing squads—which often fucked up, so the stories went—or a single pistol round in the head, as Lavrenti Beriya had done himself. Those stories, *everyone* believed. He'd seen photos of Beria, and they seemed to drip with blood. And Iron Feliks would doubtless have done it between bites of his sandwich. He was the kind of man to give ruthlessness an evil name.

But it was generally felt, if not widely spoken, that KGB was becoming more *kulturniy* in its dealings with the world. More cultured. More civilized. Kinder and gentler. Traitors, of course, were executed, but only after a trial in which they were at least given a pro forma chance to explain their actions and, if they were innocent, to prove it. It almost never happened, but only because the State only prosecuted the truly guilty. The investigators in the Second Chief Directorate were among the most feared and skilled people in the entire country. It was said they were never wrong and never fooled, like some kind of gods.

Except that the State said that there were no gods.

Men, then—and women. Everyone knew about the Sparrow School, about which the men often spoke with twisty grins and winking eyes. *Ah, to be an instructor or, better still, a quality-assurance officer there!* they dreamed. And to be paid for it. As his Irina often noted, all men were pigs. *But*, Zaitzev mused, *it could be fun to be a pig.*

Kill the Pope—why? He was no threat to this country. Stalin himself had once joked, *How many divisions does the Pope have?* So why kill the man? Even the *rezident* warned against it. Goderenko feared the political repercussions. Stalin had ordered Trotsky killed, and had dispatched a KGB officer to do it, *knowing* that he'd suffer long-term imprisonment for the task. But he'd done it, faithful to the Will of the Party, in a professional gesture that they talked about in the academy training classes—along with the more casual advice that *we really don't do that sort of thing anymore.* It was not, the instructors didn't add, *kulturniy.* And so, yes, KGB was drifting away from that sort of behavior.

Until now. Until today. And even our senior *rezident* is advising against it. Why? Because he doesn't want himself and his agency—and his country!—to be so *nekulturniy*?

Or because to do so would be worse than foolish? It would be *wrong* . . . ? "Wrong" was a concept foreign to citizens in the Soviet Union. At least, what people perceived as things that were morally wrong. Morality in his country had been replaced by what was politically correct or incorrect. Whatever served the interests of his country's political system was worthy of praise. That which did not was worthy of . . . death?

And who decided such things?

Men did.

Men did because there was no morality, as the world understood the term. There was no God to pronounce what was good and what was evil.

And yet . . .

And yet, in the heart of every man was an inborn knowledge of right and wrong. To kill another man was wrong. To take a man's life you had to have a just cause. But it was also men who decided what constituted such cause. The right men in the right place with the right authority had the ability and the right to kill because—why?

Because Marx and Lenin said so.

That was what the government of his country had long since decided.

Zaitzev buttered his last piece of bread and dipped it in the remaining gravy in his bowl before eating it. He knew he was thinking overly deep, even dangerous, thoughts. His parent society did not encourage or even permit independent thinking. You were not supposed to question the Party and its wisdom. Certainly not here. In the KGB cafeteria, you *never, ever, not even once* heard someone wonder aloud if the Party and the Motherland it served and protected were even capable of doing an incorrect act. Oh, maybe once in a while, people speculated on tactics, but even then the talk was within limits that were taller and stronger than the Kremlin's own brick walls.

His country's morality, he mused, had been predetermined by a German Jew living in London, and the son of a czarist bureaucrat who simply hadn't liked the czar much and whose overly adventurous brother had been executed for taking direct action. That man had found shelter in that most capitalistic of nations, Switzerland, then had been dispatched back to Mother Russia by the Germans in the hope that he could upset the czar's government, allowing Germany then to defeat the other Western nations on the Western Front of the First World War. All in all, it didn't sound like something ordained by any deity for some great plan for human advancement, did it? Everything Lenin had used as a model for changing his country—and through it, the entire world—had come from a book written by Karl Marx, more writings by Friedrich Engels, and his own vision for becoming the chief of a new kind of country.

The only thing that distinguished Marxism-Leninism from a religion was the lack of a godhead. Both systems claimed absolute authority over the affairs of men, and both claimed to be right a priori. Except that his country's system chose to assert that authority by exercising the power of life and death.

His country said it worked for justice, for the good of the workers and peasants all around the world. But other men, higher up in the hierarchy, decided who the workers and peasant were, and they themselves lived in ornate dachas and multiroom flats, and had automobiles and drivers . . . and privileges.

What privileges they had! Zaitzev had also dispatched messages about pantyhose and perfumes that the men in this building wanted for their women. These items were often delivered in the diplomatic bag from embassies in the West, things his own country could not produce, but which the *nomenklatura* craved, along with their West German refrigerators and stoves. When he saw the big shots racing down the center of Moscow's streets in their chauffeured Zils, then Zaitzev understood how Lenin had felt about the czars. The czar had claimed divine right as his personal deed to power. The Party chieftains claimed their positions by the will of the people.

Except that the People had never given anything to them by public acclamation. The Western democracies had elections—*Pravda* spat upon them every few years—but they *were* real elections. England was now run by a nasty-looking woman, and America by an aged and buffoonish actor, but both had been chosen by the people of their countries, and the previous rulers had been removed by popular choice. Neither leader was well-loved in the Soviet Union, and he'd seen many official messages sent out to ascertain their mental state and deeply held political beliefs; the concern in those messages had been manifest, and Zaitzev himself had his worries, but as distasteful and unstable as these leaders might be, their people had chosen them. The Soviet people had decidedly not selected the current crop of princes on the Politburo.

And now the new communist princes were thinking about murdering a Polish priest in Rome. But how did *he* threaten the *Rodina*? This Pope fellow had no military formations at his command. A political threat, then? But how? The Vatican was supposed to have diplomatic identity, but nationhood without military power was—what? If there was no God, then whatever power the Pope exercised had to be an illusion, of no more substance than a puff of cigarette smoke. Zaitzev's country had the greatest army on earth, a fact proclaimed regularly by *We Serve the Soviet Union*, the TV show that everybody watched.

So, why do they want to kill a man who poses no threat? Would he part the oceans with a wave of his staff or bring down plagues on the land? Of course not.

And to kill a harmless man is a crime, Zaitzev told himself, exercising his mind for the first time in his tenure at #2 Dzerzhinskiy Square, silently asserting his free will. He'd asked a question and come up with an answer.

It would have been helpful if he'd had someone to talk to about that, but of course that was out of the question. That left Zaitzev without a safety valve—a way to process his feelings and bring them to some kind of resolution. The laws and customs of his nation forced him to recycle his thoughts over and over, and ultimately that led in only one direction. That it was a direction of which the State would not approve was, in the end, a product of the State's own making.

On finishing his lunch, he sipped his tea and lit a cigarette, but that contemplative act didn't help the state of his mind. The hamster was still running in its wheel. No one in the huge dining room noticed. To those who saw Zaitzev, he was just one more man enjoying his after-meal smoke in solitude. Like all Soviet citizens, Zaitzev knew how to hide his feelings, and so his face gave nothing away. He just looked at the wall clock so that he wouldn't be late going back to work for his afternoon watch, just one more bureaucrat in a large building full of them.

UPSTAIRS, it was a little different. Colonel Rozhdestvenskiy hadn't wanted to interrupt the Chairman's lunch, and so he'd sat in his own office waiting for the hands on the clock to move, munching on his own sandwich but ignoring the cup of soup that had come with it. Like his Chairman, he smoked American Marlboro cigarettes, which were milder and better made than their Soviet counterparts. It was an affectation he'd picked up in the field, but as a high-ranking First Chief Directorate officer, he could shop at the special store in Moscow Centre. They were expensive, even for one paid in "certificate" rubles, but he only drank cheap vodka, so it evened out. He wondered how Yuriy Vladimirovich would react to Goderenko's message. Ruslan Borissovich was a very capable *rezident*, careful and conservative, and a man senior enough to be allowed to talk back, as it were. His job, after all, was to feed good information to Moscow Centre, and if he thought something might compromise that mission, it was his duty to warn them about it—and besides, the original dispatch had not carried an obligatory directive in it, just an instruction to ascertain a situation. So, no, Ruslan Borissovich would probably not get into any trouble from his reply. But Andropov might bark and, if he did, then he, Colonel A. N. Rozhdestvenskiy, would bear the noise, which was never fun. His place here was enviable in one way and frightening in another. He had the ear of the Chairman, but being that close meant that he had to be close to the teeth, too. In the history of KGB, it was not unknown for some people to suffer for the actions of others. But it was unlikely in this case. Though an undeniably tough man, Andropov was also a reasonably fair one. Even so, it didn't pay to be too close to a rumbling volcano. His desk phone rang. It was the Chairman's private secretary.

"The Chairman will see you now, Comrade Colonel."

"*Spasiba.*" He rose and walked down the corridor.

"We have a reply from Colonel Goderenko," Rozhdestvenskiy reported, handing it over.

For his part, Andropov was not surprised, and to Colonel Rozhdestvenskiy's invisible relief, he did not lose his temper.

"I expected this. Our people have lost their sense of daring, haven't they, Aleksey Nikolay'ch?"

"Comrade Chairman, the *rezident* gives you his professional assessment of the problem," the field officer answered.

"Go on," Andropov commanded.

"Comrade Chairman," Rozhdestvenskiy replied, choosing his words with the greatest care, "you cannot undertake an operation like the one you are evidently considering without political risks. This priest has a good deal of influence, however illusory that influence may be. Ruslan Borissovich is concerned that an attack on him might affect his ability to gather information, and that, comrade, is his primary task."

"The assessment of political risk is my job, not his."

"That is true, Comrade Chairman, but it is his territory, and it is his job to tell you what he thinks you need to know. The loss of some of his agents' services could be costly to us both in direct and indirect terms."

"How costly?"

"That is impossible to predict. The Rome *rezidentura* has a number of highly productive agents for NATO military and political intelligence information. Can we live without it? Yes, I suppose we could, but better that we should live with it. The human factors involved make prediction difficult. Running agents is an art and not a science, you see."

"So you have told me before, Aleksey." Andropov rubbed his eyes tiredly. His skin was a little sallow today, Rozhdestvenskiy noted. Was his liver problem kicking up again?

"Our agents are all people, and individual people have their individual peculiarities. There is no avoiding it," Rozhdestvenskiy explained for perhaps the hundredth time. It could have been worse; Andropov actually listened some of the time. His predecessors had not all been so enlightened. Perhaps it came from Yuriy Vladimirovich's intelligence.

"That's what I like about signals intelligence," the Chairman of KGB groused. That was what everyone in the business said, Colonel Rozhdestvenskiy noted. The problem was in getting signals intelligence. The West was better at it than his country, despite their infiltration of the West's signals agencies. The American NSA and British GCHQ, in particular, worked constantly to defeat Soviet communications security and occasionally, they worried, succeeded at it. Which was why KGB depended so absolutely on one-time pads. They couldn't trust anything else.

"HOW GOOD IS THIS?" Ryan asked Harding.

"We think it's the genuine article, Jack. Part of it comes from open sources, but most comes from documents prepared for their Council of Ministers. At that level, they don't lie to themselves much."

"Why not?" Jack asked pointedly. "Everyone else there does."

"But here you're dealing with something concrete, products that have to be delivered to their army. If they do not appear, it will be noted, and inquiries will be made. In any case," Harding went on, qualifying himself carefully, "the most important material here has to do with policy questions, and for that you gain nothing by lying."

"I suppose. I raised a little hell at Langley last month when I ripped through an economics assessment that was going on to the President's office. I said it couldn't possibly be true, and the guy who drew it up said it was just what the Politburo saw at their meetings—"

"And you said what, Jack?" Harding interrupted.

"Simon, I said, whether the big shots saw it or not, it simply could not be true. That report was total bullshit—which makes me wonder how the hell their Politburo makes policy when the data they base it on is about as truthful as Alice-in-goddamned-Wonderland. You know, when I was in the Marine Corps, we worried that Ivan Ivanovich the Russian Soldier might be ten feet tall. He isn't. There may be a lot of them, but they're actually smaller than our people because they don't eat as well as children, and their weapons suck. The AK-47's a nice rifle, but I'll take the M-16 over it any time, and a rifle is a damned sight simpler than a portable radio. So I finally get into CIA and find out the tactical radios their army uses are for shit, and so it turns out I was right about that back when I was a shavetail butter-bar in the Green Machine. Bottom line, Simon, they lie to the Politburo on what are supposed to be economic realities, and if they lie to those folks, they'll lie about anything."

"So, what happened to the report to your President?"

"They sent it to him, but with five pages of mine appended to the back. I hope he got that far. They say he reads a lot. Anyway, what I'm saying is that they base their policy on lies, and maybe we can make better policy by appreciating reality a little bit better. I think their economy's in the shitter, Simon. It can't be performing as well as their data says it is. If it were, we'd be seeing the positive results in the products they make, but we don't, do we?"

"Why be afraid of a country that can't feed itself?"

"Yep." Ryan nodded.

"In the Second World War—"

"In 1941, Russia got invaded by a country that they never liked much, but Hitler was too damned stupid to make their antipathy for their own government work for him, so he implemented racist policies that were *calculated* to drive the Russian people back into the arms of Joe Stalin. So that's a false comparison, Simon. The Soviet Union is fundamentally unstable. Why? Because it's an unjust society, and there ain't no such thing as a *stable* unjust society. Their economy . . ." He paused. "You know, there ought to be a way to make that work for us . . ."

"And do what?"

"Shake their foundations some. Maybe a mild earthquake," Ryan suggested.

"And bring them crashing down?" Harding asked. His eyebrows went up. "They do have a lot of nuclear weapons, you might want to remember."

"Okay, fine, we try to arrange a soft landing."

"Bloody decent of you, Jack."

CHAPTER 7

SIMMERING

ED FOLEY'S JOB as Press Attaché was not overly demanding in terms of the time required to stroke the local American correspondents and occasionally others. "Others" included reporters purportedly from *Pravda* and other Russian publications. Foley assumed that all of them were KGB officers or stringers—there was no difference between the two since KGB routinely used journalistic covers for its field officers. As a result, most Soviet reporters in America as often as not had an FBI agent or two in close attendance, at least when the FBI had agents to spare for the task, which wasn't all that often. Reporters and field intelligence officers had virtually identical functions.

He'd just been pinged hard by a *Pravda* guy named Pavel Kuritsyn, who was either a professional spook or sure as hell had read a lot of spy novels. Since it was easier to act dumb than smart, he'd fumbled through his Russian, smiling with apparent pride at how well he'd mastered the complex language. For his part, Kuritsyn had advised the American to watch Russian TV, the quicker to master the mother tongue. Foley had then drafted a contact report for the CIA files, noting that this Pavel Yevgeniyevich Kuritsyn smelled like a Second Chief Directorate boy who was checking *him* out, and opining that he thought he'd passed the test. You couldn't be sure, of course. For all he knew, the Russians did employ people who read minds. Foley knew that they'd experimented in almost everything, even something called remote viewing, which to his professional mind was a step down from gypsy fortune-tellers—but which had gotten the Agency to start a program of its own, much to Foley's disgust. For Ed Foley, if you couldn't hold it, then it wasn't real. But there was no telling what those pantywaists in the Directorate of Intelligence would try, just to bypass what the DO people—the *real* spooks in CIA—had to do every goddamned day.

It was enough that Ivan had eyes, and Christ knew how many ears, in the embassy, though the building was regularly swept by electronics experts. (Once they'd even succeeded in planting a bug in the ambassador's own office.) Just across the street was a former church that was used by KGB. In the U.S. Embassy, it was known as Our Lady of the Microchips, because the structure was full of microwave transmitters aimed at the embassy, their function being to interfere with all the listening devices that Station Moscow used to tap in to Soviet phone and radio systems. The amount of radiation that came in flirted with dangerous-to-your-health levels, and as a result the embassy was protected with metal sheeting in the drywall, which reflected a lot of it right back at the people across the street. The game had rules, and the Russians pretty much played within them, but the rules often didn't make a hell of a lot of sense. There had been quiet protests to the local natives about the microwaves, but these were invariably met with shrugs of "Who, us?" And that was as far as it usually went. The embassy doc said he wasn't worried—but *his* office was in the basement, shielded from the radiation by stone and dirt. Some people said you could cook a hot dog by putting it on the east-facing windowsills.

Two people who did know about Ed Foley were the ambassador and the Defense Attaché. The former was Ernest Fuller. Fuller looked like an illustration from a book about patricians: tall, slim, with a regal mane of white hair. In fact, he'd grown up on an Iowa hog farm, gotten a scholarship to Northwestern University, and then a law degree, which had taken him to corporate boardrooms, where he finally ended up as CEO of a major auto company. Along the way, he'd served three years in the U.S. Navy in World War II on the light cruiser USS *Boise* during the Guadalcanal campaign. He was regarded as a serious player and a gifted amateur by the embassy's FSOs.

The Defense Attaché was Brigadier General George Dalton. By profession an artilleryman, he got along well with his Russian counterparts. Dalton was a bear of a man with curly black hair, who'd played linebacker for West Point twenty-odd years before.

Foley had an appointment with both of them—ostensibly, to talk over relations with the American news correspondents. Even his internal embassy business needed a cover in this station.

"How's your son adjusting?" Fuller asked.

"He misses his cartoons. Before we came over, I bought one of those new tape machines—you know, the Betamax thing—and some tapes, but those only last so long, and they cost an arm and a leg."

"There's a local version of Roadrunner-Coyote," General Dalton told him. "It's called *Wait a Moment,* something like that. It's not as good as Warner Brothers, but better than that damned exercise show in the morning. The gal on that could whip a command sergeant-major."

"I noticed that yesterday morning. Is she part of their Olympic weightlifting squad?" Foley joked. "Anyway . . ."

"First impressions—any surprises?" Fuller asked.

Foley shook his head. "About what I was briefed to expect. Looks like everywhere I go, I have company. How long you suppose that will last?"

"Maybe a week or so. Take a walk around—better yet, watch Ron Fielding when he takes a walk. He does his job pretty well."

"Anything major under way?" Ambassador Fuller asked.

"No, sir. Just routine operations at the moment. But the Russians have something very large happening at home."

"What's that?" Fuller asked.

"They call it Operation RYAN. Their acronym for Surprise Nuclear Attack on the Motherland. They're worried that the President might want to nuke them, and they have officers running around back home trying to get a feel for his mental state."

"You're serious?" Fuller asked.

"As a heart attack. I guess they took the campaign rhetoric a little too seriously."

"I have had a few odd questions from their foreign ministry," the Ambassador said. "But I just wrote it off to small talk."

"Sir, we're investing a lot of money in the military, and that makes them nervous."

"Whereas, when they buy ten thousand new tanks, it's normal?" General Dalton observed.

"Exactly," Foley agreed. "A gun in my hand is a defensive weapon, but a gun in your hand is an offensive weapon. It's a matter of outlook, I suppose."

"Have you seen this?" Fuller asked, handing across a fax from Foggy Bottom.

Foley scanned it. "Uh-oh."

"I told Washington it would worry the Soviets a good deal. What do you think?"

"I concur, sir. In several ways. Most important will be the potential unrest in Poland, which could spread throughout their empire. That's the one area in which they think long-term. Political stability is their sine qua non. What are they saying in Washington?"

"The Agency just showed it to the President, and he handed it off to the Secretary of State, and he faxed it to me for comment. Can you rattle any bushes, see if they're talking about it in the Politburo?"

Foley thought for a moment and nodded. "I can try." It made him slightly uncomfortable, but that was his job, wasn't it? It meant getting a message to one or more of his agents, but that was what they were for. The troubling part was that it meant exposing his wife. Mary Pat would not object—hell, she *loved* the spy game in the field—but it always bothered her husband to expose her to danger. He supposed it was chauvinism. "What's the priority on this?"

"Washington is very interested," Fuller said. That made it important, but not quite an emergency tasking.

"Okay, I'll get on it, sir."

"I don't know what assets you're running here in Moscow—and I don't want to know. It's dangerous to them?"

"They shoot traitors over here, sir."

"This is rougher than the car business, Foley. I do understand that."

"Hell, it wasn't this rough in the Central Highlands," General Dalton noted. "Ivan plays pretty mean. You know, I've been asked about the President, too, usually over drinks by senior officers. They're really that worried about him, eh?"

"It sure looks that way," Foley confirmed.

"Good. Never hurts to rattle the other guy's confidence a little, keep him looking over his shoulder some."

"Just so it doesn't go too far," Ambassador Fuller suggested. He was relatively new to diplomacy, but he had respect for the process. "Okay, anything that I need to know about?"

"Not from my end," the COS replied. "Still getting used to things. Had a Russian reporter in today, maybe a KGB counterspook checking me out, guy named Kuritsyn."

"I think he's a player," General Dalton said at once.

"I caught a whiff of that. I expect he'll check me out through the *Times* correspondent."

"You know him?"

"Anthony Prince." Foley nodded. "And that pretty much sums him up. Groton and Yale. I bumped into him a few times in New York when I was at the paper. He's very smart, but not quite as smart as he thinks he is."

"How's your Russian?"

"I can pass for a native—but my wife can pass for a poet. She's really good at it. Oh, one other thing. I have a neighbor in the compound, Haydock, husband Nigel, wife Penelope. I presume they're players, too."

"Big-time," General Dalton confirmed. "They're solid."

Foley thought so, but it never hurt to be sure. He stood. "Okay, let me get some work done."

"Welcome aboard, Ed," the Ambassador said. "Duty here isn't too bad once you get used to it. We get all the theater and ballet tickets we want through their foreign ministry."

"I prefer ice hockey."

"That's easy, too," General Dalton responded.

"Good seats?" the spook asked.

"First row."

Foley smiled. "Dynamite."

FOR HER PART, Mary Pat was out on the street with her son. Eddie was too big for a stroller, which was too bad. You could do a lot of interesting things with a stroller, and she figured the Russians would be hesitant to mess with an infant and a diaper bag—especially when they both came with a diplomatic passport. She was just taking a walk at the moment, getting used to the environment, the sights and smells. This was the belly of the beast, and here she was, like a virus—a deadly one, she hoped. She'd been born Mary Kaminsky, the granddaughter of an equerry to the House of Romanov. Grandfather Vanya had been a central figure of her youth. From him she'd learned Russian as a toddler, and not the base Russian of today, but the elegant, literary Russian of a bygone time. She could read the poetry of Pushkin and weep, and in this she was more Russian than American, for the Russians had venerated their poets for centuries, while in America they were mainly relegated to writing pop songs. There was much to admire and much to love about this country.

But not its government. She'd been twelve, looking forward to her teens with enthusiasm, when Grandfather Vanya had told her the story of Aleksey, the crown prince of Russia—a good child, so her grandfather said, but an unlucky one, stricken with hemophilia and for that reason a fragile child. Colonel Vanya Borissovich Kaminsky, a minor nobleman in the Imperial Horse Guards, had taught the boy to ride a horse, because that was one physical skill a prince needed in that age. He'd had to be ever so careful—Aleksey often went about in the arms of a sailor in the Imperial navy, lest he trip and fall and bleed—but he'd accomplished the task, to the gratitude of Nikolay II and Czarina Alexandra, and along the way the two had become as close as, if not father and son, then uncle and nephew. Grandfather Vanya had gone to the front and fought against the Germans, but early in the war had been captured at the Battle of Tannenberg. It had been in a German prisoner-of-war camp that he'd learned of the revolution. He'd managed to come back to Mother Russia, and fought with the White Guards in the doomed counterrevolutionary effort—then learned that the czar and his entire family had been murdered by the usurpers at Ekaterinberg. He'd known then that the war was lost, and he'd managed to escape and make his way to America, where he'd begun a new life, but one in perpetual mourning for the dead.

Mary Pat remembered the tears in his eyes when he told the tale, and the tears had communicated to her his visceral hatred for the Bolsheviks. It had muted somewhat. She wasn't a fanatic, but when she saw a Russian in a uniform, or in a speeding ZIL, headed for a Party meeting, she saw the face of the enemy, an enemy that needed defeating. That communism was her country's adversary was merely sauce for the goose. If she could find a button that would bring down this odious political system, she'd push it without a blink of hesitation.

And so the appointment to Moscow had been the best of all dream assignments. Just as Vanya Borissovich Kaminsky had told her his ancient and sad story, so he had given her a mission for her life, and a passion for its achievement. Her choice to join CIA had been as natural as brushing out her honey-blond hair.

And now, walking about, for the first time in her life she really understood her grandfather's passionate love for things past. Everything was different from what she knew in America, from the pitch of the building roofs to the color of the asphalt in the streets to the blank expressions on the faces of the people. They looked at her as they passed, for in her American clothes she stood out like a peacock among crows. Some even managed a smile for little Eddie, because dour as the Russians were, they were unfailingly kind to children. For the fun of it, she asked for directions from a militiaman, as the local police were called, and he was polite to her, helping with her poor pronunciation of his language and giving directions. So that was one good thing. She had a tail, she noted, a KGB officer, about thirty-five, following behind by about fifty yards, doing his best to remain invisible. His mistake was in looking away when she turned. That's probably how he had been trained, so that his face would not become too familiar to his surveillance target.

The streets and sidewalks were wide here, but not overly crowded with people. Most Russians were at work, and there was no population of free women here, out shopping or heading to social affairs or golf outings—maybe the wives of the really important party members, that was all.

Kind of like the idle rich at home, Mary Pat reflected, if there were still such people. Her mom had always worked, at least in her memory—still did, in fact. But here working women used shovels while the men drove dump trucks. They were always fixing potholes in the streets, but never quite fixing them well enough. *Just like in Washington and New York,* she thought.

There were street vendors here, though, selling ice cream, and she bought one for little Eddie, whose eyes were taking it all in. It troubled her conscience to inflict this place and this mission on her son, but he was only four and it would be a good learning experience for him. At least he'd grow up bilingual. He'd also learn to appreciate his country more than most American kids, and that, she thought, was a good thing. So, she had a tail. How good was he? Perhaps it was time to find out. She reached into her purse and surreptitiously removed a length of paper tape. It was red in color, a bright red. Turning a corner, she stuck it to a lamppost in a gesture so casual as to be invisible and kept going. Then, fifty yards down the new block, she turned to look back as though lost . . . and she saw him walk right past that lamppost. So he hadn't seen her leave the flag signal. Had he seen her, he would at least have looked . . . and he was the only one following her; her route had been so randomly chosen that there wouldn't be anyone else assigned to her, unless there was a really major surveillance effort applied to her, and that didn't seem likely. She'd never been blown on any of her field assignments. She remembered every single moment of her training at The Farm in Tidewater, Virginia. She'd been at the top of her class, and she knew she was good—and better still, she knew that you were never so good that you could forget to be careful. But as long as you were careful, you could ride any horse. Grandfather Vanya had taught her to ride, too.

She and little Eddie would have many adventures in this city, Mary Pat thought. She'd let it wait until the KGB got tired of hanging a shadow on her, and then she could really cut loose. She wondered whom she might recruit to work for CIA, in addition to running the established agents-in-place. Yeah, she was in the belly of the beast, all right, and her job was to give the son of a bitch a bleeding ulcer.

"VERY WELL, Aleksey Nikolay'ch, you know the man," Andropov said. "What do I tell him now?"

It was a sign of the Chairman's intelligence that he didn't lash out with a scorching reply, to put the Rome *rezident* back in his place. Only a fool stomped on his senior subordinates.

"He asks for guidance—the scope of the operation and so forth. We should give it to him. This brings into question exactly what you are contemplating, Comrade Chairman. Have you thought it through to that point?"

"Very well, Colonel, what do *you* think we should do?"

"Comrade Chairman, there is an expression the Americans use which I have learned to respect: That is above my pay grade."

"Are you telling me that you do not play Chairman yourself—in your own mind?" Yuriy Vladimirovich asked, rather pointedly.

"Honestly, no, I limit my thinking to that which I understand—operational questions. I am not competent to trespass into high political confines, comrade."

A clever answer, if not a truthful one, Andropov noted. But Rozhdestvenskiy would be unable to discuss whatever high-level thoughts he might have, because no one else at KGB was cleared to discuss such things. Now, he *might* be interviewed by some very senior member of the Party's Central Committee, on orders from the Politburo, but such an order would almost have to come from Brezhnev himself. And that, Yuriy Vladimirovich thought, was not likely at this time. So, yes, the colonel would think about it in the privacy of his own mind, as all subordinates did, but as a professional KGB officer, rather than a Party flack, he would leave such thoughts right there.

"Very well, we will dispense with the political considerations entirely. Consider this a theoretical question: How would one kill this priest?"

Rozhdestvenskiy looked uneasy.

"Sit," the Chairman told his subordinate. "You have planned complex operations before. Take your time to walk through this one."

Rozhdestvenskiy took his seat before speaking. "First of all, I would ask for assistance from someone better-versed in such things. We have several such officers here in The Centre. But . . . since you ask me to think about it in theoretical terms . . ." The colonel's voice trailed off and his eyes went up and to the left. When he started speaking again, his words came slowly.

"First of all, we would use Goderenko's station only for information—reconnaissance of the target, that sort of thing. We would not want to use Station Rome's people in any active way. . . . In fact, I would advise against using Soviet personnel at all for the active parts of the operation."

"Why?" Andropov asked.

"The Italian police are professionally trained, and for an investigation of this magnitude, they would throw people into it, assign their very best men. At any event like this, there will be witnesses. Everyone on earth has two eyes and a memory. Some have intelligence. That sort of thing cannot be predicted. While on the one hand, this militates in favor of, let us say, a sniper and a long-range shot, such a methodology would point to a state-level operation. Such a sniper would have to be well-trained and properly equipped. That would mean a soldier. A soldier means an army. An army means a nation-state—and which nation-state would wish to kill the Pope?" Colonel Rozhdestvenskiy asked. "A truly black operation cannot be traced back to its point of origin."

Andropov lit a cigarette and nodded. He'd chosen well. This colonel was no man's fool. "Go on."

"Ideally, the shooter would have no ties whatsoever to the Soviet Union. We must be sure of that because we cannot ignore the possibility that he will be arrested. If he is arrested, he will be questioned. Most men talk under questioning, either for psychological or physical reasons." Rozhdestvenskiy reached into his pocket and pulled out his own cigarette. "I remember reading about a Mafia killing in America. . . ." Again, the voice tailed off and his eyes fixed on the far wall while examining something in the past.

"Yes?" the Chairman prompted.

"A killing in New York City. One of their senior people was at odds with his peers, and they decided to not merely kill him, but to do so with some degree of ignominy. They had him killed by a black man. To the Mafia, that is particularly disgraceful," Rozhdestvenskiy explained. "In any case, the shooter was immediately thereafter killed by another man, presumably a Mafia assassin who then made a successful escape—no doubt he had assistance, which proves that it was a carefully planned exercise. The crime was never solved. It was a perfect technical exercise. The target was killed and so was the assassin. The true killers—those who had planned the exercise—accomplished their mission, and gained prestige within their organization, but were never punished for it."

"Criminal thugs," Andropov snorted.

"Yes, Comrade Chairman, but a properly carried-out mission is worthy of study, even so. It does not completely apply to our task at hand, because it was *supposed* to look like a well-executed Mafia murder. But the shooter got close to his target because he was manifestly *not* a member of a Mafia gang and could not later implicate or identify those who paid him to commit the act. That is precisely what we would wish to achieve. Of course, we cannot copy this operation in full—for example, killing off our shooter would point directly to us. This cannot be like the elimination of Leon Trotsky. In that case, the origin of the operation was not really concealed. As with the Mafia killing I just cited, it was supposed to be something of a public announcement." That a Soviet state action was a direct parallel to this New York City gangster rubout did not need much elaboration in Rozhdestvenskiy's eyes. But in his operational brain, the Trotsky killing and the Mafia assassination were an interesting confluence of tactics and objectives.

"Comrade, I need some time to consider this fully."

"I'll give you two hours," Chairman Andropov responded generously.

Rozhdestvenskiy stood, came to attention, and walked out through the clothes dresser into the secretary's room.

Rozhdestvenskiy's own office was small, of course, but it was private and on the same floor as the Chairman's. A window overlooked Dzerzhinskiy Square, with all its traffic and the statue of Iron Feliks. His swivel chair was comfortable, and his desk had three telephones because the Soviet Union had somehow failed to master multiline phones. He had a typewriter of his own, which he rarely used, preferring to have a secretary come in from the executive pool. There was talk that Yuriy Vladimirovich used one of them for something other than taking dictation, but Rozhdestvenskiy did not believe it. The Chairman was too much of an aesthete for that. Corruption just wasn't his way, which appealed to him. It was hard to feel loyal to a man such as Brezhnev. Rozhdestvenskiy took the Sword and Shield motto of his agency seriously. It was his job to protect his country and its people, and they needed protecting—sometimes from the members of their own Politburo.

But why did they need protection from this priest? he asked himself.

He shook his head and applied his mind to the exercise. He tended to think with his eyes open, examining his thoughts like a film on an invisible screen.

The first consideration was the nature of the target. The Pope seemed to be a tall man in the pictures, and he usually dressed in white. One could scarcely ask for a finer shooting target than that. He rode about in an open vehicle, which made him an even better target, because it drove about slowly, so that the faithful could see him well.

But who would be the shooter? Not a KGB officer. Not even a Soviet citizen. A Russian exile, perhaps. KGB had them throughout the West, many of them sleeper agents, living their lives and awaiting their activation calls. . . . But the problem was, so many of them went native and ignored their activation notices, or called the counterintelligence service in their country of residence. Rozhdestvenskiy didn't like that sort of long-term assignment. It was too easy for an officer to forget who he was and become what his cover said he was supposed to be.

No, the shooter had to be an outsider, not a Russian national, not a non-Russian former Soviet citizen, not even a foreigner trained by KGB. Best of all would be a renegade priest or nun, but people like that didn't just fall into your lap, except in Western spy fiction and TV shows. The real world of intelligence operations was rarely that convenient.

So, what sort of shooter did he need? A non-Christian? A Jew? A Muslim? An atheist would be too easy to associate with the Soviet Union, so no, not one of those. To get a Jew to do it—that would be rich! One of the Chosen People. Best of all, an Israeli. Israel had its fair share of religious fanatics. It *was* possible . . . but unlikely. KGB had assets in Israel—many of the Soviet citizens who emigrated there were KGB sleepers—but Israeli counterintelligence was notoriously efficient. The possibility of such an operation being blown was too high, and this was one operation that could not be blown. So that left Jews out.

Maybe a madman from Northern Ireland. Certainly the Protestants there loathed the Catholic Church, and one of their chieftains—Rozhdestvenskiy couldn't remember his name, but he looked like an advertisement for a brewery—had said he wished the Pope dead. The man was even supposed to be a minister himself. But, sadly, such people hated the Soviet Union even more, because their IRA adversaries claimed to be Marxists—something Colonel Rozhdestvenskiy had trouble accepting. If they were truly Marxists, he could have used Party discipline to get one of them to undertake the operation . . . but no. What little he knew of Irish terrorists told him that getting one to put Party discipline above his ethnic beliefs was far too much to ask. Attractive as it might be in a theoretical sense, it would be too hard to arrange.

That left Muslims. A lot of them were fanatics, with as little to do with the core beliefs of their religion as the Pope did with Karl Marx. Islam was just too big, and it suffered from the diseases of bigness. But if he wanted a Muslim, where to get him? KGB did have operations in many countries, with Islamic populations, as did other Marxist nations. *Hmm,* he thought, *that's a good idea.* Most of the Soviet Union's allies had intelligence services, and most of them were under KGB's thumb.

The best of them was the DDR's Stasi, superbly operated by its director, Markus Wolf. But there were few Muslims there. The Poles were good, as well, but there was no way he would use them for this operation. The Catholics had it penetrated—and that meant the West had it penetrated as well, if only at second hand. Hungary—no, again the country was too Catholic, and the only Muslims there were foreigners in ideological training camps for terrorist groups, and those he probably ought not to use. The same was true of the Czechs. Romania was not regarded as a true Soviet ally. Its ruler, though a stern communist, played too much like the gypsy gangsters native to his country. That left . . . Bulgaria. Of course. Neighbor to Turkey, and Turkey was a Muslim country, but one with a secularized culture and a lot of good gangster material. And the Bulgars had a lot of cross-border contacts, often covered as smuggling activity, which they used to get NATO intelligence, just as Goderenko did in Rome.

So, they would use the *rezident* in Sofia to get the Bulgars to do their dirty work. They had a debt of long standing to KGB, after all. Moscow Centre had enabled them to dispose of their wayward national on Westminster Bridge in a very clever operation that been partially blown only by the worst case of bad luck.

But there was a lesson in that, Colonel Rozhdestvenskiy reminded himself. Just as with that Mafia killing, the operation could not be so clever as to point directly to KGB. No, this one had to look gangsterish in its execution. Even then, there were dangers. Western governments would have their suspicions—but with no direct or even indirect connection to Dzerzhinskiy Square, they would not be able to talk about it in public. . . .

Would that be good enough? he asked himself.

The Italians, the Americans, and the British would all wonder. They would whisper, and perhaps those whispers would find their way into the public press. Did that matter?

It depended on how important this operation was to Andropov and the Politburo, didn't it? There would be risks, but in the great political reckoning, you weighed the risks against the importance of the mission.

So Station Rome would be the reconnaissance element. Station Sofia would contract the Bulgarians to hire the shooter—it would probably have to be done with a pistol. Getting close enough to use a knife was too difficult a task to plan for seriously, and rifles were too hard to conceal, though a sub-machine gun was always the weapon of choice for something like this. And the shooter would not even be a citizen of a socialist country. No, they'd get one from a NATO country. There was some degree of complexity here. But not all that much.

Rozhdestvenskiy lit up another cigarette and mentally walked back and forth through his reasoning, looking for errors, looking for weaknesses. There were some. There were always some. The real problem would be in finding a good Turk to do the shooting. For that they had to depend on the Bulgars. Just how good were their clandestine services? Rozhdestvenskiy had never worked directly with them, and knew them only by reputation. That reputation was not entirely good. They reflected their government, which was cruder and more thuggish than Moscow, not very *kulturniy,* but he supposed that was partly Russian chauvinism on the KGB's part. Bulgaria was Moscow's little brother, politically and culturally, and big brother–little brother thinking was inescapable. They just had to be good enough to have decent contacts in Turkey, and that meant just one good intelligence officer, preferably one trained in Moscow. There would be a lot of those, and KGB's own academy would have the necessary records. The Sofia *rezident* might even know him personally.

This theoretical exercise was shaping up, Colonel Rozhdestvenskiy thought to himself, with some degree of pride. So he still knew how to set up a good field operation, despite having become a headquarters drone. He smiled as he stubbed out his smoke. Then he lifted his white phone and dialed 111 for the Chairman's office.

CHAPTER 8

THE DISH

THANK YOU, ALEKSEY NIKOLAY'CH. That is a most interesting concept. So, how do we move forward, then?"

"Comrade Chairman, we have Rome keep us updated on the Pope's schedule—as far in advance as possible. We do not let them know of the existence of any operation. They are merely a source of information. When the time comes, we might wish for one of their officers to be in the area merely to observe, but it is better for all concerned that Goderenko knows as little as possible."

"You do not trust him?"

"No, Comrade Chairman. Excuse me; I did not mean to give that impression. But the less he knows, the less he might ask questions or inadvertently ask things of his personnel that might tip matters off, even innocently. We choose our Chiefs of Station for their intelligence, for their ability to see things where others do not. Should he sense that something is happening, his professional expertise might compel him at least to keep watch—and that might impede the operation."

"Freethinkers," Andropov snorted.

"Can it be any other way?" Rozhdestvenskiy asked reasonably. "There is always that price when you hire men of intelligence."

Andropov nodded. He was not so much a fool as to ignore the lesson. "Good work, Colonel. What else?"

"Timing is crucial, Comrade Chairman."

"How long to set something like this up?" Andropov asked.

"Certainly a month, likely more. Unless you have people already in place, these things always take longer than you hope or expect," Rozhdestvenskiy explained.

"I shall need that much time to get approval for this. But we will go forward with operational planning, so that when approval comes, we can execute as rapidly as possible."

Execute, Rozhdestvenskiy thought, *was the right choice of words,* but even he found it cold. And he had said *when* approval comes, not *if,* the colonel noted. Well, Yuriy Vladimirovich was supposed to be the most powerful man on the Politburo now, and that suited Aleksey Nikolay'ch. What was good for his agency was also good for him, especially in his new job. There might be general's stars at the end of this professional rainbow, and that possibility suited him as well.

"How would you proceed?" the Chairman asked.

"I should cable Rome to assuage Goderenko's fears and tell him that his tasking for the moment is to ascertain the Pope's schedule for traveling, appearances, and so forth. Next, I will cable Ilya Bubovoy. He's our *rezident* in Sofia. Have you met him, Comrade Chairman?"

Andropov searched his memory. "Yes, at a reception. He's overweight, isn't he?"

Rozhdestvenskiy smiled. "Yes, Ilya Fedorovich has always fought that, but he's a good officer. He's been there for four years, and he enjoys good relations with the *Dirzhavna Sugurnost.*"

"Grown a mustache, has he?" Andropov asked, with a rare hint of humor. Russians often chided their neighbors for facial hair, which seemed to be a national characteristic of Bulgarians.

"That I do not know," the colonel admitted. He was not yet so obsequious as to promise to find out.

"What will your cable to Sofia say?"

"That we have an operational requirement for—"

The Chairman cut him off: "Not in a cable. Fly him here. I want security very tight on this, and flying him back and forth from Sofia will raise few eyebrows."

"By your order. Immediately?" Rozhdestvenskiy asked.

"Da. Yes, at once."

The colonel came to his feet. "Right away, Comrade Chairman. I will go to communications directly."

Chairman Andropov watched him leave. One nice thing about KGB, Yuriy Vladimirovich thought, when you gave orders here, things actually happened. Unlike the Party Secretariat.

COLONEL ROZHDESTVENSKIY took the elevator back down to the basement and headed for communications. Captain Zaitzev was back at his desk, doing his paperwork as usual—that's all he had, really—and the colonel went right up to him.

"I have two more dispatches for you."

"Very well, Comrade Colonel." Oleg Ivan'ch held out his hand.

"I have to write them out," Rozhdestvenskiy clarified.

"You can use that desk right there, comrade." The communicator pointed. "Same security as before?"

"Yes, one-time pad for both. One more for Rome, and the other for Station Sofia. Immediate priority," he added.

"That is fine." Zaitzev handed him the message form blanks and turned back to his work, hoping the dispatches wouldn't be too lengthy. They had to be pretty important for the colonel to come down here even before they were drafted. Andropov must have a real bug up his rectum. Colonel Rozhdestvenskiy was the Chairman's personal gofer. It had to be kind of demeaning for someone with the skills to be a *rezident* somewhere interesting. Travel, after all, was the one real perk KGB offered its employees.

Not that Zaitzev got to travel. Oleg Ivanovich knew too much to be allowed in a Western country. After all, he might not come back—KGB always worried about that. And for the first time, he wondered why. That was the kind of day it had been. Why did KGB worry so much about possible defections? He'd seen dispatches openly discussing the troublesome possibility, and he'd seen officers who had been brought home to "talk" about it here in The Centre and often never returned to the field. He'd always known about it, but he'd never actually thought about it for as much as thirty seconds.

They left because—because they thought their state was wrong? Could they actually think it was so bad they would do something so drastic as *betray* their Motherland? That, Zaitzev belatedly realized, was a very big thought.

And yet, what was KGB but an agency that lived on betrayal? How many hundreds—thousands—of dispatches had he read about just that? Those were Westerners—Americans, Britons, Germans, Frenchmen—all used by KGB to find out things that his country wanted to know—and they were all traitors to their mother countries, weren't they? They did it mainly for money. He'd seen a lot of those messages, too, discussions between The Centre and the *rezidenturas* discussing the amounts of payment. He knew that The Centre was always niggardly with the money it paid out, which was to be expected. The agents wanted American dollars, British pounds sterling, Swiss francs. And cash, real paper money—they always wanted to be paid in cash. Never rubles or even certificate rubles. It was the only money they trusted, clearly enough. They betrayed their country for money, but only for *their* own money. Some of them even demanded millions of dollars, not that they ever got it. The most he'd ever seen authorized was £50,000, paid out for information about British and American naval ciphers. *What would the Western powers* not *pay for the communications information in* his *mind?* Zaitzev thought idly. It was a question with no answer. He did not really have the ability to frame the question properly, much less consider the answer seriously.

"Here you go," Rozhdestvenskiy said, handing over the message blanks. "Send them out at once."

"As soon as I get them enciphered," the communicator promised.

"And the same security as before," the colonel added.

"Certainly. Same identifier tag on both?" Oleg Ivanovich asked.

"Correct, all with this number," he replied, tapping the 666 in the upper-right corner.

"By your order, Comrade Colonel. I'll see to it right now."

"And call me when they go out."

"Yes, Comrade Colonel. I have your office number," Zaitzev assured him.

There was more to it than the mere words, Oleg knew. The tone of his voice had told him much. This *was* going out under the direct order of the Chairman, and all this attention made it a matter of the highest priority, not just something of routine interest to an important man. This wasn't about ordering pantyhose for some bigwig's teenage daughter.

He walked to the cipher-book storage room to get two books, the ones for Rome and Sofia, and then he pulled out his cipher wheel and laboriously encrypted both messages. All in all, it took forty minutes. The message to Colonel Bubovoy in Sofia was a simple one: Fly to Moscow immediately for consultations. Zaitzev wondered if that would make the *rezident*'s knees wobble a little. Colonel Bubovoy could not know what the numerical identifier meant, of course. He'd find out soon enough.

The rest of Zaitzev's day went routinely. He managed to lock up his confidential papers and walk out before six in the evening.

LUNCH AT CENTURY HOUSE was good, but British-eccentric. Ryan had learned to enjoy the British Ploughman's Lunch, mainly because the bread was so uniformly excellent over here.

"So, your wife's a surgeon?"

Jack nodded. "Yeah, eye cutter. She's actually starting to use lasers for some things now. She's hoping to be a pioneer in that stuff."

"Lasers? What for?" Harding asked.

"Some of it's like welding. They use a laser to cauterize a leaky blood vessel, for instance—they did it with Suslov. Blood leaked inside the eye, so they drilled into the eyeball and drained out all the fluid—aqueous humor, I think they call it—and then used lasers to weld shut the leaky vessels. Sounds pretty yucky, doesn't it?"

Harding shuddered at the thought. "I suppose it's better than being blind."

"Yeah, I know what you mean. Like when Sally was in shock-trauma.

The idea of somebody carving up my little girl didn't exactly thrill me." Ryan remembered how fucking awful that had been, in fact. Sally still had the scars on her chest and abdomen from it, though they were fading.

"What about you, Jack? You've been under the knife before," Simon observed.

"I was asleep, and they didn't make videos of the operations—but you know, Cathy would probably be interested in seeing all three of them."

"Three?"

"Yeah, two when I was in the Marines. They stabilized me on the ship, then flew me to Bethesda for the rest of it—I was asleep practically the whole time, thank God, but the neurosurgeons there weren't quite good enough, and that left me with a bad back. Then, when Cathy and I were dating—no, we were engaged then—my back blew up again over dinner in Little Italy, and she took me into Hopkins and had Sam Rosen take a look at me. Sam fixed it all up. Good guy, and a hell of a doc. You know, sometimes it's nice to be married to a doctor. She knows some of the best people in the world." Ryan took a big bite of turkey and baguette. It was better than the burgers in the CIA cafeteria. "Anyway, that's the short version of a three-year adventure that started with a broke helicopter on Crete. It ended up with me being married, so I guess it all worked out okay."

Harding filled his pipe out of a leather pouch and lit it. "So, how's your report coming on Soviet management and practices?"

Jack set his beer down. "It's amazing how screwed up they are, especially when you compare their internal documents with the hard data we learn when our guys get hands-on with their gear. What they call quality control, we call a dog's breakfast. At Langley, I saw some stuff on their fighter planes that the Air Force got, mainly through the Israelis. The goddamned parts don't fit together! They can't even cut aluminum sheets into regular shapes. I mean, a high-school kid in shop class would have to do better or flunk out of school. We know they have competent engineers, especially the guys who work in theoretical stuff, but their manufacturing practices are so primitive that you'd expect better from third-graders."

"Not in all areas, Jack," Harding cautioned.

"And not all the Pacific Ocean's blue, Simon. There are islands and volcanoes, sure. I know that. But the rule is the ocean is blue, and the rule in the Soviet Union is shitty work. The problem is that their economic system doesn't reward people for doing good work. There's a saying in economics: 'Bad money drives out good.' That means poor performance will take over if good performance isn't recognized. Well, over there, mainly it isn't, and for their economy it's like cancer. What happens in one place gradually carries over to the whole system."

"There are some things at which they are very good indeed," Harding persisted.

"Simon, the Bolshoi Ballet isn't going to attack into West Germany. Neither is their Olympic team," Jack retorted. "Their military may be competently led at the higher levels, but their equipment is crummy, and the middle-level management is practically nonexistent. Without my gunnery sergeant and my squad leaders, I could not have used my platoon of Marines efficiently, but the Red Army doesn't have sergeants as we understand them. They have competent officers—and, again, some of their theoretical people are world-class—and their soldiers are probably patriotic Russians and all that, but without proper training at the tactical level, they're like a beautiful car with flat tires. The engine might turn over and the paint job might shine, but the car isn't going anywhere."

Harding took a few contemplative puffs. "Then what are we worried about?"

Jack shrugged. "There's a hell of a lot of them, and quantity does have a quality all its own. If we go forward with our defense buildup, however, we can stop anything they try. A Russian tank regiment is just a collection of targets if we have the right equipment and our guys are properly trained and led. Anyway, that's what my report is probably going to say."

"It's a little early for a conclusion," Simon told his new American friend. Ryan hadn't yet learned how a bureaucracy was supposed to work.

"Simon, I used to make my money in trading. You succeed in that business by seeing things a little faster than the next guy, and that means you don't wait until you have every last little crumb of information. I can see where this information is pointing me. It's bad over there, and it's getting worse. Their military is a distillation of what is good and bad in their society. Look at how badly they're doing in Afghanistan. I haven't seen your data, but I've seen what they have at Langley, and it isn't pretty. Their military is performing very poorly in that rockpile."

"I think they will ultimately succeed."

"It's possible," Jack conceded, "but it'll be an ugly win. We did a lot better in Vietnam." He paused. "You guys have ugly memories of Afghanistan, don't you?"

"My great-uncle was there in 1919. He said it was worse than the Battle of the Somme. Kipling did a poem that ends with an instruction to a soldier to blow his brains out rather than be captured there. I'm afraid some Russians have learned that lesson, to their sorrow."

"Yeah, the Afghans are courageous, but not overly civilized," Jack agreed. "But I think they're going to win. There's talk at home about giving them the Stinger SAM. That would neutralize the helicopters the Russians are using, and without those, Ivan's got a problem."

"Is the Stinger that good?"

"Never used it myself, but I've heard some nice things about it."

"And the Russian SAM-seven?"

"They kind of invented the idea of a man-portable SAM, didn't they? But we got a bunch through the Israelis in seventy-three, and our guys weren't all that impressed. Again, Ivan had a great idea, then couldn't execute it properly. That's their curse, Simon."

"Then explain KGB to me," Harding challenged.

"Same as the Bolshoi Ballet and their ice hockey teams. They load a lot of talent and money into that agency, and they get a fair return for it—but they have a lot of spooks skip over the wall, too, don't they?"

"True," Simon had to concede.

"And why, Simon?" Jack asked. "Because they fill their heads with how corrupt and messed up we are, and then when their people get here and look around, it isn't all that bad, is it? Hell, we have safe houses all over America with KGB guys in them, watching TV. Not many of them decide to go home, either. I've never met a defector, but I've read a lot of transcripts, and they all say pretty much the same thing. Our system is better than theirs, and they're smart enough to tell the difference."

"We have some living here as well," Harding admitted. He didn't want to admit that the Russians also had a few Brits—nowhere near as many, just enough to be a considerable embarrassment to Century House. "You're a hard man to debate, Jack."

"I just speak the truth, buddy. That's what we're here for, isn't it?"

"That's the theory," Harding had to admit. This Ryan fellow would never be a bureaucrat, the Brit decided, and wondered if that was a good thing or bad. The Americans took a different slant on things, and the contrast to his own organization's take was entertaining, at least. Ryan had a lot to learn . . . but he also had a few things to teach, Harding realized. "How's your book coming along?"

Ryan's face changed. "Haven't gotten much work done lately. I do have my computer set up. Hard to concentrate on that after a full day here—but if I don't make the time, the thing will never get done. At heart, I'm lazy," Ryan admitted.

"Then how did you become rich?" Harding demanded. He got a grin.

"I'm also greedy. Gertrude Stein said it, pal: 'I've been rich and I've been poor. It's better to be rich.' Truer words have never been spoken."

"I must discover that for myself someday," the British civil servant observed.

Oops, Ryan thought. *Well, it wasn't his fault, was it?* Simon was smart enough to make money in the real world, but he didn't seem to think in those terms. It made good sense to have a smart guy here in the analyst pool at Century House, even though that meant sacrificing his own well-being for his country. But that was not a bad thing, and Ryan reflected that he was doing it, too. His advantage was that he'd made his money up front and could afford to kiss this job off and go back to teaching whenever the urge struck him. It was a sort of independence that most government employees would never know. . . . *And their work probably suffered because of it,* Jack thought.

ZAITZEV MADE HIS WAY out past the various security checkpoints. Some people were frisked at random by the guards to make sure that they weren't taking anything out with them, but the checks—he'd suffered through his share of them—were too cursory to be effective, he thought. Just enough to be a nuisance, and not regular enough to be a real threat—perhaps once in thirty days—and, if you got frisked one day, you knew you were safe for at least the next five or so, because the guards knew all the faces of the people they checked out, and even here there was human contact and friendly relationships among the employees, especially at the working level—a kind of blue-collar solidarity that was in some ways surprising. As it happened, Zaitzev was allowed to pass without inspection and made his way into the capacious square, then walked to the metro station.

He didn't usually dress in the paramilitary uniform—most KGB employees did not choose to do so, as though their employment might make them seem tainted to their fellow citizens. Neither did he hide it. If anyone asked, he gave an honest answer, and the questioning usually stopped there, because everyone knew that you didn't ask questions about what went on at the Committee for State Security. There were occasional movies and TV shows about KGB, and some of them were even fairly honest, though they gave little away concerning methods and sources beyond what some fiction writer might imagine, which wasn't always all that accurate. There was a small office at The Centre that consulted on such things, usually taking things out and—rarely—putting accurate things in, because it was in his agency's interest to be fearful and forbidding to Soviet citizens and foreigners alike. *How many ordinary citizens supplement their incomes by being informers?* Zaitzev wondered. He almost never saw any dispatches about that—that sort of thing rarely went overseas.

The things that did go out of the country were troubling enough. Colonel Bubovoy would probably be in Moscow the next day. There was regular air service between Sofia and Moscow through Aeroflot. Colonel Goderenko in Rome had been told to sit down and shut up, and to forward to The Centre the Pope's appearance schedule for the indefinite future. Andropov hadn't lost interest in that bit of information.

And now the Bulgarians would be involved. Zaitzev worried about that, but he didn't need to wonder all that much. He'd seen those dispatches before. The Bulgarian State Security Service was the loyal vassal of KGB. The communicator knew that. He'd seen enough messages go to Sofia, sometimes through Bubovoy, sometimes directly, and sometimes for the purpose of ending someone's life. KGB didn't do much of that anymore, but *Dirzhavna Sugurnost* did, on occasion. Zaitzev imagined that they had a small subunit of the DS officers who were trained and skilled and *practiced* at that particular skill. And the message header had the 666 suffix, so this dispatch concerned the same thing that Rome had been initially queried on. So this was going forward.

His agency—his country—wanted to kill that Polish priest, and that, Zaitzev thought, was probably a bad thing.

He took the escalator down to the subterranean station amid the usual afterwork crowd. Usually, the crowd of people was comforting. It meant that Zaitzev was in his element, surrounded by his countrymen, people just like himself, serving one another and the State. But was that true? *What would these people think of Andropov's mission?* It was hard to gauge. The subway ride was usually quiet. Some people might talk to friends, but group discussions were rare, except perhaps for some unusual sporting event, a bad referee's call at a soccer match, or a particularly spectacular play on the hockey rink. Other than that, people were usually alone with their thoughts.

The train stopped, and Zaitzev shuffled aboard. As usual, there were no seats available. He grasped the overhead handrail and kept thinking.

Are the others on the train thinking as well? If so, about what? Jobs? Children? Wives? Lovers? Food? You couldn't tell. Even Zaitzev couldn't tell, and he'd seen these people—these *same* people—on the metro for years. He knew only a few names, mainly given names overheard in conversations. No, he knew them only by their favorite sports teams. . . .

It struck him suddenly and hard how alone he was in his society. *How many real friends do I have?* Zaitzev asked himself. The answer was shockingly few. Oh, sure, there were people at work he chatted with. He knew the most intimate details about their wives and children—but friends in whom he could confide, with whom he could talk over some troubling development, to whom he could go for guidance in a troubling situation . . . No, he didn't have any of those. That made him unusual in Moscow. Russians often made deep and close friendships, and consecrated them often enough with the deepest and sometimes the darkest of secrets, as though daring one of their intimates to be a KGB informer, as though courting a trip to the Gulag. But his job denied him that. He'd never dare to discuss the things he did at work, not even to his coworkers.

No, whatever problems he had with this 666 series of messages were ones he had to work out for himself. Even his Irina couldn't know. She might talk with her friends at GUM, and that would surely be death for him. Zaitzev let out a breath and looked around. . . .

There he was again, that American embassy official, reading *Sovietskiy Sport* and minding his own business. He was wearing a raincoat—rain had been forecast, but had not materialized—but not a hat. The coat was open, not buttoned or belted. He was less than two meters away. . . .

On an impulse, Zaitzev shifted his position from one side of the car to the other, switching hands on the overhead rail as though to stretch a stiff muscle. That move put him next to the American. And, on further impulse, Zaitzev slid his hand into the raincoat pocket. There was nothing in there, no keys or pocket change, just empty cloth. But he had established that he could reach into this American's pocket and remove his hand without notice. He backed away, sweeping his eyes around the subway car to see if anyone had noticed or had even been looking his way. But . . . no, almost certainly not. His maneuver had gone undetected, even by the American.

FOLEY DIDN'T EVEN let his eyes move as he read to the bottom of the hockey article. Had he been in New York or any other Western city, he would have thought that someone had just attempted to pick his pocket. Strangely, he didn't expect that here. Soviet citizens were not allowed to have Western currency, and so there was nothing but trouble to be gained in robbing an American on the street, much less picking his pocket. And KGB, which was probably still shadowing him, was most unlikely to do anything like that. If they wanted to lift his wallet, they'd use a two-man team, as professional American pickpockets did, one to delay and distract, and the other to make the lift. You could get almost anyone that way, unless the target was alerted, and staying alert for so long was a lot to ask, even of an expert professional spook. So you employed passive defenses, like wrapping a rubber band or two around the wallet—simple, but very effective, and one of the things they taught you at The Farm, the sort of basic tradecraft that didn't announce *"spy!"* to everyone. The NYPD advised people to do the same thing on the streets of Manhattan, and he was *supposed* to look like an American. Since he had a diplomatic passport and "legal" cover, theoretically, his person was inviolable. Not necessarily from a street thug, of course, and both the KGB and the FBI were not above having a highly trained street thug rough someone up, albeit within carefully thought-through parameters, lest things get out of control. The entire state of affairs made the Imperial Court of Byzantium look simple by comparison, but Ed Foley didn't make the rules.

Those rules now did not allow him to check his pocket or make the least sign that he knew that someone's hand had been in there. Maybe someone had dropped him a note—a notice of desire to defect, even. But why him? His cover was supposed to be as solid as a T-bill, unless someone in the embassy had made a very shrewd guess and then ratted him out. . . . But no, even then, KGB wouldn't tip their hand this quickly. They'd watch him for a few weeks at least, just to see what else he might lead them to. KGB played the game too skillfully for that sort of play, so, no, there wasn't much chance that whoever had searched his pocket was a Second Chief Directorate guy. And probably not a pickpocket, either. *Then what?* Foley wondered. He'd have to be patient to find out, but Foley knew a lot about patience. He kept on reading his newspaper. If it were someone who wanted to do a little business, why scare him off? At the very least, he'd let him feel clever. It was always useful to help other people feel smart. That way, they could continue their mistakes.

Three more stops before he got off the subway. Foley had known up front that it would be a lot more productive to ride it than to drive the car. That Mercedes was just too standout-ish for this place. It would make Mary Pat stand out, too, but to her way of thinking, that worked for her rather than against. His wife had brilliant field instincts, better than his, but she often scared him in her daring. It wasn't so much that Mary Pat was a risk-taker. Every member of the DO took risks. It was her relish for doing so that occasionally worried him. For him, playing with the Russians was part of the job. It was business, as Don Vito Corleone would have put it, not personal. But for Mary Patricia, it was as personal as hell, because of her grandfather.

She'd lusted to be part of CIA before they'd met in the Student Union at Fordham, and then again at the CIA recruiter's desk, and they'd hit it off soon after that. She'd already had her Russian-language skills. She could pass for a native. She could alter her accent for any region of the country. She could feign being an instructor in poetry at Moscow State University, and she was pretty, and pretty women had an advantage over everyone else. It was the oldest of prejudices, that the attractive among us had to be good people, that the bad people had to be ugly because they did ugly things. Men were especially deferential to pretty women, other women were less so, because they envied their looks, but even they were nice by instinct. So Mary Pat could skate on a lot of things, because she was just that pretty American girl, that ditsy blonde, because blondes were universally thought to be dumb, even here in Russia, where they were not all that uncommon. The ones here were probably natural blondes, too, because the local cosmetics industry was about as advanced as it must have been in twelfth-century Hungary, and there wasn't much Clairol Blond #100G in the local drugstores. No, the Soviet Union paid scant attention to the needs of its womenfolk, which led his mind to another question—why had the Russians stopped at only one revolution? In America there would have been hell to pay for the lack of choices in clothes and cosmetics the women had here. . . .

The train stopped at his station. Foley made his way to the door and walked to the escalator. Halfway up, his curiosity got the better of him. He rubbed his nose as though with a case of the sniffles, and fished in his pocket for a handkerchief. He rubbed his nose with it and then shoved it in his coat pocket, which, he discovered, was empty. So what had that been all about? There was no telling. Just one more random event in a life filled with them?

But Edward Foley hadn't been trained to think in terms of random events. He'd continue this regular schedule, and be sure to catch this same subway train every day for a week or so, just to see if there might be a repeat.

ALBERT BYRD SEEMED a competent eye cutter. He was shorter and older than Jack. He had a beard, black and showing hints of gray—like a lot of beards in England, she'd noted. And tattoos. More than she'd ever encountered before. Professor Byrd was a skilled clinician, good with his patients, and a very adept surgeon, liked and trusted by his nursing team—always the sign of a good doc, Cathy knew. He seemed to be a good teacher, but Cathy already knew most of what he had to teach, and knew more about lasers than he did. The argon laser here was new, but not as new as the one at Hopkins, and it would be two weeks before they even had a xenon-arc laser, for which she was Wilmer Eye Institute's best jockey at Hopkins.

The bad news was in the physical facilities. Health care in Britain was effectively a government monopoly. Everything was free—and, like everywhere in the world, you got what you paid for. The waiting rooms were far shabbier than Cathy was used to, and she remarked on it.

"I know," Professor Byrd said tiredly. "It's not a priority."

"The third case I saw this morning, Mrs. Dover, she'd been on the waiting list for eleven months—for a cataract evaluation that took me twenty minutes. My God, Albert, at home her family physician just calls my secretary and I see her in three or four days. I work hard at Hopkins, but not that hard."

"What would you charge?"

"For that? Oh . . . two hundred dollars. Since I'm an assistant professor at Wilmer, I come a little higher than a new resident." But, she didn't add, she was a damned sight smarter than the average resident, more experienced, and a faster worker. "Mrs. Dover is going to need surgery to correct it," she added. "Want me to do it?"

"Complicated?" Byrd asked.

She shook her head. "Routine procedure. About ninety minutes' work because of her age, but it doesn't look as though there should be any complications."

"Well, Mrs. Dover will go on the list."

"How long?"

"It's not an emergency procedure . . . nine to ten months," Byrd figured.

"You're kidding," Cathy objected. "That long?"

"That's about normal."

"But that's nine or ten months during which she can't see well enough to drive a car!"

"She won't ever see a bill," Byrd pointed out.

"Fine. She can't read the newspapers for the best part of a year. Albert, that's awful!"

"It's our national health-care system," Byrd explained.

"I see," Cathy said. But she didn't really. The surgeons here were proficient enough, but they did only a bit more than half the procedures she and her colleagues did at Hopkins—and she'd never felt overworked in the Maumenee Building. Sure, you worked hard. But people needed you, and her job was to restore and improve the sight of people who required expert medical care—and to Caroline Ryan, M.D., FACS, that was a religious calling. It wasn't that the local docs were lazy, it was just that the system allowed—nay, encouraged—them to take a very laissez-faire attitude toward their work. She'd arrived in a very new medical world, and it wasn't all that brave.

Neither had she seen a CAT scanner. They'd essentially been invented in Britain by EMI, but some bean counter in the British government—the Home Office, they'd told her—had decided that the country only needed a few of them, and so most hospitals lost the lottery. The CAT scan had just come into being a few years before she'd entered the Johns Hopkins University School of Medicine, but in the ensuing decade they'd become as much a part of medicine as the stethoscope. Practically every hospital in America had one. They cost a million dollars apiece, but the patient paid for the use of the things, and they paid themselves off quickly enough. She only rarely needed one—to examine tumors around the eye, for example—but when you did, you damned well needed it right now!

And at Johns Hopkins, the floors were mopped every day.

But the people had the same needs, and she was a doc, and that, Cathy decided, was that. One of her medical school colleagues had gone to Pakistan and come back with the kind of experience in eye pathologies that you couldn't get in a lifetime in American hospitals. Of course, he'd also come back with amoebic dysentery, which was guaranteed to lessen anyone's enthusiasm for foreign travel. At least that wouldn't happen here, she told herself. Unless she caught it in a doctor's waiting room.

CHAPTER 9

SPIRITS

THUS FAR, Ryan had not managed to catch the same train home as his wife, always managing to get home later than she did. By the time he got home, he'd be able to think about doing some work on his Halsey book. It was about 70 percent done, with all the serious research behind him. He just had to finish the writing. What people never seemed to understand was that this was the hard part; researching was just locating and recording facts. Making the facts seem to come together in a coherent story was the difficult part, because human lives were never coherent, especially a hard-drinking warrior like William Frederick Halsey, Jr. Writing a biography was more than anything else an exercise in amateur psychiatry. You seized incidents that happened in his life at randomly selected ages and education levels, but you could never know the little key memories that formed a life—the third-grade schoolyard fight, or the admonishment from his maiden aunt Helen that resonated in his mind for his entire life, because men rarely revealed such things to others. Ryan had such memories, and some of them appeared and disappeared in his consciousness at seemingly random intervals, when the message from Sister Frances Mary in Second Grade at St. Matthew's School leaped into his memory as though he were seven years old again. A skilled biographer seemed to have the ability to simulate such things, but it sometimes came down to making things up, to applying your own personal experiences to the life of another person and that was . . . fiction, and history wasn't supposed to be fiction. Neither was an article in a newspaper, but Ryan knew from his own experience that much purported "news" was made up from whole cloth. But nobody ever said that writing a biography was easy. His first book, *Doomed Eagles,* had been in retrospect a much easier project. Bill Halsey, Fleet Admiral, USN, had fascinated him since reading the man's own autobiography as a boy. He'd commanded naval forces in battle, and while that had seemed exciting to a boy of ten years, it was positively frightening to a man of thirty-two, because now he understood the things that Halsey didn't discuss in full—the unknowns, having to trust intelligence information without really knowing where it came from, how it was gathered, how it was analyzed and processed, how it was transmitted to him, and whether or not the enemy was listening in. Ryan was now in that loop, and having to wager his life on the work that he did himself was frightening as hell—rather more so, actually, to be wagering the lives of others whom he might or, more likely, might not know.

There was a joke he remembered from his time in the Marine Corps, Ryan thought, as the green English countryside slid past his window: The motto of the intelligence services was "We bet *your* life." That was now his business. He had to wager the lives of others. Theoretically, he might even come up with an intelligence estimate that risked the fate of his country. You had to be so damned sure of yourself and your data. . . .

But you couldn't always be sure, could you? He'd scoffed at many official CIA estimates to which he'd been exposed back at Langley, but it was a damned sight easier to spit on the work of others than it was to produce something better yourself. His Halsey book, tentatively titled *Fighting Sailor,* would upset a few conventional-wisdom apple carts, and deliberately so. Ryan thought that the conventional thinking in some areas was not merely incorrect, but stuff that could not possibly be true. Halsey had acted rightly in some cases where the all-seeing eye of hindsight had castigated him for being wrong. And that was unfair. Halsey could only be judged responsible for the information that was available to him. To say otherwise was like castigating doctors for not being able to cure cancer. They were smart people doing their best, but there were some things they didn't know yet—they were working like hell to find them out, but the process of discovery took time then, and it was still taking time now, Ryan thought. Was it ever. And Bill Halsey could only know what he was given, or what a reasonably intelligent man might deduce from that information, given a lifetime of experience and what he knew of the psychology of his enemy. And even then the enemy did not willingly cooperate in his own destruction, did he?

That's my job, all right, Ryan thought behind blank eyes. It was a quest for Truth, but it was more than that. He had to replicate for his own masters the thinking processes of others, to explain them to his own superiors, so that they, Ryan's bosses, could better understand their adversaries. He was playing pshrink without a diploma. In a way, that was amusing. It was less so when you considered the magnitude of the task and the potential consequences of failure. It came down to two words: *dead people.* In the Basic School at Quantico Marine Base, they'd hammered the same lesson home often enough. Screw up leading your platoon, and some of your Marines don't go home to their mothers and wives, and that would be a heavy burden to carry on your conscience for the rest of your life. The profession of arms attached a large price tag to mistakes. Ryan hadn't served long enough to learn that lesson for himself, but it had frightened him on quiet nights, feeling the roll of the ship on her way across the Atlantic. He'd talked it over with Gunny Tate, but the sergeant—then an "elderly" man of thirty-four—had just told him to remember his training, trust his instincts, and to think before acting if he had the time, and then warned that you didn't always have the luxury of time. And he'd told his young boss not to worry, because he seemed pretty smart for a second lieutenant. Ryan would never forget that. The respect of a Marine gunnery sergeant didn't come cheaply.

So he had the brains to make good intelligence estimates and the guts to put his name behind them, but he had to be damned sure they were good stuff before he put them out. Because he *was* betting the lives of other people, wasn't he?

The train slowed to a stop. He walked up the steps, and there were a few cabs topside. Jack imagined they had the train schedule memorized.

"Good evening, Sir John." Jack saw it was Ed Beaverton, his morning pickup.

"Hi, Ed. You know," Ryan said, getting into the front seat for a change. Better legroom. "My name is actually Jack."

"I can't call you that," Beaverton objected. "You're a knight."

"Only honorary, not a real one. I do not own a sword—well, only my Marine Corps one, and that's back home in the States."

"And you were a lieutenant, and I was only a corporal."

"And you jumped out of airplanes. Damned if I ever did anything that stupid, Eddie."

"Only twenty-eight times. Never broke anything," the taxi driver reported, turning up the hill.

"Not even an ankle?"

"Just a sprain or two. The boots help with that, you see," the cabbie explained.

"I haven't learned to like flying yet—damned sure I'll never jump out of an airplane." No, Jack was sure, he never would have opted for Force Recon. Those Marines just weren't wired right. He'd learned the hard way that flying over the beach in helicopters was scary enough. He still had dreams about it—the sudden sensation of falling, and seeing the ground rush up—but he always woke up just before impact, usually lurching up to a sitting position in the bed and then looking around the darkened bedroom to make sure he wasn't in that damned CH-46 with a bad aft rotor, falling to the rocks on Crete. It was a miracle that he and a lot of his Marines hadn't been killed. But his had been the only major injury. The rest of his platoon had gotten away with nothing worse than sprains.

Why the hell are you thinking about that? he demanded of himself. It was more than eight years in his past.

They were pulling up in front of the house in Grizedale Close. "Here we are, sir."

Ryan handed him his fare, plus a friendly tip. "The name's Jack, Eddie."

"Yes, sir. I'll see you in the morning."

"Roger that." Ryan walked off, knowing he'd never win that battle. The front door was unlocked in anticipation of his arrival. His tie went first, as he headed to the kitchen.

"Daddy!" Sally fairly screamed, as she ran to his arms. Jack scooped her up and gave and got a hug. "How's my big girl?"

"Fine."

Cathy was at the stove, fixing dinner. He set Sally down and headed to his wife for a kiss. "How is it," her husband asked, "that you're always home first? At home you're usually later."

"Unions," she replied. "Everybody clocks out on time here, and 'on time' is usually pretty early—not like Hopkins." Where, she didn't add, just about everyone on the professional staff worked late.

"Must be nice to work bankers' hours."

"Even dad doesn't leave his office this early, but everybody over here does. And lunch means a full hour—half the time away from the hospital. Well," she allowed, "the food's a little better that way."

"What's for dinner?"

"Spaghetti." And Jack saw that the pot was full of her special meat sauce. He turned to see a baguette of French bread on the counter.

"Where's the little guy?"

"Living room."

"Okay." Ryan headed that way. Little Jack was in his crib. He'd just mastered sitting up—it was a little early for that, but that was fine with his dad. Around him was a collection of toys, all of which found their way into his mouth. He looked up to see his father and managed a toothless smile. Of course, that merited a pickup, which Jack accomplished. His diaper felt dry and fresh. Doubtless, Miss Margaret had changed him before scooting off—as always, before Jack made it home from the shop. She was working out fairly well. Sally liked her, and that was the important part. He set his son back down, and the little guy resumed playing with a plastic rattle and watching the TV—especially the commercials. Jack went off to the bedroom to change into more comfortable clothes, then back to the kitchen. Then the doorbell chimed, much to everyone's surprise. Jack went to answer it.

"Dr. Ryan?" the voice asked in American English. It was a guy of Ryan's height and general looks, dressed in a jacket and tie, holding a large box.

"That's right."

"I got your STU for you, sir. I work comms at the embassy," the guy explained. "Mr. Murray said I should bring this right over."

The box was a cardboard cube about two and a half feet on a side, and blank, with no printing on it. Ryan let the man into the house and led him directly to his den. It took about three minutes to extract the oversized phone from the box. It went next to Jack's Apple IIe computer.

"You're NSA?" Ryan asked.

"Yes, sir. Civilian. Used to be in the Army Security Agency, E-5. Got out and got a pay increase as a civilian. Been over here two years. Anyway, here's your encryption key." He handed over the plastic device. "You know how these things work, right?"

"Oh yeah." Ryan nodded. "Got one on my desk downtown."

"So you know the rules about this. If anything breaks, you call me"—he handed over his card—"and nobody but me or one of my people is allowed to look at the inside. If that happens, the system self-destructs, of course. Won't start a fire or anything, but it does stink some, 'cause of the plastic. Anyway, that's it." He broke down the box.

"You want a Coke or anything?"

"No, thanks. Gotta get home." And with that, the communications expert walked back out the door to his car.

"What was that, Jack?" Cathy asked from the kitchen.

"My secure phone," Jack explained, returning to his wife's side.

"What's that for?"

"So I can call home and talk to my boss."

"Can't you do that from the office?"

"There's the time difference and, well, there are some things I can't talk about there."

"Secret-agent stuff," she snorted.

"That's right." Just like the pistol he had in his closet. Cathy accepted the presence of his Remington shotgun with some equanimity—he used it for hunting, and she was prepared to tolerate that, since you could cook and eat the birds, and the shotgun was unloaded. But she was less comfortable with a pistol. And so, like civilized married people, they didn't talk about it, so long as it was well out of Sally's reach, and Sally knew that her father's closet was off-limits. Ryan had gotten fond of his Browning Hi-Power 9mm automatic, which *was* loaded with fourteen Federal hollow-point cartridges and two spare magazines, plus tritium match sights and custom-made grips. If he ever needed a pistol again, this would be the one. He'd have to find a place to practice shooting, Ryan reminded himself. Maybe the nearby Royal Navy base had a range. Sir Basil could probably make a phone call and straighten it out. As an honorary knight, he didn't own a sword, but a pistol was the modern equivalent, and it could be a useful tool on occasion.

So could a corkscrew. "Chianti?" Ryan asked.

Cathy turned. "Okay, I don't have anything scheduled for tomorrow."

"Cath, I've never understood what a glass or two of wine tonight would have to do with surgery tomorrow—it's ten or twelve hours away."

"Jack, you don't mix alcohol with surgery," she explained patiently. "Okay? You don't drink and drive. You don't drink and cut, either. Not ever. Not once."

"Yes, doctor. So tomorrow you just set glasses prescriptions for people?"

"Uh-huh, simple day. How about you?"

"Nothing important. Same crap, different day."

"I don't know how you stand it."

"Well, it's interesting, secret crap, and you have to be a spook to understand it."

"Right." She poured the spaghetti sauce into a bowl. "Here."

"I haven't got the wine open yet."

"So work faster."

"Yes, Professor the Lady Ryan," Jack responded, taking the bowl of sauce and setting it on the table. Then he pulled the cork out of the Chianti.

Sally was too big a girl for a high chair but still small enough for a booster seat, which she carried to the chair herself. Since the dinner was "pisgetty," her father tucked the cloth napkin into her collar. The sauce would probably get to her pants anyway, but it would teach his little girl about napkins, and that, Cathy thought, was important. Then Ryan poured the wine. Sally didn't ask for any. Her father had indulged her once (over his wife's objections), and that had ended that. Sally got some Coca-Cola.

SVETLANA WAS ASLEEP, finally. She liked to stay up as long as she could, every night the same, or so it seemed, until she finally put her head down. She slept with a smile, her father saw, like a little angel, the sort that decorated Italian cathedrals in the travel books he used to read. The TV was on. Some World War II movie, it sounded like. They were all the same. The Germans attacked cruelly—well, occasionally there was a German character with something akin to humanity, usually a German communist, it would be revealed along the way, torn by conflicting loyalties to his class (working class, of course) and his country—and the Soviets resisted bravely, losing a lot of defiant men at first until turning the tide, usually outside Moscow in December 1941, at Stalingrad in January 1943, or the Kursk Bulge in the summer of 1943. There was always a heroic political officer, a courageous private soldier, a wise old sergeant, and a bright young junior officer. Toss in a grizzled general who wept quietly and alone for his men, then had to set his feelings aside and get the job done. There were about five different formulas, all of them variations of the same theme, and the only real difference was whether Stalin was seen as a wise, godlike ruler or simply wasn't mentioned at all. *That* depended on when the film had been shot. Stalin had fallen out of fashion in the Soviet film industry about 1956, soon after Nikita Sergeyevich Khrushchev had made his famous but then-secret speech revealing what a monster Stalin had been—something Soviet citizens still had trouble with, especially the cabdrivers, or so it seemed. Truth in his country was a rare commodity, and almost always one hard to swallow.

But Zaitzev wasn't watching the movie now. Oleg Ivanovich sipped at his vodka, eyes focused on the TV screen, without seeing it. It had just struck him how huge a step he'd taken that afternoon on the metro. At the time, it had almost been a lark, like a child playing a prank, reaching into that American's pocket like a sneak-thief, just to see if he could do it. No one had noticed. He'd been clever and careful about it, and even the American hadn't noticed, or else he would have reacted.

So he'd just proven that he had the ability to . . . *what?* To *do* what? Oleg Ivan'ch asked himself with surprising intensity.

What the hell had he done on the metro coach? What had he been thinking about? Actually, he hadn't really thought about it at all. It had just been some sort of foolish impulse . . . hadn't it?

He shook his head and took another sip of his drink. He was a man of intelligence. He had a university degree. He was an excellent chess player. He had a job that required the highest security clearance, that paid well, and that had just put him at the bottom entry level of the *nomenklatura*. He was a person of importance—not much, but some. The KGB trusted him with knowledge about many things. The KGB had confidence in him . . . but . . .

But what*?* he asked himself. What came after the "but" part? His mind was wandering in directions he didn't understand and could barely see. . . .

The priest. It came down to that, didn't it? Or did it? What was he thinking? Zaitzev asked himself. He didn't really know if he was thinking anything at all. It was as though his hand had developed a mind of its own, taking action without the brain's or the mind's permission, leading off in a direction that he didn't understand.

Yes, it had to be that damned priest. Was he bewitched? Was some outside force taking control of his body?

No! That is not possible! Zaitzev told himself. That was something from ancient tales, the sort of thing old women discussed—prattled about—over a boiling pot.

But why, then, did I put my hand in the American's pocket? his mind demanded of itself, but there was no immediate answer.

Do you want to be a part of murder? some small voice asked. *Are you willing to facilitate the murder of an innocent man?*

Was he innocent? Zaitzev asked himself, taking another swallow. Not a single dispatch crossing his desk suggested otherwise. In fact, he could hardly remember any mention of this Father Karol in any KGB messages during the past couple years. Yes, they'd taken note of his trip back to Poland soon after being elected Pope, but what man didn't go home after his promotion to see his friends and seek their approval of his new place in the world?

The Party was made up of men, too. And men made mistakes. He saw them every day, even from the skilled, highly trained officers of KGB, who were punished, or chided, or just remarked upon by their superiors in The Centre. Leonid Ilyich made mistakes. People chuckled about them over lunch often enough—or talked more quietly about the things his greedy children did, especially his daughter. Hers was a petty corruption, and while people talked about it, they usually spoke quietly. But he was thinking about a much larger and more dangerous kind of corruption.

Where did the legitimacy of the State come from? In the abstract, it came from the people, but the people had no say in things. The Party did, but only a small minority of the people were in the Party, and of those only a much smaller minority achieved anything resembling power. And so the legitimacy of his State resided atop what was by any logical measure . . . a fiction . . .

And that was a very big thought. Other countries were ruled by dictators, often fascists on the political Right. Fewer countries were ruled by people on the political Left. Hitler represented the most powerful and dangerous of the former, but he'd been overthrown by the Soviet Union and Stalin on one side, and by the Western states on the other. The two most unlikely of allies had combined to destroy the German threat. And who were they? They claimed to be democracies, and while that claim was consistently denigrated by his own country, the elections held in those countries were real—they had to be, since his country and his agency, the KGB, spent time and money trying to influence them—and so *there,* the Will of the People had some reality to it, or else why would KGB try to affect it? Exactly how much, Zaitzev didn't know. There was no telling from the information available in his own country, and he didn't bother listening to the Voice of America and other obvious propaganda arms of the Western nations.

So, it wasn't the people who wanted to kill the priest. It was Andropov, certainly, and the Politburo, possibly, who wished to do it. Even his workmates at The Centre had no particular bone to pick with Father Karol. There was no talk of his enmity to the Soviet Union. The State TV and radio had not called out for class hatred against him, as they did for other foreign enemies. There had been no pejorative articles about him in *Pravda* that he'd seen of late. Just some rumbles about the labor problems in

Poland, and those were not overly loud, more the sort of thing a neighbor might say about a misbehaving child next door.

But that's what it had to be all about. Karol was Polish, and a source of pride for the people there, and Poland was politically troubled because of labor disputes. Karol wanted to use his political or spiritual power to protect his people. That was understandable, wasn't it?

But was killing him understandable?

Who would stand up and say, "No, you cannot kill this man because you dislike his politics"? The Politburo? No, they'd go along with Andropov. He was the heir apparent. When Leonid Ilyich died, he'd be the one to take his chair at the head of the table. Another Party man. Well, what else could he be? The Party was the Soul of the People, so the saying went. That was about the only mention of "soul" the Party permitted.

Did some part of a man live on after death? That was what the soul was supposed to be, but here the Party was the soul, and the Party was a thing of men, and little more. And corrupt men at that.

And they wanted to kill a priest.

He'd seen the dispatches. In a very small way, he, Oleg Ivanovich Zaitzev, was helping. And that was eating at something inside him. A conscience? Was he supposed to have one of those? But a conscience was something that measured one set of facts or ideas against another and was either content or not. If not, if it found some action at fault, then the conscience started complaining. It whispered. It forced him to look and keep looking until the issue was resolved, until the wrong action was stopped, or reversed, or atoned for—

But how did you stop the Party or the KGB from doing something?

To do that, Zaitzev knew, you had, at the very least, to demonstrate that the proposed action was contrary to political theory or would have adverse political consequences, because politics was the measure of right and wrong. But wasn't politics too fleeting for that? Didn't "right" and "wrong" have to depend on something more solid than mere politics? Wasn't there some higher value system? Politics was just *tactics,* after all, wasn't it? And while tactics were important, strategy was more so, because strategy was the measure of what you used tactics for, and strategy in this case was supposed to be what was right—transcendentally right. Not just right at the moment, but right for all times—something historians could examine in a hundred or a thousand years and pronounce as correct action.

Did the Party think in such terms? How exactly did the Communist Party of the Soviet Union make its decisions? What was good for the people? But who measured that? Individuals did, Brezhnev, Andropov, Suslov, the rest of the full voting members of the Politburo, advised by the nonvoting candidate members, further advised by the Council of Ministers and the members of the Central Committee of the Party, all the senior members of the *nomenklatura*—the ones to whom the *rezident* in Paris shipped perfume and pantyhose in the diplomatic bag. Zaitzev had seen enough of those dispatches. And he'd heard the stories. Those were the ones who lavished presents and status upon their children, the ones who raced down the center lane of the broad Moscow boulevards, the corrupt Marxist princes who ruled his country with hands of iron.

Did those princes think in terms of what was good for the *narod*—the masses, as they were called—the numberless workers and peasants whom they ruled, for whose good they supposedly looked after?

But probably the minor princes under Nikolay Romanov had thought and spoken the same way. And Lenin had ordered them all shot as enemies of the people. As modern movies spoke of the Great Patriotic War, so earlier movies had portrayed them for less sophisticated audiences as evil buffoons, hardly serious enemies, easily hated and easily killed, caricatures of real people who were all so different from those men who'd replaced them, of course. . . .

As the princes of old had driven their troika-harnessed sleds over the very bodies of the peasants on their way to the royal court, so today the officers of the Moscow militia kept the center lane open for the new *nomenklatura* members who didn't have time for traffic delays.

Nothing had really changed. . . .

Except that the czars of old had at least paid lip service to a higher authority. They'd financed St. Basil's Cathedral here in Moscow, and other noblemen had financed countless other churches in lesser cities, because even the Romanovs had acknowledged a power higher than theirs. But the Party acknowledged no higher order.

And so it could kill without regret, because killing was often a political necessity, a *tactical* advantage to be undertaken when and where convenient.

Was that all this was? Zaitzev asked himself. *Were they killing the Pope just because it was more convenient?*

Oleg Ivan'ch poured himself another portion of vodka from the nearby bottle and took another swallow.

There were many inconveniences in his life. It was too long a walk from his desk to the water cooler. There were people at work whom he didn't like—Stefan Yevgeniyevich Ivanov, for example, a more senior major in communications. How he'd managed to get promoted four years ago was a mystery to everyone in the section. He was disregarded by the more senior people as a drone who was unable to do any useful work. Zaitzev supposed every business had one such person, an embarrassment to the office, but not easily removed because . . . because he was just there and that was all there was to it. Were Ivanov out of the way, Oleg could be promoted—if not in rank, then in status to chief of the section. Every single breath Ivanov took was an inconvenience to Oleg Ivan'ch, but that didn't give him the right to kill the more senior communicator, did it?

No, he'd be arrested and prosecuted, and perhaps even executed for murder. Because it was forbidden by law. Because it was *wrong.* The law, the Party, and his own conscience told him that.

But Andropov wanted to kill Father Karol, and his conscience didn't say nay. Would some other conscience do so? Another swallow of vodka. Another snort. A *conscience,* on the *Politburo?*

Even in the KGB, there were no ruminations. No debates. No open discussion. Just action messages and notices of completion or failure. Evaluations of foreigners, of course, discussions of the thinking of foreigners, real agents, or mere agents of influence—called "useful fools" in the KGB lexicon. Never had a field officer written back about an order and said, "No, comrade, we ought not to do that because it would be morally wrong." Goderenko in Rome had come closest, posing the observation that killing Karol might have adverse consequences on operations. Did that mean that Ruslan Borissovich had a troubled conscience as well? No. Goderenko had three sons—one in the Soviet navy; another, he'd heard, at the KGB's own academy out on the Ring Road; and the third in Moscow State University. If Ruslan Borissovich had any difficulties with the KGB, any action could mean, if not death, then at least serious embarrassment for his children, and few men took action like that.

So, was his the only conscience in KGB? Zaitzev took a swallow to ponder that one. Probably not. There were thousands of men in The Centre, and thousands more elsewhere, and just the laws of statistics made it likely that there were plenty of "good" men (however one defined that), but how did one identify them? It was certain death—or lengthy imprisonment—to try to go looking for them. That was the baseline problem he had. There was no one in whom he could confide his doubts. No one with whom he could discuss his worries—not a doctor, not a priest . . . not even his wife, Irina . . .

No, he had only his vodka bottle, and though it helped him think, after a fashion, it wasn't much of a companion. Russian men were not averse to shedding tears, but they wouldn't have helped either. Irina might ask a question, and he wouldn't be able to answer to anyone's satisfaction. All he had was sleep. It would not help, he was sure, and in this he was right.

Another hour and two more slugs of the vodka at least drugged him into sleepiness. His wife was dozing in front of the TV—the Red Amy had won the Battle of Kursk, again, and the movie ended at the beginning of a long march that would lead to the Reichstag in Berlin, full of hope and enthusiasm for the bloody task. Zaitzev chuckled to himself. It was more than he had at the moment. He carried his empty glass to the kitchen, then roused his wife for the trip to the bedroom. He hoped that sleep would come quickly. The quarter-liter of alcohol in his belly should help. And so it did.

"YOU KNOW, ARTHUR, there are a lot of things we don't know about him," Jim Greer said.

"Andropov, you mean?"

"We don't even know if the bastard's married," the DDI continued.

"Well, Robert, that's your department," the DCI observed, with a look at Bob Ritter.

"We think he is, but he's never brought his wife, if any, to an official function. That's usually how we find out," the DDO had to admit. "They often hide their families, like Mafia dons. They're so anal about hiding everything over there. And, yeah, we're not all that good about digging the information up, because it's not operationally important."

"How he treats his wife and kids, if any," Greer pointed out, "can be useful in profiling the guy."

"So you want me to task CARDINAL on something like that? He could do it, I'm sure, but why waste his time that way?"

"Is it a waste? If he's a wife-beater, it tells us something. If he's a doting father, it tells us something else," the DDI persisted.

"He's a thug. You can look at his photo and see that. Look how his staff acts around him. They're stiff, like you'd have expected from Hitler's staff," Ritter responded. A few months before, a gaggle of American state governors had flown to Moscow for some sub-rosa diplomacy. The governor of Maryland, a liberal Democrat, had reported back that when Andropov had entered the reception room, he'd spotted him at once as a thug, then learned that it was Yuriy Vladimirovich, Chairman of the Committee for State Security. The Marylander had possessed a good eye for reading people, and that evaluation had gone into the Andropov file at Langley.

"Well, he wouldn't have been much of a judge," Arthur Moore observed. He'd read the file, too. "At least not at the appeals level. Too interested in hanging the poor son of a bitch just to see if the rope breaks or not." Not that Texas hadn't had a few judges like that, once upon a time, but it was much more civilized now. There were fewer horses that needed stealing than men who needed killing, after all. "Okay, Robert, what can we do to flesh him out a little? Looks like he's going to be their next General Secretary, after all. Strikes me as a good idea."

"I can rattle some cages. Why not ask Sir Basil what he can do? They're better at the social stuff than we are, and it takes the heat off our people."

"I like Bas, but I don't like having him hold that many markers for us," Judge Moore answered.

"Well, James, your protégé is over there. Have him ask the question. You get him an STU at home yet?"

"Ought to have gotten there today, yes."

"So call your lad and have him ask, nice and casual-like."

Greer's eyes went to the Judge. "Arthur?"

"Approved. Lowercase this, though. Tell Ryan that it's for his personal interest, not ours."

The Admiral checked his watch. "Okay, I can do that before I head home."

"Now, Bob, any progress on MASQUE OF THE RED DEATH?" the DCI asked with amusement, just to close down the afternoon meeting. It was a fun idea, but not a very serious one.

"Arthur, let's not discount it too much, shall we? They *are* vulnerable to the right sort of bullet, once we load it in the gun."

"Don't talk that way in front of Congress. They might foul their panties," Greer warned, with a laugh. "We're supposed to enjoy peaceful coexistence with them."

"That didn't work very well with Hitler. Stalin and Chamberlain both tried to make nice with the son of a bitch. Where did it get them? They are our enemies, gentlemen, and the sad truth is that we can't have a real peace with them, like it or not. Their ideas and ours are too out of sync for that." He held up his hands. "Yeah, I know, we're not supposed to think that way, but thank God the President does, and we still work for him."

They didn't have to comment on that. All three had voted for the current President, despite the institutional joke that the two things one never found at Langley were communists and . . . Republicans. No, the new President had a little iron in his spine and a fox's instinct for opportunity. It especially appealed to Ritter, who was the cowboy of the three, if also the most abrasive.

"Okay. I have some budget work to do for that hearing with the Senate day after tomorrow," Moore announced, breaking up the meeting.

RYAN WAS AT his computer, thinking over the Battle of Leyte Gulf, when the phone rang. It was the first time for it, with its oddly trilling ringer. He reached in his pocket for the plastic key, slid it into the appropriate slot, then lifted the receiver.

"STAND BY," a mechanical voice said, "SYNCHRONIZING THE LINE; STAND

BY, SYNCHRONIZING THE LINE; STAND BY, SYNCHRONIZING THE LINE—LINE IS SECURE," it said at last.

"Hello," Ryan said, wondering who had an STU and would call him this late. It turned out to be the obvious answer.

"Hi, Jack," a familiar voice greeted him. One nice thing about the STU: The digital technology made voices as clear as if the speaker were sitting in the room.

Ryan checked the desk clock. "Kinda late there, sir."

"Not as late as in Jolly Old England. How's the family?"

"Mainly asleep at the moment. Cathy is probably reading a medical journal," which was what she did instead of watching TV, anyway. "What can I do for you, Admiral?"

"I have a little job for you."

"Okay," Ryan responded.

"Ask around—casual-like—about Yuriy Andropov. There are a few things about him we don't know. Maybe Basil has the information we want."

"What exactly, sir?" Jack asked.

"Is he married, and does he have any kids?"

"We don't know if he's married?" Ryan realized that he hadn't seen that information in the dossier, but he'd assumed it was elsewhere, and had taken no particular note of it.

"That's right. The Judge wants to see if Basil might know."

"Okay, I can ask Simon. How important is this?"

"Like I said, casual-like, like it's your own interest. Then call me back from there, your home, I mean."

"Will do, sir. We know his age, birthday, education, and stuff, but not if he's married or has any kids, eh?"

"That's how it works sometimes."

"Yes, sir." And that got Jack thinking. They knew everything about Brezhnev but his dick size. They *did* know his daughter's dress size—12—which someone had thought important enough to get from the Belgian milliner who'd sold the silken wedding dress to her doting father, through the ambassador. But they didn't know if the likely next General Secretary of the Soviet Union was married. *Christ, the guy was pushing sixty, and they didn't know? What the hell?* "Okay, I can ask. That ought not to be too hard."

"Otherwise, how's London?"

"I like it here, and so does Cathy, but she's a little dubious about their state medical-care system."

"Socialized medicine? I don't blame her. I still get everything done at Bethesda, but it helps a little that I have 'admiral' in front of my name. It's not quite as fast for a retired chief bosun's mate."

"I bet." In Ryan's case, it helped a whole lot that his wife was on the faculty at Johns Hopkins. He didn't talk to anyone in a lab coat without "professor" on his nametag, and he'd learned that in the field of medicine, the really smart ones were the teachers, unlike the rest of society.

THE DREAMS CAME after midnight, though he had no way of knowing that. It was a clear Moscow summer day, and a man in white was walking across the Red Square. St. Basil's Cathedral was behind him, and he was walking against the traffic past Lenin's mausoleum. Some children were with him, and he was talking to them in a kindly way, as a favored uncle might . . . or perhaps a parish priest. Then Oleg knew that's what he was, a parish priest. But why in white? With gold brocade, even. The children, four or five each of boys and girls, were holding his hands and looking up at him with innocent smiles. Then Oleg turned his head. Up at the top of the tomb, where they stood for the May Day parades, were the Politburo members: Brezhnev, Suslov, Ustinov, and Andropov. Andropov was holding a rifle and pointing at the little procession. There were other people around—faceless people walking aimlessly, going about their business. Then Oleg was standing with Andropov, listening to his words. He was arguing for the right to shoot the man. *Be careful of the children, Yuriy Vladimirovich,* Suslov warned. *Yes, be careful,* Brezhnev agreed. Ustinov reached over to adjust the sights on the rifle. They all ignored Zaitzev, who moved among them, trying to get their attention.

But why? Zaitzev asked. *Why are you doing this?*

Who is this? Brezhnev asked Andropov.

Never mind him, Suslov snarled. *Just shoot the bastard!*

Very well, Andropov said. He took his aim carefully, and Zaitzev was unable to intervene, despite being right there. Then the Chairman squeezed the trigger.

Zaitzev was back on the street now. The first bullet struck a child, a boy on the priest's right, who fell without a sound.

Not him, *you idiot—the priest!* Mikhail Suslov screamed like a rabid dog.

Andropov shot again, this time hitting a little blonde girl standing at the priest's left. Her head exploded in red. Zaitzev bent down to help her, but she said it was all right, and so he left her and returned to the priest.

Look out, why don't you?

Look out for what, my young comrade? The priest asked pleasantly, then he turned. *Come, children, we're off to see God.*

Andropov fired again. This time the bullet struck the priest square in the chest. There was a splash of blood, about the size and color of a rose. The priest grimaced, but kept going, with the smiling children in tow.

Another shot, another rose on the chest, to the left of the first. But still he kept going, walking slowly.

Are you hurt? Zaitzev asked.

It is nothing, the priest replied. *But why didn't you stop him?*

But I tried! Zaitzev insisted.

The priest stopped walking, turning to look him square in the face. *Did you?*

That's when the third bullet struck him right in the heart.

Did you? the priest asked again. Now the children were looking at him and not the priest.

Zaitzev found himself sitting up in the bed. It was just before four in the morning, the clock said. He was sweating profusely. There was only one thing to do. He rose from the bed and walked to the bathroom. There he urinated, then had himself a glass of water, and padded off to the kitchen. Sitting down by the sink, he lit a cigarette. Before he went back to sleep, he wanted to be fully awake. He didn't want to walk back into *that* dream.

Out the window, Moscow was quiet, the streets completely empty—not even a drunk staggering home. A good thing, too. No apartment house elevators would be working at this hour. There was not a car in view, which was a little odd, but not so much as in a Western city.

The cigarette achieved its goal. He was now awake enough to go back to sleep afresh. But even now he knew that the vision wouldn't leave him. Most dreams faded away, just like cigarette smoke, but this one would not. Zaitzev was sure of that.

CHAPTER 10

BOLT FROM THE BLUE

HE HAD A LOT of thinking to do. It was as if the decision had made itself, as if some alien force had overtaken his mind and, through it, his body, and he had been transformed into a mere spectator. Like most Russians, he didn't shower, but washed his face and shaved with a blade razor, nicking himself three times in the process. Toilet paper took care of that—the symptoms, anyway, if not the cause. The images from the dream still paraded before his eyes like that war film on television. They continued to do so during breakfast, causing a distant look in his eyes that his wife noticed but decided not to comment on. Soon enough it was time to go to work. He went along the way like an automaton, taking the right path to the metro station by rote memory, his brain both quiescent and furiously active, as though he'd suddenly split into two separate but distantly connected people, moving along parallel paths to a destination he couldn't see and didn't understand. He was being carried there, though, like a chip of wood down mountain rapids, the rock walls passing so rapidly by his left and right that he couldn't even see them. It came almost as a surprise when he found himself aboard the metro carriage, traveling down the darkened tunnels dug by political prisoners of Stalin's under the direction of Nikita Sergeyevich Khrushchev, surrounded by the quiet, almost faceless bodies of other Soviet citizens also making their way to workplaces for which they had little love and little sense of duty. But they went to them because it was how they earned the money with which they bought food for their families, minuscule cogs in the gigantic machine that was the Soviet state, which they all purported to serve and which purported to serve them and their families. . . .

But it was all a lie, wasn't it? Zaitzev asked himself. Was it? How did the murder of a priest serve the Soviet State? How did it serve all these people? How did it serve him and his wife and his little daughter? By feeding them? By giving him the ability to shop in the "closed" shops and buy things that the other workers could not even think about getting for themselves?

But he *was* better off than nearly everyone else on the subway car, Oleg Ivan'ch reminded himself. Ought he not be grateful for that? Didn't he eat better food, drink better coffee, watch a better TV set, sleep on better sheets? Didn't he have all the creature comforts that these people would like to have? *Why am I suddenly so badly troubled?* the communicator asked himself. The answer was so obvious that it took nearly a minute for him to grasp the answer. It was because his position, the one that gave him the comforts he enjoyed, also gave him knowledge, and in this case, for the first time in his life, knowledge was a curse. He knew the thoughts of the men who determined the course his country was taking, and in that knowledge he saw that the course was a false one . . . an evil one, and inside his mind was an agency that looked at the knowledge and judged it wrong. And in that judgment came the need to do something to change it. He could not object and expect to keep what passed for freedom in his country. There was no agency open to him through which he could make his judgment known to others, though others might well concur with his judgment, might ask the men who governed their country for a redress of their grievances. No, there was no way for him to act within such a system as it existed. To do that, you had to be so very senior that before you voiced doubts you had to think carefully, lest you lose your privilege, and so whatever consciences you had were tempered by the cowardice that came with having so much to lose. He'd never heard of any senior political figure in his country standing up that way, standing on a matter of principle and telling his peers that they were doing something wrong. No, the system precluded that by the sort of people it selected. Corrupted men only selected other corrupted men to be their peers, lest they have to question the things that gave them their own vast privileges. Just as the princes under the czars rarely if ever considered the effect their rule had on the serfs, so the new princes of Marxism never questioned the system that gave them their place in the world. Why? Because the world hadn't changed its shape—just its color, from czarist white to socialist red—and in keeping the shape, it kept its method of working, and in a red world, a little extra spilled blood was difficult to notice.

The metro carriage stopped at his station, and Zaitzev made his way to the sliding metal door, to the platform, left to the escalator, up to the street on a fine, clear, late-summer day, again part of a crowd, but one that dispersed as it moved. A medium-sized contingent walked at a steady pace toward the stone edifice of The Centre, through the bronze doors, and past the first security checkpoint. Zaitzev showed his pass to the uniformed guard, who checked the picture against his face and jerked his head to the right, signaling that it was all right for him to enter the vast office building. Showing the same lack of emotion as he would any other day, Zaitzev took the stone steps down to the basement level through another checkpoint and finally into the open-bay work area of the signals center.

The night crew was just finishing up. At Zaitzev's desk was the man who worked the midnight-to-eight shift, Nikolay Konstantinovich Dobrik, a newly promoted major like himself.

"Good morning, Oleg," Dobrik said in comradely greeting, accompanied by a stretch in his swivel chair.

"And to you, Kolya. How was the night watch?"

"A lot of traffic last night from Washington. That madman of a president was at it again. Did you know that we are 'the focus of evil in the modern world'?"

"He said that?" Zaitzev asked incredulously.

Dobrik nodded. "He did. The Washington *rezidentura* sent us the text of his speech—it was red meat for his party faithful, but it was incendiary even so. I expect the ambassador will get instructions from the foreign ministry about it, and the Politburo will probably have something to say. But at least it gave me a lively watch to read it all!"

"They didn't put it on the pad, did they?" A complete transmission on a one-time cipher pad would have been a nightmare job for the clerks.

"No, it was a machine job, thank God," Dobrik replied. His choice of words wasn't entirely ironic. That euphemism was a common one, even at The Centre. "Our officers are trying to make sense of his words even now. The political department will be going over it for hours—days, more likely, complete with the psychiatrists, I wager."

Zaitzev managed a chuckle. The back-and-forth between the head doctors and the field officers would undoubtedly be entertaining to read—and, like good clerks, they tended to read all of the entertaining dispatches.

"You have to wonder how such men get to rule major countries," Dobrik observed, standing up and lighting a cigarette.

"I think they call it the democratic process," Zaitzev responded.

"Well, in that case, thanks be for the Collective Will of the People as expressed through the beloved Party." Dobrik was a good Party member, despite the planned irony of his remark, as was everyone in this room, of course.

"Indeed, Kolya. In any case"—Zaitzev looked over at the wall clock. He was six minutes early—"I relieve you, Comrade Major."

"And I thank you, Comrade Major." Dobrik headed off to the exit.

Zaitzev took the seat, still warm from Dobrik's backside, and signed in on the time sheet, noting the time. Next he dumped the contents of the desk ashtray into the trash bucket—Dobrik never seemed to do that—and started a new day at the office. Relieving his colleague had been a rote process, if a pleasant one. He hardly knew Dobrik, except for these moments at the start of his day. Why anyone would volunteer for continuous night duty mystified him. At least Dobrik always left a clean desk behind, not one piled up with unfinished work, which gave Zaitzev a few minutes to get caught up and mentally organized for the day.

In this case, however, those few minutes merely brought back the images that, it seemed, were not about to go away. And so Oleg Ivanovich lit up his first work cigarette of the day and shuffled the papers on the metal desk while his mind was elsewhere, doing things that he himself didn't want to know about just yet. It was ten minutes after the hour when a cipher clerk came to him with a folder.

"From Station Washington, Comrade Major," the clerk announced.

"Thank you, comrade," Zaitzev acknowledged.

Taking the manila folder, he opened it and started leafing through the dispatches.

Ah, he thought, *this CASSIUS fellow has reported in* . . . yes, more political intelligence. He didn't know the name or face that went along with CASSIUS, but he had to be an aide to a senior parliamentarian, possibly even a senator. He delivered high-quality political intelligence that hinted at access to hard intelligence information. So a servant to a very senior American politician worked for the Soviet Union, too. He wasn't paid, which made him an ideologically motivated agent, the very best sort.

He read through the dispatch and then searched his memory for the right recipient upstairs . . . Colonel Anatoliy Gregorovich Fokin, in the political department, whose address was Washington Desk, Line PR, First Department, First Chief Directorate, up on the fourth floor.

OUTSIDE OF TOWN. Colonel Ilya Fedorovich Bubovoy walked off his morning flight from Sofia. To catch it, he'd had to arise at three in the morning, an embassy car taking him to the airport for the flight to Moscow. The summons had come from Aleksey Rozhdestvenskiy, whom he'd known for some years and who had shown him the courtesy to call the day before and assure him that nothing untoward was meant by this summons to The Centre. Bubovoy had a clear conscience, but it was nice to know, even so. You never could be sure with KGB. Like children called to the principal's office, officers were often known to have a few upper-gastric butterflies on the way into headquarters. In any case, his tie was properly knotted, and his good shoes shined properly. He did not wear his uniform, as his identity as the Sofia *rezident* was technically secret.

A uniformed sergeant of the Red Army met him at the gate and led him out to a car—in fact, the sergeant was KGB, but that wasn't for public knowledge: Who knew if CIA or other Western services had eyes at the airport? Bubovoy picked up a copy of *Sovietskiy Sport* at a kiosk on the walk out to the car. It would be thirty-five minutes in. Sofia's soccer team had just beaten Moscow Dynamo, 3–2, a few days before. The colonel wondered if the local sportswriters would be calling for the heads of the Moscow team, couched in appropriate Marxist rhetoric, of course. Good socialists always won, but the sportswriters tended to get confused when one socialist team lost to another.

FOLEY WAS ON the metro as well, running a little late this morning. A power failure had reset his alarm clock without formal notice, so he'd been awakened by sunlight through the windows instead of the usual metallic buzz. As always, he tried not to look around too much, but he couldn't help checking for the owner of the hand that had searched his pocket. But none of the faces looked back at him. He'd try again that afternoon, on the train that left the station at 17:41, just in case. In case of what? Foley didn't know, but that was one of the exciting things about his chosen line of work. If it had been just happenstance, all well and good, but for the next few days he'd be on the same train, in the same coach, standing in much the same place. If he had a shadow, the man wouldn't remark on it. The Russians actually found it comforting to trail someone who followed a routine—the randomness of Americans could drive them to distraction. So, he'd be a "good" American, and show them what they want, and they wouldn't find it strange. The Moscow Chief of Station shook his head in amazement.

Reaching his stop, he took the escalator up to the street level, and from there it was a short walk to the embassy, just across the street from Our Lady of the Microchips, and the world's largest microwave oven. Foley always liked to see the flag on the pole, and the Marines inside, more proof that he was in the right place. They always looked good, in their khaki shirts over dress-blue uniform trousers, holstered pistols, and white caps.

His office was as shabby as usual—it was part of his cover to be a little on the untidy side.

But his cover did not include the communications department. It couldn't. Heading embassy comms was Mike Russell, formerly a lieutenant colonel in the Army Security Agency—ASA was the Army's own communications-security arm—and now a civilian with the National Security Agency, which officially did the same for the entire government.

Moscow was a hardship tour for Russell. Black and divorced-single, he didn't get much female action here, since the Russians were notoriously dubious of people with dark skin. The knock on the door was distinctive.

"Come on in, Mike," Foley said.

"Morning, Ed." Russell was under six feet, and he needed to watch his eating by the look of his waist. But he was a good guy with codes and comms, and that was sufficient for the moment. "Quiet night for you."

"Oh?"

"Yeah, just this." He fished an envelope out of his coat pocket and handed it over. "Nothing important, looks like." He had also decrypted the dispatch. Even the ambassador wasn't cleared as high as the head of communications. Foley was suddenly glad for Russian racism. It made Mike that much less likely to get turned. *That* was a scary thought. Of all the people in the embassy, Mike Russell was the one guy who could rat everyone out, which was why intelligence services always tried to corrupt cipher clerks, the underpaid and spat-upon people who had enormous information power in any embassy.

Foley took the envelope and opened it. The dispatch inside was lower than routine, proof positive that CIA was just one more government bureaucracy, however important its work might be. He snorted and entered the paper into his shredder, where rotating steel wheels reduced it to fragments about two centimeters square.

"Must be nice to get your day's work done in ten seconds," Russell observed, with a laugh.

"Wasn't like that in Vietnam, I bet."

"Not hardly. I remember once one of my troops DF'd a VC transmitter at MAC-V headquarters, and that was one busy night."

"Get him?"

"Oh yeah," Russell replied with a nod. "The locals were seriously pissed about that little dink. He came to a bad end, they told me." Russell had been a first lieutenant then. A Detroit native, his father had built B-24 bombers during World War II, and had never stopped telling his son how much more satisfying that had been than making Fords. Russell detested everything about this country (they didn't even appreciate good soul music!), but the extra pay that came with duty here—Moscow was officially a hardship posting—would buy him a nice place on the Upper Peninsula someday, where he'd be able to hunt birds and deer to his heart's content. "Anything to go out, Ed?"

"Nope, not today—not yet, anyway."

"Roger that. Have a good one." And Russell disappeared out the door.

It wasn't like the spy novels—the job of a CIA officer was composed of a good deal more boredom than excitement. At least two-thirds of Foley's time as a field officer was taken up with writing reports that somebody at Langley might or might not read, and/or waiting for meets that might or might not come off. He had case officers to do most of the street work, because his identity was too sensitive to risk exposure—something about which he had to lecture his wife on occasion. Mary Pat just liked the action a little too much. It was somewhat worrying, though neither of them faced much real physical danger. They both had diplomatic immunity, and the Russians were assiduous about respecting that, for the most part. Even if things should get a little rough, it would never be really rough. Or so he told himself.

"GOOD MORNING, Colonel Bubovoy," Andropov said pleasantly, without rising.

"Good day to you, Comrade Chairman," the Sofia *rezident* replied, swallowing his relief that Rozhdestvenskiy hadn't lied to him. You could never be too careful, after all, or too paranoid.

"How go things in Sofia?" Andropov waved him to the leather seat opposite the big oak desk.

"Well, Comrade Chairman, our fraternal socialist colleagues remain cooperative, especially with Turkish matters."

"Good. We have a proposed mission to undertake and I require your opinion of its feasibility." The voice stayed entirely pleasant.

"And what might that be?" Bubovoy asked.

Andropov outlined the plans, watching his visitor's face closely for his reaction. There was none. The colonel was too experienced for that, and besides, he knew the look he was getting.

"How soon?" he asked.

"How quickly could you set things up?"

"I will need to get cooperation from our Bulgarian friends. I know who to go to—Colonel Boris Strokov, a very skillful player in the DS. He runs their operations in Turkey—smuggling and such—which gives him entrée into Turkish gangster organizations. The contacts are very useful, especially when a killing is necessary."

"Go on," the Chairman urged quietly.

"Comrade Chairman, such an operation will not be simple. Without a means of getting a gunman into the private residence of the target, it will mean making the attempt at a public appearance, at which there will necessarily be many people. We can tell our gunman that we have the means of getting him away, but that will be a lie, of course. From a tactical point of view, it would be better to have a second man present, to kill him immediately after he takes his shot—with a suppressed weapon. For the second killer, escape is far easier, since the attention of the crowd will be on the first gunman. It also alleviates the possible problem of our gunman talking to the police. The Italian police do not have a good public reputation, but this is not, strictly speaking, true. As our *rezident* in Rome can tell you, their investigative arms are quite well organized and highly professional. Thus, it is in our interest to have our gunman eliminated at once."

"But won't that suggest the involvement of an intelligence service?" Andropov asked. "Is it too elegant?"

Bubovoy leaned back and spoke judiciously. This was what Andropov wanted to hear, and he was ready to deliver it. "Comrade Chairman, one must weigh one hazard against another. The greatest danger is if our assassin talked about how he came to be in Rome. A dead man tells no tales, as they say. And a silenced voice cannot give out information. The other side can speculate, but it is merely speculation. For our part, we can easily release information through the press sources we control about Muslim animosity toward the head of the Roman church. The Western news services will pick it up and, with proper guidance, we can help shape the public understanding of what has taken place. The United States and Canada Institute has some excellent academicians for this purpose, as you know. We can use them to formulate the black propaganda, and then use people from the First Chief Directorate to propagate it. This proposed operation is not without risk, of course, but, though complex, it is not all that difficult from a conceptual point of view. The real problems will be in its execution and in operational security. That's why it's critical to eliminate the assassin immediately. The most important thing is the denial of information to the other side. Let them speculate all they wish, but without hard information, they will *know* nothing. This operation will be very closely held, I presume."

"Less than five people at present. How many more?" Andropov asked, impressed at Bubovoy's expertise and sangfroid.

"At least three Bulgarians. Then they will select the Turk—it must be a Turk, you see."

"Why?" Though Andropov figured he knew the answer.

"Turkey is a Muslim country, and there is a long-standing antipathy between the Christian churches and Islam. This way, the operation will generate additional discord between the two religious groups—consider that a bonus," the Sofia *rezident* suggested.

"And how will you select the assassin?"

"I will leave that to Colonel Strokov—his ancestry is Russian, by the way. His family settled in Sofia at the turn of the century, but he thinks like one of us. He is *nashi*," Bubovoy assured his boss, "a graduate of our own academy, and an experienced field operator."

"How long to set this up?"

"That depends more on Moscow than Sofia. Strokov will need approval from his own command, but that is a political question, not an operational one. After he gets his orders . . . two weeks, perhaps as many as four."

"And the chances of success?" the Chairman asked.

"Medium to high, I should think. The DS field officer will drive the killer to the proper place, and then kill him a moment after the mission is accomplished, before making his escape. That is more dangerous than it sounds. The assassin will probably have a pistol, and it will not be a suppressed weapon. So the crowd will be drawn to the sound. Most people will draw back, but some will leap forward into danger, hoping to detain the gunman. If he falls from a silent bullet in the back, they will still rush in, while our man, like others in the crowd, draws back. Like waves on the beach," Bubovoy explained. He could see it all happening in his mind. "Shooting a pistol is not as easy as the cinema would have us believe, though. Remember, on a battlefield, for every man killed, two or three are wounded and survive. Our gunman will get no closer than four or five meters. That's close enough for an expert, but our man will not be an expert. And then there's the complicating factor of medical care. Unless you're shot through the heart or brain, skilled surgeons can often reach into the grave and pull a wounded man back out. So, realistically, it is a fifty-percent operation. The consequences of failure, therefore, must be taken into account. That is a political question, Comrade Chairman," Bubovoy concluded, meaning that it wasn't his ass on the line, exactly. At the same time, he knew that mission success meant general's stars, which, for the colonel, was an acceptable gamble with a huge upside and little in the way of a downside. It appealed to his careerism as well as his patriotism.

"Very well. What needs to be done?"

"First of all, the DS operates under political guidance. The section that Colonel Strokov commands operates with few written records, but it is directly controlled by the Bulgarian Politburo. So we would have to get political authorization, which necessarily means approval from our own political leadership. The Bulgarians will not authorize their cooperation without an official request from our government. After that, it's actually a straightforward operation."

"I see." Andropov went silent for half a minute or so. There was a Politburo meeting the day after tomorrow. *Was it too soon to float this mission?* he wondered. How difficult might it be to make his case? He'd have to show them the Warsaw Letter, and they would not be the least bit pleased by it. He'd have to present it in such a way as to make the urgency of the matter plain and . . . frightening to them.

Would they be frightened? Well, he could help them along that path, couldn't he? Andropov pondered the question for a few more seconds and came to a favorable conclusion.

"Anything else, Colonel?"

"It hardly needs saying that operational security must be airtight. The Vatican has its own highly effective intelligence service. It would be a mistake to underestimate their capabilities," Bubovoy warned. "Therefore, our Politburo and the Bulgarians must know that this matter cannot be discussed outside of their own number. And for our side, that means no one, even in the Central Committee or the Party Secretariat. The smallest leak would be ruinous to the mission. But, at the same time," he went on, "we have much working for us. The Pope necessarily cannot isolate himself, nor can he be protected as we or any other nation-state would do with such a threat to its chief of state. In an operational sense, he is, actually, rather a 'soft' target—*if,* that is, we can find an assassin willing to risk his life to get sufficiently close to take his shot."

"So, if I can get authorization from the Politburo, and then we make the request for assistance from our Bulgarian brothers, and then you can get this Colonel Strokov moving, how long before it actually happens?"

"A month, I should think, perhaps two months, but not more than that. We would need some support from Station Rome, for issues of timing and such, but that's all. Our own hands would be entirely clean—especially if Strokov assists in eliminating the assassin immediately upon completion of his mission."

"You'd want this Strokov fellow to act personally?"

"Da." Bubovoy nodded. "Boris Andreyevich is not averse to getting his hands wet. He's done this sort of thing before."

"Very well." Andropov looked down at his desk. "There will be no written records of this operation. Once I have proper authorization, you will receive notice to proceed from my office, but only by operational code, and that is 15-8-82-666. Any complex information will be relayed by messenger or by face-to-face contact only. Is that clear?"

"It is clear, Comrade Chairman. Nothing gets written down except the operation number. I expect I will be flying a good deal between Sofia and Moscow, but that is not a problem."

"The Bulgarians are trustworthy?" Andropov asked, suddenly worried.

"Yes, they are, Comrade Chairman. We have a long-standing operational relationship with them, and they are expert at this sort of thing—more than we are, in fact. They have had more practice. When someone must die, it's often the Bulgars who take care of matters for us."

"Yes, Colonel Rozhdestvenskiy has told me that. I just have no direct knowledge of it."

"You could, of course, meet with Colonel Strokov any time you wish," Bubovoy suggested.

Andropov shook his head. "Better that I should not, I think."

"As you wish, Comrade Chairman." *That figures,* Bubovoy thought. Andropov was a party man, not used to getting his hands dirty. Politicians were all the same—bloodthirsty, but personally tidy, depending on others to carry out their nasty wishes. Well, that was his job, the colonel decided, and since politicians controlled the good things in his society, he needed to please them to get the honey from the hive. And he had as big a sweet tooth as anyone else in the Soviet Union. At the end of this mission might be general's stars, a nice flat in Moscow—even a modest dacha in the Lenin Hills. He'd be glad to return to Moscow, and so would his wife. If the price of it was the death of some foreigner who was a political inconvenience to his country, well, that was just too bad. He should have been more careful about who he was offending.

"Thank you for coming and for giving me your expertise, Comrade Colonel. You will be hearing from me."

Bubovoy stood. "I serve the Soviet Union," he said, and made his way through the hidden door.

Rozhdestvenskiy was in the secretaries' room, waiting for him.

"How did it go, Ilya?"

"I am not sure I am allowed to say" was the guarded reply.

"If this is about Operation -666, then you are allowed, Ilya Fedorovich," Rozhdestvenskiy assured him, leading him out the door into the corridor.

"Then the meeting went well, Aleksey Nikolay'ch. More than that, I can only say with the Chairman's approval." This might be a security test, after all, however much a friend Rozhdestvenskiy might be.

"I told him you could be relied upon, Ilya. This could be good for both of us."

"We serve, Aleksey, just like everybody else in this building."

"Let me get you to your car. You can make the noon flight easily." A few minutes later, he was back in Andropov's office.

"Well?" the Chairman asked.

"He says the meeting went well, but he will not say another word without your permission. Ilya Fedorovich is a serious professional, Comrade Chairman. Am I to be your contact for the mission?"

"Yes, you are, Aleksey," Andropov confirmed. "I will send a signal to that effect." Andropov didn't feel the need to run the operation himself. His was a big-picture mind, not an operational one. "What do you know of this Colonel Boris Strokov?"

"Bulgarian? The name is familiar. He's a senior intelligence officer who has in the past specialized in assassination operations. He has ample experience—and obviously Ilya knows him well."

"How does one specialize in assassinations?" the Chairman asked. It was an aspect of the KGB he hadn't been briefed in on.

"His real work is something else, obviously, but the DS has a small group of officers with experience in this sort of thing. He is the most experienced. His operational record is flawless. If memory serves, he's personally eliminated seven or eight people whose deaths were necessary—mostly Bulgarians, I think. Probably a Turk or two as well, but no Westerners that I know of."

"Is it difficult to do?" Yuriy Vladimirovich asked.

"I have no such experience myself," Rozhdestvenskiy admitted. He didn't add that he didn't especially want any. "Those who do say that their concern is not so much in accomplishing the mission as in completing it—that is, avoiding police investigation afterwards. Modern police agencies are fairly effective at investigating murders, you see. In this case, you can expect a most vigorous investigation."

"Bubovoy wants this Strokov fellow to go on the mission and then eliminate the assassin immediately afterward."

Rozhdestvenskiy nodded thoughtfully. "That makes good sense. We have discussed that option ourselves, as I recall."

"Yes." Andropov closed his eyes for a moment. Again, the image paraded itself before his mind. Certainly it would solve a lot of political problems. "Yes, my next job will be to get the Politburo's approval for the mission."

"Quickly, Comrade Chairman?" Colonel Rozhdestvenskiy asked, unable to contain his curiosity.

"Tomorrow afternoon, I think."

DOWN IN COMMUNICATIONS. Zaitzev had allowed his daily routine to absorb his consciousness. It suddenly struck him how mindless his job was. They wanted this job to be done by machines, and he'd become that machine. He had it all committed to memory, which operational designator went to which case officer upstairs and what the operations were all about. So much information slid into his mind along the way that it rather amazed him. It had happened so gradually that he'd never really noticed. He noticed now.

But it was 15-8-82-666 that kept swimming around his mind. . . .

"Zaitzev?" a voice asked. The communicator turned to see Colonel Rozhdestvenskiy.

"Yes, Comrade Colonel?"

"A dispatch for *rezident* Sofia." He handed across the message form, properly made out.

"On the machine or the pad, comrade?"

The colonel paused for a moment, weighing the two options. He came down on the side of consistency: "The pad, I think."

"As you wish, Comrade Colonel. I will have it out in a few minutes."

"Good. It will be waiting for Bubovoy when he gets back to his desk." He made the comment without thinking about it. People all over the world talk too much, and no amount of training can entirely stop them from doing so.

So, the Sofia rezident *was just here?* Zaitzev didn't have to ask. "Yes, Comrade Colonel. Shall I call you to confirm the dispatch?"

"Yes, thank you, Comrade Major."

"I serve the Soviet Union," Zaitzev assured him.

Rozhdestvenskiy made his way back upstairs, while Zaitzev went through the normal, mind-numbing routine of encryption.

MOST SECRET
IMMEDIATE AND URGENT
FROM: OFFICE OF CHAIRMAN, MOSCOW CENTRE
TO: REZIDENT SOFIA

REFERENCE: OPERATIONAL DESIGNATOR 15-8-82-666
FOR ALL FUTURE COMMUNICATIONS YOUR OPERATIONAL CONTACT WILL BE COLONEL ROZHDESTVENSKIY. BY ORDER OF THE CHAIRMAN.

It was just a housekeeping message, but coded "Immediate and Urgent." That meant it was important to Chairman Andropov, and the reference made it an operation, not just a query to some *rezident.*

They really want to do it, Zaitzev realized.

What the hell could he do about it? No one in this room—no one in the entire building—could forestall this operation. But outside the building . . . ?

Zaitzev lit a cigarette. He'd be taking the metro home as usual. Would that American be there as well?

He was contemplating treason, he thought chillingly. The crime had a fearsome sound to it, with an even more fearsome reality. But the other side of that coin was to sit here and read over the dispatches while an innocent man was killed . . . and, no, he could not do that.

Zaitzev took a message blank off a centimeter-thick pad of them on his desk. He set the single sheet of paper on the desk surface and wrote in English, using a #1 soft pencil: IF YOU FIND THIS INTERESTING, WEAR A GREEN TIE TOMORROW. That was as far as his courage stretched this afternoon. He folded the form and tucked it inside his cigarette pack, careful to do everything with normal motions, because anything the least bit unusual in this room was noticed. Next, he scribbled something on another blank form, then crumpled and tossed it into the waste can, and went back to his usual work. For the next three hours, Oleg Ivan'ch would rethink his action every time he reached in his pocket for a smoke. Every time, he'd consider taking out the folded sheet of paper and ripping it to small bits before relegating it to the waste can and then the burn bag. But every time, he'd leave it there, telling himself that he'd done nothing yet. Above all, he tried to set his mind free, to do his regular work and deliberately put himself on auto-pilot, trying to let the day go by. Finally, he told himself that his fate was in hands other than his own. If he got home without anything unusual happening, he'd take the folded form out of his cigarette pack and burn it in his kitchen, and that would be the end of it. About four in the afternoon, Zaitzev looked up at the water-stained ceiling of Communications and whispered something akin to a prayer.

Finally, the workday ended. He took the usual route at the usual pace to the usual metro stop, down the escalator, onto the platform. The metro schedule was as predictable as the coming and going of the tides, and he boarded the carriage along with a hundred others.

Then his heart almost stopped cold in his chest: There was the American, standing in exactly the same place, reading a newspaper in his right hand, with his left holding on to the overhead rail, his raincoat unbuttoned and loose around his slender frame. The open pocket beckoned to him as the Sirens had to Odysseus. Zaitzev made his way to the center of the railcar, shuffling between other riders. His right hand fished in his shirt pocket for the cigarette pack. He deftly removed the message blank from the pack and palmed it, shuffling about the car as it slowed for a station, making room for another passenger. It worked perfectly. He jostled into the American and made the transfer, then drew back.

Zaitzev took a deep breath. The deed was done. What happened now was indeed in other hands.

Was the man really an American—or some false-flag from the Second Chief Directorate?

Had the "American" seen his face?

Did that matter? Weren't his fingerprints on the message form? Zaitzev didn't have a clue. He'd been careful when tearing off the form—and, if questioned, he could always say that the pad just lay on his desk, and anyone could have taken a form—even asked him for it! It might be enough even to foil a KGB investigation if he stuck to his story. Soon enough, he was off the subway car and walking into the open air. He hoped nobody saw his hands shake as he lit up a smoke.

FOLEY'S HIGHLY TRAINED senses had failed him. With his coat loose about him, he hadn't noticed any touch, except for the usual bumps associated with the subway, whether in Moscow or New York. But as he made his way off the train, he stuck his left hand into the left-side pocket, and there was something there, and he knew that it wasn't something he'd placed there himself. A quizzical look crossed his face, which his training quickly erased. He succumbed to the temptation to look around for a tail, but instantly realized that, given his regular schedule, there'd be a fresh face here on the surface to track him, or most likely a series of cameras atop the surrounding buildings. Movie film was as cheap here as everywhere else in the world. And so he walked home, just as on any other day, nodded at the guard at the gate, and then made his way into the elevator, then through the door.

"I'm home, honey," Ed Foley announced, taking out the paper only after the door was closed. He was reasonably certain that there were no cameras in the apartment—even American technology wasn't that far along yet, and he'd seen enough of Moscow to be unimpressed with their technical capabilities. His fingers unfolded the paper, and then he stopped cold in his tracks.

"What's for dinner?" he called out.

"Come and see, Ed." Mary Pat's voice came from the kitchen.

Hamburgers were sizzling on the stove. Mashed potatoes and gravy, plus baked beans, your basic American working-class dinner. But the bread was Russian, and that wasn't bad. Little Eddie was in front of the TV, watching a *Transformers* tape, which would keep him occupied for the next twenty minutes.

"Anything interesting happen today?" Mary Pat asked from the stove. She turned for her kiss, and her husband replied with their personal code phrase for the unusual.

"Not a thing, baby." That piqued her interest enough that when he held up the sheet of paper, she took it, and her eyes went wide.

It wasn't so much the handwritten message as the printed header: STATE SECURITY OFFICIAL COMMUNICATION.

Damn. His wife's lips mouthed the word.

The Moscow COS nodded thoughtfully.

"Can you watch the burgers, honey? I have to get something."

Ed took the spatula and flipped one over. His wife was back quickly, holding a kelly green tie.

CHAPTER 11

HAND JIVE

OF COURSE, there was little to be done at the moment. Dinner was served and eaten, and Eddie went back to his VCR and cartoon tapes. Four-year-olds were easy to please, even in Moscow. His parents got down to business. Years ago, they'd seen *The Miracle Worker* on TV, in which Annie Sullivan (Anne Bancroft) taught Helen Keller (Patty Duke) the use of the manual alphabet, and they'd decided it was a useful skill to learn as a means of communicating not quickly but quietly and with their own shorthand.

W[ell], what do [yo]u think? Ed asked Mary.

This could b[e] pretty h[ot], his wife replied.

Y[ep].

Ed, this guy works in MERCURY, th[eir] version anyway! Wow!

More likely he just has access to their mess[age] forms, the Chief of Station cautioned slowly. *But I'll wear the green tie and take the same subway train for the next w[eek] or so.*

FAB, his wife agreed, which was shorthand for Fuckin' A, Bubba!

Hope it isn't a trap or a false-flag, Ed observed.

Part of the terr[itory], h[oney], MP responded. The thought of being burned didn't frighten her, though she didn't want to suffer the embarrassment. She looked for opportunities more than her husband did—he worried more. But, strangely, not this time. If the Russians had "made" him as the Chief of Station or even just as a field spook—*not likely,* Ed thought—they'd be total idiots to burn him like this, not this fast and not this amateurishly. Unless they were trying to make some sort of political point, and he couldn't see the logic of that—and the KBG was as coldly logical as Mr. Spock ever was on planet Vulcan. Even the FBI wouldn't play this loose a game. So this opportunity had to be real, unless KGB was shaking down every embassy employee it could, just to see what might fall off the tree. Possible, but damned unlikely, and therefore worth the gamble, Foley judged. He'd wear the green tie and see what happened, and be damned careful to check all the faces on the subway car.

Tell L[angley]? Mary asked next.

He just shook his head. *2 early 4 that.*

She nodded agreement. Next, Mary Pat mimed riding a horse. That meant that there was a chase and they were really in the game, finally. It was as though she were afraid that her skills were going stale. *Damned little chance of that,* her husband thought. He was willing to bet that his wife had gone all the way through parochial school without a single rap on the knuckles, because the sisters had never once caught her misbehaving. . . .

And, for that matter, Ed reflected, neither had he.

W[ell], tomor[row] will be inter[esting], he told her, getting a sexy nod as a reply.

The hard part for the rest of the evening was not dwelling on the opportunity. Even with their training, their thoughts kept coming back to the idea of working an agent in the Russian MERCURY. It was a conceptual homer in the bottom of the ninth in the seventh game of the World Series—Reggie Jackson Foley as Mister October.

Damn.

"SO, SIMON, what do we really know about the guy?"

"Not all that much on the personal level," Harding admitted. "He's a Party man first, last, and always. His horizons have been broadened, I suppose, from his chairmanship of KGB. There's talk that he prefers Western liquor to his own vodka, and stories that he enjoys American jazz, but those could be stories floated in-house by The Centre to help him appear amenable to the West—not bloody likely, in my humble opinion. The man is a thug. His Party record is not one of gentleness. One doesn't advance in that organization except by toughness—and remarkably often the high-flyers are men who have crushed their own mentors along the way. It's a Darwinian organization gone mad, Jack. The fittest survive, but they prove themselves to be the fittest by smashing those who are a threat to them, or merely smashing people to prove their own ruthlessness in the arena they've chosen."

"How smart is he?" Ryan asked next.

Another draw on the briar pipe. "He's no fool. Highly developed sense of human nature, probably a good—even a brilliant—amateur psychologist."

"You haven't compared him to someone from Tolstoy or Chekhov," Jack noted. Simon was a lit major, after all.

Harding dismissed the thought. "Too easy to do so. No, people like him most often do not appear in literature, because novelists lack the requisite imagination. There was no warning of a Hitler in German literature, Jack. Stalin evidently thought himself another Ivan the Terrible, and Sergei Eisenstein played along with his epic movie about the chap, but that sort of thing is only for those without the imagination to see people as they are instead of being like someone else they understand. No, Stalin was a complex and fundamentally incomprehensible monster, unless you have psychiatric credentials. I do not," Harding reminded him. "One need not understand them fully to predict their actions, because such people are rational within their own context. One need only understand that, or so I have always believed."

"Sometimes I think I ought to get Cathy involved in this work."

"Because she's a physician?" Harding asked.

Ryan nodded. "Yeah, she's pretty good reading people. That's why we had the docs report in on Mikhail Suslov. None of them were pshrinks," Jack reminded his workmate.

"So, no, we know remarkably little on Andropov's personal life," Harding admitted. "No one's ever been tasked to delve too deeply into it.

If he gets elevated to the General-Secretaryship, I imagine his wife will become a semipublic figure. In any case, there's no reason to think him a homosexual or anything like that. They are quite intolerant of that aberration over there, you know. Some colleague would have used it against him along the way and wrecked his career for fair. No, the closet they live in within the Soviet Union is a very deep one. Better to be celibate," the analyst concluded.

Okay, Ryan thought, *I'll call the Admiral tonight and tell him that the Brits don't know, either.* It was strangely disappointing, but somehow predictable. For all that the intelligence services knew, the frequency of holes in their knowledge was often surprising to the outsiders, but not so to those on the inside. Ryan was still new enough at the game to be surprised and disappointed. A married man would be used to compromise, to letting his wife have her way on all manner of things, because every married man is pussy-whipped to one extent or another—unless he is a total thug, and few people fit into that category. Fewer still could rise up any hierarchy that way, because in any organization you had to go along in order to get along. That was human nature, and even the Communist Party of the Soviet Union couldn't repeal that, for all their talk about the New Soviet Man that they kept trying to build over there. *Yeah,* Ryan thought, *sure.*

"Well," Harding said, checking his watch, "I think we've served Her Majesty enough for one day."

"Agreed." Ryan stood up and collected his jacket off the clothes tree. Take the tube this time to Victoria Station, and catch the Lionel home. The routine was getting to him. It would have been better to get a place in town and cut down the commute, but that way Sally wouldn't have much in the way of green grass to play on, and Cathy had been adamant about that. Renewed proof that he was indeed pussy-whipped, Jack thought on the way to the elevator. Well, it could have been worse. He did have a good wife to do the whipping, after all.

COLONEL BUBOVOY came back to the embassy on his way home from the airport. A short dispatch was waiting, which he quickly decrypted: He'd be working through Colonel Rozhdestvenskiy. No particular surprise there.

Aleksey Nikolay'ch was Andropov's lapdog. And that was probably a good job, the *rezident* thought. You just had to keep the boss happy, and Yuriy Vladimirovich was probably not the demanding bastard that Beria had been. Party people might be overly precise in their demands, but anyone who'd worked in the Party Secretariat doubtless knew how to work with people. The age of Stalin had indeed passed.

So, it looked as though he had an assassination to arrange, Bubovoy thought. He wondered how Boris Strokov would react to it. Strokov was a professional, with little in the way of excess emotion, and less in the way of a professional conscience. To him, work was work. But the magnitude of this was higher than anything he would have encountered working for the *Dirzhavna Sugurnost.* Would that frighten him or excite him? It would be interesting to see. There was a coldness to his Bulgarian colleague that both alarmed and impressed the KGB officer. His particular skills could be useful things to have in one's pocket. And if the Politburo needed this annoying Pole killed, then he would just have to die. Too bad, but if what he believed was true, then they were just sending him off to heaven as a holy martyr, weren't they? Surely that was the secret ambition of every priest.

Bubovoy's only concern was the political repercussions. Those would be epic, and so it was good that he was just a cutout in the operation. If it went bad, well, it wouldn't be his fault. That Strokov was the best man for the job, based on his curriculum vitae, was something no man could deny, something a board of inquiry, if any, could confirm. He'd warned the Chairman that a shot, however closely taken, would not necessarily be fatal. He'd have to put that in a memo to make sure the thin paper trail on operation 15-8-82-666 would have his formal evaluation in it. He'd draft it himself and send it by diplomatic bag to The Centre—and keep his own copy in his office safe, just to make sure his own backside was properly covered.

But for now he would have to wait for the authorization to come from the Politburo. Would those old women elect to go forward with this? That was the question, and one on which he would not make a wager. Brezhnev was in his dotage. Would that make him bloodthirsty or cautious? It was too hard a question for the colonel to puzzle out. They were saying that

Yuriy Vladimirovich was the heir apparent. If so, here was his chance to win his spurs.

"SO, MIKHAIL YEVGENIYEVICH, will you support me tomorrow?" Andropov asked over drinks in his flat.

Alexandrov swirled the expensive brown vodka in his glass. "Suslov will not attend tomorrow. They say his kidneys have failed, and he has no more than two weeks," the ideologue-in-waiting said, briefly dodging the issue. "Will you support me for his chair?"

"Need you ask, Misha?" the Chairman of the Committee for State Security responded. "Of course I will support you."

"Very well. So, what are the chances for success in this operation you propose?"

"About fifty-fifty, my people tell me. We will use a Bulgarian officer to set it up, but for security reasons the assassin will have to be a Turk. . . ."

"A black-ass Muslim?" Alexandrov asked sharply.

"Misha, whoever it is will almost certainly be apprehended—dead, according to our plan. It is impossible to expect a clean getaway in such a mission. Thus, we cannot use one of our own. The nature of the mission places constraints upon us. Ideally, we would use a trained sniper—from Spetsnaz, for example—from three hundred meters, but that would mark the assassination as a killing done by a nation-state. No, this must appear to be the act of a single madman, as the Americans have them. You know, even with all the evidence the Americans had, some fools over there still blamed Kennedy on us or Castro. No, the evidence we leave must be a clear sign that we were *not* involved. That limits our operational methods. I think this is the best plan we can come up with."

"How closely have you studied it?" Alexandrov asked, taking a swallow.

"It has been closely held. Operations like this must be. Security must be airtight, Mikhail Yevgeniyevich."

The Party man conceded the point: "I suppose that is so, Yuriy—but the risk of failure . . ."

"Misha, in every aspect of life, there is risk. The important thing is that the operation not be tied to us. That we can assure with certainty. If nothing else, a serious wound will at least lessen Karol's ardor for making trouble for us, will it not?"

"It should—"

"And half a chance of failure means half a chance of total success," Andropov reminded his guest.

"Then I will support you. Leonid Ilyich will go along as well. That will carry the day. How long after that to get things moving?"

"A month or so, perhaps six weeks."

"That quickly?" Party matters rarely sped along that well.

"What is the point of taking such, such—'executive action,' isn't that what the Americans call it?—if it is to take so long? If it is to be done, better that it should be done quickly, so as to forestall further political intrigue by this man."

"Who will replace him?"

"Some Italian, I suppose. His selection was a major aberration. Perhaps his death will encourage the Romans to go back to their old habits," Andropov suggested. It generated a laugh from his guest.

"Yes, they are so predictable, these religious fanatics."

"So tomorrow I will float the mission, and you will support me?" Andropov wanted that one very clear.

"Yes, Yuriy Vladimirovich. You will have my support. And you will support me for Suslov's full voting seat at the table."

"Tomorrow, comrade," Andropov promised.

CHAPTER 12

HANDOFF

THIS TIME, the alarm clock worked, and woke them both. Ed Foley rose and headed for the bathroom, quickly made way for his wife, then headed to Eddie's room to shake him loose while Mary Pat started breakfast. Their son immediately switched on the TV and got the morning exercise show that every city in the world seemed to have, starring, as everywhere in the world, a woman of impressive physique—she looked capable of waltzing through the Army's Ranger School at Fort Benning, Georgia. Because he had seen the Lynda Carter series at home on cable, Eddie called her Worker-*Womannnnnn!* Mary Pat was of the opinion that the Russian's blond hair came out of a bottle, while Ed thought it hurt just to watch the things she did. With no decent paper or sports page to read, however, he had little choice in the matter, and semi-vegetated in front of the TV while his son giggled through the end of the wake-up-and-sweat program. It was done live, the Chief of Station saw. So, whoever this broad was, she had to wake up at four in the morning, and so this was probably her morning workout as well. Well, then, at least it was honest. Her husband must have been a Red Army paratrooper, and she could probably beat the shit out of him, Ed Foley thought, waiting for the morning news.

That started at 6:30. The trick was to watch it and then try to figure out what was really happening in the world—*just like at home,* the CIA officer thought, with an early-morning grumble. Well, he'd have the *Early Bird* at the embassy for that, sent by secure fax from Washington for the senior embassy staffers. For an American citizen, living in Moscow was like being on a desert island. At least they had a satellite dish at the embassy so they could download CNN and other programming. It made them feel like real people—almost.

Breakfast was breakfast. Little Eddie liked Frosted Flakes—the milk was from Finland, because his mother didn't trust the local grocery store, and the foreigners-only store was convenient to the compound. Ed and Mary Pat didn't talk much over breakfast, in deference to the bugs that littered their walls. They never talked at home about important matters, except via hand code—and *never* in front of their son, because little kids were incapable of keeping secrets of any kind. In any case, their KGB surveillance people were probably bored with the Foleys by now, which they'd both worked hard at, inserting just enough randomness in their behavior to make them look like Americans. But a considered amount. Not too much. They'd planned it out carefully and thoroughly at Langley, with the help of a tame KGB Second Chief Directorate defector.

Mary Pat had her husband's clothes all laid out on the bed, including the green tie to go with his brown suit. Like the President, Ed looked good in brown, his wife thought. Ed would wear a raincoat again, and he would keep it unbuttoned and loose around his body should another message be passed, and his senses would be thoroughly sandpapered all day.

"What are your plans for the day?" he asked Mary Pat in the living room.

"The usual. I might get together with Penny after lunch."

"Oh? Well, say hello for me. Maybe we can get together for dinner later this week."

"Good idea," his wife said. "Maybe they can explain rugby to me."

"It's like football, honey, just the rules are a little goofy," the Station Chief explained. "Well, off to keep the reporters happy."

"Right!" Mary Pat laughed, working her eyes at the walls. "That guy from the *Boston Globe* is such an ass."

Outside, the morning was pleasant enough—just a hint of cool air to suggest the approach of autumn. Foley walked off toward the station, waving at the gate guard. The guy on morning duty actually smiled once in a while. He'd clearly been around foreigners too much, or had been trained to do so by KGB. His uniform was that of the Moscow Militia—the city police—but Foley thought he looked a little too intelligent for that. Muscovites thought of their police as a rather low form of life, and such an agency would not attract the brightest of people.

The couple blocks to the metro station passed quickly. Crossing the streets was reasonably safe here—far more so than in New York—because private cars were pretty rare. And it was a good thing. Russian drivers made the Italians look prudent and orderly. The guys driving the ubiquitous dump trucks must all have been former tank crewmen, judging by their road manners. He picked up his copy of *Pravda* at the kiosk and took the escalator down to the platform. A man of the strictest habits, he arrived at the station at exactly the same time every morning, then checked the clock hanging from the ceiling to make sure. The subway trains ran on an inhumanly precise schedule, and he walked aboard at exactly 7:43 A.M. He hadn't looked over his shoulder. It was too far into his residency in Moscow to rubberneck like a new tourist, and that, he figured, would make his KGB shadow think that his American subject was about as interesting as the kasha that Russians liked for breakfast along with the dreadful local coffee. Quality control was something the Soviets reserved for their nuclear weapons and space program, though Foley had doubts about those, based on what he'd seen in this city, where only the metro seemed to work properly. Such a strange combination of casual-klutz and Germanlike precision they were. You could tell how well things worked over here by what they were used for, and intelligence operations had the highest priority of all, lest the Soviets' enemies find out not what they had, but what they didn't have. Foley had agent CARDINAL to tell him and America what the Soviet Union had in the military realm. Generally, it was good stuff to learn, but that was mainly because the more you learned, the less you had to worry. No, it was political intelligence that counted most here because, as backward as they were, they were still big enough to cause trouble if you couldn't counter them early on. Langley was very worried about the Pope at the moment. He'd evidently done something that might be embarrassing to the Russians. And Ivan didn't like being embarrassed in the political field any more than American politicians—just that Ivan didn't go running off to *The Washington Post* to get even. Ritter and Moore were very concerned about what Ivan might do—and even more worried about what Yuriy Andropov might do. Ed Foley didn't have a feel for that particular Russian. Like most in CIA, he knew the guy only by his face, name, and his evident liver problems—that information had leaked out through a means the Station Chief didn't know. Maybe the Brits . . . *if you could trust the Brits,* Ed cautioned himself. He had to trust them, but something kept making the hackles on his neck get nervous about them. Well, they probably had doubts about CIA. Such a crazy game this was. He scanned the front page. Nothing surprising, though the piece on the Warsaw Pact was a little interesting. They still worried about NATO. Maybe they really did worry about having the German army come east again. They were certainly paranoid enough. . . . Paranoia had probably been invented in Russia. *Maybe Freud discovered it on a trip here,* he mused, lifting his eyes for a pair tracking him . . . no, none, he decided. Was it possible that the KGB *wasn't* tracking him? Well, possible, yes, but likely, no. If they had a guy—more likely a team—shadowing him, the coverage would be expert—but why put expert—but why put expert coverage on the Press Attaché? Foley sighed to himself. Was he too much of a worrier, or not paranoid enough? And how did you tell the difference? Or might he have exposed himself to a false-flag operation by wearing a green tie? *How the hell do you tell?*

If he *was* burned, then so was his wife, and that would put the brakes on two very promising CIA careers. He and Mary Pat were Bob Ritter's fair-haired pair, the varsity, the young all-pro team at Langley, and it was a reputation that had to be both protected carefully and also built upon. The President of the United States himself would read their "take" and maybe make decisions based on the information they brought in. Important decisions that could affect the policy of their country. The responsibility was not something to dwell on. It could drive you nuts, make you too cautious—so cautious that you never accomplished anything. No, the biggest problem in the intelligence business was in drawing the line between circumspection and effectiveness. If you leaned too far the one way, you never got anything useful done. If you went too far the other way, then you got yourself burned, and your agents, and over here that meant virtual certain death for people for whose lives *you* were responsible. It was a dilemma fit to drive a man to drink.

The metro stopped at his station and he went out the door, then up the escalator. He was pretty sure that nobody had fished in his pocket. On the street level, he checked. Nothing. So whomever it was, either he only rode the afternoon train or the Chief of Station had been "made" by the opposition. It would give him something to worry about all day.

"THIS ONE'S FOR YOU," Dobrik said, handing it over. "From Sofia."

"Oh?" Zaitzev responded.

"It's in the book, your-eyes-only, Oleg Ivan'ch," the night-duty officer said. "At least it's short."

"Ah," Zaitzev said, taking the message and seeing the header: 15-8-82-666. So they figured that with a number instead of a name, the header didn't need to be encrypted. He didn't react or say anything further. It just wasn't done. Surely, Kolya wondered about it—it was the office sport in Communications, wondering about the things one couldn't read. This message had come in just forty minutes after his departure. "Well, something to start my watch with. Anything else, Nikolay Konstantinovich?"

"No, aside from that, you have a clean desk." Dobrik was an efficient worker, whatever faults he might have had. "And now I am properly relieved of duty. At home I have a fresh bottle of vodka."

"You should eat first, Kolya," Zaitzev warned.

"That's what my mother says, Oleg. Perhaps I'll have a sandwich with my breakfast," he joked.

"Sleep well, Comrade Major, I relieve you," Zaitzev said, as he took his seat. Ten minutes later, he had the brief dispatch decrypted. The Sofia *rezident* acknowledged that Colonel Rozhdestvenskiy was his point of contact for Operation 15-8-82-666. So that *t* was properly crossed. And 15-8-82-666 was a full-fledged operation now. He tucked the decrypted message into a manila envelope, sealed it, and then dripped hot wax on the seal.

They're really going to do it, Oleg Ivanovich told himself with a frown. *What do I do now?*

Work his usual day, and then look for a green tie on the metro home. And pray he saw it? Or pray he didn't?

Zaitzev shook the thought off and called for a messenger to hand-deliver the dispatch to the top floor. A moment later, a basketful of dispatches landed on his desk for processing.

"OUCH," Ed Foley said aloud at his desk. The message—a lengthy one—came from Ritter and Moore, speaking for the President. He'd have to rattle some serious bushes for this.

Station Moscow didn't have a written list of agents, even by code names, and even in Foley's office safe, which in addition to a combination had a two-phase alarm built in, a keypad on the outside, and one on the inside with a different code, which Foley had set himself. The embassy's Marines had orders to respond to either alarm with drawn weapons, since the contents of this safe were about the most sensitive documents in the whole building.

But Foley had the names of every Russian citizen who worked for the Agency hard cut into his eyelids, along with their specialty areas. Twelve such agents were currently operating. They'd just lost one the week before he'd arrived in Moscow—burned. No one knew how, though Foley was concerned that the Russians might have a mole in Langley itself. It was heresy to think it, but as CIA tried to do it to KGB, so KGB tried to do it to CIA, and there was no referee on the playing field to let the players know what the score was. The lost agent, whose code name had been SOUSA, was a lieutenant colonel in the GRU and had helped identify some major leaks in the German defense ministry and other NATO sources, through which KGB had gotten political-military intelligence of a high order. But that guy was dead—still breathing, perhaps, but dead even so. Foley hoped they wouldn't load the guy alive into a furnace, as had been done with another GRU source back in the 1950s. Rather a cruel method of execution, even for the Russians under Khrushchev, and something that had kept his case officer awake for a very long time, the COS was sure.

So they'd have to get two, maybe three, of their agents working on this one. They had a good guy in KGB and another in the Party Central Committee. Maybe one of them might have heard about a possible operation against the Pope.

Damn, Foley thought, *are they* that *crazy?* It required a considerable stretch of his imagination. An Irishman by ancestry, and Roman Catholic by education and religious affiliation, Ed Foley had to make a mental effort to set aside his personal thoughts. Such a plot was beyond the pale, perhaps, but he was dealing with people who didn't recognize the concept of limits, certainly not from any outside agency. For them, God was politics, and a threat to their political world was like Lucifer himself challenging the order of heaven. Except that the simile only went so far. This was more like Michael the Archangel challenging the order of Hell. Mary Pat called it the belly of the beast, and this one was one nasty fuckin' beast.

"DADDY!" SALLY EXCLAIMED, waking up with her usual smile. He guided her to the bathroom and then downstairs, where her oatmeal was waiting. Sally still wore her bunny-rabbit sleepers, with feet and a long zipper. This one was yellow. And it was the largest size, and her feet were stretching it. She'd have to change to some other sleepwear soon, but that was Cathy's department.

The routine was set. Cathy fed Little Jack and, halfway through, her husband set down his paper and headed upstairs to shave. By the time he was dressed, she was finished with her duty, and went off to get cleaned up and dressed while Jack burped the little guy and got him into his socks to keep his feet warm, and also to give him something to pull off so that he could see if the feet tasted the same as they had the previous day, which was a newly acquired skill.

Soon the doorbell rang, and it was Margaret van der Beek, soon followed by Ed Beaverton, which allowed the parents to escape off to work. At Victoria Station, Cathy kissed her husband good-bye and headed for the tube station for the ride to Moorefields, while Jack took a different train to Century House, and the day was about to start for real.

"Good morning, Sir John."

"Hey, Bert." Ryan paused. Bert Canderton had "army" written all over him, and it was time to ask. "What regiment were you?"

"I was Regimental Sergeant Major of the Royal Green Jackets, sir."

"Infantry?"

"Correct, sir."

"I thought you guys wore red coats," Ryan observed.

"Well, that's your fault—you Yanks, that is. In your revolutionary war, my regiment took so many casualties from your riflemen that the colonel of the regiment decided a green tunic might be safer. It's been that way ever since."

"How did you end up here?"

"I'm waiting for an opening at the Tower to be a Yeoman Warder, sir. Should have a new red coat in a month or so, they tell me."

Canderton's rent-a-cop blouse had some service ribbons on it, probably not for brushing and flossing his teeth, and a regimental sergeant major in the British army was *somebody*, like a master gunnery sergeant in the Marine Corps.

"I've been there, been to the club they have," said Ryan. "Good bunch of troops."

"Indeed. I have a friend there, Mick Truelove. He was in the Queen's Regiment."

"Well, sar-major, keep the bad guys out," Ryan said, as he worked his card into the electronic slot that controlled the entry gate.

"I will do that, sir," Canderton promised.

Harding was at his desk when Ryan came in. Jack hung his jacket on the tree.

"Come in early, Simon?"

"Your Judge Moore sent a fax to Bas last night—just after midnight, as a matter of fact. Here." He handed it across.

Ryan scanned it. "The Pope, eh?"

"Your President is interested, and so is the PM, as it happens," Harding said, relighting his pipe. "Basil called us in early to go over what data we have."

"Okay, what *do* we have?"

"Not much," Harding admitted. "I can't talk to you about our sources—"

"Simon, I'm not dumb. You have somebody in close, either a confidante of a Politburo member or someone in the Party Secretariat. He's not telling you anything?" Ryan had seen some very interesting "take" in here, and it had to have come from somebody inside the big red tent.

"I can't confirm your suspicion," Harding cautioned, "but no, none of our sources have given us anything, not even that the Warsaw Letter has arrived in Moscow, though we know it must have."

"So, we don't know jackshit?"

Simon nodded soberly. "Correct."

"Amazing how often that happens."

"It's just a part of the job, Jack."

"And the PM has her panties in a wad?"

Harding hadn't heard that Americanism before, and it caused him to blink twice. "So it would seem."

"So, what are we supposed to tell her? She damned sure doesn't want to hear that we don't know."

"No, our political leaders do not like to hear that sort of thing."

Neither do ours, Ryan admitted to himself. "So, how good is Basil at a song-and-dance number?"

"Quite good, actually. In this case, he can say that your chaps do not have very much, either."

"Ask other NATO services?"

Harding shook his head. "No. It might leak out to the opposition—first, that we're interested, and second, that we don't know enough."

"How good are our friends?"

"Depends. The French SDECE occasionally turns good information, but they do not like to share. Neither do our Israeli friends. The Germans are thoroughly compromised. That Markus Wolf chap in East Germany is a bloody genius at this business—perhaps the best in the world, and under Soviet control. The Italians have some talented people, but they, too, have problems with penetration. You know, the best service on the continent might well be the Vatican itself. But if Ivan is doing anything at the moment, he's covering it nicely. Ivan is quite good at that, you know."

"So I've heard," Ryan agreed. "When does Basil have to go to Downing Street?"

"After lunch—three this afternoon, I understand."

"And what will we be able to give him?"

"Not very much, I'm afraid—worse, Basil might want me with him."

Ryan grunted. "That ought to be fun. Met her before?"

"No, but the PM has seen my analyses. Bas says she wants to meet me." He shuddered. "It'd be much better if I had something substantive to tell her."

"Well, let's see if we can come up with a threat analysis, okay?" Jack sat down. "What exactly *do* we know?"

Harding handed a sheaf of documents across. Ryan leaned back in his chair to pick through them.

"You got the Warsaw Letter from a Polish source, right?"

Harding hesitated, but it was clear he had to answer this one: "That is correct."

"So nothing from Moscow itself?" Jack asked.

He shook his head. "No. We know the letter was forwarded to Moscow, but that's all."

"We're really in the dark, then. You might want to have a beer before you go across the river."

Harding looked up from his notes. "Why, thank you, Jack. I really needed to hear that bit of encouragement."

They were silent for a moment.

"I work better on a computer," Ryan said. "How hard is it to get one in here?"

"Not easy. They have to be tempest-checked to make sure someone outside the building cannot read the keystrokes electronically. You can call administration about it."

But not today, Ryan didn't say aloud. He'd learned that the bureaucracy at Century House was at least as bad as the one at Langley, and after a few years of working in the private sector, it could drive him to distraction. *Okay,* he'd try to come up with some ideas to save Simon from getting a new asshole installed in his guts. The Prime Minister was a lady, but in terms of demands, Father Tim at Georgetown had nothing on her.

OLEG IVAN'CH got back from lunch at the KGB cafeteria and faced facts. Very soon, he would have to decide what to say to his American, and how to say it.

If he was a regular embassy employee, he would have passed the first note along to the CIA chief in the embassy—there had to be one, he knew, an American *rezident* whose job it was to spy on the Soviet Union, just as Russians spied on everyone in the world. The big question was whether they were spying on *him*. Could he have been "doubled" by the Second Chief Directorate, whose reputation would frighten the devil in hell himself? Or could this ostensible American have been a Russian bearing a "false-flag"?

So, first of all, Oleg had to make damned sure he was dealing with the real thing. How to do that . . . ?

Then it came to him. *Yes,* he thought. That was something KGB could never bring off. That would ensure that he was dealing with someone able to do what he needed done. No one could fake that. In celebration, Zaitzev lit up another cigarette and went back into the morning dispatches from the Washington *rezidentura.*

IT WAS HARD to like Tony Prince. The *New York Times* correspondent in Moscow was well-regarded by the Russians, and, as far as Ed Foley was concerned, that spoke to a weakness in his character.

"So, how do you like the new job, Ed?" Prince asked.

"Still settling in. Dealing with the Russian press is kind of interesting. They're predictable, but unpredictably so."

"How can people be unpredictably predictable?" the *Times* correspondent inquired, with a crooked smile.

"Well, Tony, you know what they're going to say, just not how they're going to ask it." *And half of them are spooks or at least stringers, anyway, in case you haven't noticed.*

Prince affected a laugh. He felt himself to be the intellectual superior.

Foley had failed as a general-beat reporter in New York, whereas Prince had parlayed his political savvy to one of the top jobs in American journalism. He had some good contacts in the Soviet government, and he cultivated them assiduously, frequently sympathizing with them over the boorish, *nekulturniy* behavior of the current regime in Washington, which he occasionally tried to explain to his Russian friends, often pointing out that *he* hadn't voted for this damned actor, and neither had anyone in his New York office.

"Have you met the new guy, Alexandrov, yet?"

"No, but one of my contacts knows him, says he's a reasonable sort, talks like he's in favor of peaceful coexistence. More liberal than Suslov. I hear *he's* pretty sick."

"I've heard that, too, but I'm not sure what's wrong with him."

"He's diabetic, didn't you hear? That's why the Baltimore docs came over to work on his eyes. Diabetic retinopathy," Prince explained, speaking the word slowly so that Foley could comprehend it.

"I'll have to ask the embassy doc what that means," Foley observed, making an obvious note on his pad. "So, this Alexandrov guy is more liberal, you think?" "Liberal" was a word that meant "good guy" to Prince.

"Well, I haven't met him myself, but that's what my sources think. They also think that when Suslov departs from this life, Mikhail Yevgeniyevich will take his place."

"Really? I'll have to drop that on the ambassador."

"And the Station Chief?"

"You know who that is? I don't," Foley said.

An eye roll. "Ron Fielding. Hell, *everybody* knows that."

"No, he isn't," Ed protested as sharply as his acting talent allowed. "He's the senior consular officer, not a spook."

Prince smiled, thinking, *You never could figure things out, could you?* His Russian contacts had fingered Fielding to him, and he knew they wouldn't lie to him. "Well, that's just a guess, of course," the reporter went on.

And if you thought it was me, you'd blurt it right out, wouldn't you? Foley thought right back at him. *You officious ass.* "Well, I'm cleared for some things, as you know, but not that one."

"I know who does know," Prince offered.

"Yeah, but I'm not going to ask the Ambassador, Tony. He'd rip my face off."

"He's just a political appointment, Ed—nothing special. This ought to be a posting for somebody who knows diplomacy, but the President didn't ask me for advice."

Thank God, the Station Chief commented inwardly.

"Fielding sees him a lot, doesn't he?" Prince went on.

"A consular officer works directly with the Ambassador, Tony. You know that."

"Yeah. Convenient, isn't it? How much do you see him?"

"The boss, you mean? Once a day, usually," Foley answered.

"And Fielding?"

"More. Maybe two or three times."

"There you have it," Prince concluded grandly. "You can always tell."

"You read too many James Bond books," Foley said dismissively. "Or maybe Matt Helm."

"Get real, Ed," Prince bristled with elegant gentleness.

"If Fielding is the head spook, who are his underlings? Damned if I know."

"Well, those are always pretty covert," Prince admitted. "No, on that I don't have a clue."

"Pity. That's one of the games you play in the embassy—who are the spooks."

"Well, I can't help you."

"It's not something I need to know anyway, I guess," Foley admitted.

You never were curious enough to be a good reporter, Prince thought, with a casual, pleasant smile. "So, does this keep you busy?"

"It's not a ball-breaker. Anyway, can we make a deal?"

"Sure," Prince replied. "What is it?"

"If you hear anything interesting, let us know here?"

"You can read about it in the *Times,* usually on the front page above the fold," he added, to make sure Foley knew how important he was, along with his penetrating analysis.

"Well, some things, you know, the Ambassador likes to get a heads-up. He told me to ask, off-the-record-like."

"That's an ethical issue, Ed."

"If I tell Ernie that, he won't be real happy."

"Well, you work for him. I don't."

"You are an American citizen, right?"

"Don't wave the flag at me, okay?" Prince responded wearily. "Okay, if I find out they're about to launch nuclear weapons, I'll let you know. But it looks to me like we're more likely to do something that stupid than they are."

"Tony, give me a break."

"This 'focus of evil in the world' crap wasn't exactly Abe Lincoln talking, was it?"

"You saying the President was wrong?" the Chief of Station asked, wondering just how far his opinion of this ass might sink.

"I know about the Gulag, okay? But that's a thing of the past. The Russians have mellowed since Stalin died, but the new administration hasn't figured that one out yet, have they?"

"Look, Tony, I'm just a worker bee here. The Ambassador asked me to forward a simple request. I take it your response is 'no'?"

"You take it correctly."

"Well, don't expect any Christmas cards from Ernie Fuller."

"Ed, my duty is to *The New York Times* and my readers, period."

"Okay, fine. I had to ask," Foley said defensively. He hadn't expected anything better from the guy, but he'd suggested this to Ambassador Fuller himself to feel Prince out, and the Ambassador had approved it.

"I understand." Prince checked his watch. "Hey, I have a meeting scheduled at the CPSU Central Committee building."

"Anything I ought to know about?"

"Like I said, you can read it in the *Times.* They fax you the *Early Bird* out of Washington, don't they?"

"Yeah, it eventually trickles down here."

"Then, day after tomorrow, you can read it," Prince advised, standing to take his leave. "Tell Ernie."

"I'll do that," Foley said, extending his hand. Then he decided he'd walk Prince to the elevator. On the way back, he'd hit the men's room to wash his hands. His next stop after that was the Ambassador's office.

"Hi, Ed. Meet with that Prince guy?"

Foley nodded his head. "Just cut him loose."

"Did he nibble at your hook?"

"Nope. Just spat it right back at me."

Fuller smiled crookedly. "What did I tell you? There used to be some patriotic reporters back when I was your age, but they've mostly grown out of it over the last few years."

"I'm not surprised. When Tony was a new kid in New York, he never liked the cops very much, but he was good at getting them to talk to him. Persuasive bastard, when he wants to be."

"Did he work on you?"

"No, sir. I'm not important enough for that."

"What did you think of the Washington request about the Pope?" Fuller asked, changing the subject.

"I'm going to have some people look into it, but—"

"I know, Ed. I don't *want* to know exactly what you're doing about it. If you find anything, will you be able to tell me about it?"

"Depends, sir," Foley answered, meaning *probably not.*

Fuller accepted that. "Okay. Anything else shaking?"

"Prince is on to something, ought to be in the papers day after tomorrow. He's on his way to the Central Committee, or so he told me. He confirmed that Alexandrov will replace Mikhail Suslov when Red Mike checks out. If they're telling him, it must be official. I think we can believe that one. Tony has good contacts with their political types, and it tracks with what our other friends tell us about Suslov."

"I've never met the guy. What gives with him?"

"He's one of the last true believers. Alexandrov is another one. He thinks Marx is the One True God, and Lenin is his prophet, and their political and economic system really does work."

"Really? Some people never learn."

"Yep. You can take that to the bank, sir. There are a few left, but Leonid Ilyich isn't one of them, and neither is his heir apparent, Yuriy

Vladimirovich. But Alexandrov is Andropov's ally. There's a Politburo meeting later today."

"When will we know what they discussed?"

"Couple of days, probably." *But exactly how we find out, you do not need to know, sir,* Foley didn't add.

He didn't have to. Ernie Fuller knew the rules of the game. The U.S. Ambassador to every country was thoroughly briefed on the embassy he was taking over. To get into Moscow involved voluntary brainwashing at Foggy Bottom and Langley. In reality, the American ambassador to Moscow was his country's chief intelligence officer in the Soviet Union, and Uncle Ernie was a pretty good one, Foley thought.

"Okay, keep me posted if you can."

"Will do, sir," the Chief of Station promised.

CHAPTER 13

COLLEGIALITY

ANDROPOV ARRIVED IN THE KREMLIN at 12:45 for the 1:00 P.M. meeting. His driver pulled the handmade ZIL through the Spasskiy Gate's towering brick structure, past the security checkpoints, past the saluting soldiers of the ceremonial Tamanskiy Guards Division stationed outside Moscow and used mainly for parades and pretty-soldier duties. The soldier saluted smartly, but the gesture went unnoticed by the people inside the car. From there it was a hundred fifty meters to the destination, where another soldier wrenched open the door. Andropov noted this salute and nodded absently to let the senior sergeant know that he was seen, then made his way inside the yellow-cream-colored building. Instead of taking the stone steps, Andropov turned right to go to the elevator for the ride to the second floor, followed by his aide, Colonel Rozhdestvenskiy, for whom this was the most interesting and about to be the most intimidating part of his official duties since joining KGB.

There was yet more security on the upper floors: uniformed Red Army officers with holstered side arms, in case of trouble. But there would be no trouble in his ascension to the General Secretaryship, Andropov thought. This would be no palace coup. He'd be elected by his political peers in the usual way that the Soviet Union handled the transition of power—awkwardly and badly, but predictably. The one with the most political capital would chair this counsel of peers, because they would trust him not to rule by force of will, but by collegial consensus. None of them wanted another Stalin, or even another Khrushchev, who might lead them on adventures. These men did not enjoy adventures. They'd all learned from history that gambling carried with it the possibility of losing, and none of them had come this far to risk losing anything at all. They were the chieftains in a nation of chess players, for whom victory was something determined by skillful maneuvers taken patiently and progressively over a period of hours, whose conclusion would seem as foreordained as the setting of the sun.

That was one of the problems today, Andropov thought, taking his seat next to Defense Minister Ustinov. Both sat near the head of the table, in the seats reserved for members of the Defense Counsel or *Soviet Orborony,* the five most senior officials in the entire Soviet government, including the Secretary for Ideology—Suslov. Ustinov looked up from his briefing papers.

"Yuriy," the minister said in greeting.

"Good day, Dmitriy." Andropov had already reached his accommodation with the Marshal of the Soviet Union. He'd never obstructed his requests for funding for the bloated and misdirected Soviet military, which was blundering around Afghanistan like a beached whale. It would probably win in the end, everyone thought. After all, the Red Army had never failed . . . unless you remembered Lenin's first assault into Poland in 1919, which had ended in an ignominious rout. No, they preferred to remember defeating Hitler after the Germans had come to within sight of the Kremlin itself, stopping only when attacked by Russia's historically most reliable ally, General Winter. Andropov was not a devotee of the Soviet military, but it remained the security blanket for the rest of the Politburo, because the army made sure the country did what they told it to do. That was not because of love, but because the Red Army had guns in large numbers. So did the KGB, and the Ministry of the Interior, in order to act as a check on the Red Army—no sense giving them ideas. Just to make sure,

KGB also had the Third Chief Directorate, whose job it was to keep an eye on every single rifle company in the Red Army. In other countries, it was called checks and balances. Here it was a balance of terror.

Leonid Ilyich Brezhnev came in last of all, walking like the aged peasant he was, his skin dropping on his once manly face. He was approaching eighty years, a number he might meet but would not surpass, by the look of him. That was both good news and bad. There was no telling what thoughts wiggled their way around the inside of his doting brain. He'd been a man of great personal power once—Andropov could remember it plainly enough. He'd been a vigorous man who'd enjoyed walking in the forests to kill elk or even bear—the mighty hunter of wild animals. But not now. He hadn't shot anything in years—except, perhaps, people, at second or third hand. But that didn't make Leonid Ilyich mellow with age. Far from it. The brown eyes were still sly, still looking for treachery, and sometimes finding it where there was none. Under Stalin, that was frequently a death sentence. But not now. Now you'd just be broken, stripped of power, and relegated to a provincial post where you'd die of boredom.

"Good afternoon, comrades," the General Secretary said, as pleasantly as his grumbly voice allowed.

At least there was no obvious bootlicking anymore, every communist courtier jousting with each other to curry favor with the Marxist emperor. You could waste half the meeting with that twaddle, and Andropov had important things to discuss.

Leonid Ilyich had been prebriefed, and after sipping his post-lunch tea, the General Secretary turned his face to the KGB Chairman. "Yuriy Vladimirovich, you have something to discuss with us?"

"Thank you, Comrade General Secretary. Comrades," he began, "something has come up which commands our attention." He waved to Colonel Rozhdestvenskiy, who quickly circulated around the table, handing out copies of the Warsaw Letter.

"What you see is a letter dispatched to Warsaw last week by the Pope of Rome." Each man had a photocopy of the original—some of them spoke Polish—plus an exact translation into literary Russian, complete with footnotes. "I feel that this is a potential political threat to us."

"I have already seen this letter," Alexandrov said from his distant "candidate" seat. In deference to the seniority of the terminally ill Mikhail Suslov, the latter's seat at Brezhnev's left hand (and next to Andropov) was empty, though his place at the table had the same collection of papers as everyone else's—maybe Suslov had read them on his deathbed, and he'd lash out one last time from his waiting niche in the Kremlin wall.

"This is outrageous," Marshal Ustinov said immediately. He was also well into his seventies. "Who does this priest think he is!"

"Well, he is Polish," Andropov reminded his colleagues, "and he feels he has a certain duty to provide his former countrymen with political protection."

"Protection from what?" the Minister of the Interior demanded. "The threat to Poland comes from their own counterrevolutionaries."

"And their own government lacks the balls to deal with them. I told you last year we needed to move in on them," the First Secretary of the Moscow Party reminded the rest.

"And if they resist our move?" the Agricultural Minister inquired from his seat at the far end of the table.

"You may be certain of that," the Foreign Minister thought out loud. "At least politically, they will resist."

"Dmitriy Fedorovich?" Alexandrov directed his question at Marshal Ustinov, who sat there in his military uniform, complete with a square foot of ribbons, and two Hero of the Soviet Union gold stars. He'd won them both for political courage, not on the battlefield, but he was one of the smartest people in the room, having earned his spurs as People's Commissar of Armaments in the Great Motherland War, and for helping shepherd the USSR into the Space Age. His opinion was predictable, but respected for its sagacity.

"The question, comrades, is whether the Poles would resist with armed force. That would not be militarily threatening, but it would be a major political embarrassment, both here and abroad. That is, they could not stop the Red Army on the battlefield, but should they make the attempt, the political repercussions would be serious. That is why I supported our move last year to bring political pressure on Warsaw—which was successfully accomplished, you will recall." At the age of seventy-four, Dmitriy Fedorovich had learned caution, at least on the level of international politics. The unspoken concern was the effect such resistance would have on the United States of America, which liked to stick its nose where it didn't belong.

"Well, this might well incite additional political unrest in Poland, or so my analysts tell me," Andropov told his colleagues, and the room got a little chilly.

"How serious is this, Yuriy Vladimirovich? How serious might it become?" It was Brezhnev speaking for the first time from beneath his bushy eyebrows.

"Poland continues to be unstable, due to counterrevolutionary elements within their society. Their labor sector, in particular, is restless. We have our sources within this 'Solidarity' cabal, and they tell us that the pot continues to boil. The problem with the Pope is that if he does what he threatens and comes to Poland, the Polish people will have a rallying point, and if a sufficient number of them become involved, the country might well try to change its form of government," the Chairman of the KGB said delicately.

"That is not acceptable," Leonid Ilyich observed in a quiet voice. At this table, a loud voice was just a man venting his stress. A quiet one was far more dangerous. "If Poland falls, then Germany falls . . ." and then the entire Warsaw Pact, which would leave the Soviet Union without its buffer zone to the West. NATO was strong, and would become more so, as the new American defense buildup began to take effect. They'd already been briefed on that troublesome subject. Already, the first new tanks were being given to line units, preparatory to shipping them to West Germany. And so were the new airplanes. Most frightening of all was the vastly increased training regimen for the American soldiers. It was as though they were actually preparing for a strike east.

The fall of Poland and Germany would mean that a trip to Soviet territory would be shortened by more than a thousand kilometers, and there was not a man at this table who did not remember the last time the Germans had entered the Soviet Union. Despite all the protestations that NATO was a defensive alliance whose entire purpose was to keep the Red Army from driving down the Champs Élysées, to Moscow NATO and all the other American alliances looked like an enormous noose designed to fit around their collective necks. They'd all considered that before at great length. And they really didn't need political instability to add to their problems. Communists—though not quite so fervent as Suslov and his ideological heir, Alexandrov—feared above all the possible turning away of their people from the True Faith, which was the source of their own very comfortable personal power. They'd all come to power at second hand to a popular peasant revolt which had overthrown the Romanov dynasty—or so they all told themselves, despite what history really said—and they had no illusions about what a revolt would do to them. Brezhnev shifted in his chair. "So, this Polish priest is a threat."

"Yes, comrades, he is," Andropov said. "His letter is a genuine and sincere thrust at the political stability of Poland, and thus of the entire Warsaw Pact. The Catholic Church remains politically powerful throughout Europe, including our fraternal socialist allies. If he were to resign the papacy and travel back to his homeland, that in itself would be a huge political statement.

"Josef Vissarionovich Stalin once asked how many army divisions the Pope had. The answer is none, of course, but we cannot disregard his power. I suppose we could try diplomatic contacts to dissuade him from this course . . ."

"A complete waste of time," the Foreign Minister observed at once. "We have had occasional diplomatic contacts in the Vatican itself, and they listen to us politely, and they speak reasonably, and then they take whatever action they want to take. No, we cannot influence him, even with direct threats to the church. They merely see threats as challenges."

And that put the matter squarely in the middle of the table. Andropov was grateful to the Foreign Minister, who was also in his camp for the issue of succession. He wondered idly if Brezhnev knew or cared about what would happen after he died—well, he'd care about his children's fate and protection, but that was easily handled. Sinecure Party posts could be found for all of them, and there would be no future marriages to require the china and tableware from the Hermitage.

"Yuriy Vladimirovich, what can KGB do about this threat?" Brezhnev inquired next. *He is so easy to manage,* Andropov reflected briefly and gratefully.

"It may be possible to eliminate the threat by eliminating the man who makes it," the Chairman replied, with an even, unemotional voice.

"To kill him?" Ustinov asked.

"Yes, Dmitriy."

"What are the dangers of that?" the Foreign Minister asked at once. Diplomats always worried about such things.

"We cannot entirely eliminate them, but we can control them. My people have come up with an operational concept, which would involve shooting the Pope at one of his public appearances. I have brought my aide, Colonel Rozhdestvenskiy, to brief us in on it. With your permission, comrades?" He received a collection of nods. Then he turned his head: "Aleksey Nikolay'ch?"

"Comrades." The colonel rose and walked to the lectern, trying to keep his shaking knees under control. "The operation has no name, and will have none for security reasons. The Pope appears in public every Wednesday afternoon. He generally parades around Saint Peter's Square in a motor vehicle, which offers him no protection against attack and comes within three or four meters of the assembled multitude." Rozhdestvenskiy had chosen his words carefully. Every man at the table knew biblical matters and terminology. You could not grow up, even here, without acquiring knowledge of Christianity—even if it was just enough to despise everything about it.

"The question then is how to get a man with a pistol to the front rank of spectators, so that he can take his shot at sufficiently close range to make a successful shot likely."

"Not 'certain'?" the Minister of the Interior asked harshly.

Rozhdestvenskiy did his best not to wilt. "Comrade Minister, we rarely deal in absolute certainties. Even a skilled pistol shot cannot guarantee a perfect shot against a moving target, and the tactical realities here will not allow a carefully aimed round. The assassin will have to bring his weapon up rapidly from a place of concealment, and fire. He will be able to get off two, possibly three, shots before the crowd collapses on him. At that point, a second officer will then kill the assassin from behind with a silenced pistol—and then make his own escape. This will leave no one behind to speak to the Italian police. For this, we will use our Bulgarian socialist allies to select the assassin, to get him to the scene, and then to eliminate him."

"How will our Bulgarian friend get away under these circumstances?" Brezhnev asked. His personal knowledge of firearms allowed him to skip over technical issues, Andropov saw.

"It is likely that the crowd will concentrate on the assassin, and will not take note of the intelligence officer's follow-up shot. It will be virtually silent and there will be a great deal of crowd noise. He will then simply back away and make his escape," Rozhdestvenskiy explained. "The officer we want on this is well experienced in operations of this kind."

"Does he have a name?" Alexandrov asked.

"Yes, comrade, and I can give it to you if you wish, but for security reasons . . ."

"Correct, Colonel," Ustinov put in. "We do not really need to know his name, do we, comrades?" Heads shook around the table. For these men, secrecy came as naturally as urination.

"Not a rifleman?" Interior asked.

"That would risk exposure. The buildings around the square are patrolled by the Vatican's own security force, Swiss mercenaries, and—"

"How good are these Swiss militiamen?" another voice asked.

"How good do they need to be to see a man with a rifle and to raise an alarm?" Rozhdestvenskiy asked, reasonably. "Comrades, when you plan an operation like this one, you try to keep the variables under strict control. Complexity is a dangerous enemy in any such undertaking. As planned, all we need to do is to insert two men into a crowd of thousands and get them close. Then it's just a matter of taking the shot. A pistol is easily concealed in loose clothing. The people there are not screened or searched in any way. No, comrades, this plan is the best we can establish—unless you would have us dispatch a platoon of Spetsnaz soldiers into the Vatican Apartments. That would obviously work, but the origin of such an operation would be impossible to conceal. This mission, if it comes off, depends only on two people, only one of whom will survive, and who will almost certainly escape cleanly."

"How reliable are the participants?" the Chairman of the Party Control Commission asked.

"The Bulgarian officer has personally killed eight men, and he has good contacts within the Turkish criminal community, from which he will select our assassin."

"A Turk?" the Party man asked.

"Yes, a Muslim," Andropov confirmed. "If the operation can be blamed on a Turkish follower of Mohammed, so much the better for us. Correct?"

"It would not hurt our purposes," the Foreign Minister confirmed. "In fact, it might well have the effect of making Islam look more barbaric to the West. That would cause America to increase its support for Israel, and that would annoy the Muslim countries from whom they buy their oil. There is an elegance to it all, which appeals to me, Yuriy."

"So, the complexity of the operation is entirely limited to its consequences," Marshal Ustinov observed, "and not to the undertaking itself."

"Correct, Dmitriy," Andropov confirmed.

"What are the chances that this operation might be linked to us?" asked the Ukrainian Party Secretary.

"If all we leave behind is a dead Turk, connections will be very difficult to establish," the KGB Chairman replied. "This operation has no name. The number of people involved is less than twenty, and most of them are in this room, right here. There will be no written records. Comrades, the security of this operation will be absolute. I must insist that none of you speak about this to anyone. Not your wives, not your private secretaries, not your political advisers. In that way, we can ensure against leaks. We must remember that the Western intelligence services are always trying to discover our secrets. In this case, that cannot be allowed to happen."

"You should have limited this discussion to the Defense Counsel," Brezhnev thought aloud.

"Leonid Ilyich, I thought of that," Andropov responded. "But the political implications of this matter command attention by the entire Politburo."

"Yes, I can see that," the General Secretary agreed with a nod. What he did not see was that Andropov had carefully followed this course so as not to be seen as an adventurer by the men who would someday soon elect him to his own head chair. "Very well, Yuriy. I cannot object to that," Brezhnev said thoughtfully.

"It's still a dangerous thing to contemplate," said the Secretary of the Russian Soviet Federated Socialist Republic. "I must say that I am not entirely comfortable with this plan."

"Gregoriy Vasil'yevich," the Ukrainian Party boss responded, "about Poland—if their government falls, there will be consequences for me that I do not find attractive. Nor should you," he warned. "If this Pole returns home, the results could be ruinous to all of us."

"I understand that, but murder of a chief of state is nothing to be undertaken lightly. I think we ought to warn him first. There are ways to get his attention."

The Minister for Foreign Affairs shook his head. "I've already said it—a waste of time. Men like this do not understand what death is. We could threaten his church members in the Warsaw Pact, but that would probably only have the opposite effect of what we desire. It would give us the worst of all worlds, the consequences of attacking the Roman Church without the option of eliminating this troublesome churchman. No." He shook his head. "If it is to be done, then it must be done properly, decisively, and speedily. Yuriy Vladimirovich, how long to accomplish this mission?"

"Colonel Rozhdestvenskiy?" the KGB Chairman asked.

All heads turned to the colonel, and he did his best to keep his voice level. This was very deep water for a mere colonel. The entire operation now rested on his shoulders, a possibility he had somehow never fully considered. But if he was to get his general's stars, he had to take this responsibility, didn't he?

"Comrade Minister, I would estimate four to six weeks, if you authorize the operation today, and so notify the Bulgarian Politburo. We will be using one of their assets, for which their permission is necessary."

"Andrey Andreyevich?" Brezhnev asked. "How cooperative will they be in Sofia?"

The Foreign Minister took a moment. "That depends on what we ask them and how we ask it. If they know the purpose of the operation, they might dally somewhat."

"Can we ask their cooperation without telling them what it is for?" Ustinov asked.

"Yes, I think so. We can just offer them a hundred new tanks or some fighter aircraft, as a gesture of socialist solidarity," the Minister for Foreign Affairs suggested.

"Be generous," Brezhnev agreed. "I'm sure they have a request floating in the Defense Ministry, yes, Dmitriy?"

"Always!" Marshal Ustinov confirmed. "It's all they ever ask for, more tanks and more MiGs!"

"Then load the tanks on a train and send them to Sofia. Comrades, we have a vote to take," the General Secretary told the Politburo. The eleven voting members felt a little bit railroaded. The seven "candidate," or nonvoting, members just watched and nodded.

As usual, the vote was unanimous. No one voted no, despite the fact that some of them had doubts concealed in their silence. In this room, one did not want to stray too far from the *kollectiv* spirit. Power here was as circumscribed as everywhere else in the world, a fact upon which they rarely reflected and on which they *never* acted.

"Very well." Brezhnev turned his head to Andropov. "KGB is authorized to undertake this operation, and may God have mercy on his Polish soul," he added, in a bit of peasant levity. "So, what is next?"

"Comrade, if I may . . ." Andropov said, getting a nod. "Our brother and friend Mikhail Andreyevich Suslov will soon depart this life, after long and devoted service to the Party we all hold dear. His chair is already empty due to his illness, and needs filling. I propose Mikhail Yevgeniyevich Alexandrov as the next Central Committee Secretary for Ideology, with full voting membership in the Politburo."

Alexandrov even managed to blush. He held up his hands and spoke with the utmost sincerity. "Comrades, my—our—friend is still alive. I cannot take his place while he still lives."

"It is good of you to put it that way, Misha," the General Secretary observed, using the affectionate abbreviation for his Christian name. "But Mikhail Andreyevich is gravely ill and has not long to live. I suggest that we table Yuriy's motion for the moment. Such an appointment must, of course, be ratified by the Central Committee as a whole." But that was less than a formality, as everyone here knew. Brezhnev had just given his blessing to Alexandrov's promotion, and that was all he needed.

"Thank you, Comrade General Secretary." And now Alexandrov could look at the empty chair at Brezhnev's left hand and know that in a few weeks it would soon be his officially. He'd weep like all the others when Suslov died, and the tears would be just as cold. And Mikhail Andreyevich would even understand. His biggest problem now was facing death, the greatest of life's mysteries, and wondering what lay on the other side of it. It was something everyone at the table would have to face, but for all of them it was sufficiently distant to be dismissed . . . for the moment. That, Yuriy Andropov thought, was one difference between them and the Pope, who was soon to die at their hands.

The meeting broke up just after four in the afternoon. The men took their leave, as always, with friendly words and shaken hands, before they went their separate ways. Andropov, with Colonel Rozhdestvenskiy in tow, headed out toward the end. Soon he would be the last to leave, as was the prerogative of the General Secretary.

"Comrade Chairman, a moment, if you would allow it," Rozhdestvenskiy said, heading for the men's room. He emerged a minute and a half later with an easier stride.

"You did well, Aleksey," Andropov told him, as they resumed their way out—the Chairman took the steps down instead of the elevator. "So, what did you make of it?"

"Comrade Brezhnev is frailer than I expected."

"Yes, he is. It didn't help him very much to stop smoking," Andropov reached into his coat pocket for his Marlboros—at the Politburo meetings, people now avoided smoking, out of deference to Leonid Ilyich, and the KGB Chairman needed a cigarette right now. "What else?"

"It was remarkably collegial. I expected more disagreement, more arguing, I suppose." Discussions between spooks at #2 Dzerzhinskiy Square were far more lively, especially when discussing operations.

"They are all cautious players, Aleksey. Those with so much power at their fingertips always are—and they should be. But they often do not take action because they fear doing anything new and different." Andropov knew that his country needed new and different things, and wondered how difficult it would be for him to bring them about.

"But, Comrade Chairman, our operation—"

"That's different, Colonel. When they feel threatened, then they can take action. They fear the Pope. And they are probably right to. Don't you think?"

"Comrade Chairman, I am a colonel only. I serve. I do not rule."

"Keep it that way, Aleksey. It's safer." Andropov entered the car and sat down, and immediately became lost in his thoughts.

AN HOUR LATER, Zaitzev was finishing up his day and awaiting his relief. Then Colonel Rozhdestvenskiy appeared at his side without warning.

"Captain, I need you to send this out to Sofia immediately." He paused. "Does anyone else see these messages?"

"No, Comrade Colonel. The message designator labels it as something to come to me only. That is in the order book."

"Good. Let's keep it that way." He handed over the blank.

"By your order, Comrade Colonel." Zaitzev watched him head off. He barely had time to get this done before taking his leave.

Most Secret
Immediate and Urgent
From: Office of Chairman, Moscow Centre
To: Rezident Sofia
Reference: Operational Designator 15-8-82-666
Operation approved. Next step intermediate approval Bulgarian Politburo. Expect full approval ten days or less. Continue planning for operation.

Zaitzev saw it telexed off, then handed the copy to a messenger to be hand-delivered to the top floor. Then he took his leave, walking a little more swiftly than usual. Out on the street, he fished out his cigarette pack to get himself another Trud before going down the escalator to the metro platform. There, he checked the ceiling clock. He'd actually walked too quickly, he saw, and so let the train go without him, fumbling with his cigarette pack as an excuse if anyone was watching him—but then again, if anyone were watching him now, he was already a dead man. The thought made his hands shake, but it was too late for that. The next train came out of the tunnel exactly on time, and he boarded the proper carriage, shuffling in with fifteen or so other workers. . . .

And there he was. Reading a newspaper, wearing an unbuttoned raincoat, his right hand on the chrome overhead bar.

Zaitzev wandered that way. In his right hand was the second note that he'd just fished out of his cigarette pack. Yes, he saw belatedly, the man was wearing a bright green tie, held in place by a gold-colored tie bar. A brown suit, a clean white shirt that looked expensive, and his face was occupied with the paper. The man did not look around. Zaitzev slid closer.

ONE OF THE things Ed Foley had studied at The Farm was how to perfect his peripheral vision. With training and practice, your eyes could actually see a wider field than the unschooled realized. At CIA camp, he'd learned by walking down the street and reading house numbers without turning his head. Best of all, it was like riding a bicycle. Once learned, it was always there if you just concentrated when you needed to. And so he noticed that someone was moving slowly toward him—white male, about five-nine, medium build, brown eyes and hair, drab clothes, needed a haircut. He didn't see the face clearly enough to remember it or to pick it out of a lineup. A Slavic face, that was all. Expressionless, and the eyes were definitely in his direction. Foley didn't allow his breathing to change, though his heart might have increased its frequency by a few extra beats.

Come on, Ivan. I'm wearing the fucking tie, just like you said. He'd gotten on at the right stop. KGB headquarters was just a block from the escalator. So, yeah, this guy was probably a spook. And not a false-flag. If this was some Second Chief Directorate guy, they would have staged it differently. This was too obvious, too amateurish, not the way KGB would do things. They would have done it at a different subway stop.

This guy's fuckin' real, Foley told himself. He forced himself to be patient, which wasn't easy, even for this experienced field officer, but he took an imperceptible deep breath and waited, telling the nerve endings in his skin to report the least shift in the weight of his topcoat on his shoulders. . . .

ZAITZEV LOOKED AROUND the car as casually as he could. There were no eyes on him, none even looking in this general direction. So his right hand slid into the open pocket, quickly but not too quickly. Then he withdrew.

BINGO, FOLEY THOUGHT, as his heart skipped two or three beats. *Okay, Ivan, what's the message this time?*

Again, he had to be patient. No sense getting this guy killed. If he was really a guy from the Russian MERCURY, then there was no telling how important this might be. Like the first nibble on a deep-sea fishing boat. Was this a marlin, a shark, or a lost boot? If a nice blue marlin, how big? But he couldn't even pull back on the fishing rod to set the hook yet. No, that would come later, if it came at all. The recruitment phase of field operations—taking some innocent Soviet citizen and making him an agent, an information-procuring asset of the CIA, a *spy*—that was harder than going to a CYO dance and getting laid. The real trick was not getting the girl pregnant—or the agent killed. No, the way the game was played, you had the first fast dance, then the first slow dance, then the first kiss, then the first grope, and then, if you got lucky, unbuttoning the blouse . . . and then . . .

The reverie stopped when the train did. Foley removed his hand from the overhead rail and looked around. . . .

And there he was, actually looking at him, and the face went into the mental photo album.

Bad tradecraft, buddy. That can get your ass killed. Never look right at your case officer in a public place, Foley thought, his eyes passing right over him, no expression at all on his own face as he walked past the guy, deliberately taking the long way to the door.

ZAITZEV WAS IMPRESSED by the American. He'd actually looked at his new Russian contact, but his eyes had revealed nothing, had not even looked at him directly, but past him to the end of the carriage. And, just that quickly, the American had walked away. *Be what I hope you are*, Oleg Ivan'ch's mind thought, just as loudly as it could.

FIFTY METERS UP on the open street, Foley refused even to let his hand go into the coat. He was certain that a hand had been there. He'd felt it, all right. And Ivan Whoever hadn't done it looking for change.

Foley walked past the gate guard, into the building, and went up in the elevator. His key went into the lock, and the door opened. Only when it was closed behind him did he reach into the pocket.

Mary Pat was there, watching his face, and she saw the unguarded flash of recognition and discovery.

Ed took the note out. It was the same blank message form and, as before, it had writing on it. Foley read it once, then again, and a third time before handing it over to his wife.

Mary Pat's eyes flared, too.

It was a fish, Foley thought. *Maybe a big one.* And he was asking for something substantive. Whoever he was, he wasn't stupid. It would not be easy to arrange what he wanted, but he'd be able to pull it off. It just meant making the gunnery sergeant angry, and more important, visibly angry, because the embassy was always under surveillance. Something like this could not appear routine, or deliberate, but it didn't have to be an Oscar-class bit of acting either. He was sure the Marines could bring it off. Then he felt Mary Pat's hand in his.

"Hey, honey," he said, for the microphones.

"Hi, Ed." Her hand entered his.

This guy's re[al], her hand said. He answered with a nod.

Tomor[row] mor[ning], she asked, and got another nod.

"Honey, I have to run back to the embassy. I left something in my desk, damn it." Her answer was a thumbs-up.

"Well, don't take too long. I have dinner on. Got a nice roast from the Finnish store. Baked potatoes and frozen corn on the cob."

"Sounds good," he agreed. "Half an hour, max."

"Well, don't be late."

"Where are the car keys?"

"In the kitchen." And they both walked that way.

"Do I have to leave without a kiss?" he asked in his best pussy-whipped voice.

"I guess not" was the playful reply.

"Anything interesting at work today?"

"Just that Price guy from the *Times.*"

"He's a jerk."

"Tell me about it. Later, honey." Foley headed for the door, still wearing his topcoat.

He waved to the gate guard on the way back out, a frustrated grimace on his face for theatrical effect. The guards would probably write down his passage—maybe even call it in somewhere—and, with luck, his drive to the embassy would be matched against the tapes from the apartment, and the Second Chief Directorate pukes would tick off whatever box they had on their surveillance forms and decide that Ed Foley had fucked up and indeed left something at the office. He'd have to remember to drive back with a manila envelope on the front seat of the Mercedes. Spooks earned their living most of all by remembering everything and forgetting nothing.

The drive to the embassy was faster than taking the metro at this time of day, but that was factored in to everything else his working routine encompassed. In just a few minutes, he pulled into the embassy gate, past the Marine sentry, and took a visitor's slot before running in, past some more Marines, and up to his office. There he lifted the phone and made a call, while he took a manila envelope and slid a copy of the *International Herald Tribune* into it.

"Yeah, Ed?" The voice belonged to Dominic Corso, one of Foley's field officers. Actually older than his boss, Corso was covered as a Commercial Attaché. He'd worked Moscow for three years and was well regarded by his Station Chief. Another New Yorker, he was a native of the Borough of Richmond—Staten Island—the son of an NYPD detective. He looked like what he was, a New York guinea, but he was a quite a bit smarter than ethnic bigots would like to have admitted. Corso had the fey brown eyes of an old red fox, but he kept his intelligence under wraps.

"Need you to do something."

"What's that?"

Foley told him.

"You're serious?" It wasn't exactly a normal request.

"Yep."

"Okay, I'll tell the gunny. He's going to ask why." Gunnery Sergeant Tom Drake, the NCO-in-Charge of the Marine detail at the embassy, knew whom Corso worked for.

"Tell him it's a joke, but it's an important one."

"Right." Corso nodded. "Anything I need to know?"

"Not right now."

Corso blinked. *Okay, this was sensitive if the COS wasn't sharing information, but that wasn't so unusual, was it?* Corso reflected. In CIA, you often didn't know what your own team was doing. He didn't know Foley all that well, but he knew enough to respect him.

"Okay, I'll go see him now."

"Thanks, Dom."

"How's the boy like Moscow?" the field officer asked his boss on the way out the door.

"He's adjusting. Be better when he can skate some. He really likes hockey."

"Well, he's in the right town for that."

"Ain't that the truth." Foley gathered his papers and stood. "Let's get this one done, Dom."

"Right now, Ed. See you tomorrow."

CHAPTER 14

DANGER SIGNAL

IF THERE IS ANYTHING CONSTANT in the business of espionage, it is a persistent lack of sleep for the players. That comes from stress, and stress is always the handmaiden of spooks. When sleep was slow in coming for Ed and Mary Pat Foley, they could at least talk with their hands in bed.

He's re[al as] h[ell], b[aby], Foley told his wife under the covers.

Y[ep], she agreed. *Have w[e] ev[er] had a g[uy] fr[om] that far in[side]?* she wondered.

N[o] way José, he replied.

Lan[gley] will flip.

B[ig]-time, her husband agreed. Bottom of the ninth, bases loaded, two outs, full count, and the pitcher had hung a curveball right over Main Street, and he was about to stroke it over the scoreboard. *Assuming we don't fuck it all up,* Foley warned himself.

Want me to get inv[olved]? she wondered next.

Need to wait n s[ee].

A sigh told him, *Yeah, I know.* Even for them, patience came hard. Foley could see that curveball, hanging right over the middle of the plate, just about belt-high, and the Louisville Slugger was tight in his hands: his eyes were locked on the ball so tight that he could see the stitches turning as it approached—and this one was going out of the park, going downfuckin'-town. He'd show Reggie Jackson who was the hitter on this playground . . .

If he didn't fuck it up, he thought again. But Ed Foley had done this kind of operation in Tehran, had developed an agent in the revolutionary community, and had been the only field officer in the station to get a feel for how bad it was for the Shah, and that series of reports had lit up his star at Langley and made him one of Bob Ritter's varsity.

And he was going to take this one deep, too.

At Langley, MERCURY was the one place that everyone was afraid of—*everybody* knew that an employee there under foreign control could damned near bring the whole building down. That was why they all went "on the box" twice a year, polygraphed by the best examiners FBI had—they didn't even trust CIA's own polygraph experts for that tasking. A bad field officer or a bad senior analyst could burn agents and missions, and that was bad for everyone involved—but a leaker in MERCURY would be like turning a female KGB officer loose on Fifth Avenue with an American Express Gold Card. She'd be able to get anything her heart desired. Hell, the KGB might even pay a million bucks for such a source. It would bust the Russian exchequer, but they would cash in one of Nikolay II's Fabergé eggs, and be glad for it. Everyone knew there had to be a KGB counterpart office to MERCURY, but nobody in any intelligence service had ever bagged a Russian national from there.

Foley found himself wondering what it was like, how the room looked. At Langley it was immense, the size of a parking garage, with no internal walls or dividers, so that everyone could see everyone else. There were seven drum-shaped cassette storage structures, named for Disney's Seven Dwarfs; they even had TV cameras on the inside, should some lunatic try to get in there, though he'd almost certainly be killed by such an adventure, since the motorized retrievers turned powerfully and without warning. Besides, only the big mainframe computers—including the fastest and most powerful one, made by Cray Research—knew which cassette had which data and lay in which storage slot. The security there was unreal, multilayered, and checked on a daily—maybe an hourly—basis. The people who worked there were occasionally and randomly followed home from work, probably by the FBI, which was pretty good at such stuff, for a bunch of gumshoed cops. It must have been oppressive for the people who worked there, but if anyone had ever complained about it, those reports hadn't come to Ed Foley. Marines had to run their three miles per day and undergo formal inspections, and CIA employees had to put up with the overpowering institutional paranoia, and that was just how things were. The polygraph was a particular pain in the ass, and the Agency even had psychiatrists who trained people in how to defeat them. He'd undergone such training, and so had his wife—and still CIA put them on the box at least once a year, whether to test their loyalty or to see if they still remembered their training, who could tell?

But did KGB do that as well? They'd be crazy not to, but he wasn't sure if they had polygraph technology, and so . . . maybe, maybe not. There was so much about KGB that he and CIA didn't know. Langley made a lot of SWAGs—stupid wild-ass guesses—mainly from people who said, "Well, we do it this way, and therefore they must, too," which was total horseshit. No two people, and damned-sure no two countries, had ever done anything exactly the same way, and that was why Ed Foley deemed himself one of the best in this crazy business. He knew better. He never stopped looking. He never did anything the same way twice, except as a ruse, to give a false impression to someone else—especially Russians, who probably (almost certainly, he figured) suffered from the same bureaucratic disease that circumscribed minds at CIA.

Wh[at] if this g[uy] wants a tick[et] out? Mary Pat asked.

First class on Pan Am, her husband answered, as fast as his fingers could move, *and he gets to screw the stew.*

U R bad, Mary Patricia responded, with the gagging sound of a suppressed laugh. But she knew he was right. If this guy wanted to play spy, it might be smarter just to yank his ass out of the USSR and fly him to Washington, and toss in a lifetime pass to Disney World for after the debrief. A Russian would go into sensory overload in the Magic Kingdom, not to mention the newly opened Epcot Center. Coming out of Space Mountain, Ed had joked that CIA ought to rent the whole place for one day and take the Soviet Politburo around, let them ride every ride and gobble down the burgers and swill the Cokes, and then, on the way out, tell them, "This is what Americans do for fun. Unfortunately, we can't show you the things we do when we're serious." And if that didn't scare the piss out of them, nothing would. But it would scare the piss out of them, both Foleys were sure. They—even the important ones with access to everything KGB got out of the Main Enemy—even they were the most insular and provincial of people. For the most part, they really did believe the propaganda because they had nothing to measure it against, because they were as much victims of their system as the poor dumb muzhiks—peasants—driving the dump trucks.

But the Foleys didn't live in a fantasy world.

So, w[e] d[o] what he says, then what? she asked next.

One step at a time, he replied, and she nodded in the darkness. Like having a baby, this couldn't be rushed unless you wanted a funny-looking kid. It told Mary Pat that her husband wasn't a total curmudgeon, though, and that elicited a kiss in the darkness.

ZAITZEV WASN'T COMMUNICATING with his wife. For him, right now, even a half liter of vodka couldn't help him sleep. He'd made his request. Only tomorrow would he know for sure if he was dealing with someone able to help him. What he'd asked wasn't entirely reasonable, but he didn't have the time or the security to be reasonable. He was secure in the knowledge that even KGB couldn't fake what he'd specified. Oh, sure, maybe they could get the Poles or the Romanians or some other socialist country to do it, but not the Americans. Even KGB had its limits.

So, again, he got to wait, but sleep didn't come. Tomorrow he would not be a very happy comrade. He could feel the hangover coming already, like an earthquake trapped and contained inside his skull. . . .

"HOW'D IT GO, SIMON?" Ryan asked.

"It could have been worse. The PM didn't rip my head off. I told her that we only have what we have, and Basil backed me up. She wants more. She said that in my presence."

"No surprise. Ever hear of a president who wanted less information, buddy?"

"Not recently," Harding admitted. Ryan saw the stress bleeding off his workmate. Damned sure he'd have a beer at the pub before heading home. The Brit analyst loaded his pipe and lit it, taking a long pull.

"If it makes you feel any better, Langley doesn't have any more than you guys do."

"I know. She asked, and that's what Basil said. Evidently, he talked to your Judge Moore before driving over."

"So we're all ignorant together."

"Bloody comforting," Simon Harding snorted.

It was far past going-home time. Ryan had waited to see what Simon would say about the meeting at 10 Downing Street, because Ryan was also here to gather intelligence on the Brits. They would understand, because that was the game they all played. He checked his watch.

"Well, I've got to boogie on home. See you tomorrow."

"Sleep well," Harding said, as Ryan headed out the door. Jack was reasonably sure that Simon would not. He knew what Harding made, as a mid-level civil servant, and it wasn't quite enough for this stressful a day. *But,* he told himself out on the street, *that's Life in the Big City.*

"WHAT DID YOU tell your people, Bob?" Judge Moore asked.

"Just what you told me, Arthur. The President wants to know. No feedback yet. Tell the Boss he's going to have to be patient."

"I said that. He was not overly pleased," the DCI responded.

"Well, Judge, I can't stop the rain from falling. We don't have power over a lot of things, and time is one of them. He's a big boy; he can understand that, can't he?"

"Yes, Robert, but he likes to get what he needs. He's worried about His Holiness, now that the Pope has kicked over the anthill—"

"Well, we think he has. The Russians might be smart enough to work through diplomatic channels and tell him to cool down and let things work out, and—"

"Bob, that wouldn't work," Admiral Greer put in. "He's not the sort of guy you can warn off with lawyer talk, is he?"

"No," Ritter admitted. This Pope was not a man to compromise on issues of great importance. He'd seen himself through all manner of unpleasantness, from Hitler's Nazis to Stalin's NKVD, and he'd kept his church together by circling the wagons, like settlers against Indian attacks in those old Western movies. He hadn't managed to keep his church alive in Poland by giving in on important issues, had he? And, by holding his ground, he'd maintained enough moral and political strength to threaten the other of the world's superpowers. No, this guy wasn't going to fold under pressure.

Most men feared death and ruin. This one didn't. The Russians would never understand why, but they would understand the respect it earned him. It was becoming clear to Bob Ritter and the other senior intelligence officers in this room that the one single response that would make sense to the Politburo was an attack on the Pope. And the Politburo had met today, though what they had discussed and concluded were frustratingly unknown.

"Bob, do we have any assets who can find out what they talked about in the Kremlin today?"

"We have a few, and they will be alerted in the next two days—or, if they come up with something important, they can decide to get the information on their own hook. If they become aware of something this hot, you'd expect them to figure it out on their own and get a packet of information out to their handlers," Ritter told the DCI. "Hey, Arthur, I don't like waiting and not knowing any more than you do, but we have to let this thing take its course. You know the dangers of a balls-to-the-wall alert to our agents as well as I do."

And all three of them did. That sort of thing had gotten Oleg Penkovskiy killed. The information he'd gotten out had probably averted a nuclear war—and had assisted in the recruitment of CIA's longest-lived agent-in-place, CARDINAL—but that hadn't done Penkovskiy much good. On his discovery, no less a figure than Khrushchev himself had demanded his blood—and gotten it.

"Yeah," Greer agreed, "and this isn't all *that* important in the great scheme of things, is it?"

"No," Judge Moore had to admit, though he didn't especially look forward to explaining that one to the President. But the new Boss did understand things once you made them clear. The really scary part was what the President might do if the Pope were to die unexpectedly. The Boss, too, was a man of principle, but also a man of emotions. It would be as enraging as waving the Soviet flag in front of a fighting bull. You couldn't let emotion get in the way of statecraft—it only called out more emotion, frequently the mourning of the newly dead. And the miracle of modern technology only served to make the number of such people all the larger. The DCI reproached himself for that thought. The new President was a thoughtful man. His emotions were the servant of his intellect, and his intellect was far larger than it was generally believed, especially by the media, who only saw the smile and the theatrical personality. But the media, like a lot of politicians, was a lot more comfortable dealing with appearances than reality. It was a lot less intellectually demanding, after all. Judge Moore looked at his principal subordinates. "Okay, but let's remember that it can be lonely facing him in the Oval Office when you don't have what he wants."

"I'm sure it is, Arthur," Ritter sympathized.

HE COULD STILL TURN BACK, Zaitzev told himself, as sleep still had not come. Next to him, Irina was breathing placidly in sleep. The sleep of the just, it was called. Not the sleeplessness of the traitor.

All he had to do was stop. That was all. He'd taken two small steps, but no more. The American might know his face, but that was easily fixed—take a different metro, walk onto a different carriage. He'd never see him again; their contact would be as broken as a water glass dropped to the floor, and his life would return to normal, and his conscience . . .

. . . would never trouble him again? He snorted. It was his conscience that had gotten him into this mess. No, that wasn't going to go away.

But the other side of that coin was perpetual worry and sleeplessness, and fear. He hadn't really tasted the fear yet. That would come, he was sure.

Treason had only one punishment. Death for the traitor, followed by ruin for his survivors. They'd be sent off to Siberia—to count trees, as the euphemism went. It was the Soviet hell, a place of eternal damnation, from which death was the only escape.

In fact, it was exactly what his conscience would do to him if he didn't follow through on his action, Zaitzev realized, finally losing his battle and sliding off into sleep.

A SECOND LATER, so it seemed to him, the alarm clock went off. At least, he hadn't been tormented with dreams. That was the only good news this morning. His head pounded, threatening to push his eyeballs out of their sockets. He staggered into the bathroom, where he splashed water onto his face and took three aspirin, which, he forlornly hoped, might ease his hangover in a few hours.

He couldn't face sausages for breakfast, since his stomach was also irritated, and so he settled for cereal and milk with some buttered bread on the side. He thought about coffee, but decided a glass of milk would be easier on his stomach.

"You drank too much last night," Irina told him.

"Yes, darling, I know that now," he managed to say, not unpleasantly. His condition wasn't her fault, and she was a good wife to him, and a good mother for Svetlana, his little *zaichik*. He knew that he'd survive this day. He just wouldn't like it much. Worst of all, he had to get going early, and this he did, shaving very badly along the way, but becoming presentable with a clean shirt and tie. He tucked four more aspirin into his coat pocket before walking out the door, and, to get his blood moving, he took the stairs down instead of the elevator. There was a mild chill in the morning air, which helped somewhat on the way to the metro. He bought a copy of *Izvestia* and smoked a Trud, and that helped move him along, too.

If anyone recognized him—well, few would. He was not in the usual carriage, and he was not on the usual train. He was usually fifteen minutes later. He was just one more anonymous face on a subway train filled with anonymous people.

And so no one would note that he was getting off at the wrong station.

The American Embassy was just a couple of blocks away, and he headed that way, checking his watch.

He knew the proper timing because he'd been here once before, as a cadet in the KGB Academy, brought here early one morning in a bus along with forty-five other members of his class. They'd even worn their official uniforms for the trip, probably to remind them of their professional identity. Even then, it had seemed a foolish waste of time, but the academy commandant back then had been a hard-liner, and now the trip served a purpose that would have outraged the man. Zaitzev lit another cigarette as the building came into view.

He checked his watch. At precisely 0730 hours every day, they raised their flag. The academy commandant, ten years before, had pointed and said, "See there, comrades, that is the enemy! That is where he lives in our fine city of Moscow. In that building live spies which those of you who enter the Second Chief Directorate will endeavor to identify and expel from our fair land. There live and work the ones who spy on our country and our people. *That* is their flag. Remember it always." And then, exactly on time, the flag had been hoisted to the top of a white pole with a bronze eagle at the top, hauled up by members of the United States Marine Corps in their pretty uniforms. Zaitzev had checked his watch in the metro station. It should be right about . . . now.

A BUGLE BLEW a tune that he didn't know. He could just make out the white caps of the Marines, barely visible above the stone parapet of the building's flat roof. He was on the other side of the street, just by the old church, which KGB had crammed full of electronic devices.

There, he thought, staring, along with a handful of other passersby on the cracked cement sidewalk.

Yes, he saw. The top part of the flag as it appeared was red and white horizontal stripes, not the blue canton with its fifty white stars. The flag was being hoisted upside down! It was unmistakably wrong. And it went all the way to the top of the pole that way.

So, they did as I asked. Quickly, Zaitzev walked to the end of the block and turned right, then right again, and back to the metro station he'd just left, and, with the payment of a large five-kopeck copper coin, he boarded another subway car for the trip to Dzerzhinskiy Square.

Just that quickly, his hangover went away, as though by magic. He scarcely even noticed until he took the escalator up to the street level.

The Americans want to help me, the communications officer told himself. *They will* help *me. Perhaps I can save the life of that Polish priest after all.* There was a spring in his step as he entered The Centre.

"SIR, what the fuck was that all about?" Gunnery Sergeant Drake asked Dominic Corso. They'd just fixed the flag back properly atop its pole.

"Gunny, I can't say," was the best Corso could do, though his eyes said a little more.

"Aye aye, sir. How do I log it?"

"You don't log it, Gunny. Somebody made a dumb mistake, and you fixed it."

"You say so, Mr. Corso." The gunnery sergeant would have to explain it to his Marines, but he'd explain it in much the same way in which it had just been explained to him, though, in his case, rather more profanely. If anyone in the Marine Embassy Regiment asked him, he'd just say he'd gotten orders from somebody in the embassy, and Colonel d'Amici would just have to deal with it. What the hell, he could hand the colonel off to Corso. They were both wops, maybe they'd understand each other, the sergeant from Helena, Montana, hoped. If not, then Colonel d'Amici would tear him and his Marines each a new and bloody asshole.

ZAITZEV TOOK HIS seat after relieving Major Dobrik. The morning traffic was a little lighter than usual, and he began his normal morning routine. Forty minutes later, that changed again.

"Comrade Major," a newly familiar voice said. Zaitzev turned to see Colonel Rozhdestvenskiy.

"Good morning, Comrade Colonel. You have something for me?"

"This." Rozhdestvenskiy handed over the message blank. "Please send it out immediately, on the pad."

"By your command. Information copy to you?"

"Correct." Rozhdestvenskiy nodded.

"I presume it's permissible to use an internal messenger to get that to your hand?"

"Yes, it is."

"Very well. I'll have it out in a few minutes."

"Good." Rozhdestvenskiy took his leave.

Zaitzev looked at the dispatch. It was agreeably short. Encryption and transmission took only fifteen minutes.

MOST SECRET
IMMEDIATE AND URGENT
FROM: OFFICE OF CHAIRMAN, MOSCOW CENTRE
TO: REZIDENT SOFIA
REFERENCE: OPERATIONAL DESIGNATOR 15-8-82-666
OPERATIONAL APPROVAL EXPECTED TODAY, VIA CHANNELS DISCUSSED IN OUR MEETING. REPORT WHEN PROPER CONTACTS ESTABLISHED.

And that meant that operation -666 was going forward. The day before, that notice had chilled Zaitzev, but not today. Today he knew he'd be doing something to prevent it. If anything bad happened now, it would be the fault of the Americans. That made a considerable difference. Now he just had to figure how to establish some sort of regular contact with them. . . .

UPSTAIRS, Andropov had the Foreign Minister in his office.

"So, Andrey, how do we go about this?"

"Ordinarily our Ambassador would meet with their First Secretary, but, in the interests of security, we might want to try another method of approach."

"How much executive authority does their First Secretary have?" the Chairman asked.

"About as much as Koba did thirty years ago. Bulgaria is run in a very tight way. Their Politburo members represent various constituencies, but only their Party First Secretary really has decision-making power."

"Ah." That was good news to Yuriy Vladimirovich. He lifted his desk phone. "Send in Colonel Rozhdestvenskiy," he told his secretary.

The colonel appeared through the dresser door in two minutes. "Yes, Comrade Chairman."

"Andrey, this is Colonel Rozhdestvenskiy, my executive assistant. Colonel, does our Sofia *rezident* talk directly to the Bulgarian head of government?"

"Rarely, comrade, but he has done so occasionally in the past." Rozhdestvenskiy was surprised that the Chairman didn't know that, but he was still learning how field operations worked. At least he had the good sense to ask questions, and he was not embarrassed to do so.

"Very well. For security reasons, we would prefer that the entire Bulgarian Politburo not know the scope of this operation -666. So, do you think we could have Colonel Bubovoy brief in their party chief and get approval by a more direct route?"

"To that end, a signed letter from Comrade Brezhnev would probably be necessary," Rozhdestvenskiy answered.

"Yes, that would be the best way to do it," the Foreign Minister agreed at once. "A good thought, colonel," he added approvingly.

"Very well. We'll get that today. Leonid Ilyich will be in his office, Andrey?"

"Yes, Yuriy. I will call ahead and tell him what is needed. I can have it drafted in my office if you wish, or would you prefer it to be done here?"

"With your permission, Andrey," Andropov said graciously, "better that we should do it. And we'll have it couriered to Sofia for delivery tomorrow or the day after."

"Better to give our Bulgarian comrade a few days, Yuriy. They are our allies, but they remain a sovereign country, after all."

"Quite so, Andrey." Every country in the world had a bureaucracy, whose entire purpose was to delay important things from happening.

"And we don't want the world to know that our *rezident* is making a highly important call on the man," the Foreign Minister added, teaching the KGB Chairman a little lesson in operational security, Colonel Rozhdestvenskiy noted.

"How long after that, Aleksey Nikolay'ch?" Andropov asked his aide.

"Several weeks, at least." He saw annoyance in his boss's eyes and decided to explain. "Comrade Chairman, selecting the right assassin will not be a matter of lifting a phone and dialing a number. Strokov will necessarily be careful in making his selection. People are not as predictable as machines, after all, and this is the most important—and most sensitive—aspect of the operation."

"Yes, I suppose that is so, Aleksey. Very well. Notify Bubovoy that a hand-delivered message is on the way."

"Now, Comrade Chairman, or after we have it signed and ready for dispatch?" Rozhdestvenskiy asked the question like a skilled bureaucrat, letting his boss know the best way without saying it out loud.

This colonel would go far, the Foreign Minister thought, taking note of his name for the first time.

"A good point, Colonel. Very well, I will let you know when the letter is ready to go."

"By your command, Comrade Chairman. Do you need me further?"

"No, that is all for now," Andropov answered, sending him on his way.

"Yuriy Vladimirovich, you have a good aide."

"Yes, there is so much for me still to learn here," Andropov admitted. "And he educates me every day."

"You are fortunate in having so many expert people."

"That is the truth, Andrey Andreyevich. That is the truth."

DOWN THE HALL in his office, Rozhdestvenskiy drew up the brief dispatch for Bubovoy. This was moving fast, he thought, but not fast enough for the Chairman of the KGB. He really wanted that priest dead. The Politburo certainly seemed fearful of political earthquakes, but Rozhdestvenskiy himself was doubtful of that. The Pope, after all, was just one person, but the colonel had tailored his advice to what his boss wanted to hear, like a good functionary, while also letting the Chairman know the things he needed to know. His job actually carried great power with it.

Rozhdestvenskiy knew that he could break the careers of officers whom he did not like and influence operations to a significant degree. If CIA ever tried to recruit him, he could be an agent of great value. But Colonel Rozhdestvenskiy was a patriot, and besides, the Americans probably had no idea who he was and what he did. The CIA was more feared than it deserved to be. The Americans didn't really have a feel for espionage. The English did, but KGB and its antecedents had enjoyed some success at infiltrating it in the past. Less so today, unfortunately. The young Cambridge communists of the 1930s were all old now, either in British prisons or drawing their government pensions in peace, or living out their years in Moscow, like Kim Philby, considered a drunk even by Muscovites. He probably drank because he missed his country—missed the place in which he'd grown up, the food and drink and football games, the newspapers with which he'd always philosophically disagree, but he'd miss them even so. *What a terrible thing it must be to be a defector,* Rozhdestvenskiy thought.

WHAT WILL I DO? Zaitzev asked himself. *What will I ask for?*

Money? CIA probably paid its spies very well—more money than he would ever be able to spend. Luxuries beyond his imagination. A videotape machine! They were just becoming available in Russia, mainly made in Hungary, patterned after Western machines. The bigger problem was in getting tapes—pornographic ones were particularly in demand. Some of his KGB coworkers spoke of such things. Zaitzev had never seen one himself, but he was curious, as any man might be. The Soviet Union was run by such conservative men. Maybe the Politburo members were just too old to enjoy sex, and so saw no need for younger citizens to indulge.

He shook his head. Enough! He had to decide what to tell the American in the metro. That was a task that he chewed on with his lunch in the KGB cafeteria.

C H A P T E R 15

MEETING PLACE

MARY PAT WAS EXPECTED to come into the embassy sometimes, to see her husband about family matters or to purchase special food items from the commissary. To do this, she always dressed up—better than she did for the Moscow streets—with her hair well-brushed and held in place by a youthful headband, and her makeup done, so that when she drove into the compound parking lot she would look like a typical air-headed American blonde. She smiled to herself. She liked being a natural blonde, and anything that made her appear dumb worked for her cover.

So she breezed in the front door, waving airily at the ever-polite Marines, and into the elevator. She found her husband alone in his office.

"Hey, baby." Ed rose to kiss her, then drew back to take in the whole picture. "Looking good."

"Well, it's an effective disguise." It had worked fine in Iran, too, especially when she'd been pregnant. That country didn't treat women especially well, but it did extend them an odd deference, especially when pregnant, she'd found, right before she'd skipped the country for good. It was one station she didn't particularly miss.

"Yeah, babe. Just gotta get you a surfboard and a nice beach, maybe the Banzai Pipeline."

"Oh, Ed, that's just so *tubular.* And Banzai Beach is in Hawaii, dummy." A quick gear change. "The flag go up wrong?"

"Yep. The TV cameras didn't show anyone on the street paying particular attention to it. But you could see it from a block away, and the security cameras don't look that far out. We'll see if our friend drops a message in my pocket on the ride home tonight."

"What did the Marines say?" she asked.

"They asked why, but Dom didn't tell them anything. Hell, he doesn't know either, does he?"

"He's a good spook, Dominic is," Mary Pat judged.

"Ritter likes him. Oh," Foley remembered. He fished a message out of his drawer and handed it across.

"Shit," his wife breathed, scanning it quickly. "The *Pope?* Those motherfuckers want to kill the Pope?" Mary Pat didn't always talk like a California blonde.

"Well, there's no information to suggest that directly, but, if they want to, we're supposed to find out."

"Sounds like a job for WOODCUTTER," who was their man in the Party Secretariat.

"Or maybe CARDINAL?" Ed wondered.

"We haven't flagged him yet," MP pointed out, but it would soon be time to check in with him. They checked his apartment every night for the light-and-blinds combination in his living room. His apartment was agreeably close to their own, and the ratline was well established, beginning with a piece of paper tape on a lamppost. Setting that flag signal was MP's job. She'd already walked Little Eddie by it half a dozen times. "Is this a job for him?" she asked.

"The President wants to know," her husband pointed out.

"Yeah." But CARDINAL was their most important agent-in-place, and not one to be alerted unless it was really critical. CARDINAL would also know to get something like this out on his own if he became aware of it. "I'd hold off on that unless Ritter says different."

"Agreed," Ed Foley conceded. If Mary Pat advised caution, then caution was justified. After all, she was the one who enjoyed taking risks and betting her skill against the house odds. But that didn't mean that his wife was a reckless player, either. "I'll sit on that one for a while."

"Be nice to see what your new contact will do next."

"Bet your cute little tushy, babe. Want to meet the Ambassador?"

"I suppose it's time," she agreed.

"SO, RECOVER FROM yesterday?" Ryan asked Harding. It was the first time he'd beaten his workmate into the office.

"Yes, I suppose I have."

"If it makes you feel any better, I haven't met the President yet, myself. And I'm not exactly looking forward to the experience. Like Mark Twain said about the guy who got himself tarred and feathered, if it weren't for the honor of the thing, he would just as soon have missed it."

Harding managed a brief laugh. "Precisely, Jack. One does go a little weak in the knees."

"Is she as tough as they say?"

"I'm not sure I'd want to play rugger against her. She's also very, very bright. Doesn't miss a thing, and asks bloody good questions."

"Well, answering them is what they pay us for, Simon," Ryan pointed out. There was no sense being afraid of people who were only doing their job as well, and who needed good information to do it properly.

"And her, too, Jack. She has to do questions in Parliament."

"On this sort of thing?" Jack asked, surprised.

"No, not this. It's occasionally discussed with the opposition, but under strict rules."

"You worry about leaks?" Jack asked, wondering. In America, there were select committees whose members were thoroughly briefed on what they could say and what they could not. The Agency did worry about leaks—they were politicians, after all—but he'd never heard of a serious one off The Hill. Those more often came from inside the Agency, and mainly from the Seventh Floor . . . or from the White House's West Wing. That didn't mean that CIA was comfortable with leaks of any kind, but at least these were more often than not sanctioned, and often they were disinformation with a political purpose behind them. It was probably the same here, especially since the local news media operated under controls that would have given *The New York Times* a serious conniption fit.

"One always wonders about them, Jack. So, anything new come in last night?"

"Nothing new on the Pope," Ryan reported. "Our sources, such as they are, have run into a brick wall. Will you be turning your field spooks loose?"

"Yes, the PM made it clear to Basil that she wants more information. If something happens to His Holiness, well—"

"—she blows a head gasket, right?"

"You Americans do have a way with words, Jack. And your President?"

"He'll be seriously pissed, and by that I do not mean hitting the booze. His dad was Catholic, and his mom raised him a Protestant, but he wouldn't be real happy if the Pope so much as catches a late-summer cold."

"You know, even if we turn some information, it is not at all certain that we'll be able to do a thing with it."

"I kinda figured that, but at least we can say something to his protective detail. We can do that much, and maybe he can change his schedule—no, he won't. He'd rather take the bullet like a man. But maybe we can interfere somehow with what the Bad Guys are planning. You just can't know until you have a few facts to rub together. But that's not really our job, is it?"

Harding shook his head, as he stirred his morning tea. "No, the field officers feed it to us, and we try to determine what it means."

"Frustrating?" Ryan wondered. Harding had been at the job much longer than he had.

"Frequently. I know the field officers sweat blood doing their jobs—and it can be physically dangerous to the ones who do not have a 'legal' cover—but we users of information can't always see it from their perspective. As a result, they do not appreciate us as much as we appreciate them. I've met with a few of them over the years, and they are good chaps, but it's a clash of cultures, Jack."

The field guys are probably pretty good at analysis themselves, when you get down to it, Ryan thought. *I wonder how often the analyst community really appreciates that?* It was something for Ryan to slip into his mental do-not-forget file. The Agency was supposed to be one big happy team, after all. Of course it wasn't, even at the Seventh Floor level.

"Anyway, we had this come in from East Germany." Jack handed the folder across. "Some rumbles in their political hierarchy last week."

"Those bloody Prussians," Harding breathed, as he took it and flipped to the first page.

"Cheer up. The Russians don't much like them either."

"I don't blame them a bit."

ZAITZEV WAS DOING some hard thinking at his desk, as his brain worked on autopilot. He'd have to meet with his new American friend. There was danger involved, unless he could find a nice, anonymous place. The good news was that Moscow abounded with such places. The bad news was that the Second Chief Directorate of the KGB probably knew all of them. But if it was crowded enough, that didn't matter.

What would he say?

What would he ask for?

What would he offer them?

Those were all good questions, weren't they? The dangers would only increase. The best possible outcome would be for him to leave the Soviet Union permanently, with his wife and daughter.

Yes, that was what he'd ask for, and if the Americans said no, he'd just melt back into his accustomed reality, knowing that he'd tried. He had things they would want, and he'd make it clear to them that the price of that information was his escape.

Life in the West, he thought. All the decadent things the State preached to everyone who could read a newspaper or watch TV, all the awful things they talked about. The way America treated its minorities. They even showed pictures on TV of the slum areas—but they also showed automobiles. If America oppressed its blacks, why, then, did it allow them to purchase so many automobiles? Why did it permit them to riot in the streets? Had that sort of thing happened in the USSR, the government would have called in armed troops. So no, the state propaganda could not be entirely true, could it? And, besides, wasn't he white? What did he care about some discontented blacks who could buy any car they wished? Like most Russians, he'd only seen black people on TV—his first reaction was to wonder if there really were such a thing as a chocolate man, but, yes, there were. KGB ran operations in Africa. But then he asked himself: Could he remember a KGB operation in America using a black agent? Not very many, perhaps one or two, and those had both been sergeants in the American army. If blacks were oppressed, how then did they get to become sergeants? In the Red Army, only the politically reliable were admitted to Sergeant School. So, one more lie uncovered—and that one only because he worked for KGB. What other lies was he being told? Why not leave? Why not ask the Americans for a ticket out?

But will they grant it? Zaitzev wondered.

Surely they would. He could tell them about all manner of KGB operations in the West. He had the names of officers and the code names of agents—traitors to the Western governments, people whom they would definitely wish to eliminate.

Was that being an accessory to murder? he asked himself.

No, it was not. Those persons were *traitors*, after all. And a traitor was a traitor. . . .

And what does that make you, Oleg Ivanovich? The little voice in his mind asked, just to torment him.

But he was strong enough now to shake it off with a simple movement of his head left and right. Traitor? No, he was *preventing* a murder, and that was an honorable thing. And he was an honorable man.

But he still had to figure a way to do it. He had to meet with an American spy and say what he wanted.

Where and how?

It would have to be a crowded place, where people could bump into each other so naturally that even a counterspy from the Second Chief Directorate would not be able to see what was happening or hear what was being said.

And suddenly he realized: His own wife worked in such a place.

So he'd write it down on another blank message form and transfer it on the metro as he'd already done twice. Then he'd see if the Americans really wanted to play his game. He was in the Chairman's seat now, wasn't he? He had something they wanted, and he controlled how they could get it, and he would make the rules in this game, and they would have to play by those rules. It was just that simple, wasn't it?

Yes, he told himself.

Wasn't this rich? He'd be doing something the KGB had always wanted to do, dictate terms to the American CIA.

Chairman for a day, the communicator told himself. The words had a delicious taste to them.

IN LONDON, Cathy watched as two local ophthalmic surgeons worked on one Ronald Smithson, a bricklayer with a tumor behind his right eye. The X-rays showed a mass about half the size of a golf ball, which had been so worrisome that Mr. Smithson had only waited five weeks for the procedure to be done. That was maybe thirty-three days longer than it would have been at Hopkins, but considerably faster than was usual over here.

The two Moorefields surgeons were Clive Hood and Geoffrey Phillips, both experienced senior residents. It was a fairly routine procedure. After exposing the tumor, a sliver was removed for freezing and dispatch to Pathology—they had a good histopathologist on duty and he would decide if the growth was benign or malignant. Cathy hoped for the former, as the malignant variety of this tumor could be troublesome for its victims. But the odds were heavily on the patient's side, she thought. On visual examination it didn't look terribly aggressive, and her eye was right about 85 percent of the time. It was bad science to tell herself that, and she knew it. It was almost superstition, but surgeons, like baseball players, knew about superstition. That was why they put their socks on the same way every morning—pantyhose, in her case—because they just fell into a pattern of living, and surgeons were creatures of habit, and they tended to translate those dumb personal habits into the outcome of their procedures. So, with the frozen section off to Pathology, it was just a matter of excising the pinkish-gray encapsulated mass. . . .

"What time is it, Geoffrey?" Dr. Hood asked.

"Quarter to one, Clive," Dr. Phillips reported, checking the wall clock. "How about we break for lunch, then?"

"Fine with me. I could use something to eat. We'll need to call in another anesthesiologist to keep Mr. Smithson unconscious," their gas-passer observed.

"Well, call and get one, Owen, would you?" Hood suggested.

"Righto," Dr. Ellis agreed. He left his chair at the patient's head and walked to the wall phone. He was back in seconds. "Two minutes."

"Excellent. Where to, Geoffrey?" Hood asked.

"The Frog and Toad? They serve a fine bacon, lettuce, and tomato with chips."

"Splendid," Hood said.

Cathy Ryan, standing behind Dr. Phillips, kept her mouth shut behind the surgical mask, but her china-blue eyes had gone wide. *They were leaving a patient unconscious on the table while they went to lunch?* Who were these guys, witch doctors?

The backup anesthesiologist came in just then, all gowned up and ready to take over. "Anything I need to know, Owen?" he asked Ellis.

"Entirely routine," the primary gas-passer replied. He pointed to the various instruments measuring the patient's vital signs, and they were all in the dead center of normal values, Cathy saw. But even so . . .

Hood led them out to the dressing room, where the four medics shucked their greens and grabbed their coats, then left for the corridor and the steps down to street level. Cathy followed, not knowing what else to do.

"So, Caroline, how do you like London?" Hood asked pleasantly.

"We like it a lot," she answered, still somewhat shell-shocked.

"And your children?"

"Well, we have a very nice nanny, a young lady from South Africa."

"One of our more civilized local customs," Phillips observed approvingly.

The pub was scarcely a block away, west on City Road. A table was quickly found. Hood immediately fished out a cigarette and lit it. He noticed Cathy's disapproving look.

"Yes, Mrs. Ryan, I know it's not healthy and bad form for a physician, but we are all entitled to one human weakness, aren't we?"

"You're seeking approval from the wrong person," she responded.

"Ah, well, I'll blow the smoke away from you, then." Hood had himself a chuckle as the waiter came over. "What sort of beer do you have here?" he asked him.

It was good that he smoked, Cathy told herself. She had trouble handling more than one major shock at a time, but at least that one gave her fair warning. Hood and Phillips both decided on John Courage. Ellis preferred Tetley's. Cathy opted for a Coca-Cola. The docs mainly talked shop, as physicians often do.

For her part, Caroline Ryan sat back in her wooden chair, observing three physicians enjoying beer, and, in one case, a smoke, while their blissfully unconscious patient was on nitrous oxide in Operating Room #3.

"So, how do we do things here? Differently from Johns Hopkins?" Hood asked, as he stubbed out his cigarette.

Cathy nearly gagged, but decided not to make any of the comments running around her brain. "Well, surgery is surgery. I'm surprised that you don't have very many CAT scans. Same for MRI and PET scanners. How can you do without them? I mean, at home, for Mr. Smithson, I wouldn't even think of going in without a good set of shots of the tumor."

"She's right, you know," Hood thought, after a moment's reflection. "Our bricklayer chum could have waited several months more if we'd had a better idea of the extent of the growth."

"You wait that long for a hemangioma?" Cathy blurted out. "At home, we take them out immediately." She didn't have to add that these things *hurt* to have inside your skull. It caused a frontal protrusion of the eyeball itself, sometimes with blurring of vision—which was why Mr. Smithson had gone to this local doctor to begin with. He'd also reported god-awful headaches that must have driven him mad until they'd given him a codeine-based analgesic.

"Well, here things operate a little differently."

Uh-huh. That must be a good way to practice medicine, by the hour instead of by the patient. Lunch arrived. The sandwich was okay—better than the hospital food she was accustomed to—but she still couldn't get over these guys drinking *beer!* The local beer was about double the potency of American stuff, and they were drinking a full pint of it—*sixteen ounces! What the* hell *was this?*

"Ketchup for your chips, Cathy?" Ellis slid the bottle over. "Or should I say Lady Caroline? I hear that His Highness is your son's godfather?"

"Well, sort of. He agreed to it—Jack asked him on the spur of the moment in the hospital at the Naval Academy. The real godparents are Robby and Sissy Jackson. Robby's a Navy fighter pilot. Sissy plays concert piano."

"Was that the black chap in the papers?"

"That's right. Jack met him when they were both teachers at the Naval Academy, and they're very close friends."

"Quite so. So the news reports were correct? I mean—"

"I try not to think about it. The only good thing that happened that night was that Little Jack arrived."

"I quite understand that, Cathy," Ellis responded around his sandwich. "If the news accounts were accurate, it must have been a horrid evening."

"It wasn't fun." She managed a smile. "The labor and delivery was the good part."

The three Brits had a good laugh at that remark. All had kids, and all had been there for the deliveries, which were no more fun for British women than for American women. Half an hour later, they headed back to Moorefields. Hood smoked another cigarette along the way, though he had the good manners do stay downwind of his American colleague. Ten more minutes, and they were back in the OR. The pinch-hitting gas-passer reported that nothing untoward had taken place, and surgery resumed.

"Want me to assist now?" Cathy asked hopefully.

"No, thank you, Cathy," Hood replied. "I have it," he added, bending over his patient, who, being soundly asleep, wouldn't smell the beer on his breath.

Caroline Ryan, M.D., FACS, thought to congratulate herself for not screaming her head off, but mostly she leaned in as closely as she could to make sure these two Englishmen didn't screw up and remove the patient's ear by mistake. *Maybe the alcohol would help steady their hands,* she told herself. But she had to concentrate to keep her own hands from trembling.

THE CROWN AND CUSHION was a delightful, if typical, London pub. The sandwich was just fine, and Ryan enjoyed a pint of John Smith Ale while talking shop with Simon. He thought vaguely about serving beer at the CIA cafeteria, but that would never fly. Someone in Congress would find out and raise hell in front of the C-Span cameras, while enjoying a glass of Chardonnay with his lunch in the Capitol Building, of course, or something a little stronger in his office. The culture was just different here, and *vive la difference,* he thought, walking across Westminster Bridge Road toward Big Ben—the bell, not the bell *tower*, which was, in fact, St. Mary's Bell Tower, tourist errors to the contrary. The Parliamentarians there had three or four pubs right there in the building, Ryan was sure. And they probably didn't get any drunker than their American colleagues.

"You know, Simon, I think everyone's worried about this."

"It's a pity he had to send that letter to Warsaw, isn't it?"

"Could you expect him not to?" Ryan countered. "They are his people. It is his homeland, after all, isn't it? It's his parish the Russians are trying to stomp on."

"That is the problem," Harding agreed. "But the Russians will not change. Impasse."

Ryan nodded. "Yeah. What's the chance that the Russians will back off?"

"Absent a solid reason to, not a very great chance. Will your President try to warn them off?"

"Even if he could, he wouldn't. Not on something like this, buddy."

"So we have two sides. One is driven by what it deems to be the proper moral course of action—and the other by political necessity, by fear of not acting. As I said, Jack, it's a bloody impasse."

"Father Tim at Georgetown liked to say that wars are begun by frightened men. They're afraid of the consequences of war, but they are more afraid of not fighting. Hell of a way to run a world," Ryan thought out loud, opening the door for his friend.

"August 1914 as the model, I expect."

"Right, but at least those guys all believed in God. The second go-round was a little different in that respect. The players in that one—the Bad Guys, anyway—didn't live under that particular constraint. Neither do the guys in Moscow. You know, there have to be some limits on our actions, or we can turn into monsters."

"Tell that to the Politburo, Jack," Harding suggested lightly.

"Yeah, Simon, sure." Ryan headed off to the men's room to dump some of his liquid lunch.

THE EVENING DIDN'T come quickly enough for either of the players. Ed Foley wondered what was coming next. There was no guarantee that this guy would follow up on what he'd started. He could always get cold feet—actually, it'd be rather a sensible thing for him to do. Treason was dangerous outside the U.S. Embassy. He was still wearing a green tie—the other one; he had only two—for luck, because he'd gotten to the point where luck counted. Whoever the guy was, just so he didn't get cold feet.

Come on, Ivan, keep coming and we'll give you the joint, Foley thought, trying to reach out with his mind. *Lifetime ticket to Disney World, all the football games you can handle. Oleg Penkovskiy wanted to meet Kennedy and, yeah, we can probably swing that with the new President. Hell, we'll even throw in a movie in the White House theater.*

AND ACROSS TOWN, Mary Pat was thinking exactly the same thing. If this went one more step, she'd play a part in the opening drama. If this guy worked in the Russian MERCURY, and if he wanted a ticket out of Mother Russia, then she and Ed would have to figure a way to make that happen. There *were* ways, and they'd been used before, but they weren't what you'd call "routine." Soviet border security wasn't exactly perfect, but it was pretty tight—tight enough to make you sweat playing with it, and though she had the sort of demeanor that often worked well while playing serious games, it didn't make you feel comfortable. And so she started kicking some ideas around, just in her head, as she worked around the apartment and little Eddie took his afternoon nap, and the hours crept by, one lengthy second at a time.

ED FOLEY HADN'T sent any messages off to Langley yet. It wasn't time. He had nothing substantive to report, and there was no sense getting Bob Ritter all excited over something that hadn't developed yet. It happened often enough: People made approaches to CIA and then felt a chill inside their shoes and backed away. You couldn't chase after them. More often than not, you didn't even know who they were and, if you did, and if they decided not to play, the sensible thing for the other guy was to report you to KGB. That fingered you as a spook—rendering your value to your country as approximately zero—and covered his ass nicely as a loyal and vigilant Soviet citizen, doing his duty to the Motherland.

People didn't realize that CIA almost never recruited its agents. No, those people came to you—sometimes cleverly, sometimes not. That left you open to be fooled by a false-flag operation. The American FBI was particularly good at that sort of play, and KGB's Second Chief Directorate was known to use the gambit, too, just to identify spooks on the embassy staff, which was always something worth doing. If you knew who they were, you could follow them and watch them service their dead-drops, and then camp out on the drop site to see who else stopped off there. Then you had your traitor, who could lead you to other traitors, and with luck you could roll up a whole spy ring, which earned you a gold star—well, a nice red star—in your copybook. Counterespionage officers could make their whole careers on one such case, both in Russia and in America, and so they worked pretty hard at it. The Second Directorate people were numerous—supposedly, half of KGB's personnel were in there—and they were smart, professional spooks with all sorts of resources, and the patience of a vulture circling over the Arizona desert, sniffing the air for the smell of a dead jackrabbit, then homing in to feast on the carcass.

But KGB was more dangerous than a vulture. A vulture didn't actively hunt. Ed Foley could never be sure if he had a shadow as he traveled around Moscow. Oh, sure, he might spot one, but that could just be a deliberate effort to put a clumsy—or an exceedingly clever—officer on his tail to see if he'd try to shake him. All intelligence officers were trained in surveillance and countersurveillance, and the techniques were both universally valid and universally recognized, and so Foley *never* used them. Not ever. Not even once. It was too dangerous to be clever in this game, because you could never be clever enough. There were other countermoves to use when necessary, like the preplanned brush-pass known to every spook in the world, but very difficult to spot even so, because of its very simplicity. No, when that failed, it was usually because your agent got rattled. It was a lot harder to be an agent than a field officer. Foley had diplomatic cover. The Russians could have movie film of him buggering Andropov's pet goat and not be able to do a thing about it. He was technically a diplomat, and protected by the Vienna Convention, which made his person inviolable—even in time of war, though things got a little dicier then. But that, Foley judged, was not a problem. He'd be fried like everyone else in Moscow then, and so would not be lonely in whatever afterlife spies inhabited.

He wrenched his mind away from the irrelevancies, entertaining though they might be. It came down to one thing: Would his friend Ivan take the next step, or would he just fade back into the woodwork, taking satisfaction that he'd managed to make the U.S. Embassy dance to his tune one cool Moscow morning? To find that out, you had to turn over the cards. Would it be blackjack, or just a pair of fours?

That's why you got into this business, Ed, Foley reminded himself—the thrill of the chase. It sure as hell was a thrill, even if the game disappeared into the mists of the forest. It was more fun skinning the bear than smelling it.

Why was this guy doing what he was doing? Money? Ideology? Conscience? Ego? Those were the classic reasons, as summarized by the acronym MICE. Some spies just wanted the mayonnaise jar full of one-hundred-dollar bills. Some came to believe in the politics of the foreign countries they served with the religious fervor of the newly converted. Some were troubled because their Motherland was doing something they couldn't abide. Some just knew they were better men than their bosses, and this was a way to get even with the sons-of-bitches.

Historically, ideological spies were the most productive. Men would put their lives on the betting line for their beliefs—which was why religious wars were so bloody. Foley preferred the monetarily motivated. They were always rational, and they'd take chances, because the bigger the risk, the greater their reward. Ego-driven agents were touchy and troublesome. Revenge was never a pretty motive for doing anything, and those people were usually unstable. Conscience was almost as good as ideology. At least they were driven by a principle of sorts. The truth of the matter was that CIA paid its agents well, just out of the spirit of fair play if nothing else, and besides, it didn't hurt to have that word out on the street. Knowing that you'd be properly compensated made for one hell of a tiebreaker for those who had trouble making up their minds. Whatever your baseline motivation, being paid was always attractive. The ideological needed to eat, too. So did the conscience-driven. And the ego types saw that living well was indeed a pretty good form of revenge.

Which one are you, Ivan? Foley wondered. *What is driving you to betray your country?* The Russians were a ferociously patriotic people. When Stephen Decatur said, "Our country, right or wrong," he could well have been speaking as a Russian citizen. But the country was so badly run—tragically so. Russia had to be the world's unluckiest nation—first too large to be governed efficiently; then taken over by the hopelessly inept Romanovs; and then, when even they couldn't hold back the vitality of their nation, dropped screaming into the bloody maw of the First World War, suffering such huge casualties that Vladimir Ilyich Ulyanov—Lenin—had been able to take over and set in place a political regime calculated to do destruction to itself; then handing the wounded country over to the most vicious psychopath since Caligula, in the person of Josef Stalin. The accumulation of that sort of abuse was beginning to shake the faith of the people here. . . .

Your mind sure is wandering, Foley, the Chief of Station told himself. Another half hour. He'd leave the embassy on time and catch the metro, with his topcoat open and loose around him, and just wait and see. He headed off to the men's room. Occasionally, his bladder got as excited as his intellect.

ACROSS TOWN. Zaitzev took his time. He'd be able to write on only one message blank—throwing one away in plain view was too dangerous, the burn bag could not be trusted, and he could hardly light one up in his ashtray—and so he mentally composed his message, then rethought the words, then rethought them again, and again, and again.

The process took him more than an hour in full, and then he was able to write it up surreptitiously, fold it, and tuck it into his cigarette pack.

LITTLE EDDIE SLID his favorite *Transformers* tape into the VCR. Mary Pat watched idly, behind her son's rapt attention on the living room floor. Then it hit her.

That's what I am, she realized. *I transform myself from ditsy blonde housewife to CIA spy. And I do it seamlessly.* The thought appealed to her. She was giving the Soviet Bear a peptic ulcer, hopefully a bleeding one that wouldn't be fixed by drinking milk and taking Rolaids. *In another forty minutes, Ed will find out if his new friend really wants to play and, if he wants to play, I'll have to work the agent. I'll hold his hand and lead him along and take his information and send it off to Langley.*

What will he give us? she wondered. *Something nice and juicy? Does he work in their communications center, or does he just have access to a blank message pad? Probably a lot of those in The Centre . . . well, maybe, depending on their security procedures.* Those would be pretty stringent. Only a very few people would be trusted with KGB signals. . . .

And that was the worm dangling on the hook, she knew, watching a Kenworth diesel tractor turn into a two-legged robot. This Christmas, they'd have to start buying those toys. She wondered if Little Eddie would need help transforming them.

THE TIME CAME. Ed would leave the embassy door exactly on time, which would be a comfort to his shadow, if any. If there was, he'd notice a green tie again, and think that the earlier one was not all that unusual—not unusual enough to be any sort of signal for an agent he might be working. *Even the KGB couldn't think every embassy employee was a spook,* Foley told himself. Despite the paranoia that was pandemic in the Soviet Union, even they knew the rules of the game, and his friend from the *The New York Times* had probably told his own contacts that Foley was a dumb son of a bitch who hadn't even made it as a police reporter in the Big Apple, where the busy police made that field about as difficult as watching TV on a weekend. The best possible cover for a spook was to be too dumb, and what better person to set it up for him than that arrogant ass, Anthony—*never* just plain Tony—Prince.

Out on the street, the air was cool with approaching autumn. Ed wondered if the Russian winter was all it was cracked up to be. If so, you could always dress for cold weather. It was heat that Foley detested, though he remembered playing stickball out on the streets, and the sprinklers on the tops of some of the fire hydrants. The innocence of youth was far behind him. A damned far way behind, the chief of station reflected, checking his watch as he entered the metro station. As before, the efficiency of the metro worked for him, and he entered the usual subway car.

THERE, ZAITZEV THOUGHT, maneuvering that way. His American friend was doing everything exactly as before, reading his paper, his right hand on the grab rail, his raincoat hanging loose around him . . . and in a minute or two, he was standing next to him.

FOLEY'S PERIPHERAL VISION was still working, The shape was there, dressed exactly as before. *Okay, Ivan, make your transfer. . . . Be careful, boy, be very careful,* his mind said, knowing that this sort of thing was going to be too dangerous to sustain. No, they'd have to set up a dead-drop somewhere convenient. But first they'd have to do a meet, and he'd let Mary Pat handle that one for him, probably. She just had a better disguise. . . .

ZAITZEV WAITED UNTIL the train slowed. Bodies shifted as it did so, and he reached quickly in and out of the offered pocket. Then he turned away, slowly, not so far as to be obvious, just a natural motion easily explained by the movement of the metro car.

YES! WELL DONE, IVAN. Every fiber of his being wanted to turn and eyeball the guy, but the rules didn't allow that. If there was a shadow in the car, those people noticed that sort of thing, and it wasn't Ed Foley's job to be noticed. So he waited patiently for his subway stop, and this time he turned right, away from Ivan, and made his way off the car, onto the platform, and up to the cool air on the street.

He didn't reach into his pocket. Instead, he walked all the way home, as normal as a sunset on a clear day, into the elevator, not reaching in even then, because there could well be a video camera in the ceiling.

Not until he got into his flat did Foley pull out the message blank. This time it was anything but blank, covered with black ink letters—as before, written in English. Whoever Ivan was, Foley reflected, he was educated, and that was very good news, wasn't it?

"Hi, Ed." A kiss for the microphones. "Anything interesting happen at work?"

"The usual crap. What's for dinner?"

"Fish," she answered, looking at the paper in her husband's hand and giving an immediate thumbs-up.

Bingo! They both thought. They had an agent. A no-shit spy in KGB. Working for *them.*

CHAPTER 16

A FUR HAT FOR THE WINTER

THEY DID WHAT?" Jack asked.

"They broke for lunch in the middle of surgery and went to a pub and had a beer each!" Cathy replied, repeating herself.

"Well, so did I."

"You weren't doing *surgery!*"

"What would happen if you did that at home?"

"Oh, nothing much," Cathy said. "You'd probably lose your license to practice medicine—after Bernie amputated your fucking hands with a chain saw!"

That got Jack's attention. Cathy didn't talk like that.

"No shit?"

"I had a bacon, lettuce, and tom-AH-to sandwich with chips—that's french fries for us dumb colonials. *I* had a Coke, by the way."

"Glad to hear it, doctor." Ryan walked over to give his wife a kiss. She appeared to need it.

"I've never seen anything like it," she went on. "Oh, maybe out in Bumfuck, Montana, they do stuff like that, but not in a real hospital."

"Cathy, settle down. You're talking like a stevedore."

"Or maybe a foulmouthed ex-Marine." She finally managed a smile. "Jack, I didn't say anything. I didn't know what to say. Those two eye cutters are technically senior to me, but if they *ever* tried that sort of shit at home, they'd be finished. They wouldn't even let them work on dogs."

"Is the patient okay?"

"Oh, yeah. The frozen section came back cold as ice—totally benign, not malignant—and we took out the growth and closed him back up. He'll be just fine—four or five days for recovery. No impairment to his sight, no more headaches, but those two bozos operated on him with booze in their systems!"

"No harm, no foul, babe," he suggested, lamely.

"Jack, it isn't supposed to be that way."

"So report them to your friend Byrd."

"I ought to. I really ought to."

"And what would happen?"

That lit her up again: "I don't know!"

"It's a big deal to take the bread off somebody's table, and you'd be branded as a troublemaker," Jack warned.

"Jack, at Hopkins, I'd've called them on it right then and there, and there would have been hell to pay, but over here—over here I'm just a guest."

"And the customs are different."

"Not *that* different. Jack, it's grossly unprofessional. It's potentially harmful to the patient, and that's a line you *never* cross. At Hopkins, if you have a patient in recovery, or you have surgery the next day, you don't even have a glass of wine with dinner, okay? That's because the good of the patient comes before everything else. Okay, sure, if you're driving home from a party and you see a hurt person on the side of the road, and you're the only one around, you do what you can, and get him to a doc who's got it all together, and you probably tell that doc that you had a couple before you saw the emergency. I mean, sure, during internship, they work you through impossible hours so you can train yourself to make good decisions when you're not fully functional, but there's *always* somebody to back you up if you're not capable, and you're supposed to be able to tell when you're in over your head. Okay? I had that happen to me once on pediatric rotation, and it scared the hell out of me when that little kid stopped breathing, but I had a good nurse backing me up and we got the senior resident down in one big fucking hurry, and we got him going again with no permanent damage, thank God. But, Jack, you don't go creating a suboptimal situation. You don't go looking for them. You deal with them when they happen, but you don't voluntarily jump into the soup, okay?"

"Okay, Cath, so, what are you going to do?"

"I don't *know.* At home, I'd go right to Bernie, but I'm not at home. . . ."

"And you want my advice?"

Her blue eyes fixed on her husband's. "Well, yes. What do you think?"

What he thought didn't really matter, Jack knew. It was just a question of guiding her to her own decision. "If you do nothing, how will you feel next week?"

"Terrible. Jack, I saw something that—"

"Cathy." He hugged her. "You don't need me. Go ahead and do what you think is right. Otherwise, well, it'll just eat you up. You're never sorry for doing the right thing, no matter what the adverse consequences are. Right is right, my lady."

"They said *that,* too. I'm not comfortable with—"

"Yeah, babe. Every so often at work, they call me Sir John. You roll with the punch. It's not like it's an insult."

"Over here, they call a surgeon Mr. Jones or Mrs. Jones, not *Doctor* Jones. What the hell is that all about?"

"Local custom. It goes back to the Royal Navy in the eighteenth century. A ship's doctor was usually a youngish lieutenant, and aboard ship that rank is called mister rather than *lef*tenant. Somehow or other it carried over to civilian life, too."

"How do you know that?" Cathy demanded.

"Cathy you are a doctor of medicine. I am a doctor of history, remember? I know a lot of things, like putting a Band-Aid on a cut, after that painful Merthiolate crap. But that's as far as my knowledge of medicine goes—well, they taught us a little at the Basic School, but I don't expect to patch up a bullet wound any time soon. I'll leave that to you. Do you know how?"

"I patched you up last winter," she reminded him.

"Did I ever thank you for that?" he asked. Then he kissed her. "Thanks, babe."

"I have to talk to Professor Byrd about it."

"Honey, when in doubt, do what you think is right. That's why we have a conscience, to remind us what the right thing is."

"They won't like me for it."

"So? Cathy, *you* have to like you. Nobody else. Well, me, of course," Jack added.

"Do you?"

A very supportive smile: "Lady Ryan, I worship your dirty drawers."

And finally she relaxed. "Why, thank you, Sir John."

"Let me go upstairs and change." He stopped in the doorway. "Should I wear my formal sword for dinner?"

"No, just the regular one." And now she could smile, too. "So, what's happening in your office?"

"A lot of learning the things we don't know."

"You mean finding out new stuff?"

"No, I mean realizing all the stuff we don't know that we should know. It never stops."

"Don't feel bad. Same in my business."

And Jack realized that the similarity between both businesses was that if you screwed up, people might die. And that was no fun at all.

He reappeared in the kitchen. By now Cathy was feeding Little Jack. Sally was watching TV, that great child pacifier, this time some local show instead of a Roadrunner-Coyote tape. Dinner was cooking. Why an assistant professor of ophthalmology insisted on cooking dinner herself like a truck driver's wife baffled her husband, but he didn't object—she was good at it. Had they had cooking lessons at Bennington? He picked a kitchen chair and poured himself a glass of white wine.

"I hope this is okay with the professor."

"Not doing surgery tomorrow, right?"

"Nothing scheduled, Lady Ryan."

"Then it's okay." The little guy went to her shoulder for a burp, which he delivered with great gusto.

"Damn, Junior. Your father is impressed."

"Yeah." She took the edge of the cloth diaper on her shoulder to wipe his mouth. "Okay, how about a little more?"

John Patrick Ryan, Jr. did not object to the offer.

"What things don't you know? Still worried about that guy's wife?" Cathy asked, cooled down somewhat.

"No news on that front," Jack admitted. "We're worried what they might do on something."

"Can't say what it is?" she asked.

"Can't say what it is," he confirmed. "The Russians, as my buddy Simon says, are a rum bunch."

"So are the Brits," Cathy observed.

"Dear God, I married Carrie Nation." Jack took a sip. It was Pinot Grigio, a particularly good Italian white that the local liquor stores carried.

"Only when I cut somebody open with a knife." She liked saying it that way, because it always gave her husband chills.

He held up his glass. "Want one?"

"When I'm finished, maybe." She paused. "Nothing you can talk about?"

"Sorry, babe. It's the rules."

"And you never break them?"

"Bad habit to get into. Better not to start."

"What about when some Russian decides to work for us?"

"That's different. Then he's working for the forces of Truth and Beauty in the world. We," Ryan emphasized, "are the Good Guys."

"What do they think?"

"They think they are. But so did a guy named Adolf," he reminded her. "And he wouldn't have liked Bernie very much."

"But he's long dead."

"Not everybody like him is, babe. Trust me on that one."

"You're worried about something, Jack. I can see it. Can't say, eh?"

"Yes. And no, I can't."

"Okay." She nodded. Intelligence information didn't interest her beyond her abstract desire to learn what was going on in the world. But as a physician there were many things she really wanted to know—like the cure for cancer—but didn't, and, reluctantly, she'd come to accept that. But medicine didn't allow much in the way of secrets. When you found something that helped patients, you published your discovery in your favorite medical journal so the whole world could know about it right away. Damned sure CIA didn't do that very often, and part of that offended her. Another tack, then. "Okay, when you do find out something important, what happens then?"

"We kick it upstairs. Here, it goes right to Sir Basil, and I call it in to Admiral Greer. Usually a phone call over the secure phone."

"Like the one upstairs?"

"Yep. Then we send it over by secure fax or, if it's really hot, it goes by diplomatic courier out of the embassy, when we don't want to trust the encryption systems."

"How often does that happen?"

"Not since I've been here, but I don't make those decisions. What the hell, the diplomatic bag goes over in eight or nine hours. Damned sight faster than it used to happen."

"I thought that phone thingee upstairs was unbreakable?"

"Well, some things you do are nearly perfect, too, but you still take extra care with them, right? Same with us."

"What would that be for? Theoretically speaking, that is." She smiled at her cleverness.

"Babe, you know how to phrase a question. Let's say we got something, oh, on their nuclear arsenal, something from an agent way the hell inside, and it's really good stuff, but losing it might ID the agent for the opposition. That is what you send via the bag. The name of the game is protecting the source."

"Because if they ID the guy—"

"He's dead, maybe in a very unpleasant way. There's a story that once they loaded a guy into a crematorium alive and then turned on the gas—and they made a film of it, *pour encourager les autres,* as Voltaire put it."

"Nobody does that anymore!" Cathy objected immediately.

"There's a guy at Langley who claims to have seen the film. The poor bastard's name was Popov, a GRU officer who worked for us. His bosses were very displeased with him."

"You're serious?" Cathy persisted.

"As a heart attack. Supposedly, they used to show the film to people in the GRU Academy as a warning about not crossing the line—it strikes me as bad psychology but, like I said, I've met a guy who says he saw the film. Anyway, that's one of the reasons we try to protect our sources."

"That's a little hard to believe."

"Oh, really? You mean, like a surgeon breaking for lunch and having a beer?"

"Well . . . yes."

"It's an imperfect world we live in, babe." He'd let things go. She'd have all weekend to think things over, and he'd get some work done on his Halsey book.

BACK IN MOSCOW, fingers were flying. *How u gonna tell Lan*[*gley*], she asked.

N[ot] sure, he replied.

Cour[ier], she suggested. *This could be re[ally] hot.*

Ed nodded agreement. *Rit[ter] will be exci[ted].*

D[amn] st[raight], she agreed. *Want m[e] 2 han[dle] the me[et]?* she asked.

Y[our] Ru[ssian] is pre[etty] g[ood], he agreed.

This time she nodded. She spoke an elegant literary Russian reserved to the well-educated over here, Ed knew. The average Soviet couldn't believe that a foreigner spoke his language that well. When walking the street or conversing with a shop clerk, she never let that skill slip, instead stumbling over complex phrases. To do otherwise would have been noticed at once, and so avoiding it was an important part of her cover, even more than her blond hair and American mannerisms. It would finger her immediately to their new agent.

When? she asked next.

Iv[an] sez tom[orrow]. Up 4 it? he responded.

She patted his hip and gave a cute, playful smile, which translated to *bet your ass.*

Foley loved his wife as fully as a man could, and part of that was his respect for her love of the game they both played. Paramount Central

Casting could not have given him a better wife. They'd be making love tonight. The rule in boxing might be no sex before a fight, but for Mary Pat the rule was the reverse, and if the microphones in the walls noticed, well, *fuck 'em,* the Chief of Station Moscow thought, with a sly smile of his own.

"WHEN DO YOU leave, Bob?" Greer asked the DDO.

"Sunday. ANA to Tokyo, and from there on to Seoul."

"Better you than me. I hate those long flights," the DDI observed.

"Well, you try to sleep about half the way," and Ritter was good at that. He had a conference scheduled with the KCIA, to go over things on both North Korea and the Chinese, both of which he was worried about—as were the Koreans. "Nothing much happening in my shop at the moment, anyway."

"Smart of you to skip town while we have the President chewing my backside about the Pope," Judge Moore thought aloud.

"Well, I'm sorry about that, Arthur," Ritter retorted, with an ironic smile. "Mike Bostock will be handling things in my absence." Both senior executives knew and liked Bostock, a career field spook and an expert on the Soviets and the Central Europeans. He was a little too much of a cowboy to be trusted on The Hill, though, which everyone thought was a pity. Cowboys had their uses—like Mary Pat Foley, for example.

"Still nothing out of the Politburo meeting?"

"Not yet, Arthur. Maybe they just talked about routine stuff. You know, they don't always sit there and plan the next nuclear war."

"No." Greer chuckled. "They think we're always doing that. Jesus, they're a paranoid bunch."

"Remember what Henry said: 'Even paranoids have enemies.' And that *is* our job," Ritter reminded them.

"Still ruminating over your MASQUE OF THE RED DEATH plan, Robert?"

"Nothing specific yet. The in-house people I've talked to about it—damn it, Arthur, you tell our people to think outside of the box, and what do they do? They build a better box!"

"We don't have many entrepreneur types here, remember. Government agency. Pay caps. Tends to militate against creative thinking. That's what we're for," Judge Moore pointed out. "How do we change that?"

"We have a few people from the real world. Hell, I've got one on my team—he doesn't know how to think *inside* the box."

"Ryan?" Ritter asked.

"That's one of them," Jim Greer confirmed with a nod.

"He's not one of us," the DDO observed at once.

"Bob, you can't have it both ways," the DDI shot back. "Either you want a guy who thinks like one of our bureaucrats, or a guy who thinks creatively. Ryan knows the rules, he's an ex-Marine who even knows how to think on his feet, and pretty soon he's going to be a star analyst." Greer paused. "He's about the best young officer I've seen in a few years, and what your beef with him is, Robert, I do not understand."

"Basil likes him," Moore added to the conversation, "and Basil's a hard man to fool."

"Next time I see Jack, I'd like to let him know about RED DEATH."

"Really?" Moore asked. "It's way over his pay grade."

"Arthur, he knows economics better than anyone I have in the DI. I didn't put him in my economics section only because he's too smart to be limited that way. Bob, if you want to wreck the Soviet Union—without a war—the only way to do it is to cripple their economy. Ryan made himself a pile of money because he knows all that stuff. I'm telling you, he knows how to separate the wheat from the chaff. Maybe he can figure a way to burn down a wheat field. Anyway, what does it hurt? Your project is entirely theoretical, isn't it?"

"Well?" the DCI turned to Ritter. Greer was right, after all.

"Oh, what the hell, okay," the DDO conceded the point. "Just so he doesn't talk about this to *The Washington Post.* We don't need that idea out in the open. Congress and the press would have a meltdown."

"Jack, talk to the press?" Greer asked. "Not likely. He doesn't curry favor with people, including us. He's one guy I think we can trust. The whole Russian KGB doesn't have enough hard currency to buy him off. That's more than I can say for myself," he joked.

"I'll remember you said that, James," Ritter promised, with a thin smile of his own. Such jokes were usually limited to the Seventh Floor at Langley.

A DEPARTMENT STORE was a department store anywhere in the world, and GUM was supposedly Moscow's counterpart to Macy's in New York. *Theoretically,* Ed Foley thought, walking in the main entrance. Just like the Soviet Union was theoretically a voluntary union of republics, and Russia theoretically had a constitution that existed over and above the will of the Communist Party of the Soviet Union. And there was theoretically an Easter Bunny, too, he thought, looking around.

They took the escalator to the second floor—the escalator was of the old sort, with thick wooden runners instead of the metal type which had long since taken over in the West. The fur department was over on the right, toward the back, and, on initial visual inspection, the selection there wasn't all that shabby.

Best of all, so was Ivan, wearing the same clothes that he'd worn on the metro. *Maybe his best suit?* Foley wondered. If so, he'd better get his ass to a Western country as soon as possible.

Other than the at-best-mediocre quality of the goods here, a department store was a department store, though here the departments were semi-independent shops. But their Ivan was smart. He'd suggested a meet in a part of the place where there would certainly be high-quality goods. For millennia, Russia had been a place of cold winters, a place where even the elephants had needed fur coats, and since 25 percent of the human blood supply goes to the brain, men needed hats. The decent fur hats were called *shapkas,* roughly tubular fur head coverings that had little in the way of precise shape, but did serve to keep the brain from freezing. The really good ones were made out of muskrat—mink and sable went only to the most expensive specialty stores, and those were mainly limited to well-to-do women, the wives and/or mistresses of Party bosses. But the noble muskrat, a swamp creature that smelled—well, the smell was taken out of the skin somehow, lest the wearer of the hat be mistaken for a tidal wetland garbage dump—had very fine fur or hair or whatever it was, and was a good insulator. So, fine, a rat with a high R rating. But that wasn't the important part, was it?

Ed and Mary Pat could also communicate with their eyes, though the bandwidth was pretty narrow. The time of day helped. The winter hats had just been stocked in the store, and the fall weather didn't have people racing to buy new ones yet. There was just one guy in a brown jacket, and Mary Pat moved in that direction, after shooing her husband away, as though to buy him something as a semi-surprise.

The man was shopping, just as she was, and he was in the hat department. *He's not a dummy, whoever he is,* she thought.

"Excuse me," she said in Russian.

"Yes?" His head turned. Mary Pat checked him out; he was in his early thirties, but looked older than that, as life in Russia tended to age people more rapidly, even more rapidly than New York City. Brown hair, brown eyes—rather smart-looking in the eyes. That was good.

"I am shopping for a winter hat for my husband, as you suggested," she added in her very best Russian, "on the metro."

He didn't expect it to be a girl, Mrs. Foley saw at once. He blinked hard and looked at her, trying to square the perfect Russian with the fact that she had to be an American.

"On the metro?"

"That's right. My husband thought it better that I should meet you, rather than he. So . . ." She lifted a hat and riffled the fur, then turned to her new friend, as though asking his opinion. "So, what do you wish of us?"

"What do you mean?" he blurted back at her.

"You have approached an American and requested a meeting. Do you want to assist me in buying a hat for my husband?" she asked very quietly indeed.

"You are CIA?" he asked, his thought now back under semicontrol.

"My husband and I work for the American government, yes. And you work for KGB."

"Yes," he replied, "in communications, Central Communications."

"Indeed?" She turned back to the gable and lifted another *shapka. Holy shit,* she thought, but was he telling the truth, or did he just want a cheap ticket to New York?

"Really? How can I be sure of that?"

"I say it is so," he replied, surprised and slightly outraged that his honesty should come into question. Did this woman think he was risking his life as a lark? "Why do you talk to me?"

"The message blanks you passed on the metro did get my attention," she said, holding up a dark brown hat and frowning, as though it were too dark.

"Madam, I work in the Eighth Chief Directorate."

"Which department?"

"Simple communications processing. I am not part of the signals intelligence service. I am a communications officer. I transmit outgoing signals to the various *rezidenturas,* and when signals come to my desk from out in the field, I forward them to the proper recipients. As a result, I see many operational signals. Is that sufficient to your purpose?" He was at least playing the game properly, gesturing to the *shapka* and shaking his head, then pointing to another, its fur dyed a lighter brown, almost a blond color.

"I suppose it might be. What do you ask of us?"

"I have information of great importance—very great importance. In return for that information, I require passage to the West for myself, my wife, and my daughter."

"How old is your daughter?"

"Three years and seven months. Can you deliver what I require?"

That question shot a full pint of adrenaline into her bloodstream. She'd have to make this decision almost instantly, and with that decision she was committing the whole power of CIA onto a single case. Getting three people out of the Soviet Union was not going to be a picnic.

But this guy works in MERCURY, Mary Pat realized. He'd know things a hundred well-placed agents couldn't get to. Ivan here was custodian of the Russian Crown Jewels, more valuable even than Brezhnev's balls, and so—

"Yes, we can get you and your family out. How soon?"

"The information I have is very time-sensitive. As soon as you can arrange. I will not reveal my information until I am in the West, but I assure you the information is a matter of great importance—it is enough to force me into this action," he added as an additional dangle.

Don't overplay your hand, Ivan, she thought. An ego-driven agent would tell them he had the launch codes for the Russian Strategic Rocket Forces, when he just had his mother's recipe for borscht, and getting the bastard out would be a waste of resources that had to be used with the greatest care. But, against that possibility, Mary Pat had her eyes. She looked into this man's soul, and saw that whatever he was, "liar" probably wasn't among them.

"Yes, we can do this very quickly if necessary. We need to discuss place and methods. We cannot talk any longer here. I suggest a meeting place to discuss details."

"That is simple," Zaitzev replied, setting the place for the following morning.

You're in a hurry. "What name do I call you?" she finally asked.

"Oleg Ivan'ch," he answered automatically, then realized he'd spoken the truth, in a situation where dissimulation might have served him better.

"That is good. My name is Maria," she replied. "So, which *shapka* would you recommend?"

"For your husband? This one, certainly," Zaitzev said, handing over the dirty-blond one.

"Then I shall buy it. Thank you, comrade." She fussed over the hat briefly, then walked off, checking the price tag, 180 rubles, more than a month's pay for a Moscow worker. To effect the purchase, she handed the *shapka* over to one clerk, then walked to a cash register, where she paid her cash—the Soviets hadn't discovered credit cards yet—and got a receipt in return, which she handed to the first clerk, who gave her the hat back.

So, it was true—the Russians really were more inefficient than the American government. Amazing that it was possible, but seeing was believing, she told herself, clutching the brown-paper bag and finding her husband, whom she quickly walked outside.

"So, what did you buy me?"

"Something you'll like," she promised, holding up the bag, but her sparkling blue eyes said it all. Then she checked her watch. It was just 3:00 A.M. in Washington and, if they phoned this one in, it was too early. This wasn't something for the night crew, even the trusted people in MERCURY. She'd just learned that one the hard way. No, this one would get written up, encrypted, and put in the diplomatic bag. Then it was just a matter of getting approval from Langley.

THEIR CAR HAD just been swept by an embassy mechanic the previous day—everybody in the embassy did it routinely, so this didn't finger them as spooks, and the telltales on door and hood hadn't been disturbed the previous night. The Mercedes 280 also had a fairly sophisticated alarm. So Ed Foley just turned up the sound on the radio–tape player. In the slot was a Bee Gees tape sure to offend anyone listening to a bug, and easily loud enough to overpower it. In her passenger seat, Mary Pat danced to the music, like a good California girl.

"Our friend needs a ride," she said, just loudly enough to be heard by her husband. "Him, wife, and daughter, age three and a half."

"When?" Ed wanted to know.

"Soon."

"How?"

"Up to us."

"He's serious?" Ed asked his wife, meaning, *Worth our time?*

"Think so."

You couldn't be sure, but MP had a good eye for reading people, and he was willing to wager on those cards. He nodded. "Okay."

"Any company?" she asked next.

Foley's eyes were about equally divided between the street and the mirrors. If they were being followed, it was by the Invisible Man. "Nope."

"Good." She turned the sound down some. "You know, I like it, too, Ed, but easy on the ears."

"Fine, honey. I have to go back to the office this afternoon."

"What for?" she asked in the semiangry voice every husband in the world knows.

"Well, I have some paperwork from yesterday—"

"And you want to check the baseball scores," she huffed. "Ed, why can't we get satellite TV in our apartment block?"

"They're working on getting it for us, but the Russians are making a little trouble. They're afraid it might be a spy tool," he added in a disgusted voice.

"Yeah," she observed. "Sure. Give me a break." Just in case KGB had a very clever black-bag guy who prowled the parking lot at night. Maybe the FBI could pull that one off but, though they had to guard against the possibility, she doubted that the Russians had anybody that clever. Their radios were just too bulky. Even so, yes. They were paranoid, but were they paranoid *enough?*

CATHY TOOK SALLY and Little Jack outside. There was a park just a block and a half away, off Fristow Way, where there were a few swings that Sally liked and grass for the little guy to pull at and try to eat. He'd just figured out how to use his hands, badly and awkwardly, but whatever found its way into his little fist immediately thereafter found its way to his mouth, a fact known by every parent in the world. Still and all, it was a chance to get the kids some sun—the winter nights would be long and dark here—and it got the house quiet for Jack to get some work done on his Halsey book.

He'd already taken out one of Cathy's medical textbooks, *Principles of Internal Medicine,* to read up on shingles, the skin disease that had tormented the American admiral at a very inconvenient time. Just from reading the subchapter on the ailment—related to chicken pox, it turned out—it must have been like medieval torture to the then elderly naval aviator. Even more so that his beloved carrier battle group, *Enterprise* and *Yorktown,* would have to sail into a major engagement without him. But he'd taken it like a man—the only way William Frederick Halsey, Jr., had ever taken anything—and recommended his friend Raymond Spruance to take his place. The two men could scarcely have been more different. Halsey the profane, hard-drinking, chain-smoking former football player. Spruance, the nonsmoking, teetotaling intellectual reputed never to have raised his voice in anger. But they'd become the closest of friends, and would later in the war switch off command of the Pacific Fleet, renaming it from

Third Fleet to Fifth Fleet and back again when command was exchanged. *That,* Ryan thought, *was the most obvious clue that Halsey had been the intellectual, too, and not the blustering hell-for-leather aggressor that the contemporary newspapers had proclaimed him to be.* Spruance the intellectual would not have befriended a knuckle-dragger. But their staffs had snarled at each other like tomcats fighting over a tabby in heat, probably the military equivalent of "my daddy can whip your daddy," engaged in by children up to the age of seven or so—and no more intellectually respectable.

He had Halsey's own words on the illness, though what he'd really said must have been muted by his editor and cowriter, since Bill Halsey really had spoken like a Chief Bosun's Mate with a few drinks under his belt—probably one of the reasons reporters had liked him so much. He'd made such good copy.

His notes and some source documents were piled next to his Apple IIe computer. Jack used WordStar as his word-processing program. It was fairly complicated, but a damned sight better than using a typewriter. He wondered which publisher would be right for the book. The Naval Institute Press was after him again, but he found himself wondering whether to switch over to a big-league publisher. But he had to finish the damned book first, didn't he? And so, back into Halsey's complex brain.

But he was hesitating today. That was unusual. His typing—three fingers and a thumb (two thumbs on a good day)—was the same, but his brain wasn't concentrating properly, as though it wanted to look at something else. This was an occasional curse of his CIA analysis work. Some problems just wouldn't go away, forcing his mind to go over the same material time and again until he stumbled upon the answer to a question that often enough made little sense in and of itself. The same thing had occasionally happened during his time at Merrill Lynch, when he'd investigated stock issues, looking for hidden worth or danger in the operations and finances of some publicly traded company. That had occasionally put him at odds with the big boys up in the New York office, but Ryan had never been one to do something just because a superior told him to. Even in the Marine Corps, an officer, however junior, was expected to think, and a stockbroker with clients was entrusted by them to safeguard their money as though it were his own. Mostly, he'd succeeded. After putting his own funds into Chicago and North Western Railroad, he'd been hammered by his supervisors, but he'd stood his ground, and those clients who'd listened to him had cashed in rather nicely—which had earned him a crowd of new clients. So Ryan had learned to listen to his instincts, to scratch the itches he couldn't quite see and could barely feel. This was one of those, and "this" was the Pope. The information he had did not form a complete picture, but he was used to that. In the stock-trading business, he'd learned how and when to bet his money on incomplete pictures, and nine times out of ten he'd been right.

He had nothing to bet on this one but his itch, however. Something was happening. He just didn't know what. All he'd seen was a copy of a warning letter sent to Warsaw, and certainly forwarded to Moscow, where a bunch of old men would look upon it as a threat.

That wasn't much to go on, was it? Ryan asked himself. He found himself wishing for a cigarette. Such things helped his thinking process sometimes, but there'd be hell to pay if Cathy smelled smoke in their house. But chewing gum, even bubble gum, just didn't cut it at times like this.

He needed Jim Greer. The Admiral often treated him like a surrogate son—his own son had been killed as a Marine lieutenant in Vietnam, Ryan had learned along the way—giving him the occasional chance to talk through a problem. But he wasn't that close to Sir Basil Charleston, and Simon was too near to him in age, if not quite in experience. And this was not a problem to be kicked around alone. He wished he could discuss it with his wife—doctors, he knew, were pretty smart—but that wasn't allowed, and, anyway, Cathy didn't really know the situation well enough to understand the threats. No, she'd grown up in a more privileged environment, daughter of a millionaire stock-and-bonds trader, living in a large Park Avenue apartment, all the best schools, her own new car for her sixteenth birthday, and all the hazards of life held off well beyond arm's length. Not Jack. His dad had been a cop, mostly a homicide investigator, and, while his father hadn't brought work home, Jack had asked enough questions to understand that the real world could be a place of unpredictable danger and that some people just didn't think like real people. They were called Bad Guys—and they could be pretty goddamned bad. He'd never lived without a conscience. Whether he'd picked that up in distant childhood or Catholic schools, or it had been part of his genetic makeup, Jack didn't know. He did know that breaking the rules was rarely a good thing, but he also knew that the rules were a product of reason, and reason was paramount, and so the rules *could* be broken if you had a good—a very goddamned good—reason for doing so. That was called judgment, and the Marines, oddly enough, had nurtured that particular flower. You made an estimate of the situation and thought through the options, and then you acted. Sometimes you had to do it in a very big hurry—and that was why officers were paid more than sergeants, though you were always well advised to listen to your gunny if you had the time.

But Ryan had none of those things now, and that was the bad news. There was no immediately identifiable threat in view, and that was the good news. But now he was in an environment in which the threats were not always readily visible, and it was his job to find them out by piecing the available information together. But there wasn't much of that now either. Just a possibility, which he had to apply to the minds of people he didn't know and would never meet, except as paper documents written up by other people he didn't know. It was like being the navigator on a ship in Christopher Columbus's little fleet, thinking land might be out there, but not knowing where or when he might come upon it—and hoping to God it wouldn't be at night, in a storm, and that the land would not appear as a barrier reef to rip the bottom of his ship out. His own life was not in danger, but, as he'd been compelled by professional obligation to treat the money of his clients as his own, so he had to regard the life of a man in potential danger as having the importance of the life of his own child.

And that was where the itch came from. He could call Admiral Greer, Ryan thought, but it wasn't even seven in the morning in Washington yet, and he'd be doing his boss no favor by waking him up to the trilling sound of his home STU. Especially as he had nothing to tell, just a few things to ask. So he leaned back in his chair and stared at the green screen of his Apple monitor, looking for something that just wasn't there.

CHAPTER 17

FLASH TRAFFIC

ED FOLEY WROTE IN HIS OFFICE:

PRIORITY: FLASH
TO: DDO/CIA
CC: DCI, DDI
FROM: COS MOSCOW
SUBJECT: RABBIT
TEXT FOLLOWS:
WE HAVE A RABBIT, A HIGHLY PLACED WALK-IN, CLAIMS TO BE COMMO OFFICER IN KGB CENTRE, WITH INFORMATION OF INTEREST TO USG. ESTIMATION: HE IS TRUTHFUL. 5/5.
URGENTLY REQUEST AUTHORIZATION FOR IMMEDIATE EXFILTRATION FROM REDLAND. PACKAGE INCLUDES RABBIT WIFE AND DAUGHTER (3).
5/5 PRIORITY REQUESTED.
ENDS

There, Foley thought, *that's concise enough.* The shorter the better with messages like this one—it provided less opportunity for the opposition to work on the text and crack the cipher, in the event they got their hands on it.

But the only hands that would touch this one were CIA. He was betting a lot on this op-dispatch. 5/5 meant that the estimated importance of the information available, as well as its presumed accuracy and the priority for his proposed action, was class-5, the highest. He gave an identical evaluation for the accuracy of the subject. Four aces—not the sort of dispatch you sent out every day. It was the classification he'd give to a message from Oleg Penkovskiy, or from Agent CARDINAL himself, and that was about as hot a potato as they came. He thought for a moment, wondering if he was guessing correctly, but, over his career, Ed Foley had learned to go with his instincts. He'd also measured his own thoughts against those of his wife, and her instincts were just as finely tuned. Their Rabbit—the CIA term of art for a person wanting a fast ticket out of whatever bad place he found himself in—claimed a lot, but he gave every sign of being what he claimed: the possessor of some very hot information. That made him a conscience defector, and thus pretty reliable. If he were a plant, a false-flag, he would have asked for money, because that's how KGB thought defectors thought—and CIA had never done anything to disabuse them of that notion.

So, it just *felt* right, though "feels right" isn't something you send by Diplomatic Courier to the Seventh Floor. They'd have to play along with this. They had to trust him. He was Chief of Station in Moscow, the CIA's top field posting, and with that came a truckload of credibility. They'd have to weigh it against whatever misgivings they were feeling. If a summit meeting were scheduled, then that might queer the deal, but the President had no such plans, nor did SecState. So there was nothing in the way of Langley approving some form of action—if they thought he was right. . . .

Foley didn't even know why he was questioning himself. He was The Man in Moscow, and that, by God, was that. He lifted the phone and punched three buttons.

"Russell," a voice said.

"Mike, this is Ed. I need you here."

"Right."

It took a minute and a half. The door opened.

"Yeah, Ed?"

"Something for the bag."

Russell checked his watch. "Not much margin, guy."

"It's short. I'll have to come down with you on this one."

"Well, let's get it on, then, bro." Russell walked out the door, with Foley in pursuit. Fortunately, the corridor was empty, and his office was not far.

Russell sat down in his swivel chair and lit up his cipher machine. Foley handed the sheet over. Russell clipped it to a fixture right over the keyboard. "Short enough," he said approvingly, and started typing. He was nearly as skillful as the Ambassador's own secretary, and he finished the job in a minute, including some padding—sixteen surnames taken at random from the Prague telephone book. When the new page came out of the machine, Foley took it, folded it, tucked it in a manila envelope, and sealed it. Wax was dripped over the closure, and Foley handed the envelope back to Russell.

"Back in five, Ed," the communications officer said on his way out the door. He took the elevator down to the first floor. The diplomatic courier was there. His name was Tommy Cox, a former Army warrant officer/helicopter pilot who'd been shot down four times in the Central Highlands as part of the First Cavalry Division, and a man who had only the most negative feelings for his country's adversaries. The Diplomatic Bag was a canvas carry-on–type bag that would be handcuffed to his wrist during transit. He was already booked on a Pan Am 747 direct flight to New York's Kennedy International, a flight of eleven hours, during which he would neither drink nor sleep, though he did have three paperback mysteries to read along the way. He'd be leaving the embassy in an official car in ten minutes, and his diplomatic credentials meant he wouldn't be troubled with security or immigration procedures. The Russians were actually fairly cordial about that, though they probably drooled over the chance of seeing what was inside the canvas bag. For sure, it wasn't Russian perfume or pantyhose for a friend in New York or Washington.

"Good flight, Tommy."

Cox nodded. "Roger that, Mike."

Russell headed back to Foley's office topside. "Okay, it's in the bag. Flight leaves in an hour and ten minutes, man."

"Good."

"Is a Rabbit what I think it is?"

"Can't say, Mike," Foley pointed out.

"Yeah, I know, Ed. Excuse my question." Russell wasn't one to break the rules, though he had as much curiosity as the next man. And he knew what a Rabbit was, of course. He'd spent his entire life inside the black world in one capacity or another, and the jargon wasn't all that hard to pick up. But the black world had walls, and that was that.

Foley took his copy of the message, tucked it in his office safe, and set both the combination and the alarm. Then he headed down to the embassy cafeteria, where a TV was tuned in to ESPN. There he learned that his Yankees had lost another one—three straight, and in a pennant race! *Is there no fairness in the world?* he grumbled.

MARY PAT WAS doing housework, which was boring, but a good opportunity for her to put her brain in neutral while her imagination ran wild. Okay, she'd be meeting Oleg Ivanovich again. It would be up to her to figure a way to get the "package"—yet another CIA term of art, meaning the material or person(s) to be taken out of the country—to a safe place. There were many ways to do such a thing. They were all dangerous, but she and Ed and other CIA field spooks were trained to do dangerous things. Moscow was a city of millions, and in such an environment three people on the move were just part of the background noise, like one single leaf falling in an autumn forest, one more buffalo in the herd in Yellowstone National Park, one more car on the L.A. Freeway during rush hour. That wasn't hard, was it?

Well, actually, it was. In the Soviet Union, every aspect of personal life was subject to control. As applied to America, sure, the package was just one more car on the L.A. Freeway, but going to Las Vegas meant crossing a state line, and you had to have a reason for that. Nothing was easy here in the sense that everything was easy in America.

And there was something else. . . .

It would be better, Mary Pat thought, *that the Russians didn't know he was gone.* After all, it was not a murder if there wasn't a corpse to let everyone know that somebody had died. And it wasn't a defection unless they knew that one of their citizens had turned up somewhere else—where he wasn't supposed to be. *So, how much the better . . . was it possible . . . ?* she wondered.

Wouldn't that *be a kick in the ass? But how to make it happen?* It was something to speculate on while she vacuumed the living room rug. And, oh, by the way, vacuuming would invalidate whatever bugs the Russians had implanted in the walls. . . . And so she stopped at once. Why waste that chance? She and Ed could communicate with their hands, but the bandwidth was like maple syrup in January.

She wondered if Ed would go for this. *He might,* she thought. It wasn't the sort of thing he'd think up. Ed, for all his skills, wasn't a cowboy. Though he had his talents, and good ones they were, he was more a bomber pilot than a fighter pilot. But Mary Pat thought like Chuck Yeager in the X-1, like Pete Conrad in the lunar module. She was just better at thinking long-ball.

The idea also had strategic implications. If they could get their Rabbit out unknown to the opposition, then they could make indefinite use of whatever he knew, and that possibility, if you could figure out how to make it happen, was very enticing indeed. It wouldn't be easy, and it might be a needless complication—and if so, it could be discarded—but it was worth thinking about, if she could get Ed's brain into it. She'd need his planning talents and his reality-checking ability, but the basic idea set her head abuzz. It would come down to available assets. . . . And that would be the hard part. But "hard" didn't mean "impossible." And, for Mary Pat, "impossible" didn't mean "impossible" either, did it? she asked herself.

Hell, no.

THE PAN AM FLIGHT rolled off on time, lurching across the lumpy taxiways of Sheremetyevo Airport, which was famous in the world of aviation for its roller-coaster paving. But the runways were adequate, and the big JT-9D Pratt and Whitney turbofan engines pushed the airframe to rotation speed, and the aircraft took flight. Tommy Cox, in seat 3-A, noted with a smile the usual reaction when an American airliner departed Moscow:

The passengers all cheered and/or applauded. There was no rule, and the flight crew didn't encourage it. It just happened all on its own—that's how impressed Americans were with Soviet hospitality. It appealed to Cox, who had no love for the people who'd supplied the machine guns that had splashed his Huey four times and, by the way, earned him a total of three Purple Heart medals, a miniature ribbon of which decorated the lapels of all his suitcoats, along with the two repeat stars. He looked out the window, watching the ground fall away to his left and, when he heard the welcome *ding,* fished out a Winston to light with his Zippo. It was a pity he couldn't drink or sleep on these flights, but the movie was one he hadn't seen, remarkably enough. In this job you learned to appreciate the small things. Twelve hours to New York, but a direct flight was better than having to stop over in Frankfurt or Heathrow. Such places were just an opportunity for him to drag this fucking canvas bag around, sometimes without benefit of a cart or trolley. Well, he had a full pack of smokes, and the dinner menu didn't look too bad. And the government actually paid him to sit down for twelve hours, baby-sitting a piece of cheap luggage. It was better than flying his Huey around the Central Highlands. Cox was long past wondering what important information he transported in his bag. And if other people were that interested, that was their problem.

RYAN HAD GOTTEN a hot three pages done—not a very productive day, and he couldn't claim that the artistry of his prose demanded a slow writing pace. His language was literate—he'd learned his grammar from priests and nuns for the most part, and his word mechanics were serviceable—but not particularly elegant. In his first book, *Doomed Eagles,* every bit of artistic language he'd attempted to put into his manuscript had been edited out, to his quiet and submissive fury. And so the few critics who had read and commented on his historical epic had faintly praised the quality of his analysis, but then tersely noted that it might be a good textbook for academic students of history, but not something on which a casual reader might wish to waste his money. And so the book had netted 7,865 copies sold—not much to show for two and a half years' work, but that, Jack reminded himself, was just his first outing, and maybe a new publisher would get him an editor who was more an ally than an enemy. He could hope, after all.

But the damned thing would not get done until he did it, and three pages wasn't much to show for a full day in his den. He was time-sharing his brain with another problem, and that wasn't a useful productivity tool.

"How did it go?" Cathy asked, suddenly appearing at his shoulder.

"Not too bad," he lied.

"Where are you up to?"

"May. Halsey is fighting off his skin disease."

"Dermatitis? That can be nasty, even today," Cathy noted. "It can drive the poor patients crazy."

"Since when are you a dermatologist?"

"M.D., Jack, remember? I may not know it all, but I know most of it."

"All that, and humble, too." He made a face.

"Well, when you get a cold, don't I take good care of you?"

"I suppose." She did, actually. "How are the kids?"

"Fine. Sally had a good time on the swings, and she made a new friend, Geoffrey Froggatt. His father's a solicitor."

"Great. Isn't there anything but lawyers around here?"

"Well, there's a doctor and a spook," Cathy pointed out. "Trouble is, I can't tell people what you do, can I?"

"So what *do* you tell them?" Jack asked.

"That you work for the embassy." Close enough.

"Another desk-sitting bureaucrat," he grumped.

"Well, you want to go back to Merrill Lynch?"

"Ugh. Not in this lifetime."

"Some people like making tons of money," she pointed out.

"Only as a hobby, babe." Were he to go back to trading, his father-in-law would gloat for a year. No, not in this lifetime. He'd served his time in hell, like a good Marine. "I have more important things to do."

"Like what?"

"I can't tell you," he countered.

"I know that," his wife responded, with a playful smile. "Well, at least it isn't insider trading."

Actually, it was, Ryan couldn't say—the nastiest sort. Thousands of people working every day to find out things they weren't supposed to know, and then taking action they weren't supposed to take.

But both sides played that game—played it diligently—because it wasn't about money. It was about life and death, and those games were as nasty as they got. But Cathy didn't lose any sleep over the cancer tissue she consigned to the hospital incinerator and probably those cancer cells wanted to live, too, but that was just too damned bad, wasn't it?

COLONEL BUBOVOY HAD the dispatch on his desk and read it. His hands didn't shake, but he lit a cigarette to help his contemplation. So, the Politburo was willing to go forward with this. Leonid Ilyich himself had signed the letter to the Bulgarian Party chairman. He'd have the ambassador call Monday morning to set up the meeting, which ought not to take too long. The Bulgarians were lapdogs of the Soviet Union, but occasionally useful lapdogs. The Soviets had assisted in the murder of Georgiy Markov on Westminster Bridge in London—KGB had supplied the weapon, if you could call it that, an umbrella to deliver the poison-filled metal miniball to transfer the ricin, and so silence the annoying defector who'd talked too much on BBC World Service. That had been a while, and such debts had no expiration date, did they? Not at this level of statecraft. So Moscow was calling in the debt. Besides that, there was the agreement from 1964, when it had been agreed that DS would handle KGB's wet work in the West. And Leonid Ilyich was promising to transfer a full battalion's worth of the new version of the T-72 main-battle tank, which was always the sort of thing to make a communist chief of state feel better about his political security. And it was cheaper than the MiG-29s the Bulgarians were asking for. As though a Bulgarian pilot could handle such an aircraft—the Russian joke was that they had to tuck their mustaches into the flight helmet before closing the visor, Bubovoy reminded himself. Mustaches or not, the Bulgarians were regarded as the children of Russia—an attitude that went back to the czars. And, for the most part, they were obedient children, though like them they had little appreciation of right and wrong, so long as they weren't caught. So he'd show proper respect for this chief of state and be received cordially as the messenger of a greater power, and the Chairman would hem and haw a little bit and then agree. It would be as stylized as a performance of ballet dancer Aleksander Gudonov, and just as predicable in its conclusion.

And then he'd meet with Boris Strokov and get an idea how quickly the operation might proceed. Boris Andreyevich would find the prospect exciting. This would be the biggest mission of his life, like playing in the Olympics, not so much daunting as exhilarating, and there was a sure promotion to be had for its successful completion—perhaps a new car for Strokov and/or a nice dacha outside Sofia. Or even both. *And for myself?* the KGB officer wondered. *A promotion, certainly.* General's stars and a return to Moscow, a plush office at The Centre, a nice flat on Kutusovskiy Prospekt. Going back to Moscow appealed to the *rezident,* who'd spent a lot of years outside the borders of the *Rodina. Enough,* he thought. *More than enough.*

"WHERE'S THE COURIER?" Mary Pat asked, vacuuming the living room rug.

"Over Norway by now," her husband thought out loud.

"I have an idea," she said.

"Oh?" Ed asked with no small degree of trepidation.

"What if we can get the Rabbit out and they don't know?"

"How the hell do we do that?" her husband asked, in surprise. What was she thinking about now? "Getting him and his family out in the first place won't exactly be easy."

She told him the idea she'd evolved in her tricky little head, and an original one it was.

Trust you to come up with something like that, he thought, with a neutral expression. But then he started thinking about it. "Complicated," the Chief of Station observed tersely.

"But doable," she countered.

"Honey, that's a big thought." But he was thinking about it, Mary Pat saw in his eyes.

"Yeah, but if we can pull it off, what a coup," she said, getting under the sofa. Eddie slid himself closer to the TV so that he could hear what the Transformer robots were saying. A good sign. If Eddie couldn't hear, then neither would the KGB microphones.

"It's worth thinking about," Ed conceded. "But doing it—damn."

"Well, they pay us to be creative, don't they?"

"No way in hell we could pull that one off here"—not without involving a whole lot of assets, some of whom might not be entirely reliable, which was, of course, their greatest fear, and one they couldn't easily defend against. That was one of the problems in the spook business. If the counterspies in KGB ID'd one of their assets, they were very often clever about how they handled it. They could, for example, have a little chat with the guy and tell him to keep operating, and then, maybe, he'd live to the end of the year. Their agents were trained to give a danger-wave-off signal, but who was to say that the agent would do it? It demanded a lot from the supposed dedication of their assets, more than some—most—of them would probably give.

"So, there are other places they can go. Eastern Europe, for example. Get them out that way," she suggested.

"I suppose it's possible," he conceded again. "But the mission here *is* to get them out, not score style points from the East German judge."

"I know, but think about it. If we can get him away from Moscow, that gives us a lot more flexibility in our options, doesn't it?"

"Yes, honey. It also means communications problems." And that meant the risk of screwing everything up. The KISS principle—"keep it simple, stupid"—was as much a part of the CIA ethos as the trench coat and fedora hat that people used in bad movies. Too many cooks fucked up the soup.

Yet what she'd suggested had real merit. Getting the Rabbit out in a way that made the Soviets think him dead would mean that they'd take no precautions. It would be like sending Captain Kirk into KGB headquarters by transporter—and invisible—and extracting him without anyone knowing he'd been there, along with tons of hot information. It would be as close to the perfect play as anything that had ever happened. *Hell,* Ed thought, *as perfect a play as* never *happened in the real world.* He reflected for a moment that he was blessed to have a wife as creative in her work as she was in bed.

And that was pretty damned good.

Mary Pat saw her husband's face, and she knew how to read his mind. He was a cautious player, but she'd pushed a very sensitive button, and he was smart enough to see the merit in it. Her idea was a complication . . . but maybe not that great of one. Getting the package out of Moscow would be no day at the beach under the best of circumstances. The hard part would be in crossing the Finnish border—it was always Finland, and everyone knew it. There were ways to do it, and it mostly involved trick cars with hidden passenger accommodations. The Russians had trouble countering that tactic, because if the driver of the car had diplomatic credentials, then international convention limited their search options. Any diplomat who wanted to make fast money could make a small pile by smuggling drugs—and some did, she was sure, and few of them ever got caught. With a get-out-of-jail-free card, you could accomplish a lot. But even that was not an entirely free pass. If the Soviets knew this guy was missing, then rules might get broken because the data inside his head was so valuable. The other side of the diplomatic-rules violation was that it would result only in a protest, muddled up by the public disclosure that an accredited foreign diplomat was spying—and if some of their diplomats got roughed up in the process, well, the Soviets had been known to sacrifice large numbers of military forces for a political end and just think of it as a price of doing business. For the information the Rabbit had, they'd gladly shed blood—including some of their own. Mary Pat wondered how well this guy understood the danger he was in, and how formidable the forces were arrayed against him. What it came down to was whether or not the Sovs knew something was afoot. If not, their routine surveillance procedures, no matter how thorough, were predictable. If alerted, however, they could put the entire city of Moscow under lockdown.

But everything they did in the CIA's Clandestine Service was done carefully, and there were backup procedures for when things went wrong, as well as other measures, some desperate, that had proven to be effective when you put them in play. You just tried to avoid doing that.

"Finishing up," she warned her husband.

"Okay, Mary Pat, you have me thinking." And with that his formidable mind started sifting through ideas. *Sometimes he needs a little push,* Mary Pat thought, but once you had him going in the right direction, he was like George Patton with the bit in his teeth. She wondered how much sleeping Ed would be doing tonight. Well, she'd be able to tell, wouldn't she?

"BASIL LIKES YOU," Murray said. The womenfolk were in the kitchen. Jack and Dan were out in the garden, pretending to inspect the roses.

"Really?"

"Yeah, a lot."

"Damned if I know why," Ryan said. "I haven't turned much work out yet."

"Your roomie reports to him about you every day. Simon Harding is a comer, in case nobody told you. That's why he went with Bas to Number Ten."

"Dan, I thought you were Bureau, not Agency," Jack noted, wondering just how far the Legal Attaché spread himself.

"Well, the guys down the hall are pals, and I interface with the local spooks some." *The guys down the hall* was Dan's way of saying CIA people. Yet again Jack wondered just which branch of the government Murray actually belonged to. But everything about him said "cop" to one who knew what to look for. Was this some elaborate kind of disguise, too? No, not possible. Dan had been the personal troubleshooter for Emil Jacobs, the quiet, competent FBI Director, and that was far too elaborate for a government cover. Besides, Murray didn't run agents in London, did he?

Did he? Nothing was ever what it seemed to be. Ryan hated that aspect of his CIA job, but he had to admit that it kept his mind fully awake. Even drinking a beer in his backyard.

"Well, nice to hear, I suppose."

"Basil's hard to impress, my boy. But he and Judge Moore like each other. Jim Greer, too. Basil just plain loves his analytical ability."

"He's pretty smart," Ryan agreed. "I've learned a lot from him."

"He's making you one of his stars."

"Really?" It didn't always seem that way to Ryan.

"Haven't you noticed how quick he's moving you up? Like you were a professor from Harvard or something, fella."

"Boston College and Georgetown, remember?"

"Yeah, well, us Jesuit products run the world—we're just humble about it. They don't teach 'humble' at Harvard."

For sure they don't encourage their graduates to do anything as plebeian as police work, Ryan thought. He remembered the Harvard kids in Boston, many of whom thought they owned the world—because daddy had bought it for them. Ryan preferred to make the purchase himself, doubtless because of his working-class background. But Cathy wasn't like those upper-class snots, and she *had* been born with a golden spoon in her mouth. Of course, nobody was ever disgraced to point to his son or daughter the doctor, and certainly not to a graduate of Johns Hopkins. *Maybe Joe Muller wasn't so bad a guy after all,* Ryan thought briefly. He'd helped raise a pretty good daughter. Too bad he was an overbearing asshole to his son-in-law.

"So, you like it at Century House?"

"Better than Langley. Too much like a monastery out there. At least in London you live in a city. You can step out for a beer or do some shopping over lunch."

"Shame the building's coming apart. It's the same trouble they've had in some other buildings in London—the mortar or grout, whatever you call it, it's defective. So the façade's peeling off. Embarrassing, but the contractor's gotta be long dead. Can't take a corpse to court."

"You never have?" Jack asked, lightheartedly.

Murray shook his head. "No, I've never popped a cap on anyone. Came close once, but stopped short. Good thing, too. Turned out the mutt wasn't armed. Would have been embarrassing to explain that to the judge," he added, sipping his beer.

"So, how are the local cops doing?" It was Murray's job to interface with them after all.

"They're pretty good, really. Well organized, good investigators for the major stuff. Not much street crime for them to worry about."

"Not like New York or D.C."

"Not hardly. So, anything interesting shaking at Century House?" he asked.

"Not really. Mainly, I've been looking over old stuff, back-checking old analysis against newly developed data. Nothing worth writing home about—but I have to do that anyway. The Admiral is keeping me on a long leash, but it's still a leash."

"What do you think of our cousins?"

"Basil is pretty smart," Ryan observed. "But he's careful about what he shows me. That's fair, I suppose. He knows that I'm reporting back to Langley, and I really don't need to know much about sources. . . . But I can make some guesses. 'Six' has gotta have some good people in Moscow." Ryan paused. "Damned if I'd ever play that game. Our prisons are pretty nasty. I don't even want to think about what the Russian ones are like."

"You wouldn't live long enough to find out, Jack. They're not the most forgiving people in the world, especially on espionage. You're a lot safer whacking a cop right in front of the precinct station than playing spy."

"And with us?"

"It's amazing—how patriotic convicts are, that is. Spies do very hard time in the Federal prisons. Them and child molesters. They get a lot of attention from Bubba and his armed-robber friends—you know, honest crooks."

"Yeah, my dad talked about that once in a while, how there's a hierarchy in prison, and you don't want to be on the bottom.

"Better to be a pitcher than a catcher." Murray laughed.

It was time for a real question: "So, Dan, just how tight are you with the spook shops?"

Murray surveyed the horizon. "Oh, we get along pretty nicely" was all he was willing to say.

"You know, Dan," Jack observed, "if there's anything I've learned to worry about over here, it's understatement."

Murray liked that one. "Well, then you're living in the wrong place, son. They all talk like that over here."

"Yeah, especially in the spook shops."

"Well, if we talked like everybody else, then the mystique would be gone, and people would understand how screwed up everything really is." Murray had a sip and grinned broadly. "We couldn't maintain the confidence of the people that way. I bet it's the same with doctors and stockbrokers," the FBI rep suggested.

"Every business has its own insiders language." The supposed reason was that it offered more speedy and efficient communications to those inside the fold—but the truth of the matter, of course, was that it denied knowledge and/or access to outsiders. But that was really okay if you were one of the people on the inside.

THE BAD NEWS happened in Budapest, and it resulted from pure bad luck. The agent wasn't even all that important. He provided information on the Hungarian Air Force, but that was an organization that no one took very seriously at best, along with the rest of the Hungarian military, which had rarely distinguished itself on the field of battle. Marxism-Leninism had never really taken firm root here anyway, but the state did have a hardworking, if not especially competent, intelligence/counterintelligence service, and not all of them were stupid. Some of them were even KGB-trained, and if there was anything the Soviets knew, it was intelligence and counterintelligence. This officer, Andreas Morrisay, was just sitting, drinking his morning coffee in a shop on Andrassy Utca, when he saw someone make a mistake. He would not have caught it had he not been bored with his newspaper, but there it was. A Hungarian national—you could tell from his clothing—dropped something. It was about the size of a tin of pipe tobacco. He quickly bent down to pick it up, and then, remarkably enough, he stuck it to the underside of his table. And, Andreas saw, it didn't fall off. It must have some sort of adhesive on the side. And that sort of thing was not only unusual, but also one of the things he'd been shown in a training film at the KGB Academy outside Moscow. It was a very simple and obsolete form of dead-drop, something used by enemy spies to transfer information. It was, Andreas thought, like walking unexpectedly into the cinema and watching a spy film and knowing what was happening just on pure instinct. His immediate reaction was to walk off to the men's room, where there was a pay phone. There he dialed his office and spoke for less than thirty seconds. Next he made use of the men's room, because this might take a while, and he was suddenly excited. No harm was done. The head office of his agency was only a half-dozen blocks away, and two of his coworkers came in, took their seats, and ordered their coffee, talking with apparent animation about something or other. Andreas was relatively new in his job—just two years—and he'd yet to catch anyone doing anything. But this was his day, the officer knew. He was looking at a spy. A Hungarian national who was working for some foreign power, and even if he were giving information to the Soviet KGB, he was committing a crime for which he could be arrested—though in that case, it would be cleared up quickly by the KGB liaison officer. After another ten minutes, the Hungarian rose and walked out, with one of the two other officers in trail.

What followed was, well, nothing, for more than an hour. Andreas ordered some strudel—every bit as tasty here as it was in Vienna, three hundred kilometers away, and this despite the Marxist government in the country, because the Hungarians loved their food, and Hungary was a productive agricultural country, despite the command economy imposed on the farmers to the east. Andreas lit up a string of cigarettes, read his newspaper, and just waited for something to happen.

Presently, it did. A man dressed a little too well to be a Hungarian citizen took his seat at the table next to his, lit a cigarette of his own, and read *his* newspaper.

Here it worked for Andreas that he was badly nearsighted. His glasses were so thick that it took a few seconds for anyone to see where his eyes were pointed, and he remembered his training enough not to allow his eyes to linger on any one spot more than a few brief seconds. Mainly he appeared to be reading his paper, like half a dozen others in this elegant little shop, which had somehow survived the Second World War. He watched the American—Andreas had it fixed in his mind that this one had to be an American—sip his own coffee and read his own paper, until he set his coffee cup down in the saucer, then reached into his hip pocket for a handkerchief, which he used to wipe his nose, and then replaced in the pocket. . . .

But first he retrieved the tobacco tin from under the table. It was a move so skillfully done that only a trained counterintelligence officer could have spotted it, but, Andreas told himself, that was exactly what he was. And it was his pride that generated his first and most costly mistake of the day.

The American finished his coffee and took his leave, with Andreas in close pursuit. The foreigner walked toward the underground station a block away and nearly made it. But not quite. He turned in surprise when he felt a hand on his upper arm.

"Could I see the tobacco tin that you took from the table?" Andreas said, politely, because this foreigner was probably, technically speaking, a diplomat.

"Excuse me?" the foreigner said, and his accent made him either British or American.

"The one in your pants pocket," Andreas clarified.

"I do not know what you are talking about, and I have business to do." The man started to walk away.

He didn't get far. Andreas pulled out his pistol. It was a Czech Agrozet Model 50 and it effectively ended the conversation. But not quite.

"What is this? Who are you?"

"Papers." Andreas held out his hand, keeping his pistol in close. "We already have your contact. You are," he added, "under arrest."

In the movies, the American would have drawn his own side arm and tried to make his escape down the twenty-eight steps into the ancient metro. But the American's fear was that this guy had seen too many movies himself, and it might make him nervous enough to pull the trigger on his Czech piece-of-shit handgun. So he reached into his coat pocket, very slowly and deliberately, lest he scare the idiot, and withdrew his passport. It was a black one, the sort issued to diplomats, and instantly recognizable to lucky asses like this stupid, fucking Hunky. The American's name was James Szell, and he was by ancestry Hungarian, one of the many minorities welcomed to the America of the previous century.

"I am an American diplomat, properly accredited to your government. You will take me to my embassy immediately." Inwardly, Szell was seething. His face didn't show it, of course, but his five years in the field had just come to a screeching halt. All this over a rookie second-rate agent furnishing second-rate information about a third-rate communist air force. *Goddamn it!*

"First you will come with me," Andreas told him. He motioned with his pistol. "This way."

THE PAN AM 747 LANDED at Kennedy half an hour early due to favorable winds. Cox put his books back in his carry-on and stood, managing to be the first passenger off, with a little help from the stewardess. From there, it was a quick walk through customs—his canvas bag told everyone who and what he was—and from there to the next shuttle to Washington National. A total of ninety minutes later, he was in the back of a cab to the State Department at Foggy Bottom. Inside that capacious building, he opened the Diplomatic Bag and parceled out the various contents. The envelope from Foley was handed to a courier, who drove up the George Washington Parkway to Langley, where things also move fairly fast.

The message was hand-carried to MERCURY, the CIA's message center, and, once decrypted and printed up, hand-delivered to the Seventh Floor. The original was put in the burn bag, and no hard copies were kept, though an electronic one was transferred to a VHS cassette, which ended up in a slot in Sneezy.

Mike Bostock was in his office, and when he saw the envelope from Moscow, he decided that everything else could wait. It surely could, he saw at once, but when he checked his watch he knew that Bob Ritter was over eastern Ohio and heading west on an All Nippon Airlines 747. So he called Judge Moore at home, and requested that he come in to the office. Grumbling, the DCI agreed to do so, at once, also telling Bostock to call Jim Greer as well. Both lived agreeably close to CIA headquarters, and they came out of the executive elevator just eight minutes apart.

"What is it, Mike?" Moore asked on his arrival.

"From Foley. Looks like he has something interesting." Cowboy or not, Bostock was one to understate things.

"Damn," the DCI breathed. "And Bob's already gone?"

"Yes, sir, just an hour ago."

"What is it, Arthur?" Admiral Greer asked, wearing a cheap golf shirt.

"We got us a Rabbit." Moore handed the message over.

Greer took his time going over it. "This could be very interesting," he thought, after a moment's reflection.

"Yes, it could." Moore turned to the deputy of the Operations Directorate. "Mike, talk to me."

"Foley thinks it's hot. Ed's as good a field officer as anybody we have, and so's his wife. He wants to exfiltrate this guy and his family soonest. We pretty much have to go with his instincts on this one, Judge."

"Problems?"

"The question is: How do we accomplish the mission? Ordinarily, we leave that to the people in the field, unless they try to pull something crazy, but Ed and Mary are too smart for that." Bostock took a breath and looked out the floor-length windows to the Potomac Valley, out beyond the VIP parking lot. "Judge, Ed seems to think this guy has some very hot information. We can't question him on that. The obvious supposition is that the Rabbit's pretty far inside, and he wants to get the hell out of Dodge City. Adding the wife and daughter to the package is a serious complication. Again, we pretty much have to go with the instincts of our field personnel. It would be nice if we could run the guy as an agent, have him deliver information on a continuing basis, but for some reason either that isn't feasible, or Ed thinks he has what we need and want already."

"Why couldn't he tell us more?" Greer observed, still holding the dispatch.

"Well, it's possible that he was time-limited on getting this to the bagman, or he didn't trust the courier system with stuff that could ID the guy to the opposition. Whatever this guy has, Ed didn't want to trust normal communications channels, and that, gentlemen, is a message in and of itself."

"So, you say approve the request?" Moore asked.

"Not a hell of a lot else we can do," Bostock pointed out rather obviously.

"Okay—approved," the DCI said officially. "Get it off to him, right now."

"Yes, sir." And Bostock left the room.

Greer had himself a chuckle. "Bob's going to be pissed."

"What can be so important that Foley would want to short-circuit procedures this abruptly?" Moore wondered aloud.

"We're just going to have to wait to find out."

"I suppose, but you know, patience has never been my long suit."

"Well, think of this as a chance to acquire a virtue, Arthur."

"Great." Moore stood. He could go home now and grumble all day, like a kid on Christmas Eve, wondering what was going to be under the tree—if Christmas was really going to happen this year.

CHAPTER 18

CLASSICAL MUSIC

THE BOUNCE-BACK SIGNAL arrived after midnight in Moscow, where it was printed up and walked to Mike Russell's desk by the night communications officer and promptly forgotten. Due to the eight-hour time difference from Washington, this was often the busiest time for inbound signals, and that one was just another piece of paper with gibberish on it, one which he was not allowed to decrypt.

AS MARY PAT had expected, Ed hadn't gotten any sleep to speak of, but had done his best not to roll around too much, lest he disturb his wife. Doubts were also part of the espionage game. Was Oleg Ivan'ch a false-flag, some random attempt from the KGB on which he'd bitten down a little too fast and a little too hard? Had the Soviets just gone fishing at random and landed a big blue marlin on the first try? Did KGB play such games? Not according to his lengthy mission briefing at Langley. They'd played similar games in the past, but those had been targeted deliberately toward people whom they knew to be players, from whom they could get a line on other agents just by following them around to check out drop sites. . . .

But you didn't play it this way. You didn't ask for a ticket out on the first go-round unless you really wanted something specific, like the neutralization of a particular target—and that couldn't be it. He and Mary Pat hadn't *done* much of anything yet. Hell, only a handful of people at the embassy knew who and what he was. He hadn't recruited new agents yet, nor worked any existing ones. That wasn't, strictly speaking, his job. The Chief of Station wasn't supposed to work the field. He was supposed to direct and supervise those who did, like Dom Corso and Mary Pat and the rest of his small but expert crew.

And if Ivan knew who he was, why tip its hand so quickly—it would only tell CIA more than it knew now, or could easily learn. You didn't play the spy game that way.

Okay, what if the Rabbit was a throwaway, whose job it was to ID Foley and then give over useless or false information—what if the whole job had as its objective nothing more than to ID the COS Moscow? But they couldn't have targeted him without knowing who he was, could they? Even KGB didn't have the assets to shotgun such a mission and ping on every embassy staffer—it was way too clumsy and was certain to alert embassy personnel to something very strange under way.

No, KGB was too professional for that.

So they couldn't target him without knowing, and if they knew, they'd want to hide that information, lest they alert CIA to a source or method that they'd be far better advised to conceal.

So Oleg Ivanovich couldn't be a false-flag, and that was that.

So, he *had to be* the real thing. Didn't he?

For all his intelligence and experience, Foley could not come up with a construct that made the Rabbit anything but the genuine item. The problem was that it made little sense.

But what in espionage ever made sense?

What *did* make sense was the necessity of getting this guy out. They had a Rabbit, and the Rabbit needed to run away from the Bear.

"YOU CAN'T SAY what's bothering you?" Cathy asked.

"Nope."

"But it's important?"

"Yep." He nodded. "Yeah, it sure is, but the problem is that we don't know how serious."

"Something for me to worry about?"

"Well, no. It's not World War Three or anything like that. But I really can't talk about it."

"Why?"

"You know why—it's classified. You don't tell me about your patients, do you? That's because you have rules of ethics, and I have rules of classification." Smart as Cathy was, she still hadn't fully grasped that one yet.

"Isn't there any way I can help?"

"Cathy, if you were cleared for this, maybe you could offer insights. But maybe not. You're not a pshrink, and that's the medical field that applies to this—how people respond to threats, what their motivations are, how they perceive reality, and how those perceptions determine their actions. I've been trying to get inside the heads of people I haven't met to figure out what they're going to do about something. I've been studying how they think for quite a while, even before I joined the Agency, but you know—"

"Yeah, it's hard to look inside somebody's brain. And you know what?"

"What's that?"

"It's harder with the sane ones than the crazy ones. People can think rationally and still do crazy things."

"Because of their perceptions?"

She nodded. "Partially that, but partially because they've chosen to believe totally false things—for entirely rational reasons, but the things they believe in are still false."

This struck Ryan as worth pursuing. "Okay. Tell me about . . . Josef Stalin, for instance. He killed a lot of people. Why?"

"Part of it was rational, and part of it was wild paranoia. When he saw a threat, he dealt with it decisively. But he tended to see threats that weren't there or weren't serious enough to merit deadly force. Stalin lived on the borderline between madness and normality, and he crossed back and forth like a guy on a bridge who couldn't make up his mind about where he lived. In international affairs, he was supposed to be just as rational as everybody else, but he had a ruthless streak and nobody ever said 'no' to him. One of the docs at Hopkins wrote a book on the guy. I read it when I was in med school."

"What did it say?"

Mrs. Dr. Ryan shrugged. "It wasn't all that satisfactory. The current thinking is that it's chemical imbalances in the brain that cause mental illness, not whether your dad slapped you around too much or you saw your mom in bed with a goat. But we can't test Stalin's blood chemistry now, can we?"

"Not hardly. I think they finally burned him up and put him in—where? I don't remember," Jack admitted. It wasn't the Kremlin wall, was it? Or maybe they just buried the pine box instead of burning it all up. It wasn't worth finding out, was it?

"It's funny. A lot of historical figures did the stuff they did because they were mentally unstable. Today, we could fix them with lithium or other stuff we've learned about—mainly in the last thirty years or so—but back then, all they had was alcohol and iodine. Or maybe an exorcism," she added, wondering if those were real.

"And Rasputin had a bad chemical imbalance, too?" Jack wondered aloud.

"Maybe. I don't know much about that, except he was supposed to be a crazy kinda priest, wasn't he?"

"Not a priest, some kinda mystic civilian. I suppose today he'd be a TV evangelist, right? Whatever he was, he brought down the House of Romanov—but they were pretty useless anyway."

"And then Stalin took over?"

"Lenin first, then Stalin. Vladimir Ilyich checked out from strokes."

"Hypertensive, maybe, or just cholesterol buildup and he clotted in the brain and that did him. And Stalin was worse, right?"

"Lenin was no day at the beach, but Stalin was pretty amazing—Tamerlane come back to the twentieth century, or maybe one of the Caesars. When the Romans reconquered a rebellious city, they killed everything there was, right down to the dogs."

"Really?"

"Yeah, but the Brits always spared the dogs. Too sentimental about them," Jack added.

"Sally misses Ernie," Cathy reminded him in female fashion—almost, but not totally irrelevant to the conversation. Ernie was their dog back home.

"So do I, but he's going to have a lot of fun this fall—duck season soon. He'll get to retrieve all the dead birds out of the water."

Cathy shivered. She'd never hunted anything more alive than the hamburger at the local supermarket—but she carved up human beings with knives. *Like* that *makes any sense,* Ryan thought with a wry smile. But the world had no rule that required logic on its surface—not the last time he'd checked.

"Don't worry, babe. Ernie will like it. Trust me."

"Yeah, sure."

"He loves to go swimming," Jack pointed out, extending the needle. "So, what interesting eyeball problems at the hospital next week?"

"Just routine stuff—checking eyes and prescribing glasses all week."

"No fun stuff, like cutting some poor bastard's left eye in half and then sewing it back together?"

"That's not a procedure," she pointed out.

"Babe, I could never cut into a person's eyeball with a knife without tossing my cookies—or maybe fainting." The very thought of it made him shiver.

"Wimp" was all she had to say about that admission. She didn't understand that this was a skill not covered in the Marine Corps Basic School at Quantico, Virginia.

MARY PAT COULD feel that her husband was still awake, but it wasn't a time to talk, even with their personal hand-jive technique. Instead she was thinking about operations—how to get the package out. Moscow would be too hard. Other parts of the Soviet Union were no easier, because Moscow Station didn't have all that many assets it could use elsewhere in this vast country—intelligence operations tended to be centered in national capitals because that was where you could place "diplomats" who were truly wolves in sheep's clothing. The obvious counter for that was to use your government capital just for strictly government-related administrative services, distanced from military and other sensitive affairs, but nobody would do that, for the simple reason that government big shots wanted all their functionaries within arm's length so that *they*—the big shots—could enjoy their exercise of power. And that was what they all lived for, whether it was in Moscow, Hitler's Berlin, or Washington, D.C.

So, if not out of Moscow, then where? There were only so many places the Rabbit was free to go. Nowhere west of the wire, as she thought of the Iron Curtain that had fallen across Europe in 1945. And there were few places where a man like him could plausibly want to go that were convenient to CIA. The beaches at Sochi, perhaps. Theoretically, the Navy could get a submarine there and make the snatch, but you couldn't just whistle up a submarine, and the Navy would have a cow over that, just for having it asked of them.

That left the fraternal socialist states of Eastern Europe, which were about as exciting as tourist spots as central Mississippi in the summer: a good place to go if you got off on cotton plantations and blazing heat, but otherwise why bother? Poland was out. Warsaw had been rebuilt after the Wehrmacht's harsh version of urban renewal, but Poland right now was a very tight place due to its internal political troubles, and the easiest exit point, Gdansk, was now as tightly guarded as the Russian-Polish border. It hadn't helped that the Brits had arranged for the purloining of a new Russian T-72 main battle tank there. Mary Pat hoped the stolen tank was useful to somebody, but some idiot in London had bragged about it to the newspapers and the story had broken, ending Gdansk's utility as a port of exit for the next few years. The DDR, perhaps? But few Russians cared a rat's ass about Germany, and there was little there for them to want to see. Czechoslovakia? An interesting city supposedly, landmarked with imperial architecture, and a good cultural life. Their symphonies and ballet were almost on a class with the Russians' own, and the art galleries were supposedly excellent. But the Czech-Austrian border was also very tightly guarded.

That left . . . Hungary.

Hungary, she thought. Budapest was also an old imperial city, once ruled sternly by the Austrian Hapsburg dynasty, conquered by the Russians in 1945 after a nasty, prolonged battle with the German SS, probably rebuilt to whatever former glory it had enjoyed a hundred years before. It was not enthusiastically communist, as they'd demonstrated in 1956, before being harshly put down by the Russians, at Khrushchev's personal orders, and then under Andropov's stewardship as USSR Ambasssador reestablished as a happy socialist brotherhood, though one more loosely governed after the brief and bloody rebellion. The head rebels had all been hanged, shot, or otherwise disposed of. Forgiveness had never been a Marxist-Leninist virtue.

But a lot of Russians took the train to Budapest. It was the neighbor of Yugoslavia, the communist San Francisco, a place where Russians could not go without permission, but Hungary traded freely with Yugoslavia, and so Soviet citizens could purchase VCRs, Reebok running shoes, and Fogal pantyhose there. Typically, Russians went there with one suitcase full and two or three empty, and a shopping list for all their friends.

Soviets could travel there with reasonable freedom, because they had Comecon rubles, which all socialist countries were required to honor by the socialist Big Brother in Moscow. Budapest was, in fact, the boutique of the Eastern Bloc. You could even get X-rated tapes for the tape machines that were manufactured there—rip-offs of Japanese designs, reverse-engineered and made in their own fraternal socialist factories. The tapes were smuggled in from Yugoslavia and copied—everywhere, everything from *The Sound of Music* to *Debbie Does Dallas.* Budapest had decent art galleries and historical sites, good orchestras, and the food was supposed to be pretty good. An entirely plausible place for the Rabbit to go, with every ostensible intention of going back to his beloved *Rodina.*

That's the beginning of a plan, Mary Pat thought. That was also enough lost sleep for one night.

"SO, WHAT HAPPENED?" the Ambassador asked.

"An AVH spook was having coffee one table away from where my agent made a drop," Szell explained in the Ambassador's private office. It was located on the top floor, in the corner—in fact, in the quarters once occupied by Jozsef Cardinal Mindszenty during his lengthy residency at the U.S. Embassy. A beloved figure both in the eyes of the American staffers and the Hungarian people, he'd been imprisoned by the Nazis, released by the arriving Red Army, and promptly returned to prison for not being enthusiastic enough over the advent of the New Faith of Russia, though, technically, he'd been imprisoned on the far-fetched charges of being a raging royalist who wished to return the House of Hapsburg to imperial rule. The local communists hadn't been overly strong on creative writing. Even at the turn of the twentieth century, the Hapsburgs had been about as popular in Budapest as a bargeload of plague rats.

"Why were you doing it, Jim?" Ambassador Peter "Spike" Ericsson asked. He'd have to reply to the venomous, but entirely predictable, communiqué that had arrived with the Station Chief, which was now sitting in the center of his desk.

"Bob Taylor's wife—she's pregnant, remember?—had some plumbing problems, and they flew 'em both off to Second Army General Hospital up at Kaiserslauten to get checked out."

Ericsson grunted. "Yeah, I forgot."

"Anyway, the short version is, I blew it," Szell had to admit. It just wasn't his way to cover things up. It would cause a major hiccup in his CIA career, but that couldn't be helped. Damned sure it was a lot rougher right now for that poor clumsy bastard who'd screwed up the transfer. The Hungarian State Security Authority—*Allavedelmi Hatosag,* or AVH—officers who'd interrogated him evidently hadn't had a good gloat in some time, and had made a point of telling him how easily he'd been bagged. *Fucking amateurs,* Szell raged. But the end of the game was that he was now PNG'd, declared *persona non grata* by the Hungarian government, and requested to leave the country in forty-eight hours—preferably, with his tail tucked firmly between his legs.

"Sorry to lose you, Bob, but there's nothing much I can do."

"And I'm pretty useless to the team now anyway. I know." Szell let out a long and frustrated breath. He'd been here long enough to set up a pretty good little spy shop, providing fairly good political and military information—none of it overly important, because Hungary was not an overly important country, but you just never knew when something of interest would happen, even in Lesotho—which might well be his next posting, Szell reflected. He'd have to buy some sunblock and a nice bush jacket. . . . At least he'd get to catch the World Series back at home.

But for now, Station Budapest was out of business. *Not that Langley would really miss it,* Szell consoled himself.

The signal about this would go to Foggy Bottom via embassy telex—encrypted, of course. Ambassador Ericsson drafted his reply to the Hungarian Foreign Ministry, rejecting out of hand the absurd allegation that James Szell, Second Secretary to the Embassy of the United States of America, had done anything inconsistent with his diplomatic status, and lodging an official protest in the name of the U.S. Department of State. Perhaps in the next week, Washington would send some Hungarian diplomat back—whether he was a sheep or a goat would be decided in Washington. Ericsson thought it would be a sheep. Why let on that the FBI had ID'd a goat, after all? Better to let the goat continue to munch away in whatever garden it had invaded—under close observation. And so the game went on. The Ambassador thought it a stupid game, but every member of his staff played it with greater or lesser enthusiasm.

THE MESSAGE ABOUT SZELL, it turned out, was sufficiently under the radar so that when it was forwarded to CIA headquarters, it was tucked into routine traffic as not worthy of interfering with the DCI's weekend—Judge Moore got a morning brief every single day anyway, of course, and this item would wait until 8:00 A.M. Sunday, the watch officers collectively decided, because judges liked an orderly life. And Budapest wasn't all that important in the Great Scheme of Things, was it?

SUNDAY MORNING IN Moscow was much the same as Sunday morning everywhere else, albeit with fewer people getting dressed up for church. That was true for Ed and Mary Pat, also. A Catholic priest celebrated mass at the U.S. Embassy on Sunday mornings, but most of the time they didn't make it—though they were both Catholic enough to feel guilt for their slothful transgressions. They both told themselves that their guilt was mitigated by the fact that they were both doing God's own work right in the center of the land of the heathen. So the plan for today was to take Eddie for a walk in the park, where he might meet some kids to play with. At least, that was Eddie's mission brief. Ed rolled out of bed and headed to the bathroom first, followed by his wife and then by little Eddie. No morning paper, and the Sunday TV programming was every bit as bad as it was the rest of the week. So they actually had to talk over breakfast, something many Americans find hard to do. Their son was still young and impressionable enough to find Moscow interesting, though nearly all of his friends were Americans or Brits: inmates, like his entire family, in the compound/ghetto, guarded by MGB or KGB—opinions were divided on that question, but everyone knew it made little real difference.

The meeting was set for 11:00. Oleg Ivan'ch would be easy to spot—as would she, Mary Pat knew. Like a peacock among crows, her husband liked to say (even though the peacock was actually a male bird). She decided to play it down today. No makeup, just casually brushed-out hair, jeans, and a pullover shirt. She couldn't change her figure very much—the local aesthetic preferred women of her height to be about ten kilograms heavier. Diet, she supposed. Or maybe when you had food available in what was largely a hungry country, you ate it. Maybe the fat layer you acquired made the winters more comfortable? Whatever, the level of fashion for the average Russian female was like something from a Dead End Kids movie. You could tell the wives of important people easily, because their clothes looked almost middle-class, as opposed to the more normal Appalachia class of dress. But that was grossly unfair to the people of Appalachia, Mary Pat decided.

"You coming, Ed?" she asked after breakfast.

"No, honey. I'll clean up the kitchen and get into this new book I got last week."

"The truck driver did it," she offered. "I've read that guy before."

"Thanks a bunch," her husband grumbled.

And with that, she checked her watch and headed out. The park was just three of the long blocks to the east. She waved to the gate guard—definitely KGB, she thought—and headed to the left, holding little Eddie's hand. The traffic on the street was minimal by American standards, and it was definitely getting cooler out. She was glad she'd dressed her son in a long-sleeve shirt. A turn to look down at him revealed no obvious tail. There could, of course, be binoculars in the apartments across the street, but somehow she thought not. She'd pretty well established herself as a dumb American blonde, and just about everyone bought it. Even Ed's press contacts thought her dumber than him—and they thought him to be an ass—which could not have suited her any better. Those chattering blackbirds repeated everything she and Ed said to one another, until the word was as uniformly spread as the icing on one of her cakes. It all got back to KGB as quickly as any rumor could go—damned near the speed of light in that community, because reporters did intellectual incest as a way of life—and the Russians listened to them and put everything in their voluminous dossiers until it became something that "everybody knows." A good field officer always used others to build his or her cover. Such a cover was random-sounding—just as real life always was—and that made it plausible, even to a professional spook.

The park was about as bleak as everything else in Moscow. A few trees, some badly trodden grass. Almost as though KGB had had all the parks trimmed to make them bad contact points. That it would also limit places for young Muscovites to rendezvous and trade some kisses probably would not have troubled the consciences at The Centre, which were probably about the Pontius Pilate level on a reflective day.

And there was the Rabbit, a hundred meters or so away, nicely located, near some play items that would appeal to a three-year-old—or a four-year-old. Walking closer, she saw again that Russians doted on their little ones, and, in this case, maybe a little more—the Rabbit was KGB, and so he had access to better consumer goods than the average Russian, which, like a good parent in any land, he lavished on his little girl. That was a good sign for his character, Mary Pat decided. Maybe she could even like this guy, an unexpected gift for a field officer. So many agents were screwed up as badly as a South Bronx street mugger. He didn't observe her approach any more than to turn and scan the area in boredom, as men walking their children did. The two Americans headed the right way in what would surely appear to be a random act.

"Eddie, there's a little girl you can say hello to. Try out your Russian on her," his mommy suggested.

"Okay!" and he raced off in the manner of toddlers. Little Eddie ran right up to her and said "Hello."

"Hello."

"My name is Eddie."

"My name is Svetlana Olegovna. Where do you live?"

"That way." Eddie pointed back to the foreigners' ghetto.

"That is your son?" the Rabbit asked.

"Yes, Eddie Junior. Edward Edwardovich to you."

"So," Oleg Ivan'ch said next, without amusement, "is he also CIA?"

"Not exactly." Almost theatrically, she extended her hand to him. She had to protect him, just in case cameras were about. "I am Mary Patricia Foley."

"I see. Does your husband like his *shapka*?"

"Actually, he does. You have good taste in furs."

"Many Russians do." Then he switched gears. It was time to go back to business. "Have you decided that you can help me or not?"

"Yes, Oleg Ivan'ch, we can. Your daughter is darling. Her name is Svetlana?"

The communications officer nodded. "Yes, that is my little *zaichik*."

The irony of that was positively eerie. Their Rabbit called his little girl his bunny. It generated a brilliant smile. "So, Oleg, how do we get you to America?"

"You ask me this?" he asked with no small degree of incredulity.

"Well, we need some information. Your hobbies and interests, for example, and your wife's."

"I play chess. More than anything else, I read books on old chess matches. My wife is more classically educated than I. She loves music—classical music, not the trash you make in America."

"Any particular composer?"

He shook his head. "Any of the classical composers, Bach, Mozart, Brahms—I do not know all of the names. It is Irina's passion. She studied piano as a child, but wasn't quite good enough to get official state training. That is her greatest regret, and we do not have a piano for her to practice on," he added, knowing that he had to give her this kind of information to assist in her efforts to save him and his family. "What else do you require?"

"Do any of you have any health problems—medications, for example?" They were speaking in Russian again, and Oleg noted her elegant language skills.

"No, we are all quite healthy. My Svetlana has been through all the usual childhood diseases, but without complications of any sort."

"Good." *That simplifies a lot of things,* Mary Pat thought. "She's a lovely little girl. You must be very proud of her."

"But will she like life in the West?" he worried aloud.

"Oleg Ivan'ch, no child has ever had reason to dislike life in America."

"And how does your little Edward like things in the Soviet Union?"

"He misses his friends, of course, but right before we came over, we took him to Disney World. He still talks a lot about that."

Then came a surprise: "Disney World? What is that?"

"It is a large commercial business made for the pleasure of children—and for adults who remember their childhood. It's in Florida," she added.

"I've never heard of it."

"You will find it remarkable and most enjoyable. More so for your daughter." She paused. "What does your wife think of your plans?"

"Irina knows nothing of this," Zaitzev said, surprising the hell out of his American interlocutor.

"What did you say?" *Are you out of your fucking mind?* MP wondered at once.

"Irina is a good wife to me. She will do what I tell her to do." Russian male chauvinism was of the aggressive variety.

"Oleg Ivan'ch, that is most dangerous for you. You must know that."

"The danger to me is being caught by KGB. If that happens, I am a dead man, and so is someone else," he added, thinking a further dangle was in his interest.

"Why are you leaving? What convinced you that it is necessary?" she had to ask.

"KGB is planning to kill a man who does not deserve to die."

"Who?" And she had to ask that one, too.

"That I will tell you when I am in the West."

"That is a fair response," she had to say in reply. *Playing a little cagey, aren't we?*

"One other thing," he added.

"Yes?"

"Be very careful what items you transmit to your headquarters. There is reason to believe your communications are compromised. You should use one-time pads, as we do at The Centre. Do you understand what I am telling you?"

"All communications about you were first encrypted and then dispatched by Diplomatic Bag to Washington." When she said that, the relief on his face was real, much as he tried to hide it. And the Rabbit had just told her something of very great importance. "Are we penetrated?"

"That, also, is something I will discuss only in the West."

Oh, shit, Mary Pat thought. *They have a mole somewhere, and he might be in the White House Rose Garden for all we know. Oh, shit . . .*

"Very well, we will take the utmost security with your case," she promised. But that meant that there'd be a two-day minimum turnaround time for important signals. It was back to World War One procedures with this guy. Ritter would just love that. "Can you tell me what methods might be safe?"

"The British changed their cipher machines about four months ago. We have as yet had no success in cracking them. That I know. Exactly which of your signals are compromised, I do not know, but I do know that some are fully penetrated. Please keep this in mind."

"That I will do, Oleg Ivan'ch." This guy had information that CIA needed—big-time. Cracked communications were the most dangerous things that could happen to any covert agency. Wars had been won and lost over such things as that. The Russians lacked American computer technology, but they did have some of the world's finest mathematicians, and the brain between a person's ears was the most dangerous instrument of all, and a damned site more competent that the ones that sat on a desk or a floor. Did Mike Russell have any of the old one-time pads at the embassy? CIA had used them once upon a time, but their cumbersome nature had caused them to be discarded. NSA told everybody who'd listen that on his best day, Seymour Cray couldn't brute-force their ciphers, even with his brand-new CRAY-2 supercomputer on amphetamines. If they were wrong, it could hurt America in ways too vast to comprehend. But there were many cipher systems, and those who cracked one could not necessarily crack another. Or so everybody said . . . but communications security was not her area of expertise. Even she had to trust someone and something once in a while. But this was like being shot in the back by the starting gun in a hundred-meter race and having to run for the tape anyway. Damn.

"It is an inconvenience, but we will do what is necessary to protect you. You want to be taken out soon."

"This week would be very helpful—not so much for my needs as for the needs of a man whose life is in danger."

"I see," she said, not quite seeing. This guy might be laying a line on her, but if so, he was doing it like a real pro, and she wasn't getting that signal from this guy. No, he didn't read like an experienced field spook. He was a player, but not her kind of player.

"Very well. When you get to work tomorrow, make a contact report," she told him.

That one surprised him: "Are you serious?"

"Of course. Tell your supervisor that you met an American, the wife of a minor embassy official. Describe me and my son—"

"And tell them you are a pretty but shallow American female who has a handsome and polite little boy," he surmised. "And your Russian needs a little work, shall we say?"

"You learn quickly, Oleg Ivan'ch. I bet you play a good game of chess."

"Not good enough. I will never be a Grand Master."

"We all have our limitations, but in America you will find them far more distant than they are in the Soviet Union."

"By the end of the week?"

"When my husband wears his bright red tie, you set the time and place for a meeting. Possibly by tomorrow afternoon you will get your signal, and we will make the arrangements."

"Good day to you, then. Where did you learn your Russian?"

"My grandfather was equerry to Aleksey Nikolayevich Romanov," she explained. "In my childhood, he told me many stories about the young man and his untimely death."

"So, your hatred for the Soviet Union runs deep, eh?"

"Only for your government, Oleg. Not for the people of this country. I would see you free."

"Someday, perhaps, but not soon."

"History, Oleg Ivan'ch, is made not of a few big things but of many small things." That was one of her core beliefs. Again, for the cameras that might be there or not, she shook his hand and called her son. They walked around the park for another hour before heading back home for lunch.

But for lunch instead they all drove to the embassy, talking on the way about nothing more sensitive than the admirably clear weather. Once there, they all had hot dogs in the embassy canteen, and then Eddie went to the day-care room. Ed and Mary Pat went to his office.

"He said what?" the Chief of Station snapped.

"He said his wife—named Irina, by the way—doesn't know his plans," Mary Pat repeated.

"Son of a *bitch!*" her husband observed at once.

"Well, it does simplify some of our exposure. At least she can't let anything slip." His wife was always the optimist, Ed saw.

"Yeah, baby, until we try to make the exfiltration, and she decides not to go anywhere."

"He says she'll do what he says. You know, the men here like to rule the roost."

"That wouldn't work with you," the Chief of Station pointed out. For several reasons, not the least of which was that her balls were every bit as big as his.

"I'm not Russian, Eddie."

"Okay, what else did he say?"

"He doesn't trust our comms. He thinks some of our systems are compromised."

"Jesus!" He paused. "Any other good news?"

"The reason he's skipping town is that KGB wants to kill somebody who, he says, doesn't deserve to be killed."

"Did he say who?"

"Not until he breathes free air. But there is good news. His wife is a classical music buff. We need to find a good conductor in Hungary."

"Hungary?"

"I was thinking last night. Best place to get him out from. That's Jimmy Szell's station, isn't it?"

"Yeah." They both knew Szell from time at The Farm, CIA's training installation in Tidewater, Virginia, off Interstate 64, a few miles from Colonial Williamsburg. "I always thought he deserved something bigger." Ed took a second to think. "So, out of Hungary via Yugoslavia, you're thinking?"

"I always knew you were smart."

"Okay . . ." His eyes fixed on a blank part of the wall while his brain went to work. "Okay, we can make that work."

"Your flag signal's a red tie on the metro. Then he slips you the meeting arrangement, we do that, and the Rabbit skips out of town, along with Mrs. Rabbit and the Bunny—oh, you'll love this, he already calls his daughter *zaichik*."

"Flopsy, Mopsy, and Cotton-tail?" Ed exercised his sense of humor.

"I like that. Call it Operation BEATRIX," she suggested. Both of them had read Mrs. Potter's *Peter Rabbit* as kids. Who hadn't?

"The problem's going to be getting Langley's approval. If we can't use normal comm channels, coordinating everything is going to be a major pain in the ass."

"They never told us at The Farm that this job was easy. So remember what John Clark told us. Be flexible."

"Yeah, like linguine." He let out a long breath. "With the communications limitations, it essentially means we plan it and run it out of this office, with no help from the Home Office."

"Ed, that's the way it's supposed to be anyway. All Langley does is tell us we can't do what we want to do"—which was, after all, the function of every home office in every business in the world.

"Whose comms can we trust?"

"The Rabbit says the Brits just set up a new system they can't crack—yet, anyway. Do we have any one-time pads left here?"

The COS shook his head. "Not that I know of." Foley lifted his phone and punched the right numbers. "Mike? You're in today? Want to come over here? Thanks."

Russell arrived in a couple minutes. "Hey, Ed—hello, Mary. What are you doing in the shop today?"

"Got a question."

"Okay."

"Got any one-timers left?"

"Why do you ask?"

"We just like the extra security," she replied. The studiedly casual reply didn't work.

"You telling me my systems aren't secure?" Russell asked in well-hidden alarm.

"There is reason to believe some of our encryption systems are not fully secure, Mike," Ed told the embassy Communications Officer.

"Shit," he breathed, then turned with some embarrassment. "Oh, sorry, Mary."

She smiled. "It's okay, Mike. I don't know what the word means, but I've heard it spoken before." The joke didn't quite get to Russell. The previous revelation was too earthshaking for him to see much humor at the moment.

"What can you tell me about that?"

"Not a thing, Mike," the Station Chief said.

"But you think it's solid?"

"Regrettably, yes."

"Okay, back in my safe I do have a few old pads, eight or nine years old. I never got rid of them—you just never know, y'know?"

"Michael, you're a good man." Ed nodded his approval.

"They're good for maybe ten dispatches of about a hundred words each—assuming they still have matching pads at Fort Meade, but the guys I report to don't throw much away. They will have to dig them out of some file drawer, though."

"How hard to use them?"

"I hate the goddamned things. You know why. Damn it, guys, the new STRIPE cipher is just a year old. The new Brit system is an adaptation of it. I know the team in Z-Division who developed it. I'm talking 128-bit keying, plus a daily key that's unique to the individual machines. No way in hell you can crack that."

"Unless they have an agent-in-place at Fort Meade, Mike," Ed pointed out.

"Then let me get my hands on him, and I'll skin the motherfucker alive with my Buck hunting knife." The very thought had jacked up his blood pressure enough that he didn't apologize to the lady present for his vulgarity. This black man had killed and skinned his share of white-tailed deer, but he still had a hankering to convert a bear into a rug, and a big ol' Russian brown bear would suit him just fine. "Okay, I can't tell The Fort about this?"

"Not with STRIPE you can't," Foley answered.

"Well, when you hear a big, angry shout from the West, you'll know what it is."

"Better you don't discuss this with anybody right now, Mike," Mary Pat thought out loud. "They'll find out soon enough through other channels."

That told Russell that the Rabbit signal he'd dispatched the other day was about somebody they wanted to get out in a hurry, and now he figured he knew why. Their Rabbit was a communications specialist, and damned sure when you got one of those, you got him the hell on the first train out of Dodge. *Soon enough* meant right the hell now, or as close to it as you could arrange.

"Okay, get me your signal. I'll encrypt it on my STRIPE machine and then one-time-pad it. If they're reading my signals"—he managed not to shudder—"will that tell them anything?"

"You tell me," Ed Foley replied.

Russell thought for a moment, then shook his head. "No, it shouldn't. Even when you can crack the other guy's systems, you never get more than a third of the traffic. The systems are too complex for that—unless the other guy's agent-in-place is reading the cleartext on the far end. Ain't no defense against that, least not from my point of view."

And that was the *other* very scary thought. It was, after all, the same game they played and the same objective they were constantly trying to achieve. Get a guy all the way inside who could get the all-the-way-inside information back out. Like their agent CARDINAL, a word they *never* spoke aloud. But that was the game they'd chosen and, while they knew the other side was pretty good, they figured that they were better. And that was the name of that tune.

"Okay, Mike. Our friend believes in one-time pads. I guess everybody does."

"Ivan sure as hell does, but it must drive their troops crazy, having to go through every signal one letter at a time."

"Ever work the penetration side?" Ed Foley asked him.

Russell shook his head at once. "Not smart enough. Good thing, too. A lot of those guys end up in rubber rooms cutting out paper dolls with blunted scissors. Hey, I know a lot of the guys in Z-Division. The boss guy there just turned down the chair in math at Cal Tech. He's pretty smart," Russell estimated. "Damned sight smarter than I'll ever be. Ed Popadopolous's—his name is Greek—father used to run a restaurant up in Boston. Ask me if I want his job."

"No, eh?"

"Not even if they threw in Pat Cleveland as a fringe benefit." And that was one fine-looking lady, Ed Foley knew. Mike Russell really did need a woman in his life. . . .

"Okay, I'll get you a dispatch in about an hour. Okay?"

"Cool." Russell headed out.

"Well, I think we rattled his cage pretty hard," MP thought aloud.

"Admiral Bennett at Fort Meade ain't going to be real happy either. I got a signal to draft."

"Okay, I'll see how Eddie's doing with his crayons." And Mary Patricia Kaminsky Foley took her leave as well.

JUDGE ARTHUR MOORE'S morning briefing normally happened at 7:30 in the morning, except on Sunday, when he slept late, and so it took place at 9:00. His wife even recognized the knock of the National Intelligence Officer who delivered the daily intelligence news, always in the private study of his Great Falls house, which was swept weekly by the Agency's best debugging expert.

The world had been relatively quiet the previous day—even communists liked to relax on weekends, he'd learned on taking the job.

"Anything else, Tommy?" the Judge asked.

"Some bad news from Budapest," the NIO answered. "Our Station Chief, James Szell, got burned by the opposition making a pickup. Details unknown, but he got himself PNG'd by the Hungarian government. His principal deputy, Robert Taylor, is out of the country on personal business. So Station Budapest is out of business for the moment."

"How bad is that?" Not too bad, the DCI thought.

"Not a major tragedy. Nothing much seems to happen in Hungary. Their military is pretty much a minor player in the Warsaw Pact, and their foreign policy, aside from the things they do in their immediate neighborhood, is just a mirror image of Moscow's. The station's been passing us a fair amount of military information, but the Pentagon doesn't worry too much about it. Their army doesn't train enough to be a threat to much of anybody, and the Soviets regard them as unreliable," the NIO concluded.

"Is Szell somebody to screw up?" Moore asked. He vaguely remembered meeting the guy at an Agency get-together.

"Actually, Jimmy is well regarded. As I said, sir, we don't have any details yet. He'll probably be home by the end of the week."

"Okay. That does it?"

"Yes, sir."

"Nothing new on the Pope?"

"Not a word, sir, but it'll take time for our people to shake all their trees."

"That's what Ritter says."

IT TOOK FOLEY almost an hour to write up his dispatch. It had to be short but comprehensive, and that taxed his writing ability. Then he walked it down to Mike Russell's office. He sat there and watched a grumbling chief communications officer one-time-pad the words one goddamned letter at a time, pad it with more Czech surnames, then super-encrypt on his STRIPE encryption machine. With that done, it went on the secure fax machine, which, of course, encrypted the text one more time, but in a graphics fashion rather than an alphanumeric one. The fax encryption was relatively simple, but since the opposition—which was assumed to monitor the embassy's satellite transmitter—could not tell if the signal was graphics or text, that was just one more hoop for their decryption people to jump through. The signal went up to a geosynchronous satellite and back down to different downlinks, one at Fort Belvoir, Virginia, another at Sunnyvale, California, and, of course, one at Fort Meade, Maryland, to which the other stations sent their "take" via secure fiber-optic landlines.

The communications people at Fort Meade were all uniformed noncomms, and when one of them, an Air Force E-5, ran it through his decoding machine, he was surprised to see the notation that said the super-encryption was on a one-time pad, NHG-1329.

"Where the hell is that?" he asked his watch supervisor, a Navy senior chief.

"Damn," the chief commented. "I haven't seen one of those in a long time." He had to open a three-ring binder and root through it until he found the storage site inside the big communications vault at the far corner of the room. That was guarded by an armed Marine staff sergeant whose sense of humor, like that of all the Marines who worked here, had been surgically removed at Bethesda Naval Medical Center prior to his assignment to Fort Meade.

"Hey, Sarge, gotta go inside for something," he told the jarhead.

"You gotta see the Major first," the sergeant informed him. And so the senior chief walked to the desk of the USAF major who was sitting at his desk, reading the morning paper.

"Morning, Major. I need to get something out of the vault."

"What's that, Chief?"

"A one-time pad, NHG-1329."

"We still have any of them?" the major asked in some surprise.

"Well, sir, if not, you can use this to start a fire on your grill with." He handed the dispatch over.

The Air Force officer inspected it. "Tell me about it. Okay." He scribbled an authorization on a pad in the corner of his desk. "Give this to the Marine."

"Aye aye, sir." The senior chief walked back to the vault, leaving the Air Force puke to wonder why the squids always talked so funny.

"Here you go, Sam," the chief said, handing over the form.

The Marine unlocked the swinging door, and the senior chief headed inside. The box the pad was in wasn't locked, presumably because anyone who could get past the seven layers of security required to get to this point was probably as trustworthy as the President's wife.

The one-time pad was a small-ring binder. The Navy chief signed for it on the way out, then went back to his desk. The Air Force sergeant joined him, and together they went through the cumbersome procedure of decrypting the dispatch.

"Damn," the young NCO observed about two-thirds of the way through. "Do we tell anybody about that?"

"That's above our pay grade, sonny. I expect the DCI will let the right people know. And forget you ever heard that," he added. But neither really would, and both knew it. With all the wickets they had to pass through to be here, the idea that their signal systems were not secure was rather like hearing that their mother was turning tricks on Sixteenth Street in D.C.

"Yeah, Chief, sure," the young wing-wiper replied. "How do we deliver this one?"

"I think a courier, sonny. You want to whistle one up?"

"Aye aye, sir." The USAF sergeant took his leave with a smile.

The courier was an Army staff sergeant, driving a tan Army Plymouth Reliant, who took the sealed envelope, tucked it into the attaché case on his front seat, and drove down the Baltimore-Washington Parkway to the D.C. Beltway, and west on that to the George Washington Parkway, the first right off of which was CIA. At that point, the dispatch—whatever the hell it was, he didn't know—ceased being his responsibility.

The address on the envelope sent it to the Seventh Floor. Like many government agencies, CIA never really slept. On the top floor was Tom Ridley, a carded National Intelligence Officer, and the very one who handled Judge Moore's weekend briefings. It took him about three seconds to see that this one had to go to the judge right now. He lifted his STU secure phone and hit speed-dial button 1.

"This is Arthur Moore," a voice said presently.

"Judge, Tom Ridley here. Something just came in." "Something" means it was really something.

"Now?"

"Yes, sir."

"Can you come out here?"

"Yes, sir."

"Jim Greer, too?"

"Yes, sir, and probably Mr. Bostock also."

That made it interesting. "Okay, call them and then come on out." Ridley could almost hear the *God damn it, don't I* ever *get a day off!* at the other end before the line went dead. It took another few minutes to call the two other senior Agency officials, and then Ridley went down to his car for the drive out, pausing only to make three Xerox copies.

IT WAS LUNCHTIME in Great Falls. Mrs. Moore, ever the perfect hostess, had lunch meats and soft drinks set out for her unexpected guests before retiring to her sitting room upstairs.

"What is it, Tommy?" Moore asked. He liked the newly appointed NIO. A graduate of Marquette University, he was a Russian expert and had been one of Greer's star analysts before fleeting up to his present post. Soon he'd be one of the guys who always accompanied the President on Air Force One.

"This came in late this morning via Fort Meade," Ridley said, handing out the copies.

Mike Bostock was the fastest reader of the group: "Oh, Lord."

"This will make Chip Bennett happy," James Greer predicted.

"Yeah, like a trip to the dentist," Moore observed last of all. "Okay, people, what does this tell us?"

Bostock took it first. "It means we want this Rabbit in our hutch in one big hurry, gentlemen."

"Through Budapest?" Moore asked, remembering his morning brief.

"Uh-oh," Bostock observed.

"Okay." Moore leaned forward. "Let's get our thinking organized. First, how important is this information?"

James Greer took it. "He says KGB's going to kill somebody who doesn't deserve it. That kinda suggests the Pope, doesn't it?"

"More importantly, he says our communications systems might be compromised," Bostock pointed out. "That's the hottest thing I see in this signal, James."

"Okay, in either case, we want this guy on our side of the wire, correct?"

"Judge, you can bet your bench on that," the Deputy DDO shot back. "As quickly as we can make it happen."

"Can we use our own assets to accomplish it?" Moore asked next.

"It won't be easy. Budapest has been burned down."

"Does that change the importance of getting his cute little cottontail out of Redland?" the DCI asked.

"Nope." Bostock shook his head.

"Okay, if we can't do it ourselves, do we call in a marker?"

"The Brits, you mean?" Greer asked.

"We've used them before. We have good relations with them, and Basil does like to generate debts with us," Moore reminded them. "Mike, can you live with that?" he asked Bostock.

A decisive nod. "Yes, sir. But it might be nice to have one of our people around to keep an eye on things. Basil can't object to that."

"Okay, we need to decide which of our assets we can send. Next," Moore went on, "how fast?"

"How does tonight grab you, Arthur?" Greer observed to general amusement. "The way I read this, Foley's willing to run the operation out of his own office, and he's pretty hot to trot, too. Foley's a good boy. I think we let him run with it. Budapest is probably a good exit point for our Rabbit."

"Concur," Mike Bostock agreed. "It's a place a KGB officer can get to, like on vacation, and just disappear."

"They'll know he's gone pretty fast," Moore thought out loud.

"They knew when Arkady Shevchenko skipped, too. So what? He still gave us good information, didn't he?" Bostock pointed out. He'd helped oversee that operation, which had really been ramrodded by the FBI in New York City.

"Okay. What do we send back to Foley?" Moore asked.

"One word: 'Approved.' " Bostock *always* backed his field officers.

Moore looked around the room. "Objections? Anybody?" Heads just shook.

"Okay, Tommy. Back to Langley. Send that to Foley."

"Yes, sir." The NIO stood and walked out. One nice thing about Judge Moore. When you needed a decision, you might not like what you got, but you always got it.

CHAPTER 19

CLEAR SIGNAL

THE TIME DIFFERENCE was the biggest handicap in working his station, Foley knew. If he waited around the embassy for a reply, he might have to wait for hours, and there was no percentage in that. So, right after the signal went out, he'd collected his family and gone home, with Eddie conspicuously eating another hot dog on the way out to the car, and a facsimile copy of the New York *Daily News* in his hand. It was the best sports page of the New York papers, he'd long thought, if a little lurid in its headlines. Mike Lupica knew his baseball better than the rest of the wannabe ballplayers, and Ed Foley had always respected his analysis. He might have made a good spook if he'd chosen a useful line of work. So now he could see why the Yankees had fallen on their asses this season. It looked as though the goddamned Orioles were going to take the pennant, and that, to his New York sensibilities, was a crime worse than how the Rangers looked this year.

"So, Eddie, you looking forward to skating?" he asked his son, belted in the back seat.

"Yeah!" the little guy answered at once. Eddie Junior was his son, all right, and maybe here he'd really learn how to play ice hockey the right way.

Waiting in his father's closet was the best pair of junior hockey skates that money could buy, and another pair for when his feet got bigger. Mary Pat had already checked out the local junior leagues, and those, her husband thought, were about the best this side of Canada, and maybe better.

On the whole, it was a shame he couldn't have an STU in his house, but the Rabbit had told him that they might not be entirely secure, and besides, it would have told the Russians that he wasn't just the embassy officer who baby-sat the local reporters.

Weekends were the dullest time for the Foley family. Neither minded the time with the little guy, of course, but they could have done that at their now-rented Virginia home. They were in Moscow for their work, which was a passion for both of them, and something their son, they hoped, would understand someday. So for now his father read some books with him. The little guy was picking up on the alphabet, and seemed to read words, though as calligraphic symbols rather than letter constructs. It was enough for his father to be pleased about, though Mary Pat had a few minor doubts. After thirty minutes of that, Little Eddie talked his dad through a half hour of *Transformers* tapes, to the great satisfaction of the former and the bemusement of the latter.

The Station Chief's mind, of course, was on the Rabbit, and now it returned to his wife's suggestion of getting the package out without KGB's knowing they were gone. It was during the *Transformers* tape that it came back to him. You couldn't have a murder without a body, but with a body you damned sure had a murder. But what if the body wasn't the right one?

The essence of magic, he'd once heard Doug Henning say, was controlling the perception of the audience. If you could determine what they saw, then you could also dictate what they thought they saw, and from that precisely what they would remember seeing, and what they would then tell others. The key to *that* was in giving them something that they expected to see, even if it was unbelievable. People—even intelligent people—believed all manner of impossible things. It was sure as hell true in Moscow, where the rulers of this vast and powerful country believed in a political philosophy as out of tune with contemporary reality as the Divine Right of Kings. More to the point, they knew it was a false philosophy, and yet they commanded themselves to believe it as though it were Holy Scripture written in gold ink by God's own hand. So these people *could* be fooled. They worked pretty hard to fool themselves, after all.

Okay, how to fool them? Foley asked himself. Give the other guy something he expected to see, and he'd see it, whether it was really there or not. They wanted the Sovs to believe that the Rabbit and his family had . . . not skipped town, but had . . . died?

Dead people, so Captain Kidd had supposedly said, tell no tales. And neither did the *wrong* dead people.

The Brits did this once in World War II, didn't they? Foley wondered. Yes, he'd read the book in high school, and even then, at Fordham Prep, the operational concept had impressed him. Operation MINCEMEAT, it had been called. That concept had been very elegant indeed, as it had involved making the opposition feel smart, and people everywhere loved to feel smart. . . .

Especially the dumb ones, Foley reminded himself. And the German intelligence services in World War II hadn't been worth the powder to blow them to hell. They were so inept that the Germans would have been better advised to do without them entirely—Hitler's astrologer would have been just as good, and probably a lot cheaper in the long run.

But the Russians, on the other hand, were pretty damned smart—smart enough that you wanted to be very careful playing head games with them, but not so smart that if they found something they expected to find, they would toss it in the trash can and go looking for what they *didn't* expect. No, that was just human nature, and even the New Soviet Man they kept trying to build was subject to human nature, much as the Soviet government tried to breed it out of him.

So, how would we go about that? he wondered quietly, as on the television a diesel truck-tractor changed into a two-legged robot, the better to fight off the forces of evil—whoever they were. . . .

Oh. Yeah. It was pretty obvious, wasn't it? You just had to give them what they needed to see to prove that the Rabbit and his little hutchmates were dead, to give them what dead people always left behind. *That* would be a major complication, but not so vast of one as to be impossible to arrange. But they'd need assistance. That thought did not make Ed

Foley feel secure. In his line of work, you trusted yourself more than you trusted anyone or anything else—and after that, maybe, others of your own organization, but as few of them as possible. After *that,* when it became necessary to trust people in some other organization, you really gritted your teeth. Okay, sure, on his premission brief at Langley, he'd been told that Nigel Haydock could be relied upon as a very tame—and very able—Brit, and a pretty good field spook working for a closely allied service, and, okay, sure, he liked the look of the guy, and, okay, sure, they'd hit it off fairly well. But, God damn it, he wasn't Agency. But Ritter had told him that, in a pinch, Haydock could be relied upon for a helping hand, and the Rabbit himself had told him that Brit comms hadn't been cracked yet, and he had to trust the Rabbit to be an honest player. Foley's life wasn't riding on that, but damned sure his career was.

Okay, but what—no, *how*—to work this one. Nigel was the Commercial Attaché at the Brit Embassy, right across the river from the Kremlin itself, a station that went back to the czars, and one that had supposedly pissed Stalin off royally, to see the Union Jack every morning from his office window. And the Brits had helped recruit, and had later run GRU Colonel Oleg Penkovskiy, the agent who'd prevented World War III and, along the way, recruited CARDINAL, the brightest jewel in CIA's crown. So if he had to trust anyone, it would have to be Nigel. Necessity was the mother of many things, and if the Rabbit came to grief, well, they'd know that SIS was penetrated. Again. He realized he'd have to apologize to Nigel just for thinking this way, but this was business, not personal.

Paranoia, Eddie, the COS told himself. *You can't suspect everybody.*

The hell I can't!

But, probably, he knew, Nigel Haydock thought the same thing about him. That was just how the game was played.

And if they got the Rabbit out, it was proof positive that Haydock was straight. No way in hell that Ivan would let this bunny skip town alive. He just knew too much.

Did Zaitzev have any idea at all of the danger he was walking into? He *trusted* CIA to get him and his family out of Dodge City alive. . . .

But with all the information to which he had access, wasn't he making an informed judgment?

Jesus, there were enough interlocking wheels in this to make a bicycle factory, weren't there?

The tape ended, and Master Truck Robot—or whatever the hell his name was—transformed himself back into a truck and motored off to the sound of "Transformers, more than meets the eye . . ." It was sufficient to the moment that Eddie liked it. So, he'd arranged some quality time with his son and some good think time for himself—not a bad Sunday evening on the whole.

"SO, WHAT'S THE PLAN, Arthur?" Greer asked.

"Good question, James," the DCI answered. They were watching TV in his den, the Orioles and the White Sox playing in Baltimore. Mike Flanagan was pitching, and looked to be on his way to another Cy Young Award, and the rookie shortstop the Orioles had just brought up was playing particularly well, and looked to have a big-league future. Both men were drinking beer and eating pretzels, as though they were real people enjoying a Sunday afternoon of America's pastime. That was partly true.

"Basil will help. We can trust him," Admiral Greer opined.

"Agreed. Whatever problems he had are a thing of the past, and he'll compartmentalize it as tight as the Queen's jewel box. But we'll want one of our people involved at his end."

"Who, do you suppose?"

"Not the COS London. Everybody knows who he is, even the cabdrivers." There was no disputing that. The London Station Chief had been in the spook business for a very long time, and was more an administrator now than an active field officer. The same could be said of most of his people, for whom London was a sinecure job, and mainly a sunset posting for people looking forward to retirement. They were good men all, of course, just ready to hang up the spikes. "Whoever it is, he'll have to go to Budapest, and he'll have to be invisible."

"So, somebody they don't know."

"Yep." Moore nodded as he took a bite of his sandwich and reached for some chips. "He won't have to do very much, just let the Brits know he's there. Keep 'em honest, like."

"Basil's going to want to interview this guy."

"No avoiding that," Moore agreed. "And he's entitled to dip his beak, too." That was a line he had picked up as a judge on a rare organized-crime appeals case. He and his fellow jurists in Austin, Texas, had laughed about it for weeks, after rejecting the appeal, 5–0.

"We'll want one of our people in for that, too."

"Bet your bippy, James," Moore agreed again.

"And better that our guy is based over there. Timing might get a little tough."

"You bet."

"How about Ryan?" Greer asked. "He's way the hell under the radar. Nobody knows who he is—he's one of mine, right? He doesn't even look like a field officer."

"His face has been in the papers," Moore objected.

"You think KGB reads the society page? At most they might have noticed him as a rich wannabe writer, and if he has a file, it's in some sub-basement at The Centre. That ought not to be a problem."

"You think so?" Moore wondered. For sure, this would give Bob Ritter a bellyache. But that wasn't entirely a bad thing. Bob had visions of taking over all CIA operations, and, good man that he was, he would never be DCI, for any number of reasons, not the least of which was that Congress didn't much like spooks with Napoleonic complexes. "Is he up to it?"

"The boy's an ex-Marine and he knows how to think on his feet, remember?"

"He *has* paid his dues, James. He doesn't take a leak sitting down," the DCI conceded.

"And all he has to do is keep an eye on our friends, not play spook on enemy soil."

"Bob will have a conniption fit."

"It won't hurt our purposes to keep Bob in his place, Arthur." *Especially,* he didn't add, *if this works out.* And work out it should. Once out of Moscow, it ought to be a fairly routine operation. Tense, of course, but routine.

"What if he screws things up?"

"Arthur, Jimmy Szell dropped the ball in Budapest, and he's an experienced field officer. I know, probably not even his fault, probably just bad luck, but it proves the point. A lot of this racket is just luck. The Brits will be doing all the real work, and I'm sure Basil will pick a good team."

Moore weighed the thought quietly. Ryan was very new at CIA, but he was a rising star. What helped was his adventure, not yet a year old, where twice he'd faced loaded guns and gotten it done anyway. One nice thing about the Marine Corps, they didn't turn out many pussies. Ryan *could* think and act on his feet, and that was a nice thing to have in your pocket. Better yet, the Brits liked him. He'd seen the comments from Sir Basil Charleston on Ryan's tenure at Century House—he was taking quite a liking to the young American analyst. So this was a chance to bring a new talent along, and though he wasn't a graduate of The Farm, that didn't mean he was a babe in the woods. Ryan had been through the woods, and he'd killed himself a couple of wolves along the way, hadn't he?

"James, it's a little outside the box, but I won't say no for that reason. Okay, cut him loose. I hope your boy doesn't wet his pants."

"What did Foley call this operation?"

"BEATRIX, he said. You know, like *Peter Rabbit.*"

"Foley, that boy is going places, Arthur, and his wife, Mary Patricia, she is a real piece of work."

"There we surely agree, James. She'd make a great rodeo rider, and he'd be a pretty good town marshal west of the Pecos," the DCI said. He liked to see some of the young talent the Agency was producing. Where they all came from—well, they came from a lot of different places, but they all seemed to have the same fire in the belly that he'd had thirty years before, working with Hans Tofte. They weren't terribly different from the Texas Rangers he'd learned to admire as a little boy—the smart, tough people who did what had to be done.

"How do we get the word to Basil?"

"I called Chip Bennett last night, told him to have his people gin up some one-timers. Ought to be at Langley this evening. We'll fly them to London on the 747 tonight, and shoot some on from there to Moscow. So we'll be able to communicate securely, if not conveniently."

THAT, IN FACT, was just about done. A computer system used for taking down the dot-dash signals of International Morse Code was connected to a highly sensitive radio tuned to a frequency used by no human agency, transforming the garbage noise into Roman letters. One of the technicians at Fort Meade remarked along the way that the intergalactic noise they were copying down was the residual static produced by the Big Bang, for which Penzias and Miller had collected a Nobel Prize a few years before, and that was as random as things got—unless you could decode it to learn what God thought, which was beyond the skills even of NSA's Z-division. A dot-matrix printer put the letters to carbon-paper sets—three copies of each, the original to the originators, and a copy each for CIA and NSA. They all contained enough letters to transcribe the first third of the Bible, and each page and each line were alphanumerically identified to make decryption possible. Three people separated the pages, made sure that the sets were properly arranged, and then slipped them into ring binders for some semblance of ease of use. Then two were handed off to an Air Force NCO, who drove the CIA copies off to Langley. The lead technician wondered what was so goddamned important to require such massive one-time pads, which NSA had long before gotten past with its institutional worship of electronic technology, but his was not—ever—to reason why, was it? Not at Fort Meade, Maryland, it wasn't.

RYAN WAS WATCHING TV, trying to get used to the British sitcoms. He'd grown to like British humor—they'd invented Benny Hill, after all. That guy had to be mentally disabled to do some of the things he did—but the regular series TV took a little getting used to. The signals were just different, and though he spoke English as well as any American, the nuances here—exaggerated, of course, on TV—had a subtle dimension that occasionally slipped by him. But not his wife, Jack observed. His wife was laughing hard enough to gag, and at things he barely comprehended. Then came the trilling note of his STU in his upstairs den. He trotted upstairs to get it. It wouldn't be a wrong number. Whoever had set his number up—British Telecom, a semiprivate corporation that did exactly what the government told it to do—would have chosen a number so far off the numerical trail that only an infant could dial his secure phone by mistake.

"Ryan," he said, after his phone mated up with the one at the other end.

"Jack, Greer here. How's Sunday evening in Jolly Old England?"

"It rained today. I didn't get to cut the grass," Ryan reported. He didn't mind much. He *hated* cutting grass, having learned as a child that however much you sliced it down, the goddamned stuff just grew back in a few days to look scraggly again.

"Well, here the Orioles are leading the White Sox five-two after six innings. I think your team looks good for the pennant."

"Who in the National League?"

"If I had to bet, I'd say the Phillies all the way, my boy."

"I got a buck says you're wrong, sir. My O's look good from here." *Which isn't* there, *damn it.* Since losing the Colts, he'd transferred his loyalty to baseball. The game was more interesting, tactically speaking, though lacking the manly combat of NFL football. "So, what's happening in Washington on a Sunday afternoon, sir?"

"Just wanted to give you a heads-up. There's a signal on its way to London that's going to involve you. New tasking. It'll take maybe three or four days."

"Okay." It perked his interest, but he'd have to see what it was before he got overly excited about it. Probably some new analysis that they wanted him for. Those were usually economics, because the Admiral liked his way of working through the numbers games. "Important?"

"Well, we're interested in what you can do with it" was all the DDI wanted to say.

This guy must teach foxes how to outsmart dogs and horses. Good thing he wasn't a Brit. The local aristocracy would shoot him for ruining their steeplechases, Ryan told himself. "Okay, sir, I'll be looking for it. I don't suppose you can give me a play-by-play?" he asked with a little hope in his voice.

"That new shortstop—Ripken, is it?—just doubled down the left-field line, drove in run number six, one out, bottom of the seventh."

"Thank you for that, sir. It beats *Fawlty Towers.*"

"What the hell is that?"

"It's what they call a comedy over here, Admiral. It's funny if you can understand it."

"Brief me in next time I come over," the DDI suggested.

"Aye aye, sir."

"Family okay?"

"We're all just fine, sir, thank you for asking."

"Okay. Have a good one. See ya."

"What was that?" Cathy asked in the living room.

"The boss. He's sending me something to work on."

"What exactly?" She never stopped trying.

"He didn't say, just a heads-up that I have something new to play with."

"And he didn't tell you what it was?"

"The Admiral likes his surprises."

"Hmph" was her response.

THE COURIER SETTLED into his first-class seat. The package in his carry-on bag was tucked under the seat in front, and he had a collection of magazines to read. Since he was covert, not an official diplomatic courier, he could pretend to be a real person, a disguise that he'd shed at Heathrow's Terminal Four immigration desk, there to catch an embassy car for the ride into Grosvenor Square. Mainly he looked forward to a nice pub and some Brit beer before he flew back home in a day and a half. It was a waste of talent and training for the newly hatched field officer, but everyone had to pay his dues, and this, for a guy fresh out of The Farm, was just that. He consoled himself with the thought that whatever it was, it had to be a little bit important. Sure, Wilbur. If it were all that important, he'd be on the Concorde.

ED FOLEY WAS sleeping the sleep of the just. The next day, he'd find an excuse to head over to the British Embassy and have a sit-down with Nigel and plan the operation. If that went well, he'd wear his reddest tie and take the message from Oleg Ivan'ch, set up the next face-to-face and go forward with the operation. *Who is it*, he wondered, *who the KGB is trying to kill? The Pope?* Bob Ritter had his knickers in a twist over that. *Or somebody else?* The KGB had a very direct way of dealing with people it didn't like. CIA did not. They hadn't actually killed anyone since the fifties, when President Eisenhower had used CIA—actually quite skillfully—as an alternative to employing uniformed troops in an overt fashion. But that skill hadn't been conveyed to the Kennedy Administration, which had screwed up nearly everything it touched. Too many James Bond books, probably. Everything in fiction was simpler than the real world, even fiction written by a former field spook. In the real world, zipping your zipper could be hard.

But he was planning a fairly complex operation and telling himself that it wasn't all *that* complex. Was he making a mistake? Foley's mind wandered while the rest of his consciousness slept. Even asleep, he kept going over and over things. In his dreams, he saw rabbits running around a green field while foxes and bears watched. The predators didn't move on them, perhaps because they were too fast and/or too close to their rabbit holes for them to waste a chase. But what happened when the rabbits got too far away from their holes? Then the foxes could catch them, and the bears could move in to swallow them whole. . . . And his job was to protect the little bunnies, wasn't it?

Even so, in his dream the foxes and bears just watched while he, the eagle, circled high and looked down. He, the eagle, had sworn off rabbits, though a fox might be a nice morsel to rip apart, if his talons got it properly, just behind the head to snap the neck, and leave him for the bear to eat, because bears didn't really care whom they ate. No, Mr. Bear didn't care one little bit. He was just a big old bear, and his belly was always empty. He'd even eat an eagle if he got the chance, but the eagle was too swift and too smart, wasn't he? Only so long as he kept his eyes open, the noble eagle told himself; he had great abilities and fine sight, but even he had to be careful. And so the eagle soared aloft, riding the thermals and watching. He couldn't enter the fray, exactly. At most, he could swoop down and warn the cute little bunnies that there was danger about, but the bunnies were proverbially dumb bunnies, munching their grass and not looking around as much as they ought to. That was his job, the noble eagle told himself, to use his superb eyesight to make sure he knew everything he needed to know. The bunny's job was to run when he needed to run, and with help from the eagle, to run to a different field, one without foxes and bears around it, so that he could be free to raise more cute little bunnies and live happily ever after, like Beatrix Potter's little Flopsy, Mopsy, and Cotton-tail.

Foley rolled over, and the dream ended, the eagle watching for danger, and the rabbits eating their grass, and the foxes and bears a good way off, just watching but not moving, because they didn't know which bunny would stray too far from its safe little hole.

THE ALARM CLOCK'S deliberately annoying buzz caused Foley's eyes to snap open, and he rolled over to switch it off. Then he jerked himself out of bed and into the bathroom. He suddenly missed his house in Virginia. It had more than one bathroom—two and a half, in fact, which allowed some degree of flexibility should an emergency occur. Little Eddie got up when summoned, then almost immediately sat on the floor in front of the TV set and called out "Worker-womannnn!" when the exercise show came on. That generated a smile from his mom and dad. Even the KGB guys on the other end of the bug wires probably had a little chuckle at that.

"Anything important planned for the office today?" Mary Pat asked in the kitchen.

"Well, ought to be the usual weekend traffic from Washington. I have to run over to the Brit Embassy before lunch."

"Oh? What for?" his wife asked.

"I want to stop over and see Nigel Haydock about a couple of things," he told her, as she set the bacon frying. Mary Pat always did bacon and eggs on the day of important spook work. He wondered if their KGB listeners would ever tumble to that. Probably not. Nobody was that thorough, and American eating habits probably interested them only insofar as foreigners usually ate better than Russians.

"Well, say hello for me."

"Right." He yawned and took a sip of coffee.

"We need to have them over—maybe next weekend?"

"Works for me. Roast beef and the usual?"

"Yeah, I'll try to get some frozen corn on the cob." Russians grew corn you could buy in the open farmers' markets, and it was okay, but it wasn't the Silver Queen that they'd come to love in Virginia. So they usually settled for the frozen corn the Air Force flew in from Rhein-Main, along with the Chicago Red hot dogs that they served in the embassy canteen and all the other tastes of home that became so important on a posting like this one. *It was probably just as true in Paris,* Ed thought. Breakfast went quickly, and half an hour later, he was almost dressed.

"Which tie today, honey?"

"Well, in Russia, you should wear red once in a while," she said, handing the tie over with a wink, along with the lucky silver tie bar.

"Um-hmm," he agreed, looking in the mirror to snug it into his collar. "Well, here is Edward Foley, Senior, foreign-service officer."

"Works for me, honey." She kissed him, a little loudly.

"Bye, Daddy," Junior said as his father headed for the door. A high five instead of a kiss. He'd gotten a little too old for the sissy stuff.

The rest of the trip was stultifyingly routine. Walk to the metro. Buy his paper at the kiosk and catch the exact same train for the same five-kopeck fare, because if he caught the same one going home, so as to be marked by KGB as a creature of strict routine, then he had to mirror-image morning and afternoon habits. At the embassy, he entered his office and waited for Mike Russell to bring in the morning message traffic. More than usual, he saw at once, flipping through the messages and checking the headers.

"Anything about what we talked about?" the communications officer asked, lingering for a moment.

"Doesn't look like it," Foley replied. "Got you a little torqued?"

"Ed, getting secure stuff in and out is my only job, y'know?"

"Look at it from my side, Mike. If they tumble to me, I'm as useless as tits on a boarhog. Not to mention the guys who get killed because of it."

"Yeah, I hear you." Russell paused. "I just can't believe they can crack my systems, Ed. Like you said, you'd be losing people left and right."

"I want to agree with you, but we can't be too careful, can we?"

"Roger that, man. I catch anybody dicking around in my shop, they won't live long enough to talk to the FBI," he promised darkly.

"Don't get too carried away."

"Ed, when I was in Vietnam, nonsecure signals got soldiers killed. That's as important as things get, y'know?"

"If I hear anything, I'll make sure you know about it, Mike."

"Okay." Russell headed out, not quite trailing smoke out of his ears.

Foley organized his message traffic—it was addressed to the Chief of Station, of course, not to anyone's name—and started reading through it. There was still concern about KGB and the Pope, but, aside from the Rabbit, he had nothing new to report, and it was only hope that told him the Flopsy had anything to report on that subject. A lot of interest in last week's Politburo meeting, but for that he'd have to wait for his sources to report in. Questions about Leonid Brezhnev's health, but while they knew the names of his physicians—a whole team of them—none of them talked to CIA directly. You could see the picture on TV and know that Leonid Ilyich wasn't going to be running the marathon in the next Olympics. But people like that could linger for years, good news and bad news. Brezhnev wasn't going to be doing anything new and different, but, as he became increasingly irrational, there was no telling what dumbass things he might try—damned sure he wasn't going to be pulling out of Afghanistan. He didn't care a rap about the lives of young Russian soldiers, not when he heard Death's footsteps approaching his own door. The succession was of interest to CIA, but it was fairly settled that Yuriy Vladimirovich Andropov would be the next guy at the seat at the head of the table, absent a sudden death or a major foot put wrong in a political sense. Andropov was too canny a political operator for that, however. No, he was the current czarevich, and that was that. Hopefully, he wouldn't be too vigorous—and he wouldn't if the stories about his liver disease were true. Every time Foley saw him on Russian TV, he looked for the yellow tinge on his skin that announced that particular ailment—but makeup could hide that, if they used makeup on their political chieftains. . . . *Hmm, how to check that?* he wondered. Something to send back to the Science and Technology Directorate at Langley, maybe.

ZAITZEV TOOK HIS SEAT, after relieving Kolya Dobrik, and looked over his message traffic. He decided to memorize as much as possible, and so he took a little longer than usual forwarding the messages to their end-recipients. There was one from Agent CASSIUS again, routed for political-intelligence people upstairs, and also at the U.S.–Canada Institute, where the academicians read the tea leaves for The Centre as a backup. There was one from NEPTUNE, requesting money for the agent who was giving KGB such good communications intelligence. NEPTUNE suggested the sea, didn't it? Zaitzev searched his memory for previous signals from that source. Wasn't it mainly about the American navy? And *he* was the reason he worried about American signals security. Surely KGB was paying him a *huge* amount of money, hundreds of thousands of dollars in American cash, something KGB had a problem getting ahold of—it was far easier for the Soviet Union to pay in diamonds, since it could mine for diamonds in eastern Siberia. They'd paid some Americans in diamonds, but they'd been caught by the vigilant American FBI, and KGB had never tried to negotiate their release . . . so much for loyalty. The Americans tried to do that, he knew, but most of the time the people they tried to get out had already been executed—a thought that stopped his thoughts cold in their tracks.

But there was no turning back now, and CIA was competent enough that KGB feared it, and didn't *that* mean that he was in good hands?

Then he remembered one other thing he had to do today. In his drawer was a pad of contact reports. Mary had suggested he report their meeting, and so he did. He described her as pretty, in her late twenties or early thirties, mother of a fairly nice little son, and none too bright—*very American in mannerisms,* he wrote—with modest language skills, good vocabulary but poor syntax and pronunciation, which made her Russian understandable but stilted. He didn't make an evaluation of her likelihood to be an intelligence officer, which, he figured, was the smart thing to do. After fifteen minutes of writing, he walked it over to the department security officer.

"This was a waste of time," he said, handing it to the man, a captain passed over for promotion twice.

The security officer scanned it. "Where did you meet her?"

"It's right there." He pointed to the contact form. "I took my *zaichik* for a walk in the park, and she showed up with her little boy. His name is Eddie, actual name is evidently Edward Edwardovich—Edward Junior, as the Americans say it—age four, I think she said, a nice little boy. We talked a few minutes about not very much, and the two of them walked away."

"Your impression of her?"

"If she is a spy, then I am confident of the victory of socialism," Zaitzev replied. "She is rather pretty, but far too skinny, and not overly bright. What I suppose is a typical American housewife."

"Anything else?"

"It's all there, Comrade Captain. It took longer to write that up than it did to speak with her."

"Your vigilance is noted, Comrade Major."

"I serve the Soviet Union." And Zaitzev headed back to his desk. *It was a good idea on her part,* he thought, *to cross this* t *so assiduously.* There might have been a shadow on her, after all, and if not, then there would be a new entry in her KGB file, reported by a KGB officer, certifying that she was no threat to world socialism.

Back at his desk, he returned to making extra-careful mental notes of his daily work. The more he gave CIA, the better he'd be paid. Maybe he would take his daughter to that Disney Planet amusement park, and maybe his little *zaichik* would enjoy herself there. His signals included other countries, too, and he memorized those as well. One code-named MINISTER in England was interesting. He was probably in their Foreign Ministry, and provided excellent political/diplomatic intelligence that they loved upstairs.

FOLEY TOOK AN embassy car for the drive to the British Embassy. They were cordial enough once he showed his ID, and Nigel came down to meet him in the grand foyer, which was indeed quite grand.

"Hello, Ed!" He gave a hearty handshake and a smile. "Come this way." They went up the marble stairs and then right to his office. Haydock closed the door and pointed him to a leather chair.

"What can I do for you?"

"We got a Rabbit," Foley said, skipping the preliminaries.

And that said it all. Haydock knew that Foley was a spook—a "cousin" in the British terminology.

"Why are you telling me?"

"We're going to need your help getting him out. We want to do that through Budapest, and our station there just got burned down. How's your shop there?"

"The chief is Andy Hudson. Former officer in the Parachute Regiment, able chap. But do back up, Edward. What can you tell me, and why is this so important?"

"He's a walk-in, I guess you'd say. He seems to be a communications guy. He feels real as hell, Nigel. I've requested permission to bust him right out, and Langley has green-lighted it. Pair of fives, man," he added.

"So, high priority and high reliability on this chappie?"

Foley bobbed his head. "Yep. Want the good news?"

"If there is any."

"He says our comms may be compromised, but your new system hasn't been cracked yet."

"Good to hear. So, that means I can communicate freely, but you cannot?"

Another nod. "I learned this morning that a communications aid is on its way to me—perhaps they ginned up a couple of pads for me to use. I'll find out later today, maybe."

Haydock leaned back in his chair and lit up a smoke, a low-tar Silk Cut. He'd switched to them to make his wife happy.

"You have a plan?" the Brit spook asked.

"I figure he takes the train to Budapest. For the rest of it, well . . ." Foley outlined the idea he and Mary Pat had figured out.

"That *is* creative, Edward." Haydock thought. "When did you read up on MINCEMEAT? It's part of the syllabus at our academy, you know."

"Back when I was a kid. I always thought it was pretty clever."

"In the abstract, not a bad idea—but, you know, the pieces you need are not something you pick up at the ironmongers."

"I kinda figured that, Nigel. So, if we want to make the play, better that we get moving on it right quick."

"Agreed." Haydock paused. "Basil will want to know a few things. What else can I tell him?"

"He ought to get a hand-carried letter from Judge Moore this morning. All I can really say is, this guy looks pretty real."

"You said he's a communications officer—in The Centre, is it?"

"Yep."

"That could be very valuable indeed," Haydock agreed. "Especially if he's a mail clerk." He pronounced it *clark*. The invocation of the name of Foley's training officer almost caused him to smile . . . but not quite.

It was a slower nod this time, with Foley's eyes locked in on his host. "That's what we're thinking, guy."

It finally got home. "Bloody hell," Haydock breathed. "That would be valuable. And he's just a walk-in?"

"Correct. A little more complicated than that, but that's what it comes down to, bud."

"Not a trap, not a false-flag?"

"I've thought about that, of course, but it just doesn't make sense, does it?" Foley asked. The Brit knew he was Agency, but didn't know he was Station Chief. "If they've ID'd me, why tip their hand this early?"

"True," Nigel had to agree. "That would be clumsy. So, Budapest, is it? Easier than out of Moscow—at least there's that."

"There's bad news, too. His wife isn't in on the plan." Foley had to tell him that.

"You must be joking, Edward."

"Wish I was, man. But that's how it's going down."

"Ah. Well, what's life without a few complications? Any preferences how to get your Rabbit out?" He asked, not quite letting Foley know what he was thinking.

"That's for your guy Hudson in Budapest, I suppose. It's not my turf, not my place to tell him how to run his operation."

Haydock just nodded. It was one of those things that went without saying but had to be said anyway. "When?" he asked.

"Soon, as soon as possible. Langley's almost as hot for this as I am." And, he didn't add, it was sure as hell a way for him to make an early mark as Chief of Station Moscow.

"Rome, you're thinking? Sir Basil has been rattling my windows about that."

"Your Prime Minister interested?"

"About as much as your President, I should imagine. That play might well muddy the waters rather thoroughly."

"Big-time," Foley agreed. "Anyway, I wanted to give you a heads-up. Sir Basil will probably have a signal for you later today."

"Understood, Edward. When that arrives, I'll be able to begin taking action." He checked his watch—too soon to offer his guest a beer in the embassy pub. Pity.

"When you get authorization, give me a call. Okay?"

"Certainly. We shall get things sorted out for you, Ed. Andy Hudson's a good officer, and he runs a tight operation in Budapest."

"Great." Foley stood.

"How about a dinner soon?" Haydock asked.

"I guess we'd better do it soon. Penny looks about due. When will you be flying her home?"

"A couple of weeks. The little bugger is rolling about and kicking all the time now."

"Always a good sign, man."

"And we have a good physician right here in the embassy, should he be a little early." Just that the embassy doc didn't really want to deliver a baby. They never did.

"Well, if it's a boy, Eddie will lend you his *Transformers* tapes," Ed promised.

"*Transformers*? What's that?"

"If it's a boy, you'll find out," Foley assured him.

CHAPTER 20

STAGING

THE JUNIOR FIELD OFFICER arrived in London's Heathrow Terminal Four just before seven in the morning. He breezed through immigration and customs and headed out, where he saw his driver holding the usual sign card, this one in a false name, of course, since CIA spooks only used their real names when they had to. The driver's name was Leonard Watts. Watts drove an embassy Jaguar, and, since he had a diplomatic passport and tags on the car, he wasn't all that concerned with speed limits.

"How was the flight?"

"Fine. Slept most of the way."

"Well, welcome to the world of field operations," Watts told him. "The more sleep you get, the better."

"I suppose." It was his first overseas assignment, and not a very demanding one. "Here's the package." And his cover wasn't enhanced by the fact that he was traveling with only the courier package and a small bag that had spent the trip in the overhead bin, with a clean shirt, clean underwear, and shaving kit.

"Name's Len, by the way."

"Okay, I'm Pete Gatewood."

"First time in London?"

"Yeah," Gatewood answered, trying to get used to sitting in the left front seat without a steering wheel to protect him, and being driven by a NASCAR reject. "How long to get to the embassy?"

"Half hour." Watts concentrated on his driving. "What are you carrying?"

"Something for the COS, is all I know."

"Well, it isn't routine. They woke me up for it," Watts groused.

"Where have you worked?" Gatewood asked, hoping to get this maniac to slow down some.

"Oh, around. Bonn, Berlin, Prague. Getting ready to retire, back to Indiana. We got a football team to watch now."

"Yeah, and all the corn, too," Gatewood observed. He'd never been to Indiana, and had no particular wish to tour the farming state, which did, he reminded himself, turn out some fairly good basketball players.

Soon enough, or nearly so, they were passing a large green park on the left, and a few blocks after that, the green rectangle of Grosvenor Square. Watts stopped the car to let Gatewood out. He dodged around the "flower pots" designed to keep car bombers from getting too close to the concrete that surrounded the surpassingly ugly building, and walked it. The Marines inside checked his ID and made a call. Presently, a middle-aged woman came into the entrance foyer and led him to an elevator that took him to the third floor, just next door to the technical group that worked closely with the British GCHQ at Cheltenham. Gatewood walked into the proper corner office and saw a middle-aged man sitting at an oaken desk.

"You're Gatewood?"

"Yes, sir. You're . . . ?"

"I'm Randy Silvestri. You have a package for me," the COS London announced.

"Yes, sir." Gatewood opened the zipper on his bag and pulled out the large manila envelope. He handed it over.

"Interested in what's in it?" Silvestri asked, eyeing the youngster.

"If it concerns me, I expect you'll tell me, sir."

The Station Chief nodded his approval. "Very good. Annie will take you downstairs for breakfast if you want, or you can catch a cab for your hotel. Got some Brit money?"

"A hundred pounds, sir, in tens and twenties."

"Okay, that'll handle your needs. Thanks, Gatewood."

"Yes, sir." And Gatewood left the office.

Silvestri ripped open the package after determining that the closure hadn't been disturbed beforehand. The flat ring binder had what looked like forty or fifty printed sheets of paper—all space-and-a-half random letters. So, a one-time-cipher pad—for Station Moscow, the cover note said. He'd have that couriered to Moscow on the noon British Airways flight. And two letters, one for Sir Basil, with hand delivery indicated. He'd have a car drive him to Century House after calling ahead. The other one was for that Ryan kid that Jim Greer liked so much, also for hand delivery via Basil's office. He wondered what was up. It had to be nontrivial for this sort of handling. He picked up his phone and hit speed-dial #5.

"This is Basil Charleston."

"Basil, it's Randy. Something just came in for you. Can I bring it over?"

A sound of shuffling papers. Basil would know this was important. "Say, ten o'clock, Randy?"

"Right. See you then." Silvestri sipped his coffee and estimated the time required. He could sit here for about an hour before heading over. Next he punched his intercom button.

"Yes, sir?"

"Annie, I have a package to be couriered to Moscow. We got a bagman on deck?"

"Yes, sir."

"Okay, could you take this down to him?"

"Yes, sir." CIA secretaries are not paid to be verbose.

"Good. Thanks." Silvestri hung up.

JACK AND CATHY were on the train, passing through Elephant and Castle—and he'd still not learned how the damned place had gotten *that* name, Jack reminded himself. The weather looked threatening. *England wasn't broad enough for a storm system to linger*, Ryan thought. Maybe there was just a series of rain clouds coming across the Atlantic? In any case, between yesterday and today, his personal record of fair weather over here seemed to be ending. Too bad.

"Just glasses this week, babe?" he asked his wife, her head buried as usual in a medical journal.

"All week," she confirmed. Then she looked up. "It's not as exciting as surgery, but it's still important, you know."

"Cath, if you do it, it must be important."

"And you can't say what you'll be doing?"

"Not until I get to my desk." And probably not then, either. Whatever it was, it had doubtless been transmitted via secure printer or fax line overnight . . . unless it was something really important, and had been sent via courier. The time difference actually made that fairly convenient. The early 747 from Dulles usually got in between six and seven in the morning, and then it was forty minutes more to his desk. The government could work more efficiently than Federal Express when it wanted to. Another fifteen minutes of his *Daily Telegraph* and her *NEJM* and they parted company at Victoria. Cathy perversely took the tube. Ryan opted for a cab. It hustled past the Palace of Westminster, then hopped across the Thames. Ryan paid the four pounds fifty and added a healthy tip. Ten seconds later, he was inside.

"Good morning, Sir John," Bert Canderton called in greeting.

"Howdy, Sar-Major," Ryan said in reply, sliding his pass through the gate, then to the elevator and up to his floor.

Simon was already in his seat, going over message traffic. His eyes came up when Jack entered. "Morning, Jack."

"Hey, Simon. How was the weekend?"

"Didn't get any gardening done. Bloody rain."

"Anything interesting this morning?" He poured himself a cup of coffee. Simon's English Breakfast Tea wasn't bad for tea, but tea just didn't make it for Jack, at least not in the morning. They didn't have bear claws here, either, and Jack had neglected to get his croissant on the way in.

"Not yet, but something's coming in from America."

"What is it?"

"Basil didn't say, but when something comes in by hand on a Monday morning, it's usually interesting. Must be Soviet-related. He's told me to stand by for it."

"Well, might as well start the week with something interesting." Ryan sipped his coffee. It wasn't quite up to what Cathy made, but better than tea. "When's it coming in?"

"About ten. Your Station Chief, Silvestri, is driving it over."

Ryan had only met him once. He'd seemed competent enough, but you expected that of a COS, even one in a sunset posting.

"Nothing new from Moscow?"

"Just some new rumors about Brezhnev's health. It seems that stopping smoking did him precious little good," Harding said, lighting his pipe. "Nasty old bugger," the Brit analyst added.

"What about this stuff from Afghanistan?"

"Ivan's getting cleverer. Those Mi-24 helicopters seem to be rather effective. Bad news for the Afghans."

"How do you think that's going to play out?"

Harding shrugged. "It's a question of how many casualties Ivan is willing to take. They have the firepower they need to win, and so it's a matter of political will. Unfortunately for the Mujahideen, the leadership in Moscow doesn't trouble itself very much with casualties."

"Unless something changes the equation," Ryan thought out loud.

"Like what?"

"Like an effective surface-to-air missile to neutralize their helos. We have the Stinger. Never used it myself, but the write-up's pretty good."

"But can a mob of illiterate savages use a missile properly?" Harding asked dubiously. "A modern rifle, certainly. A machine gun, sure. But a missile?"

"The idea is to make a new weapon soldier-proof, Simon. You know, simple enough that you don't have to think while you're dodging bullets. There's not much time to think then, and you make the steps as short as you can. Like I said, I've never used that one, but I've played with anti-tank weapons, and they're pretty simple."

"Well, your government will have to decide to give them the SAMs, and they haven't yet. Hard for me to get overly excited about it. Yes, they are killing Russians, and I reckon that's good, but they are bloody savages."

And they killed a lot of Brits once, Ryan reminded himself, *and Brit memories are as long as anyone else's.* There was also the issue of having Stingers fall into Russian hands, which would not make the United States Air Force terribly happy. But that was well above his pay grade. There were some rumbles in Congress about it, though.

Jack settled into his seat, sipped his coffee, and read his message traffic. After that he'd get back to his real job of analyzing the Soviet economy. That would be like drafting a road map of a plateful of spaghetti.

SILVESTRI'S JOB in London was not a secret. He'd been in the spook business too long, and while he hadn't been burned per se, the East Bloc had pretty much guessed which government agency he worked for by the end of his stay in Warsaw, where he'd run a very tight shop and winkled out a lot of good political intelligence. This was to be his final tour of duty—the same was true of most of his officers—and since he was respected by various allied services, he'd drawn the London posting, where his main job was interfacing with the British Secret Intelligence Service. So he had an embassy Daimler drive him over across the river.

He didn't even need a pass to get through security. Sir Basil himself was waiting for him at the entrance, where hands were cordially shaken before the trip upstairs.

"What's the news, Randy?"

"Well, I have a package for you, and one for that Ryan guy," Silvestri announced.

"Indeed. Should I call him in?"

The London COS had read the cover sheet and knew what was in the packages. "Sure, Bas, no problem. Harding, too, if you want."

Charleston lifted his phone and made the summons. The two analysts arrived in less than two minutes. They had all met at least once. Ryan, in fact, was the least familiar with the other American. Sir Basil pointed them to seats. He'd already ripped his envelope open. Silvestri handed Ryan his own message.

For his part, Jack was already thinking *oh, shit.* Something unusual was in the offing, and he'd learned not to trust new and different things at CIA.

"This *is* interesting," Charleston observed.

"Do I open this now?" Ryan asked. Silvestri nodded, so he took out his

Swiss Army Knife and sliced through the heavy manila paper. His message was only three pages, personally signed by Admiral Greer.

A Rabbit, he saw. He knew the terminology. Somebody wanted a ticket out of . . . Moscow . . . and CIA was providing it, with the help of SIS because Station Budapest was currently out of business. . . .

"Tell Arthur that we will be pleased to assist, Randy. We will, I assume, get a chance to speak with him before you fly him off to London?"

"It's only fair, Bas," Silvestri confirmed. "How hard to pull this one off, you suppose?"

"Out of Budapest?" Charleston thought for a moment. "Not all that difficult, I should think. The Hungarians have a rather nasty secret-police organization, but the country as a whole is not devoutly Marxist—oh, this Rabbit says that KGB may have compromised your communications. *That* is what Langley is excited about."

"Damned straight, Basil. If that's a hole, we have to plug it up fast."

"This guy's in their MERCURY? Jesus Christ," Ryan breathed.

"You got that one right, sonny," Silvestri agreed.

"But what the hell am I going into the field for?" Jack demanded next. "I'm not a field officer."

"We need one of ours to keep an eye on things."

"I quite understand, Randy," Charleston observed, his head still down in his briefing papers. "And you want someone whom the opposition doesn't know?"

"So it seems."

"But why me?" Ryan persisted.

"Jack," Sir Basil soothed, "your only job will be to watch what happens. It's just pro forma."

"But what about my cover?"

"We'll give you a new diplomatic passport," C answered. "You will be quite safe. The Vienna Convention, you know."

"But . . . but . . . it'll be fake."

"They won't know that, dear boy."

"What about my *akzint*?" It was painfully obvious that his accent was an American's, not a Brit's.

"In Hungary?" Silvestri asked with a smile.

"Jack, with their bloody language, I seriously doubt they will notice the difference, and in any case, with your new documents, your person is quite inviolable."

"Relax, kid. It's better than your little girl's teddy bear. Trust me on that one, okay?" Silvestri assured him.

"And you'll have a security officer with you at all times," Charleston added.

Ryan had to sit back and take a breath. He couldn't allow himself to appear to be a wuss, not in front of these guys and not before Admiral Greer. "Okay, excuse me. It's just that I've never been in the field before. It's all kinda new to me." He hoped that was adequate backpedaling. "What exactly will I be doing, and how do I go about it?"

"We'll fly you into Budapest out of Heathrow. Our chaps will pick you up at the airport and take you to the embassy. You will sit it out there—a couple of days, I expect—and then watch how Andy gets your Rabbit out of Redland. Randy, how long would you expect?"

"To get this moving? End of the week, maybe a day or two longer," Silvestri thought. "The Rabbit will fly or take the train to Budapest, and your man will figure how to get him the hell out of Dodge City."

"Two or three days for that," Sir Basil estimated. "Mustn't be too quick."

"Okay, that keeps me away from home for four days. What's my cover story?"

"For your wife?" Charleston asked. "Tell her that you have to go to—oh, to Bonn, shall we say, on NATO business. Be vague on the time factor," he advised. He was inwardly amused to have to explain this to the Innocent American Abroad.

"Okay," Ryan conceded the point. *Not like I have a hell of a lot of choice in the matter, is there?*

UPON GETTING BACK to the embassy, Foley walked to Mike Barnes's office. Barnes was the Cultural Attaché, the official expert on artsy-fartsy stuff. That was a major assignment in Moscow. The USSR had a fairly rich cultural life. The fact that the best part of it dated back to the czars didn't seem to matter to the current regime, probably, Foley thought, because all Great Russians wanted to appear *kulturniy,* and superior to Westerners, especially Americans, whose "culture" was far newer and far crasser than the country of Borodin and Rimsky-Korsakov. Barnes was a graduate of the Juilliard School and Cornell, and especially appreciated Russian music.

"Hey, Mike," Foley said in greeting.

"How's keeping the newsies happy?" Barnes asked.

"The usual. Hey, got a question for you."

"Shoot."

"Mary Pat and I are thinking about traveling some, maybe to Eastern Europe. Prague and like that. Any good music to be heard that way?"

"The Prague symphony hasn't opened up yet. But Jozsef Rozsa is in Berlin right now, and then he's going to Budapest."

"Who's he? I don't know the name," Foley said, as his heart nearly leapt out of his chest.

"Hungarian native, cousin of Miklos Rozsa, Hollywood composer—*Ben Hur,* and like that. Musical family, I guess. He's supposed to be excellent. The Hungarian State Railroad has four orchestras, believe it or not, and Jozsef is going to conduct number one. You can go there by train or fly, depends on how much time you have."

"Interesting," Foley thought aloud. *Fascinating,* he thought inside.

"You know, the Moscow State Orchestra opens up beginning of next month. They have a new conductor, guy named Anatoliy Sheymov. Haven't heard him yet, but he's supposed to be pretty good. I can get you tickets easy. Ivan likes to show off to us foreigners, and they really are world-class."

"Thanks, Mike, I'll think about it. Later, man." Foley took his leave.

And he smiled all the way back to his office.

"BLOODY HELL," Sir Basil observed, reading over the newest cable from Moscow. "What bloody genius came up with this idea?" he asked the air. Oh, he saw. The American officer, Edward Foley. *How the hell will he make this come about?* the Director General wondered.

He'd been about to leave for lunch at Westminster Palace across the river, and he couldn't break that one off. Well, it would be something to ruminate over with his roast beef and Yorkshire pudding.

"LUCKY ME," Ryan observed, back in his office.

"Jack, it will be less dangerous than crossing the street"—which could be a lively exercise in London.

"I can take care of myself, Simon," Ryan reminded his workmate. "But if I screw up, somebody else takes the fall."

"You'll not be responsible for any of that. You'll just be there to observe. I don't know Andy Hudson myself, but he has an excellent professional reputation."

"Great," Ryan commented. "Lunchtime, Simon, and I feel like a beer."

"Duke of Clarence all right?"

"Isn't that the guy who drowned in a barrel of malmsey wine?"

"Worse ways to go, Sir John," Harding observed.

"What is malmsey anyway?"

"Strong and sweet, rather like a Madeira. It now comes from those islands, in fact."

One more piece of trivia learned, Ryan thought, going to get his coat.

IN MOSCOW, Zaitzev checked his personnel file. He'd accrued twelve days of vacation time. He and his family hadn't gotten a time slot at Sochi the previous summer—the KGB quota had been filled in July and August—and so they had gone without. It was easier to schedule a vacation with a preschool child, as in any other country—you got to run away from town whenever you wished. Svetlana was in state-provided day care, but missing a few days of blocks and crayons was a lot easier to arrange than a week or two of state primary school, which was frowned upon.

UPSTAIRS, Colonel Rozhdestvenskiy was going over the latest message from Colonel Bubovoy in Sofia, just brought in by courier. So the Bulgarian premier had agreed to Moscow's request with a decent lack of annoying questions. The Bulgars knew their place. The chief of state of a supposedly sovereign nation knew how to take his orders from a field-grade officer of Russia's Committee for State Security. *Which was just as it should be,* the colonel thought. And now Colonel Strokov of the *Dirzhavna Sugurnost* would be out picking his shooter, undoubtedly a Turk, and Operation -666 could go forward. He would report this to Chairman Andropov later in the day.

"THREE *HUMAN* BODIES?" Alan Kingshot asked in considerable surprise. He was Sir Basil's most senior field officer, a very experienced operator who'd worked the streets of every major European city, first as a "legal" officer and later as a headquarters troubleshooter, in his thirty-seven years of service to Queen and Country. "Some sort of switch, is it?"

"Yes. The chap who suggested it is a fan of MINCEMEAT, I imagine," Basil responded.

Operation MINCEMEAT was a World War II legend. It had been designed to give Germany the impression that the next major Allied operation would not be the planned Operation HUSKY, the invasion of Sicily, and so it had been decided to suggest to German intelligence that Corsica was the intended invasion target. To do this, the Germans were given the body of a dead alcoholic who'd been transformed after a death of dissipation into a major of the Royal Marines, putatively a planning officer for the fictitious operation to seize Corsica. The body had been dropped in the water off the Spanish coast by the submarine HMS *Seraph*, from which it had washed to shore, been duly picked up, delivered to the local police, autopsied, and the document case handcuffed to the cadaver's wrist handed over to the local *Abwehr* officer. He'd fired the papers off to Berlin, where they'd had the intended effect, moving several German divisions to an island with no more military significance than the fact that it was Napoleon's birthplace. The story was called *The Man Who Never Was,* the subject of a book and a movie, and further proof of the wretched performance of German intelligence, which couldn't tell the difference between the body of a dead drunk and that of a professional soldier.

"What else do we know? I mean," Kingshot pointed out, "what age and gender, sir?"

"Yes, and hair color and so forth. The manner of death will also be important. We do not know those things yet. So the initial question is a broad one: Is it possible to do this?"

"In the abstract, yes, but before we can go forward with it, I shall need a lot of specifics. As I said, height, weight, hair and eye color, gender to be sure. With that, we can go forward."

"Well, Alan, get thinking about it. Get me a specific list of what you need by tomorrow noon."

"What city will this be in?"

"Budapest probably."

"Well, that's something," the field spook thought aloud.

"Damned grisly business," Sir Basil muttered after his man left.

ANDY HUDSON WAS sitting in his office, relaxing after his Ploughman's Lunch in the embassy's pub, along with a pint of John Courage beer. Not a tall man, he had eighty-two parachute jumps under his belt, and had the bad knees to prove it. He'd been invalided out of active service eight years before, but because he liked a little excitement in his life, he'd opted to join the Secret Intelligence Service, and worked his way rapidly up the ladder mainly on the strength of his superior language skills. Here in Budapest, he needed those. The Hungarian language is known as Indo-Altaic to philologists. Its nearest European neighbor is Finnish and, after that, Mongolian. It has no relationship at all with any European language, except for some Christian names, which were conveyed when the Magyar people succumbed to Christianity, after killing off enough missionaries to become bored with doing so. Along the way, they'd also lost whatever warrior ethos they'd once had. The Hungarians were about the most unwarlike people on the continent.

But they were pretty good at intrigue, and, like any society, they had a criminal element—but theirs had mainly gone into the Communist Party and power apparat. The Secret Police here, the *Allavedelmi Hatosag,* could be as nasty as the Cheka had been under Iron Feliks himself. But nasty wasn't quite the same as efficient. It was as though they tried to make up for their inbred inefficiency by viciousness against those whom they blundered into catching. And their police were notoriously stupid—there was a Hungarian aphorism, "As stupid as six pairs of policeman's boots," which Hudson had largely found to be true. They weren't the Metropolitan Police, but Budapest wasn't London, either.

In fact, he found life pleasant here. Budapest was a surprisingly pretty city, very French in its architecture, and surprisingly casual for a communist capital. The food was remarkably good, even in the government-run worker canteens that dotted every street corner, where the fare was not elegant but tasty. Public transportation was adequate to his purposes, which were mainly political intelligence. He had a source—called PARADE—inside the Foreign Ministry who fed him very useful information about the Warsaw Pact and East Bloc politics in general, in return for cash, and not very much cash at that, so low were his expectations.

Like the rest of Central Europe, Budapest was an hour ahead of London. The embassy messenger knocked on Hudson's door, then reached in to toss an envelope onto his desk. Hudson set down his small cigar and lifted it. From London, he saw. Sir Basil himself . . .

Bloody hell, Hudson thought. His life was about to get a little bit more interesting.

"More details to follow," it ended. About right. You never knew it all until you had to do it. Sir Basil wasn't a bad chap to work for but, like most spymasters, he greatly enjoyed being clever, which was something never fully appreciated out in the field, where the worker bees had wasps to worry about. Hudson had a staff of three, including himself. Budapest wasn't a major station, and for him it was a way station until something more important opened up. As it was, he was young to be a Station Chief. Basil was giving him the chance to stretch his legs. That suited Hudson. Most Station Chiefs sat in their offices like spiders in their web, which looked dramatic but could actually be quite boring, since it involved writing endless reports. He ran field tasks himself. That ran the risk of his being burned, as Jim Szell had been—bloody awful luck, nothing more than that, Hudson had learned from a source named BOOT, who was right inside the AVH. But in the danger came the charm of the job. It was less dangerous than jumping out the back of a Lockheed Hercules with sixty pounds of weapons and rations strapped to your back. Also less dangerous than patrolling Belfast with Provos about. But it was the skills learned in the city streets of Ulster that gave him his street smarts as a spook. As with everything else in life, you took the bitter with the sweet. But better, he told himself, to take his bitter by the pint.

He had a rabbit coming out. That ought not to be difficult, though this rabbit had to be an important one, so much so that CIA was asking for assistance from "Six," and that didn't happen every day. Only when the bloody Yanks buggered things up, which was, Hudson thought, not too infrequent.

There was nothing for him to do as yet. He could not know what needed to be done until he had a lot more specifics, but in the abstract he knew how to get people out of Hungary. It wasn't all that hard. The Hungarians were insufficiently wedded to Marxism to be that serious an adversary. So, he sent off a "message received" dispatch to Century House and awaited further developments.

THE BRITISH AIRWAYS noon flight to Moscow was a Boeing 737 twin-engine jet. The flight took about four hours, depending on winds, which were fairly calm today. On arriving at Sheremetyevo Airport, the Diplomatic Courier walked out the forward door and breezed through immigration control on the strength of his canvas bag and diplomatic passport, then walked to the waiting embassy car for the drive into town. The courier had been there and done that many times, enough so that his driver and the embassy guards knew him by sight, and he knew his own way around the embassy. With his delivery made, he headed down to the canteen for a hot dog and a beer, and settled into his newest paperback book. It occurred to him that he needed to exercise some, since his job was entirely occupied with sitting down, in cars and mainly in airplanes. It couldn't be healthy, he thought.

MIKE RUSSELL LOOKED over the monstrous one-time pad he'd been sent, hoping that he wouldn't have to use it all in one day. The sheer drudgery of transposing random letters was enough to drive a man mad, and there had to be an easier way. That was what his KH-7 encrypting machines were for, but Foley had suggested to him that the -7 was not fully secure, which thought outraged the professional in him. The KH-7 was the most sophisticated encryption machine ever made, easy to use, and utterly impossible—so he thought—to crack. He knew the design team of mathematicians who'd figured out the algorithms. The algebraic formulas used in the -7 were sufficiently over his head that he had to strain to see the bottom. . . . But what one mathematician could make, another, in theory, could break, and the Russians had good ones. And from that fact came the nightmare: The communications that it was his job to protect were being read by the enemy.

And that just wouldn't do.

So, he had to use this pad for super-critical communications, inconvenient or not. It wasn't as though he had much of a social life in Moscow. Ordinary Russian citizens viewed his dark skin as an indication of some relationship with some tree-climbing African monkey, which was so offensive to Russell that he never talked about it to anyone, just let it generate rage in his heart, the sort of deep-soul anger that he'd felt for the Ku Klux Klan before the FBI had put those ignorant crackers out of business. Maybe they still hated him, but a steer could lust after a lot of things without being able to fuck them, and so it was with those bigoted idiots who'd forgotten that Ulysses Simpson Grant had defeated Bobby Lee, after all. They could hate all they wanted, but the prospect of Leavenworth Federal Pen kept them in their dark little holes. *The Russians are just as bad*, Russell thought, *racist cocksuckers.* But he had his books and his tape player for cool jazz, and the extra pay that came with this hardship post. And for now he'd show Ivan a signal he couldn't crack, and Foley would get his Rabbit out. He lifted his phone and dialed the proper numbers.

"Foley."

"Russell. Want to come down to my office for a minute?"

"On the way," the Station Chief replied. Four minutes. "What is it, Mike?" he asked, coming through the door.

Russell held up the ring binder. "Only three copies of this. Us, Langley, and Fort Meade. You want secure, my man, you got secure. Just try to keep the messages short, okay? This shit can really jack up my blood pressure."

"Okay, Mike. Shame there isn't a better way of doing that."

"Maybe someday. Ought to be a way to do it with a computer—you know, put the pad on a floppy disk. Maybe I'll write to Fort Meade about it," Russell thought. "This stuff can make you cross-eyed."

Better you than me, Foley couldn't say. "Okay, I'll have something for you later today."

"Right." Russell nodded. He didn't have to add that it would also be enciphered on his KH-7 and *then* super-encrypted with the pad. He hoped that Ivan would intercept the signal and give his cryptanalysts the document to work on. Thinking about those bastards going nuts over one of his signals was one of the things he liked to smile about. Fine, give their world-class math aces this stuff to fool with.

But there was no telling. If KGB had managed, for example, to plant a bug in the building, it would be powered not by an internal battery, but rather by microwave emanations from Our Lady of the Microchips across the street. He had two permanent staff people who roamed the embassy, searching for unexplained RF signals. Every so often, they found one and dug the bug out, but the last of those had been twenty months before. Now they said that the embassy was fully swept and fully clean. But nobody believed that. Ivan was just too clever. Russell wondered how Foley kept his identity a secret, but that was not his problem. Keeping the comms secure was hard enough.

BACK IN HIS OFFICE, Foley drafted his next signal to Langley, trying to keep it as short as possible to make it easy for Russell. It would surely open some eyes on the Seventh Floor. He hoped that the Brits hadn't gotten word on the idea to Washington yet. That would be seen as a major impropriety, and senior officials everywhere got their noses out of joint on trivial crap like that. But with some things you just didn't have time to run it through channels, and as a senior Station Chief, it was expected that he would show some initiative once in a while.

And along with initiative, maybe a little panache.

Foley checked his watch. He was wearing his reddest tie, and he was an hour and a half from taking the metro home, and the Rabbit needed to see him and the flag signal. A little voice was telling Foley to get BEATRIX moving as fast as practicable. Whether it was danger to the Rabbit or something else, he couldn't tell, but Foley was one to trust his instincts.

CHAPTER 21

VACATION

IT WASN'T EASY, really, to make sure one took the right subway train. Both the Rabbit and Foley were using the inhuman efficiency of what had to be the only aspect of Soviet life that actually functioned properly, and the remarkable thing was that the trains ran on a schedule that was as regular and predictable as the setting of the sun, just far more frequent. Foley got his dispatch into Mike Russell's hands, then put his raincoat on and walked out the embassy front door at exactly the right moment, walked at exactly the usual pace, and got to the subway platform at exactly the right time, then turned to verify it with the clock that hung on the ceiling of the station. Yeah, he'd done it again. The train pulled in, just as the previous train pulled out, and Foley walked aboard the usual car, turning to see . . . yes, the Rabbit was there. Foley unfolded his paper. His unbuttoned raincoat hung loosely on his shoulders.

Zaitzev was actually surprised to see the red tie, but he could hardly complain. As usual, he inched his way in the proper direction.

It was almost routine now, the COS thought. He felt the hand surreptitiously enter his pocket and withdraw. Then his acute senses felt the man take a step away. Hopefully, there would be little more of this. It was safe for Foley, but decidedly unsafe for the Rabbit, however skillful he might have become at this exercise. The presence of others on this subway car—some faces he recognized from repetition—could well represent people of the Second Chief Directorate. There could be intermittent surveillance on him, using a bunch of different officers. That would be a sensible tactic for the opposition to use, on and off, to diminish the chance that he'd spot them.

In due course, as before, the train arrived at the appointed stop, and Foley walked off. In a few more weeks, he'd have to put the lining in his coat, and maybe even wear the *shapka* Mary Pat had bought him. He had to start thinking about what would happen *after* they got the Rabbit out. If BEATRIX worked all the way, he'd have to maintain his cover activities for a time—or maybe switch to driving to the embassy, a change in routine that the Russians would not note as unusual. He was an American, after all, and Americans were famous for driving everywhere. The metro was getting tedious. Too crowded, often with people who didn't know what a shower was for. The things he did for his country, Foley thought. No, he corrected himself, the things he did *against* his country's enemies. That was what made it worthwhile. *Giving the big ol' Bear a bellyache—maybe even stomach cancer,* he mused, walking to his apartment.

"YES, ALAN?" Charleston asked, looking up from his desk.

"This is a major operation, I take it?" Kingshot asked.

"Major in its objective, yes," the Director General confirmed. "As routine as possible in its operation. We only have three people in Budapest, and it would not be overly brilliant to fly in a goon squad."

"Anyone else going?"

"Jack Ryan, the American," Sir Basil said.

"He's no field officer," Kingshot objected immediately.

"It's fundamentally an American operation, Alan. They reasonably requested that one of their people go along to observe. In return, we'll have a day or two to debrief their Rabbit at a safe house of our choosing. He will doubtless have a good deal of useful information, and we'll get the first chance to speak with him."

"Well, I hope this Ryan fellow doesn't queer the pitch for us."

"Alan, he's shown himself to be fairly levelheaded in time of trouble, hasn't he?" Sir Basil asked, reasonable as ever.

"Must be his Marine training," Kingshot observed with dark generosity.

"And he's very clever, Alan. He's been giving us excellent work on his analysis project."

"If you say so, sir. To get the three bodies, I need to get some help from Special Branch, and then spend time on my knees hoping for something dreadful to happen."

"What are you thinking?"

Kingshot explained his nascent operational concept. It was really the only way to make something like this happen. And, as Sir Basil had observed earlier in the day, it was as grisly as an autopsy.

"How likely is such a thing to happen?" Basil asked.

"I need to talk with the police to answer that one."

"Who's your contact there?"

"Chief Superintendent Patrick Nolan. You've met him."

Charleston closed his eyes for a moment. "The huge chap, arrests rugby forwards for light exercise?"

"That's Nolan. They call him 'Tiny' on the force. I think he eats barbells with his porridge. Am I free to discuss this Operation BEATRIX with him?"

"Just in terms of our needs, Alan."

"Very good, sir," Kingshot agreed, and left the room.

"YOU WANT *WHAT?*" Nolan asked over a pint in a pub a block from New Scotland Yard, just after four in the afternoon.

"You heard me, Tiny," Kingshot said. He lit a cigarette to fit in with the rest of the bar's patrons.

"Well, I must say I've heard a lot of strange things in my time with the Yard, but never that." Nolan was a good six-four and two hundred thirty pounds, very little of it fat. He spent at least an hour, three times a week, in the Yard's exercise room. He rarely carried a handgun on duty. He'd never needed one to help a felon see the futility of resistance. "Can you say what this is for?" he asked.

"Sorry, not allowed to. All I can say is that's it's a matter of some importance."

A long pull on his beer. "Well, you know that we do not keep such things in cold storage, even in the Black Museum."

"I was thinking a traffic smash. They happen all the time, don't they?"

"Yes, they do, Alan, but not to a family of three."

"Well, how often *do* such things happen?" Kingshot asked.

"Perhaps twenty such incidents in an average year, and their occurrence is wholly irregular. You cannot depend on it in any given week."

"Well, we'll just have to hope for good luck, and if it doesn't happen, then it simply does not happen." That would be an inconvenience. Perhaps it would be better to enlist the help of the Americans. They killed at least fifty thousand people per year on their highways. He'd suggest that to Sir Basil in the morning, Kingshot decided.

"Good luck? Not sure I'd call it that, Alan," Nolan pointed out.

"You know what I mean, Tiny. All I can say is that it's bloody important."

"And if it happens out on the M4, then what?"

"We collect the bodies—"

"And the survivors of the deceased?" Nolan asked.

"We substitute weighted bags for the bodies. The condition of the corpses will preclude an open-casket ceremony, won't it?"

"Yes, there is that. Then what?"

"We'll have our people deal with the bodies. You really do not need to know the details." The SIS had a close and cordial relationship with the Metropolitan Police, but it went only so far.

Nolan finished his pint. "Yes, I'll leave the nightmares to you, Alan." He managed not to shiver. "I should start keeping my eyes open at once, is it?"

"Immediately."

"And we should consider taking the leavings from more than one such incident?"

"Obviously." Kingshot nodded. "Another round?"

"Good idea, Alan," Nolan agreed. And his host waved to the barman. "You know, someday I'd love to know what you are using me for."

"Someday after we're both retired, Patrick. You'll be pleased to know what you are helping with. That I can promise you, old man."

"If you say so, Alan." Nolan conceded the point. For now.

"WHAT THE HELL?" Judge Moore observed, reading the latest dispatch from Moscow. He handed the fresh copy over to Greer, who scanned it and passed it along to Mike Bostock.

"Mike, your boy Foley has a lively imagination," the Admiral commented.

"This sounds more like Mary Pat. She's the cowboy—well, cow*girl*, I suppose you'd say. It *is* original, guys."

"Original isn't the word," the DCI said, rolling his eyes somewhat. "Okay, Mike, is it doable?"

"Theoretically, yes—and I like the operational concept. To get a defector and keep Ivan ignorant of the fact. That's style, gentlemen," Bostock said admiringly. "The ugly part is that you need three bodies, one of them a child."

The three intelligence executives managed not to shudder at the thought. It was easiest, oddly, for Judge Moore, who'd managed to get his hands wet thirty years earlier. But that had been in time of war, when the rules were a lot looser. But not loose enough for him to keep from having regrets. That was what had gotten him back into the law. He couldn't take back the things he'd done wrong, but he could make sure they wouldn't happen again. *Or something like that,* he told himself now. *Something like that.*

"Why a car crash?" Moore asked. "Why not a house fire? Doesn't that suit the tactical purposes better?"

"Good point," Bostock agreed at once. "Less physical trauma to have to explain away."

"I'll shoot that off to Basil." Even the most brilliant of people, Moore realized, could be limited in their thinking. Well, that was why he kept telling people to think outside the box. And every so often, someone managed to do that. Just not often enough.

"You know," Mike Bostock said, after a little thinking. "This will be something if we can pull it off."

" 'If' can be a very large word, Mike," Greer cautioned.

"Well, maybe this time the glass is half full," the Deputy DDO suggested. "Fine. The main mission is getting this guy out, but the goose can use a little sauce once in a while."

"Hmph," Greer observed dubiously.

"Well, I'll call Emil over at the Bureau and see what he has to say about this," Moore said. "More his turf than ours."

"And if some lawyer gets hold of it, then what, Arthur?"

"James, there are ways of dealing with lawyers."

A pistol is often useful, Greer didn't say. He nodded concurrence. One bridge to cross at a time was always a good rule, especially in this crazy business.

"HOW DID THINGS go today, honey?" Mary Pat asked.

"Oh, the usual" was the reply for the microphones in the ceiling. More significant was the double thumbs-up, followed by the pass of the note from his coat pocket. They had a meeting place and a time. MP would handle that. She read the note and nodded. She and Eddie would take another walk to meet little Svetlana, the *zaichik*. Then it was just a matter of getting the Rabbit out of town, and since he was KGB, it ought not to be overly hard. That was one advantage of having him work at The Centre. They were taking out a minor nobleman, after all, not just another *muzhik* from the widget factory.

Dinner, he saw, was steak, the usual celebratory meal. MP was as psyched about this as he was—probably more so. With just a little luck, this Operation BEATRIX would make their reputation, and a good field rep was something they both wanted.

RYAN TOOK THE usual train back to Chatham. He'd missed his wife again, but she'd had a routine day, so she'd probably left early, like all the government-employed docs with whom she worked. He wondered if this bad habit would carry over when they went home to Peregrine Cliff. Probably not. Bernie Katz liked to have his desk clean, and waiting lists at zero, and the local work habits were driving his wife to drink. The good news was that, with no surgery scheduled this week, they'd be able to have wine that evening with dinner.

He wondered how long he'd be away from home. It wasn't something he was used to. One advantage of being an analyst was that he did all of his work at the office, then drove home. He'd rarely slept away from his wife in all the time they'd been married, a rule almost sacred in their marriage. He liked it when he woke up at three in the morning and could roll over and kiss her in mid-dream, then see her smile in her sleep. His marriage to Cathy was the anchor to his life, the very center of his universe. But now duty would take him away from her for several days—not something he looked forward to. Nor did he look forward to flying on another goddamned airplane into a communist country with false identity papers and overseeing a black operation there—he didn't know shit about them, just what he'd picked up talking to the occasional field spook at Langley . . . and from his own experiences here in London, and at home over the Chesapeake, when Sean Miller and his terrorists had come to his house with guns blazing. It was something he tried very hard to forget. It might have been different had he stayed in the Marine Corps, but there he would have been surrounded by fellow warriors. He'd have been able to bathe in their respect, to remember his feat of arms with pride at having done the right thing at the right time, to recount his deeds to the interested, to pass along the tactical lessons learned the hard way on the field of demibattle over beers at the O-club, even to smile about something that one didn't ordinarily smile about. But he'd left the Marine Corps with a bad back, and had had to endure his combat as a very frightened civilian. Courage, though, he'd once been told, was being the only one who knew how terrified you were. And, yeah, he supposed, he'd shown that quality when it had counted. And his job in Hungary would be only to watch, and then, the important part, to sit in while Sir Basil's boys interviewed the Rabbit at some safe house in London, or wherever, before the Air Force, probably, flew them to Washington in their own special-mission KC-135 out of RAF Bentwaters, with nice food and plenty of liquor to ease the flight fright.

He walked off the train and up the steps, and caught a cab for Grizedale Close, where he found that Cathy had sent Miss Margaret away and was busy in the kitchen, assisted, he saw, by Sally.

"Hey, babe." Kiss. He lifted Sally for the usual hug. Little girls give the best hugs.

"So, what was the important message about?" Cathy asked.

"No big deal. Kinda disappointing, actually."

Cathy turned to look her husband in the eye. Jack couldn't lie worth a damn. It was one of the things she liked about him, actually. "Uh-huh."

"Honest, babe," Ryan said, knowing the look, and then deepening the hole in which he was standing. "I didn't get shot at or anything."

"Okay," she acknowledged, meaning, *We'll talk about it later.*

Blew it again, Jack, Ryan told himself. "How's the glasses business?"

"Saw six people, had time for eight or nine, but that's all I had on my list."

"Have you told Bernie about working conditions here?"

"Called him today, right after I got home. He had himself a good laugh and told me to enjoy the vacation."

"What about the guys who had a brewski during a procedure?"

Cathy turned. "He said, and I quote, 'Jack's in the CIA, isn't he? Have him shoot the bastards.' End of quote." She turned back to her cooking.

"You need to tell him that we don't do that sort of thing." Jack managed a smile. This, at least, wasn't a lie, and he hoped she could tell.

"I know. You'd never be able to carry it on your conscience."

"Too Catholic," he confirmed.

"Well, at least I know you'll never fool around on me."

"May God strike me dead with cancer if I ever do." It was the one imprecation about cancer that she almost approved of.

"You'll never have reason to, Jack." And that was true enough. She didn't like guns and she didn't like bloodshed, but she did love him. And that was sufficient to the moment.

Dinner turned out okay, followed by the usual evening activities, until it was time for their four-year-old to put on her yellow sleeper and climb into her big-girl bed.

With Sally in bed and Little Jack dozing as well, there was time for the usual mindless TV watching. Or so Jack hoped, until . . .

"Okay, Jack, what's the bad news?"

"Nothing much," he answered. The worst possible answer. Cathy was just too good at reading his mind.

"What's that mean?"

"I have to go on a little trip—to Bonn," Jack remembered the advice from Sir Basil. "It's a NATO thing I got stuck with."

"Doing what?"

"I can't say, babe."

"How long?"

"Three or four days, probably. They think I am uniquely suited to this for some damned reason or other."

"Uh-huh." Ryan's semi-truthfulness was just oblique enough to foil her mind reading for once.

"You're not going to be carrying a gun or anything?"

"Honey, I am an analyst, not a field officer, remember? That sort of thing is not my job. For that matter, I don't think field spooks carry guns very much anyway. Too hard to explain away if somebody notices."

"But—"

"James Bond is in the movies, babe, not real life."

Ryan returned his attention to the TV. ITV was doing a repeat of *Danger—UXB,* and again Jack found himself wondering if Brian would survive his job of defusing unexploded bombs and then marry Suzy when he returned to civilian life. EOD, now *there* was a miserable job, but, if you made a mistake, at least it wouldn't hurt for very long.

"HEARD ANYTHING FROM BOB?" Greer asked just before six in the evening.

Judge Moore stood up from his expensive swivel chair and stretched. Too much time sitting down, and not enough moving around. Back in Texas, he had a small ranch—called that because he owned three quarter horses; you couldn't be a prominent citizen in Texas unless you owned a horse or two—and three or four times a week, he'd saddle Aztec up and ride around for an hour or so, mainly to get his head clear, to allow himself to think outside his office. That was how he tended to get his best thinking done. Maybe, Moore thought, that's why he felt so goddamned unproductive here. An office just wasn't a very good place for thinking, but every executive in the world pretended it was. Christ knew why. That's what he needed at Langley—his own stable. There was plenty of room on the Langley campus—a good five times what he had in Texas. But if he ever did that, the stories would spread around the world: The American DCI liked to ride horses with his black Stetson hat—that went along with the horse—and probably a Colt .45 on his hip—that was optional—and *that* just wouldn't look good to the TV crews that would sooner or later appear at the perimeter fence with their minicams. And so, for reasons of personal vanity, he had to deny himself the chance to do some good creative thinking. It was totally asinine, the former judge told himself, to allow such considerations to affect the way he did his work. Over in England, Basil could chase foxes on the back of a nice hunter-thoroughbred, and would anyone over there care? Hell, no. He'd be admired for it, or at worst thought a tiny bit eccentric, in a country where eccentricity was an admirable quality. But in the Land of the Free, men were enslaved by customs imposed on them by news reporters and elected officials who screwed their secretaries. Well, there was no rule that the world had to make sense, was there?

"Nothing important. Just a cable that said his meetings with our Korean friends were going well," Moore reported.

"You know, those people scare me a little," Greer observed. He didn't have to explain why. The KCIA occasionally had its field personnel deal a little too directly with employees of the other Korean government. The rules were a little different over there. The ongoing state of war between North and South was still a very real thing and, in time of war, some people lost their lives. CIA hadn't done such things in almost thirty years. Asian people hadn't adopted Western ideas of the value of human life. Maybe because their countries were just too crowded. Maybe because they have different religious beliefs. Maybe a lot of things, but for whatever reason they were just a little different in the operational parameters they felt free to work within—or without.

"They're our best eye on North Korea and China, James," Moore reminded him. "And they are very faithful allies."

"I know, Arthur." It was nice to hear things about the People's Republic of China once in a while. Penetrating *that* country was one of CIA's most frustrating tasks. "I just wish they weren't so cavalier about murder."

"They operate within fairly strict rules, and both sides seem to play by them."

And on both sides, killings had to be authorized at a very high level. Not that this would matter all that much to the corpse in question. "Wet" operations interfered with the main mission, which was gathering information. That was something people occasionally forgot, but something that CIA and KGB mainly understood, which was why both agencies had gotten away from it.

But when the information retrieved frightened or otherwise upset the politicians who oversaw the intelligence services, then the spook shops were ordered to do things that they usually preferred to avoid—and so, then, they took their action through surrogates and/or mercenaries, mainly. . . .

"Arthur, if KGB wants to hurt the Pope, how do you suppose they'd go about it?"

"Not one of their own," Moore thought. "Too dangerous. It would be a political catastrophe, like a tornado going right through the Kremlin. It would sure as hell kibosh Yuriy Vladimirovich's political career and, you know, I don't see him taking that much risk for any cause. Power is just too important to him."

The DDI nodded. "Agreed. I think he's going to resign his chairmanship soon. Has to. They wouldn't even let him jump from KGB boss to the General Secretaryship. That's a little too sinister even for them. They still remember Beria—the ones who sit around that table do, anyway."

"That's a good point, James," Moore said, turning back from the window. "I wonder how much longer Leonid Illyich has." Ascertaining Brezhnev's health was a constant CIA interest—hell, it was a matter of interest to everyone in Washington.

"Andropov is our best indicator on that. We're pretty sure he's Brezhnev's replacement. When it looks like Leonid Illyich is heading for the last roundup, then Yuriy Vladimirovich changes jobs."

"Good point, James. I'll float that to State and the White House."

Admiral Greer nodded. "It's what they pay us for. Back to the Pope," he suggested.

"The President is still asking questions," Moore confirmed.

"If they do anything, it won't be a Russian. Too many political pitfalls, Arthur."

"Again, I agree. But what the hell does that leave us?"

"They use the Bulgarians for wet work," Greer pointed out.

"So, look for a Bulgarian shooter?"

"How many Bulgars make pilgrimages to Rome, you suppose?"

"We can't tell the Italians to look into that, can we? It would leak sure as hell, and we can't have that. It would look pretty stupid in the press. It's just something we can't do, James."

Greer let out a long breath. "Yeah, I know, not without something firm."

"Firmer than what we have now—and that's air, James, just plain damned air." *It would be nice,* Judge Moore thought, *if CIA were as powerful as the movies and the critics think we are. Not all the time. Just once in a while.* But they weren't, and that was a fact.

THE NEXT DAY started in Moscow before it started anywhere else. Zaitzev awoke at the ringing of his windup alarm clock, grumbled and cursed like every workingman in the world, then stumbled off to the bathroom. Ten minutes later, he was drinking his morning tea and eating his black bread and butter.

Less than a mile away, the Foley family was doing much the same thing. Ed decided on an English muffin and grape jelly with his coffee for a change, joined by Little Eddie, who took a break from Worker Woman and his *Transformers* tapes. He was looking forward to the preschool that had been set up for Western children right there in the ghetto, where he showed great promise with crayons and the newly arrived Hot Wheels tricycles, plus being champion at the Sit 'n Spin.

He told himself that he could relax today. The meeting would be in the evening, and MP would handle that. In another week or so . . . maybe . . . BEATRIX would be all over, and he could relax again, letting his field officers do the running around this damned ugly city. Sure enough, the goddamned Baltimore Orioles were in the playoffs, and looking to go head to head with the Philadelphia Phillies, relegating his Bronx Bombers to the Hot Stove League yet again. What was with the new ownership, anyway? How could rich people be so stupid?

He'd have to keep to his metro routine. If KGB had him shadowed, it would be unusual—or would it?—for them to mark the specific train he was getting on. There was a question for him. If they did a one-two tail, the number two guy would stay on the platform and, after the train left, write down the time off the clock in the station—that was the only one that made sense, since it was the one that governed the trains themselves. KGB was thorough and professional, but would they be *that* good? That sort of precision was positively Germanic, but if the bastards could make the trains run that precisely, then probably KGB could take note of it, and the precise timing was what had enabled *him* to contact the Rabbit.

God damn this life, anyway! Foley raged briefly. But he'd known that before he'd accepted the posting to Moscow, and it was *exciting* here, wasn't it? *Yeah, like Louis XVI was probably excited on the cart ride to the guillotine,* Ed Sr. thought.

Someday he'd lecture on this down at The Farm. He hoped they'd appreciate just how hard it had been to write the lesson plan for his Operation BEATRIX lecture. Well, they might be a little impressed.

Forty minutes later, he purchased his copy of *Izvestia* and rode down the interminable escalator to the platform, as usual not noting the sideways looks of Russians looking at a real, live American as though he were a creature in the zoo. It would never have happened to a Russian in New York, where every ethnic group could be found, especially behind the wheel of a yellow cab.

THE MORNING ROUTINE was set in concrete by now. Miss Margaret was hovering over the kids, and Eddie Beaverton was outside the door. The kids were duly hugged and kissed, and the parents headed off to work. If there was anything Ryan hated, it was this routine. If only he'd been able to persuade Cathy to buy a flat in London, then every work day would have been a good two hours shorter—but, no, Cathy wanted green stuff around for the kids to play on. And soon they wouldn't see the sun until they got to work, and soon thereafter, hardly even then.

Ten minutes later, they were in their first-class compartment rolling northwest for London, Cathy in her medical journal and Jack in his *Daily Telegraph.* There was an article about Poland, and this reporter was unusually well-informed, Ryan saw at once. The articles in Britain tended to be a lot less long-winded than in *The Washington Post,* and for once Jack found himself regretting that. This guy had been well-briefed and/or he was pretty good at analysis. The Polish government was really caught between a rock and a hard place, and was getting squeezed, and there was talk, he saw, that the Pope was making some rumbles about the welfare of his homeland and his people, and *that,* the reporter noted, could upset a lot of apple carts.

Ain't that the truth, Jack thought. The really bad news was that it was in the open now. Who'd leaked it? He knew the reporter's name. He was a specialist in foreign affairs, mainly European. So, who'd leaked this? Somebody in the Foreign Office? Those people were, on the whole, pretty smart, but, like their American counterparts at Foggy Bottom, they occasionally spoke without thinking, and over here that could happen over a friendly pint in one of the thousands of comfortable pubs, maybe in a quiet corner booth, with a government employee paying off a marker or just wanting to show the media how smart he was. Would a head roll over this one? he wondered. Something to talk about with Simon.

Unless Simon had been the leaker. He was senior enough and well liked by his boss. Maybe Basil had authorized the leak? Or maybe they both knew a guy in Whitehall and had authorized him to have a friendly pint with a guy from Fleet Street.

Or maybe the reporter was smart enough to put two and two together all by himself. Not all the smart guys worked at Century House. Damned sure not all the smart ones in America worked at Langley. Generally speaking, talent went to where the money was, because smart people wanted large houses and nice vacations just like everyone else did. Those who went into government service knew that they could live comfortably, but not lavishly—but the best of them also knew that they had a mission to fulfill in life, and that was why you found very good people wearing uniforms or carrying guns and badges. In his own case, Ryan had done well in the trading business, but he finally found it unsatisfying. And so not all talented people sought after money. Some found themselves on some sort of quest.

Is that what you're doing, Jack? he asked himself, as the train pulled into Victoria Station.

"What deep thoughts this morning?" his wife asked.

"Huh?" Jack responded.

"I know the look, honey," she pointed out. "You're chewing over something important."

"Cathy, are you an eye cutter or a pshrink?"

"With you, I'm a pshrink," she replied, with a playful smile.

Jack stood and opened the compartment door. "Okay, my lady. You have eyeballs to regulate, and I have secrets to figure out." He waved his wife out the door. "What new things did you learn from *The Asshole and Armpit Monthly Gazette* on the way in?"

"You wouldn't understand."

"Probably," Jack conceded, heading off to the cabstand. They took a robin's-egg-blue one instead of the usual black.

"Hammersmith Hospital," Ryan told the driver, "and then One Hundred Westminster Bridge Road."

"MI-Six, is it, sir?"

"Excuse me?" Ryan replied innocently.

"Universal Export, sir, where James Bond used to work." He chuckled and pulled off.

Well, Ryan reflected, the CIA exit off the George Washington Parkway wasn't marked NATIONAL HIGHWAY ADMINISTRATION anymore. Cathy thought it was pretty funny. There was no keeping secrets from London cabdrivers. Cathy hopped out in the large underpass at Hammersmith, and the driver U-turned and went the last few blocks to Century House. Ryan went through the door, past Sergeant Major Canderton, and up to his office.

Coming in the door, he dropped the *Telegraph* on Simon's desk before doffing his raincoat.

"I saw it, Jack," Harding said at once.

"Who's talking?"

"Not sure. Foreign Office, probably. They've been briefed in on this. Or perhaps someone from the PM's office. Sir Basil is not pleased," Harding assured him.

"Nobody called the paper?"

"No. We didn't know about this until it was published this morning."

"I thought the local papers had a more cordial relationship with the government over here."

"Generally, they do, which leads me to believe it was the PM's office that did the leak." Harding's face was innocent enough, but Jack found himself trying to read it. That was something his wife was far better at. He had the feeling that Harding was not being entirely truthful, but he had no real reason to complain about that, did he?

"Anything new from the overnights?"

Harding shook his head. "Nothing of great interest. Nothing on this BEATRIX operation, either. Tell your wife about your impending trip?"

"Yeah, and I didn't tell you that she's pretty good at reading my mind."

"Most wives can, Jack." Harding had a good laugh at that.

ZAITZEV HAD THE same desk and the same pile of message traffic, always different in exact details, but always the same really: reports from field officers transmitting data from foreign nationals on all manner of subjects. He had hundreds of operation names memorized, and untold thousands of details resident between his ears, including the actual names of some of the agents and the code names of many, many others.

As on the previous workdays, he took his time, reading over all the morning traffic before sending it upstairs, trusting his trained memory to record and file away all of the important details.

Some, of course, contained information that was hidden in multiple ways. There was probably a penetration agent within CIA, for example, but his code name—TRUMPET—was all Zaitzev knew. Even the data he transmitted were concealed by the use of layered super-encryption, including a one-time pad. But the data went to a colonel on the sixth floor who specialized in CIA investigations and worked closely with the Second Chief Directorate—so, by implication, TRUMPET was giving KGB something in which the Second Directorate was interested, and *that* meant agents operating *for* CIA right here in Moscow. Which was enough to give him chills, but the Americans he'd talked to—he'd warned them about communications security, and that would flag any dispatch about him to a very limited number of people. And he knew that TRUMPET was being paid huge amounts of money, and so, probably he was not a senior CIA official, who, Zaitzev judged, were probably very well paid. An ideological agent would have given him cause to worry, but there were none of them in America whom he knew about—and he would know, wouldn't he?

In a week, perhaps less, the communicator told himself, he'd be in the West and safe. He hoped his wife would not go totally amok when he told her his plans, but probably she would not. She had no immediate family. Her mother had died the previous year, to Irina's great sorrow, and she had neither brothers nor sisters to hold her back, and she was not happy working at GUM because of all the petty corruption there. And he would promise to get her the piano she longed to have, but which even his KGB post couldn't get for her, so meager was the supply.

So he shuffled his papers, perhaps more slowly than usual, but not greatly so, he thought. There were few really hard workers, even in KGB. The cynical adage in the Soviet Union was "As long as they pretend to pay us, we will pretend to work," and the principle applied here as well. If you exceeded your quota, they'd just increase it the following year without any improvement in your working conditions—and so, few worked hard enough to be noticed as Heroes of Socialist Labor.

Just after 11:00, Colonel Rozhdestvenskiy appeared in the comms room. Zaitzev caught his eye and waved him over.

"Yes, Comrade Major?" the colonel asked.

"Comrade Colonel," he said quietly, "there have been no recent communications about six-six-six. Is there anything I need to know?"

The question took Rozhdestvenskiy aback. "Why do you ask?"

"Comrade Colonel," Zaitzev went on humbly, "it was my understanding that this operation is important and that I am the only communicator cleared for it. Have I acted improperly in any way?"

"Ah." Rozhdestvenskiy relaxed. "No, Comrade Colonel, we have no complaints with your activities. The operation no longer requires communications of this type."

"I see. Thank you, Comrade Colonel."

"You look tired, Major Zaitzev. Is anything the matter?"

"No, comrade. I suppose I could use a vacation. I didn't get to go anywhere during the summer. A week or two off duty would be a blessing, before the winter hits."

"Very well. If you have any difficulties, let me know, and I'll try to smooth things out for you."

Zaitzev managed a grateful smile. "Why, thank you, Comrade Colonel."

"You do good work down here, Zaitzev. We're all entitled to some time off, even State Security people."

"Thank you again, Comrade Colonel. I serve the Soviet Union."

Rozhdestvenskiy nodded and took his leave. As he walked out the door, Zaitzev took a long breath and went back to work memorizing dispatches . . . but not for the Soviet Union. *So,* he thought, *-666 was being handled by courier now.* He'd learn no more about it, but he'd just learned that it was going forward on a high-priority basis. They were really going to do it. He wondered if the Americans would get him out quickly enough to forestall it. The information was in his hands, but the ability to do anything about it was not. It was like being Cassandra of old, daughter of King Priam of Troy, knowing what was going to happen, but unable to get anyone to do anything about it. Cassandra had angered the gods somehow or other and received that curse as a result, but what had *he* done to deserve it? Zaitzev wondered, suddenly angry at CIA's inefficiency. But he couldn't just board a Pan American flight out of Sheremetyevo International Airport, could he?

CHAPTER 22

PROCUREMENTS AND ARRANGEMENTS

THE SECOND FACE-TO-FACE meeting was back at GUM department store, where a certain Little Bunny needed some fall/winter clothing, which her father wanted to get her—which was something of a surprise for Irina Bogdanova, but a pleasant one. Mary Pat, the supreme expert on shopping in the Foley family, wandered about looking at the various items on sale, surprised to see that they weren't all Soviet schlock. Some were even attractive . . . though not quite attractive enough to buy. She dawdled again in the fur department—the furs here might have sold fairly well in New York, though they were not quite on a par with Fendi. There weren't enough Italian designers in Russia. But the quality of the furs—that is, the animal skins themselves—wasn't too shabby. The Soviets just didn't know how to sew them together properly. *That was too bad, really,* she thought. The saddest thing about the Soviet Union was how the government of that gray country prevented its citizens from actually accomplishing much. There was so little originality here. The best things to buy were all old, pre-revolutionary art works, usually small ones, almost always religious pieces, sold at impromptu flea markets to raise needed money for some family or other. She'd already purchased several pieces, trying not to feel like a thief in doing so. To assuage her conscience, she never haggled, almost always paying the price asked instead of trying to chisel it down by a few percent. That would have been like armed robbery, she thought, and her ultimate mission in Moscow—this was a core belief for her—was to help these people, though in a way they could hardly have understood or approved. But, for the most part, Muscovites liked her American smile and friendliness. And certainly they liked the blue-stripe certificate rubles she paid with, cash money that would give them access to luxury items or, almost as good, cash that they could exchange at a rate of three or four to one.

She wandered about for half an hour, then saw her target in the children's clothing area. She maneuvered that way, taking time to lift and examine various items before coming up behind him.

"Good evening, Oleg Ivan'ch," she said quietly, handling a parka meant for a girl of three or four.

"Mary, is it?"

"That is correct. Tell me, do you have any vacation days available to you?"

"Yes, I do. Two weeks of it, in fact."

"And you told me that your wife likes classical music?"

"That is also correct."

"There is a fine conductor. His name is Jozsef Rozsa. He will start performing in the main concert hall in Budapest on Sunday evening. The best hotel for you to check in to is the Astoria. It is a short distance from the train station, and is popular with Soviet guests. Tell all your friends what you are doing. Arrange to buy them things in Budapest. Do everything that a Soviet citizen does. We will handle the rest," she assured him.

"All of us," Zaitzev reminded her. "All of us come out?"

"Of course, Oleg. Your little *zaichik* will see many wonders in America, and the winters are not so fierce as they are here," MP added.

"We Russians enjoy our winters," he pointed out, with a little amour propre.

"In that case, you will be able to live in an area as cold as Moscow. And if you desire warm weather in February, you can drive or fly to Florida and relax on a sunny beach."

"You are tourist agent, Mary?" the Rabbit asked.

"For you, Oleg, I am just that. Are you comfortable passing information to my husband on the metro?"

"Yes."

You shouldn't be, Mary Pat thought. "What is your best necktie?"

"A blue one with red stripes."

"Very well, wear that one two days before you take the train to Budapest. Bump into him and apologize, and we will know. Two days before you leave Moscow, wear your blue-striped tie and bump into him on the metro," she repeated. You had to be careful doing this. People could make the goddamnedest mistakes in the simplest of matters, even when—no, *especially* when—their lives were on the line. That was why she was making it as easy as possible. Only one thing to remember. Only one thing to do.

"*Da,* I can do that easily."

Optimistic bastard, aren't you? "Excellent. Please be very careful, Oleg Ivan'ch." And with that, she went on her way. But then she stopped five or six meters away and turned. In her purse was a Minox camera. She shot five frames, and then walked away.

"WELL, DIDN'T YOU see anything worth getting?" her husband asked, out in their used Mercedes 280.

"No, nothing really worthwhile. Maybe we should try a trip up to Helsinki to get some winter stuff," she suggested. "You know, take the train, like. Ought to be fun to do it that way. Eddie should like it."

The Station Chief's eyebrow went up. *Probably better to take the train,* he thought. *Doesn't look rushed or forced. Carry lots of suitcases, half of them empty to bring back all the shit you'll buy there with your Comecon rubles,* Ed Foley thought. *Except you don't come back . . . and if Langley and London get their shit together, maybe we can make it a real home-run ball. . . .*

"Home, honey?" Foley asked. Wouldn't it be a hoot if KGB *didn't* have their home and car bugged, and they were doing all this secret-agent crap for no reason at all? he thought idly. Well, at worst, it was good practice, wasn't it?

"Yeah, we've done enough for one day."

"BLOODY HELL," Basil Charleston breathed. He lifted his phone and punched three buttons.

"Yes, sir?" Kingshot asked, coming into the room.

"This." C handed the dispatch across.

"Shit," Kingshot breathed.

Sir Basil managed a smile. "It's always the obvious, simple things, isn't it?"

"Yes, sir. Even so, does make one feel rather thick," he admitted. "A house fire. Works better than what we originally thought."

"Well, something to remember. How many house fires do we have in London, Alan?"

"Sir Basil, I have not a clue," the most senior field spook in the SIS admitted. "But find out I shall."

"Get this to your friend Nolan as well."

"Tomorrow morning, sir," Kingshot promised. "At least it improves our chances. Are CIA working on this as well?"

"Yes."

AS WAS THE FBI. Director Emil Jacobs had heard his share of oddball requests from the folks on "the other side of the river," as CIA was sometimes called in official Washington. But this was positively gruesome. He lifted his phone and punched his direct line to the DCI.

"There's a good reason for this, I presume, Arthur?" he asked without preamble.

"Not over the phone, Emil, but yes."

"Three Caucasians, one male in his early thirties, one female same age, and a little girl age three or four," Jacobs said, reading it off the hand-delivered note from Langley. "My field agents will think the Director's slipped a major gear, Arthur. We'd probably be better off asking local police forces for assistance—"

"But—"

"Yes, I know, it would leak too quickly. Okay, I can send a message to all my SACs and have them check their morning papers, but it won't be easy to keep something like this from leaking out."

"Emil, I understand that. We're trying to get help from the Brits on this as well. Not the sort of thing you can just whistle up, I know. All I can say is that it's very important, Emil."

"You due on The Hill anytime soon?"

"House Intelligence Committee tomorrow at ten. Budget stuff," Moore explained. Congress was always going after that information, and Moore always had to defend his agency from people on The Hill, who would just as soon cut CIA off at the ankles—so that they could complain about "intelligence failures" later on, of course.

"Okay, can you stop off here on the way? I gotta hear this cock-and-bull story," Jacobs announced.

"Eight-forty or so?"

"Works for me, Arthur."

"See you then," Moore promised.

Director Jacobs replaced his phone, wondering what could be so goddamned important as to request the Federal Bureau of Investigation to play grave robber.

ON THE METRO HOME, after buying his little *zaichik* a white parka with red and green flowers on it, Zaitzev thought over his strategy. When would he tell Irina about their impromptu vacation? If he sprang it on her as a surprise, there would be one sort of problem—Irina would worry about her accounting job at GUM, but the office was, by her account, so loosely run that they'd hardly notice a missing body. But if he did give her too much warning, there would be another problem—she'd try to micromanage everything, like every wife in the known world, since, in her mind, he was unfitted to figure out anything. That was rather amusing, Oleg Ivan'ch thought, given the current circumstances.

So, then, no, he would not tell her ahead of time, but instead spring this trip on her as a surprise, and use this Hungarian conductor as the excuse. Then the big surprise would come in Budapest. He wondered how she'd react to that piece of news. Perhaps not well, but she was a Russian wife, trained and educated to accept the orders of her man, which, all Russian men thought, was as it should be.

Svetlana loved riding the metro. That was the thing with little children, Oleg had learned. To them everything was an adventure to take in with their wide children's eyes, even something as routine as riding the underground train. She didn't walk or run. She pranced, like a puppy—or like a bunny, her father thought, smiling down at her. Would his little *zaichik* find better adventures in the West?

Probably so . . . if I get her there alive, Zaitzev reminded himself. There was danger involved, but somehow his fear was not for himself, but for his daughter. How odd that was. Or was it? He didn't know anymore. He knew that he had a mission of sorts, and that was all that he actually saw before him. The rest of it was just a collection of intermediate steps, but at the end of the steps was a bright, shining light, and that was all he could really see. It was very strange how the light had grown brighter and brighter since his first doubts about Operation -666 until now, when it occupied all his mental eyes could see. Like a moth drawn to a light, he kept circling in closer and closer, and all he could really hope was that the light was not a flame that would kill him.

"Here, Papa!" Svetlana said, recognizing their stop, taking his hand, and dragging him forward to the sliding doors. A minute later, she jumped on the moving steps of the escalator, excited by that ride as well. His child was like an American adult—or how Russians supposed them to be, always seeing opportunities and possibilities and the fun to be had, instead of the dangers and threats that careful, sober Soviet citizens saw everywhere. But if Americans were so foolish, why were Soviets always trying—and failing—to catch up with them? Was America really right where the USSR was so often wrong? It was a deeper question that he'd scarcely considered. All he knew of America was the obvious propaganda he saw every night on television or read about in the official State newspapers. He knew that had to be wrong, but his knowledge was unbalanced, since he did not really know true information. And so his leap to the West was fundamentally a leap of faith. If his country was so wrong, then the alternative superpower had to be right. It was a big, long, and dangerous leap, he thought, walking down the sidewalk and holding his little girl's hand. He told himself that he ought to be more fearful.

But it was too late to be frightened, and turning back would have been as harmful to him as going forward. Above everything else, it was a question of who would destroy him—his country or himself—if he failed to carry out his mission. And on the other side, would America reward him for trying to do what he deemed the right thing? It seemed that he was like Lenin and the other revolutionary heroes: He saw something that was objectively wrong, and he was going to try to prevent it. Why? Because he had to. He had to trust that his country's enemies would see right and wrong as he did. Would they? While the American President had denounced his nation as the focus of all the evil in the world, his country said much the same thing of America. Who was right? Who was wrong? But it was *his* country and *his* employer that was conspiring to murder an innocent man, and that was as far as he could see into the right/wrong question.

As Oleg and Svetlana turned left to go into their apartment building, he recognized one final time that his course was set. He could not change it, but could only toss the dice and wait to see how they came up.

And where would his daughter grow up? That also rested on the flying dice.

IT HAPPENED FIRST in York, the largest city in northern England. Fire-safety engineers tell everyone who will listen that the least important thing about fires is what causes them to start, because they always start for the same reasons. In this case, it was the one that firefighters most hate to discover. Owen Williams, after a friendly night at his favorite pub, The Brown Lion, managed to down six pints of dark beer, which, added to a lengthy and tiring day working his job as a carpenter, had made him rather sleepy by the time he got to his third-floor flat, but that didn't stop him from switching on the TV in his bedroom and lighting a final cigarette of the day. His head propped up on a plumped pillow, he took a few puffs before fading out from the alcohol and the day's hard work. When that happened, his hand relaxed, and the cigarette fell onto the bedclothes. There it smoldered for about ten minutes before the white cotton sheets started to burn. Since Williams was unmarried—his wife had divorced him a year before—there was no one nearby to take note of the acrid, evil smell, and gradually the smoke wafted up to the ceiling as the low-level fire progressively consumed the bedclothes and then the mattress.

People rarely die from fire, and neither did Owen Williams. Instead, he started breathing in the smoke. Smoke—engineers often use the term "fire gas"—mainly consists of hot air, carbon monoxide, and soot particles, which are unburned material from the fire's fuel. Of these, the carbon monoxide is often the deadliest component, since it forms a bond with the red blood cells. This bond is actually stronger than the bond that hemoglobin forms with the free oxygen that the blood conveys to the various parts of the human body. The overall effect on the human consciousness is rather like that of alcohol—euphoria, like being pleasantly drunk, followed by unconsciousness and, if it goes too far, as in this case, death from oxygen starvation of the brain. And so, with a fire all around him, Owen Williams never woke, only fell deeper and deeper into a sleep that took him peacefully into eternity at the age of thirty-two years.

It wasn't until three hours later that a shift worker who lived on the same floor came home from work and noticed a smell in the third-floor corridor that lit up his internal alarm lights. He pounded on the door, and, getting no response, ran to his own flat and dialed 999.

There was a firehouse only six blocks away, and there, as with any other such house in the world, the firefighters rolled out of their military-style single beds, pulled on their boots and their turn-out coats, slid down the brass rail to the apparatus floor, punched the button to lift the automatic doors, and raced out on the street in their Dennis pumper, followed by a ladder truck. The drivers both knew the streets as well as any taxi driver and arrived at the apartment building less than ten minutes after their bells had chimed them awake. The pumper crew halted their vehicle, and two men dragged the draft hoses to the corner fire hydrant, charging the line in a skillful and well-practiced drill. The ladder men, whose primary job was search and rescue, raced inside to find that the concerned citizen who'd called in the alarm had already pounded on every door on the third floor and gotten his neighbors awake and out of their apartments. He pointed the lead fireman to the correct door, and that burly individual knocked it down with two powerful swings of his axe. He was greeted by a dense cloud of black smoke, the smell of which got past his air mask and immediately announced "mattress" to his experienced mind. This was followed by a quick prayer that they'd gotten here in time, and then instant dread that they had not. Everything, including the time of day, was against them in the dark, early morning. He ran into the back bedroom, smashed out the windows with his steel axe to vent the smoke outside, and then turned to see what he'd seen thirty or more times before—a human form, nearly hidden by the smoke and not moving. By then, two more of his colleagues were in the room. They dragged Owen Williams out into the corridor.

"Oh, shit!" one of them observed. The senior paramedic on the crew put an oxygen mask on the colorless face and started hitting the button to force pure oxygen into the lungs, and a second man began pounding on the victim's chest to get his heart restarted while, behind them, the enginemen snaked a two-and-a-half-inch hose into the flat and started spraying water.

All in all, it was a textbook exercise. The fire was snuffed out in less than three minutes. Soon thereafter, the smoke had largely cleared, and the firemen took off their protective air masks. But, out in the corridor, Owen Williams showed not a flicker of life. The rule was that nobody was dead until a physician said so, and so they carried the body like a large and heavy limp rag to the white ambulance sitting on the street. The paramedic crew had their own battle drill, and they followed it to the letter, first putting the body on their gurney, then checking his eyes, then his airway—it was clear—and using their ventilator to get more oxygen into him, plus more CPR to get the heart moving. The peripheral burns would have to wait. The first thing to be done was to get the heart beating and lungs breathing, as the driver pulled out onto the darkened streets for Queen Victoria Hospital, just more than a mile away.

But by the time they got there, the paramedics in the back knew that it was just a waste of their highly valuable time. The casualty-receiving area was ready for them. The driver reversed direction and backed in, the rear doors were wrenched open, and the gurney was wheeled out, with a young doctor observing but not touching anything yet.

"Smoke inhalation," the fireman-paramedic said, on coming in the swinging doors. "Severe carbon monoxide intoxication." The extensive but mainly superficial burns could wait for the moment.

"How long?" the ER doc asked at once.

"Don't know. It does not look good, doctor. CO poisoning, eyes fixed and dilated, fingernails red, no response to CPR or oxygen as yet," the paramedic reported.

The medics all tried. You don't just kiss off the life of a man in his early thirties, but an hour later it was clear that Owen Williams would not open his blue eyes ever again, and, on the doctor's command, lifesaving efforts were stopped and a time of death announced, to be typed in on the death certificate. The police were there, also, of course. They mostly chatted with the firemen until the cause of death was established. The blood chemistry was taken—they'd drawn blood immediately to check blood gasses—and after fifteen minutes, the lab reported that the level of carbon monoxide was 39 percent, deep into the lethal range. He'd been dead before the firemen had rolled off their cots. And that was that.

It was the police rather than the firemen who took it from there. A man had died, and it had to be reported up the chain of command.

That chain ended in London in the steel-and-glass building that was New Scotland Yard, with its revolving triangular sign that made tourists think that the name of the London police force was, in fact, Scotland Yard, when actually that had been a street name years before for the old headquarters building. There, a Post-it note on a teletype machine announced that Chief Superintendent Nolan of Special Branch wanted to be informed at once of any death by fire or accident, and the teletype operator lifted a phone and called the appropriate number.

That number was to the Special Branch watch officer, who asked a few questions, then called York for further information. Then it was his job to awaken "Tiny" Nolan just after four in the morning.

"Very well," the Chief Superintendent said, after collecting himself. "Tell them to do nothing whatsoever with the body—nothing at all. Make sure they understand, nothing at all."

"Very well, sir," the sergeant in the office confirmed. "I will relay that."

And seven miles away, Patrick Nolan went back to sleep, or at least tried to, while his mind wondered again what the hell SIS wanted a roasted human body for. It had to be something interesting, just that it was also quite disgusting to contemplate—enough that it denied him sleep for twenty minutes or so, before he faded back out.

THE MESSAGES WERE flying back and forth across the Atlantic and Eastern Europe all that night, and all of them were processed by the signals specialists in the various embassies, the underpaid and overworked clerical people who, virtually alone, were needed to transmit all of the most sensitive information from originators to end-users, and so, virtually alone, were the people who knew it all but did nothing with it. They were also the ones whom enemies tried so hard to corrupt, and who were, as a result, the most carefully watched of all staffers, whether at headquarters or in the various embassies, though for all the concern, there was usually no compensating solicitude for their comfort. But it was through these so often unappreciated but vital people that the dispatches found their way to the proper desks.

One recipient was Nigel Haydock, and it was to him that the most important of the morning's messages went, because only he, at this moment, knew the scope of BEATRIX, there in his office, where he was covered as Commercial Attaché to Her Britannic Majesty's Embassy, on the eastern bank of the Moscow River.

Haydock usually took his breakfast at the embassy, since with his wife so gravidly pregnant, he felt it improper for him to have her fix the morning meal for him—and besides, she was sleeping a lot, in preparation for not sleeping at all when the little bugger arrived, Nigel thought. So there he was at his desk, drinking his morning tea and eating a buttered muffin when he got to the dispatch from London.

"Bloody hell," he breathed, then paused to think. It was brilliant, this American play on MINCEMEAT—nasty and grisly, but brilliant. And it appeared that Sir Basil was going forward with it. That tricky old bugger. It was the sort of thing Bas would like. The current C was a devotee of the old school, one who liked the feel of devious operations. *His over-cleverness might be the downfall of him someday, but,* Haydock thought, *one has to admire his panache.* So get the Rabbit to Budapest and arrange his escape from there. . . .

ANDY HUDSON PREFERRED coffee in the morning, accompanied by eggs, bacon, fried tomatoes, and toast. "Bloody brilliant," he said aloud. The audacity of this operation appealed to his adventurous nature. So they'd have to get three individuals—an adult male, an adult female, and a little girl—all out of Hungary covertly. Not overly difficult, but he'd have to check his rat line, because this was one operation he didn't want to bollix up, especially if he had thoughts of promotion in the future. The Secret Intelligence Service was singular among British government bureaucracies insofar as, while it rewarded success fairly well, it was singularly unforgiving of failure—there was no union at Century House to protect the worker bees. But he'd known that going in, and they couldn't take his pension away in any case—once he had the seniority to qualify for one, Hudson cautioned himself. But while this operation wasn't quite the World Cup, it would be rather like scoring the winning goal for Arsenal against Manchester United at Wembly Stadium.

So his first task of the day was to see after his cross-border connections. *Those were reliable,* he thought. He'd spent a good deal of time setting them up, and he'd checked them out before. But he'd check them out again, starting today. He'd also check in with his AVH contact . . . or would he? Hudson wondered. What would that get him? It could allow him to find out if the Hungarian secret police force was on a state of alert or looking for something, but if that were true, the Rabbit would not be leaving Moscow. His information had to be highly important for an operation of this complexity to be run by CIA through SIS, and KGB was too careful and conservative an agency to take any sort of chances with information of that importance. The other side was never predictable in the intelligence business. There were just too many people with slightly different ideas for everyone to operate in lockstep. So, no, AVH wouldn't know very much, if anything at all. KGB trusted no one at all, absent direct oversight, preferably with guns.

So the only smart thing for him to do would be to look in on his escape procedures, and even to do that circumspectly, and otherwise wait for this Ryan chap to arrive from London to look over his shoulder. . . . *Ryan,* he thought, *CIA.* The same one who—no chance of that. Just a coincidence. Had to be. That Ryan was a bootneck—an *American* bootneck. *Just too much of a coincidence,* the COS Budapest decided.

RYAN HAD REMEMBERED his croissants, and this time he'd taken them with him in the cab from Victoria to Century House, along with the coffee. He arrived to see Simon's coat on the tree, but no Simon. *Probably off with Sir Basil,* he decided, and sat down at his desk, looking at the pile of overnights to go through. The croissants—he'd pigged out and bought three of them, plus butter and grape-jelly packets—were sufficiently flaky that he risked ending up wearing them instead of eating them, and this morning's coffee wasn't half bad. He made a mental note to write to Starbucks and suggest that they open some outlets in London. The Brits needed good coffee to get them off their damned tea, and this new Seattle company might just pull it off, assuming they could train people to brew it up right. He looked up when the door opened.

"Morning, Jack."

"Hey, Simon. How's Sir Basil this morning?"

"He's feeling very clever indeed with this Operation BEATRIX. It's under way, in a manner of speaking."

"Can you fill me in on what's happening?"

Simon Harding thought for a moment, then explained briefly.

"Is somebody out of his fucking mind?" Ryan demanded at the conclusion of the minibrief.

"Jack, yes, it is creative," Harding agreed. "But there should be little in the way of operational difficulties."

"Unless I barf," Jack responded darkly.

"So take a plastic bag," Harding suggested. "Take one from the airplane with you."

"Funny, Simon." Ryan paused. "What is this, some sort of initiation ceremony for me?"

"No, we don't do that sort of thing. The operational concept comes from your people, and the request for cooperation comes from Judge Moore himself."

"Fuck!" Jack observed. "And they dump me in the shitter, eh?"

"Jack, the objective here is not merely to get the Rabbit out, but to do so in such a way as to make Ivan believe he's dead, not defected, along with his wife and daughter."

Actually, the part that bothered Ryan was the corpses. What could be more distasteful than that? *And he doesn't even know the nasty part yet,* Simon Harding thought, glad that he'd edited that part out.

ZAITZEV WALKED INTO the administrative office on The Centre's second floor. He showed his ID to the girl and waited a few minutes before going into the supervisor's office.

"Yes?" the bureaucrat said, only half looking up.

"I wish to take my vacation days. I want to take my wife to Budapest. There's a conductor there she wants to hear—and I wish to travel there by train instead of by air."

"When?"

"In the next few days. As soon as possible, in fact."

"I see." The KGB's travel office did many things, most of them totally mundane. The travel agent—what else could Zaitzev call him?—still didn't look up. "I must check the availability of space on the train."

"I want to travel International Class, compartments, beds for three—I have a child, you see."

"That may not be easy," the bureaucrat noted.

"Comrade, if there are any difficulties, please contact Colonel Rozhdestvenskiy," he said mildly.

That name caused him to look up, Zaitzev saw. The only question was whether or not he'd make the call. The average desk-sitter did not go out of his way to become known to a senior official, and, like most people in The Centre, he had a healthy fear of those on the top floor. On the one hand, he might want to see if someone were taking the colonel's name in vain. On the other hand, calling his attention to that senior officer as an officious little worm in Administration would do him little good. He looked at Zaitzev, wondering if he had authorization to invoke Rozhdestvenskiy's name and authority.

"I will see what I can do, Comrade Captain," he promised.

"When can I call you?"

"Later today."

"Thank you, comrade." Zaitzev walked out and down the corridor to the elevators. So that was done, thanks to his temporary patron on the top floor. To make sure everything was all right, he had his blue striped tie folded and in his coat pocket. Back at his desk, he went back to memorizing the content of his routine message traffic. A pity, he thought, that he could not copy out of the one-time-pad books, but that was not practical, and memorizing them was a sheer impossibility even for his trained memory.

UNDERWAY WAS THE single word on the message from Langley, Foley saw. So they were going forward. That was good. Headquarters was hot to trot on BEATRIX, and that was probably because the Rabbit had warned them about general communications security, the one thing sure to cause a general panic on the Seventh Floor at headquarters. But could it possibly be true? No. Mike Russell didn't think so, and, as he'd already observed, were it true, some of his agents would have been swept up like confetti after a parade, and that hadn't happened . . . unless KGB was really being clever and had doubled his agents, operating them under Soviet control, and he'd be able to determine that, wouldn't he? *Well, probably,* Foley judged. Certainly they could not all be double agents. Some things were just impossible to hide, unless KGB's Second Chief Directorate had the cleverest operation in the history of espionage, and while that was theoretically possible, it was the tallest of tall orders, and something that they'd probably avoid since the quality of some information going out would have to be good—too good to let go voluntarily. . . .

But he couldn't entirely discount that possibility. For sure, NSA would be taking steps right now to examine their KH-7 and other cipher machines, but Fort Meade had a very active Red Team whose only job was to crack their own systems, and while Russian mathematicians were pretty smart—always had been—they weren't aliens from another planet . . . unless they had an agent of their own deep inside Fort Meade, and that was a worry that everyone had. How much would KGB pay for that sort of information? Millions, perhaps. They didn't have all *that* much cash to pay their people and, in addition to being niggardly, KGB was singularly disloyal to its people, regarding them all as expendable assets. Oh, sure, they got Kim Philby out and safely ensconced in Moscow. The Western spy agencies knew where he lived and had even photographed the turncoat bastard. They even knew how much he drank—a lot, even by Russian standards. But when the Russians lost an agent to arrest, did they ever try to bargain for him, do a trade? No, not since CIA had bargained for Francis Gary Powers, the unlucky U-2 pilot whom they'd shot down in 1961 and then traded for Rudolf Abel, but Abel had been one of their own officers, a colonel and a pretty good one, operating in New York. That *had to be* a deterrent to any American national in the spook business who had illusions of getting rich off Mother Russia's bank account. And traitors did hard time in the federal prison system, which had to be one hell of a deterrent.

But traitors were real, however misguided they were. At least the age of the ideological spy was largely ended. Those had been the most productive and the most dedicated, back when people really had believed that communism was the leading wave of human evolution, but even Russians no longer believed in Marxism-Leninism, except for Suslov—who was just about dead—and his successor-to-be, Alexandrov. So, no, KGB agents in the West were almost entirely mercenary bastards. Not the freedom fighters Ed Foley ran on the streets of Moscow, the COS told himself. That was an illusion all CIA officers held dearly, even his wife.

And the Rabbit? He was mad about something. A murder, he said, a proposed killing. Something that offended the sense of an honorable and decent man. So, yes, the Rabbit was honorable in his motivations, and therefore worthy of CIA's attention and solicitude.

Jesus, Ed Foley thought, *the illusions you have to have to carry on this stupid fucking business.* You had to be psychiatrist, loving mother, stern father, close friend, and father confessor to the idealistic, confused, angry, or just plain greedy individuals who chose to betray their country. Some of them drank too much; some of them were so enraged that they endangered themselves by taking grotesque risks. Some were just plain mad, demented, clinically disturbed. Some became sexual deviants—hell, some started off that way and just got worse. But Ed Foley had to be their social worker, which was such an odd job description for someone who thought of himself as a warrior against the Big Ugly Bear. *Well,* he told himself, *one thing at a time.* He'd knowingly chosen a profession with barely adequate pay, virtually no credit ever to be awarded, and no recognition for the dangers, physical and psychological, that attended it, serving his country in a way that would never be appreciated by the millions of citizens he helped to protect, despised by the news media—whom he in turn despised—and never being able to defend himself with the truth of what he did. What a hell of a life.

But it did have its satisfactions, like getting the Rabbit the hell out of Dodge City.

If BEATRIX worked.

Foley told himself that now, once more, he knew what it was like to pitch in the World Series.

ISTVAN KOVACS LIVED a few blocks from the Hungarian parliamentary palace, an ornate building reminiscent of the Palace of Westminster, on the third floor of a turn-of-the-century tenement, whose four toilets were on the first floor of a singularly dreary courtyard. Hudson took the local metro over to the government palace and walked the rest of the way, making sure that he didn't have a tail. He'd called ahead—remarkably, the city's phone lines were secure, uncontrolled mainly because of the inefficiency of the local phone systems.

Kovacs was so typically Hungarian as to deserve a photo in the nonexistent tourist brochures: five-eight, swarthy, a mainly circular face with brown eyes and black hair. But he dressed rather better than the average citizen because of his profession. Kovacs was a smuggler. It was almost an honored livelihood in this country, since he traded across the border to a putatively Marxist country to the south, Yugoslavia, whose borders were open enough that a clever man could purchase Western goods there and sell them in Hungary and the rest of Eastern Europe. The border controls on Yugoslavia were fairly loose, especially for those who had an understanding with the border guards. Kovacs was one such person.

"Hello, Istvan," Andy Hudson said, with a smile. "Istvan" was the local version of Steven, and "Kovacs" the local version of Smith, for its ubiquity.

"Andy, good day to you," Kovacs replied in greeting. He opened a bottle of Tokaji, the local tawny wine made of grapes with the noble rot, which afflicted them every few years. Hudson had come to enjoy it as the local variant of sherry, with a different taste but an identical purpose.

"Thank you, Istvan." Hudson took a sip. This was good stuff, with six baskets of nobly rotten grapes on the label, indicating the very best. "So, how is business?"

"Excellent. Our VCRs are popular with the Yugoslavs, and the tapes they sell me are popular with everyone. Oh, to have such a prick as those actors do!" He laughed.

"The women aren't bad, either," Hudson noted. He'd seen his share of such tapes.

"How can a *kurva* be so beautiful?"

"The Americans pay their whores more than we do in Europe, I suppose. But, Istvan, they have no heart, those women." Hudson had never paid for it in his life—at least not up front.

"It's not their hearts that I want." Kovacs had himself another hearty laugh. He'd been hitting the Tokaji already this day, so he wasn't making a run tonight. Well, nobody worked all the time.

"I may have a task for you."

"Bringing what in?"

"Nothing. Bringing something out," Hudson clarified.

"That is simple. What trouble the *határ rség* give us is when we come in, and then not much." He held up his right hand, rubbing thumb and forefinger together in the universal gesture for what the border guards wanted—money or something negotiable.

"Well, this package might be bulky," Hudson warned.

"How bulky? A tank you want to take out?" The Hungarian army had just taken delivery of new Russian T-72s, and that had made the TV, in an attempt to buck up the fighting spirit of the troops. *A waste of time,* Hudson thought. "That might be hard, but it can be done, for a price." But the Poles had already given one of those to SIS, a fact not widely known.

"No, Istvan, smaller than that. About my size, but three packages."

"Three people?" Kovacs asked, getting a dull stare in return. He got the message. "Bah, a simple task—*baszd meg*!" he concluded: Fuck it.

"I thought I could count on you, Istvan," Hudson said with a smile. "How much?"

"For three people into Yugoslavia . . ." Kovacs pondered that for a moment. "Oh. Five thousand d-mark."

"Ez kurva drága!" Hudson objected, or ostensibly so. It was cheap at the price, hardly a thousand quid. "Very well, you thief! I'll pay it because you are my friend—but just this one time." He finished his drink. "You know, I could just fly the packages out," Hudson suggested.

"But the airport is the one place where the *határ rség* are alert," Kovacs pointed out. "The poor bastards are always in the light, with their senior officers about. No chance for them to be open to . . . negotiations."

"I suppose that is so," Hudson agreed. "Very well. I will call you to keep track of your schedule."

"That is fine. You know where to find me."

Hudson stood. "Thanks for the drink, my friend."

"It lubricates the business," Kovacs said, as he opened the door for his guest. Five thousand West German marks would cover a lot of obligations and buy him a lot of goods to resell in Budapest for a handsome profit.

CHAPTER 23

ALL ABOARD

ZAITZEV CALLED THE TRAVEL OFFICE at 1530. He hoped that this didn't show an unusual eagerness, but everyone was interested in their vacation arrangements, he figured.

"Comrade Major, you are on the train day after tomorrow. It leaves Kiev Station at thirteen hours thirty and arrives in Budapest two days later at fourteen hours exactly. You and your family are booked into Carriage nine-oh-six in compartments A and B. You are also booked into Budapest's Hotel Astoria, Room three-oh-seven, for eleven days. The hotel is directly across the street from the Soviet Culture and Friendship House, which is, of course, a KGB operation with a liaison office, should you need any local assistance."

"Excellent. Thank you very much for your help." Zaitzev thought for a moment. "Is there anything I might purchase for you in Budapest?"

"Why, thank you, comrade." His voice just lit up. "Yes, perhaps some pantyhose for my wife," the functionary said in a furtive voice.

"What size?"

"My wife is a real Russian," he replied, meaning decidedly not anorexic.

"Very good. I will find something—or my wife will assist me."

"Excellent. Have a grand trip."

"Yes, I shall," Zaitzev promised him. With that settled, Oleg Ivan'ch left his desk and went to his watch supervisor to announce his plans for the coming two weeks.

"Isn't there some upstairs project that only you are cleared for?" the lieutenant colonel asked.

"Yes, but I asked Colonel Rozhdestvenskiy, and he said not to be concerned about it. Feel free to call him to confirm that, comrade," Zaitzev told him.

And he did, in Zaitzev's presence. The brief call ended with a "thank you, comrade," and then he looked up at his subordinate. "Very well, Oleg Ivan'ch, you are relieved of your duties beginning this evening. Say, while you are in Budapest . . ."

"Certainly, Andrey Vasili'yevich. You may pay me for them when I get back." Andrey was a decent boss, who never screamed, and helped his people when asked. A pity he worked for an agency that murdered innocent people.

And then it was just a matter of cleaning up his desk, which wasn't difficult. KGB regulations dictated that every desk be set up exactly the same way, so that a worker could switch desks without confusion, and Zaitzev's desk was arranged exactly according to office specifications. With his pencils properly sharpened and lined up, his message log up to the moment, and all his books properly in place, he dumped his trash and walked to the men's room. There he selected a stall, removed his brown tie, and replaced it with his striped one. He checked his watch. He was actually a little early. So Zaitzev took his time on the way out, smoked two cigarettes instead of one, and took a moment to enjoy the clear afternoon, stopping off to get a paper along the way, and, to pamper himself, six packs of Krasnopresnensky, the premium cigarette smoked by Leonid Brezhnev himself, for two rubles forty. Something nice to smoke on the train. Might as well spend his rubles now, he decided. They'd be valueless where he was going. Then he walked down to the metro station and checked the clock. The train, of course, came right on time.

FOLEY WAS IN the same place, doing the same thing in exactly the same way, his mind racing as the train slowed to a stop at *this* station. He felt the tiny vibration from the boarding passengers and the grunts of people bumping into one another. He straightened up to turn the page. Then the train lurched off. The engineers—or motormen, whatever the hell you called them—were always a little heavy on the throttle. A moment later, there was a presence to his left. Foley didn't see it, but he could feel it. Two minutes later, the subway train slowed for another station. It lurched to a stop, and someone bumped into him. Foley turned slightly to see who it was.

"Excuse me, comrade," the Rabbit said. He was wearing a blue tie with red stripes.

"No problem," Foley responded dismissively, as his heart leapt inside his chest.

Okay, two days from now, Kiev Station. The train to Budapest. The Rabbit moved a step or two away, and that was that. The signal had been passed.

Skyrockets in flight. Foley folded his paper, and made his way to the sliding doors. The usual walk to his apartment. Mary Pat was fixing dinner.

"Like my tie? You didn't tell me this morning."

MP's eyes lit up. *Day after tomorrow,* she realized. They'd have to get the word out, but that was just a procedural thing. She hoped Langley was ready. BEATRIX was going a little fast, but why dawdle?

"So, what's for dinner?"

"Well, I wanted to get a steak, but I'm afraid you'll have to settle for fried chicken today."

"That's okay, honey. Steak for day after tomorrow, maybe?" she asked.

"Sounds good to me. Honey, where's Eddie?"

"Watching *Transformers,* of course." She pointed to the living room.

"That's my boy," Ed observed, with a smile. "He knows the important stuff." Foley kissed his wife tenderly.

"Later, tiger," Mary Pat breathed back. But a successful operation merited a discreet celebration. Not that this one was successful yet, but it was certainly headed that way, and it was their first in Moscow. "Got the pictures?" she whispered.

He pulled them out of his jacket pocket. They were not exactly magazine-cover quality, but they did give good representations of the Rabbit and his little bunny. They didn't know what Mrs. Rabbit looked like, but this would have to do. They'd get the shots to Nigel and Penny. One of them would cover the train station to make sure the Rabbit family got going on time.

"Ed, there's a problem with the shower," Mary Pat said. "The spray thingee isn't right."

"I'll see if Nigel has the right tools." Foley walked out the door and down the hall. In a few minutes, they were back, Nigel carrying his toolbox.

"Hello, Mary." Nigel waved on his way to the bathroom. Once there, he made a fuss about opening his toolbox, then turning on the water, and now any bug the KGB might have here was jammed.

"Okay, Ed, what is it?"

Ed handed over the photos. "The Rabbit and the Bunny. We have nothing on Mrs. Rabbit yet. They'll all be taking the one P.M. train to Budapest, day after tomorrow."

"Kiev Station," Haydock said, with a nod. "You'll want me to get a picture of Mrs. Rabbit."

"Correct."

"Very well. I can do that." The wheels started turning at once. As Commercial Attaché, he could come up with a cock-and-bull story to cover it, Haydock reasoned. He'd get a tame reporter to accompany him and make it look like a news story—something about tourism, perhaps. Paul Matthews of the *Times* would play along. Easily done. He'd have Matthews bring a photographer and take professional photos of the whole Rabbit family for London and Langley to use. And Ivan shouldn't suspect a thing. However important the Rabbit's information might be, the Rabbit himself was just a cipher, one of many thousands of KGB employees not important enough to be taken any note of. So tomorrow morning Haydock would call the Soviet state railroad and say that the Soviets' sister service in Britain—which was also state-owned—was interested in how the Russians ran theirs, and so . . . yes, that would work. There was nothing the Soviets liked better than others wanting to learn from their glorious system. Good for their egos. Nigel reached over to turn off the water.

"There, I think that has it fixed, Edward."

"Thanks, pal. Any good places in Moscow to buy tools?"

"I don't know, Ed. I've had these since I was a lad. Belonged to my father, you see."

Then Foley remembered what had happened to Nigel's father. Yeah, he wanted BEATRIX to succeed. He wanted to take every opportunity to shove a big one up the Bear's hairy ass. "How's Penny?"

"The baby hasn't dropped yet. So at least another week, probably more. Strictly speaking, she isn't due for another three weeks, but—"

"But the docs *never* get that one right, buddy. Never," Foley told his friend. "Best advice, stay close. When you planning to fly home?"

"Ten days should be about right, the embassy physician tells us. It's only a two-hour flight, after all."

"Your doc is an optimist, pal. These things never go according to plan. I don't suppose you want a little Englishman to be born in Moscow, eh?"

"No, Edward, we don't."

"Well, keep Penny off the trampoline," Foley suggested with a wink.

"Yes, I will do that, Ed." American humor could be rather crass, he thought.

This could be interesting, Foley thought, walking his friend to the door. He'd always thought Brit children were born at the age of five and sent immediately off to boarding school. Did they raise them the same way Americans did? He'd have to see.

THE BODY OF Owen Williams was never collected—it turned out he had no immediate family, and his ex-wife had no interest in him at all, especially dead. The local police, on receipt of a telex from Chief Superintendent Patrick Nolan of London's Metropolitan Police, transferred the body to an aluminum casket, which was loaded in a police van and driven south toward London. But not quite. The van stopped at a preselected location, and the aluminum box was transferred to another, unmarked, van for the drive into the city. It ended up in a mortuary in the Swiss Cottage district of north London.

The body was not in very good shape, and, since it had not yet seen a mortician, it had also not been treated in any way. The unburned underside was a blue-crimson shade of postmortem lividity. Once the heart stops, the blood is pulled by gravity to the lower regions of the body—in this case, the back—where, lacking oxygen, it tends to turn the caucasian body a pale bluish color, leaving the upper side with a disagreeable ivory pallor. The mortician here was a civilian who occasionally contracted specialty work to the Secret Intelligence Service. Along with a forensic pathologist, he examined the body for anything unusual. The worst thing was the smell of roasted human meat, but their noses were covered with surgical masks to attenuate the odor.

"Tattoo, underside of the forearm, partially but not entirely burned off," the mortician reported.

"Very well." The pathologist lit the flame of a propane blowtorch and applied it to the arm, burning all evidence of the tattoo off the body. "Anything else, William?" he asked a couple minutes later.

"Nothing I can see. The upper body is well charred. Hair is mainly gone"—the smell of burned human hair is particularly vile—"and one ear nearly burned off. I presume this chap was dead before he burned."

"Ought to have been," the pathologist said. "The blood gasses had the CO well spiked into lethal range. I doubt this poor bugger felt a thing." Then he burned off the fingerprints, lingering to sear both hands with the torch so that it would not appear to have been a deliberate mutilation of the body.

"There," the pathologist said finally. "If there's a way to identify this body, I do not know what it is."

"Freeze it now?" the undertaker asked.

"No, I don't think so. If we chill it down to, oh, two or three degrees Celsius, no noticeable decomposition ought to take place."

"Dry ice, then."

"Yes. The metal casket is well insulated and it seals hermetically. Dry ice doesn't melt, you know. It goes directly from a solid to a gas. Now we need to get it dressed." The doctor had brought the underclothing with him. None of it was British in origin, and all of it was badly damaged by fire. All in all, it was a distasteful job, but one that pathologists and morticians get used to very early in their professions. It was just a different way of thinking for a different kind of job. But this was unusually gruesome, even for these two. Both would have an extra drink before turning in that night. When they finished, the aluminum box was reloaded on the van and driven to Century House. There would be a note on Sir Basil's desk in the morning to let him know that Rabbit A was ready for his last flight.

LATER THAT NIGHT and three thousand miles away, in Boston, Massachusetts, there was a gas explosion on the second floor of a two-story frame dwelling overlooking the harbor. Three people were there when it happened. The two adults were not married, but both were drunk, and the woman's four-year-old daughter—not related to the male resident—was already in bed. The fire spread quickly, too quickly for the two adults to respond to it through their intoxication. The three deaths didn't take long, all of them from smoke inhalation rather than incineration. The Boston Fire Department responded within ten minutes, and their search-and-rescue ladder men battled their way through the flames under cover of two hose streams, found the bodies, and dragged them out, but they knew that they'd been too late again. The captain of the responding company could tell almost instantly what had gone wrong. There had been a gas leak in the kitchen from the old stove that the landlord hadn't wanted to replace, and so three people had died of his parsimony. (He'd gladly collect the insurance check, of course, and say how sorry he was about the tragic incident.) This was not the first such case. It wouldn't be the last, either, and so he and his men would have some nightmares about the three bodies, especially the little girl's. But that just went with the job.

The story was early enough to make the eleven o'clock news on the rule that "If it bleeds, it leads." The Special Agent in Charge of the FBI's Boston field division was up and watching, actually waiting for coverage of the baseball playoffs—he'd been at an official dinner and missed the live broadcast on NBC—and saw the story and instantly remembered the lunatic telex he'd gotten earlier in the day. That caused a curse to be muttered and a phone to be lifted.

"FBI," said the young agent guarding the phones when he picked up.

"Get Johnny up," the SAC ordered. "A family got burned up in a fire on Hester Street. He'll know what to do. Have him call me at home if he has to."

"Yes, sir." And that was that, except for Assistant Special Agent in Charge John Tyler, who'd been reading a book in his bed—a native of South Carolina, he preferred college football to professional baseball—when the phone rang. He managed to grumble on the way to the bathroom, then collected his side arm and car keys for the ride south. He'd seen the telex from Washington, too, and wondered what sort of drugs Emil Jacobs was taking, but his was not to reason why.

NOT TOO LONG after that, but five time zones to the east, Jack Ryan rolled out of bed, got his paper, and switched on the TV. CNN also carried the fire story from Boston—it was a slow news night at home—and he breathed a quiet prayer for the victims of the fire, followed by speculation about the gas pipe connection in his own stove. His house, though, was a lot newer than the standing lumberyard that defined a house in south Boston. When they went, they went big, and they went fast. Too fast for those people to get out, evidently. He remembered his father often saying how much he respected firemen, people who ran *into* burning buildings instead of away from them. The worst part of the job had to be what they found unmoving on the inside. He shook his head as he opened his morning paper and reached for his coffee, while his physician wife saw the tail end of the fire story and thought her own thoughts. She remembered treating burn victims in her third year of medical school and the horrid screams that went with debriding burned tissue off the underlying wounds, and there wasn't a damned thing you could do about it. But those people in Boston were dead now, and that was that. She didn't like it, but she'd seen a lot of death, because sometimes the Bad Guy won, and that was just how things worked. It was not a pleasant thought for a parent, especially since the little girl in Boston had been Sally's age and now would never get older. She sighed. At least she'd be doing some surgery that morning, something that really made a difference with somebody's health.

SIR BASIL CHARLESTON lived in an expensive townhouse in London's posh Belgravia district south of Knightsbridge. A widower whose grown children had long since moved away, he was accustomed to living alone, though he had a discreet security detail in attendance at all times. He also had a maid service which came in three times a week to straighten up, though he didn't bother with a cook, preferring to dine out or even fix small meals for himself. He had, of course, the usual accoutrements of a king spook: three different sorts of secure phones, a secure telex, and a new secure fax machine. There was no live-in secretary, but when the office was busy and he wasn't there, a courier service kept him apprised of the printed material circulating in Century House. Indeed, since he had to assume that the "opposition" kept an eye on his home, he deemed it smarter to remain at home in time of crisis, the better to project the image of calmness. It really didn't matter. He was firmly tied to the SIS by an electronic umbilical cord.

And so it was this morning. Someone at Century House had decided to let him know that SIS had an adult male body to use in Operation BEATRIX: just the sort of thing he needed with breakfast, Basil noted, with a twisted expression. They needed three, though, one of them a female child, which was *really* not something to contemplate with his morning tea and Scottish oatmeal.

However, it was hard not to get excited about this BEATRIX operation. If their Rabbit was speaking the truth—not all of them did—this chap would have all manner of useful information in his head. The most useful of all, of course, would be if he could identify Soviet agents within Her Majesty's government. That was properly the job of the Security Service—erroneously called MI-5—but the two agencies cooperated closely, more closely than CIA and FBI did in America, or so it appeared to Charleston. Sir Basil and his people had long suspected a high-level leak somewhere in the Foreign Office, but they'd been unable to close in on him or her. So, if they got their Rabbit out—it wasn't done until it was done, he reminded himself—that was certainly one question his people would be asking in the safe house they used outside of Taunton in the rolling hills of Somerset.

"NOT GOING TO work today?" Irina asked her husband. He ought to have left for the office by now, surely.

"No, and I have a surprise for you," Oleg announced.

"What is that?"

"We're going to Budapest tomorrow."

That snapped her head around. "What?"

"I decided to take my vacation days, and there's a new conductor in Budapest now, Jozsef Rozsa. I knew you liked classical music, and I decided to take you and *zaichik* there, dear."

"Oh," was all she had to say. "But what about my job at GUM?"

"Can't you get free of that?"

"Well, yes, I suppose," Irina admitted. "But why Budapest?"

"Well, the music, and we can buy some things there. I have a list of items to get for people at The Centre," he told her.

"Ah, yes . . . we can get some nice things for Svetlana," she thought out loud on reflection. Working at GUM, she knew what was available in Hungary that she'd never get in Moscow, even in the "closed" stores. "Who is this Rozsa, anyway?"

"He's a young Hungarian conductor touring Eastern Europe. He has a fine reputation, darling. The program is supposed to be Brahms and Bach, I think—one of the Hungarian state orchestras and," he added, "a lot of good shopping." There wasn't a woman in all the world who wouldn't respond favorably to that opportunity, Oleg judged. He waited patiently for the next objection:

"I don't have anything to wear."

"My dear, that is why we're going to Budapest. You will be able to buy anything you need there."

"Well . . ."

"And remember to pack everything you need in one bag. We'll take empty bags for all the things we're buying for ourselves and our friends."

"But—"

"Irina, think of Budapest as one big consumer-goods store. Hungarian VCRs, Western jeans and pantyhose, real perfume. You will be the envy of your office at GUM," he promised her.

"Well . . ."

"I thought so. My darling, we are going on vacation!" he told her, a little manly force in his voice.

"If you say so," she responded, with the hint of an avaricious smile. "I will call in to the office later and let them know. I suppose they won't miss me too badly."

"The only people they miss in Moscow are the Politburo members, and they only miss them for the day and a half it takes to replace them," he announced.

And so that was settled. They were taking the train to Hungary. Irina started thinking about what to pack. Oleg would leave that to her. *Inside a week or ten days, we will all have much better clothes,* the KGB communications officer told himself. And maybe in a month or two, they would go to that Disney Planet place in the American province of Florida. . . .

He wondered if CIA knew how much trust he was putting in them, and he prayed—an unusual activity for a KGB officer—that they would perform as well as he hoped.

"GOOD MORNING, JACK."

"Hey, Simon. What's new in the world?" Jack set his coffee down before taking his coat off.

"Suslov died last night," Harding announced. "It will be in their afternoon papers."

"What a pity. Another bat found his way back into hell, eh?" *At least he died with good eyesight, thanks to Bernie Katz and the guys from Johns Hopkins,* Ryan thought. "Complications of diabetes?"

Harding shrugged. "Plus being old, I should imagine. Heart attack, our sources tell us. Amazing that the nasty old bugger actually had a heart. In any case, his replacement will be Mikhail Yevgeniyevich Alexandrov."

"And he's not exactly a day at the beach. When will they plant Suslov?"

"He's a senior Politburo member. I would expect a full state funeral, marching band, the lot, then cremation and a slot in the Kremlin wall."

"You know, I've always wondered, what does a real communist think about when he knows he's dying? You suppose they wonder if it was all a great big fucking mistake?"

"I have no idea. But Suslov was evidently a true believer. He probably thought of all the good he'd done in his life, leading humanity to the 'Radiant Future' they like to talk about."

Nobody's that dumb, Ryan wanted to retort, but Simon was probably right. Nothing lingered longer in a man's mind than a bad idea, and certainly Red Mike had held his bad ideas close to whatever heart had finally cashed in. But a communist's best-case scenario for after death corresponded with Ryan's worst, and if the communist was wrong, then, quite literally, there was hell to pay. *Tough luck, Mishka, hope you took some sunblock with you.*

"Okay, what's up for today?"

"The PM wants to know if this will have any effect on Politburo policy."

"Tell her no, it won't. In political terms, Alexandrov might as well be Suslov's twin brother. He thinks Marx is God, and Lenin is his prophet, and Stalin was mostly right, just a little too *nekulturniy* in his application of political theory. The rest of the Politburo doesn't really believe that stuff anymore, but they have to pretend that they do. So call Alexandrov the new conductor of the ideological symphony orchestra. They don't much like the music anymore, but they dance to it anyway, 'cause it's the only dance they know. I don't think he will affect their policy decisions a dot. I bet they listen when he talks, but they let it go in one ear and out the other; they pretend to respect him, but they really don't."

"It's a little more complex than that, but you've caught the essentials," Harding agreed. "The thing is, I have to find a way to produce ten double-spaced pages that say it."

"Yeah, in bureaucratese." Ryan had never quite mastered that language, which was one of the reasons Admiral Greer liked him so much.

"We have our procedures, Jack, and the PM—indeed, all of the Prime Ministers—like to have it in words they understand."

"The Iron Lady understands the same language as a stevedore, I bet."

"Only when she speaks those words, Sir John, not when others try to speak them to her."

"I suppose. Okay," Ryan had to concede the point. "What documents do we need?"

"We have an extensive dossier file on Alexandrov. I've already called down for it."

So this day would be occupied with creative writing, Ryan decided. It would have been more interesting to look into their economy, but instead he'd have to help do a prospective, analytical obituary for a man whom nobody had liked, and who'd probably died intestate anyway.

THE PREPARATION WAS even easier than he'd hoped. Haydock had expected the Russians to be pleased, and, sure enough, one call to his contact in the Ministry of Transportation had done the trick. At ten the next morning, he, Paul Matthews, and a *Times* photographer would be at the Kiev station to do a story about Soviet state rail and how it compared to British Rail, which needed some help, most Englishmen thought, especially in upper management.

Matthews probably suspected that Haydock was a "six" person, but had never let on, since the spook had been so helpful feeding stories to him. It was the usual way of creating a friendly journalist—even taught at the SIS Academy—but it was officially denied to the American CIA. *The United States Congress passes the most remarkable and absurd laws to hamstring its intelligence services,* the Brit thought, though he was sure the official rules were broken on a daily basis by the people in the field. He'd violated a few of the much looser rules of his own mother service. And had never been caught, of course. Just as he had never been caught working agents on the streets of Moscow. . . .

"HI, TONY." Ed Foley extended a friendly hand to the Moscow correspondent of *The New York Times.* He wondered if Prince knew how much Ed despised him. But it probably went both ways. "What's happening today?"

"Looking for a statement by the Ambassador on the death of Mikhail Suslov."

Foley laughed. "How about he's glad the nasty old cocksucker is dead?"

"Can I quote you on that?" Prince held up his scribble pad.

Time to back up. "Not exactly. I have no instructions in that matter, Tony, and the boss is tied up on other things at the moment. No time loose to see you until later afternoon, I'm afraid."

"Well, I need *something,* Ed."

" 'Mikhail Suslov was an important member of the Politburo, and an important ideological force in this country, and we regret his untimely passing.' That good enough?"

"Your first quote was better and a lot more truthful," the *Times* correspondent observed.

"You ever meet him?"

Price nodded. "Couple of times, before and after the Hopkins docs worked on his eyes—"

"Is that for real? I mean, I heard a few stories about it, but nothing substantive." Foley acted the words out.

Prince nodded again. "It was true enough. Glasses like Coke-bottle bottoms. Courtly gent, I thought. Well-mannered and all that, but there was a little 'tough guy' underneath. I guess he was the high priest of communism, like."

"Oh, took vows of poverty, chastity, and obedience, did he?"

"You know, there was something of the aesthete about him, like he really was a priest of a sort," Prince said, after a moment's reflection.

"Think so?"

"Yeah, something otherworldly about the guy, like he could see things the rest of us couldn't, like a priest or something. He sure enough believed in communism. Didn't apologize for it, either."

"Stalinist?" Foley asked.

"No, but thirty years ago he would have been. I can see him signing the order to kill somebody. Wouldn't lose any sleep over it—not our Mishka."

"Who's going to replace him?"

"Not sure," Prince admitted. "My contacts say they don't know."

"I thought he was tight with another Mike, that Alexandrov guy," Foley offered, wondering if Prince's contacts were as good as he thought they were. Fucking with Western reporters was a game for the Soviet leadership. It was different in Washington, where a reporter had power to use over politicians. That didn't apply here. The Politburo members didn't fear reporters at all—much the reverse, actually.

Prince's contacts weren't all that great: "Maybe, but I'm not sure. What's the talk here?"

"Haven't been to the lunch room yet, Tony. Haven't heard the gossip yet," Foley parried. *You don't* really *expect a tip from me, do you?*

"Well, we'll know by tomorrow or day after."

But it would look good for you if you were the first reporter to make the prediction, and you want me to help you, right? Not is this lifetime, Foley thought, but then he had to reconsider. Prince would not be a particularly valuable friend, but perhaps a usable one, and it never made sense to make enemies for the fun of it. On the other hand, to be too helpful to the guy might suggest either that Foley was a spook or knew who the spooks were, and Tony Prince was one of those guys who liked to talk and tell people how smart he is. . . . *No, it's better for Prince to think I'm dumb, because he'll tell everyone he knows how smart* he *is and how dumb* I *am.*

The best cover of them all, he'd learned at The Farm, was to be thought a dullard, and while it was a little hurtful to his ego to play that game, it was helpful to the mission, and Ed Foley was a mission-oriented guy. So . . . *fuck Prince and what he thinks.* I'm *the guy in this city who makes a difference.*

"Tell you what, I'll ask around—see what people think."

"Fair enough." *Not that I expected anything useful from you,* Prince thought a little too loudly.

He was less skillful than he thought at concealing his feelings. He would never be a good poker player, the Chief of Station thought, seeing him out the door. He checked his watch. Lunchtime.

LIKE MOST EUROPEAN stations, Kiev's was a pale yellow—just like a lot of old royal palaces, in fact, as if in the early nineteenth century there had been a continent-wide surplus of mustard, and some king or other had liked the color, and so everyone had painted his palace that way. *It never happened in Britain, thank God,* Haydock thought. The ceiling was glass set in iron frames to let the light in but, as in London, the glass was rarely, if ever, cleaned, and was instead coated with soot from long-gone steam engines and their coal-fired boiler fires.

But Russians were still Russians. They came to the platform carrying their cheap suitcases, and they were almost never alone, mostly in family groups, even if only one of them was leaving, so that proper goodbyes could be experienced, with passionate kisses, male-to-female, and male-to-male, which always struck the Englishman as peculiar. But it was a local custom, and all local customs were peculiar to visitors. The train to Kiev, Belgrade, and Budapest was scheduled to leave at 1:00 P.M. on the dot, and the Russian railroads, like the Moscow Metro, kept to a fairly precise schedule.

Just a few feet away, Paul Matthews was conversing with a representative of the Soviet state railway, talking about the motive power—it was all electric, since Comrade Lenin had decided to bring electricity and eliminate lice all across the USSR. The former, strangely, had proved easier than the latter.

The big VL80T locomotive, two hundred tons of steel, sat at the head of the train on Track Three, with three-day coaches, a dining car, and six international class sleepers, plus three mail cars just behind the engine. On the platform were the various conductors and stewards, looking rather surly, as Russians in service-related jobs tended to do.

Haydock was looking around, the photos of the Rabbit and the Bunny seared into his memory. The station clock said it was 12:15, and that tallied with his wristwatch. Would the Rabbit show? Haydock usually preferred to be early for a flight or a train, perhaps from a fear of being late left over from his childhood. Whatever the reason, he'd have been here by now for a one o'clock train. But not everyone thought that way, Nigel reminded himself—his wife, for example. He was slightly afraid that she'd deliver the baby in their car on the way to the hospital. It would make a hell of a mess, the spook was sure, while Paul Matthews asked his questions, and the photographer shot his Kodak film. Finally . . .

Yes, that was the Rabbit, along with Mrs. Rabbit and the little Bunny. Nigel tapped the shoulder of the photographer.

"This family approaching now. Lovely little girl," he observed, for anyone close enough to listen. The photographer fired off ten frames at once, then switched to another Nikon and fired off ten more. *Excellent,* Haydock thought. He'd have them printed up before the embassy closed down for the night, get several printed off to—no, he'd personally hand them to Ed Foley, and make sure the others went by Queen's Messenger—the Brits' rather more dignified term for a diplomatic courier—so they'd be sure to be in Sir Basil's hands before he turned in. He wondered how they would arrange for hiding the fact of the Rabbit's defection—it certainly meant getting cadavers. Distasteful, but possible. He was glad he didn't have to figure out all the details.

As it turned out, the Rabbit family walked within ten feet of him and his reporter friend. No words were exchanged, though the little girl, like little girls everywhere, turned to look at him as she passed. He gave her a wink and got a little smile in return. And then they passed by, walked up to the attendant, and showed their paper ticket forms.

Matthews kept on asking his questions and got very polite answers from the smiling Russian trainman.

At 12:59:30, the conductor—or at least so Haydock assumed, from the shabby uniform—walked up and down the side of the train and made sure all the doors but one were secure. He blew a whistle and waved a paddle-like wand to let the engineer know it was time to move off, and at 1:00 on the dot, the horn sounded, and the train started inching away from the platform, gaining speed slowly as it headed west into the capacious railyard, heading for Kiev, Belgrade, and Budapest.

CHAPTER 24

ROLLING HILLS

IT WAS AN ADVENTURE for Svetlana most of all, but actually for all of them, since none of the Zaitzev family had ever taken an intercity train. The railyards on the way out were like any railyards: miles of parallel and converging and diverging track packed with box- and flatcars carrying who-knew-what to who-knew-where. The roughness of the tracks only seemed to increase the apparent speed. Oleg and Irina both lit cigarettes and looked with casual interest out the large but grubby windows. The seats were not unreasonable, and Oleg could see how the beds folded down from the overhead.

They had two compartments, in fact, with a connecting door. The paneling was wood—birch, by the look of it—and each compartment, remarkably, had its own lavatory, and so *zaichik* would have her very own, for the first time in her life, a fact she had yet to appreciate.

Five minutes after leaving the station, the conductor came by for their tickets, which Zaitzev handed over.

"You are State Security?" the conductor asked politely. *So the KGB travel office called ahead for me,* Zaitzev thought. *Good of them.* That desk-sitter probably really wanted the pantyhose for his wife.

"I am not permitted to discuss that, comrade," Oleg Ivan'ch answered, with a hard look, making sure that the trainman appreciated his importance. That was one way to ensure proper service. A KGB officer wasn't quite as good as a Politburo member, but it beat the hell out of being a mere factory manager. It wasn't so much that people dreaded KGB, but that they just didn't want to go out of their way to come to the agency's adverse notice.

"Yes, of course, comrade. If you need anything, please call for me. Supper is at eighteen hours, and the dining car is the next one forward." He pointed the way.

"How is the food?" Irina decided to ask. Surely, being the wife of a KGB officer had its advantages. . . .

"It is not bad, comrade," the conductor answered politely. "I eat there myself," he added, which said something, Oleg and Irina both thought.

"Thank you, comrade."

"Enjoy your trip with us," he said, and he took his leave.

Oleg and Irina both took out books. Svetlana pressed her nose to the window to watch the world passing by, and so the trip began, with only one of them knowing the final destination. Western Russia is mostly a region of rolling plains and distant horizons, not unlike Kansas or eastern Colorado. It was boring to everyone but their *zaichik*, for whom everything was new and exciting, especially the cattle that were mainly munching on grass. *Cows,* she thought, *are pretty cool.*

BACK IN MOSCOW, Nigel Haydock thanked the bureaucrat from the Transport Ministry for his splendid help, along with Paul Matthews, and then they made their way off to the British Embassy. The embassy had a photo lab, and the photographer went that way, while Matthews followed Nigel to his office.

"So, Paul, is there a useful story in that?"

"I suppose there might be. Is it important that there should be?"

"Well, it's valuable to me that the Sovs should think I can bring attention to the glory of their country," Haydock explained with a chuckle.

You are a -6 chap, aren't you? Matthews thought without voicing his suspicion. "I suppose I can generate something. God knows British Rail needs a boost. Maybe this will encourage the exchequer to send some more money their way."

"Not a bad idea at all," Nigel agreed. It was clear that his guest had his suspicions but had the good grace to keep them quiet, perhaps until a later day, when Nigel was back at a desk in Century House, and they were at a Fleet Street pub.

"You want to see our photos?"

"Would you mind?"

"Not at all. We throw most of them away, as you know."

"Excellent," Haydock announced. Then he reached into the credenza behind his desk. "Drink, Paul?"

"Thank you, Nigel. Yes, a sherry would be nice."

Two sherries later, the photographer came in with a folder full of prints. Haydock took it and leafed through them. "You do excellent work. You know, when I use my Nikon, I never quite get the light right. . . ." he said. There, a nice family shot of the Rabbit—and, most important, Mrs. Rabbit. There were three, each one better than the last. He slid them into his drawer and handed the folder back. Matthews took his cue.

"Well, must get back to my office and write this story up. Thanks for the lead, Nigel."

"My pleasure, Paul. See your own way out?"

"Not a problem, old man." And Matthews and his photographer disappeared into the corridor. Haydock returned his attention to the photos. Mrs. Rabbit was typically Russian, with her round, Slavic face—she could have had a million identical sisters throughout the Soviet Union. She needed to lose a few pounds and get a makeover in the West . . . *if they make it that far,* he cautioned himself. Height, about five feet four or so; weight, about a hundred forty pounds, not at all unpleasant. The child, he saw, was darling with her lively blue eyes and happy expression—too young to learn to hide her feelings behind a blank mask, as nearly all the adults here did. No, children were the same everywhere in their innocence and insatiable curiosity. But, most important, they now had high-quality photos of the Rabbit family.

The courier was on the top floor, near the office of the Ambassador, Sir John Kenny. Haydock passed him a manila envelope sealed by metal clasp, glue, and wax over the flap. The address on the front designated the Foreign Office box that went straight to Century House across the Thames from Whitehall. The courier's bag was an expensive leather attaché case with the coat of arms of the Royal House of Windsor embossed on both sides. There was also a pair of handcuffs for him to secure it to his wrist, despite the stern rules of the Vienna Convention. The Queen's Messenger had a car waiting to take him to Sheremetyevo International Airport for the British Airways 737 afternoon return flight to Heathrow. The photos would be in Sir Basil's hand before he went home for the evening, and surely some Century House experts would be staying late that night to go over them. That would be the last official check to see if the Rabbit was genuine. His face would be compared with those of known KGB field and security officers—and if there was a hit, then Ed and Mary Foley were in for a bad time. But Haydock didn't expect that to happen. He agreed with his CIA counterparts. This one looked and felt real. But then, so did good Directorate Two people, didn't they? His last stop was at Communications to get a quick message off to SIS Headquarters that an important message was en route via courier on Operation BEATRIX. That would perk up everyone's eyeballs, and an SIS man would be waiting at the mailroom in Whitehall for this particular envelope. *As laggardly as a government bureaucracy could be,* Haydock thought, *when you had something important to do, it usually got done quickly, at least in the SIS.*

THE FLIGHT TOOK two hours and twenty minutes—a little late due to adverse winds—before arriving at Heathrow's Terminal Three. There, a Foreign Office representative whisked the courier off to downtown London in a black Jaguar saloon car, and the Queen's Messenger made his delivery and went off to his own office. Before he even got there, an SIS officer had taken the package and hustled down to Westminster Bridge and across the Thames.

"You have it?" Sir Basil asked.

"Here, sir." The messenger passed over the envelope. Charleston checked the closures and, satisfied that it had not been tampered with, slit it open with his paper knife. Then, for the first time, he saw what the

Rabbit looked like. Three minutes later, Alan Kingshot walked in. C handed over the color prints.

Kingshot took the top photo and gave it a long look. "So, this is our Rabbit, is it?"

"Correct, Alan," Sir Basil confirmed.

"He looks ordinary enough. His wife, as well. The little girl is rather cute," the senior field spook thought out loud. "On the way to Budapest now, are they?"

"Left Kiev Station five and a half hours ago."

"Fast work from Nigel." Kingshot gave the faces a closer look, wondering what information lay in the brain behind the man's face, and whether or not they'd get to use it. "So, BEATRIX goes forward. Do we have the bodies?"

"The male from York is close enough. We'll need to burn his face off, I'm afraid," C observed distastefully.

"No surprise there, sir," Kingshot agreed. "What about the other two?"

"Two candidates from America. Mother and daughter killed in a house fire in Boston, I believe. The FBI is working on that as we speak. We need to get this photo to them at once to make sure the bodies match up properly."

"I'll take care of that now if you wish, sir."

"Yes, Alan, please do that."

The machine downstairs was a color-photo transmitter like the one used by newspapers—relatively new and, its operator told Kingshot, very easy to use. He gave the photo only a cursory look. Transmission to an identical machine made by Xerox and located at Langley took less than two minutes. Kingshot took the photo back and returned to C's office.

"Done, sir." Sir Basil waved him to a seat.

Charleston checked his watch, giving it five minutes because CIA headquarters was a large building, and the communications people were in the basement. Then he called Judge Arthur Moore on the secure, dedicated line.

"Afternoon, Basil," Moore's voice said over the digitized circuit.

"Hello, Arthur. You have the photo?"

"Just got here. Looks like a nice little family," the DCI observed. "This is from the train station?"

"Yes, Arthur, they are en route as we speak. They will arrive in Budapest in about twenty—no, nineteen hours."

"Okay. Ready at your end, Basil?"

"We soon will be. There is the matter of those unfortunate people from Boston, however. We have the male body. It appears on first inspection that it will serve our needs quite well."

"Okay, I'll have the FBI expedite things here," Moore replied. He'd have to get this photo to the Hoover Building ASAP. *Might as well share this grisly business with Emil,* he thought.

"Very good, Arthur. I shall keep you posted."

"Great, Bas. See you."

"Excellent." Charleston hung up his phone, then looked over at Kingshot. "Have our people prepare the body for transport to Budapest."

"Timing, sir?"

"Three days should be about right," Sir Basil thought out loud.

"Right." Kingshot left the room.

C thought for a moment and decided it was time to warn the American. He punched another button on his phone. This took only a minute and a half.

"Yes, sir," Ryan said, entering his office.

"Your trip to Budapest, three days from today—perhaps four, but more likely three."

"Where do I leave from?"

"There's a morning British Airways flight from Heathrow. You can leave from here, or just take a taxi from Victoria Station. You'll be accompanied on the flight by one of our people, and met in Budapest by Andy Hudson, he's our Chief of Station there. Good man. Runs a good little station."

"Yes, sir," Ryan said, not knowing what the hell else to say in preparation for his first field mission as a spook. Then it was time for a question. "What, exactly, is going to happen, sir?"

"I'm not sure yet, but Andy has good connections with local smugglers.

I would expect him to arrange a crossing into Yugoslavia, and then home from there by commercial aircraft."

Great. More fucking airplanes, Ryan thought. *Couldn't we take the train?* But ex-Marines weren't supposed to show fear. "Okay, I guess that works."

"You may speak with our Rabbit—discreetly," Charleston warned. "And then you'll be allowed to sit in on our initial debriefing out in Somerset. Finally, I rather expect you'll be one of the chaps to escort him back to the States, probably on U.S. Air Force transport out of RAF Bentwaters."

Better and better, Jack thought. His hatred for flying was something he'd have to get over, and intellectually he knew that sooner or later he'd do it. It was just that he hadn't quite gotten over it *yet.* Well, at least he wouldn't be flying anywhere in a CH-46 with a fluky transmission. He drew the line there.

"My total time away from home?" *And sleeping apart from my wife,* Ryan thought.

"Four days, perhaps as many as seven. It depends on how things work out in Budapest," C replied. "That is difficult to predict."

NONE OF THEM had ever eaten at sixty miles per hour. The adventure for their little girl just got better and better. Dinner was adequate. The beef was about average for the Soviet Union, and so they could not be disappointed by it, along with potatoes and greens, and, of course, a carafe of vodka, one of the better brands, to erase the pain of travel. They were heading into the setting sun, now in country used exclusively for farming. Irina leaned across the table to cut the *zaichik*'s meat for her, watching their little angel eat her dinner, like the big girl she proclaimed herself to be, along with a glass of cold milk.

"So, looking forward to the trip now, my dear?" Oleg asked his wife.

"Yes, especially the shopping." Of course.

Part of Oleg Ivan'ch was calm—in fact, the calmest he'd been in weeks. It was really happening. His treason—part of his consciousness thought of it that way—was under way. How many of his countrymen, he wondered—indeed, how many of his coworkers at The Centre—would take the chance if they had the courage to do so? You couldn't know. He lived in a country and worked at an office where everyone concealed their inner thoughts. And at KGB, even the Russian custom of sanctifying especially close friendships by speaking things that could put you in prison, trusting that a true friend would never denounce you—no, a KGB officer didn't do such things. KGB was founded on the dichotomous balance of loyalty and betrayal. Loyalty to the state and its principles, and betrayal of any who violated them. But since he didn't believe in those principles anymore, he had turned to treason to save his soul.

And now the treason was under way. If the Second Chief Directorate knew of his plans, they would have been mad to allow him on this train. He could leave it at any intermediate stop—or just jump off the train when it slowed, approaching some preplanned point—and escape to Western hands, which could be waiting anywhere for him. No, he was safe, at least as long as he was on this train. And so he could be calm for now, and he'd let the days come as they would and see what happened. He kept telling himself that he was doing the right thing, and from that knowledge came his feeling, however illusory, of personal safety. If there were a God, surely He would protect a man on the run from evil.

DINNER IN THE Ryan house was spaghetti again. Cathy had a particularly good recipe for sauce—from her mom, who didn't have a single drop of Italian blood in her veins—and her husband loved it, especially with good Italian bread, which Cathy had found at a local bakery in downtown Chatham. No surgery tomorrow, so they had wine with dinner. Time to tell her.

"Honey, I have to travel in a few days."

"The NATO thing?"

" 'Fraid so, babe. Looks like three or four days—maybe a little more."

"What's it about, can you say?"

"Nope, not allowed."

"Spook business?"

"Yep." He was allowed to say that.

"What's a spook?" Sally asked.

"It's what daddy does," Cathy said, without thinking.

"Spook, like in the *Wizzerdaboz*?" Sally went on.

"What?" her father asked.

"The Cowardly Lion says he believes in spooks, remember?" Sally pointed out.

"Oh, you mean the *Wizard of Oz*." It was her favorite movie so far this year.

"That's what I *said,* Daddy." How could her daddy be so stupid?

"Well, no, Daddy isn't one of those," Jack told his daughter.

"Then why did Mommy say so?" Sally persisted. *She has the makings of a good FBI agent,* Jack thought at that moment.

It was Cathy's turn. "Sally, Mommy was just making a joke."

"Oh." Sally went back to work on her *pisghetti.* Jack gave his wife a look. They couldn't talk about his work in front of his daughter—not ever. Kids never kept secrets for more than five minutes, did they? So, he'd learned, never say anything in front of a kid that you didn't want on the first page of *The Washington Post.* Everyone on Grizedale Close thought that John Patrick Ryan worked at the U.S. Embassy and was lucky enough to be married to a surgeon. They didn't need to know that he was an officer of the Central Intelligence Agency. Too much curiosity. Too many jokes.

"Three or four days?" Cathy asked.

"That's what they tell me. Maybe a little longer, but not too much, I think."

"Important?" Sally had gotten her inquisitive nature from her mother, Jack figured . . . and maybe a little bit from himself.

"Important enough that they're throwing my ass on an airplane, yeah." That actually worked. Cathy knew of her husband's hatred for air travel.

"Well, you have your Valium prescription. Want a beta-blocker, too?"

"No thanks, babe, not this time."

"You know, if you got airsick, it would be easier to understand." And easier to treat, she didn't have to add.

"Babe, you were there when my back went out, remember? I have some bad memories from flying. Maybe when we go home, we can take the boat," he added, with some hope in his voice. But, no, it wouldn't work out that way. It never did in the real world.

"Flying is fun," Sally protested. She definitely got that from her mother.

TRAVEL IS INEVITABLY TIRING, and so the Zaitzev family was agreeably surprised to see their beds turned out when they got back to their compartments. Irina got her daughter changed into her little yellow nightgown with flowers on what would have been the bodice. She gave her parents the usual good-night kiss and climbed onto her bed all by herself—she insisted on doing that—and slid under the covers. Instead of sleeping, she propped her head on the pillow and looked out the window at the darkened countryside passing by. Just a few lights from buildings on the collective farms but, for all that, fascinating to the little girl.

Her mother and father left the connecting door partly open, lest she have a nightmare or other sudden need to get a reassuring hug. Before going to bed, Svetlana had looked under the bed to see if there might be a hiding place for a big black bear, and she was satisfied that no such hiding place existed. Oleg and Irina opened books and gradually nodded off to the rocking of the train.

"BEATRIX IS RUNNING," Moore told Admiral Greer. "The Rabbit and his family are on the train, probably crossing into the Ukraine right about now."

"I hate waiting like this," the DDI observed. It was easier for him to admit it. He'd never gone into the field on an intelligence mission. No, his job had always been at a desk, looking over important information. It was times like this that reminded him of the simple pleasures of standing watch on a ship of war—mainly submarines, in his case—where you could look at wind and wave, feel the breeze on your face and, merely by speaking a few words, change the course and speed of your ship instead of waiting to see what the ocean and distant enemy might do to you. You had the illusion there of being master of your fate.

"Patience is the hardest of the virtues to acquire, James, and the higher you get, the more you need the bastard. For me, this is like sitting on the bench, waiting for the lawyers to get to the damned point. It can take forever, especially when you know what the fools are going to say," Moore admitted. He'd also been there and done that, out in the field. But so much of that job was composed of waiting, too. No man controlled his fate, a knowledge that came late in life. You just tried to muddle along from one point to another, making as few mistakes as possible.

"Tell the President about this one yet?"

Moore shook his head. "No sense getting him overly excited. If he thinks this guy has information that he doesn't have—hell, why disappoint him? We do enough of that here, don't we?"

"Arthur, we never have enough information, and the more we get, the more we appreciate what we need and don't have."

"James, my boy, neither one of us is educated to be a philosopher."

"Comes with the gray hair, Arthur." Then Mike Bostock walked in.

"Couple more days and BEATRIX goes into the history books," he announced with a smile.

"Mike, where the hell did you learn to believe in Santa Claus?" the DCI asked.

"Judge, it's like this: We got us a defector who's defecting right now. We have a good team to get him out of Redland. You trust your troops to do the job you send them out to do."

"But they're not all our troops," Greer pointed out.

"Basil runs a good shop, Admiral. You know that."

"True," Greer admitted.

"So, you just wait to see what's under the Christmas tree, Mike?" Moore asked.

"I sent Santa my letter, and Santa always delivers. Everybody knows that." He was beaming at the possibilities. "What are we going to do with him when he arrives?"

"The farmhouse out at Winchester, I imagine," Moore thought out loud. "Give him a nice place to depressurize—let him travel around some on day trips."

"What stipend?" Greer inquired.

"Depends," Moore said. He was the one who controlled that out of the Agency's black budget. "If it's good information . . . oh, as much as a million, I imagine. And a nice place to work after we tickle all of it out of him."

"Where, I wonder?" Bostock put in.

"Oh, we let him decide that."

It was both a simple and a complex process. The arriving Rabbit family would have to learn English. New identities. They'd need new names, for starters, probably make them Norwegian immigrants to explain away the accents. CIA had the power to admit a total of one hundred new citizens every year through the Immigration and Naturalization Service (and they'd never used them all up). The Rabbits would need a set of Social Security numbers, driver's licenses—probably driving lessons beforehand, maybe for both, certainly for the wife—from the Commonwealth of Virginia. (The Agency had a cordial relationship with the state government. Richmond never asked too many questions.)

Then came the psychological help for people who'd walked away from everything they'd ever known and had to find their footing in a new and grossly different country. The Agency had a Columbia University professor of psychology on retainer to handle that. Then they'd get some older defectors to hand-walk them through the transition. None of this was ever easy on the new immigrants. For Russians, America was like a toy store for a child who'd never known such a thing as a toy store existed—it was overwhelming in every respect, with virtually no common points of comparison, almost like a different planet. They had to make it as comfortable for the defectors as possible. First, for the information, and second, to make sure they didn't want to go back—it would be almost certain death, at least for the husband, but it had happened before, so strong was the call of home for every man.

"If he likes a cold climate, send him to Minneapolis–Saint Paul," Greer suggested. "But, gentlemen, we are getting a little bit ahead of ourselves."

"James, you are always the voice of sober counsel," the DCI observed with a smile.

"Somebody has to be. The eggs haven't hatched yet, people. *Then* we count the chicks."

And what if he doesn't know squat? Moore thought. *What if he's just a guy who wants a ticket out?*

God damn this business! the DCI completed the thought.

"Well, Basil will keep us posted, and we have your boy Ryan looking out for our interests."

"That's great news, Judge. Basil must be laughing into his beer about that."

"He's a good boy, Mike. Don't underestimate him. Those who did are in Maryland State Penitentiary now, waiting for the appeals process to play out," Greer said, in defense of his protégé.

"Well, yeah, he was a Marine once," Bostock conceded. "What do I tell Bob when he calls in?"

"Nothing," the DCI said at once. "Until we find out from the Rabbit what part of our comms are compromised, we are careful what goes out on a wire. Clear?"

Bostock nodded his head like a first-grader. "Yes, sir."

"I've had S and T go over our phone lines. They say they're clean. Chip Bennett is still raising hell and running in circles at Fort Meade." Moore didn't have to say that this alleged claim from the Rabbit was the scariest revelation to Washington since Pearl Harbor. But maybe they'd be able to turn it around on Ivan. Hope sprang eternal at Langley, just like everywhere else. It was unlikely that the Russians knew anything his Directorate of Science and Technology didn't, but you had to pay to see the cards.

RYAN WAS QUIETLY packing his things. Cathy was better at it, but he didn't know what he'd need. How did one pack for being secret-agent man? Business suit. His old Marine utilities? (He still had them, butter bar on the collar and all.) Nice leather shoes? Sneaks? That, he thought, sounded appropriate. He ended up deciding on a middle-of-the-road suit and two pairs of walking shoes, one semiformal, one informal. And it all had to fit in one bag—for that, an L.L. Bean canvas two-suiter that was easy to carry and fairly anonymous. He left his passport in the desk drawer. Sir Basil would be giving him a nice new British one, another diplomatic or fuck-you passport. Probably a new name to go with it. *Damn,* Jack thought, *a new name to remember and respond to.* He was used to having only one.

One nice thing about Merrill Lynch: You always knew who the hell you were. *Sure,* Jack's mind went on, *let the whole damned world know you were a flunky of Joe Muller. Not in this lifetime.* Any opinionated asshole could make money, and his father-in-law was one of them.

"Finished?" Cathy asked from behind him.

"Just about, babe," Jack answered.

"It's not dangerous, what you're doing, is it?"

"I don't expect it to be, babe." But Jack couldn't lie, and his uncertainty conveyed just enough.

"Where are you going?"

"I told you, remember, Germany." *Uh-oh. She caught me again.*

"Some NATO thing?"

"That's what they tell me."

"What do you do in London, Jack? Century House, that's intelligence stuff, and—"

"Cathy, I've told you before. I'm an analyst. I go over information from various sources, and I try to figure out what it means, and I write reports for people to read. You know, it's not all that different from what I did at Merrill Lynch. My job is to look at information and figure out what it really means. They think I'm good at it."

"But nothing with guns?" Half a question and half an observation. Jack supposed it was from her work in the Emergency Room at Hopkins. As a group, doctors didn't much care for firearms, except the ones who liked hunting birds in the fall. She didn't like the Remington shotgun in his closet, unloaded, and she liked the Browning Hi-Power hidden on the shelf in his closet, loaded, even less.

"Honey, no, no guns, not at all. I'm not that kind of spook."

"Okay," she semi-conceded. She didn't believe him completely, but she knew he couldn't say what he was doing any more than she could discuss her patients with him. In that understanding came her frustration. "Just so you're not away too long."

"Babe, you know I hate being away from you. I can't even sleep worth a damn unless you're next to me."

"So take me with you?"

"So you can go shopping in Germany? For what? Dirndls for Sally?"

"Well, she likes the Heidi movies." It was a weak offering.

"Nice try, babe. Wish you could, but you can't."

"Oh, damn," Lady Ryan observed.

"We live in an imperfect world, babe."

She especially hated *that* aphorism of his, and her reply was an ungrammatical grunt. But, really, there was no reply she could make.

Minutes later, in bed, Jack wondered what the hell he would be doing. Reason told him that it would be routine in every respect, except for the location. But except for one little thing, Abe Lincoln had enjoyed that play at Ford's Theater. He'd be on foreign soil—no, *hostile* foreign soil. He was already living in a foreign place, and, friendly as the Brits were, only home was home. But the Brits liked him. The Hungarians wouldn't. They might not take a shot at him, but neither would they give him the key to the city. And what if they found out he was traveling on a false passport? What did the Vienna Convention say about *that*? But he couldn't wimp out on this one, could he? He *was* an ex-Marine. He was *supposed* to be fearless. Yeah, sure. About the only good thing that had happened at his house a few months back was that he'd made a head call before the bad guys had crashed the party, and so hadn't been *able* to wet his pants with a gun to his head. He'd gotten it done, but he damned sure didn't feel heroic. He'd managed to survive, managed to kill that one guy with the Uzi, but the only thing he felt good about was *not* killing that bastard Sean Miller. No, he'd let the State of Maryland handle that one, by the numbers, unless the Supreme Court stepped in again, and that didn't strike him as very likely in this particular case, with a bunch of Secret Service agents dead. The courts didn't ignore dead cops very often.

But what would happen in Hungary? He'd just be a watcher, the semiofficial CIA officer overseeing the evacuation of some fool Russian who wanted to move out of his place in Moscow. *Damn, why the hell does this sort of thing always seem to happen to me?* Jack wondered. It was like hitting the devil's lottery, and his number kept coming up. Would that ever stop? He was paid to look into the future and make his predictions, but inside he knew that he couldn't do it worth a damn. He needed other people to tell him what *was* happening, so that then he could compare it with things that everyone knew *had* happened, and then combine the two into a wild-ass guess on what somebody *might* do. And, sure, he'd done okay at that in the trading business, but nobody ever got killed over a few shares of common stock. And now, maybe, *his* cute little ass would be on the line. Great. Just fucking great. He stared at the ceiling. Why were they always white?

Wouldn't black be a better color for sleeping? You could always see white ceilings, even in a darkened room. Was there a reason for that?

Was there a reason why he couldn't sleep? Why was he asking damned-fool questions with no answers? However this played out, he'd almost certainly be okay. Basil wouldn't let anything happen to him. It would look very bad to Langley, and the Brits couldn't afford that—too embarrassing. Judge Moore wouldn't forget, and it would become part of CIA's institutional memory, and that would be bad for the next ten years or more. So, no, SIS wouldn't let anything bad happen to him.

On the other hand, they wouldn't be the only players on the field and, as in baseball, the problem was that both teams played to win, and you needed the right timing to send that 95-mph fastball out to the cheap seats.

But you can't wimp out, Jack, he told himself. Others, whose opinions he valued, would be ashamed of him—worse, he'd be ashamed of himself. So, like it or not, he had to suit up and go out on the field and hope he didn't drop the damned ball.

Or just go back to Merrill Lynch, but, no, he'd rather face bayonets than do that. *I really would,* Ryan realized, in considerable surprise. Did that make him brave, or just hardheaded? *There's a question,* he thought. And the only answer had to come from someone else, someone who would only see one side of the equation. You could only see the physical part, never the thought that went into it. And that wasn't enough to judge from, much as newsmen and historians tried to shape reality in that way, as though they really understood such things at a distance of miles or years. Yeah, sure.

In any case, his bags were packed, and with luck the worst part of this trip would be the airplane ride. Much as he hated it, it was fairly predictable . . . unless a wing fell off.

"WHAT THE *FUCK* is this all about?" John Tyler asked nobody in particular. The telex in his hand only gave orders, not the reasons behind them.

The bodies had been transported to the city coroner, with a request for no action to be taken with them. Tyler thought for a moment and then called the Assistant U.S. Attorney he usually worked with.

"You want *what*?" Peter Mayfair asked in some incredulity. He'd graduated third in his Harvard Law School class three years before and was racing up the career ladder at the U.S. Attorney's office. People called him Max.

"You heard me."

"What is this all about?"

"I don't know. I just know it comes straight from Emil's office. It sounds like stuff from the other side of the river, but the telex doesn't say beans. How do we do it?"

"Where are the bodies?"

"Coroner's office, I guess. There's a note on them—mother and daughter—that says don't post them. So I suppose they're in the freezer."

"And you want them raw, like?"

"Frozen, I suppose, but yeah, raw." *What a hell of a way to put it,* the Assistant Special Agent in Charge thought.

"Any families involved?"

"The police haven't located any yet that I know of."

"Okay, we hope it stays that way. If there's no family to say no, we declare them indigent and get the coroner to release them to federal custody, you know, like a dead drunk on the street. They just put them in a cheap box and bury them in Potter's Field. Where you going to take them?"

"Max, I don't know. Guess I send a reply telex to Emil and he'll tell me."

"Fast?" Mayfair asked, wondering what priority went on this.

"Last week, Max."

"Okay, if you want, I'll drive down to the coroner's right now."

"Meet you there, Max. Thanks."

"You owe me a beer and dinner at Legal Seafood," the U.S. Attorney told him.

"Done." He'd have to deliver on this one.

CHAPTER 25

EXCHANGING THE BOGIES

THE BODIES WERE LOADED in cheap aluminum boxes, the sort used for transporting bodies by air, and then loaded on a van used by the FBI and driven to Logan International Airport. Special Agent Tyler called Washington to ask what came next, and fortunately his car radio was encrypted.

FBI Director Emil Jacobs, it turned out, hadn't thought things all the way through quite yet either, and he had to call Judge Moore at CIA, where more rapid dancing was done, until it was decided to load them on the British Airways 747 scheduled to leave Boston for London Heathrow, so that Basil's people could collect them. This was done with alacrity because BA cooperated readily with American police agencies, and Flight 214 rolled away from the gate on time at 8:10 and soon thereafter climbed to altitude for the three-thousand-mile hop to Heathrow's Terminal Four.

IT WAS APPROACHING five in the morning when Zaitzev awoke in his upper bunk, not sure why he had done so. He rolled a little to look out the window when it hit him: The train was stopped at a station. He didn't know which one—he didn't have the schedule memorized—and he felt a sudden chill. What if some Second Chief Directorate men had just boarded? In the daylight, he might have shaken it off, but KGB had the reputation of arresting people in the middle of the night, when they'd be less likely to resist effectively, and suddenly the fear came back. Then he heard feet walking down the corridor . . . but they passed him by, and moments later the train started moving again, pulling away from the wooden station building, and presently the view outside was just darkness again. *Why did this frighten me?* Zaitzev asked himself. Why now? Wasn't he safe now? *Or almost so,* he corrected himself. The answer was, no, not until his feet stood on foreign soil. He had to remind himself of that fact, until he stood on foreign, nonsocialist soil. And he wasn't there yet. With that reminder refixed in his mind, he rolled back and tried to get back to sleep. The motion of the train eventually overcame his anxiety, and he returned to dreams that were not the least bit reassuring.

THE BRITISH AIRWAYS 747 also flew through darkness, its passengers mainly asleep while the flight crew monitored its numerous instruments and sipped their coffee, taking time to enjoy the night stars, and watched the horizon for the first hint of dawn. That usually came over the west coast of Ireland.

RYAN AWOKE EARLIER than usual. He slipped out of bed without disturbing his wife, dressed casually, and went outside. The milkman was driving into the cul-de-sac at the end of Grizedale Close. He stopped his truck and got out with the half-gallon of whole milk his kids drank like a Pratt & Whitney engine guzzled jet fuel, and a loaf of bread. He was halfway to the house before he noticed his customer.

"Anything amiss, sir?" the milkman asked, thinking perhaps a child was ill, the usual reason for the parents of young children to be up and about at this time of day.

"No, just woke up a little early," Ryan replied with a yawn.

"Anything special you might need?"

"Just a cigarette," Ryan replied, without thinking. Under Cathy's iron rule, he hadn't had one since arriving in England.

"Well, here, sir." The man extended a pack with one shaken loose.

It surprised the hell out of Ryan. "Thanks, buddy." But he took it anyway, along with the light from a butane lighter. He coughed with the first drag, but got over it pretty fast. It was a remarkably friendly feeling in the still, predawn air, and the wonderful thing about bad habits was how quickly one picked them back up. It was a strong cigarette, like the Marlboros he'd smoked in his senior year of high school, part of the ascension to manhood back in the late 1960s. *The milkman ought to quit,* Jack thought, *but he probably wasn't married to a Hopkins surgeon.*

He didn't often get to talk to his customers, either. "You like living here, sir?"

"Yes, I do. The people here are very friendly."

"We try to be, sir. Have a good day, then."

"Thanks, buddy. You, too," Ryan said, as the man walked back to his truck. Milkmen had mostly gone extinct in America, victims of supermarkets and 7-Eleven stores. *A pity,* Jack thought. He remembered Peter Wheat bread and honey-dipped donuts when he'd been a little kid. Somehow it had all gone away without his noticing it around the seventh grade or so. But the smoke and the quiet air wasn't at all a bad way to wake up. There was no sound at all. Even the birds were still asleep. He looked up to see the lights of aircraft high in the sky. People traveling to Europe, probably Scandinavia, by the apparent courses they were flying—out of Heathrow, probably. *What poor bastard has to get up this early to make a meeting?* he wondered. Well . . . he finished the cigarette and flicked it out on the lawn, wondering if Cathy might spot it. Well, he could always blame it on somebody else. A pity the paperboy hadn't come yet. So Jack went inside and turned on the kitchen TV to get CNN. He caught the sports. The Orioles had won again and would be going to the World Series against the Phillies. That was good news, or nearly so. Had he been home, he would have gotten tickets to catch a game or two at Memorial Stadium and seen the rest on TV. Not this year. His cable system didn't have a single channel to catch baseball games, though the Brits were starting to watch

NFL football. They didn't really get it, but for some reason they enjoyed watching it. *Better than their regular TV*, Ryan thought with a snort. Cathy liked their comedy, but for some reason it just didn't click with him. But their news programming was pretty good. It was just taste, he assumed. *Non est disputandum*, as the Romans had said. Then he saw dawn coming, the first hint of light on the eastern horizon. It'd be more than an hour before morning actually began, but coming it was, and even the desire for more sleep would not hold it back.

Jack decided to get the coffee going—just a matter of flipping the switch on the drip machine he'd gotten Cathy for her birthday. Then he heard the *flop* of the paper on the front step, and he went to get it.

"Up early?" Cathy said, when he got back.

"Yeah. Didn't see any sense in rolling back over." Jack kissed his wife. She got a funny look on her face after the kiss but shook it off. Her tobacco-sniffing nose had delivered a faint message, but her intellect had erroneously dismissed it as too unlikely.

"Got the coffee going?"

"Flipped the button," Jack confirmed. "I'll let you do the rest."

"What do you want for breakfast?"

"I get a choice?" Ryan asked, somewhat incredulously. She was on another health kick of late. No donuts.

"GOOD MORNING, *ZAICHIK*!" Oleg said to his daughter.

"Papa!" She reached both her arms out with that smile kids have when they awaken. It was something they lost long before adulthood, and something universally astonishing to parents while it lasted. Oleg lifted her from the bed and gave her a hug. Her little bare feet went down on the carpeted floor, and then she took two steps to her private toilet. Irina came in to lay her clothes out, and both withdrew to the adult side of the accommodations. Within ten minutes, they were on their way to the dining car. Oleg looked over his shoulder to see the attendant hustling forward to make up their compartments first. Yes, there were advantages to being KGB, even if it was just for another day.

Somewhere during the night, the train had stopped at a state farm and taken on fresh milk, which Svetlana loved for her morning meal. The adults in the party had mediocre (at best) coffee and buttered bread. (The kitchen was out of eggs.) At least the bread and butter were fresh and tasty. There was a stack of newspapers at the back end of the car. Oleg picked up a *Pravda* and sat down to read it—the usual lies. One other thing about being KGB was that you knew better than to believe what was in the papers. Izvestia *at least had stories about real people, some of which were even true,* he thought. But a Soviet train would, of course, carry only the most politically correct newspapers, and "Truth" was it, Zaitzev snorted.

RYAN MAINTAINED TWO complete sets of shaving and grooming things for the occasional exigencies of travel. His Bean bag was hanging by its large brass hook in his closet, ready for whenever Sir Basil dispatched him to Budapest. He looked at it while knotting his tie, wondering when he'd be going. Then Cathy reentered the bedroom and got herself dressed. Her white lab coat doubtless hung on a hook on her office door—both of them, probably, Hammersmith and Moorefields, with the appropriate name tags.

"Cath?"

"Yeah?"

"Your office coat—did you keep your Hopkins name tag, or did you get new ones?" He'd never bothered to ask.

"Local ones. Too hard to explain it to every new patient who might notice." But some asked about her accent anyway, or would ask why the name tag proclaimed her to be Lady Caroline Ryan, M.D., FACS. The "Lady" part appealed to her woman's vanity. Jack watched her brush her hair out, something that always gave him pleasure. She would have been an absolute knockout with somewhat longer hair, but she never let it grow, saying that the surgical caps ruined whatever set she might have gotten. That would change the next time they got invited to a formal dinner. They were due for one. The Queen liked both of them, and so did the Prince of Wales, and they were on the local version of the A-list. You had to accept such invitations, though Cathy had an excuse if she was doing surgery the next day. Spooks, on the other hand, were expected to be delighted at the honor, even if it meant three short hours of sleep before the next day at work.

"What's on the agenda for today?"

"Giving a lecture on the xenon-arc laser. They're going to be buying one soon, and I'm the only person in London who knows how to use it right."

"My wife, the laser jockey."

"Well, at least I can talk about what I do," she responded, "secret-agent man."

"Yes, dear," Ryan sighed. *Maybe I should pack my Browning today just to piss her off.* But if anyone on the train noticed, he'd at best be regarded as unclean, and at worst would be asked by a police constable what he was doing with such a thing on his person. And even his diplomatic status would not entirely protect him from the resulting hassle.

FIFTEEN MINUTES LATER, Jack and Cathy were in their compartment, heading northwest to London, she again reading her medical journals, and he going through the *Telegraph.* John Keegan had a column on the inside and he was a historian for whom Ryan had considerable respect as an analyst of complex information. Why Basil hadn't recruited him for Century House was a mystery to Jack. Maybe Keegan was just doing too well as an historian, able to spread his ideas to the masses—well, at least the smart civilians out there. That made sense. Nobody ever got rich as a British civil servant, and the anonymity—well, it was nice once in a while to get a pat on the head for doing something especially well. Bureaucrats were denied that all over the world.

ABOUT THE TIME their express train passed by the Elephant and Castle station, Flight 214 rolled to an early stop at Heathrow's Terminal Four. It didn't come to a jetway. Instead it came to a halt where the shuttle buses waited to take people to Immigration and Customs. No sooner had the wheels been chocked than the cargo hatch came open. The last two items loaded at Logan had been the two coffins, and they became the first items of baggage to be manhandled off. The tags on one corner of each told the handlers where to send them, and two anonymous men from Century House were there to watch the process anyway. Placed on a four-wheel cart—called a trolley in England—they were pulled off to an area for parked cars and small trucks, where the boxes were quickly loaded on a small four-wheeled truck with no marking on its sides at all. The two men from SIS hopped aboard and drove off, easterly for London, entirely without a clue what this job was all about. It was often that way.

The truck arrived at 100 Westminster Bridge Road forty minutes later. There the boxes were removed and placed on another trolley for a ride to the freight elevator and a trip down to the second-level basement.

Two more men were waiting there. The boxes were duly opened, and both men thanked fate that there was a goodly supply of dry ice inside and the bodies were not yet venting the particularly foul smell of dead and mortifying human tissue. Wearing rubber gloves, they lifted the bodies—neither was especially heavy—and transferred them to stainless-steel tables. Neither body was clothed and, in the case of the little girl, their job was particularly sad.

It would get more so. Comparing the bodies with the *Times*-generated photograph, it was determined, unsurprisingly, that the child's face didn't match the picture. The same was true of the grown woman, though her body mass and configuration were about right. Her face was virtually untouched by the fire, the toxic gasses of which had ended her life. And so both of them would have to be grossly disfigured to be usable for Operation BEATRIX. This was done with propane blowtorches. First, the senior of the two turned on the powerful exhaust fan in the ceiling. Both then donned fire-protective coveralls and lit their torches. These were heartlessly applied to both faces. Hair color was wrong in both cases, and so that was burned off first of all. Then the torches were applied at close range to both faces. It went quickly, but not quickly enough for the two SIS employees. The one doing the little girl breathed a series of prayers for her child's soul, knowing that she was wherever innocent children went. That which remained was just cold meat, of no value to its previous owner, but of some value to the United Kingdom—and doubtless the United States of America as well, else they would not be doing such ghoulish work as this. It was when the little girl's left eye exploded from internal pressure that her tormentor had to turn away and vomit. But it had to be done. Her eyes were the wrong color.

Hands and feet had to be well-charred, and both bodies were examined for tattoos, scars, or other distinguishing characteristics, but none were found, not even an appendectomy scar.

All in all, it took ninety minutes before they were satisfied with their work. Then the bodies had to be dressed. Clothing of Soviet origin was maneuvered onto the bodies, and then *that* had to be burned so that the fibers would be enmeshed with the surface burns. With all this grisly work done, the bodies were reloaded into their transport boxes, and more dry ice was added to keep them cool enough to retard decay. The boxes were set near a third identical such box in the corner of the room. By then it was lunchtime, but neither of them cared much for food at the moment. A few shots of whiskey were more what they needed, and there were plenty of pubs within walking distance.

"JACK?" Sir Basil stuck his head through the door to find Ryan going over his documents, like a good analyst.

"Yes, sir," Ryan responded, looking up.

"Are you packed?"

"My stuff is at home, but yes, sir."

"Good. You're on the BA flight from Heathrow Terminal Three at eight this evening. We'll have a car to run you home to pick up your things—say, about three-thirty?"

"I haven't gotten my passport and visa yet," Ryan told C.

"You'll have it after lunch. Your overt cover is as an auditor from the Foreign Office. As I recall, you had an accountant's charter once upon a time. Perhaps you can look over the books while you're there." This was funny, Charleston thought.

Ryan tried to return the favor. "Probably more interesting than the local stock market. Anyone going with me?"

"No, but you'll be met at the airport by Andy Hudson. He's our Station Chief in Budapest. Good man," Sir Basil promised. "Stop in to see me before you head off."

"Will do, sir." And Basil's head vanished back into the corridor.

"Simon, how about a pint and a sandwich?" Ryan said to his workmate.

"Fine idea." Harding stood and got his coat. They walked off to the Duke of Clarence.

LUNCH ON THE TRAIN was pleasant: borscht, noodles, black bread, and a proper dessert—strawberries from some farm or other. The only problem was that Svetlana didn't care for borscht, which was odd for a Russian native, even a child. She picked at the sour cream topping, then later attacked the noodles with gusto and positively devoured the late-season strawberries. They'd just climbed through the low Transylvanian mountains on the Bulgarian border. The train would pass through Sofia, then turn northwest for Belgrade, Yugoslavia, and finally Hungary.

The Zaitzevs lingered over lunch, Svetlana peering out the windows as the train approached Sofia.

Oleg Ivanovich did the same, puffing on his cigarette. Passing through Sofia, he found himself wondering which building housed the *Dirzhavna Sugurnost.* Was Colonel Bubovoy there, working on his plot, probably with that Colonel Strokov? How far along might they be? Was the Pope's life in immediate danger? How would he feel if the Polish priest was murdered before he could get his warning out? Could he or should he have moved faster? *These damned questions*, and no one in whom he could confide them! *You are doing your best, Oleg Ivan'ch*, he told himself, *and no man can do more than that!*

The Sofia station looked like a cathedral, an impressive stone building with an almost religious purpose. Somehow he wasn't worried now about a KGB arrest team boarding the train. His only thoughts were to press on, get to Budapest, and see what the CIA did there . . . and hope they were competent. KGB could do a job like this with consummate professionalism, almost like stage magicians. Was CIA also that good? On Russian TV, they were frequently portrayed as evil but bumbling adversaries—but that wasn't what they said at The Centre. No, at #2 Dzerzhinskiy Square, they were thought to be evil spirits, always on the prowl, clever as the devil himself, the most deadly of enemies. So, which was true? Certainly he'd find out quickly enough—one way or another. Zaitzev stubbed out his cigarette and led his family back to their compartments.

"LOOKING FORWARD TO the mission, Jack?" Harding asked.

"Yeah, like the dentist. And don't tell me how easy it'll be. You've never gone out in the field either."

"Your own people suggested this, you know."

"So, when I get home—if I get home—I'll slug Admiral Greer," Ryan responded, half—but only half—joking. "I'm not trained for this, Simon, remember?"

"How many people are trained to deal with a direct physical attack? You've done that," Simon reminded him.

"Okay, I was a marine lieutenant once, for—what was it?—eleven months or so, before the helicopter crunched on Crete and I got my back broke. Shit, I don't even like roller-coasters. My mom and dad loved the goddamned things; they were always taking me up in them at Gwynn Oak Amusement Park when I was a little kid. Expected me to like the damned things, too. Dad," Ryan explained, "was a paratrooper in the One hundred first Airborne, back forty years ago. Falling out of the sky didn't worry him too much." That was followed by a snort. One nice thing about the Marine Corps, they didn't make you jump out of an airplane. *Well, damn,* Jack thought suddenly. Was he more worried about this than the airline flight? That caused a downward look and an ironic chuckle. "Do your field officers carry weapons?"

That generated a laugh. "Only in the movies, Jack. They're bloody heavy to lug about, and they can be difficult to explain. There are no double-o people in SIS—at least not to my knowledge. The French occasionally kill people, and they are actually rather good at it. So are the Israelis, but people do make mistakes, even trained professionals, and that sort of thing can be difficult to explain to the press."

"You can't invoke a D-notice?"

"Theoretically, yes, but they can be difficult to enforce. Fleet Street has its own rules, you see."

"So does *The Washington Post*, as Nixon found out. So I ought not to kill anyone."

"I would try to avoid it," Simon agreed, munching on his turkey sandwich.

BELGRADE—BEOGRAD TO its natives—also had a fine station. In the previous century, evidently, architects had worked hard to outdo each other, like the pious ones who'd built cathedrals in the Middle Ages. The train was several hours late, he saw with surprise. He couldn't see why. The train hadn't stopped for any length of time anywhere. Perhaps it wasn't traveling as fast as it was supposed to. Leaving Belgrade, it snaked up some modest hills, and none too quickly at that. He imagined this country would be pretty in winter. Wasn't there an upcoming Olympiad hereabouts? The winter probably came here about the same time it did in Moscow. It was a little late this year, but that usually meant it would be unusually harsh when it arrived. He wondered what winter would be like in America. . . .

"READY, JACK?" Charleston asked in his office.

"I suppose." Jack looked at his new passport. Since it was a diplomatic one, it was a little more ornate than the usual, and bound in red leather, with the Royal Coat of Arms on the front cover. He paged through it to see the stamps of all the places he had *not* visited. Thailand, the People's Republic of China. *Damn*, Jack thought, *I really do get around.* "Why this visa?" he asked. The U.K. didn't require them for anybody.

"Hungary controls movement in and out rather sternly. They require an entry and exit visa. You'll not be needing the latter, I expect," C observed. "Hudson will probably be taking you out in a southerly direction. He has good relations with the local smugglers."

"Walking over any mountains?" Ryan asked.

Basil shook his head. "No, we don't often do that. Car or truck, I should think. Ought not to be any problem at all, my boy." He looked up. "It really is quite routine, Jack."

"You say so, sir." *It damned sure isn't for me.*

Charleston stood. "Good luck, Jack. See you back in a few days."

Ryan took his hand. "Roger that, Sir Basil." Semper fi, *pal.*

There was a car waiting on the street. Jack hopped in the left-front seat, and the driver headed east. The ride took about fifty minutes with the light afternoon traffic, almost as fast as the train would have been.

On getting to Chatham, Ryan found his daughter napping, Little Jack playing with his feet—fascinating things they were—in the playpen, and Miss Margaret sitting with a magazine in the living room.

"Dr. Ryan, I didn't expect—"

"That's okay, I have to take a business trip." He walked to the wall phone in the kitchen and tried calling Cathy, only to learn that she was giving her damned lecture on her laser toy. *It was the one she used for welding blood vessels back shut,* he thought. Something like that. Frowning, he went upstairs for his bag. He'd try to call her from the airport. But, just in case, he scribbled a note.

OFF TO BONN. TRIED TO CALL. WILL TRY AGAIN. LOVE, JACK. This one found its way to the refrigerator door. Ryan bent down to give Sally a kiss and then reached down to lift his son for a hug, a sloppy one, as it turned out. The little guy dribbled the way a car engine dripped oil. That necessitated a paper towel on the way out.

"Have a good trip, Dr. Ryan," the nanny called.

"Thanks, Margaret. See ya." As soon as the car pulled off, she called Century House to let people know Sir John was on the way to Heathrow. Then she went back to her magazine, this month's *Tattler.*

THE TRAIN CAME to an unexpected halt in a yard right at the Hungarian frontier, near the town of Zombor. Zaitzev hadn't known about this, and the surprise was soon compounded. There were cranes on their side of the train, and no sooner had the train stopped than a crowd of coveralled workmen appeared.

The Hungarian State Railway operated on standard gauge, the tracks 1,435 milimeters—4 feet, 8½ inches—apart, which was the world's standard, and which incongruously dated back to the two-horse chariots used by the

Romans. But the Russian train gauge was five feet, or 1,524 millimeters—for some reason no one remembered. The solution to that here was to lift the train bodies off the Russian tracks—the wheel sets—and lower them onto a different set. That took about an hour, but it was efficiently done, for all that. It utterly fascinated Svetlana, and it even impressed her father that the task was performed so routinely. An hour and twenty minutes later, they were moving almost due north on narrower tracks behind a new electric locomotive, crossing the rich agricultural soil of Hungary. Almost at once, Svetlana chirped at the sight of men in local dress riding horses, which struck both parents and child as quite exotic.

THE AIRCRAFT WAS a fairly new Boeing 737 and, for this trip, Ryan decided to take a friend. He bought a pack of cigarettes at the airport and lit one up at once on the concourse.

The good news was that he'd been give a first-class window seat, 1-A. The scenery up in the sky was the only good part of flying, with the additional bonus that nobody could see the fear in your face, except maybe the stewardess, because like doctors they could probably also smell fear. But up front the booze was free, and so Ryan tried to order whiskey, only to find that the selection was Scotch (which he didn't like), vodka (which he didn't like), or gin (which he could not stand in his presence). It was the wrong airline for Jack Daniel's, but the wine list was okay, and, climbing to cruise altitude, the no-smoking light *ding*ed off, and Ryan lit up another smoke. Not as good as a nice bourbon, but better than nothing at all. At least it enabled him to lean back and pretend to relax behind closed eyes, occasionally looking out to see if the stuff under the aircraft was green or blue. The flight was agreeably smooth, with only a few bumps to make him grab for the armrests, and three glasses of a decent French white helped smooth his anxiety out. About halfway there, over Belgium, he got back to thinking. How many people hated flying? Maybe a third, maybe half? How many of them detested it as much as he did? Half of those? So, probably, he wasn't alone. Fearful people tried to hide it, and a look around showed faces much the same as his probably was. So at least he probably wasn't the only wimp on the airplane. And the wine was nice and fruity.

And if the ULA hadn't been able to punch his ticket with Uzis right in his home on the Chesapeake Bay, then random chance was probably on his side as well. So he might as well relax and enjoy the ride—he was stuck here one way or another, after all, and the Boeing cruised along at 500 knots or so.

There were a few bumps in the descent, but for Ryan this was the one part of the flight during which he felt safe—when the aircraft was returning to earth. Intellectually, he knew that this was actually the most dangerous part, but somehow his gut didn't see it that way. He heard the whine of various servos, and then the whooshing sound that announced the open landing-gear doors, and then felt safe enough to see the ground rushing toward him. The landing was bumpy, but Jack welcomed it. He was back on the ground, where you could stand up and ambulate all by yourself at a reasonably safe speed. Good.

THEY WERE IN another train yard, packed with boxcars and cattle cars, and their train car jostled back and forth through switches and turns. Once more, *zaichik* had her nose against the glass, and finally they passed under a glass roof and the train jerked to a stop in Eastern Station. Semi-uniformed and rather scruffy-looking porters drew up by the baggage car. *Zaichik* practically leaped off the car to look around, almost outracing her mother, who fumbled after her with their carry-on bags. Oleg walked to the baggage car and oversaw the transfer of his bags to the two-wheel hand truck. They walked away from the train, through the old and rather seedy ticket room, and from there outside to the cabstand. There were a lot of cabs, all of them Russian-made Ladas—the Soviet version of an old Fiat—and all the same color, which might have been beige under the dirt. Zaitzev tipped the porter one Comecon ruble and supervised the loading of their bags into the car. The trunk of the diminutive taxicab was far too small. Three bags went to the front seat, and Svetlana would have to sit in her mother's lap for the ride to the hotel. The cab pulled away, made a swift and legally dubious U-turn, and then raced at breakneck speed down what appeared to be a major shopping street.

The Astoria Hotel was only four minutes from the station. It seemed to be an impressive structure, looking almost like a grand hotel of another age. The lobby was modest in size, though not in appointments, and much carved oak was in evidence. The desk clerk expected them, and greeted them with a smile. Soon after giving Zaitzev the room key, he pointed across the street to the Soviet-Hungarian Culture and Friendship Center, which was so obviously a KGB operation that it might as well have had a statue of Iron Feliks in front. The bellman led them to the tiny elevator and then to the third floor, turning right for Room 307, a corner room that would be their home for the next ten days, or so everyone but Oleg thought. He also got a ruble for his trouble and withdrew, leaving the family in a room little larger than the combined space of their train accommodations, and with only a single bathroom, albeit one with a bath/shower, which all three of them needed. Oleg let his wife and daughter go first.

As shabby as the room was by Western standards, however, by Soviet ones it was almost palatial. There was a chair by the window, and Zaitzev sat down and surveyed the streets for a CIA officer. That, he knew, was a fool's errand, but he could hardly resist the temptation.

THE MEN HE was looking for were not Americans at all, but rather Tom Trent and Chris Morton, both of whom worked for Andy Hudson. Both had dark hair and hadn't washed that day so that they could appear to be working-class Hungarians. Trent had staked out the train station and spotted them coming in, while Morton had camped out in the hotel. With good photographic prints provided by the *Times* photographer in Moscow, identifying the Zaitzev family had been simplicity itself. As a final check, Morton, who spoke flawless Russian, walked to the reception desk and verified his "old friend's" room number at the desk, in return for a twenty-florint banknote and a wink. Then he wandered down to the bar, while surveying the hotel's ground floor for future reference. So far, they decided on the subway ride back to the embassy, things were going remarkably well. The train had arrived late, but their information on the hotel had been bang-on for once.

ANDY HUDSON WAS a man of average height and appearance, except his sandy hair marked him as a foreigner in a land where everyone looked pretty much alike. *Certainly at the airport they all did,* Ryan thought.

"Can we talk?" Ryan asked on the way away from the airport.

"Yes, the car is clean." Like all such vehicles, it was regularly swept and parked in a secure location.

"How sure are you of that?"

"The opposition doesn't break the rules of diplomatic conduct. Strange, but true. And besides, the car has a very sophisticated alarm. Not sure I could fiddle it myself, as a matter of fact. In any case, welcome to Budapest, Sir John." He pronounced the city's name as *Byudapesht*, as opposed to the way Ryan thought it was spoken.

"So, you know who I am?"

"Yes, I was home in London last March. I was in town when you performed your heroics—bloody fool, you ought to have gotten yourself killed, except for the stupid bloody Irish."

"I've said that to myself many times, Mr. Hud—"

"Andy," Hudson suggested at once.

"Fine. My name is Jack."

"Good flight?"

"Any flight you walk off of is a good one, Andy. So, tell me about the mission and how you're going to go about it."

"Entirely routine. We observe the Rabbit and his family—we'll keep them under intermittent surveillance—and when the time is right, we'll whisk them out of the city and into Yugoslavia."

"How?"

"Car or truck, haven't decided yet," Hudson answered. "Hungary is the only possible problem. The Yugoslavs care sod-all about people crossing their border—they have a million citizens working overseas in various capacities. And our relations with the border guards is very cordial indeed," Andy assured him.

"Payoffs?"

Hudson nodded as he took a turn around a modest-sized park. "It's a good way for them to outfit their families with fashionable items. I know people who smuggle hard drugs in—I make no use of them, of course. Drugs are one thing the locals at least pretend to care about, but some border guards are more open to negotiation than others—hell, they probably all are, or damned nearly all. It's remarkable what you can get for some hard currency or a pair of Reebok running shoes. The black market here is a lively one, and since it often brings hard currency into the country, the political leadership will look the other way so long as it doesn't get too out of hand, you see."

"Then how did the CIA station get clobbered?"

"Bad bloody luck." Hudson went on to explain for a minute or two. "Like being run over by a lorry on an empty road."

"Damn, does that sort of thing really happen?"

"Not often, rather like winning a state lottery."

"You gotta play to win," Ryan murmured. It was the motto for the Maryland State Lottery, which was just one more form of tax for those dumb enough to partake, just one that was a little more cynical than the other kinds.

"Yes, that's right. It's a chance we all take."

"And how does that apply to getting the Rabbit and his family out?"

"One in ten thousand."

To Ryan, those sounded like betting odds, but there was one other hang-up to worry about. "Have they told you his wife and kid don't know how extended his vacation is?"

That made Hudson's head turn. "You're bloody joking."

"Nope. That's what he told our people in Moscow. Complication?"

His hands flexed on the wheel. "Only if she's noisy. I suppose we can handle that if we must." But it was plain on his face that it was something to worry about.

"European women, they tell me, are less assertive than American ones."

"They are, as a matter of fact," Hudson agreed. "Particularly true of the Russians, I believe. Well, we shall see."

One last turn onto Harm Utca, and they were at the British Embassy. Hudson parked the car and got out.

"That building there is the *Budapesti Rendõrfõkápitanság,* the police headquarters. Good to be in a secure location—they are little threat to us. The local police are not very highly regarded. The local language is bloody impossible. Indo-Altaic, philologists call it. Origin is somewhere in Mongolia, if you can believe it. Unrelated to any language you've ever heard about. Not too many people here speak English, but some German, because Austria is the next country over. Not to worry, you'll have one of us with you at all times. I'll take you on a walkabout tomorrow morning. Don't know about you, but traveling always tires me out."

"Yeah," Ryan agreed at once. "I call it travel shock."

"So, we'll get you settled in your quarters upstairs. The embassy canteen is quite adequate, and your quarters will be comfortable if not elaborate. Let me get your bag."

You couldn't knock the hospitality, Jack thought ten minutes later. A bed, private bath, a TV, and a VCR with a dozen or so tapes. He decided on *The Cruel Sea* with Jack Hawkins, and he made it to the end before fading off to sleep.

CHAPTER 26

TOURISTS

ALL OF THEM WOKE UP about the same time. Little *zaichik* was first, quickly followed by her mother and finally her father. The Hotel Astoria even had room service, an unheard-of luxury for Soviet citizens. Their room had a telephone, and Irina, after taking down the orders, called it in to the right extension, then was told that their food would arrive in about thirty minutes.

"I could fix it faster," Irina observed, with a hint of sourness. But even she had to admit that not having to fix it wasn't a bad deal for her at all. And so they all took turns in the bathroom in anticipation of their morning meal.

RYAN GOT HIMSELF showered and found his way to the embassy canteen about a quarter to eight. Evidently, the Brits liked their luxuries as much as American foreign service officers. He got himself a pile of scrambled eggs and bacon—Ryan loved English bacon, though their most popular sausages seemed to him to use sawdust as a filler—and four slices of white toast, figuring that he'd need a big breakfast to make it through this day.

The coffee wasn't all that bad. On asking, he found out that it was Austrian in origin, which explained the quality.

"The Ambassador insisted on that," Hudson said, sitting down across the table from his American guest. "Dickie loves his coffee."

"Who?" Jack asked.

"Richard Dover. He's the Ambassador—back in London at the moment, just left day before yesterday. Too bad. He'd enjoy meeting you. Good boss, he is. So, sleep well?"

"No complaints. What the hell, only one hour's worth of time difference. Is there a way for me to call London? I didn't get a chance to talk to my wife before I left yesterday. Don't want her to worry," Jack explained.

"Not a problem, Sir John," Hudson told him. "You can do that from my office."

"She thinks I'm in Bonn on NATO business."

"Really?"

"Cathy knows I'm Agency, but she doesn't know much about what I do—and besides, *I* don't know what the hell I'm doing here anyway. Analyst," Ryan explained, "not an operations guy."

"So the signal about you said. Bollocks," the field officer observed tersely. "Think of this as a new experience for your collection."

"Thanks a bunch, Andy." Ryan looked up with a very crooked smile. "I got plenty already, pal."

"Well, then, the next time you do a memo, you'll have a better appreciation for how things are at the sharp end."

"Fine with me, just so I don't get blunted by a brick wall."

"It's my job to prevent that."

Ryan took a long sip of the coffee. It wasn't up to Cathy's but, for industrial coffee, not too shabby. "What's the plan for today?"

"Finish breakfast, and I'm your tour guide. We'll get you a feel for the land and start thinking about how we complete Operation BEATRIX."

THE ZAITZEV FAMILY was agreeably surprised by the quality of the food. Oleg had heard good things about Hungarian cuisine, but the proof of the pudding is always in the eating, and the surprise was a pleasant one. Eager to see the new city, they finished, got dressed, and asked for directions. Since Irina was the one most interested in the local opportunities, she asked for the best shopping street. This, the desk clerk said, was Váci Utca, to which they could take the local metro, which, he told them, was the oldest in Europe. And so they walked to Andrassy Utca and walked down the steps. The Budapest Metro, they saw, was really an ordinary streetcar tram, just underground. Even the tram car was of wooden construction, with the same overhead catenary you usually found over the street. But it was underground, if barely so, and it moved efficiently enough. Barely ten minutes after boarding, they were at Vorosmarty Tér, or Red Marty Square, a short walk from Váci Street. They didn't notice the man who accompanied them at a discreet distance—Tom Trent—who was quite amazed to see them walking directly toward the British Embassy on Harm Utca.

RYAN WENT BACK to his room to get his raincoat—Hudson had advised a topcoat for the morning's jaunt—and then hustled down to the foyer, then outside onto the street. The weather was broken clouds, which suggested rain later in the day. Hudson nodded at the security officer at the door and led Ryan out, rather to his surprise when he got there. Hudson's first look was to the left at police headquarters, but there was Tom Trent, not seventy-five yards away. . . .

Following the Rabbit family?

"Uh, Jack?"

"Yeah, Andy?"

"That's our bloody Rabbit, Mrs. Rabbit, and the little Bunny."

Ryan turned to look, and was startled to see the three people from the photos walking right toward him. "What the hell . . . ?"

"Must be going shopping on the next block. It's a tourist area—shops and everything. Bloody strange coincidence," Hudson observed, wondering what the hell this might mean.

"Follow them?" Jack asked.

"Why not?" Hudson asked rhetorically. He lit a smoke of his own—he liked small cigars—and waited for his companion to ignite a cigarette as the Rabbits passed. They waited for Trent to pass by before heading that way as well.

"Does this mean anything?" Ryan asked.

"I do not know," Hudson answered. But while he wasn't visibly uneasy, the tone of his voice carried a message of its own. They followed anyway.

Things were clear almost immediately. Within minutes, it was apparent that the Rabbits were shopping, with Mrs. Rabbit taking the lead, as all mama rabbits usually do.

Váci Street was seemingly an old one, though the buildings must have been restored after World War II, Ryan thought. This city had been fought for, and viciously so, in early 1945. Ryan looked in the shop windows and saw the usual variety of goods, though of poorer quality, and lesser quantities than one saw in America or London. Certainly they were impressive to the Rabbit family, whose matriarch gestured with enthusiasm at every window she passed.

"Woman thinks she's on Bond Street," Hudson observed.

"Not quite." Jack chuckled back. He'd already dropped a fair bit of his personal exchequer there. Bond Street was perhaps the finest shopping street in all the world, if you could afford to walk the sidewalk there. But what was Moscow like, and how did this shopping area look to a Russian?

All women, it seemed to Jack, were alike in one respect. They liked window shopping, until the strain of not buying things drove them over the edge. In Mrs. Rabbit's case, it lasted about 0.4 blocks before she walked into a clothing store, dragging little Bunny with her, while Mr. Rabbit went in last, with visible reluctance.

"This is going to be a while," Ryan predicted. "Been there, done that, got the T-shirt."

"What's that, Jack?"

"You married, Andy?"

"Yes."

"Kids?"

"Two boys."

"You're lucky. Girls require more expensive upkeep, buddy." They walked forward to eyeball the store in question. Women's and girls' stuff. *Yeah,* Jack thought, *they'll be a while.*

"Well, good, we know what they look like. Time for us to be off, Sir John." Hudson waved up and down Váci Utca as though describing it to a new visitor to Budapest, and then led his guest back to the embassy, his eyes sweeping like radar antennae. He kept gesturing out of sync with his words. "So, we know what they look like. I don't see any obvious coverage. That is good. If this were one of your sting operations, they would not have let the bait come so near to us like this—at least, I would not do it that way, and KGB is fairly predictable."

"Think so?"

"Oh, yes. Ivan is very good, but predictable, rather like they play football, or chess, I suppose: a very straightforward game with excellent execution, but little in the way of originality or flair. Their activities are always circumscribed. It's their culture. They do not encourage people to stand out from the crowd, do they?"

"True, but their leaders often have."

"That one died thirty years ago, Jack, and they do not want another one."

"Concur." No sense arguing the point. The Soviet system did not encourage individualism of any sort. "Now where?"

"The concert hall, the hotel, points of interest. We've had enough surprises for one morning, I think."

LITTLE BOYS GENERALLY detest shopping, but that is not ordinarily true of little girls. It was certainly not true of *zaichik*, who had never seen such a variety of brightly colored clothing, even in the special shops to which her parents had recently achieved access. With her mother selecting and watching, Svetlana tried on a total of six coats, ranging from forest green to an incandescent red with a black velvet collar, and while she tried two after that one, the red one was the one they purchased, and which *zaichik* insisted on wearing right away. The next stop was for Oleg Ivan'ch, who bought three videocassette recorders, all unlicensed Hungarian copies of Sony Betamax machines from Japan. This shop, he learned, would deliver them to his hotel room—visiting Westerners shopped there—and this purchase took care of half of his office shopping list. He decided to toss in some tapes also, the sort that he didn't want his daughter to see, but which would have gone over well with his friends at The Centre. And so, Zaitzev parted with nearly two thousand Comecon rubles, for which he would have little use in the West anyway.

The shopping expedition continued nearly to lunch, by which time they were carrying more goods than it was comfortable to lug about, and so they walked back to the ancient metro and headed back to their hotel to dump them off before doing something for their daughter.

HEROES SQUARE WAS a place built by the Hapsburgs to honor their royal (but not entirely willing) possession of Hungary at the end of the previous century, with statues of previous Hungarian kings, back to St. Stephen—"Istvan" in the Magyar language—whose crown Jimmy Carter had returned to the country just a few years before, the one with the bent cross on the top.

"That happened, so they say," Hudson explained, "when Stephen slammed his crown atop the other one. Returning it was probably a clever move on Carter's part. It's a symbol of their nationhood, you see. The communist regime could not very well reject it, and in accepting it, they had to acknowledge that the history of the country long predates Marxism-Leninism. I am not really a fan of Mr. Carter, but that was, I think, a subtle move on his part. The Hungarians mainly detest communism, Jack. The nation is fairly religious."

"There *are* a lot of churches," Ryan observed. He'd counted six or seven on the way to this park.

"That's the other thing that gives them a sense of political identity. The government doesn't like it, but it's too big and too dangerous a thing to destroy, and so there's rather an uneasy peace between the two."

"If I had to bet, I'd put my money down on the church."

Hudson turned. "As would I, Sir John."

Ryan looked around. "Hell of a big square." It looked like more than a square mile of pavement.

"That goes back to 1956," Hudson explained. "The Sovs wanted this to be large enough to bring in troop carriers. You can land an AN-ten Cub right here, which makes it quicker to bring in airborne troops if the locals ever revolt again. You could bring, oh, say ten or twelve Cubs, a hundred and fifty soldiers each, and they would defend the center of the city against the counterrevolutionaries and wait for the tanks coming in from the east. It's not a brilliant plan, but that is how they think."

"But what if you park two city buses here and shoot the tires out?"

"I didn't say it was perfect, Jack," Hudson replied. "Even better, a few land mines. Might as well kill a few of the bastards and start a nice little fire. No way a pilot would be able to see them on his approach. And transport pilots are the blindest and dumbest lot going."

And Ivan figures he'd insert his troops before things really got out of hand. Yeah, it made sense, Ryan thought.

"You know who the Soviet ambassador was in 'fifty-six?"

"No—wait a minute, I do . . . wasn't it Andropov?"

Hudson nodded. "Yuriy Vladimirovich himself. It explains why he is so beloved of the locals. A bloody great lot of people lost their lives in that adventure."

Ryan remembered being in grammar school then—too young to appreciate the complications: It was the fall of a presidential election year, and at the same time Britain and France had decided to invade Egypt to protect their rights with the Suez Canal. Eisenhower had been hamstrung by two simultaneous crises, and had perforce been unable to do much of anything. But America had gotten a good bunch of immigrants out of it. Not a total loss.

"And the local Secret Police?"

"Just down Andrassy Utca from here, Number sixty. It's an ordinary-looking building that positively drips with blood. Not as bad now as it used to be. The original lot there were devotees of Iron Feliks, more ruthless than Hitler's Gestapo. But after the failed rebellion, they moderated somewhat and changed their name from *Allamvedelmi Osztaly* to *Allavedelmi Hivatal.* State Security *Bureau* instead of State Security *Section.* The former boss was replaced, and they got gentler. Formerly, they had a deserved reputation for torture. Supposedly, that is a thing of the past. The reputation alone is enough to make a suspect crumble. Good thing to have a diplomatic passport," Andy concluded.

"How good are they?" Jack asked next.

"Oafish. Perhaps they recruited competent people once, but that is well in the past. Probably a lingering effect of how evil they were in the forties and fifties. Good people don't want to work there and there's no real benefit from doing so, of the kind that KGB can offer its recruits. In fact, this country has some superb universities. They turn out remarkably good engineers and people in the sciences. And the Semmelweis medical school is first-rate."

"Hell, half the guys in the Manhattan Project were Hungarians, weren't they?"

Hudson nodded. "Indeed they were, and many of them Hungarian Jews. Not too many of those left, though in the big war the Hungarians saved about half of theirs. The Chief of State, Admiral Horthy, was probably killed over that—he died under what are euphemistically called 'mysterious circumstances.' Hard to say what sort of chap he actually was, but there is a school of thought that says he was a rabid anti-Communist, but decidedly not a pro-Nazi. Perhaps just a man who picked a bad place and time to be born. We may never know for sure." Hudson enjoyed being a tour guide for a change. Not a bad change of pace from being a king—well, maybe prince—spook.

But it was time to get back to business. "Okay, how are we going to do this?" Jack asked. He was looking around for a tail, but if there was one about, it was invisible to him, unless there was a team of the ubiquitous—dirty—Lada automobiles following them about. He'd have to trust Hudson to scan for that possibility.

"Back to the car. We'll go see the hotel." It was just a few minutes of driving time down Andrassy Utca, a route of remarkably French-style architecture. Ryan had never been to Paris, but, closing his eyes, he thought he might well have been.

"There, that's it," Hudson said, pulling over. One nice thing about communist countries: It wasn't hard to find a parking space.

"Nobody watching us?" Ryan wondered, trying not to look too obvious in his turning around.

"If so, he's being very clever about it. Now, right there across the street is the local KGB station. The Soviet Cultural and Friendship House, sadly lacking in culture or friendship, but we reckon thirty or forty KGB types there—none interested in us," Hudson added. "The average Hungarian would probably rather catch gonorrhea than go inside. Hard to tell you how detested the Soviets are in this country. The locals will take their money and perhaps even shake hands after the money is exchanged, but not much more than that. They remember 1956 here, Jack."

The hotel struck Ryan as something from what H. L. Mencken had called the gilded age—champagne ambition on a beer budget.

"I've stayed in better," Jack observed. It wasn't the Plaza in New York or London's Savoy.

"Our Russian friends probably have not."

Damn. If we get them to America, they're going to be in hog heaven, Jack thought at once.

"Let's go inside. There's a rather nice bar," Hudson told him.

And so there was, off to the right and down some steps, almost like a New York City disco bar, though not quite as noisy. The band wasn't there yet, just some records playing, and not too loudly. The music, Jack noted, was American. How odd. Hudson ordered a couple glasses of Tokaji.

Ryan sipped his. It wasn't bad.

"It's bottled in California, too, I think. Your chaps call it Tokay, the national drink of Hungary. It's an acquired taste, but better than grappa."

Ryan chuckled. "I know. That's Italian for 'lighter fluid.' My uncle Mario used to love it. *De gustibus*, as they say." He looked around. There was nobody within twenty feet. "Can we talk?"

"Better just to look about. I'll come here tonight. This bar closes after midnight, and I need to see what the staff is like. Our Rabbit is in Room 307. Third floor, corner. Easy access via the fire stairs. Three entrances, front and either side. If, as I expect, there's only a single clerk at the desk, it's just a matter of distracting him to get our packages up and the Rabbit family out."

"Packages up?"

Hudson turned. "Didn't they tell you?"

"Tell me what?"

Bloody hell, Hudson thought, *they* never *get the necessary information out to everyone who needs it. Never changes.*

"We'll talk about it later," he told Ryan.

Uh-oh, Ryan thought at once. Something was up that he wouldn't like. Sure as hell. Maybe he should have brought his Browning with him. *Oh, shit.* He finished his drink and went looking for the men's room. The symbology helped. The room had not been recently scrubbed, and it was a good thing he didn't need to sit down. He emerged to find Andy waiting for him, and followed him back outside. Soon they were back in his car.

"Okay, can we discuss that little problem now?" Jack asked.

"Later," Hudson told him. It just made Ryan worry a little more.

THE PACKAGES WERE just arriving at the airport—three rather large boxes with diplomatic stickers on them—and an official from the embassy was at the ramp to make sure they weren't tampered with. Someone had made sure to put them in identifying boxes from an electronics company—the German company Siemens, in this case—thus making it seem that they were coding machines or something else bulky and sensitive. They were duly loaded in the embassy's own light truck and driven downtown with nothing more than curiosity in their wake. The presence of an embassy officer had prevented their being x-rayed, and that was important. That might have damaged the microchips inside, of course, the customs people at the airport thought, and so made up their official report to the *Belügyminisztérium.* Soon it would be reported to everyone interested, including the KGB, that the U.K. Budapest Embassy had taken on some new encryption gear. The information would be duly filed and forgotten.

"ENJOY YOUR TOUR?" Hudson asked, back in his office.

"Beats doing a real audit. Okay, Andy," Ryan shot back. "You want to walk me through this?"

"The idea comes from your people. We're to get the Rabbit family out in such a way that KGB think them dead, and hence not defectors who will cooperate with the West. To that end, we have three bodies to put into the hotel room after we get Flopsy, Mopsy, and Cotton-tail out."

"Okay, that's right," Ryan said. "Simon told me about it. Then what?"

"Then we torch the room. The three bodies are victims of domestic fires. They ought to have arrived today."

All Ryan could still feel was a visceral disgust. His face showed it.

"This is not always a tidy business, Sir John," the SIS COS informed his guest.

"Christ, Andy! Where are the bodies from?"

"Does that matter to anyone?"

A long breath. "No, I suppose not." Ryan shook his head. "Then what?"

"We drive them south. We'll meet with an agent of mine, Istvan Kovacs, a professional smuggler who is being well paid to get us over the border into Yugoslavia. From there into Dalmatia. Quite a few of my countrymen like to get some sun there. We put the Rabbit family aboard a commercial airliner to take them—and you—back to England, and the operation is concluded to everyone's satisfaction."

"Okay." *What else can I say?* Jack thought. "When?"

"Two or three days, I think."

"Are you going to be packing?" he wondered next.

"A pistol, you mean?"

"Not a slingshot," Ryan clarified.

Hudson just shook his head. "Not really very useful things, guns. If we run into trouble, there will be trained soldiers with automatic rifles, and a pistol is useless to anyone, except to cause the opposition to fire at us with rather a higher probability of hitting us. No, should that happen, you're better off talking your way out of it, using the diplomatic papers. We already have British passports for the Rabbits." He lifted a large envelope from his desk drawer. "Mr. Rabbit reportedly speaks good English. That should suffice."

"It's all thought through, eh?" Ryan wasn't sure if it seemed that way to him or not.

"It's what they pay me for, Sir John."

And I don't have standing to criticize, Ryan realized. "Okay, you're the pro here. I'm just a fucking tourist."

"Tom Trent reported in." There was a message on Hudson's desk. "He did not see any coverage on the Rabbit family. So the operation looks entirely unremarkable to this point. I would say things are going very well indeed." *Except for the frozen burned bodies in the embassy basement,* he didn't add. "Seeing them this morning helped. They look entirely ordinary, and that helps. At least we're not trying to smuggle Grace Kelly out of the country. People like that get noticed, but women like Mrs. Rabbit do not."

"Flopsy, Mopsy, and Cotton-tail . . ." Ryan whispered.

"Just a matter of moving them to a different hutch."

"You say so, man," Ryan responded dubiously. This guy just lived a different sort of life from his own. Cathy cut up people's eyeballs for a living, and that would have made Jack faint dead away like a broad confronting a rattlesnake in the bathtub. Just a different way of earning a living. It sure as hell wasn't his.

TOM TRENT WATCHED them take the long walk from the hotel to the local zoo, which was always a good place for children. The male lion and tiger were both quite magnificent, and the elephant house—built in a drunken Arabian pastel style—housed several adequate pachyderms. With an ice cream cone bought for the little girl, the tourist part of the day came to its end. The Rabbit family walked back to the hotel, with the father carrying the sleeping child for the last half kilometer or so. This was the hardest part for Trent, for whom staying invisible on a square mile of cobblestone landing field taxed even his professional skills, but the Rabbit family was not all that attentive, and on getting back to the Astoria, he ducked into a men's room to switch his reversible coat to change at least his outward colors. Half an hour later, the Zaitzevs walked out again, but turned immediately to enter the people's restaurant just next door. The food there was wholesome if not especially exciting and, more to the point, quite inexpensive. As he watched, they piled their plates high with the local cuisine and sat down to devour it. They all saved room for apple strudel, which in Budapest was just as fine as a man could eat in Vienna, but for about a tenth of the price. Another forty minutes, and they looked thoroughly tired and well stuffed, not even taking a postprandial walk around the block to settle their stomachs before riding the elevator back to the third floor and, presumably, their night's sleep. Trent took half an hour to make sure, then caught a cab for Red Marty Park. He'd had a long day and now needed to write up his report for Hudson.

THE COS AND RYAN were drinking beer in the canteen when he arrived back at the embassy. Introductions were made, and another pint of beer secured for Trent.

"Well, what do you think, Tom?"

"It certainly appears that they are just what we've been told to expect. The little girl—the father calls her *zaichik;* means 'bunny,' doesn't it?—seems a very sweet child. Other than that, an ordinary family doing ordinary things. He purchased three TV tape machines over on Váci Street. The store delivered them to the hotel. Then they went on a bimble."

"A what?"

"A walkabout, just wandering around as tourists do," Trent explained. "To the zoo. The little girl was properly impressed by the animals, but most of all by a new red coat with a black collar they bought this morning. All in all, they seem rather a pleasant little family," the spook concluded.

"Nothing out of the ordinary?" Hudson asked.

"Not a thing, Andy, and if there is any coverage on them, I failed to see it. The only surprise of the day was in the morning when they walked right past the embassy here on the way to shopping. *That* was rather a tender moment, but it seems to have been entirely coincidental. Váci Utca is the best shopping area for Easterners and Westerners. I expect the desk clerk told them to take the underground here."

"Pure vanilla, eh?" Jack asked, finishing his beer.

"So it would appear," Trent replied.

"Okay, when do we make our move?" the American asked next.

"Well, that Rozsa chap opens his concert series tomorrow night. Day after, then? We give Mrs. Rabbit a chance to hear her music. Can we get tickets for ourselves?" Hudson asked.

"Done," Trent answered. "Box six, right side of the theater, fine view of the entire building. Helps to be a diplomat, doesn't it?"

"The program is . . . ?"

"J. S. Bach, the first three Brandenberg concerti, then some other opuses of his."

"Ought to be pleasant enough," Ryan observed.

"The local orchestras are actually quite good, Sir John."

"Andy, enough of that knighthood shit, okay? My name is Jack. John Patrick, to be precise, but I've gone by 'Jack' since I was three years old."

"It is an honor, you know."

"Fine, and I thanked Her Majesty for it, but we don't do that sort of thing where I live, okay?"

"Well, wearing a sword can be inconvenient when you try to sit down," Trent sympathized.

"And caring for the horse can be such a bother." Hudson had himself a good laugh. "Not to mention the expense of jousting."

"Okay, maybe I had that coming," Ryan admitted. "I just want to get the Rabbit the hell out of Dodge."

"Which we shall do, Jack," Hudson assured him. "And you will be there to see it."

"EVERYBODY'S IN BUDAPEST," Bostock reported. "The Rabbit and his family are staying in a no-tell motel called the Astoria."

"Isn't there a part of New York by that name?" the DCI asked.

"Queens," Greer confirmed. "What about the hotel?"

"Evidently, it suits our purposes," the Deputy DDO informed them. "Basil says the operation is nominal to this point. No surveillance on our subjects has been spotted. Everything looks entirely routine. I guess our cousins have a competent Station Chief in Budapest. The three bodies arrived there today. Just a matter of crossing the t's and dotting the i's."

"Confidence level?" the DDI asked.

"Oh, say, seventy-five percent, Admiral," Bostock estimated. "Maybe better."

"What about Ryan?" Greer asked next.

"No beefs from London on how he's doing. I guess your boy is handling himself."

"He's a good kid. He ought to."

"I wonder how unhappy he is," Judge Moore wondered.

The other two each had a smile and a head shake at that. Bostock spoke first. Like all DO people, he had his doubts about members of the far more numerous DI.

"Probably not as comfortable as he is at his desk with his comfy swivel chair."

"He'll do fine, gentlemen," Greer assured them, hoping he was right.

"I wonder what this fellow has for us . . . ?" Moore breathed.

"We'll know in a week," Bostock assured them. He was always the optimist. And three out of four constituted betting odds, so long as your own ass wasn't on the line.

Judge Moore looked at his desk clock and added six hours. People would be asleep in Budapest now, and almost there in London. He remembered his own adventures in the field, mostly composed of waiting for people to show up for meets or filling out contact reports for the at-home bureaucrats who still ran things at CIA. You just couldn't get free of the fact that the Agency was a government operation, subject to all of the same restrictions and inefficiencies that attended that sad reality. But this time, for this BEATRIX operation, they *were* making things happen speedily for once . . . only because this Rabbit person said that government communications were compromised. *Not* because he'd said he had information about an innocent life that might be lost. The government had its priorities, and they did not always correspond to the needs of a rational world. He was Director of Central Intelligence, supposedly—and by federal law—in command of the entire intelligence-gathering and -analysis operations of the government of the United States of America. But getting this bureaucracy to operate efficiently was the functional equivalent of beaching a whale and commanding it to fly. You could scream all you wanted, but you couldn't fight gravity. Government was a thing made by men, and so it ought to be possible for men to change it, but in practice that just didn't happen. So, three chances out of four, they'd get their Russian out and get to debrief him in a comfortable safe house in the Virginia hills, pick his brain clean, and maybe they'd find out some important and useful things, but the game wouldn't change and neither, probably, would CIA.

"Anything we need to say to Basil?"

"Nothing comes to mind, sir," Bostock answered. "We just sit as still as we can and wait for his people to carry out the mission."

"Right," Judge Moore conceded.

DESPITE THE THREE PINTS of dark British beer, Ryan did not sleep well. He couldn't think of anything that he might be missing. Hudson and his crew seemed competent enough, and the Rabbit family had looked ordinary enough on the street the previous morning. There were three people, one of whom really wanted out of the USSR, which struck Ryan as something entirely reasonable . . . though the Russians were some of the most rabidly patriotic people in all the world. But every rule had exceptions, and evidently this man had a conscience and felt the need to stop . . . something. Whatever it was, Jack didn't know, and he knew better than to guess. Speculation wasn't analysis, and good analysis was what they paid him his meager salary for.

It would be interesting to find out. Ryan had never spoken directly with a defector. He'd read over their stuff, and had sent written questions to some of them to get answers to specific inquiries, but he'd never actually looked one in the eye and watched his face when he answered. As in playing cards, it was the only way to read the other guy. He didn't have the ability at it that his wife had—there was something to be said for medical training—but neither was he a three-year-old who'd believe anything. No, he wanted to see this guy, talk to him, and pick his brain apart, just to evaluate the reliability of what he said. The Rabbit could be a plant, after all. KGB had done that in the past, Ryan had heard. There'd been one defector who'd come out after the assassination of John Kennedy who'd proclaimed to the very heavens that KGB had taken no part in that act. It was, in fact, sufficient to make the Agency wonder if maybe KGB had done precisely that. KGB could be tricky, but like all clever, tricky people, they inevitably overplayed their hand sooner or later—and the later they did it, the worse they overplayed it. They understood the West and how its people really thought things through. No, Ivan wasn't ten feet tall, and neither was he a genius at everything, despite what the frightmongers in Washington—and even some at Langley—thought.

Everyone had the capacity for making mistakes. He'd learned that from his father, who'd made a living catching murderers, some of whom thought themselves very clever indeed. No, the only difference between a wise man and a fool was in the magnitude of his mistakes. To err was human, and the smarter and more powerful you were, the greater the scope of your screwup. Like LBJ and Vietnam, the war Jack had barely avoided due to his age—a colossal screwup foisted on the American people by the most adroit political tactician of his age, a man who'd thought his political abilities would translate to international power politics, only to learn that an Asian communist didn't think the same way that a senator from Texas did. All men had their limitations. It was just that some were more dangerous than others. And while genius knew it had limits, idiocy was always unbounded.

He lay in his bed, smoking a cigarette and looking at the ceiling, wondering what would come tomorrow. Another manifestation of Sean Miller and his terrorists?

Hopefully not, Jack thought, still wondering why Hudson wouldn't have a gun close by for the coming adventures. Had to be some European thing, he decided. Americans on hostile soil liked to have at least one friend around.

CHAPTER 27

RABBIT RUN

ONE MORE DAY *in a strange city,* Zaitzev thought, as the sun began to rise in the east, two hours earlier than in Moscow. At home he'd still be sleeping, Oleg Ivan'ch told himself. In due course, he hoped, he'd be waking up somewhere else, in an altogether different time zone yet again. But for now he just lay still, savoring the moment. There was virtually no sound outside, perhaps a few delivery trucks on the streets. The sun was not quite yet above the horizon. It was dark, but no longer night; brightening up, but not yet morning; the middle part of the early day. It could be a pleasant moment. It was a time children could like, a magical time when the world belonged only to those few who were awake, and all others were still unseen in their beds, and the kids could walk around like little kings, until their mothers caught them and dragged them back into their beds.

But Zaitzev just lay there, hearing the slow breathing of his wife and daughter, while he was now fully awake, free to think entirely alone.

When would they contact him? What would they say? Would they change their minds? Would they betray his trust?

Why was he so goddamned uneasy about everything? Wasn't it time to trust the CIA just a little bit? Wasn't he going to be a huge asset to them?

Would he not be valuable to them? Even KGB, as stingy as a child with the best toys, gave comfort and prestige to its defectors. All the alcohol Kim Philby could drink. All the *zhopniki* Burgess could ass-fuck, or so the stories went. In both cases, the stories went, the appetites were fairy large. But such stories always grew with the telling, and they depended at least partly on the Soviet antipathy for homosexuals.

He wasn't one of those. He was a man of principle, wasn't he? Zaitzev asked himself. Of course he was. For principle he was taking his own life in his hands and juggling it. Like knives in the circus. And like that juggler, only he would be hurt by a misjudgment. Oleg lit his first smoke of the day, trying to think things through for the hundredth time, looking for another viable course of action.

He *could* just go to the concerts, continue his shopping, take the train back to Kiev Station, and be a hero to his workmates for getting them their tape machines and pornographic movies, and the pantyhose for their wives, and probably a few things for himself. And KGB would never be the wiser.

But then the Polish priest will die, at Soviet hands . . . hands you have the power to forestall, and then *what sort of man will you see in the mirror, Oleg Ivan'ch?*

It always came back to the same thing, didn't it?

But there was little point in going back to sleep, so he smoked his cigarette and lay there, watching the sky brighten outside his hotel window.

CATHY RYAN DIDN'T really wake up until her hand found empty bed where it ought to have found her husband. That automatically, somehow, caused her to come fully awake in an instant and just as quickly to remember that he was out of town and out of the country—theirs *and* this one—and that as a result she was alone, effectively a single mother, which was not something she'd bargained for when she'd married John Patrick Ryan, Sr. She wasn't the only woman in the world whose husband traveled on business—her father did it often enough, and she'd grown up with that. But this was the first time for Jack, and she didn't like it at all.

It wasn't that she was unable to cope. She had to cope on a daily basis with worse tribulations than this one. Nor was she concerned that Jack might be getting a little on the side while he was away. She'd often enough wondered that about her father on his trips—her parents' marriage had occasionally been a rocky one—and didn't know what her mother (now deceased) had wondered about. But with Jack, no, that ought not to be a problem. But she loved him, and she knew that he loved her, and people in love were supposed to be together. Had they met while he was still an officer in the Marine Corps, it would have been a problem with which she would have had to deal—and worse, she might someday have had to deal with a husband who'd gone in harm's way, and that, she was sure, was the purest form of hell to live with. But no, she'd not met him until after all that. Her own father had taken her to dinner, bringing Jack along as an afterthought, a bright young broker with keen instincts, ready to move from the Baltimore office up to New York, only to be surprised—pleasantly at first—by the interest they'd instantly found in each other, and then had come the revelation that Jack wanted to take his money and go back to teaching history, of all things. It was something she had to deal with more than Jack, who barely tolerated Joseph Muller, Senior Vice President of Merrill Lynch Pierce Fenner and Smith, plus whatever acquisitions they'd made in the past five years. Joe was still "Daddy" to her and "him" (which translated to "that pain in the ass") to Jack.

What the hell is he working on? she wondered. *Bonn? Germany? NATO stuff?* The goddamned intelligence business, looking at secret stuff and making equally secret observations on it that went to other people who might or might not read it and think about it. She, at least, was in an honest line of work, making sick people well, or at least helping them to see better. But not Jack.

It wasn't that he did useless things. He'd explained it to her earlier in the year. There were bad people out there, and somebody had to fight against them. Fortunately, he didn't do that with a loaded gun—Cathy hated guns, even the ones that had prevented her kidnapping and murder at their home in Maryland on the night that had ended blessedly with Little Jack's birth. She'd treated her share of gunshot wounds in the emergency room during her internship, enough to see the harm they inflicted, though not the harm they might have prevented in other places. Her world was somewhat circumscribed in that respect, a fact she appreciated, which was why she *allowed* Jack to keep a few of the damned things close by, where the kids could not reach them, even standing on a chair. He'd once tried to teach her how to use them, but she'd refused even to touch the things. Part of her thought that she was overreacting, but she was a woman, and that was that. . . . And Jack didn't seem to mind that very much.

But why isn't he here? Cathy asked herself in the darkness. What could be so damned important as to take her husband away from his wife and children?

He couldn't tell her. And *that* really made her angry. But there was no fighting it, and it wasn't as if she were dealing with a terminal cancer patient. And it wasn't as if he were boffing some German chippie on the side. But . . . damn. She just wanted her husband back.

EIGHT HUNDRED MILES AWAY, Ryan was already awake, out of the shower, shaved, brushed, and ready to face the day. Something about travel made it easy for him to wake up in the morning. But now he had nothing to do until the embassy canteen opened. He looked at the phone by his bed and thought about calling home, but he didn't know how to dial out on this phone system, and he probably needed Hudson's permission—and assistance—to accomplish the mission. Damn. He'd awakened at three in the morning, thinking to roll over and give Cathy a kiss on the cheek—it was something Jack liked to do, even though she never had any memory of it. The good news was that she always kissed back. She really did love him. Otherwise, the return kiss would not have come. People can't dissimulate while asleep. It was an important fact in Ryan's personal universe.

There was no use turning on the bedside radio. Hungarian—actually Magyar—was a language probably found on the planet Mars. For damned sure, it didn't belong on Planet Earth. He'd not heard one, not even one, word that he recognized from English, German, or Latin, the three languages he'd studied at one time or another in his life. The locals also spoke as quickly as a machine gun, adding to the difficulty on his part. Had Hudson dropped him off anywhere in this city, he would have been unable to find his way back to the British Embassy, and *that* was a feeling of vulnerability he hadn't had since he was four years old. He might as well have been on an alien planet, and having a diplomatic passport wouldn't help, since he was accredited *by* the wrong country *to* this alien world. Somehow he'd not fully considered that on the way in. Like most Americans, he figured that with a passport and an American Express card he could safely travel the entire world in his shorts, but that world was only the capitalist world, where somebody would speak enough English to point him to a building with the American flag on the roof and U.S. Marines in the lobby. Not in this alien city. He didn't know enough to find the men's room—well, he'd found one in a bar the previous day, Ryan admitted to himself. The feeling of helplessness was hovering at the border of his consciousness like the proverbial monster under the bed, but he was a grown-up American male citizen, over thirty, formerly a commissioned officer in the U.S. Marine Corps. It wasn't the way he usually felt about things. And so he watched the numbers change on his digital clock radio, bringing him closer to his personal date with destiny, whatever the hell that was going to be, one red-lit number at a time.

ANDY HUDSON WAS already up and about. Istvan Kovacs was preparing for one of his normal smuggling runs, this time bringing Reebok running shoes into Budapest from Yugoslavia. His hard cash was in a steel box under his bed, and he was drinking his morning coffee and listening to music on the radio when a knock on the door made him look up. He walked to answer it in his underwear.

"Andy!" he said in surprise.

"Did I wake you, Istvan?"

Kovacs waved him inside. "No, I've been up for half an hour. What brings you here?"

"We need to move our package tonight," Hudson replied.

"When, exactly?"

"Oh, about two in the morning."

Hudson reached into his pocket and pulled out a wad of banknotes. "Here is half of the agreed sum." There was no point in paying this Hungarian what they were really worth. It would alter the whole equation.

"Excellent. Can I get you some coffee, Andy?"

"Yes, thank you."

Kovacs waved him to the kitchen table and poured a cup. "How do you want to go about it?"

"I will drive our package to near the border, and you will take them across. I presume you know the border guards at the crossing point."

"Yes, it will be Captain Budai Laszlo. I've done business with him for years. And Sergeant Kerekes Mihály, good lad, wants to go to university and be an engineer. They do twelve-hour shifts at the crossing point, midnight to noon. They will already be bored, Andy, and open to negotiation." He held up his hand and rubbed a thumb over his forefinger.

"What is the usual rate?"

"For four people?"

"Do they need to know our package is people?" Hudson asked in return.

Kovacs shrugged. "No, I suppose not. Then some pairs of shoes. The Reeboks are very popular, you know, and some Western movie tapes. They already have all the tape-player machines they need," Kovacs explained.

"Be generous," Hudson suggested, "but not too generous." *Mustn't make them suspicious*, he didn't have to add. "If they are married, perhaps something for their wives and children. . . ."

"I know Budai's family well, Andy. That will not be a problem." Budai had a young daughter, and giving something for little Zsóka would cause no problems for the smuggler.

Hudson made a calculation for distance. Two and a half hours to the Yugoslav border should be about right at that time of night. They'd be using a small truck for the first part of the journey. Istvan would handle the rest in his larger truck. And if anything went wrong, Istvan would expect to be shot by the British Secret Service officer. That was one benefit of the world-famous James Bond movies. But, more to the point, five thousand d-mark went a very long way in Hungary.

"I will be driving to what destination?"

"I will tell you tonight," Hudson answered.

"Very well. I shall meet you at Csurgo at two tomorrow morning without fail."

"That is very good, Istvan." Hudson finished his coffee and stood. "It is good to have such a reliable friend."

"You pay me well," Kovacs observed, defining their relationship.

Hudson was tempted to say how much he trusted his agent, but that wasn't strictly true. Like most field spooks, he didn't trust anybody—not until after the job was completed. Might Istvan be in the pay of the AVH? Probably not. No way they could afford five thousand West German marks on anything approaching a regular basis, and Kovacs liked the good life too much. If the communist government of this country ever fell, he'd be among the first to become a millionaire, with a nice house in the hills of Pest on the other side of the Danube, overlooking Buda.

TWENTY MINUTES LATER, Hudson found Ryan at the front of the line in the embassy canteen.

"Like your eggs, I see," the COS observed.

"Local, or do you truck it in from Austria?"

"The eggs are local. The farm products here are actually quite good. But we like our English bacon."

"Developed a taste for it myself," Jack reported. "What's happening?" he asked. Andy's eyes had a certain excitement in them.

"It's tonight. First we go to the concert hall, and then we make our pickup."

"Giving him a heads-up?"

Hudson shook his head. "No. He might act differently. I prefer to avoid that complication."

"What if he's not ready? What if he has second thoughts?" Jack worried.

"In that case, it's a blown mission. And we disappear into the mists of Budapest, and come tomorrow morning many faces will be red in London, Washington, and Moscow."

"You're pretty cool about this, buddy."

"In this job, you take things as they come. Getting excited about them doesn't help at all." He managed a smile. "So long as I take the Queen's shilling and eat the Queen's biscuit, I shall do the Queen's work."

"Semper fi, man," Jack observed. He added cream to his coffee and took a sip. Not great, but good enough for the moment.

SO WAS THE food in the state-run cafeteria next door to the Hotel Astoria. Svetlana had chosen and positively inhaled a cherry Danish pastry, along with a glass of whole milk.

"The concert is tonight," Oleg told his wife. "Excited?"

"You know how long it has been since I've been to a proper concert?" she retorted. "Oleg, I shall never forget this kindness on your part." She was surprised by the look on his face, but made no comment on it.

"Well, my dear, today we have more shopping to do. Ladies' things. You will have to handle that for me."

"Anything for myself?"

"To that end, we have eight hundred and fifty Comecon rubles, just for you to spend," Oleg Ivan'ch told her, with a beaming smile, wondering if anything she bought would be in use by the end of the week.

"YOUR HUSBAND STILL off on business?" Beaverton asked.

"Unfortunately," Cathy confirmed.

Too bad, the former Para didn't say. He'd become a good student of human behavior over the years, and her unhappiness with the current situation was plain. Well, Sir John was doubtless off doing something interesting. He'd taken the time to do a little research on the Ryans. She, the papers said, was a surgeon, just as she'd told him weeks before. Her husband, on the other hand, despite his claim to be a junior official at the American Embassy, was probably CIA. It had been hinted at by the London papers back when he'd had that run-in with the ULS terrorists, but that supposition had *never* been repeated. Probably because someone had asked Fleet Street—politely—not to say such a thing ever again. That told Eddie Beaverton everything he needed to know. The papers had also said he was, if not rich, certainly comfortably set, and that was confirmed by the expensive Jaguar in their driveway. So, Sir John was away on secret business of some sort or other. There was no sense in wondering what, the cabdriver thought, pulling up to the miniature Chatham train station. "Have a good day, mum," he told her when she got out.

"Thanks, Eddie." The usual tip. It was good to have such a generous steady customer.

For Cathy it was the usual train ride into London, with the company of a medical journal, but without the comfort of having her husband close by, reading his *Daily Telegraph* or dozing. It was funny how you could miss even a sleeping man next to you.

"THAT'S THE CONCERT HALL."

Like Ryan's old Volkswagen Rabbit, the Budapest Concert Hall was well made in every detail, but little, hardly filling the city block it sat upon, its architecture hinting at the Imperial style found in better and larger form in Vienna, two hundred miles away. Andy and Ryan went inside to collect the tickets arranged by the embassy through the Hungarian Foreign Ministry. The foyer was disappointingly small. Hudson asked for permission to see where the box was, and, by virtue of his diplomatic status, an usher took them upstairs and down the side corridor to the box.

Inside, it struck Ryan as similar to a Broadway theater—the Majestic, for example—not large, but elegant, with its red-velvet seating and gilt plaster, a place for the king to come when he deigned to visit the subject city far from his imperial palace up the river in Vienna. A place for the local big shots to greet their king and pretend they were in the big leagues, when they and their sovereign knew differently. But for all that, it was an earnest effort, and a good orchestra would cover for the shortcomings. The acoustics were probably excellent, and that was what really mattered. Ryan had never been to Carnegie Hall in New York, but this would be the local equivalent, just smaller and humbler—though grudgingly so.

Ryan looked around. The box was admirably suited for that. You could scan just about every seat in the theater.

"Our friends' seats—where are they?" he asked quietly.

"Not sure. Tom will follow them in and see where they sit before he joins us."

"Then what?" Jack asked next.

But Hudson cut him off with a single word: "Later."

BACK AT THE EMBASSY, Tom Trent had his own work to do. First of all, he got two gallons of pure grain alcohol, 190 proof, or 95 percent pure. It was technically drinkable, but only for one who wanted a very fast and deep drunk. He sampled it, just a taste to make sure it was what the label said. This was not a time to take chances. One millimetric taste was enough for that. This was as pure as alcohol ever got, with no discernible smell, and only enough taste to let you know that it wasn't distilled water. Trent had heard that some people used this stuff to spike the punch at weddings and other formal functions to . . . liven things up a bit. Surely this would accomplish that task to a fare-thee-well.

The next part was rather more distasteful. It was time to inspect the boxes. The embassy basement was now off-limits to everyone. Trent cut loose the sealing tape and lifted off the cardboard to reveal . . .

The bodies were in translucent plastic bags, the sort with handles, used by morticians to transport bodies. The bags even came in more than one size, he saw, probably to accommodate the bodies of children and adults of various dimensions. The first body he uncovered was that of a little girl. Blessedly, the plastic obscured the face, or what had once been a face. All he could really see was a blackened smudge, and for the moment, that was good. He didn't need to open the bag, and that, too, was good.

The next boxes were heavier but somehow easier. At least these bodies were adults. He manhandled them onto the concrete floor of the cellar and left them there, then moved the dry ice to the opposite corner, where the frozen CO_2 would evaporate on its own without causing harm or distraction to anyone. The bodies would have about fourteen hours to thaw out, and that, he hoped, would be enough. Trent left the basement, being careful to lock the door.

Then he went to the embassy's security office. The British legation had its own security detail of three men, all of them former enlisted servicemen. He'd need two of them tonight. Both were former sergeants in the British army, Rodney Truelove and Bob Small, and both were physically fit.

"Lads, I need your help tonight with something."

"What's that, Tom?" Truelove asked.

"We'll just need to move some objects, and do it rather covertly," Trent semi-explained. He didn't bother telling them it would be something of great importance. These were men for whom everything was treated as a matter of some importance.

"Sneak in and sneak out?" Small asked.

"Correct," Trent confirmed to the former color sergeant in the Royal Engineers. Small was from the Royal Regiment of Wales, the men of Harlech.

"What time?" Truelove inquired next.

"We'll leave here about oh-two-hundred. Ought not to take more than an hour overall."

"Dress?" This was Bob Small.

And that was a good question. To wear coats and ties didn't feel right, but to wear coveralls would be something a casual observer might notice. They'd have to dress in such a way as to be invisible.

"Casual," Trent decided. "Jackets but no coats. Like a local. Shirts and pants, that should be sufficient. Gloves, too." *Yeah, they'll surely want to wear gloves,* the spook thought.

"No problem with us," Truelove concluded. As soldiers, they were accustomed to doing things that made no sense and taking life as it came. Trent hoped they'd feel that way the following morning.

FOGAL PANTYHOSE WERE French in origin. The packaging proclaimed that. Irina nearly fainted, holding the package in her hand. The contents were real but seemed not to be, so sheer as to be a manufactured shadow and no more substantial than that. She'd heard about these things, but she'd never held them in her hand, much less worn any. And to think that any woman in the West could own as many as she needed. The wives of Oleg's Russian colleagues would swoon wearing them, and how envious her own friends at GUM would be! And how careful they'd be putting them on, afraid to create a run, careful not to blunder into things with their legs, like children who bruised every single day. These hose were far too precious to endanger. She had to get the right size for the women on Oleg's list . . . plus six pairs for herself.

But what size? To buy any article of clothing that was too large was a deadly insult to a woman in any culture, even Russia, where women tended more to the Rubenesque than to a starving waif in the Third World . . . or Hollywood. The sizes shown on the packages were A, B, C, and D. This was an additional complication, since in Cyrillic, "B" corresponded to the Roman "V" and "C" to "S," but she took a deep breath and bought a total of twenty pairs of size C, including the six for herself. They were hideously expensive, but the Comecon rubles in her purse were not all hers, and so with another deep breath she paid cash for the collection, to the smile of the female salesclerk, who could guess what was going on. Walking out of the store with such luxuries made her feel like a czarist princess, a good sensation for any female in the world. She now had 489 rubles left to spend on herself, and that almost produced a panic. So many nice things. So little money. So little closet space at home.

Shoes? A new coat? A new handbag?

She left out jewelry, since that was Oleg's job, but, like most men, he didn't know a thing about what women wore.

What about foundation garments? Irina wondered next. A Chantarelle brassiere? Did she dare purchase something that elegant? That was at least a hundred rubles, even at this favorable exchange rate. . . . And it would be something only she knew she had on. Such a brassiere would feel like . . . hands. Like the hands of your lover. Yes, she had to get one of those.

And cosmetics. She had to get cosmetics. It was the one thing Russian women always paid attention to. She was in the right city for that. Hungarian women cared about skin care as well. She'd go to a good store and ask, comrade to comrade. Hungarian women—their faces proclaimed to the world that they cared about their skin. In this the Hungarians were most *kulturniy*.

It took another two hours of utter bliss, so pleasant that she didn't even notice her husband and daughter waiting about. She was living every Soviet woman's dream, spending money in—well, if not the West, then the next best thing. And it was wonderful. She'd wear the Chantarelle to the concert tonight, listen to Bach, and pretend she was in another time and another place, where everyone was *kulturniy* and it was a good thing to be a woman. It was a pity that no such place existed in the Soviet Union.

OUTSIDE THE SUCCESSION of women's stores, Oleg just stood around and smoked his cigarettes like any other man in the world, intensely bored by the details of women's shopping. How they could enjoy the process of picking and comparing, picking and comparing, never making a decision, just sucking in the ambience of being surrounded by things they couldn't wear and didn't really like? They always took the dress and held it up to their necks and looked in a mirror and decided *nyet*, not this one. On and on and on, past the sunset and into the night, as though their very souls depended on it. Oleg had learned patience with his current life-threatening adventure, but one thing he'd never learned, and never expected to learn, was how to watch a woman shop . . . without wishing to throttle her. Just standing there like a fucking beast of burden, holding the things she'd finally decided to purchase—then waiting while she decided to change her mind or not. Well, it couldn't last forever. They did have tickets to the concert that night. They had to go back to the hotel, try to get a sitter for *zaichik*, get dressed, and go to the concert hall. Even Irina would appreciate that.

Probably, Oleg Ivan'ch thought bleakly. As though he didn't have enough to worry about. But his little girl wasn't concerned about a thing, Oleg saw. She ate her ice cream and looked around at this different place with its different sights. There was much to be said for a child's innocence. A pity one lost it—and why, then, did children try so hard to grow up and leave their innocence behind? Didn't they know how wonderful the world was for them alone? Didn't they know that, with understanding, the wonders of the world only became burdens? And pain.

And doubts, Zaitzev thought. *So many doubts.*

But no, *zaichik* didn't know that, and by the time she found out, it would be too late.

Finally, Irina walked outside, with a beaming smile such as she'd not had since delivering their daughter. Then she really surprised him—she came up to him for a hug and a kiss.

"Oh, Oleg, you are so good to me!" And another passionate kiss of a woman sated by shopping. Even better than one sated by sex, her husband suddenly thought.

"Back to the hotel, my dear. We must dress for the concert."

The easy part was the ride on the metro, then into the Astoria and up to Room 307. Once there, they decided more or less by default to take Svetlana with them. Getting a sitter would have been an inconvenience—Oleg had thought about a female KGB officer from the Culture and Friendship House across the street, but neither he nor his wife felt comfortable with such arrangements, and so *zaichik* would have to behave herself during the concert. His tickets were in the room, Orchestra Row 6, seats A, B, and C, which put him right on the aisle, where he preferred to be. Svetlana would wear her new clothes this evening, which, he hoped, would make her happy. It usually did, and these were the best clothes she'd ever had.

The bathroom was crowded in their room. Irina worked hard and long to get her face right. It was easier for her husband, and easier still for their daughter, for whom a wet washcloth across her grimacing face was enough. Then they all got dressed in their best clothing. Oleg buckled his little girl's shiny black shoes over the white tights to which she'd taken an immediate love. Then she put on the red coat with the black collar, and the little Bunny was all ready for the adventures of the evening. They took the elevator down to the lobby and caught a cab outside.

FOR TRENT IT was a little awkward. Staking out the lobby ought to have been difficult, but the hotel staff seemed not to notice him, and so when the package left, it was a simple matter of walking out to his car and following their cab to the concert hall, just a mile down the street. Once there, he found a parking place close by and walked quickly to the entrance. Drinks were being served there, and the Zaitzevs availed themselves of what looked like Tokaji before heading in. Their little girl was as radiant as ever. *Lovely child,* Trent thought. He hoped she'd like life in the West. He watched them head into the theater to their seats, and then he turned to go up the stairs to his box.

RYAN AND HUDSON were already there, sitting on the old chairs with their velvet cushions.

"Andy, Jack," Trent said in greeting. "Sixth row, left side of center, just on the aisle."

Then the houselights started flickering. The curtain drew back, the meandering tones of musicians tuning their various instruments trailed off, and the conductor, Jozsef Rozsa, appeared from stage right. The initial applause was little more than polite. It was his first concert in the series, and he was new to this audience. That struck Ryan as odd—he was a Hungarian, a graduate of their own Franz Liszt Academy. Why wasn't their greeting more enthusiastic? He was a tall and thin guy with black hair and the face of an aesthete. He bowed politely to the audience and turned back to the orchestra. His little baton stick—whatever it was called, Ryan didn't know—was there on the little stand, and when he lifted it, the room went dead still, and then his right arm shot out to the string section of the Hungarian State Railroad Orchestra #1.

Ryan was not the student of music that his wife was, but Bach was Bach, and the concerto built in majesty almost from the first instant. Music, like poetry or painting, Jack told himself, was a means of communication, but he'd never quite figured out what composers were trying to say. It was easier with a John Williams movie score, where the music so perfectly accompanied the action, but Bach hadn't known about moving pictures, and so he must have been "talking about" things that his original audiences would have recognized. But Ryan wasn't one of those, and so he just had to appreciate the wonderful harmonies. It struck him that the piano wasn't right, and only when he looked did he see that it wasn't a piano at all, but rather an ancient harpsichord, played, it seemed, by an equally ancient virtuoso with flowing white hair and the elegant hands of . . . a surgeon, Jack thought. Jack did know piano music. Their friend Sissy Jackson, a solo player with the Washington Symphony, said Cathy was too mechanical in her playing, but Ryan only noted that she never missed a key—you could always tell—and to him that was sufficient. *This guy,* he thought, watching his hands and catching the notes through the wonderful cacophony, *didn't miss a single note,* and every one, it seemed, was precisely as loud or soft as the concert required, and so precisely timed as to define perfection. The rest of the orchestra seemed about as well practiced as the Marine Corps Silent Drill Team, everything as precise as a series of laser beams.

The one thing Ryan couldn't tell was what the conductor was doing. Wasn't the concerto written down? Wasn't conducting just a matter of making sure—beforehand—that everybody knew his part and did it on time? He'd have to ask Cathy about it, and she'd roll her eyes and remark that he really was a Philistine. But Sissy Jackson said that Cathy was a mechanic on the keyboard, lacking in soul. So there, Lady Caroline!

The string section was also superb, and Ryan wondered how the hell you ran a bow along a string and made the exact noise you wanted to. *Probably because they do it for a living,* he told himself, and he sat back to enjoy the music. It was only then that he watched Andy Hudson, whose eyes were on the package. He took the moment to look that way as well.

The little girl was squirming, doing her best to be good, and maybe taking note of the music, but it couldn't be as good as a tape of *The Wizard of Oz,* and that couldn't be helped. Still and all, she was behaving well, the little Bunny sitting between Ma and Pa Rabbit.

Mama Rabbit was watching the concert with rapt attention. Papa Rabbit was being politely attentive. Maybe they should call ahead to London and get Irina a Walkman, Jack thought, along with some Christopher Hogwood tapes. . . . Cathy seemed to like him a lot, along with Nevile Marriner.

In any case, after about twenty minutes, they finished the Menuetto, the orchestra went quiet, and when Conductor Rozsa turned to face the audience . . .

The concert hall went berserk with cheering and shouts of *"Bravo!"* Jack didn't know what he'd done differently, but evidently the Hungarians did. Rozsa bowed deeply to the audience and waited for the noise to subside before turning back and commanding quiet again as he raised his little white stick to start Brandenberg #2.

This one started with a brass and strings, and Ryan found himself entranced by the individual musicians more than whatever the conductor had done with them. *How long do you have to study to get that good?* he wondered. Cathy played two or three times a week at home in Maryland—their Chatham house wasn't big enough for a proper grand piano, rather to her disappointment. He'd offered to get an upright, but she'd declined, saying that it just wasn't the same. Sissy Jackson said that she played three hours or more every single day. But Sissy did it for a living, while Cathy had another and somewhat more immediate passion in her professional life.

The second Brandenberg concerto was shorter than the first, ending in about twelve minutes, and the third followed at once. Bach must have loved the violins more than any other instrument, and the local string section was pretty good. In any other setting Jack might have given himself over to the moment and just drunk in the music, but he did have something more important planned for this evening. Every few seconds, his eyes drifted left to see the Rabbit family. . . .

BRANDENBERG #3 ENDED roughly an hour after #1 had begun. The houselights came on, and it was time for the intermission. Ryan watched Papa Rabbit and Mrs. Rabbit leave their seats. The reason was plain. The Bunny needed a trip to the little girls' room, and probably Papa would avail himself of the local plumbing as well. Hudson saw that and leapt to his feet, back out of the box, into the private corridor, closely followed by Tom Trent, and down the steps to the lobby and into the men's room, while Ryan stayed in the box and tried to relax. The mission was now fully under way.

NOT FIFTY YARDS AWAY, Oleg Ivan'ch was standing in the line to use the men's room. Hudson managed to get right behind him. The lobby was filled with the usual buzz of small talk. Some people went to the portable bar for more drinks. Others were puffing on cigarettes, while twenty men or so were waiting to relieve their bladders. The line moved fairly rapidly—men are more efficient at this than women are—and soon they were in the tiled room.

The urinals were as elegant as everything else, seemingly carved from Carerra marble for this noble purpose. Hudson stood like everyone else, hoping that his clothing did not mark him as a foreigner. Just inside the wood-and-glass door, he took a breath and, leaning forward, called on his Russian.

"Good evening, Oleg Ivanovich," Hudson said quietly. "Do not turn around."

"Who are you?" Zaitzev whispered back.

"I am your travel agent. I understand you wish to take a little trip."

"Where might that be?"

"Oh, in a westerly direction. You are concerned for the safety of someone, are you not?"

"You are CIA?" Zaitzev could not utter the acronym in anything but a hiss.

"I am in an unusual line of work," Hudson confirmed. No sense confusing the chap at the moment.

"So, what will you do with me?"

"This night you will sleep in another country, my friend," Hudson told him, adding, "along with your wife and your lovely little daughter." Hudson watched his shoulders slump—with relief or fear, the British spook wondered. Probably both.

Zaitzev cleared his throat before whispering again. "What must I do?"

"First, you must tell me that you wish to go forward with your plan."

Only the briefest hesitation before: "*Da.* We will proceed."

"In that case, just do your business in here—" they were approaching the head of the line "—and then enjoy the rest of the concert, and return to your hotel. We shall speak again there at one-thirty or so. Can you do that?"

Just a curt nod and a gasping single syllable: "*Da.*" Oleg Ivan'ch really needed to use the urinal now.

"Be at ease, my friend. All is planned. All will go well," Hudson said to him. The man would need assurance and confidence now. This had to be the most frightening moment of his life.

There was no further reply. Zaitzev took the next three steps to the marble urinal, unzipped, and relieved himself in more than one way. He turned to leave without seeing Hudson's face.

But Trent saw his, as he stood there and sipped a glass of white wine. If he'd made any signal to a fellow KGB spook in the room, the British officer hadn't seen it. No rubbing the nose or adjusting his tie, no physical sign at all. He just walked back through the swinging door and back to his seat. BEATRIX was looking better and better.

THE AUDIENCE WAS back in its seats. Ryan was doing his best to look like just one more classical music fan. Then Hudson and Trent reentered the box.

"Well?" Ryan rasped.

"Bloody good music, isn't it?" Hudson replied casually. "This Rozsa chap is first-rate. Amazing that a communist country can turn out anything better than a reprise of the *Internationale*. Oh, after it's over," Hudson added, "how about a drink with some new friends?"

Jack let out a very long breath. "Yeah, Andy, I'd like that." *Son of a bitch*, Ryan thought. *It's really going to happen*. He had lots of doubts, but they'd just subsided half a step or so. It wasn't really very much, but it was a damned sight better than it could have been.

THE SECOND HALF of the concert started with more Bach, the Toccata and Fugue in D Minor. Instead of strings, this one was a celebration of brass, and the lead cornet here might have taught Louis Armstrong himself something about the higher notes. This was as much Bach as Ryan had ever heard at one time, and that old German composer had really had his shit wired, the former Marine thought, for the first time relaxing enough to enjoy it somewhat. Hungary was a country that respected its music, or so it seemed. If there was anything wrong with this orchestra, he didn't notice it, and the conductor looked as though he were in bed with the love of his life, so transfixed he was by the joy of the moment. Jack wondered idly if Hungarian women were any good at that. There was an earthy look to them, but not much smiling. . . . Maybe that was the communist government. Russians were not known for smiling, either.

"SO, ANY NEWS?" Judge Moore asked.

Mike Bostock handed over the brief dispatch from London. "Basil says his COS Budapest is going to make his move tonight. Oh, you'll love this part. The Rabbit is staying in a hotel right across the street from the KGB *rezidentura*."

Moore's eyes flared a bit. "You have to be kidding."

"Judge, do you think I'd say that for the fun of it?"

"When does Ritter get back?"

"Later today, flying back on Pan Am. From what he sent to us from Seoul, everything went pretty well with the KCIA meetings."

"He'll have a heart attack when he finds out about BEATRIX," the DCI predicted.

"It *will* get his eyes opened," the Deputy DDO agreed.

"Especially when he finds out that this Ryan boy is in on it?"

"On that, sir, you can bet the ranch, the cattle, and the big house."

Judge Moore had himself a good chuckle at that one. "Well, I guess the Agency is bigger than any one individual, right?"

"So they tell me, sir."

"When will we know?"

"I expect Basil will let us know when the plane takes off from Yugoslavia. It's going to be a long day for our new friends, though."

THE NEXT SELECTION was Bach's "Sheep May Safely Graze." Ryan recognized it as the tune played in a Navy recruiting commercial. It was a gentle piece, very different from that which had preceded it. He wasn't sure if this evening's performance was a showcase for Johann Sebastian or for the conductor. In either case, it was pleasant enough, and the audience was wildly appreciative, noisier than for the concert selection. One more piece. Ryan had a program, but hadn't bothered looking at it, since it was printed in Magyar, and he couldn't read Martian any better than he could decipher the spoken form.

The last selection was Pachelbel's Canon, a justly famous piece, one that had always struck Ryan like a movie of a pretty girl saying her prayers back in the seventeenth century, trying to concentrate on her devotions instead of thinking about the handsome boy down the lane from her farmhouse—and not quite succeeding.

WITH THE END, Jozsef Rozsa turned to the audience, which leapt again to its feet and howled its approval for endless minutes. Yeah, Jack thought, the local boy had gone away, but he'd come home to make good, and the home boys from the old days were glad to have him back. The conductor hardly smiled, as though exhausted from running the marathon. And he was sweating, Jack saw. Was conducting that hard? If you were that far into it, maybe it was. He and his Brit companions were standing and applauding as much as everyone else—no sense standing out—before, finally, the noise stopped. Rozsa waved to the orchestra, which caused the cheering to continue, and then to the concertmaster of the orchestra, the first fiddle. It seemed gracious of Rozsa, but probably the thing you had to do if you wanted the musicians to put out their best for you. And then, at long last, it was time for the crowd to break up.

"Enjoy the music, Sir John?" Hudson asked with a sly grin.

"It beats what they play on the radio at home," Ryan observed. "Now what?"

"Now we get a nice drink in a quiet place." Hudson nodded to Trent, who made his own way off, and took Ryan in tow.

The air was cool outside. Ryan immediately lit a cigarette, along with every other man in view and most of the women. Hungarians didn't plan to live all that long, or so it seemed. He felt as tied to Hudson as a child to his mother, but that wouldn't last too much longer. The street had mostly apartment-type buildings. In a Western city, it would have been condos, but those probably didn't exist here. Hudson waved for Ryan to follow and they walked two blocks to a bar, ending up following about thirty people leaving the concert. Andy got a corner booth from which he could scan the room, and a waiter came with a couple glasses of wine.

"SO, WE GO?" Jack asked.

Hudson nodded. "We go. I told him we'd be to the hotel about one-thirty."

"And then?"

"And then we drive to the Yugoslav border."

Ryan didn't ask further. He didn't have to.

"The security to the south is trivial. Different the other way," Andy explained. "Near the Austrian border, it's fairly serious, but Yugoslavia, remember, is a sister communist state—that's the local fiction in any case. I'm no longer sure what Yugoslavia is, politically speaking. The border guards on the Hungarian side do well for themselves—many friendly arrangements with the smugglers. That is a growth industry, but the smart ones don't grow too much. Do that and the Belügyminisztérium, their Interior Ministry, might take notice. Better to avoid that," Hudson reminded him.

"But if this is the back door into the Warsaw Pact—hell, KGB's gotta know, right?"

Hudson completed the question. "So, why don't they shut things down? I suppose they could, but the local economy would suffer, and the Sovs get a lot of the things they like here, too. Trent tells me that our friend has made some major purchases here. Tape machines and pantyhose—bloody pantyhose, their women kill for the things. Probably most are overtly intended for friends and colleagues back in Moscow. So, if KGB intervened, or forced the AVH to do so, then they would lose a source of things they themselves want. So a little corruption doesn't do any major damage, and it supplies the greed of the other side. Never forget that they have their weaknesses, too. Probably more than we do, in fact, much as people argue to the contrary. They want the things we have. Official channels can't work very well, but the unofficial ones do. There's a saying in Hungarian that I like: *A nagy kapu mellett, mindig van egy kis kapu.* Next to the big gate, there is always a little door. That little door is what makes things work over here."

"And I'm going through it."

"Correct." Andy finished his wine and decided against another. He had a ways to drive tonight, in the dark, over inferior roads. Instead, he lit one of his cigars.

Ryan lit a smoke of his own. "I've never done this before, Andy."

"Frightened?"

"Yeah," Jack admitted freely. "Yeah, I am."

"First time is never easy. I've never had people with machine guns come into my home."

"I don't recommend it as after-dinner entertainment," Jack replied, with a twisted smile. "But we managed to luck our way out of it."

"I don't really believe in luck—well, sometimes, perhaps. Luck does not go about in search of a fool, Sir John."

"Maybe so. Kinda hard to notice from the inside." Ryan thought back, again, to that dreadful night. The feel of the Uzi in his hands. Having to get that one shot right. No second chance in that ballgame. And he'd dropped to one knee, taken aim, and gotten it right. He'd never learned the name of the guy in the boat he'd stitched up. *Strange,* he reflected. *If you kill a man right by your home, you should at least know his name.*

But, yeah, if he could do that, he could damned well do this. He checked his watch. It would be a while still, and he wasn't driving tonight, and another glass of wine seemed a good idea. But he'd stop it there.

BACK AT THE ASTORIA, the Zaitzevs got their little Bunny to bed, and Oleg ordered some vodka to be brought up. It was the generic Russian vodka brand that the working class drank, a half-liter bottle with a foil closure at the top that essentially forced you to drink it all in one sitting. Not an altogether bad idea for this night. The bottle arrived in five minutes, and by then *zaichik* was asleep. He sat on the bed. His wife sat in the one upholstered chair. They drank from tumblers out of the bathroom.

Oleg Ivan'ch had one task yet to perform. His wife didn't know his plan. He didn't know how she'd react to it. He knew she was unhappy. He knew that this trip was the high point of their marriage. He knew she hated her job at GUM, that she wanted to enjoy the finer things in life. But would she willingly leave her motherland behind?

On the plus side of the ledger, Russian women did not enjoy much in the way of freedom, within their marriages or without. They usually did what their husbands told them to do—the husband might pay for it later, but only later. And she loved him and trusted him, and he'd shown her the best of good times in the past few days, and so, yes, she'd go along.

But he'd wait before telling her. Why spoil things by taking a risk right now? Right across the street was the KGB's Budapest *rezidentura.* And if they got word of what he had planned, then he was surely a dead man.

BACK AT THE British Embassy, sergeants Bob Small and Rod Truelove lifted the plastic bags and carried them to the embassy's nondescript truck—the license tags had already been switched. Both tried to ignore the contents, then went back to get the alcohol containers, plus a candle and a cardboard milk carton. Then they were ready. Neither had so much as a glass of beer that night, though both wished otherwise. They drove off just after midnight, planning to take their time to scout the objective before committing to a course of action. The hard part would be getting the right parking place, but, with more than hour to pick it, they were confident that one would appear in due course.

THE BAR WAS emptying out, and Hudson didn't wish to be the last one in there. The bar bill was fifty forints, which he paid, not leaving a tip, because it wasn't the local custom, and it wouldn't do to be remembered. He motioned to Ryan and headed out but, on second thought, made his way to the loo. The thought struck Ryan as very practical, too.

Outside, Ryan asked what came next.

"We take a stroll up the street, Sir John," Hudson answered, using the knightly title as an unfair barb. "Thirty-minute stroll to the hotel, I think, will be about right." The exercise would also give them a chance to make sure they weren't being followed. If the opposition were onto their operation, they'd be unable to resist the temptation to shadow the two intelligence officers, and, on mainly empty city streets, it wouldn't be too difficult to "make" them along the way . . . unless the opposition consisted of KGB. They were cleverer than the locals by a sizable margin.

ZAITZEV AND HIS WIFE had the comfortable glow of three very stiff drinks each. Oddly, his wife showed little sign of approaching sleep, however. Too excited by the night's fine entertainment, Oleg thought. Maybe it was for the better. Just that one more worry to go—except for how the CIA planned to get them out of Hungary. What would it be? A helicopter near the border, flying them under Hungarian radar coverage? That was what he would have chosen. Would CIA be able to hop them from inside Hungary to Austria? Just how clever were they? Would they let him know? Might it be something really clever and daring? And frightening? he wondered.

Would it succeed? If not . . . well, the consequences of failure did not bear much contemplation.

But neither would they go entirely away. Not for the first time, Oleg considered that his own death might result from this adventure, and prolonged misery for his wife and child. The Soviets would not kill them, but it would mark them forever as pariahs, doomed to a life of misery. And so they were hostages to *his* conscience as well. How many Soviets had stopped short of defection just on that basis? Treason, he reminded himself, was the blackest of crimes, and the penalties for it were equally forbidding.

Zaitzev poured out the remainder of the vodka and gunned it down, waiting the last half hour before the CIA arrived to save his life . . .

Or whatever they planned to do with him and his family. He kept checking his watch while his wife finally dozed off and back, smiling and humming the Bach concert with a head that lolled back and forth. At least he'd given her as fine a night as he'd ever managed to do. . . .

THERE WAS A parking place just by the hotel's side door. Small drove up to it and backed in neatly. Parallel parking is an art form in England that he still remembered how to perform. Then they sat, Small with a cigarette and Truelove with his favorite briar pipe, looking out at empty streets, just a few pedestrians in the distance, with Small keeping an eye on the rearview mirror for activity at the KGB residency. There were some lights on up on the second floor, but nothing moving that he could see. Probably some KGB chap had just forgotten to flip the switch on the way out.

THERE IT WAS, Ryan saw, just three blocks, on the right-hand side of the street.

Showtime.

The remaining walk passed seemingly in an instant. Tom Trent, he saw, was by the corner of the building. People were coming out of the building, probably from the basement bar Hudson had shown him, about right for closing time, just in twos and threes, nobody leaving alone. *Must be a saloon for the local singles crowd,* Jack thought, *setting up one-night stands for the terminally lonely.* So, they had them in communist countries too, eh?

As they approached, Hudson flicked a finger across his nose. That was the sign for Trent to go inside and distract the desk clerk. How he did that, Ryan would never know, but minutes later when they walked in the door, the lobby was totally empty.

"Come on." Hudson hurried over to the stairs, which wrapped around the elevator shaft. Getting to the third floor took less than a minute. And there was Room 307. Hudson turned the knob. The Rabbit had not locked it. Hudson opened it slowly.

Zaitzev saw the door open. Irina was mostly asleep now. He looked at her to be sure, then stood.

"Hello," Hudson said in quiet greeting. He extended his hand.

"Hello," Zaitzev said, in English. "You are travel agent?"

"Yes, we both are. This is Mr. Ryan."

"Ryan?" Zaitzev asked. "There is KGB operation by that name."

"Really?" Jack asked, surprised. He hadn't heard about that one yet.

"We can discuss that later, Comrade Zaitzev. We must leave now."

"Da." He turned to shake his wife awake. She started violently when she saw the two unexpected men in her room.

"Irina Bogdanova," Oleg said with a touch of sternness in his voice. "We are taking an unexpected trip. We are leaving right now. Get Svetlana ready."

Her eyes came fully open in surprise. "Oleg, what is this? What are we doing?"

"We are leaving right now for a new destination. You must get moving now."

Ryan didn't understand the words, but the content was pretty clear. Then the woman surprised him by coming to her feet and moving like an automaton. The daughter was on a small children's bed. Mother Rabbit lifted the sleeping child to semi-wakefulness and got her clothes organized.

"What are we doing exactly?" the Rabbit asked.

"We are taking you to England—tonight," Hudson emphasized.

"Not America?"

"England first," Ryan told him. "Then I will take you to America."

"Ah." He was in a very tense state, Ryan saw, but that was to be expected. This guy had laid his life on the craps table, and the dice were still in the air. It was Ryan's job to make sure they didn't come up snake eyes. "What do I bring?"

"Nothing," Hudson said. "Not a bloody thing. Leave all your papers here. We have new ones for you." He held up three passports with a lot of faked stamps on the inside pages. "For now I will hold these for you."

"You are CIA?"

"No, I am British. Ryan here is CIA."

"But—why?"

"It's a long story, Mr. Zaitzev," Ryan said. "But right now we must leave."

The little girl was dressed now, but still sleepy, as Sally had been on that horrible night at Peregrine Cliff, Jack saw.

Hudson looked around, suddenly delighted to see the empty vodka bottle on the night table. Bloody good luck that was. Mother Rabbit was still confused, by the combination of three or four drinks and the post-midnight earthquake that had exploded around her. It had taken less than five minutes and everyone looked ready to leave. Then she saw her pantyhose bag, and moved toward it.

"Nyet," Hudson said in Russian. "Leave them. There are many of those where we are taking you."

"But—but—but . . ."

"Do what he says, Irina!" Oleg snarled, his equilibrium upset by the drink and the tension of the moment.

"Everyone ready?" Hudson asked. Next, Irina scooped her daughter up, her face a mass of utter confusion, and they all went to the door. Hudson looked out into the corridor, then waved for the others to follow. Ryan took the rear, closing the door, after making sure it was unlocked.

The lobby was still vacant. They didn't know what Tom Trent had done, but whatever it was, it had worked. Hudson led the others out the side door and onto the street. There was the embassy car Trent had brought over, and Hudson had the spare set of keys. On the way, he waved at the truck for Small and Truelove. The car was a Jaguar, painted a dark blue, with left-hand drive. Ryan loaded them into the backseat, closed the door, and hopped in the front. The big V-8 started instantly—the Jag was lovingly maintained for purposes like this one—and Hudson started driving.

THEIR TAILLIGHTS WERE still visible as Small and Truelove stepped out of their truck, hustling to the back. Each took one of the adult bags and headed in the side door. The lobby was still empty, and they raced up the stairs, each with a heavy and limp burden. The upstairs corridor was also empty. The two retired soldiers moved as stealthily as possible into the room. There they unzipped the bags, and with gloved hands removed the bodies. That was a hard moment on each of them. Professional soldiers that they were, both with combat experience, the immediate sight of a burned human body was hard to take without a deep breath and an inner command to take charge of their feelings. They laid the man's and the woman's bodies from different countries and continents side by side on the double bed. Then they left the room to return to the truck, taking the empty body bags with them. Small got the smallest of the bags out of the truck, while Truelove got the rest of the necessary gear, and back in they went.

Small's job proved the hardest; removing the little girl's body from the plastic bag was something he'd work hard to erase from his memory. She went on the cot, as he thought of it, in her nearly incinerated nightgown. He might have patted her little head had her hair not been entirely burned off with a blowtorch, and all he could do was whisper a prayer for her innocent little soul before his stomach nearly lost control, and to prevent that he turned abruptly away.

THE FORMER ROYAL Engineer was already into his own task. He made sure they'd left nothing. The last of the plastic bags was folded and tucked into his belt. They both still had their work gloves, and so there was nothing they'd brought to be left in the room. He took his time looking around, and then waved Small out into the corridor.

Then he tore the top off the milk carton—it had been washed clean and dried beforehand. He lit the candle with his butane lighter and dripped a dollop of hot wax into the bottom of the carton, to make sure it would have a good place to stand. Then he blew out the candle and made sure it was secure in its place.

THEN CAME THE dangerous part. Truelove opened the top of the alcohol container, first pouring nearly a quart into the carton, to within just less than an inch of the top of the candle. Next he poured the alcohol on the adult bed, and more onto the child's cot. The remainder went on the floor, much of it around the milk carton. Finished, he tossed the empty alcohol container to Bob Small.

Okay, Truelove thought, fully a gallon of pure grain alcohol soaked into the bedclothes and another on the cheap rug on the floor. A demolitions expert—in fact, he had many fields of technical expertise, like most military engineers—he knew to be careful for the next part. Bending down, he flicked his lighter again and lit the candle wick with the same care a heart surgeon might have exercised in a valve replacement. He didn't waste a second leaving the room, except to make sure the door was properly locked and the do-not-disturb card hung on the knob.

"TIME TO LEAVE, Robert," Rodney said to his colleague, and in thirty seconds they were out the side door and off to the street.

"How long on the candle?" Small asked by the truck.

"Thirty minutes at most," the Royal Engineer sergeant answered.

"That poor little girl—you suppose?" he almost asked.

"People die in house fires every day, mate. They didn't do it special for this lot."

Small nodded to himself. "I reckon."

Just then Tom Trent appeared in the lobby. They'd never found the camera he lost in an upstairs room, but he tipped the desk clerk for his effort. It turned out that he was the only employee on duty until five in the morning.

Or so the chap thinks, Trent told himself, getting into the truck.

"Back to the embassy, lads," the spook told the security men. "There's a good bottle of single-malt Scotch whiskey waiting for us all."

"Good. I could use a dram," Small observed, thinking of the little girl. "Or two."

"Can you say what this adventure is all about?"

"Not tonight. Perhaps later," Trent replied.

CHAPTER 28

BRITISH MIDLANDS

THE CANDLE BURNED NORMALLY, not knowing the part it was playing in the night's adventures, consuming wick and wax at a slow pace, gradually burning down to the still surface of the alcohol—soon to play the part of an accelerant in an arson fire. All in all, it took thirty-four minutes before the surface of the flammable fluid ignited. What started then is called a class-B fire by professionals—a flammable-liquid event. The alcohol burned with an enthusiasm hardly less than that of gasoline—this was why the Germans had used alcohol rather than kerosene in their V-2 missile—and rapidly consumed the cardboard of the milk carton, releasing the burning quart of alcohol onto the floor. That ignited the soaked surface of the hotel room's rug. The blue wave of the fire-front raced across the room's floor in a matter of seconds, like a living thing, a blue line followed by an incandescent white mass as the fire reached up to consume the available oxygen in the high-ceilinged room. Another moment and both beds ignited as well, enveloping the bodies in them with flames and searing heat.

The Hotel Astoria was an old one, lacking both smoke detectors and automatic sprinklers to warn of danger or extinguish the blaze before it got too dangerous. Instead the flames climbed almost immediately to the water-stained white ceiling, burning off paint and charring the underlying plaster, plus attacking the cheap hotel furniture. The inside of the room turned into a crematorium for three human beings already dead, eating their bodies like the carnivorous animal the ancient Egyptians thought a fire to be. The worst of the damage took just five minutes, but while the fire died down somewhat after its first glut of consumption, it didn't die just yet.

The desk clerk in the lobby had a more complex job than one might have expected. At two-thirty every morning, he placed a please-wait-back-in-a few-minutes sign on the desk, and took the elevator to the top floor to walk the corridors. He found the usual—nothing at all in this floor, and all the others, until getting to number three.

Coming down the steps, he noticed an unusual smell. That perked his senses, but not all that much until his feet touched the floor. Then he turned left and saw a wisp of smoke coming out from under the door to 307. He took the three steps to the door, and touched the knob, finding it hot, but not painfully so. That was when he made his mistake.

Taking the passkey from his pocket, he unlocked the door, and without feeling the wooden portion to see if that was hot, he pushed the door open.

The fire had largely died down, starved of oxygen, but the room remained hot, the hotel walls insulating the incipient blaze as efficiently as a barbecue pit. Opening the door admitted a large volume of fresh air and oxygen to the room, and barely had he had the chance to see the horror within when a phenomenon called flashover happened.

It was the next thing to an explosion. The room reignited in a blast of flame and a further intake of air, sufficiently strong that it nearly pulled the clerk off his feet and into the room even as an outward blast of flame pushed him the other way—and saved his life. Slapping his hands to his flash-burned face, he fell to his knees and struggled to the manual-pull alarm on the wall next to the elevator—without pulling 307's door back shut. That sounded alarm bells throughout the hotel and also reported to the nearest firehouse, three kilometers away. Screaming with pain, he walked, or fell, down the stairs to the lobby, where he first threw a glass of water on his burned face, then called the emergency number next to the phone to report the fire to the city fire department. By this time people were coming down the stairs. For them, getting past the third floor had been harrowing, and the clerk, burned as he was, got an extinguisher to spray on them, but he was unable to climb back to use the fire hose in its little cabinet on the involved floor. It would not have mattered anyway.

The first fire truck arrived less than five minutes after the pull alarm had sounded. Hardly needing to be told—the fire was visible from outside, since the room's windows had shattered from the heat of the renewed blaze—they forced their way past the escaping hotel guests. Within a minute after arriving, the first seventy-millimeter hose was spraying water into the room. It took less than five minutes to knock the fire down, and through the smoke and horrid smell, the firemen forced their way inside to find what they feared—a family of three, dead in their beds.

The fire lieutenant in command of the first responders cradled the dead child in his arms and ran down and out onto the street, but he could see it was a waste. The child had roasted like a piece of meat in an oven. Hosing her body down only exposed the ghastly effect a fire has on a human body, and there was nothing for him to do but say a prayer for her. The lieutenant was the brother of a priest and a devout Catholic in this Marxist country, and he prayed to his God for mercy for the little girl's soul, not knowing that the very same thing had happened over four thousand miles away and ten days earlier.

THE RABBITS WERE out of the city in a matter of minutes. Hudson drove carefully, within the posted speed limits, lest there be a cop around, though there was virtually no traffic in evidence, merely the occasional truck, commercial ones with canvas sides, carrying who knew what to who knew where. Ryan was in the right-front seat, half turned to look in the back. Irina Zaitzev was a mask of tipsy confusion, not comprehending enough to be frightened. The child was asleep, as children invariably were at this time of night. The father was trying to be stoic, but the edge of fear was visible on his face, even in the darkness. Ryan tried to put himself in his place, but found it impossible to do so. To betray one's country was too great a leap of imagination for him. He knew there were those who stabbed America in the back, mainly for money, but he didn't pretend to understand their motivation. Sure, back in the '30s and '40s there had been those for whom communism looked like the leading wave of human history, but those thoughts were all as dead as V. I. Lenin was today. Communism was a dying idea, except in the minds of those who needed it to be the source of their personal power. . . . And perhaps some still believed in it because they'd never been exposed to anything else, or because the idea had been too firmly planted in their distant youth, as a minister or priest believed in God. But the words of Lenin's *Collected Works* were not Holy Writ to Ryan and never would be. As a new college graduate, he'd sworn his oath to the Constitution of the United States and promised to "bear true faith and allegiance to the same" as a second lieutenant of the United States Marine Corps, and that was that.

"How long, Andy?"

"A little over an hour to Csurgo. Traffic ought not to be a problem," Hudson answered.

And it wasn't. In minutes, they were outside the boundaries of Hungary's capital, and then the lights of houses and businesses just stopped as though someone had flipped the master switch for electricity to the region. The road was two-lane blacktop, and none too wide at that. Telephone poles, no guardrails. *And this is a major commercial highway?* Ryan wondered. They might as well have been driving across central Nevada. Perhaps one or two lights every kilometer, farmhouses where people liked to have one on to help find their way to the bathroom. Even the road signs looked decrepit and not very helpful—not the mint-green highway signs of home or the friendly blue ones of England. It didn't help that the words on them were in Martian. Otherwise they were the European sort, showing the speed limit in black numbers on a white disc within a red circle.

Hudson was a competent driver, puffing away on his cigars and driving as though he were on his way to Covent Garden in London. Ryan thanked God that he'd made a trip to the head before walking to the hotel—otherwise he might lose control of his bladder. Well, probably his face didn't show how nervous he was, Jack hoped. He kept telling himself that his own life wasn't on the line, but those of the people in the back were, and they were now his responsibility, and something in him, probably something learned from his policeman father, made that a matter of supreme importance.

"What is your full name?" Oleg asked him, breaking the silence unexpectedly.

"Ryan, Jack Ryan."

"What sort of name is Ryan?" the Rabbit pressed on.

"My ancestry is Irish. John corresponds to Ivan, I think, but people call me Jack, like Vanya, maybe."

"And you are in CIA?"

"Yes, I am."

"What is your job in CIA?"

"I am an analyst. Mostly I sit at a desk and write reports."

"I also sit at desk in Centre."

"You are a communications officer?"

A nod. "*Da*, that is my job in Centre." Then Zaitzev remembered that his important information was not for the back of a car, and he shut back up.

Ryan saw that. He had things to say, but not here, and that was fair enough for the moment.

The trip went smoothly. Four cigars for Hudson, and six cigarettes for Ryan, until they approached the town of Csurgo.

Ryan had expected something more than this. Csurgo was barely a wide place in the road, with not even a gas station in evidence, and surely not an all-night 7-Eleven. Hudson turned off the main road onto a dirt track, and three minutes later there was the shape of a commercial truck. It was a big Volvo, he saw in a moment, with a black canvas cover on the back and two men standing next to it, both smoking. Hudson pulled around it, finding concealment behind some nondescript sort of shed a few yards from it, and stopped the Jaguar. He hopped out, and motioned to the rest to do the same.

Ryan followed the Brit spook to the two men. Hudson walked right up to the older of the two and shook his hand.

"Hello, Istvan. Good of you to wait for us."

"Hello, Andy. It is a dull night. Who are your friends?"

"This is Mr. Ryan. These are the Somerset family. We're going across the border," Hudson explained.

"Okay," Kovacs agreed. "This is Jani. He's my driver for tonight. Andy, you can ride in front with us. The rest will be in the back. Come," he said, leading the way.

The truck's tailgate had ladder steps built in. Ryan climbed up first, and bent down to lift the little girl—Svetlana, he remembered, was her name—and watched her mother and father climb up. In the cargo area, he saw, were some large cardboard boxes, perhaps containers for the tape machine Hungarians made. Kovacs climbed up also.

"You all speak English?" he asked, and got nods. "It is a short way to the border, just five kilometer. You will hide in boxes here. Please make no noise. Is important. You understand? Make no noise." He got more nods, noting that the man—definitely not an Englishman, he could see—translated to his wife. The man took the child, Kovacs saw also. With his cargo hidden away, he closed the tailgate and walked forward.

"Five thousand d-mark for this, eh?" Istvan asked.

"That is correct," Hudson agreed.

"I should ask more, but I am not a greedy man."

"You are a trusted comrade, my friend," Hudson assured him, briefly wishing that he had a pistol in his belt.

The Volvo's big diesel lit up with a rumbling roar and the truck jerked off, back to the main road, with Jani at the large, almost flat steering wheel.

It didn't take long.

And that was a good thing for Ryan, crouching in the cardboard box in the back. He could only guess how the Russians felt, like unborn babies in a horrible womb, one with loaded guns outside it.

Ryan was afraid even to smoke a final cigarette, fearing someone might smell the smoke over the pungent diesel exhaust, which was altogether unlikely.

"So, Istvan," Hudson asked in the cab, "what is the routine?"

"Watch. We usually travel at night. Is more—dramatic, you say? I know the Határ-rség here many years now. Captain Budai Laszlo is good man to do business with. He has wife and little daughter, always want present for daughter Zsóka. I have," Kovacs promised, holding up a paper bag.

The border post was sufficiently well lighted that they could see it three kilometers off, and blessedly there was little traffic this time of night. Jani drove up normally, slowing and stopping there when the private of the border guards, the *Határ-rség,* waved for them to halt.

"Is Captain Budai here?" Kovacs asked at once. "I have something for him." The private headed into the guardhouse and returned instantly with a more senior man.

"Laszlo! How are you this cold night?" Kovacs called in Magyar, then jumped down from the cab with the paper shopping bag.

"Istvan, what can I say, it is dull night," the youngish captain replied.

"And your little Zsóka, she is well?"

"Her birthday is next week. She will be five."

"Excellent!" the smuggler observed. He handed over the bag. "Give her these."

"These" were a pair of candy-apple-red Reebok sneakers with Velcro closures.

"Lovely," Captain Budai observed, with genuine pleasure. He took them out to look at them in the light. Any female child in the world loved the things, and Laszlo was as happy as his daughter would be in four days. "You are a good friend, Istvan. So, what do you transport tonight?"

"Nothing of value. I'm making a pickup this morning in Beograd, though. Anything you need?"

"My wife would love some tapes for the Walkman you got her last month." The amazing thing about Budai was that he was not an overly greedy man. That was one of the reasons Kovacs liked to travel across the border on his watch.

"What groups?"

"The Bee Gees, I think she called them. For me, some show tunes, if you don't mind."

"Anything in particular? The music from American movies, like *Star Wars,* perhaps."

"I have that one, but not the new one, the *Empire Attacks Back,* perhaps?"

"Done." They shook hands. "How about some Western coffee?"

"What kind?"

"Austrian or American, maybe? There's a place in Beograd that has American Folgers coffee. It is very tasty," Kovacs assured him.

"I have never tried that."

"I'll get you some and you can try it—no charge."

"You are a good man," Budai observed. "Have a good night. Pass," he concluded, waving to his corporal.

And it was just that easy. Kovacs walked back around and climbed into his truck. He wouldn't have to part with the present he had for Sergeant Kerekes Mikaly, and that was good, too.

Hudson was surprised. "No paper check?"

"Laszlo just runs the name through the teletype to Budapest. Some people there are also on my payroll. They are more greedy than he is, but is not major expense. Jani, go," he said to the driver, who started up and pulled across the line painted on the pavement. And just that easily, the truck left the Warsaw Pact.

In the back, Ryan had rarely felt so good to feel a vehicle start to move. It stopped again in a minute, but this was a different border.

And going into Yugoslavia, Jani handled it, just trading a few words with the guard, not even killing the engine, before being waved forward and into the semi-communist country. He drove three kilometers before being told to pull off onto a side road. There, after a few bumps, the Volvo stopped. Yugoslavian border security, Hudson saw, was sod-all.

Ryan was already out of his cardboard box and standing at the back when the canvas cover was flipped aside.

"We're here, Jack," Hudson said.

"Where is that exactly?"

"Yugoslavia, my lad. The nearest town is Légrád, and here we part company."

"Oh?"

"Yes, I'm turning you over to Vic Lucas. He's my counterpart in Belgrade. Vic?" Hudson beckoned.

The man who came into view might have been Hudson's twin, except for the hair, which was black. He was also two or three inches taller, Jack decided on second inspection. He went forward to get the Rabbits out of the boxes. That happened in a hurry, and Ryan helped them down, handing the little girl—remarkably, still asleep—to her mother, who looked more confused than ever.

Hudson walked them to a car, a station wagon—"estate wagon" to the Brits—which would at least have ample room for everyone.

"Sir John—Jack, that is—well done, and thanks for all your help."

"I didn't do shit, Andy, but you handled this pretty damned well," Ryan said, taking his hand. "Come see me in London for a pint sometime."

"That I shall do," Hudson promised.

The estate wagon was a British Ford. Ryan helped the Rabbits into their seats and then took the right-front again.

"Mr. Lucas, where do we go now?"

"To the airport. Our flight is waiting," the Belgrade COS replied.

"Oh? Special flight?"

"No, the commercial aircraft is experiencing 'technical difficulties' at the moment. I rather expect they will be cleared up about the time we get aboard."

"Good to know," Ryan observed. Better this than a real broken airplane, then he realized that one more harrowing adventure lay ahead. His hatred of flying was suddenly back, now that they were in semi-free country.

"Right, let's be off," Lucas said, starting his engine and pulling off.

Whatever sort of spook Vic Lucas was, he must have thought himself Stirling Moss's smarter brother. The car rocketed down the road into the Yugoslavian darkness.

"So, how has your night been, Jack?"

"Eventful," Ryan answered, making sure his seat belt was properly fastened.

The countryside here was better lit and the road better engineered and maintained, or so it seemed, flashing by at what felt like seventy-five miles per hour, rather fast for a strange road in the dark. Robby Jackson drove like this, but Robby was a fighter pilot, and therefore invincible while at the controls of any transportation platform. This Vic Lucas must have felt the same way, calmly looking forward and turning the wheel in short, sharp increments. In the back, Oleg was still tense, and Irina still trying to come to terms with some new and incomprehensible reality, while their little daughter continued to sleep like a diminutive angel. Ryan was chain-smoking. It seemed to help somewhat, though if Cathy smelled it on his breath there would be hell to pay. Well, she'd just have to understand, Jack thought, watching telephone poles flash by the car like fence pickets. He was doing Uncle Sam's business.

Then Ryan saw a police car sitting by the side of the road, its officers sipping coffee or sleeping through their watch.

"Not to worry," Lucas said. "Diplomatic tags. I am the senior political counselor at Her Britannic Majesty's Embassy. And you good people are my guests."

"You say so, man. How much longer?"

"Half an hour, roughly. Traffic's been very kind to us so far. Not much truck traffic. This road can be crowded, even late at night with cross-border trade. That Kovacs chap's been working with us for years. I could make quite a good living in partnership with him. He often brings those Hungarian tape machines this way. They're decent machines, and they're giving the bloody things away, what with the labor costs in Hungary. Surprising they don't try to sell them in the West, though I expect they'd have to pay the Japanese for the patent infringements. Not too scrupulous about such things on the other side of the line, you see." Lucas took another high-speed turn.

"Jesus, guy, how fast do you go in daylight?"

"Not much faster than this. Good night vision, you see, but the suspension on this car slows me down. American design, you see. Too soft for proper handling."

"So buy a Corvette. Friend of mine has one."

"Lovely things, but made out of plastic." Lucas shook his head and reached for a cigar. Probably a Cuban one, Ryan was sure. They loved the things in England.

Half an hour later, Lucas congratulated himself. "There it is. Just on time."

Airports are airports all over the world. The same architect probably designed them all, Ryan thought. The only differences were the signs for the rest rooms. In England they called them toilets, which had always struck him as a little crude in an otherwise gentle country. Then he got a surprise. Instead of driving to the terminal, Lucas took the path through the open gate right onto the flight line.

"I have an arrangement with the airport manager," he explained. "He likes single malts." Still and all, Lucas stayed on the yellow-lined car path, right to a lonely aircraft jetway with an airliner parked next to it. "Here we are," the Brit spook announced.

They all stepped out of the car, this time with Mrs. Rabbit holding the Bunny. Lucas led them up the exterior stairs into the jetway's control booth, and from there right into the aircraft's open door.

The captain, hatless but wearing four stripes on his shoulders, was standing right there. "You're Mr. Lucas?"

"That is correct, Captain Rogers. And here are your extra passengers." He pointed to Ryan and the Rabbit family.

"Excellent." Captain Rogers turned to his lead stew. "We can board the aircraft now."

The second-ranking flight attendant took them to the four front-row first-class seats, where Ryan was singularly surprised to be happy belting himself in to 1-B, the aisle seat just behind the front bulkhead. He watched thirty or so working-class passengers come aboard after sunning themselves on the Dalmatian Coast—a favorite for Brits of late—none of them looking very happy for the three-hour delay on what was already supposed to be the day's last flight to Manchester. Things happened quickly after that. He heard both engines start up, and then the BAC-111—the British counterpart to the Douglas DC-9—backed away from the jetway and taxied out on the ramp.

"What now?" Oleg asked, in what was almost a normal voice.

"We fly to England," Ryan replied. "Two hours or so, I guess, and we'll be there."

"So easy?"

"You think this was easy?" Ryan asked, with no small amount of incredulity in his voice. Then the intercom turned on.

"Ladies and gentlemen, this is Captain Rogers speaking. I am glad to say that we finally got the electronic problem repaired. Thank you ever so much for your patience, and after we lift off, the drinks will be free to all passengers." That evoked a cheer from the back of the aircraft. "For the moment, please pay attention to the flight attendants for your safety message."

Put your seat belts on, dummies, and they work like this, *for those of you stupid enough not to notice that you have the fucking things in your personal automobiles, too.* And then in three more minutes the British Midlands airliner clawed its way into the sky.

As promised, before they'd gotten to ten thousand feet, the no-smoking light *ding*ed off and the drink cart arrived. The Russian asked for vodka and got three miniatures of Finlandia. Ryan got himself a glass of wine and the promise of more. He wouldn't sleep on this flight, but he wouldn't worry as much as usual, either. He was leaving the communist world behind at five hundred miles per hour, and that was probably the best way to do it.

Oleg Ivan'ch, he saw, drank vodka as though it were water after a hot day of cutting the grass. His wife, over in 1-C, was doing the same. Ryan felt positively virtuous sipping gently at his French wine.

"SIGNAL IN FROM BASIL," Bostock reported over the phone. "The Rabbit is in the air. ETA Manchester in ninety minutes."

"Great," Judge Moore breathed, relieved as always when a black operation worked out as planned. Better still, they'd run it without Bob Ritter, who, though a good man, was not entirely indispensable.

"Three more days and we can debrief him," Bostock said next. "The nice house out by Winchester?"

"Yeah, we'll see if he likes horse country." The house even had a Steinway piano for Mrs. Rabbit to play and lots of green for the kid to run around on.

ALAN KINGSHOT WAS just pulling into the parking area at the Manchester airport, along with two subordinates. There would be a large back Daimler automobile to take the arriving defectors out to Somerset in the morning. He hoped they didn't mind driving. It would be nearly a two-hour drive.

For the moment, they'd be quartering at a nice country house just a few minutes from the airport. They'd probably done quite enough traveling for the moment, with still more to come before the end of the week. But then he started thinking about it. Might that be too hard on them? The question gave him something to ponder at one of the airport's bars.

RYAN WAS PRETTY well potted. Maybe alcohol interacted with anxiety, he thought, taking a moment to go to the forward rest room on the airliner, and feeling better when he got back and was strapped in. He almost never took his seat belt off. The food served was just sandwiches—English ones, with their unnatural affection for a weed called watercress. What he really wanted now was a good corned beef, but the Brits didn't even know what corned beef was, thinking it the canned junk that looked like dog food to most Americans. In fact, the Brits probably fed better stuff to their dogs, as enthralled as they were with their pets. The lights passing underneath the airliner proved that they were overflying Western Europe. The Eastern part was never well lit, as he'd learned coming south from Budapest.

BUT ZAITZEV wasn't sure. What if this was a very elaborate ruse to get him to spill the beans? What if the Second Chief Directorate had staged a huge *maskirovka* village for his brief benefit?

"Ryan?"

Jack turned. "Yes?"

"What will I see in England when we get there?"

"I don't know what the plan is after we get to Manchester," Ryan reported.

"You are CIA?" the Rabbit asked again.

"Yes." Jack nodded.

"How can I be sure of this?"

"Well . . ." Ryan fished out his wallet. "Here are my driver's license, credit cards, some cash. My passport is fake, of course. I'm an American, but they fixed me up with a British one. Oh," Ryan realized, "you're worried that this is all faked?"

"How can I be sure?"

"My friend, in less than an hour, you will be certain it is not. Here—" He opened his wallet again. "This is my wife, my daughter, and our new son. My address at home—in America, that is—is here on my driver's license, 5000 Peregrine Cliff Road, Anne Arundel County, Maryland. That is right on the Chesapeake Bay. It takes me about an hour to drive from there to CIA Headquarters at Langley. My wife is an eye surgeon at Johns Hopkins Hospital in Baltimore. It is world-famous. You must have heard of it."

Zaitzev just shook his head.

"Well, a couple years ago, three docs from Hopkins fixed the eyes of Mikhail Suslov. I understand he just died. His replacement, we think, will be Mikhail Yevgeniyevich Alexandrov. We know a little about him, but not enough. In fact, we don't know enough about Yuriy Vladimirovich."

"What do you not know?"

"Is he married? We've never seen a picture of his wife, if any."

"Yes, everyone knows this. His wife is Tatiana, elegant woman, my wife says she has noble features. But no children for them," Oleg concluded.

Well, there's factoid #1 from the Rabbit, Ryan thought.

"How is it possible that you do not know this?" Zaitzev demanded.

"Oleg Ivan'ch, there are many things we do not know about the Soviet Union," Jack admitted. "Some are important, and some are not."

"Is this true?"

"Yes, it is."

Something rattled loose in Zaitzev's head. "You say your name Ryan?"

"That's right."

"Your father policeman?"

"How did you know that?" Ryan asked in some surprise.

"We have small dossier on you. Washington *rezidentura* do it. Your family attacked by hooligans, yes?"

"Correct." *KGB is interested in me, eh?* Jack thought. "Terrorists, they tried to kill me and my family. My son was born that night."

"And you join CIA after that?"

"Again, yes—officially, anyway. I've done work for the Agency for several years." Then curiosity took full hold. "What does my dossier say about me?"

"It say you are rich fool. You were officer in naval infantry, and your wife is rich and you marry her for that reason. To get more money for self."

So, even the KGB is a prisoner of its own political prejudices, Jack thought. *Interesting.*

"I am not poor," Jack told the Rabbit. "But I married my wife for love, not money. Only a fool does that."

"How many capitalists are fools?"

Ryan had himself a good laugh. "A lot more than you might think. You do not need to be very smart in America to become rich." New York and Washington in particular were full of rich idiots, but Ryan thought the Rabbit needed a little while before he learned that lesson. "Who did the dossier on me?"

"Reporter in Washington *rezidentura* of *Izvestia* is junior KGB officer. He do it last summer."

"And how did you come to know about it?"

"His dispatch come to my desk, and I forward to America–Canada Institute—is KGB office. You know that, yes?"

"Yes," Jack confirmed. "That is one we do know." That was when his ears popped. The airliner was descending. Ryan gunned down the last of his third white wine and told himself it would all be over in a few minutes. One thing he'd learned from Operation BEATRIX: This field work wasn't for him.

The no-smoking sign *ding*ed back on. Ryan brought his chair to its full upright position, and then the lights of Manchester appeared through the windows, the car headlights and the airport fence, and in a few more seconds . . . *thump,* the wheels touched down in Merry Old England. It might not be the same as America, but for the moment it would do.

Oleg, he saw, had his face against the window, checking out the tail colors of the aircraft. There were too many for this to be a Soviet Air Force base and a huge *maskirovka.* He visibly started to relax.

"We welcome you to Manchester," the pilot said over the intercom. "The time is three-forty, and the temperature outside is fifty-four degrees Fahrenheit. We appreciate your patience earlier today, and we hope to see you again soon in British Midlands Airways."

Yeah, Jack thought. *In your dreams, skipper.*

Ryan sat and waited as the aircraft taxied to the international-arrivals area. A truck-borne stairway came to the front door, which the lead stew duly opened. Ryan and the Rabbit family were first off and down the steps, where they were guided to some cars instead of the waiting transfer bus.

Alan Kingshot was there to take his hand. "How was it, Jack?"

"Just like a trip to Disney World," Ryan answered, without a trace of audible irony in his voice.

"Right. Let's get you all loaded and off to a comfortable place."

"Works for me, pal. What is it, quarter of three?" Ryan hadn't changed his watch back yet. Britain was an hour behind the rest of Europe.

"That's right," the field spook confirmed.

"Damn," Jack reacted. Too damned late to call home and tell Cathy he was back. But, then, he wasn't really back. Now he had to play CIA representative for the first interview of the Red Rabbit. Probably Sir Basil had him doing this because he was too junior to be very effective. Well, maybe he'd show his British host just how dumb he was, Ryan growled to himself. But first it was time for sleep. Stress, he'd learned, was about as tiring as jogging—just harder on the heart.

BACK IN BUDAPEST, the three bodies were at the city morgue, an institution as depressing behind the Iron Curtain as in front of it. When Zaitzev's identity as a Russian citizen had been confirmed, a call had been made to the Soviet Embassy, where it was speedily established that the man in question was a KGB officer. *That* generated interest in the *rezidentura,* just across the street from the hotel where he'd ostensibly died, and more telephone calls were made.

Before five in the morning, Professor Zoltán Bíró was awakened in his bed by the AVH. Bíró was professor of pathology at the Ignaz Semmelweis Medical College. Named for one of the fathers of the germ theory that had transformed the science of medicine in the nineteenth century, it remained a good one, even attracting students from West Germany, none of whom would attend the postmortem examinations ordered by the country's Belügyminisztérium, which would also be attended by the physician-in-residence at the Soviet Embassy.

The first done would be the adult male. Technicians took blood samples from all three bodies for analysis in the adjacent laboratory.

"This is the body of a male Caucasian, approximately thirty-five years of age, length approximately one hundred seventy-five centimeters, weight approximately seventy-six kilograms. Color of hair cannot be determined due to extensive charring from a domestic fire. Initial impression is death by fire—more probably from carbon monoxide intoxication, as the body shows no evidence of death throes." Then the dissection began with the classical Y incision to open the body cavity for viewing of the internal organs.

He was examining the heart—unremarkable—when the lab reports came in.

"Professor Bíró, carbon monoxide in all three blood samples are well into lethal range," the voice on the speaker said, giving the exact numbers.

Bíró looked over at his Russian colleague. "Anything else you need? I can do a full postmortem on all three victims here, but the cause of death is determined. This man was not shot. We will do fuller blood-chemistry checks, of course, but it's unlikely that they were poisoned, and there is clearly no bullet wound or other penetrating trauma in this man. They were all killed by fire. I will send you the full laboratory report this afternoon." Bíró let out a long breath. *"A kurva életbe!"* he concluded with a popular Magyar epithet.

"Such a pretty little girl," the Russian internist observed. Zaitzev's wallet had somehow survived the fire, along with its family photos. The picture of Svetlana had been particularly engaging.

"Death is never sentimental, my friend," Bíró told him. As a pathologist, he knew that fact all too well.

"Very well. Thank you, Comrade Professor." And the Russian took his leave, already thinking through his official report to Moscow.

CHAPTER 29

REVELATION

THE SAFE HOUSE WAS palatial, the country home of somebody with both money and taste, built in the previous century by the look of it, with stucco and the sort of heavy oaken timbers used to build ships like HMS *Victory* once upon a time. But landlocked, it was about as far from blue water as one could get on this island kingdom.

Evidently, Alan Kingshot knew it well enough, since he drove them there and then got them settled inside. The two-person staff that ran the place looked like cops to Ryan, probably married and retired from the Police Force of the Metropolis, as the London Constabulary was officially known. They kindly escorted their new guests to a rather nice suite of rooms. Irina Zaitzev's eyes were agog at the accommodations, which were impressive even by Ryan's standards. All Oleg Ivanovich did was set his shaving kit in the bathroom, strip off his clothes, and collapse onto the bed, where alcohol-aided sleep proved to be less than five minutes away.

WORD GOT TO Judge Moore just before midnight that the package was safely ensconced in a very secure location, and with that information he also went to bed. All that remained was to tell the Air Force to get a KC-

135 or a similar aircraft ready to fly the package home, and that would take a mere telephone call to an officer in the Pentagon. He wondered what the Rabbit would say, but he could wait for that. Patience, once the dangerous stuff was behind, was not all that difficult for the Director of Central Intelligence. It was like Christmas Eve, and while he wasn't exactly sure what would be under the tree, he could be confident that it wouldn't be anything bad.

FOR SIR BASIL Charleston at his Belgravia house, the news came before breakfast, when a messenger from Century House arrived with the word. *An altogether pleasant way to start a working day,* he thought, certainly better than some others he'd had. He left home for the office just before seven A.M., ready for his morning brief to outline the success of Operation BEATRIX.

RYAN WAS AWAKENED by traffic noise. Whoever had built this magnificent country home hadn't anticipated the construction of a motorway just three hundred yards away, but somehow Ryan had avoided a hangover from all the drinks on the flight in, and the lingering excitement of the moment had gotten him fully awake after a mere six and a half hours of slumber. He washed up and made his way to the pleasant not-so-little breakfast room. Alan Kingshot was there, working on his morning tea.

"Probably coffee for you, eh?"

"If you have any."

"Only instant," Kingshot warned.

Jack stifled his disappointment. "Better than no coffee at all."

"Eggs Benedict?" the retired woman cop asked.

"Ma'am, for that I will forgive the absence of Starbucks," Jack replied, with a smile. Then he saw the morning papers, and he thought that reality and normality had finally returned to his life. Well, almost.

"Mr. and Mrs. Thompson run this house for us," Kingshot explained. "Nick was a homicide detective with the Yard, and Emma was in administration."

"That's what my dad used to do," Ryan observed. "How did you guys get working for SIS?"

"Nick worked on the Markov case," Mrs. Thompson answered.

"And did a damned good job of it, too," Kingshot told Ryan. "He would have been a fine field officer for us."

" 'Bond, James Bond'?" Nick Thompson said, walking into the kitchen. "I think not. Our guests are moving about. It sounds as though the little girl got them up."

"Yeah," Jack observed. "Kids will do that. So, we do the debrief here or somewhere else?"

"We were planning to do it in Somerset, but I decided last night not to drive them around too much. Why stress them out?" Kingshot asked rhetorically. "We just took title to this house last year, and it's as comfortable a place as any. The one in Somerset—near Taunton—is a touch more isolated, but these people ought not to bolt, you think?"

"If he goes home, he's one dead Rabbit," Ryan thought out loud. "He has to know that. On the plane, he was worried that we were KGB and this was all an elaborate *maskirovka* setup, I think. His wife did a lot of shopping in Budapest. Maybe we have somebody take her shopping around here?" the American wondered. "Then we can talk to him in comfort. His English seems okay. Do we have anybody here with good Russian?"

"My job," Kingshot told Ryan.

"First thing we want to know, why the hell did he decide to skip town?"

"Obviously, but then, what's all this lot about compromised communications?"

"Yeah." Ryan took a deep breath. "I imagine people are jumping out windows about that one."

"Too bloody right," Kingshot confirmed.

"So, Al, you've worked Moscow?"

The Brit nodded. "Twice. Good sport it was, but rather tense the whole time I was there."

"Where else?"

"Warsaw and Bucharest. I speak all the languages. Tell me, how was Andy Hudson?"

"He's a star, Al. Very smooth and confident all the way—knows his turf, good contacts. He took pretty good care of me."

"Here's your coffee, Sir John," Mrs. Thompson said, bringing his cup of Taster's Choice. The Brits were good people, and their food, Ryan thought, was wrongly maligned, but they didn't know beans about coffee, and that was that. But it was still better than tea.

The Eggs Benedict arrived shortly thereafter, and at that dish, Mrs. Thompson could have given lessons. Ryan opened his paper—it was the *Times*—and relaxed to get reacquainted with the world. He'd call Cathy in about an hour when he was at work. With luck, he might even see her in a couple days. In a perfect world, he'd have a copy of an American paper, or maybe the *International Tribune*, but the world was not yet perfect. There was no sense asking how the World Series was going. It was going to start tomorrow, wasn't it? How good were the Phillies this year? Well, as usual, you played the games to find out.

"So, how was the trip, Jack?" Kingshot asked.

"Alan, those field officers earn every nickel they make. How you deal with the constant tension, I do not understand."

"Like everything else, Jack, you get used to it. Your wife is a surgeon. The idea of cutting people open with a knife is not at all appealing to me."

Jack barked a short laugh. "Yeah, me too, pal. And she does eyeballs. Nothing important, right?"

Kingshot shuddered visibly at the thought, and Ryan reminded himself that working in Moscow, running agents—and probably arranging rescue missions like they'd done for the Rabbit—could not have been much more fun than a heart transplant.

"Ah, Mr. Somerset," Ryan heard Mrs. Thompson say. "Good morning, and welcome."

"*Spasiba*," Oleg Ivan'ch replied in a sleepy voice. Kids could get you up at the goddamnedest hours, with their smiling faces and lovely dispositions. "That is my new name?"

"We'll figure something more permanent later," Ryan told him. "Again, welcome."

"This is England?" the Rabbit asked.

"We're eight miles from Manchester," the British intelligence officer replied. "Good morning. In case you don't remember, my name is Alan Kingshot. This is Mrs. Emma Thompson, and Nick will be back in a few minutes." Handshakes were exchanged.

"My wife be here soon. She see to *zaichik*," he explained.

"How are you feeling, Vanya?" Kingshot asked.

"Much travel, much fear, but I am safe now, yes?"

"Yes, you are entirely safe," Kingshot assured him.

"And what would you like for breakfast?" Mrs. Thompson asked.

"Try this," Jack suggested, pointing at his plate. "It's great."

"Yes, I will—what is called?"

"Eggs Benedict," Jack told him. "Mrs. Thompson, this hollandaise sauce is just perfect. My wife needs your recipe, if I may impose." And maybe Cathy could teach her about proper coffee. *That would be an equitable trade,* Ryan thought.

"Why, certainly, Sir John," she replied with a beaming smile. No woman in all the world objects to praise for her cooking.

"For me also, then," Zaitzev decided.

"Tea or coffee?" she asked her guest.

"You have English Breakfast tea?" the Rabbit asked.

"Of course," she answered.

"Please for me, then."

"Certainly." And she disappeared back into the kitchen.

It was still a lot for Zaitzev to take. Here he was, in the breakfast room of a manor house fit for a member of the old nobility, surrounded by a green lawn such as one might see at Augusta National, with monstrous oak trees planted two hundred years before, a carriage house, and stables in the distance. It was something he might have imagined as worthy of Peter the Great, the things of books and museums, and he was in it as an honored guest?

"Nice house, isn't it?" Ryan asked, finishing off the Eggs Benny.

"Is amazing," Zaitzev responded, wide eyes sweeping around.

"Belonged to a ducal family, bought by a textiles manufacturer a hundred years ago, but his business fell on hard times, and the government bought it last year. We use it for conferences and as a safe house. The heating system is a little primitive," Kingshot reported. "But that is not a problem at the moment. We've had a very pleasant summer, and the fall looks promising as well."

"At home, there'd be a golf course around this place," Jack said, looking out the windows. "A big one."

"Yes," Alan agreed. "It would be splendid for that."

"When I go America?" the Rabbit asked.

"Oh, three or four days," Kingshot answered. "We would like to talk with you a little, if you don't mind."

"When do we start?"

"After breakfast. Take your time, Mr. Zaitzev. You are no longer in the Soviet Union. We shall not pressure you at all," Alan promised.

My ass, Ryan thought. *Buddy, they're going to suck your brain out of your head and strain it for your thoughts one molecule at a time.* But the Rabbit had just gotten a free ride out of Mother Russia, with the prospect of a comfortable life for him and his family in the West, and everything in life had its price.

He loved his tea. Then the rest of the family came out and, over the next twenty minutes, Mrs. Thompson nearly ran out of Hollandaise sauce, while the arriving Russians ensured steady employment for the local egg farmers.

Irina left the breakfast room to tour the house and was greatly excited to see a concert grand Bösendorfer piano, turning like a kid at Christmas to ask if she might tickle the keys. She was years out of practice, but the look on her face was like a return of childhood as she struggled through "On the Bridge at Avignon," which had been her favorite exercise tune many years before—and which she still remembered.

"A friend of mine plays professionally," Jack said, with a smile. It was hard not to appreciate her joy of the moment.

"Who? Where?" Oleg asked.

"Sissy—actually, Cecilia Jackson. Her husband and I are friends. He's a fighter pilot for the U.S. Navy. She is number-two piano soloist at the Washington Symphony. My wife plays, too, but Sissy is really good."

"You are good to us," Oleg Ivan'ch said.

"We try to take decent care of our guests," Kingshot told him. "Shall we talk in the library?" He pointed the way.

The chairs were comfortable. The library was another stellar example of nineteenth-century woodwork, with thousands of books and three rolling ladders—it isn't a proper English library without a ladder. The chairs were plush. Mrs. Thompson brought in a tray of ice water and glasses, and business began.

"So, Mr. Zaitzev, can you begin to tell us about yourself?" Kingshot asked. He was rewarded by name, ancestry, place of birth, and education.

"No military service?" Ryan asked.

Zaitzev shook his head. "No, KGB spot me and they protect me from army time."

"And that was in university?" Kingshot asked for clarity. A total of three tape recorders were turning.

"Yes, that is correct. My first year they speak to me for first time."

"And when did you join KGB?"

"Immediately I leave Moscow State University. They take me into communications department."

"And how long there?"

"Since, well, for nine and half years in total, set aside my time in academy and other training."

"And where do you work now?" Kingshot led him on.

"I work in Central Communications in basement of Moscow Centre."

"And what exactly did you do there?" Alan finally asked.

"During my watch, all dispatches come in from field to my desk. My job is to maintain security, to be sure proper procedures followed, and then I forward to action officers upstairs. Or to United States–Canada Institute sometimes," Oleg said, gesturing to Ryan.

Jack did his best not to let his mouth fall open. This guy really *was* an escapee from the Soviet counterpart to CIA's Mercury. This guy saw it all. Everything, or damned near. He'd just helped a gold mine escape from behind the wire. *Son of a bitch!*

Kingshot did a somewhat better job of concealing his feelings, but he let his eyes slip over to Ryan's, and that expression said it all.

Bloody hell.

"So, do you know the names of your field officers and their agents?" Kingshot asked.

"KGB officer names—I know many names. Agents, the names I know very few, but I know code names. In Britain, our best agent is code-named MINISTER. He give us high-value diplomatic and political intelligence for many years—twenty years, I think, perhaps more."

"You said KGB has compromised our communications," Ryan observed.

"Yes, somewhat. That is agent NEPTUNE. How much he give, I am not sure, but I know KGB read much of American naval communications."

"What about other communications?" Jack asked immediately.

"Naval communications, that I am sure. Others, I am not sure, but you use same cipher machines for all, yes?"

"Actually not," Alan told him. "So, you say British communications are secure?"

"If broken, I do not know it," Zaitzev replied. "Most American diplomatic and intelligence information we get come from Agent CASSIUS. He is aide to senior politician in Washington. He give us good information on what CIA do and what CIA learn from us."

"But you said he's not part of CIA?" Ryan asked.

"No, I think he is politician aide, helper, member of staff—like that," Zaitzev said rather positively.

"Good." Ryan lit up a smoke and offered one to Zaitzev, who took it at once.

"I run out of my *Krasnopresnenskiye,*" he explained.

"I should give you all of mine. My wife wants me to quit. She's a doctor," Jack explained.

"Bah," the Rabbit responded.

"So, why did you decide to leave?" Kingshot asked, taking a sip of tea. The reply nearly made him drop the cup.

"KGB want to kill Pope."

"You're serious?" It was the more experienced man who asked that question, not Ryan.

"Serious? I risk my life, my wife life, my daughter life. *Da,* I am serious," Oleg Ivanovich assured his interlocutors with an edge on his voice.

"Fuck," Ryan breathed. "Oleg, we need to know about this."

"It start in August. Fifteen August it start," Zaitzev told them, spinning out his tale without interruption for five or six minutes.

"No name for the operation?" Jack asked when he stopped.

"No name, just dispatch number fifteen-eight-eighty-two-six-six-six. That is date of first message from Andropov to *rezidentura* Rome, and number of message, yes? Yuriy Vladimirovich ask how get close to Pope. Rome say bad idea. Then Colonel Rozhdestvenskiy—he is main assistant to chairman, yes?—he send signal to *rezidentura* Sofia. Operation go from Sofia. So, operation -six-six-six probably run for KGB by *Dirzhavna Sugurnost.* I think officer name is Strokov, Boris Andreyevich."

Kingshot had a thought and rose, leaving the room. He came back with Nick Thompson, a former detective superintendent of the Metropolitan Police.

"Nick, does the name Boris Andreyevich Strokov mean anything to you?"

The former cop blinked hard. "Indeed it does, Alan. He's the chappie we think killed Georgiy Markov on Westminster Bridge. We had him under surveillance, but he flew out of the country before we had enough cause to pick him up for questioning."

"Wasn't he under diplomatic cover?" Ryan asked, and was surprised by Thompson's answer.

"Actually not. He came in undocumented and left the same way. I saw him myself at Heathrow. But we didn't put the pieces together quickly enough. Dreadful case it was. The poison they gave Markov was horrific stuff."

"You eyeballed this Strokov guy?"

Thompson nodded. "Oh, yes. He might have noticed me. I wasn't being all that careful under the circumstances. He's the one who killed Markov. I'd stake my life on it."

"How can you be sure?"

"I chased murderers for near on twenty years, Sir John. You get to know them in all that time. And that's what he was, a murderer," Thompson said with total confidence. Ryan could remember his father being like this, even on frustrating cases when he knew what he needed but couldn't quite prove it to a jury.

"The Bulgarians have a sort of contract with the Soviets," Kingshot explained. "Back in 1964 or so, they agreed to handle all the 'necessary' eliminations for the KGB. In return, they get various perks, mostly political.

Strokov, yes, I've heard that name before. Did you get a photo of the chap, Nick?"

"Fifty or more, Alan," Thompson assured him. "I'll never forget that face. He has the eyes of a corpse—no life in them at all, like a doll's eyes."

"How good is he?" Ryan asked.

"As an assassin? Quite good, Sir John. Very good indeed. His elimination of Markov on the bridge was expertly done—it was the third attempt. The first two would-be assassins bungled the job, and they called Strokov in to get it right. And that he did. Had things gone just a little differently, we would not have realized it was a murder at all."

"We think he's worked elsewhere in the West," Kingshot said. "But very little good information. Just gossip really. Jack, this is a dangerous development. I need to get this information to Basil soonest." And with that, Alan left the room to get to a secure phone. Ryan turned back to Zaitzev.

"And that's why you decided to leave?"

"KGB want kill innocent man, Ryan. I see plot grow. Andropov himself say do this. I handle the messages. How can man stop KGB?" he asked. "I cannot stop KGB, but I will not help KGB kill priest—he is innocent man, yes?"

Ryan's eyes looked down at the floor. "Yes, Oleg Ivan'ch, he is." *Dear God in heaven.* He checked his watch. He had to get this information out PDQ, but nobody was awake at Langley yet.

"BLOODY HELL," Sir Basil Charleston said into his secure phone. "Is this reliable information, Alan?"

"Yes, sir, I believe it to be entirely truthful. Our Rabbit seems a decent chap, and a rather clever one. He seems to be motivated exclusively by his conscience." Next, Kingshot told him about the first revelation of the morning, MINISTER.

"We need to get 'five' looking into that." The British Security Service—once known as MI-5—was the counterespionage arm of their government. They'd need a little more specific information to run that putative traitor down, but they already had a starting point. Twenty years, was it?

What a productive traitor that fellow had to be, Sir Basil thought. Time for him to see Parkhurst Prison on the Isle of Wight. Charleston had spent years cleaning up his own shop, once a playground for the KGB. But no more, and never bloody again, the Knight Commander of the Bath swore to himself.

WHOM DO I TELL? Ryan wondered. Basil would doubtless call Langley—Jack would make sure of that, but Sir Basil was a supremely reliable guy. Next came a more difficult question: *What the hell can I/we do about this?*

Ryan lit another smoke to consider that one. It was more police work than intelligence work. . . .

And the central issue would be classification.

Yeah, that's going to be the problem. If we tell anybody, the word will get out somehow, and then somebody will know we have the Rabbit—and guess what, Jack? The Rabbit is now more important to the CIA than the life of the Pope.

Oh, shit, Ryan thought. It was like a trick of jujitsu, like a sudden reversal of polarity on the dial of a compass. North was now south. Inside was now outside. And the needs of American intelligence might now supersede the life of the Bishop of Rome. His face must have betrayed what he was thinking.

"What is amiss, Ryan?" the Rabbit asked. It seemed to Jack a strange word for him to know.

"The information you just gave us. We've been worrying about the safety of the Pope for a couple of months, but we had no specific information to make us believe his life was actually at risk. Now you have given that information to us, and someone must decide what to do with it. Do you know anything at all about the operation?"

"No, almost nothing. In Sofia the action officer is the *rezident*, Colonel Bubovoy, Ilya Fedorovich. Senior colonel, he is—Ambassador, can I say? To Bulgarian DS. This Colonel Strokov, this name I know from old cases. He is officer assassin for DS. He do other things, too, yes, but when man need bullet, Strokov deliver bullet, yes?"

This struck Ryan as something from a bad movie, except that in the movies the big, bad CIA was the one with a special assassination department, like a cupboard with vampire bats inside. When the director needed somebody killed, he'd open the door, and one of the bats flew out and made its kill, then flew back docilely to the cupboard and hung upside down until the next man needed killing. Sure, Wilbur. Hollywood had everything figured out, except that government bureaucracies all ran on paper—nothing happened without a written order of some sort, because only a piece of white paper with black ink on it would cover somebody's ass when things went bad—and if somebody really needed killing, someone inside the system had to sign the order, and who would sign *that* kind of order? That sort of thing became a *permanent* record of something bad, and so the signature blank would be bucked all the way to the Oval Office, and once there it just wasn't the sort of paper that would find its way into the Presidential Library that memorialized the person known inside the security community as National Command Authority. And nobody in between would sign the order, because government employees never stuck their necks out—that wasn't the way they were trained.

Except me, Ryan thought. But he wouldn't kill someone in cold blood. He hadn't even killed Sean Miller in very hot blood, and while that was a strange thing to be proud of, it beat the hell out of the alternative.

But Jack wasn't afraid of sticking it out. The loss of his government paycheck would be a net profit for John Patrick Ryan. He could go back to teaching, perhaps at a nice private university that paid halfway decently, and he'd be able to dabble with the stock market on the side, something with which his current job interfered rather badly. . . .

What the hell am I going to do? The worst part of all was that Ryan considered himself to be a Catholic. Maybe he didn't make it to mass every week. Maybe they'd never name a church after him, but, God damn it, the Pope was someone he was compelled by his lengthy education—Catholic schools all the way, including almost twelve years of Jesuits—to respect. And added to that was something equally important—the education he'd received at the gentle hands of the United States Marine Corps at Quantico's Basic School. They'd taught him that when you saw something that needed doing, you damned well did it, and you hoped that your senior officers would bless it afterward, because decisive action had saved the day more than once in the history of the Corps. "It's a lot easier to get forgiveness than permission" was what the major who'd taught that particular class had said, then added with a smile, "But don't you people ever quote me on that." You just had to apply judgment to your action, and such judgment came with experience—but experience often came from bad decisions.

You're over thirty now, Jack, and you've had experience that you never wanted to get, but be damned if you haven't learned a hell of a lot from it. He would have been at least a captain by now, Jack thought. Maybe even a junior major, like Billy Tucker, who'd taught that class. Just then, Kingshot walked back into the room.

"Al, we have a problem," Ryan told him.

"I know, Jack. I just told Sir Basil. He's thinking about it."

"You're a field spook. What do you think?"

"Jack, this is well over my level of expertise and command."

"You turn your brain off, Al?" Ryan asked sharply.

"Jack, we cannot compromise our source, can we?" Kingshot shot back. "That is the paramount consideration here and now."

"Al, we know that somebody is going to try to whack the head of my church. We know his name, and Nick has a photo album on the fucker, remember?" Ryan took a deep breath before going on. "I am not going to sit here and do nothing about it," Ryan concluded, entirely forgetting the presence of the Rabbit for the moment.

"You do nothing? I risk my life for this and you do nothing?" Zaitzev demanded, catching on to the rapid-fire English exchanged in front of him. His face showed both outrage and puzzlement.

Al Kingshot handled the answer. "That is not for us to say. We cannot compromise our source—you, Oleg. We must protect you as well."

"Fuck!" Ryan stood and walked out of the room. But what the hell could he actually do? Jack asked himself. Then he went looking for the secure phone and dialed a number from memory.

"Murray," a voice said after the STUs married up.

"Dan, it's Jack."

"Where you been? I called two nights ago and Cathy said you were in Germany on NATO business. I wanted to—" Ryan just cut him off.

"Stick it, Dan. I was somewhere else doing something else. Listen up. I need some information and I need it in a hurry," Jack announced, lapsing briefly back into the voice of an officer of Marines.

"Shoot," Murray replied.

"I need to know the Pope's schedule for the next week or so." It was Friday. Ryan hoped the Bishop of Rome didn't have anything hopping for the weekend.

"What?" The FBI official's voice communicated predictable puzzlement.

"You heard me."

"What the hell for?"

"Can't tell you—oh, shit," Ryan swore, and then went on. "Dan, we have reason to believe there's a contract out on the Pope."

"Who?" Murray asked.

"It ain't the Knights of Columbus," was all Ryan felt comfortable saying.

"Shit, Jack. Are you serious?"

"What the hell do you think?" Ryan demanded.

"Okay, okay. Let me make some phone calls. What exactly am I free to say?"

That question stopped Ryan cold in his tracks. *Think, boy, think.* "Okay, you're a private citizen and a friend of yours is going to Rome and he wants to eyeball His Holiness. You want to know what's the best way to accomplish that mission. Fair enough?"

"What's Langley say about this?"

"Dan, frankly, I don't care a rat's ass right now, okay? Please, get me that information. I'll call back in an hour. Okay?"

"Roger that, Jack. One hour." Murray hung up. Ryan knew he could trust Murray. He was himself a Jesuit product, like so many FBI agents, in his case a Boston College alum, just like Ryan, and so whatever additional loyalties he had would work in Ryan's favor. Breathing a little easier, Ryan returned to the ducal library.

"Whom did you call, Jack?" Kingshot asked.

"Dan Murray at the embassy, the FBI rep. You ought to know him."

"The Legal Attaché—yes, I do. Okay, what did you ask?"

"The Pope's schedule for the coming week."

"But we don't know anything yet," Kingshot objected.

"Does that make you feel any better, Al?" Jack inquired delicately.

"You did not compro—"

"Compromise our source? You think I'm that stupid?"

The Brit spook nodded to the logic of the moment. "Very well. No harm done, I expect."

The next hour of the first interview returned to routine things. Zaitzev fleshed out for the Brits what he knew about MINISTER. It was sufficiently juicy to give them a good start on IDing the guy. It was immediately clear that Kingshot wanted his hide on the barn door. There was no telling how much good information KGB was getting from him—it was definitely a him, Zaitzev made clear, and "him" was probably a senior civil servant in Whitehall, and soon his residence would be provided by Her Majesty's Government for the indefinite future—"at the Queen's pleasure" was the official phrase. But Jack had more pressing concerns. At 2:20 in the afternoon, he went back to the STU in the next room.

"Dan, it's Jack."

The Legal Attaché spoke without preamble. "He has a busy week ahead, the embassy in Rome tells me, but the Pope is always in the open on Wednesday afternoons. He parades around in his white jeep in St. Peter's Square, right in front of the cathedral, for the people to see him and take his blessing. It's an open car, and, if you want to pop a cap, that sounds to me like a good time to try—unless they have a shooter infiltrated all the way inside. Maybe a cleaning man, plumber, electrician, hard to say, but you have to assume that the inside staff is pretty loyal, and that people keep an eye on them."

Sure, Jack thought, *but those are the guys best suited to do something like this. Only the people you trust can really duck you. Damn.* The best people to look into this were with the Secret Service, but he didn't know anybody in there, and even if he did, getting them into the Vatican bureaucracy—the world's oldest—would require divine intervention.

"Thanks, pal. I owe you one."

"*Semper fi,* bud. Will you be able to tell me more? This sounds like a major case you're working on."

"Probably not, but it's not for me to say, Dan. Gotta run. Later, man." Ryan hung up and reentered the library.

The sun was over the yardarm, and a wine bottle had just appeared, a French white from the Loire Valley, probably a nice old one. There was dust on the bottle. It had been there for a while, and the cellar downstairs would not be stocked with Thunderbird and Wild Irish Rose.

"Zaitzev here has all manner of good information on this MINISTER chap." *Just a matter of dredging it up,* Kingshot didn't add. But tomorrow they'd have skilled psychologists sitting in, using their pshrink skills to massage his memories—maybe even hypnosis. Ryan didn't know if that actually worked or not; though some police forces believed in the technique, a lot of defense lawyers foamed at the mouth over it, and Jack didn't know who was right on that issue. On the whole, it was a shame that the Rabbit wasn't able to come out with photos taken of KGB files, but it would have been asking a lot to request that the guy place his neck not so much on the block as inside the guillotine head-holder and shout for the operator to come over. And so far, Zaitzev had impressed Ryan with his memory.

Might he be a plant, a false defector sent West to give the Agency and others false information? It was possible, but the proof of that pudding would lie in the quality of the agents he identified to the Western counterintelligence services. If MINISTER was really giving out good information, the quality of it would tell the Security Service if he were that valuable an agent. The Russians were never the least bit loyal to their agents—they'd *never*, not once, tried to bargain for an American or British traitor rotting away in prison, as America had often done, sometimes successfully. No, the Russians considered them expendable assets, and such assets were . . . expended, with little more than a covert decoration that would never be worn by its "honored" recipient. It struck Ryan as very strange. The KGB was the most professional of services in so many ways—didn't they know that showing loyalty to an agent would help make other agents willing to take greater chances? Perhaps it was a case of national philosophy overruling common sense. A lot of that went on in the USSR.

By 4:00 local time, Jack could be sure that somebody would be at work at Langley. He asked one more question of the Rabbit.

"Oleg Ivan'ch, do you know if KGB can crack our secure phone systems?"

"I think not. I am not sure, but I know that we have an agent in Washington—code name CRICKET—whom we have asked to get information on your STU telephones for us. As yet he has not been able to provide what our communications people wish. We are afraid that you can read our telephone traffic, however, and so we mainly avoid using telephones for important traffic."

"Thanks." And Ryan went back to the STU in the next room. The next number was another he had memorized.

"This is James Greer."

"Admiral, this is Jack."

"I am told the Rabbit is in his new hutch," the DDI said by way of a greeting.

"That is correct, sir, and the good news is that he believes our comms are secure, including this one. The earlier fears appear to have been exaggerated or misinterpreted."

"Is there bad news?" the DDI asked warily.

"Yes, sir. Yuriy Andropov wants to kill the Pope."

"How reliable is that assertion?" James Greer asked at once.

"Sir, that's the reason he skipped. I'll have chapter and verse to you in a day or two at most, but it's official, there is a no-shit KGB operation to assassinate the Bishop of Rome.We even have the operation designator. You will want to let the Judge in on that, and probably NCA will want to know as well."

"I see," Vice Admiral Greer said from thirty-four hundred miles away. "That's going to be a problem."

"Damned straight it is." Ryan took a breath. "What can we do about it?"

"That's the problem, my boy," the DDI said next. "First, can we do anything about it? Second, do we want to do anything about it?"

"Admiral, why would we *not* want to do something about it?" Ryan asked, trying to keep his voice short of insubordinate. He respected Greer as a boss and as a man.

"Back up, son. Think it all the way through. First, our mission in life is to protect the United States of America, and no one else—well, allies, too, of course," Greer added for the tape recorders that had to be on this line. "But our primary duty is to our flag, not to any religious figure. We *will* try to help him if we can, but if we cannot, then we cannot."

"Very well," Ryan responded through gritted teeth. *What about right and wrong?* He wanted to ask, but that would have to wait a few moments.

"We do not ordinarily give away classified information, and you can imagine how tightly held this defection is going to be," Greer went on.

"Yes, sir." But at least it wasn't going to be NoForn—not for distribution to foreigners. The Brits were foreigners, and they already knew all about Beatrix and the Rabbit, but the Brits weren't big on sharing, except, sometimes, with America, and usually with a big quid pro quo tacked onto it. It was just how things worked. Similarly, Ryan wasn't allowed to discuss a single thing about some operations he was cleared into. Talent Keyhole was the code name: the reconnaissance satellites, though CIA and the Pentagon had fallen all over themselves giving the raw data to the British during the Falklands War, plus every intercept the National Security Agency had from South America. Blood was still thicker than water. "Admiral, how will it look in the papers if it becomes known that the Central Intelligence Agency had data on the threat to the Pope and we just sat on our hands?"

"Is that a—"

"Threat? No, sir, not from me. I play by the rules, sir, and you know it. But somebody there will leak the information just because he's pissed about it, and you know that, and when that happens, there'll be hell to pay."

"Point taken," Greer agreed. "Are you proposing anything?"

"That's above my pay grade, sir, but we have to think hard about possible action of some sort."

"What else are we getting from our new friend?"

"We have the code names of three major leaks. One is Minister, sounds like a political and foreign policy leak in Whitehall. Two for our side of the ocean: Neptune sounds naval, and that's the source of our communications insecurity. Somebody in Redland is reading the Navy's mail, sir. And there's one in D.C. called Cassius. Sounds like a leaker on The Hill, top-drawer political intelligence, plus stuff about our operations."

"Our—you mean CIA?" the DDI asked, with sudden concern in his voice. No matter how old a player you were, no matter how much experience you had, the idea that your parent agency might be compromised scared the living hell out of you.

"Correct," Ryan answered. He didn't need to press that button very hard. Nobody at Langley was entirely comfortable with all the information that went to the "select" intelligence committees in the House and Senate. Politicians talked for a living, after all. Hell, there were few things harder than making a political figure keep his mouth shut. "Sir, this guy is a fantastically valuable source. We'll get him cut loose from over here in three days or so. I think the debriefing process will take months. I've met his wife and daughter. They seem nice enough—the little girl is Sally's age. I think this guy's the real deal, sir, and there's gold in them thar hills."

"How comfortable is he?"

"Well, they're all probably in sensory overload at the moment. I'd think hard about getting a pshrink assigned to them to help with the transition. Maybe more than one. We want to keep him settled down—we want him confident in his new life. That might not be easy, but it'll damned sure pay off for us."

"We have a couple of guys for that. They know how to talk them through the transition part. Is the Rabbit a flight risk?"

"Sir, I see nothing to suggest that, but we have to remember that he's made one hell of a broad jump, and the stuff he landed in isn't exactly what he's used to."

"Noted. Good call, Jack. What else?"

"That's all for the moment. We've only been talking to the guy about five and a half hours, just preliminary stuff so far, but the waters look pretty deep."

"Okay. Arthur is on the phone with Basil right now. I'm going to head over that way and give him your read. Oh, Bob Ritter just got back from Korea—jet-lagged all to hell and gone. We're going to tell him about your adventure in the field. If he tries to bite your head off, it's our fault, mine and the Judge's."

Ryan took a long look down at the carpet. He didn't quite understand why Ritter disliked him, but they didn't swap Christmas cards, and that was a fact. "Gee, thanks, sir."

"Don't sweat it. From what I understand, it sounds like you acquitted yourself pretty well."

"Thanks, Admiral. I didn't trip over my own feet. That's all I'm going to claim, if that's okay with you."

"Fair enough, my boy. Get your write-up completed and fax it to me PDQ."

IN MOSCOW, the secure fax went into the office of Mike Russell. Oddly, it was a graphic, the first-edition cover of *Peter Rabbit* by Beatrix Potter. The address on the cover sheet told him who was supposed to get it. And on the page was a handwritten message: "Flopsy, Mopsy, and Cotton-tail have moved to a new hutch."

So, Russell thought, *they did have a Rabbit case, and it had been successfully run.* Nothing he could claim to know for certain, but he knew the language spoken in the community. He walked down to Ed Foley's office and knocked on the door.

"Come," Foley's voice called.

"This just came in from Washington, Ed." Russell handed the fax across.

"Well, that's good news," the COS observed. He folded the signal into his jacket pocket for Mary Pat. "There's an additional message in this fax, Mike," Foley said.

"What's that?"

"Our comms are secure, pal. Otherwise it would not have come in this way."

"Well, thank the Good Lord for that," Russell said.

CHAPTER 30

FLAVIAN AMPHITHEATER

RYAN? HE DID *WHAT*?" Bob Ritter growled.

"Bob, you want to settle down? It's nothing to get your tits in a flutter about," James Greer said, half soothingly and half an indirect challenge in the CIA's in-house power playground. Judge Moore looked on in amusement. "Jack went into the field to observe an operation for which we had no available field officer. He didn't step on his crank with the golf shoes, and the defector is in a safe house in the English Midlands right now, and from what I hear, he's singing like a canary."

"Well, what's he telling us?"

"For starters," Judge Moore answered, "it seems that our friend Andropov wants to assassinate the Pope."

Ritter's head snapped around. "How solid is that?"

"It's what made the Rabbit decide to take a walk," the DCI said. "He's a conscience defector, and that set him off."

"Okay, good. What does he know?" the DDO asked.

"Bob, it seems that this defector—his name is Oleg Ivanovich Zaitzev, by the way—was a senior watch officer in The Centre's communications, their version of our MERCURY."

"*Shit,*" Ritter observed an instant later. "This is for real?"

"You know, sometimes a guy puts a quarter in the slot and pulls the handle and he really does get the jackpot," Moore told his subordinate.

"Well, damn."

"I didn't think you'd object. And the good part," the DCI went on, "is that Ivan doesn't know he's gone."

"How the hell did we do that?"

"It was Ed and Mary Pat who twigged to that possibility." Then Judge Moore explained how it had been carried out. "They both deserve a nice pat on the head, Bob."

"And all while I was out of town," Ritter breathed. "Well, I'll be damned."

"Yes, there's a bunch of attaboy letters to be drawn up," Greer said next. "Including one for Jack."

"I suppose," the DDO conceded. He went quiet for a moment, thinking over the possibilities of Operation BEATRIX. "Anything good so far?"

"Aside from the plot against the Pope? Two code names of penetration agents they have working: NEPTUNE—he sounds like somebody working in the Navy—and CASSIUS. He's probably on The Hill. More to come, I expect."

"I talked to Ryan a few minutes ago. He's pretty excited about this guy, says his knowledge is encyclopedic, says there's gold in these hills, to quote the boy."

"Ryan does know a thing or two about gold," Moore thought out loud.

"Fine, we'll make him our portfolio manager, but he isn't a field officer," Ritter groused.

"Bob, he succeeded. We don't punish people for that, do we?" the DCI asked. This had gone far enough. It was time for Moore to act like the appeals-court judge he had been until a couple years before: the Voice of God.

"Fine, Arthur. You want me to sign the letter of commendation?" Ritter saw the freight train coming, and there was no sense in standing in its way. What the hell, it would just go into the files anyway. CIA commendations almost never saw the light of day. The Agency even classified the names of field officers who'd died heroically thirty years before. It was like a back door into heaven, CIA style.

"Okay, gentlemen, now that we've settled the administrative issues, what about the plot to kill the Pope?" Greer asked, trying to bring order back to the meeting of supposed sober senior executives.

"How solid is the information?" Ritter wanted to know.

"I talked to Basil a few minutes ago. He thinks we need to take it seriously, but I think we need to talk to this Rabbit ourselves to quantify the danger to our Polish friend."

"Tell the President?"

Moore shook his head. "He's tied up all day today with legislative business, and he's flying out to California late this afternoon. Sunday and Monday, he'll be giving speeches in Oregon and Colorado. I'll see him Tuesday afternoon, about four." Moore could have asked for an urgent meeting—he could break into the President's schedule on really vital matters—but until they had the chance to speak face-to-face with the Rabbit, that was out of the question. The President might even want to speak to the guy himself. He was like that.

"What kind of shape is Station Rome in?" Greer asked Ritter.

"The Chief of Station is Rick Nolfi. Good guy, but he retires in three months. Rome's his sunset post. He asked for it. His wife, Anne, likes Italy. Six officers there, mainly working on NATO stuff—two pretty experienced, four rookies," Ritter reported. "But before we get them alerted we need to think this threat through, and a little Presidential guidance won't hurt. The problem is, how the hell do we tell people about this in such a way as not to compromise the source? Guys," Ritter pointed out, "if we went to all the trouble of concealing the defection, it doesn't make much sense to broadcast the information we get from him out to the four winds, y'know?"

"That is the problem," Moore was forced to agree.

"The Pope doubtless has a protective detail," Ritter went on. "But they can't have the same latitude that the Secret Service does, can they? And we don't know how secure they are."

"IT'S THE OLD STORY," Ryan was saying at the same time in Manchester. "If we use the information too freely, we compromise the source and lose all of its utility. But if we don't use it for fear of compromising it, then we might as well not have the fucking source to begin with." Jack finished off his wine and poured another glass. "There's a book on this, you know."

"What's that?"

"*Double-Edged Secrets.* A guy named Jasper Holmes wrote it. He was a U.S. Navy crippie in World War Two, worked signals intelligence in FRUPAC with Joe Rochefort and his bunch. It's a pretty good book on how the intelligence business works down where the rubber meets the road."

Kingshot made a mental note to look that book up. Zaitzev was out on the lawn—a very plush one—with his wife and daughter at the moment. Mrs. Thompson wanted to take them all shopping. They had to have their private time—their bedroom suite was thoroughly bugged, of course, complete to a white-noise filter in the bathroom—and keeping the wife and kid happy was crucial to the entire operation.

"Well, Jack, whatever the opposition has planned, it will take time for them to set it up. The bureaucracies over there are even more moribund than ours, you know."

"KGB, too, Al?" Ryan wondered. "I think that's the one part of their system that actually works, and Yuriy Andropov isn't known for his patience, is he? Hell, he was their ambassador in Budapest in 1956, remember? The Russians worked pretty decisively back then, didn't they?"

"That was a serious political threat to their entire system," Kingshot pointed out.

"And the Pope isn't?" Ryan fired back.

"You have me there," the field spook admitted.

"Wednesday. That's what Dan told me. He's all the way in the open every Wednesday. Okay, the Pope can appear at that porch he uses to give blessings and stuff, and a halfway good man with a rifle can pop him doing that, but a man with a rifle is too visible to even a casual observer, and a rifle says 'military' to people, and 'military' says 'government' to everybody. But those probably aren't scheduled very far in advance—at least they're irregular, but every damned Wednesday afternoon he hops in his jeep and parades around the Piazza San Pietro right in the middle of the assembled multitude, Al, and that's pistol range." Ryan sat back in his chair and took another sip of the French white.

"I am not sure I'd want to fire a pistol at that close a range."

"Al, once upon a time they got a guy to do Leon Trotsky with an ice axe—engagement range maybe two feet," Ryan reminded him. "Sure, different situation now, but since when have the Russians been reticent about risking their troops—and this will be that Bulgarian bastard, remember? *Your* guy called him an expert killer. It's amazing what a real expert can do. I saw a gunnery sergeant at Quantico—that guy could write his name with a forty-five at fifty feet. I watched him do it once." Ryan had never really mastered the big Colt automatic, but that gunny sure as hell had.

"You're probably being overly concerned."

"Maybe," Jack admitted. "But I'd feel a hell of a lot better if His Holiness wore a Kevlar jacket under his vestments." He wouldn't, of course. People like that didn't scare the way civilians did. It wasn't the sense of invincibility that some professional soldiers had. It was just that to them death wasn't something to be afraid of. Any really observant Catholic was supposed to feel that way, but Jack wasn't one of those. Not quite.

"As a practical matter, what can one do? Look for one face in a crowd, and who's to say it's the right face?" Kingshot asked. "Who's to say Strokov hasn't hired someone else to do the actual shooting? I can see myself shooting someone, but not in a crowd."

"So, you use a suppressed weapon, a big can-type silencer. Cut down the noise, and you remove a lot of the danger of being identified. All the eyes are going to be on the target, remember, not looking sideways into the crowd."

"True," Al conceded.

"You know, it's too damned easy to find reasons to do nothing. Didn't Dr. Johnson say that doing nothing is in every man's power?" Ryan asked forlornly. "That's what we're doing, Al, finding reasons not to do anything. Can we let the guy die? Can we just sit here and drink our wine and *let* the Russians kill the man?"

"No, Jack, but we cannot go off like a loose hand grenade, either. Field operations have to be planned. You need professionals to think things through in a professional way. There are many things professionals can do, but first they have orders to do them."

But that was being decided elsewhere.

"PRIME MINISTER, we have reason to believe that the KGB has an operation under way to assassinate the Pope of Rome," C reported. He'd come over on short notice, interrupting her afternoon political business.

"Really?" she asked Sir Basil in dry reply. She was used to hearing the strangest of things from her Intelligence Chief, and had cultivated the habit of not responding too violently to them. "What is the source for that information?"

"I told you several days ago about Operation BEATRIX. Well, we and the Americans have got him out successfully. We even managed to do it in such a way that the Sovs think him dead. The defector is in a safe house outside Manchester right now," C told his chief of government.

"Have we told the Americans?"

Basil nodded. "Yes, Prime Minister. He's their fox, after all. We'll let him fly to America next week, but I discussed the case briefly earlier today with Judge Arthur Moore, their Director of Central Intelligence. I expect he'll brief the President in early next week."

"What action do you suppose they will take?" she asked next.

"Difficult to say, ma'am. It's a rather dicey proposition, actually. The defector—his name is Oleg—is a most important asset, and we must work very hard to protect his identity, and also knowledge of the fact that he is now on our side of the Curtain. Exactly how we might warn the Vatican of the potential danger is a complex issue, to say the least."

"This is a real operation the Soviets have under way?" the PM asked again. It was rather a lot to swallow, even for them, who she believed capable of almost anything.

"It appears so, yes," Sir Basil confirmed. "But we do not know the priority, and, of course, we know nothing of the schedule."

"I see." The Prime Minister fell quiet for a moment. "Our relations with the Vatican are cordial but not especially close." That fact went all the way back to Henry VIII, though the Roman Catholic Church had gradually come to letting bygones be bygones over the intervening centuries.

"Regrettably, that is so," C agreed.

"I see," she said again, and thought some more before speaking again. When she leaned forward, she spoke with dignity and force. "Sir Basil, it is not the policy of Her Majesty's Government to stand idly by while a friendly Chief of State is murdered by our adversaries. You are directed to look into any possible action that might forestall this eventuality."

Some people shot from the hip, Sir Basil thought. Others shot from the heart. For all her outward toughness, the United Kingdom's Chief of Government was one of the latter.

"Yes, Prime Minister." The problem was that she didn't say how the hell he was supposed to do this. Well, he'd coordinate with Arthur at Langley. But for right now he had a mission that would be difficult at best. What exactly was he supposed to do, deploy a squadron of the Special Air Service to St. Peter's Square?

But you didn't say no to this Prime Minister, at least not in a 10 Downing Street conference room.

"Anything else this defector has told us?"

"Yes, ma'am. He has identified by code name a Soviet penetration agent, probably in Whitehall. The code name is MINISTER. When we get more information about the man in question, we'll have the Security Service root about after him."

"What does he give them?"

"Political and diplomatic intelligence, ma'am. Oleg tells us that it is high-level material, but he has not as yet given us information that would directly identify him."

"Interesting." It was not a new story. This one could be one of the Cambridge group that had been so valuable to the USSR back in the war years and then all the way into the 1960s, or perhaps a person recruited by them. Charleston had been instrumental in purging them out of SIS, but Whitehall wasn't quite his patch. "Do keep me posted on that." A casual order from her had the force of a granite slab hand-delivered from Mt. Sinai.

"Of course, Prime Minister."

"Would it be helpful if I spoke to the American President on this matter with the Pope?"

"Better to let CIA brief him first, I think. It wouldn't do to short-circuit their system. This defector was, after all, mainly an American operation, and it's Arthur's place to speak to him first."

"Yes, I suppose so. But when I do talk to him, I want him to know that we are taking it with the utmost seriousness, and that we expect him to take some substantive action."

"Prime Minister, I should think he will not take it lying down, as it were."

"I agree. He's such a good chap." The full story on America's covert support for the Falkland Islands War would not see the light of day for many years. America had to keep her fences with South America well mended, after all. But neither was the PM one to forget such assistance, covert or not.

"This BEATRIX operation, it was well executed?" she asked C.

"Flawlessly, ma'am," Charleston assured her. "Our people did everything exactly by the book."

"I trust you will look after those who carried it out."

"Most certainly, ma'am," C assured her.

"Good. Thank you for coming over, Sir Basil."

"A pleasure as always, Prime Minister." Charleston stood, thinking that that Ryan fellow would have called her his sort of broad. As, indeed, she was. But all the way back to Century House, he worried about the operation he now had to get under way. What, exactly, would he be doing about it? Figuring such things out, of course, was why he was so lavishly paid.

"HI, HONEY," Ryan said.

"Where are you?" Cathy asked at once.

"I can't say exactly, but I'm back in England. The thing I had to do on the continent—well, it developed into something I have to look after here."

"Can you come home and see us?"

" 'Fraid not." One major problem was that, although his Chatham home was actually within driving distance, he wasn't confident enough yet to drive that far without crunching himself on a side road. "Everybody okay?"

"We're fine, except that you aren't here," Cathy responded, with an edge of anger/disappointment in her voice. One thing she was sure of: Wherever Jack had been, it sure as hell hadn't been Germany. But she couldn't say that over the phone. She understood the intelligence business that much.

"I'm sorry, babe. I can tell you that what I'm doing is pretty important, but that's all."

"I'm sure," she conceded. And she understood that Jack wanted to be home with his family. He wasn't one to skip town for the fun of it.

"How's work?"

"I did glasses all day. Got some surgery tomorrow morning, though. Wait a minute, here's Sally."

"Hi, Daddy," a new and small voice said.

"Hi, Sally. How are you?"

"Fine." What kids *always* said.

"What did you do today?"

"Miss Margaret and I colored."

"Anything good?"

"Yeah, cows and horses!" she reported with considerable enthusiasm. Sally especially liked pelicans and cows.

"Well, I need to talk to Mommy."

"Okay." And Sally would think of this as a deep and weighty conversation, as she went back to the *Wizzerdaboz* tape in the living room.

"And how's the little guy?" Jack asked his wife.

"Chewing on his hands, mostly. He's in the playpen right now, watching the TV."

"He's easier than Sally was at that age," Jack observed with a smile.

"He's not colicky, thank God," Mrs. Dr. Ryan agreed.

"I miss you," Jack said, rather forlornly. It was true. He *did* miss her.

"I miss you, too."

"Gotta get back to work," he said next.

"When will you be home?"

"Couple of days, I think."

"Okay." She had to surrender to that unhappy fact. "Call me."

"Will do, babe."

"Bye."

"See you soon. Love ya."

"I love you, too."

"Bye."

"Bye, Jack."

Ryan put the phone back in the cradle and told himself that he wasn't designed for this kind of life. Like his father before him, he wanted to sleep in the same bed as his wife—had his father ever slept away from home? Jack wondered. He couldn't remember such a night. But Jack had chosen a line of work in which that was not always possible. It was supposed to have been. He was an analyst who worked at a desk and slept at home, but somehow it wasn't working out that way, God damn it.

Dinner was beef Wellington with Yorkshire pudding. Mrs. Thompson could have been head chef at a good restaurant. Jack didn't know where the beef came from, but it seemed more succulent than the usual grass-fed British sort. Either she got the meat in a special place—they still had specialty butcher shops over here—or she really knew how to tenderize it, and the Yorkshire pudding was positively ethereal. Toss in the French wine, and this dinner was just plain brilliant—an adjective popular in the U.K.

The Russians attacked the food rather as Georgiy Zhukov had attacked Berlin, with considerable gusto.

"Oleg Ivan'ch, I have to tell you," Ryan admitted in a fit of honesty, "the food in America is not always of this quality." He'd timed this for Mrs. Thompson's appearance at the dining-room door. Jack turned to her. "Ma'am, if you ever need a recommendation as a chef, you just call me, okay?"

Emma had a very friendly smile. "Thank you, Sir John."

"Seriously, ma'am, this is wonderful."

"You're very kind."

Jack wondered if she'd like his steaks on the grill and Cathy's spinach salad. The key was getting good corn-gorged Iowa beef, which wasn't easy here, though he could try the Air Force commissary at Greenham Commons. . . .

It took nearly an hour to finish dinner, and the after-dinner drinks were excellent. They even served Starka vodka, in a gesture of additional hospitality to their Russian guests. Oleg, Jack saw, really gunned it down.

"Even the Politburo does not eat so well," the Rabbit observed, as dinner broke up.

"Well, we raise good beef in Scotland. This was Aberdeen Angus," Nick Thompson advised, as he collected the plates.

"Fed on corn?" Ryan asked. They didn't have that much corn over here, did they?

"I do not know. The Japanese feed beer to their Kobe beef," the former cop observed. "Perhaps they do that up in Scotland."

"That would explain the quality," Jack replied with a chuckle. "Oleg Ivan'ch, you must learn about British beer. It's the best in the world."

"Not American?" the Russian asked.

Ryan shook his head. "Nope. That's one of the things they do better than us."

"Truly?"

"Truly," Kingshot confirmed. "But the Irish are quite good as well. I do love my Guinness, though it's better in Dublin than in London."

"Why waste the good stuff on you guys?" Jack asked.

"Once a bloody Irishman, always a bloody Irishman," Kingshot observed.

"So, Oleg," Ryan asked, lighting up an after-dinner smoke, "is there anything different we ought to be doing—to make you comfortable, I mean?"

"I have no complaints, but I expect CIA will not give me so fine a house as this one."

"Oleg, I am a millionaire and don't live in a house this nice," Ryan confirmed with a laugh. "But your home in America will be more comfortable than your apartment in Moscow."

"Will I get car?"

"Sure."

"Wait how long?" Zaitzev asked.

"Wait for what? To buy a car?"

Zaitzev nodded.

"Oleg, you can pick from any of hundreds of car dealerships, pick the car you like, pay for it, and drive it home—we usually let our wives pick the color," Jack added.

The Rabbit was incredulous. "So easy?"

"Yep. I used to drive a Volkswagen Rabbit, but I kinda like the Jaguar now. I might get one when I get home. Nice engine. Cathy likes it, but she might go back to a Porsche. She's been driving them since she was a teenager. Of course, it's not real practical with two kids," Ryan added hopefully. He didn't like the German two-seater that much. Mercedes seemed to him a much safer design.

"And buy house, also easy?"

"Depends. If you buy a new house, yes, it's pretty easy. To buy a house that somebody already owns, first you have to meet the owner and make an offer, but the Agency will probably help you with that."

"Where will we live?"

"Anywhere you want." *After we pick your brain clean,* Ryan didn't add. "There's a saying in America: 'It's a free country.' It's also a big country. You can find a place you like and move there. A lot of defectors live in the Washington area. I don't know why. I don't much like it. The summers can be miserable."

"Beastly hot," Kingshot agreed. "And the humidity is awful."

"You think it's bad there, try Florida," Jack suggested. "But a lot of people love it down there."

"And travel from one part to another, no papers?" Zaitzev asked.

For a KGB puke, this guy doesn't know shit, Jack thought. "No papers," Ryan assured him. "We'll get you an American Express card to make that easy." Then he had to explain credit cards to the Rabbit. It took ten minutes, it was so alien a concept to a Soviet citizen. By the end, Zaitzev's head was visibly swimming.

"You do have to pay the bill at the end of the month," Kingshot warned him. "Some people forget that, and they can get into serious financial trouble as a result."

C WAS IN HIS Belgravia townhouse, sipping some Louis XIII brandy and chatting with a friend. Sir George Hendley was a colleague of thirty years' standing. By profession a solicitor, he'd worked closely with the British government for most of his life, often consulting quietly with the Security Service and the Foreign Office. He had a "Most Secret" clearance, plus one into compartmented information. He'd been a confidant of several prime ministers over the years, and was considered as reliable as the Queen herself. He thought it just came along with the Winchester school tie.

"The Pope, eh?"

"Yes, George," Charleston confirmed. "The PM wants us to look into protecting the man. Trouble is, I haven't a clue at the moment. We can't contact the Vatican directly about it."

"Quite so, Basil. One can trust their loyalty, but not their politics. Tell me, how good do you suppose their own intelligence service is?"

"I'd have to say it's top-drawer in many areas. What better confidant than a priest, after all, and what better way to transfer information than inside the confessional? Plus all the other techniques that one can use. Their political intelligence is probably as good as ours—perhaps even better. I would imagine they know everything that happens in Poland, for example. And Eastern Europe probably has few secrets from them as well. One cannot underestimate their ability to call on a man's highest loyalty, after all. We've kept an ear on their communications for decades."

"Is that so?" Hendley asked.

"Oh, yes. During World War Two, they were very valuable to us. There was a German cardinal in the Vatican back then, chap named Mansdorf—odd, isn't it? Sounds like a Jewish name. First name Dieter, archbishop of Mannheim, then promoted to the Vatican diplomatic service. Traveled a lot. Kept us posted on the inner secrets of the Nazi Party from 1938 through to the end of the war. He didn't much care for Hitler, you see."

"And their communications?"

"Mansdorf actually gave us his own cipher book to copy. They changed it after the war, of course, and so we got little more in the way of their private mail later on, but they never changed their cipher system, and the chaps at GCHQ have occasional success listening in. Good man, Dieter Cardinal Mansdorf. Never got recognized for his service, of course. Died in 'fifty-nine, I think."

"So how do we know that the Romans don't know about this operation already?" Not a bad question, Charleston thought, but he'd long since considered that one.

"It is being held very closely, our defector tells us. Hand-delivered messages, not going out on their machine ciphers, that sort of thing. And a bare handful of people involved. The one important name we do know is a Bulgarian field officer, Boris Strokov, colonel in the DS. We suspect he's the chap who killed Georgiy Markov just up the road from my office." Which Charleston considered an act of lèse-majesté, perhaps even executed as a direct challenge to the Secret Intelligence Service. CIA and KGB had an informal covenant: Neither service ever killed in the other's capital. SIS had no such agreement with anyone, a fact that might have cost Georgiy Markov his life.

"So, you think he might be the prospective assassin?"

C waved his hands. "It's all we have, George."

"Not much," Hendley observed.

"Too thin for comfort, but it's better than nothing. We have numerous photos of this Strokov fellow. The Yard was close to arresting him when he flew out of Heathrow—for Paris, actually, and from there on to Sofia."

"Perhaps he was in a hurry to leave?" Hendley suggested.

"He's a professional, George. How many chances do such people take? In retrospect, it's rather amazing that the Yard got a line on him at all."

"So, you think he might be in Italy." A statement, not a question.

"It's a possibility, but whom can we tell?" C asked. "The Italians have criminal jurisdiction to a point. The Lateran Treaty gives them discretionary jurisdiction, subject to a Vatican veto," Charleston explained. He'd had to look into the legalities of the situation. "The Vatican has its own security service—the Swiss Guards, you know—but however good the men are, it's necessarily a thin reed, what with the restrictions imposed on them from above. And the Italian authorities cannot flood the area with their own security forces, for obvious reasons."

"So, the PM has saddled you with an impossible task."

"Yes, again, George," Sir Basil had to agree.

"So, what can you do?"

"All I can really come up with is to put some officers in the crowd and look for this Markov fellow."

"And if they see him?"

"Ask him politely to depart the area?" Basil wondered aloud. "It would work, probably. He is a professional, and being spotted—I suppose we'd ostentatiously take photographs of him—would give him serious pause, perhaps enough to abandon the mission."

"Thin." Hendley thought of that idea.

"Yes, it is," C had to agree. But it would at least give him something to tell the Prime Minister.

"Whom to send?"

"We have a good Station Chief in Rome, Tom Sharp. He has four officers in his shop, plus we could send a few more from Century House, I suppose."

"Sounds reasonable, Basil. Why did you call me over?"

"I was hoping you'd have an idea that's eluded me, George." A final sip from the snifter. As much as he felt like some more brandy for the night, he demurred.

"One can only do what one can," Hendley sympathized.

"He's too good a man to be cut down this way—at the hands of the bloody Russians. And for what? For standing up for his own people. That sort of loyalty is supposed to be rewarded, not murdered in public."

"And the PM feels the same way."

"She is comfortable taking a stand." For which the PM was famous throughout the world.

"The Americans?" Hendley asked.

Charleston shrugged. "They haven't had a chance to speak to the defector yet. They trust us, George, but not that much."

"Well, do what you can. This KGB operation probably will not happen in the immediate future, anyway. How efficient are the Soviets, anyway?"

"We shall see" was all C had to say.

IT WAS QUIETER HERE than in his own house, despite the nearby presence of the motorway, Ryan thought, rolling out of bed at 6:50. The sink continued the eccentric British way of having two faucets, one hot and one cold, making sure that your left hand boiled while the right one froze when you washed your hands. As usual, it felt good to shave and brush and otherwise get yourself ready for the day, even if you had to start it with Taster's Choice.

Kingshot was already in the kitchen when Jack got there. Funny how people slept late on Sunday but frequently not on Saturday.

"Message from London," Al said by way of greeting.

"What's that?"

"A question. How would you feel about a flight to Rome this afternoon?"

"What's up?"

"Sir Basil is sending some people to the Vatican to suss things out. He wants to know if you want to go. It's a CIA op, after all."

"Tell him yes," Jack said without a moment's thought. "When?" Then he realized he was being impetuous again. Damn.

"Noon flight out of Heathrow. You ought to have time to go home and change clothes."

"Car?"

"Nick will drive you over," Kingshot told him.

"What are you going to tell Oleg?"

"The truth. It ought to make him feel more important," Al thought aloud. It was always a good thing for defectors.

RYAN AND THOMPSON left within the hour, with Jack's bags in the "boot."

"This Zaitzev chap," Nick said out on the motorway. "He seems rather an important defector."

"Bet your ass, Nick. He's got all kinds of hot information between his ears. We're going to treat him like a hod full of gold bricks."

"Good of CIA to let us talk to him."

"It'd be kinda churlish not to. You guys got him out for us, and covering the defection up was pretty slick." Jack couldn't say too much more. As trusted as Nick Thompson was, Jack couldn't know how much clearance he had.

The good news was that Thompson knew what not to ask. "So, your father was a police officer?"

"Detective, yeah. Mainly homicide. Did that more than twenty years. He topped out at lieutenant. Said captains never got to do anything more than administrative stuff, and dad wasn't into that. He liked busting bad guys and sending them to the joint."

"The what?"

"Prison. The Maryland State Prison is one evil-looking structure in Baltimore, by Jones Falls. Kinda like a medieval fortress, but more forbidding. The inmates call it Frankenstein's Castle."

"Fine with me, Sir John. I've never had much sympathy for murderers."

"Dad didn't talk about them much. Didn't bring his work home. Mom didn't like hearing about it. Except once, a father killed his son over a crab cake. That's like a little hamburger made out of crab meat," Jack explained. "Dad said it seemed like a shitty thing to get killed over. The father—the killer—copped right out, all broken up about it. But it didn't do his son much good."

"Amazing how many murderers react that way. They gather up the rage to take a life, then afterwards they are consumed by remorse."

"Too soon old, too late smart," Jack quoted from the Old West.

"Indeed. The whole business can be so bloody sad."

"What about this Strokov guy?"

"Different color of horse, entirely," Thompson replied. "You don't see many of those. For them it's part of the job, ending a life. No motive in the usual sense, and they leave little behind in the way of physical evidence. They can be very difficult to find, but mainly we do find them. We have time on our side, and sooner or later someone talks and it gets to our ear. Most criminals talk their own way into prison," Nick explained. "But people like this Strokov fellow, they do not talk—except when he gets home and writes up his official report. But we never see those. Getting a line on him was plain luck. Mr. Markov remembered being poked by the umbrella, remembered the color suit the man was wearing. One of our constables saw him wearing the same suit and thought there was something odd about him—you know, instead of flying right home, he waited to make sure Markov died. They'd bungled two previous attempts, you see, and so they called him in because of his expertise. Good professional, Strokov. He wanted to be completely sure, and he waited to read the death notice in the newspapers. In that time, we talked to the staff at his hotel and started assembling information. The Security Service got involved, and they were helpful in some ways but not in others—and the government got involved. The government was worried about creating an international incident, and so they held us up—cost us two days, I reckon. On the first of those two days, Strokov took a taxi to Heathrow and flew off to Paris. I was on the surveillance team. Stood within fifteen feet of him. We had two detectives with cameras, shot a lot of pictures. The last was of Strokov walking down the jetway to the Boeing. Next day, the government gave us permission to detain him for questioning."

"Day late and a dollar short, eh?"

Thompson nodded. "Quite. I would have liked to put him in the dock at the Old Bailey, but that fish got away. The French shadowed him at De Gaulle International, but he never left the international terminal, never talked with anyone. The bugger showed no remorse at all. I suppose for him it was like chopping firewood," the former detective said.

"Yeah. In the movies you make your hit and have a martini, shaken not stirred. But it's different when you kill a good guy."

"All Markov ever did was broadcast over BBC World Service," Nick said, gripping the wheel a little tightly. "I imagine the people in Sofia were somewhat put out with what he said."

"The people on the other side of the Curtain aren't real big on Freedom of Speech," Ryan reminded him.

"Bloody barbarians. And now this chap is planning to kill the Pope? I am not a Catholic, but he is a man of God, and he seems rather a good chap. You know, the most vicious criminal hesitates before trifling with a man of the clergy."

"Yeah, I know. Doesn't do to piss God off. But they don't believe in God, Nick."

"Fortunate for them that I am not God."

"Yeah, it would be nice to have the power to right all the wrongs in the world. The problem is, that's what Markov's bosses think they're doing."

"That is why we have laws, Jack—yes, I know, they make up their own."

"That's the problem," Jack agreed as they came into Chatham.

"This is a pleasant area," Thompson said, turning up the hill on City Way.

"Not a bad neighborhood. Cathy likes it. I would have preferred closer to London, but, well, she got her way."

"Women usually do." Thompson chuckled, turning right onto Fristow Way and then left on Grizedale Close. And there was the house. Ryan got out and retrieved his bags.

"Daddy!" Sally screamed when he walked in the door. Ryan dropped his bags and scooped her up. Little girls, he'd long since learned, gave the best hugs, though their kisses tended to be a little sloppy.

"How's my little Sally?"

"Fine." It was oddly like a cat, coming out of her mouth.

"Oh, hello, Dr. Ryan," Miss Margaret said in greeting. "I didn't expect you."

"Just making a low pass. Have to change cleans for dirties and head back out."

"You going away *again*?" Sally asked with crushing disappointment in her voice.

"Sorry, Sally. Daddy has business."

Sally wriggled out of his arms. "Phooey." And she went back to the TV, putting her father firmly in his place.

Jack took the cue to go upstairs. Three—no, four—clean shirts, five sets of underwear, four new ties, and . . . yes, some casual wear, too. Two new jackets, two pairs of slacks. His Marine tie bar. That about did it. He left the pile of dirties on the bed and, with his bags packed, headed back down. Oops. He set his bags down and went back upstairs for his passport. No sense using the fake Brit one anymore.

"Bye, Sally."

"Bye, Daddy." But then she thought again and jumped to her feet to give him another hug. She wouldn't grow up to break hearts, but to rip them out and cook them over charcoal. But that was a long way off, and for now her father had the chance to enjoy her. Little Jack was asleep on his back in the playpen, and his father decided not to disturb him.

"See ya, buddy," Ryan said as he turned to the door.

"Where are you going?" Miss Margaret asked.

"Out of the country. Business," Jack explained. "I'll call Cathy from the airport."

"Good trip, Dr. Ryan."

"Thanks, Margaret." And back out the door.

"How are we on time?" Ryan asked, back in the car.

"No problem," Thompson thought out loud. If they were late, this airliner, too, would have a minor mechanical problem.

"Good." Jack adjusted his seat to lean back and get a few winks.

He awoke just outside Heathrow Terminal Three. Thompson drove up to where a man in civilian clothes was standing. He looked like some sort of government worker.

He was. As soon as Ryan alighted from the car, the man came over with a ticket envelope.

"Sir, your flight leaves in forty minutes, Gate Twelve," the man reported. "You'll be met in Rome by Tom Sharp."

"What's he look like?" Jack asked.

"He will know you, sir."

"Fair enough." Ryan took the tickets and headed to the back of the car for his bags.

"I'll take care of that for you, sir."

This sort of traveling had its possibilities, Jack thought. He waved at Thompson and headed into the terminal, looking for Gate Twelve. That proved easy enough. Ryan took a seat close by the gate and checked his ticket—1-A again, a first-class ticket. The SIS must have had a comfortable understanding with British Airways. Now all he had to do was survive the flight.

He boarded twenty minutes later, sitting down, strapping in, and turning his watch forward one hour. He endured the usual rigmarole of useless safety briefing and instructions on how to buckle his seat belt, which, in Jack's case, was already clicked and snugged in.

The flight took two hours, depositing Jack at Leonardo da Vinci Airport at 3:09 local time. Jack walked off the aircraft and looked for the Blue Channel to get his diplomatic passport stamped after a wait of about five seconds—one other diplomat had been ahead of him, and the bonehead had forgotten which pocket his passport was in.

With that done, he retrieved his bags off the carousel and headed out. A man with a gray and brown beard seemed to be eyeballing him.

"You're Jack Ryan?"

"You must be Tom Sharp."

"Correct. Let me help you with your bags." Why people did this, Ryan didn't know, though on reflection, he'd done it himself often enough, and the Brits were the world champions at good manners.

"And you are?" Ryan asked.

"Station Chief Rome," Sharp replied. "C called to say you were coming in, Sir John, and that I ought to meet you personally."

"Good of Basil," Jack thought out loud.

Sharp's car was, in this case, a Bentley sedan, bronze in color, with left-hand driver's seat in deference to the fact that they were in a barbarian country.

"Nice wheels, fella."

"My cover is Deputy Chief of Mission," Sharp explained. "I could have had a Ferrari, but it seemed a little too ostentatious. I do little actual field work, you see, just administrative things. I actually *am* the DCM of the embassy. Too much diplomatic work—that can drive one mad."

"How's Italy?"

"Lovely place, lovely people. Not terribly well organized. They say we Brits muddle through things, but we're bloody Prussians compared to this lot."

"Their cops?"

"Quite good, actually. Several different police forces. Best of the lot are the Carabinieri, paramilitary police of the central government. Some of them are excellent. Down in Sicily they're trying to get a handle on the Mafia—pig of a job that is, but, you know, eventually I think they will succeed."

"You briefed in on why they sent me down?"

"Some people think Yuriy Vladimirovich wants to kill the Pope? That's what my telex said."

"Yeah. We just got a defector out who says so, and we think he's giving us the real shit."

"Any details?"

" 'Fraid not. I think they sent me down here to work with you until somebody figures out the right thing to do. Looks to me like an attempt might be made Wednesday."

"The weekly appearance in the square?"

Jack nodded. "Yep." They were on the highway from the airport to Rome. The country looked odd to Ryan, but it took a minute to figure out why. Then he got it. The pitch of the roofs was different—shallower than what he was used to. They probably didn't get much snow here in winter. Otherwise the houses looked rather like sugar cubes, painted white to reject the heat of the Italian sun. Well, every country had its unique architecture.

"Wednesday, eh?"

"Yeah. We're also looking for a guy named Boris Strokov, colonel in the Bulgarian DS. Sounds like a professional killer."

Sharp concentrated on the road. "I've heard the name. Wasn't he a suspect in the Georgiy Markov killing?"

"That's the guy. They ought to be sending some photos of him."

"Courier on your flight," Sharp reported. "Taking a different way into the city."

"Any ideas on what the hell to do?"

"We'll get you settled at the embassy—my house, actually, two blocks away. It's rather nice. Then we'll drive down to Saint Peter's and look around, get a feel for things. I've been there to see the artwork and such—the Vatican art collection is on a par with the Queen's—but I've never worked there per se. Ever been to Rome?"

"Never."

"Very well, let's take a drive-about first instead, give you a quick feel for the place."

Rome seemed a remarkably disorganized place—but so did a street map of London, whose city fathers had evidently not been married to the city mothers. And Rome was older by a thousand years or so, built when the fastest thing going was a horse, and they were slower in real life than in a John Ford Western. Not many straight lines for the roads, and a meandering river in the middle. Everything looked old to Ryan—no, not old but *old,* as though dinosaurs had once walked the streets. That was a little hard to reconcile with the automobile traffic, of course.

"That's the Flavian Amphitheater. It was called the Coliseum because the Emperor Nero had built a large statue of himself right there"—Sharp pointed—"and the people took to calling the stadium by that name, rather to the annoyance of the Flavian family, which built the place out of proceeds from the Jewish rebellion that Josephus wrote about."

Jack had seen it on TV and in the movies, but that wasn't quite the same as driving past it. Men had built that with nothing more than sweat power and hemp ropes. Its shape was strangely reminiscent of Yankee Stadium in New York. But Babe Ruth had never spilled a guy's guts out in the Bronx. A lot of that had happened here. It was time for Ryan to make an admission.

"You know, if they ever invent a time machine, I think I might like to come back and see what it was like. Makes me a barbarian, doesn't it?"

"Just their version of rugby," Sharp said. "And the football here can be pretty tough."

"Soccer is a girl's game," Jack snorted.

"You *are* a barbarian, Sir John. Soccer," he explained in his best accent, "is a gentleman's game played by thugs, while rugby is a thug's game played by gentlemen."

"I'll take your word for it. I just want to see the *International Tribune.* My baseball team's in the World Series, and I don't even know how it's going."

"Baseball? Oh, you mean rounders. Yes, that is a girl's game," Sharp announced.

"I've had this talk before. You Brits just don't understand."

"As you do not understand proper football, Sir John. In Italy it's even more a national passion than at home. They tend to play a fiery game, rather different from the Germans, for example, who play like great bloody machines."

It was like listening to the distinction between a curveball and a slider or a screwball and a forkball. Ryan wasn't all that good a baseball fan to be able to grasp all the distinctions; it depended on the TV announcer, who probably just made it up anyway. But he knew that there wasn't a player in baseball who could smack a good curveball on the outside corner.

Saint Peter's Basilica was five minutes after that.

"Damn!" Jack breathed.

"Big, isn't it?"

It wasn't big; it was *vast.*

Sharp went to the left side of the cathedral, ending up in what looked like an area of shops—jewelry, it seemed—where he parked.

"Let's take a look, shall we?"

Ryan took the chance to leave the car and stretch his legs, and he had to remind himself that he was not here to admire the architecture of Bramante and Michelangelo. He was here to scout the terrain for a mission, as he had been taught to plan for at Quantico. It wasn't really all that hard if you spoke the language.

From above, it must have looked like an old-fashioned basketball key. The circular part of the piazza looked to be a good two hundred yards in diameter, then narrowed down to perhaps a third of that as you got away from the monstrous bronze doors to the church itself.

"When he sees the crowd, he boards his car—rather like a cross between a jeep and a golf trolley—just there, and he follows a cleared path in the crowd along this way," Sharp explained, "around there, and back. Takes about, oh, twenty minutes or so, depending on whether he stops the car for—what you Americans call pressing the flesh. I suppose I shouldn't compare him to a politician. He seems a very decent chap, a genuinely good man. Not all the popes have been so, but this one is. And he's no coward. He's had to live through the Nazis and the communists, and that never turned him a single degree from his path."

"Yeah, he must like riding the point of the lance," Ryan murmured in reply. There was just one thing occupying his mind now. "Where's the sun going to be?"

"Just at our backs."

"So, if there's a bad guy, he'll stand just about here, sun behind him, not in his eyes. People looking that way from the other side have the sun in *their* eyes. Maybe it's not all that much, but when your ass is on the line, you play every card in your hand. Ever been in uniform, Tom?"

"Coldstream Guards, *lef*tenant through a captaincy. Saw some action in Aden, but mainly served in the BOAR. I agree with your estimate of the situation," Sharp said, turning to do his own evaluation. "And professionals are somewhat predictable, since they all study out of the same syllabus. But what about a rifle?"

"How many men you have to use for this?"

"Four, besides myself. C might send more down from London, but not all that many."

"Put one up there?" Ryan gestured to the colonnade. Seventy feet high? Eighty? About the same height as the perch Lee Harvey Oswald had used to do Jack Kennedy . . . *with an Italian rifle,* Jack reminded himself. That was good for a brief chill.

"I can probably get a man up there disguised as a photographer." And long camera lenses made for good telescopes.

"How about radios?"

"Say, six civilian-band walkie-talkies. If we don't have them at the embassy, I can have them flown in from London."

"Better to have military ones, small enough to conceal—we had one in the Corps that had an earpiece like from a transistor radio. Also better if it's encrypted, but that might be hard." *And such systems,* Ryan didn't add, *are not entirely reliable.*

"Yes, we can do that. You have a good eye, Sir John."

"I wasn't a Marine for long, but the way they teach lessons in the Basic School, it's kinda hard to forget them. This is one hell of a big place to cover with six men, fella."

"And not something SIS trains us to do," Sharp added.

"Hey, the U.S. Secret Service would cover this place with over a hundred trained agents—shit, maybe more—plus try to get intel on every hotel, motel, and flophouse in the area." Jack let out a breath. "Mr. Sharp, this is not possible. How thick are the crowds?"

"It varies. In the summer tourist season, there are enough people here to fill Wembley Stadium. This coming week? Certainly thousands," he estimated. "How many is hard to reckon."

This mission is a real shitburger, Ryan told himself.

"Any way to hit the hotels, try to get a line on this Strokov guy?"

"More hotels in Rome than in London. It's a lot to cover with four field officers. We can't get any help from the local police, can we?"

"What guidance on that from Basil?" Ryan inquired, already guessing the answer.

"Everything is on close hold. No, we cannot let anyone know what we're doing."

He couldn't even call for help from CIA's local station, Jack realized. Bob Ritter would never sanction it. *Shitburger* was optimistic.

CHAPTER 31

BRIDGE BUILDER

SHARP'S OFFICIAL RESIDENCE was as impressive in its way as the safe house outside Manchester. There was no guessing what—whom—it had been built for, and Ryan was tired of asking anyway. He had a bedroom and a private bathroom, and that was enough. The ceilings were high in every room, presumably defense against the hot summers Rome was known for. It had been about 80 during the afternoon drive, warm, but not too bad for someone from the Baltimore-Washington area, though to an Englishman it must have seemed like the very boiler room of hell. *Whoever had written about mad dogs and Englishmen must have lived in another age,* Jack thought. In London, people started dropping dead in the street when it got to 75. As it was, he thought he had three days to worry, and one in which to execute whatever plan he and Sharp managed to come up with—in the hope that nothing at all would happen, and that CIA would come up with a way to warn His Holiness's security troops that they needed to firm up their means of seeing to his physical safety. Christ, the guy even wore white, the better to make a perfect sight picture for whatever gun the bad guy might use—like a great big paper target blank for the bad guy to put his rounds into. George Armstrong Custer hadn't walked into a worse tactical environment, but at least he'd done it with open eyes, albeit clouded by lethal pride and faith in his own luck. The Pope didn't live under that illusion. No, he believed that God would come and collect him whenever it suited His purpose, and that was *that.* Ryan's personal beliefs were not all that different from the Polish priest's, but he figured that God had given him brains and free will for a reason—did that make Jack an instrument of God's will? It was too deep a question for the moment, and besides, Ryan wasn't a priest to dope that one out. Maybe it was a lack of faith. Maybe he believed in the real world too much. His wife's job was to fix health problems, and were those problems visited upon people by God Himself? Some thought so. Or were those problems things God merely allowed to happen so that people like Cathy could fix them, and thus do His work? Ryan tended to this view, and the Church must have agreed, since it had built so many hospitals across the world.

But for damned sure, the Lord God didn't approve of murder, and it was now Jack's mission to stop one from happening, if that was possible. Certainly he wasn't one to stand by and ignore it. A priest would have to limit himself to persuasion or, at most, passive interference. Ryan knew that if he saw a criminal drawing a bead on the Pope—or, for that matter, anyone else—and he had a gun in his hand, he wouldn't hesitate more than a split second to interrupt the act with a pistol bullet of his own. Maybe that was just how he was made up, maybe it was the things he'd learned from his dad, maybe it was his training in the Green Machine, but for whatever reason, the use of physical force would not make him faint away—at least not until after he'd done the act. There were a few people in hell to prove that fact. And so Jack started the mental preparation for what he'd have to do, maybe, if the Bad Guys were in town and he saw them. Then it hit him that he wouldn't even have to answer for it—not with diplomatic status. The State Department had the right to withdraw his protection under the Vienna Convention, but, no, not in a case like this they wouldn't. So whatever he did could be a freebie, and that wasn't so bad a deal, was it?

The Sharps took him out for dinner—just a neighborhood place, but the food was brilliant, renewed proof that the best Italian restaurants are often the little mom-and-pop places. Evidently, the Sharps ate there often, the staff was so friendly to them.

"Tom, what the hell are we going to do?" Jack asked openly, figuring that Annie had to know what he did for a living.

"Churchill called it KBO—keep buggering on." He shrugged. "We do the best we can, Jack."

"I suppose I'd feel a hell of a lot better with a platoon of Marines to back my play."

"As would I, my boy, but one does the best one can with what one has."

"Tommy," Mrs. Sharp said. "What exactly are you two talking about?"

"Can't say, my dear."

"But you are CIA," she said next, looking at Jack.

"Yes, ma'am," Ryan confirmed. "Before that, I taught history at the Naval Academy in Annapolis, and before that I traded stocks, and before that I was a Marine."

"Sir John, you're the one who—"

"And I'll never live it down, either." Why the hell, Jack wondered, hadn't he just kept his wife and daughter behind that tree on the Mall in London and let Sean Miller do his thing? Cathy would have gotten some pictures and that would have helped with the police, after all. No good—or dumb—deed ever went unpunished, he supposed. "And you can stop the Sir John stuff. I do not own a horse or a steel shirt." And his only sword was the Mameluke that the Marine Corps gave to its officers upon graduation at Quantico.

"Jack, a knight is ceremonially one who will take up arms in protection of the sovereign. You've done that twice, if memory serves. You are, therefore, entitled to the honorific," Sharp pointed out.

"You guys never forget, do you?"

"Not something like that, Sir John. Courage under fire is one of the things worth remembering."

"Especially in nightmares, but in those the gun never works, and, yeah, sometimes I have them," Jack admitted, for the first time in his life. "What are we doing tomorrow, Tom?"

"I have embassy work in the morning. Why don't you scout the area some more, and I can join you for lunch."

"Fair enough. Meet where?"

"Just inside the Basilica, to the right, is Michelangelo's *Pietá.* Just there at one fifteen exactly."

"Fair enough," Jack agreed.

"SO, WHERE IS RYAN?" the Rabbit asked.

"Rome," Alan Kingshot answered. "He's looking into what you told us." All of this day had been occupied with uncovering what he knew of KGB operations in the UK. It turned out to be quite a lot, enough that the three-man Security Service team had positively drooled as they took their notes. Ryan had been wrong, Kingshot thought over dinner. This fellow wasn't a gold mine. No, he was Kimberly, and the diamonds just spilled out from his mouth. Zaitzev was relaxing a little more, enjoying his status. *As well he might,* Alan thought. Like the man who'd invented the computer chip, this Rabbit was set for life, all the carrots he could eat, and men with guns would protect his hole in the ground against all bears.

The Bunny, as he thought of her, had discovered Western cartoons today. She especially liked "Roadrunner," immediately noting the similarity to the Russian "Hey, Wait a Minute," and laughing through every one of them.

Irina, on the other hand, was rediscovering her love for the piano, playing the big Bösendorfer in the home's music room, making mistakes but learning from them, and starting to recover her former skills, to the admiring looks of Mrs. Thompson, who'd never learned to play herself, but who'd found reams of sheet music in the house for Mrs. Zaitzev to try her hand at.

This family, Kingshot thought, *will do well in the West.* The child was a child. The father had tons of good information. The mother would breathe free and play her music to her heart's content. They would wear their newfound freedom like a loose and comfortable garment. They were, to use the Russian word, *kulturniy,* or cultured people, fit representatives of the rich culture which had long predated communism. Good to know that not all defectors were alcoholic ruffians.

"LIKE A CANARY on amphetamines, Basil says," Moore told his senior people in the den of his home. "He says this guy will give us more information than we can easily use."

"Oh, yeah? Try us," Ritter thought out loud.

"Indeed, Bob. When do we get him over here?" Admiral Greer asked.

"Basil asked for two more days to get him over. Say, Thursday afternoon. I'm having the Air Force send a VC-137 over. Might as well do it first class," the Judge observed generously. It wasn't *his* money, after all. "Basil's alerted his people in Rome, by the way, just in case KGB is running fast on their operation to whack the Pope."

"They're not that efficient," Ritter said with some confidence.

"I'd be careful about that, Bob," the DDI thought out loud. "Yuriy Vladimirovich isn't noted for his patience." Greer was not the first man to make that observation.

"I know, but their system grinds slower than ours."

"What about the Bulgarians?" Moore asked. "They think the shooter is a guy named Strokov, Boris Strokov. He's probably the guy who killed Georgiy Markov on Westminster Bridge. Experienced assassin, Basil thinks."

"It figures they'd use the Bulgars," Ritter observed. "They're the Eastern Bloc's Murder Incorporated, but they're still communists, and they're chess players, not high-noon types. But we still haven't figured out how to warn the Vatican. Can we talk to the Nuncio about this?"

They'd all had a little time to think through that question, and now it was time to face it again. The Papal Nuncio was the Vatican's ambassador to the United States, Giovanni Cardinal Sabatino. Sabatino was a longtime member of the Pope's own diplomatic service and was well regarded by the State Department's career foreign-service officers, both for his sagacity and his discretion.

"Can we do it in such a way as not to compromise the source?" Greer wondered.

"We can say some Bulgarian talked too much—"

"Pick that fictional source carefully, Judge," Ritter warned. "Remember, the DS has that special subunit. It reports directly to their Politburo, and they don't write much down, according to what sources we have over there. Kinda like the commie version of Albert Anastasia. This Strokov guy is one of them, or so we have heard."

"We could say their party chairman talked to a mistress. He has a few," Greer suggested. The Director of Intelligence had all manner of information on the intimate habits of world leaders, and the Bulgarian party boss was a man of the people in the most immediate of senses. Of course, if this ever leaked, life might get difficult for the women in question, but adultery had its price, and the Bulgarian chairman was such a copious drinker that he might not remember to whom he'd (never) said what would be attributed to him. That might serve to salve their consciences a little.

"Sounds plausible," Ritter opined.

"When could we see the Nuncio?" Moore asked.

"Middle of the week, maybe?" Ritter suggested again. They all had a full week before them. The Judge would be on The Hill doing budget business until Wednesday morning.

"Where?" They couldn't bring him here, after all. The churchman wouldn't come. Too much potential unpleasantness if anyone noticed. And Judge Moore couldn't go to the Nuncio. His face, also, was too well known by the Washington establishment.

"Foggy Bottom," Greer thought out loud. Moore went to see the Secretary of State often enough, and the Nuncio wasn't exactly a stranger there.

"That'll work," the DCI decided. "Let's get it set up." Moore stretched. He hated having to do work on a Sunday. Even a judge of the appeals court got weekends off.

"There's still the issue of what they can actually do with the information," Ritter warned them. "What is Basil doing?"

"He's got his Rome Station rooting around, only five of them, but he's going to send some more troops from London tomorrow just in case they try to make their hit on Wednesday—that's when His Holiness appears in public. I gather he has a pretty busy work schedule, too."

"Shame he can't call off the ride around the plaza, but I guess he wouldn't listen if anybody asked."

"Not hardly," Moore agreed. He didn't bring up the word from Sir Basil that Ryan had been dispatched to Rome. Ritter would just throw another conniption fit, and Moore wasn't up to that on a Sunday.

RYAN AROSE EARLY, as usual, had his breakfast, and caught a taxi to St. Peter's. It was good to walk around the square—which was almost entirely round, of course—just to stretch his legs. It seemed odd that here, inside the capital of the Italian Republic, was a titularly sovereign state whose official language was Latin. He wondered if the Caesars would have liked that or not, the last home of their language also being the home of the agency that had brought down their world-spanning empire, but he couldn't go to the Forum to ask whatever ghosts lived there.

The church commanded his attention. There were no words for something that large. The funds to build it had necessitated the indulgence selling that had sparked Martin Luther to post his protest on the cathedral door and so start the Reformation, something the nuns at St. Matthew's had not approved of, but for which the Jesuits of his later life had taken rather a broader view. The Society of Jesus also owed its existence to the Reformation—they'd been founded to fight against it.

That didn't much matter at the moment. The basilica beggared description, and it seemed a fit headquarters for the Roman Catholic Church. He walked in and saw that, if anything, the interior seemed even more vast than the outside. You could play a football game in there. A good hundred yards away was the main altar, reserved for use by the Pope himself, under which was the crypt where former popes were buried, including, tradition had it, Simon Peter himself. "Thou art Peter," Jesus was quoted in the Gospel, "and upon this rock I shall build my church." Well, with the help of some architects and what must have been an army of workers, they'd certainly built a church here. Jack felt drawn into it as though it were God's own personal house. The cathedral in Baltimore would scarcely have been an alcove here. Looking around, he saw the tourists, also staring at the ceiling with open mouths. *How had they built this place without structural steel?* Jack wondered. It was all stone resting on stone. *Those old guys really knew their stuff,* Ryan reflected. The sons of those engineers now worked for Boeing or NASA. He spent a total of twenty minutes walking around, then reminded himself that he wasn't, after all, a tourist.

This had once been the site of the original Roman Circus Maximus. The big racetrack for chariots, like those in the movie *Ben-Hur*, had then been torn down and a church built here, the original St. Peter's, but over time that church had deteriorated, and so a century-plus-long project to build this one had been undertaken and was finished in the sixteenth century, Ryan remembered. He went back outside to survey the area once again. Much as he looked for alternatives, it seemed that his first impression had been the correct one. The Pope got in his car *there*, drove around *that way*, and the place of greatest vulnerability was . . . *right about there.* The problem was that *there* was a semicircular space perhaps two hundred yards long.

Okay, he thought, *time to do some analysis.* The shooter would be a pro. A pro would have two considerations: one, getting a good shot off; and two, getting the hell out of here alive.

So Ryan turned to see potential exit routes. To the left, closest to the façade of the church, people would really pile up there in their desire to get the first look at the Pope as he came out. Farther down, the open vehicle path widened somewhat, increasing the range of the shot—something to be avoided. But the shooter still needed to get his ass out of Dodge City, and the best way to do that was toward the side street where Sharp had parked the day before. You could stash a car there, probably, and if you made it that far, you'd go pedal-to-the-metal and race the hell off to wherever you had a backup car parked—a backup, because the cops would sure as hell be looking for the first one, and Rome had a goodly supply of police officers who'd run through fire to catch whoever had popped a cap on the Pope.

Back to the shooting place. He wouldn't want to be in the thickest part of the crowd, so he wouldn't want to be too close to the church. But he'd want to boogie out through *that* arch. Maybe sixty or seventy yards. Ten seconds, maybe? With a clear path, yeah, about that. Double it, just to be sure. He'd probably yell something like *"There he goes!"* as a distraction. It might make him easier to identify later, but Colonel Strokov will be figuring to sleep Wednesday night in Sofia. *Check flight times*, Jack told himself. *If he takes the shot and gets away, he won't be swimming home, will he? No, he'll opt for the fastest way out—unless he has a really deep hidey-hole here in Rome.*

That was a possibility. The problem was that he was dealing with an experienced field spook, and he could have a lot of things planned. But this was reality, not a movie, and professionals kept things simple, because even the simplest things could go to shit in the real world.

He'll have at least one backup plan. Maybe more, but sure as hell he'll have one.

Dress up like a priest, maybe? There were a lot of them in evidence. Nuns, too—more than Ryan had ever seen. *How tall is Strokov?* Anything over five-eight and he'd be too tall for a nun. But if he dressed as a priest, you could hide a fucking RPG in a cassock. That was a pleasant thought. But how fast could one run in a cassock? That was a possible downside.

You have to assume a pistol, probably a suppressed pistol. A rifle—no, its dangers lay in its virtues. It was so long that the guy standing next to him could bat the barrel off target, and he'd never get a good round off. An AK-47, maybe, able to go rock-and-roll? But, no, it was only in the movies that people fired machine guns from the hip. Ryan had tried it with his M-16 at Quantico. It felt real John Wayne, but you just couldn't hit shit that way. The sights, the gunnery sergeants had all told his class at the Basic School, are there for a reason. Like Wyatt Earp shooting on TV—draw and fire from the hip. It just didn't work unless your other hand was on the fucker's shoulder. The sights are there for a reason, to tell you where the weapon is pointed, because the bullet you're shooting is about a third of an inch in diameter, and you are, in fact, shooting *at* a target just that small, and a hiccup could jerk you off target, and under stress your aim just gets worse . . . unless you're used to the idea of killing people. Like Boris Strokov, colonel of the *Dirzhavna Sugurnost.* What if he was one of those who just didn't rattle, like Audie Murphy of the Third Infantry Division in WWII? But how many people like that were around? Murphy had been one in eight million American soldiers, and nobody had seen that deadly quality in him before it just popped out on the battlefield, probably surprising even him. Murphy himself probably never appreciated how different he was from everybody else.

Strokov is a pro, Jack reminded himself. *And so he'll act like a pro. He'll plan every detail, especially the getaway.*

"You must be Ryan," a British voice said quietly. Jack turned to see a pale man with red hair.

"Who are you?"

"Mick King," the man replied. "Sir Basil sent the four of us down. Sussing the area out?"

"How obvious am I?" Ryan worried suddenly.

"You could well be an architecture student." King blew it off. "What do you think?"

"I think the shooter would stand right about here, and try to boogie on out that way," Jack said, pointing. King looked around before speaking.

"It's a dicey proposition, however one plans it, with all the people sure to be here, but, yes, that does look the most promising option," the spook agreed.

"If I were planning to do it myself, I'd want to use a rifle from up there. We'll need to have somebody topside to handle that possibility."

"Agreed. I'll have John Sparrow go up there. The chap with short hair over there. He brought a ton of cameras with him."

"One more man to camp out in the street that way. Our bird will probably have a car to skip town with, and that's where I'd park it."

"A little too convenient, don't you think?"

"Hey, I'm an ex-Marine, not a chess master," Ryan replied. But it was good to have somebody second-guessing him. There were a lot of tactical possibilities here, and everybody read a map a little differently, and Bulgarians might well study out of a different playbook altogether.

"It's a pig of a mission they've given us. Best hope is that this Strokov fellow doesn't show up. Oh, here he is," King said, handing Ryan an envelope.

It was full of eight-by-ten prints, actually of pretty good quality.

"Nick Thompson told me he has lifeless eyes," Ryan said, looking at one of them.

"Does seem rather a cold chap, doesn't he?"

"When we come here Wednesday, we going to be carrying?"

"I certainly shall be," King said positively. "Nine-millimeter Browning. There ought to be a few more at the embassy. I know you can shoot accurately under pressure, Sir John," he added, with casual respect.

"It doesn't mean I like to, pal." And the best engagement range for any pistol was contact range, holding the gun right against the other bastard. Kinda hard to miss that way. It would even cut the noise down, too. Plus, it was a hell of a good way to tell someone not to do anything untoward.

For the next two hours, the five men walked the piazza, but they kept coming back to the same place.

"We can't cover it all, not without a hundred men," Mick King finally said. "And if you can't be strong everywhere, you might as well pick one place and be strong there."

Jack nodded, remembering how Napoleon had ordered his generals to come up with a plan for protecting France from invasion, and when a senior officer had spread his troops evenly along the borders, he'd heartlessly inquired if the guy was trying to protect against smuggling. So, yeah, if you couldn't be strong *everywhere*, then you planned to be strong *somewhere*, and prayed that you'd picked the right spot. The key, as always, was to put yourself into the other guy's head, just as they'd taught him to do as an intelligence analyst. Think the way your adversary thinks, and stop him that way. It sounded so good and so easy theoretically. It was rather different in the field, however.

They caught Tom Sharp walking into the basilica, and together they went off to a restaurant for lunch and a talk.

"Sir John is right," King said. "The best spot is over on the left side. We have photos of the bugger. We put you, John"—he said to Sparrow—"atop the colonnade with your cameras. Your job will be to sweep the crowd and try to spot the bastard, and radio your information to us."

Sparrow nodded, but his face showed what he thought of the job as the beers arrived.

"Mick, you had it right from the beginning," Sparrow said. "It's a pig of a job. We ought to have the whole bloody SAS regiment here, and even *that* would not be enough." The 22nd Special Air Service Regiment was actually just a company or two in size, brilliant troopers that they were.

"Ours is not to reason why, lad," Sharp told them all. "So good to know that Basil knows his Tennyson." The resulting snorts around the lunch table told the tale.

"What about radios?" Jack asked.

"On the way by courier," Sharp answered. "Small ones, they'll fit in a pocket, and they have ear pieces, but not small microphones, unfortunately."

"Shit," Ryan observed. The Secret Service would have exactly what they needed for this mission, but you couldn't just call them up and have them delivered. "What about the Queen's protective detail? Who does that?"

"The Metropolitan Police, I believe. Why—"

"Lapel mikes," Ryan answered. "It's what the Secret Service uses at home."

"I can ask," Sharp responded. "Good idea, Jack. They might well have what we need."

"They ought to cooperate with us," Mick King thought aloud.

"I'll see to it this afternoon," Sharp promised.

Yeah, Ryan thought, *we'll be the best-equipped guys ever to blow a mission.*

"They call this beer?" Sparrow asked after his first sip.

"Better than American canned piss," another of the new arrivals thought aloud.

Jack didn't rise to the bait. Besides, you went to Italy for the wine, not the beer.

"What do we know about Strokov?" Ryan asked.

"They faxed me the police file on him," Sharp reported. "Read it this morning. He's five-eleven, about fifteen stone. Evidently, he likes to eat too much. So, not an athlete—certainly not a sprinter. Brown hair, fairly thick. Good language skills. Speaks accented English, but reportedly speaks French and Italian like a native. Thought to be an expert with small arms. He's been in the business twenty years—age forty-three or so. Selected for the special DS assassination unit about fifteen years ago, with eight kills attributed to him, possibly more—we don't have good information on that."

"Delightful chap, sounds like," Sparrow thought aloud. He reached for one of the photos. "Ought not to be difficult to spot. Better to get some of these prints reduced to pocket size, so that we can all carry them with us."

"Done," Sharp promised. The embassy had its own little photo lab, mainly for his use.

Ryan looked around the table. At least it was good to be surrounded by professionals. Given the chance to perform, they probably wouldn't blow it—like a good bunch of Marines. It was not all that much, but it was something.

"What about side arms?" Ryan asked next.

"All the nine-millimeter Brownings we need," Tom Sharp assured him.

Ryan wanted to ask if they had hollow-point ammunition, but they probably just had military-issue hardball. That Geneva Convention bullshit. The nine-millimeter Parabellum cartridge was thought by Europeans to be powerful, but it was hardly a BB compared to the .45 Colt with which he'd been trained. So, then, why did he own a Browning Hi-Power? Jack asked himself. But the one he had at home was loaded with Federal 147-grain hollow-points, regarded by the American FBI as the only useful bullet to shoot out of the thing, good both for penetration and for expanding to the diameter of a dime inside the target's body, to make him bleed out in a hurry.

"He'd better be bloody close," Mick King announced. "I haven't fired one of the things in years." Which reminded Jack that England did not have the gun culture America has, even in their security services. James Bond was someone from the movies, Ryan had to remember. Ryan himself was probably the best pistol shot in the room, and he was a long way from being an expert. The pistols Sharp would hand out would be military-issue, the ones with invisible sights and crummy grips. The one Ryan owned had Pachmayr grips that fit his hand so nicely that it might have been a custom-made glove. Damn, nothing about this job was going to be easy.

"Okay. John, you'll be atop the colonnade. Find out how you get there, and arrange to get up there Wednesday morning early."

"Right." He had press credentials to make that easy. "I'll recheck the timing for everything as well."

"Good," Sharp replied. "We'll spend the afternoon going over the ground more. Look for things we may have overlooked. I'm thinking we put one man over on the side street to try and spot our friend Strokov coming in. If we spot him, we shadow him all the way in."

"Not stop him out there?" Ryan asked.

"Better to get him in closer," Sharp thought out loud. "More of us, less chance for him to bolt. If we're onto him, Jack, he won't be doing anything untoward, will he? We'll see to that."

"Will he be that predictable?" Jack worried.

"He's doubtless been here already. Indeed, we could just spot him today or tomorrow, couldn't we?"

"I wouldn't bet the ranch on it," Jack shot back.

"We play the card we are dealt, Sir John," King said. "And hope for luck."

There was no arguing with that, Ryan realized.

"If I were planning this operation, I'd be trying very hard to keep it simple. The most important preparation he'll be making is up here." Sharp tapped the side of his head. "He, too, will be somewhat tense, no matter how experienced he is in this business. Yes, he's a clever bugger, but he is not bloody Superman. The key to his success is surprise. Well, he doesn't really have that, does he? And blown surprise is the worst nightmare of a field officer. Lose that and everything comes apart like a wrecked watch. Remember, if he sees one thing that he doesn't like, he will probably just walk away and plan to come back again. There is no clock on this mission from his point of view."

"Think so?" Ryan wasn't the least bit sure of that.

"Yes, I do. If there were, from an operational standpoint, they would well have executed the mission already, and the Pope would already be chatting directly with God. According to what I've heard from London, this mission has been in planning for more than six weeks. So, clearly he's taking his time. I'll be very surprised if it happens day after tomorrow, but we must act as though it will."

"I wish I had your confidence, man."

"Sir John, field officers think and act like field officers, whatever their nationality," Sharp said with confidence. "Our mission is a difficult one, yes, but we speak his language, as it were. If this were a balls-out mission, it would have been done already. Agreed, gentlemen?" he asked, and got nods from around the table, except from the American.

"What if we're missing something?" Ryan wondered.

"That is a possibility," Sharp admitted, "but it's a possibility we have to both live with and discount. We have only the information we have, and we must design our plan around that."

"Not much choice for us, is it, Sir John?" Sparrow asked. "We have only what we have."

"True," Ryan admitted, rather miserably. There had come the sudden thought that other things might be happening as well. What if there were a diversion? What if somebody tossed firecrackers—to draw eyes toward the noise and away from the real action? *That*, he suddenly thought, was a real possibility.

Damn.

"WHAT'S THIS ABOUT RYAN?" Ritter asked, storming into Judge Moore's office.

"Basil thought that since BEATRIX was a CIA operation from the get-go, why not send one of our officers down there to take a look at things? I don't see that it can hurt anything," Moore told his DDO.

"Who the hell does Ryan think he's working for?"

"Bob, why don't you just settle down? What the hell can he do to hurt things?"

"Damn it, Arthur—"

"Settle down, Robert," Moore shot back in the voice of a judge used to having his own way on everything from the weather on down.

"Arthur," Ritter said, calming down a whisker, "it's not a place for him."

"I see no reason to object, Bob. None of us think anything's going to happen anyway, do we?"

"Well . . . no, I suppose not," the DDO admitted.

"So he's just broadening his horizons, and from what he learns, he'll be a better analyst, won't he?"

"Maybe so, but I don't like having some desk-sitter playing field spook. He isn't trained for this."

"Bob, he used to be a Marine," Moore reminded him. And the U.S. Marine Corps had its own cachet, independent of the CIA. "He's not going to wet his pants on us, is he?"

"I suppose not."

"And all he's going to do is look around at nothing happening, and the exposure to some field officers will not do his education any harm, will it?"

"They're Brits, not our guys," Ritter objected weakly.

"The same guys who brought the Rabbit out for us."

"Okay, Arthur, I'll give you this one."

"Bob, you throw a hell of a conniption fit, but why not use them for something important?"

"Yes, Judge, but the DO is my shop to run. You want me to get Rick Nolfi into this?"

"You think it's necessary?"

Ritter shook his head. "No, I expect not."

"Then we let the Brits run this mini-op and keep it cool here at Langley until we can interview the Rabbit and quantify the threat to the Pope, all right?"

"Yes, Arthur." And the Deputy Director (Operations) of the Central Intelligence Agency headed back to his office.

DINNER WENT WELL. The Brits made good company, especially when the talk turned to non-mission-related things. All were married. Three had kids, with one expecting his first shortly.

"You have two, as I recall?" Mick King asked Jack.

"Yeah, and number two arrived on a busy night."

"Too bloody right!" Ray Stones, one of the new arrivals, agreed with a laugh. "How did the missus take it?"

"Not too bad after Little Jack arrived, but the rest of the evening was subpar."

"I believe it," King observed.

"So, who told us that the Bulgarians want to kill the Pope?" Sparrow asked.

"It's KGB that wants his ass," Jack replied. "We just got a defector out.

He's in a safe house, and he's singing like the girl in *Aida.* This is the most important thing so far."

"Reliable information?" King inquired.

"We think it's gold-plated and copper-bottomed, yeah. Sir Basil has bought into it. That's why he flew you guys down," Jack let them know, in case they hadn't already figured that one out. "I've met the Rabbit myself, and I think he's the real deal."

"CIA operation?" This was Sharp.

Jack nodded. "Correct. We had an operational problem, and you guys were kind enough to help us out. I'm not cleared to say much more, sorry."

They all understood. They didn't want their asses exposed by loose talk about a black operation.

"This must go to Andropov himself—the Pope's giving them trouble in Poland, is it?"

"It would seem so. Maybe he has command of more divisions than they appreciate."

"Even so, this seems a little extreme—how will the world see the assassination of His Holiness?" King wondered aloud.

"Evidently, they fear that less than a total political collapse in Poland, Mick," Stones thought out loud. "And they're afraid that he might be able to bring that about. The sword and the spirit, as Napoleon said, Mick. The spirit always wins in the end."

"Yes, I reckon so, and here we are at the epicenter of the world of the spirit."

"My first time here," Stones said. "It *is* bloody impressive. I must bring the family down here sometime."

"They do know their food and wine," Sparrow observed, going through his veal. "What about the local police?"

"Rather good, actually," Sharp told him. "Pity we can't enlist their assistance. They know the territory—it is their patch, after all."

But these guys are the pros from Dover, Ryan thought, with some degree of hope. Just that there weren't enough of them. "Tom, you talk to London about the radios?"

"Ah, yes, Jack. They're sending us ten. Earpieces and lapel microphones to speak into. Sideband, rather like what the army use. I don't know if they're encrypted, but fairly secure in any case, and we'll use proper radio discipline. So at least we'll be able to communicate clearly. We'll practice with them tomorrow afternoon."

"And Wednesday?"

"We'll arrive about nine in the morning, pick our individual surveillance areas, and mill about while the crowd arrives."

"This isn't what they trained me for in the Corps," Ryan thought aloud.

"Sir John," Mick King responded, "this isn't what they trained any of us for. Yes, we are all experienced intelligence officers, but this really is a job for someone in the protective services, like the police constables who guard Her Majesty and the PM or your Secret Service chaps. Hell of a way to earn a living, this is."

"Yes, Mick, I expect we'll all appreciate them a little more after this lot," Ray Stones observed, to general agreement around the table.

"John." Ryan turned to Sparrow. "You've got the most important job, spotting this motherfucker for the rest of us."

"Lovely," Sparrow replied. "All I have to do is examine five-thousand-plus faces for the one that might or might not be there. Lovely," the spook repeated.

"What will you be using?"

"I have three Nikon cameras and a good assortment of lenses. I think tomorrow I might buy some seven-by-fifty binoculars also. I just hope I can find a good perch to scan from. The height of the parapet worries me. There's a dead space extending out from the base of the columns about thirty yards or so that I can't see at all. That limits what I can do, lads."

"Not much choice," Jack thought out loud. "You can't see shit from ground level."

"That is the problem we have," Sparrow agreed. "Our best choice would be two men, one—actually, more than one—on each side with good spotting glasses. But we lack the manpower, and we'd have to get permission from the Pope's own security people, which is, I gather, quite out of the question."

"Getting them involved would be useful, but—"

"But we can't let the whole world know about the Rabbit. Yeah, I know.

The Pope's life is secondary to that consideration. Isn't that just great?" Ryan growled.

"What is the security of your country worth, Sir John, and ours also?" King asked rhetorically.

"More than his life," Ryan answered. "Yeah, I know, but that doesn't mean I have to like it."

"Has any Pope ever been murdered?" Sharp asked. Nobody knew the answer.

"Somebody tried once. The Swiss Guards fought a stonewall action to protect his retreat. Most of them went down hard, but the Pope escaped alive," Ryan said, remembering something from a comic book he'd read at St. Matthew's in the—what was it? Fourth grade or so?

"I wonder how good they are, those Swiss chaps?" Stones asked.

"They're pretty enough in the striped uniforms. Probably well motivated. Question of training, really," Sharp observed. "That's the difference between a civilian and a soldier—training. The chaps in plainclothes are probably well briefed, but if they carry pistols, are they allowed to use them? They work for a church, after all. Probably not trained to shoot people outright."

"You had that guy jump out from a crowd and fire off a starter pistol at the Queen—on the way to Parliament, wasn't it?" Ryan remembered. "There was a cavalry officer on a horse right there. I was surprised he didn't cut the asshole in half with his sabre—that would have been my instinct—but he didn't."

"Parade sword, just for ceremonial occasions. You probably couldn't cut cold butter with it," Sparrow said. "Nearly trampled the bastard with his horse, though."

"The Secret Service would have dropped him on the spot. Sure, the gun was loaded with blanks," Ryan said, "but it damned sure looked and sounded like the real thing. Her Majesty kept her head screwed on pretty tight. I would have shit myself."

"I'm sure Her Majesty availed herself of the proper facilities at Westminster Palace. She has her own loo there, you know," King told the American.

"In the event, he was some disturbed fellow, doubtless cutting out paper dolls in a mental hospital now," Sharp said, but, like every other British subject, his heart had stopped cold watching the incident on TV, and he, too, had been surprised that the lunatic had survived the event. Had one of the Yeomen of the Tower been there with his ceremonial fighting spear—called a partisan—he surely would have been pinned to the pavement like a butterfly in a collection box. Perhaps God did look after fools, drunks, and little children after all. "So, if Strokov does show up, and does take his shot, you suppose the local Italians will do for him?"

"One can hope," King said.

Wouldn't that be just great? Jack thought. The professionals can't protect the Pope, but local waiters and clothing salesmen beat the fucker to death. That'll look great on *NBC Nightly News.*

BACK IN MANCHESTER, the Rabbit and his family finished yet another superb dinner from Mrs. Thompson.

"What does an ordinary English worker eat?" Zaitzev asked.

"Not quite this well," Kingshot admitted. He sure as hell didn't. "But we try to take decent care of our guests, Oleg."

"Have I told you enough about MINISTER?" he asked next. "Is all I know." The Security Service had picked his brain pretty thoroughly on the subject that afternoon, going over every single fact at least five times.

"You've been most helpful, Oleg Ivan'ch. Thank you." In fact, he'd given the Security Service quite a lot. Most often, the way you caught such penetration agents was by identifying the information he'd transferred. Only a limited number of people would have access to all of it, and the "Five" people would observe all of them until one did something difficult to explain. Then they would see who arrived at the dead-drop site to retrieve the package, and from that they'd get the bonus of identifying his KGB control officer, and get two breaks for the price of one—or perhaps even more, because the case officer would be working more than one agent, and the discoveries could branch out like the limbs of a tree. Then you tried to arrest a peripheral agent before going after the main target, because then the KGB could not know how their main penetration agent had been exposed, and *that* would protect the primary source, Oleg Zaitzev, from discovery. The counterintelligence business was as baroque as medieval-court intrigue and was both loved and hated by the players for its intricacy, but that just made the apprehension of a real Bad Guy that much more rewarding.

"And what of the Pope?"

"As I said the other day, we have a team in Rome right now to look into the matter," Kingshot answered. "Not much we can say—in fact, not much we can really do, but we are taking action based on your information, Oleg."

"That is good," the defector thought out loud, hoping it hadn't all been for nothing. He'd not really looked forward to exposing Soviet agents throughout the West. He'd do that, to safeguard his own position in his new home, of course, and for the money he'd get for turning traitor to his Motherland, but his highest concern was in saving that one life.

TUESDAY MORNING. Ryan slept later than usual, arising just after eight, figuring he'd need to bankroll his rest for the following day. He'd sure as hell need it then.

Sharp and the rest of the team were already up.

"Anything new?" Jack asked, coming into the dining room.

"We have the radios," Sharp reported. There was, indeed, one at every place at the table. "They're excellent—the very same sort your Secret Service use—same manufacturer, Motorola. Brand new, and they are encrypted. Lapel microphones and earpieces."

Ryan looked at his. The earpiece was clear plastic, curled up like a phone cord, and nearly invisible. That was good news. "Batteries?"

"Brand new, and two sets of replacements for each. Good to know that Her Majesty is well looked after."

"Okay, so nobody can listen in, and we can swap information," Ryan said. It was one more piece of good news set against a big black pile of the bad sort. "What's the plan for the day?"

"Back to the piazza, do some more looking, and hope we see our friend Strokov."

"And if we do?" Ryan asked.

"We follow him back to his accommodations and try to see if there's a way to speak with the chap this evening."

"If we get that far, just talk to him?"

"What do you suppose, Sir John?" Sharp replied with a cold look.

You really willing to go that far, Mr. Sharp? Jack didn't ask. Well, the bastard was a multiple murderer, and as civilized as the Brits were, under all the good manners and world-class hospitality, they knew how to do business, and while Jack wasn't entirely sure that he'd be able to go all the way, these guys probably didn't have his inhibitions. Ryan figured he could live with that, as long as he wasn't the trigger man himself. Besides, they'd probably give him a chance to change countries first. Better a talking defector than a silent corpse.

"Would that give anything away?"

Sharp shook his head. "No. He's the chappie who killed Georgiy Markov, remember? We can always say it is a case of visiting Her Majesty's justice on someone who needed to learn about it."

"We don't approve of murder at home, Jack," John Sparrow advised. "It would indeed be a pleasure to have him answer for that."

"Okay." Ryan could live with that, too. He was certain his dad would approve.

Oh, yeah.

THE REST OF the day, they all played tourist and tested their radios. It turned out that the radios worked both inside and outside the basilica, and, better yet, inside to outside the immense stone structure. Each man would use his own name as an identifier. It made more sense than setting up numbers or code names that they'd all have to remember—one more confusing factor that they wouldn't need if the shit hit the fan. All the while, they looked around for the face of Boris Strokov, hoping for a miracle, and reminding themselves that miracles did occasionally happen. People really did hit the lottery—they had one in Italy, too—and the football pools every week, and so it *was* possible, just damned unlikely, and this day, it did not happen.

Nor did they find a better or more likely place from which to take a shot at a man in a slow-moving vehicle. It seemed to them all that Ryan's first impression of the tactical realities of the place was correct. That felt good to Jack until he realized that if he'd blown it, then it was his fault, not theirs.

"You know," Ryan said to Mick King—Sharp was back doing Deputy-Chief-of-Mission business for the British ambassador—"more than half the crowd is going to be in the middle there."

"Works for us, Jack. Only a fool would take the shot from in there, unless he plans to have Scotty beam him up to the starship *Enterprise*. No escape possible from that place."

"True," Jack agreed. "What about inside somewhere, get the Pope on the way to the car?"

"Possible," Mick agreed. "But that would mean that somehow Strokov or someone under his control is already inside the Papal administration—household, whatever one calls it—and is thus free to make his killing whenever he wishes. Somehow I think that infiltrating that organization would be difficult. It would mean maintaining a difficult psychological disguise for an extended period of time. No." He shook his head. "I would discount that possibility."

"Hope you're right, man."

"So do I, Jack."

They all left at about four, each catching a separate cab to within a few blocks of the Brit Embassy and walking the rest of the way.

Dinner was quiet that night. Each of them had his own worries, and everyone hoped that whatever the hell Colonel Strokov of the DS had in mind, it wasn't for this week, and that they could all fly back to London the following evening none the worse off for the experience. One thing Ryan had learned: Experienced field spooks that they were, they were no more comfortable with this mission than he was. It was good not to be alone in his anxiety. Or was that just schadenfreude? What the hell, was this how it felt the night before D-Day? No, there was no German Army waiting for them. Their job was to prevent a possible murder, and the danger was not even to themselves. It was to someone else who either didn't know or didn't care about the danger to himself, and so they had assumed responsibility for his life. Mick King had gotten it right from his first impression the day before. It was a pig of a mission.

"MORE STUFF FROM the Rabbit," Moore reported at the usual evening get-together.

"What's that?"

"Basil says there's a deep-penetration agent in their Foreign Office, and the Rabbit gave them enough information to narrow him down to four potential individuals. 'Five' is already looking at them. And he gave them some more on this CASSIUS guy over here. He's been working for them just over ten years. Definitely a senior aide to a senator on the Intelligence Committee—sounds like a political adviser. So it's probably somebody who's been briefed in and has a clearance. That cuts it down to eighteen people for the Bureau to check out."

"What's he giving them, Arthur?" Greer asked.

"Sounds like whatever we tell The Hill about KGB operations gets back to Dzerzhinskiy Square in less than a week."

"I want that son of a bitch," Ritter announced. "If that's true, then we've lost agents because of him." And Bob Ritter, whatever his faults, looked after his agents like a mama grizzly bear with her cubs.

"Well, he's been doing this long enough that he's probably pretty comfortable in his fieldcraft."

"He told us about a Navy guy—NEPTUNE, wasn't it?" Greer remembered.

"Nothing new there, but we'll be sure to ask him about it. That could be anybody. How careful is the Navy with their crypto gear?"

Greer shrugged. "Every single ship has communications people, petty officers, and a commissioned communications officer. They're supposed to destroy the setting sheets and circuit boards on a daily basis, and toss them over the side—and not just one. Two people have to see it, supposedly. And they're all cleared—"

"But only people with clearances can fuck us in the ass," Ritter reminded them.

"Only the people you trust with your money can steal from you," Judge Moore observed. He'd seen enough criminal cases along that score. "That's the problem. Imagine how Ivan's going to feel if he finds out about the Rabbit."

"That," Ritter said, "is different."

"Very good, Bob," the DCI reacted with a laugh. "My wife says that to me all the time. It must be the war cry of women all over the world—*that's different.* The other side thinks they're the forces of Truth and Beauty, too, remember."

"Yeah, Judge, but we're going to whip 'em."

It was good to see such confidence, especially in a guy like Bob Ritter, Moore thought.

"Still thinking about THE MASQUE OF THE RED DEATH, Robert?"

"Putting some ideas together. Give me a few weeks."

"Fair enough."

IT WAS JUST one in the morning in Washington when Ryan awoke on Italian time. The shower helped get him alert, and the shave got his face smooth. By seven-thirty, he was heading down for breakfast. Mrs. Sharp fixed coffee in the Italian style, which surprisingly tasted as though someone had emptied an ashtray into the pot. Jack wrote that off to differing national tastes. The eggs and (English) bacon were just fine, as was the buttered toast. Someone had decided that men going into action needed full bellies. A pity the Brits didn't know about hash brown potatoes, the most filling of unhealthy breakfast foods.

"All ready?" Sharp asked, coming in.

"I guess we all have to be. What about the rest of the crew?"

"We rendezvous at the front of the basilica in thirty-five minutes." And it was only a five-minute drive from there. "Here's a friend for you to take along." He handed over a pistol.

Jack took it and slid the slide back. It was, fortunately, empty.

"You may need this, too." Sharp handed over two loaded magazines. Sure enough, they were hardball—full-metal-jacketed—cartridges, which would go right through the target, making only a nine-millimeter hole in and out. But Europeans thought you could drop an elephant with them. *Yeah, sure,* Jack thought, wishing for a .45 Colt M1911A1, which was much better suited for putting a man on the ground and leaving him there until the ambulance crew arrived. But he'd never mastered the big Colt, though he had, barely, qualified with it. It was with a rifle that Ryan could really shoot, but nearly anyone could shoot a rifle. Sharp didn't provide a holster. The Browning Hi-Power would have to go in his belt, and he'd have to keep his jacket buttoned to conceal it. The bad thing about carrying a pistol was that they were heavy damned things to port around with you, and without a proper holster he'd have to keep adjusting it in his belt to make sure it didn't fall out or slide down his pants. That just wouldn't do. It would also make sitting down a pain in the gut, but there wouldn't be much of that today. The spare magazine went into his coat pocket. He pulled the slide back, locked it in place, and slid the loaded one into the butt, then dropped the locking lever to release the slide. The weapon was now loaded and "in battery," meaning ready to fire. On reflection, Ryan carefully dropped the hammer. A safety might have sufficed, but Ryan had been trained not to trust safeties. To fire the weapon, he'd have to remember to cock the hammer, something he'd fortunately forgotten to do with Sean Miller. But this time, if the worst happened, he would not.

"Time to boogie?" Jack asked Sharp.

"Does that mean go?" the Chief of Station Rome asked. "I meant to ask the other time you said that."

"Yeah, like, boogie on down the road. It's an Americanism. 'Boogie' used to be a kind of dance, I think."

"And your radio." Sharp pointed. "It clips on the belt over your wallet pocket. On/off switch"—he demonstrated—"earpiece fastens to your collar, and the microphone onto your collar. Clever bit of kit, this."

"Okay." Ryan got everything arranged properly, but left the radio off. The spare batteries went into his left-side coat pocket. He didn't expect to need them, but safe was always better than sorry. He reached behind to find the on/off switch and flipped it off and on. "What's the range on the radios?"

"Three miles—five kilometers—the manual says. More than we need. Ready?"

"Yeah." Jack stood, set his pistol snugly on the left side of his belt, and followed Sharp out to the car.

Traffic was agreeably light this morning. Italian drivers were not, from what he'd seen so far, the raving maniacs he'd heard them to be. But the people out now would be people heading soberly to work, whether it was selling real estate or working in a warehouse. One of the difficult things for a tourist to remember was that a city was just another city, not a theme park set in place for his personal amusement.

And damned sure this morning Rome wasn't here for anything approaching that, was it? Jack asked himself coldly.

Sharp parked his official Bentley about where they expected Strokov to park. There were other cars there, people who worked in the handful of shops, or perhaps early shoppers hoping to get their buying done before Wednesday's regularly scheduled chaos.

In any case, this most expensive of British motorcars had diplomatic tags, and nobody would fool with it. Getting out, he followed Sharp into the piazza and reached back with his right hand to flip his radio on without exposing his pistol.

"Okay," he said into his lapel. "Ryan is here. Who else is on the net?"

"Sparrow in place on the colonnade," a voice answered immediately.

"King, in place."

"Ray Stones, in place."

"Parker, in place," Phil Parker, the last of the arrivals from London, reported from his spot on the side street.

"Tom Sharp here with Ryan. We'll do a radio check every fifteen minutes. Report immediately if you see the least thing of interest. Out." He turned to Ryan. "So, that's done."

"Yeah." He checked his watch. They had hours to go before the Pope appeared. What would he be doing now? He was supposed to be a very early riser. Doubtless the first important thing he did every day was to say Mass, like every Catholic priest in the world, and it was probably the most important part of his morning routine, something to remind himself exactly what he was—a priest sworn to God's service—a reality he'd known and probably celebrated within his own mind through Nazi and communist oppression for forty-odd years, serving his flock. But now his flock, his parish, straddled the entire world, as did his responsibility to them, didn't it?

Jack reminded himself of his time in the Marine Corps. Crossing the Atlantic on his helicopter-landing ship—unknowingly on his way to a life-threatening helicopter crash—on Sunday they'd held church services, and at that moment the church pennant had been run up to the truck. It flew *over* the national ensign. It was the U.S. Navy's way of acknowledging that there was *one* higher loyalty than the one a man had for his country. That loyalty was to God Himself—the one power higher than that of the United States of America, and his country acknowledged that. Jack could feel it, here and now, carrying a gun. He could feel that fact like a physical weight on his shoulders. There were people who wanted the Pope—the Vicar of Christ on earth—dead. And that, suddenly, was massively offensive to him. The worst street criminal gave a priest, minister, or rabbi a free pass, because there might really be a god up there, and it wouldn't do to harm His personal representative among the people. How much more would God be annoyed by the murder of His #1 Representative on Planet Earth. The Pope was a man who'd probably never hurt a single human being in his life. The Catholic Church was not a perfect institution—nothing with mere people in it was or ever could be. But it was founded on faith in Almighty God, and its policies rarely, if ever, strayed from love and charity.

But those doctrines were seen as a threat by the Soviet Union. What better proof of who the Bad Guys were in the world? Ryan had sworn as a Marine to fight his country's enemies. But here and now he swore to himself to fight against God's own enemies. The KGB recognized no power higher than the Party it served. And, in proclaiming that, they defined themselves as the enemy of all mankind—for wasn't mankind made in God's own image? Not Lenin's. Not Stalin's. God's.

Well, he had a pistol designed by John Moses Browning, an American, perhaps a Mormon—Browning had come from Utah, but Jack didn't know what faith he'd adhered to—to help him see about that.

Time passed slowly for Ryan. Constant reference to his watch didn't help. People were arriving steadily. Not in large numbers, but rather like a baseball crowd, arriving single, or in pairs, or in small family groups. Lots of children, infants carried by their mothers, some escorted by nuns—school trips, almost certainly—to see the Pontifex Maximus. That term, too, came from the Romans, who with remarkably clarity likened a priest to a *pontifex*—bridge builder—between men and what was greater than men.

Vicar of Christ on earth was what kept repeating in Jack's mind. This Strokov bastard—hell, he would have killed Jesus Himself. A new Pontius Pilate—if not an oppressor himself, then certainly the representative of the oppressors, here to spit in God's face. It wasn't that he could harm God, of course. Nobody was that big, but in attacking one of God's institutions and God's personal representative—well, that was plenty bad enough. God was supposed to punish such people in His own good time . . . and maybe the Lord chose His instruments to handle that for Him . . . maybe even ex-Marines from the United States of America . . .

Noon. It would be a warm day. What had it been like to live here in Roman times without air-conditioning? Well, they hadn't known the difference, and the body adapted itself to the environment—something in the medulla, Cathy had told him once. It would have been more comfortable to take his jacket off, but not with a pistol stuck in his belt. . . . There were street vendors about, selling cold drinks and ice cream. *Like money changers in the Temple?* Jack wondered. *Probably not.* The priests in evidence didn't chase them away. *Hmm, a good way for the bad guy to get close with his weapon?* he suddenly wondered. But they were a good way off, and it was too late to worry about that, and none of them matched the photos he had. Jack had a small print of Strokov's face in his left hand, and looked down at it every minute or so. The bastard might be wearing a disguise, of course. He'd be stupid not to, and Strokov probably wasn't stupid. Not in his business. Disguises didn't cover everything. Hair length and color, sure. But not height. It took major surgery to do that. You could make a guy look heavier, but not lighter. Facial hair? *Okay, look for a guy with a beard or mustache.* Ryan turned and scanned the area. Nope. Nothing obvious, anyway.

Half an hour to go. The crowd was buzzing now, people speaking a dozen or more languages. He could see tourists and the faithful from many lands. Blond heads from Scandinavia, African blacks, Asians. Some obvious Americans . . . but no obvious Bulgarians. What did Bulgarians look like? This new problem was that the Catholic Church was supposed to be universal, and that meant people of every physical description. Lots of possible disguises.

"Sparrow, Ryan. See anything likely?" Jack asked his lapel.

"Negative," the voice in his ear answered. "I'm scanning the crowd around you. Nothing to report."

"Roger," Jack acknowledged.

"If he's here, he's bloody invisible," Sharp said, standing next to Ryan. They were eight or ten yards from the interlocking steel barriers brought in for the Pope's weekly appearance. They looked heavy. *Two men to put them on the truck, or four?* Jack wondered. He discovered that the mind liked to wander at times like this, and he had to guard against that. *Keep scanning the crowd,* he told himself.

There's too many goddamned faces! the self responded angrily. *And as soon as the fucker gets into place, he'll be looking away.*

"Tom, how about we edge forward and sweep along the railing?"

"Good idea," Sharp agreed at once.

The crowd was difficult, but not impossible, to slip through. Ryan checked his watch. Fifteen minutes. People were now edging against the barriers, wanting to get close. There was a belief from medieval times that the mere touch of a king could cure the ill or bring good fortune, and evidently that belief lingered—and how much more true if the man in question was the Pontifex Maximus? Some of the people here would be cancer victims, entreating God for a miracle. Maybe some miracles actually happened. Docs called that spontaneous remission and wrote it off to biological processes they didn't yet understand. But maybe they really were miracles—to the recipients they certainly were exactly that. It was just one more thing Ryan didn't understand.

People were leaning forward more, heads were turning to the face of the church.

"Sharp/Ryan, Sparrow. Possible target, twenty feet to your left, standing three ranks back of the barrier. Blue coat," Jack's earpiece crackled. He headed that way without waiting for Sharp. It was hard pressing through the crowd, but it wasn't a New York subway crush. Nobody turned to curse at him. Ryan looked forward. . . .

Yes . . . right there. He turned to look at Sharp and tapped his nose twice.

"Ryan is on the target," he said into his lapel. "Steer me in, John."

"Forward ten feet, Jack, immediately left of the Italian-looking woman in the brown dress. Our friend has light brown hair. He is looking to his left."

Bingo, Jack thought in silent celebration. It took two more minutes and he was standing right behind the cocksucker. *Hello, Colonel Strokov.*

Hidden in the thickness of the crowd, Jack unbuttoned his jacket.

The man was farther back than he would have done it, Jack thought. His field of fire was limited by the bodies around him, but the woman directly in front of him was short enough that he could easily draw and fire right over her, and his field of view was fairly unrestricted.

Okay, Boris Andreyevich, if you want to play, this game's going to surprise you some. If the Army or the Navy ever look on heaven's scenes/They will find the streets are guarded by United States Marines, motherfucker.

Tom Sharp took the chance to slide through the crowd in front of Strokov, brushing past as he went. On the other side, he turned in Ryan's direction and reached up with his fist into the sky. Strokov was armed.

The noise of the crowd rose in frequency, and the languages all melded into one murmuring hiss of noise that suddenly went dead still. A bronze door had opened out of Ryan's view.

Sharp was four feet away, just one person, an adolescent boy, between him and Strokov . . . easy for him to dart right and get his hands on the man.

Then a cavalcade of screams erupted. Ryan inched back and pulled out his pistol, thumbing the hammer back, putting his pistol fully in battery. His eyes were locked on Strokov.

"King, the Pope is coming out now! Vehicle is in view."

But Ryan couldn't answer. Neither could he see the Popemobile.

"Sparrow, I see him. Ryan/Sharp, he will enter your field of view in a few seconds."

Unable to say a word, unable to see His Holiness approach, Jack's eyes were locked on his target's shoulders. You can't move your arm without having them move, too, and when he did that . . .

Shooting a man in the back is murder, Jack. . . .

In his peripheral vision, Ryan saw the front-left corner of the white jeep/golf cart slowly moving left to right. The man in front of him was looking in that general direction . . . but not quite . . . why?

But then his right shoulder moved ever so slightly. . . . At the bottom of Ryan's field of view, his right elbow came into view, meaning that his forearm was now parallel to the ground.

And then his right foot moved back, ever so slightly. The man was getting ready to—

Ryan pressed the muzzle of his pistol against the base of his spine. He could feel the vertebrae of his backbone on the muzzle of his Browning. Jack saw his head rock back, just a few millimeters. Ryan leaned forward and rasped a whisper into his ear.

"If that gun in your hand goes off, you'll be pissing into a diaper the rest of your life. Now, real slow, with your fingertips, hand it back to me, or I will shoot you where you stand."

Mission accomplished, Ryan's brain announced. *This fucker isn't going to kill anybody. Go ahead, resist if you want. Nobody's that fast.* His finger was so tight on the trigger that if Strokov turned suddenly, the pistol would go off on its own accord, and sever his spine for all time to come.

The man hesitated, and surely his mind was running at the speed of light through various options. There were drills for what to do when someone had a gun in one's back, and he'd even practiced them in his intelligence academy, but here, now, twenty years later, with a real pistol against his spine, those lessons with play guns seemed a very distant thing, and could he bat the gun away so fast to keep it from destroying a kidney? Probably not. And so, his right hand came back just as he'd just been told. . . .

Ryan jumped at the sound of one-two-three pistol shots, not fifteen feet away. It was the sort of moment in which the world stops its turning, hearts and lungs stop functioning, and every mind has an instant of total clarity. Jack's eyes were drawn to the sound. There was the Holy Father, and on his snow-white cassock was a spot of red, the size of a half-dollar, in the chest, and on his handsome face was the shock of something too fast for him yet to feel the pain, but his body was already collapsing, slumping and turning to the left, folding into itself as he started to go down.

It required all of Ryan's discipline not to squeeze the trigger. His left hand snatched the pistol out of his subject's hand.

"Stand still, you motherfucker. Don't take a step, don't turn, don't do anything. Tom!" he called loudly.

"Sparrow, they have him, they have the gunman. The gunman is down on the pavement, must be ten people on him. The Pope took two, possibly three, hits."

The reaction of the crowd was almost binary in character. Those closest to the shooter jumped on him like cats on a single unlucky mouse, and whoever the shooter was, he was invisible under a mound of tourists, perhaps ten feet from where Ryan, Sharp, and Strokov stood. The people immediately around Ryan were drawing away—rather slowly, actually. . . .

"Jack, let's get our friend away from here, shall we?" And the three men moved into the escape arch, as Ryan had come to think of it.

"Sharp to all. We have Strokov with us. Leave the area separately and rendezvous at the embassy."

A minute later, they were in Sharp's official Bentley. Ryan got in back with the Bulgarian.

Strokov was clearly feeling better about things now. "What is this? I am member of Bulgarian embassy and—"

"We'll remember you said that, old man. For now, you are a guest of Her Britannic Majesty's government. Now, be a good chap and sit still, or my friend will kill you."

"Interesting tool of diplomacy, this." Ryan lifted the gun he'd taken from Strokov—East Bloc issue, with a large and awkward can-type silencer screwed on the business end. Sure as hell he'd been planning to shoot somebody.

But whom? Suddenly, Ryan wasn't sure.

"Tom?"

"Yes, Jack?"

"Something was more wrong than we thought."

"I think you're right," Sharp agreed. "But we have someone to clear that up for us."

The drive back to the embassy illustrated what had been to Ryan a hidden talent. The Bentley had an immensely powerful engine, and Sharp knew how to use it, exploding away from the Vatican like a drag-racing top fuel eliminator. The car screeched to a halt in the small parking lot next to the embassy, and the three of them went in through a side door, and from there to the basement. With Ryan covering, Sharp handcuffed the Bulgarian and sat him in a wooden chair.

"Colonel Strokov, you must answer for Georgiy Markov," Sharp told him. "We've been after you for some years now."

Strokov's eyes went as wide as doorknobs. As fast as the Bentley had gone, Tom Sharp's mind had been driving faster still.

"What do you mean?"

"I mean, we have these photos of you leaving Heathrow Airport after killing our good friend on Westminster Bridge. The Yard was onto you, old boy, but you left minutes before they got permission to arrest you. That's your bad luck. So, now, it was our job to arrest you. You will find us rather less civilized that the Yard, Colonel. You murdered a man on British soil. Her Majesty the Queen does not approve of that sort of thing, Colonel."

"But—"

"Why are we bothering to talk with this bastard, Tom?" Ryan asked, catching on. "We have our orders, don't we?"

"Patience, Jack, patience. He's not going anywhere at the moment, is he?"

"I want to have a phone to call my embassy," Strokov said—rather weakly, Ryan thought.

"Next he'll want a lawyer," Sharp observed humorously. "Well, in London you could have a solicitor to assist you, but we are not *in* London, are we, old boy?"

"And we are not Scotland Yard," Jack added, taking his lead from Sharp. "I should have just done him at the church, Tom."

Sharp shook his head. "Too noisy. Better we just let him . . . disappear, Jack. I'm sure Georgiy would understand."

It was clear from Strokov's face that he was not accustomed to having men discuss his own fate in the way that he had so often determined for himself the fates of others. It was easier to be brave, he was finding, when he was the fellow holding the gun.

"Well, I wasn't going to kill him, Tom, just sever his spine below the waist. You know, put him in a wheelchair the rest of his life, make him as incontinent as a baby. How loyal you suppose his government will be to him?"

Sharp nearly gagged on the thought. "Loyal, the *Dirzhavna Sugurnost*? Please, Jack. Be serious. They'd just put him in a hospital, probably a mental hospital, and they'll wipe his ass once or twice a day if he's lucky."

That one went through the hoop, Ryan saw. None of the East Bloc services were big on loyalty-down, even to those who'd shown a lot of loyalty-up. And Strokov knew it. No, once you screwed the pooch, you were in very deep shit, and your friends evaporated like the morning mist—and somehow Strokov didn't strike Ryan as one who had all that many friends anyway. Even in his own service he'd be like an attack dog—valuable, perhaps, but not loved or trusted around the kids.

"In any case, while Boris and I discuss the future, you have a flight to catch," Sharp told him. It was just as well. Ryan was running out of impromptu lines. "Give my regards to Sir Basil, will you?"

"You bet, Tommy." Ryan left the room and took a deep breath. Mick King and the rest were waiting out there for him. Someone at Sharp's official residence had packed his bags, and there was an embassy minibus waiting to take them all to the airport. There, a British Airways Boeing 737 was waiting, and they caught it just in time, all with first-class tickets. Ryan was next to King for the flight.

"What the hell," Jack asked, "are we going to do with him?"

"Strokov? Good question," Mick replied. "Are you sure you want to know the answer?"

CHAPTER 32

MASQUED BALL

ON THE TWO-HOUR FLIGHT back to Heathrow, Ryan availed himself of three miniatures of single-malt scotch, mainly because it was the only hard stuff they had. Somehow, his fear of flying receded into the background—it helped that the flight was so smooth that the aircraft might as well have been sitting still on the ground, but Ryan also had a head full of other thoughts.

"What went wrong, Mick?" Ryan asked over the Alps.

"What went wrong was that our friend Strokov wasn't planning to do the assassination himself. He got someone else to do the actual shooting."

"Then why was he carrying a pistol with a silencer on the front end?"

"You want a guess? I'd wager he was hoping to kill the assassin himself and then blend into the crowd and make his escape. You can't read everyone's mind, Jack," King added.

"So, we failed," Ryan concluded.

"Perhaps. It depends on where the bullets went. John said there was one hit in the body, one perhaps in the hand or arm, and one other that might have gone wild, or at worst was a peripheral strike. So, whether the man survives or not is up to whatever surgeon is working on him now." King shrugged. "Out of our hands, my friend."

"Fuck," Ryan breathed quietly.

"Did you do your best, Sir John?"

That snapped his head around. "Yes—I mean, of course. We all did."

"And that is all a man can do, isn't it? Jack, I've been in the field for, what? Twelve years. Sometimes things go according to plan. Sometimes they do not. Given the information we had and the manpower we were able to deploy, I don't see how we could have done any better. You're an analyst, aren't you?"

"Correct."

"Well, for a desk boffin, you acquitted yourself well, and now you know a good deal more about field operations. There are no guarantees in this line of work." King took another swallow of his drink. "I can't say that I like it, either. I lost an agent in Moscow two years ago. He was a young captain in the Soviet army. Seemed a decent sort. Wife and a young son. They shot him, of course. Lord only knows what happened to his family. Maybe she's in a labor camp, or maybe in some godforsaken town in Siberia, for all I know. You never find that out, you know. Nameless, faceless victims, but victims still."

"THE PRESIDENT IS PISSED," Moore told his senior executives, his right ear still burning from a conversation ten minutes before.

"That bad?" Greer asked.

"That bad," the DCI confirmed. "He wants to know who did it and why, and he'd prefer to know before lunch."

"That's not possible," Ritter said.

"There's the phone, Bob. You call him and tell him that," the Judge suggested. None of them had ever seen the President angry. It was, for the most part, something people tried to avoid.

"So, Jack was right?" Greer offered.

"He might have made a good guess. But he didn't stop it from happening, either," Ritter observed.

"Well, it gives you something to say, Arthur," Greer said, with a little hope in his voice.

"Maybe so. I wonder how good Italian doctors are."

"What do we know?" Greer asked. "Anything?"

"One serious bullet wound in the chest. The President ought to be able to identify with that," Moore thought out loud. "Two other hits, but not serious ones."

"So, call Charlie Weathers up at Harvard and ask him what the likely prognosis is." This was from Ritter.

"The President's already talked to the meatball surgeons at Walter Reed. They're hopeful but noncommittal."

"I'm sure they all say, 'If I was on it, it'd be okay.' " Greer had experience with military doctors. Fighter pilots were shrinking violets next to battlefield surgeons.

"I'm going to call Basil and have the Rabbit flown here as soon as the Air Force can get a plane ready. If Ryan's available—they ought to be flying him back from Rome right now, if I know Basil—I want him on the aircraft, too."

"Why?" Ritter asked.

"So he can brief us—maybe the President, too—on his threat analysis prior to the event."

"Christ, Arthur." Greer nearly exploded. "They told us about the threat four, five days ago."

"But we wanted to interview the guy ourselves," Moore acknowledged. "I know, James, I know."

RYAN FOLLOWED MICK KING off the airliner. At the bottom of the steps was somebody who had to be from Century House. Ryan saw that the man was staring right at him.

"Dr. Ryan, could you come with me, please? We'll have a man get your bags," the fellow promised.

"Where now?"

"We have a helicopter to take you to RAF Mildenhall, and—"

"My ass. I don't do helicopters since one nearly killed me. How far is it?"

"An hour and a half's drive."

"Good. Get a car," Jack ordered. Then he turned. "Thanks for the try, guys." Sparrow, King, and the rest shook his hand. They had indeed all tried, even though no one would ever know about their effort. Then Jack wondered what Tom Sharp would be doing with Strokov, and decided that Mick King was right. He really didn't want to know.

RAF MILDENHALL is just north of Cambridge, the home of one of the world's great universities, and Ryan's driver was in another Jaguar, and didn't much care about whatever speed limits there were on British roads. When they pulled past the RAF Ground Defense Regiment's security troops, the car didn't go to the aircraft waiting there on the ramp, but rather to a low building that looked like—and was—a VIP terminal. There, a man handed Ryan a telex that took about twenty seconds to read and resulted in a muttered "Great." Then Jack found a phone and called home.

"Jack?" his wife said when she recognized his voice. "Where the hell are you?" She must have been exercised. Cathy Ryan didn't ordinarily talk like that.

"I'm at RAF Mildenhall. I have to fly back to Washington."

"Why?"

"Let me ask you this, honey: How good are Italian doctors?"

"You mean—the Pope?"

"Yep." She couldn't see his tired but curt nod.

"Every country has good surgeons—Jack, what's going on? Were you there?"

"Cath, I was about forty feet away, but I can't tell you any more than that, and you can't repeat it to anybody, okay?"

"Okay," she replied, with wonder and frustration in her voice. "When will you be home?"

"Probably in a couple of days. I have to talk to some people at headquarters, and they'll probably send me right back. Sorry, babe. Business. So, how good are the docs in Italy?"

"I'd feel better if Jack Cammer was working on him, but they have to have some good ones. Every big city does. The University of Padua is about the oldest medical school in the world. Their ophthalmologists are about as good as we are at Hopkins. For general surgery, they must have some good people, but the guy I know best for this is Jack." John Michael Cammer was Chairman of Hopkins' Department of Surgery, holder of the prestigious Halstead Chair, and one hell of a good man with a knife. Cathy knew him well. Jack had met him once or twice at fund-raisers and been impressed by his demeanor, but wasn't a physician and couldn't evaluate the man's professional abilities. "It's fairly straightforward to treat a gunshot wound, mostly. Unless the liver or spleen is hit. The real problem is bleeding. Jack, it's like when Sally got hurt in the car with me. If you get him there fast, and if the surgeon knows his stuff, you have a good chance of surviving—unless the spleen's ruptured or the liver is badly lacerated. I saw the TV coverage. His heart wasn't hit—wrong angle. I'd say better than even money he'll recover. He's not a young man, and that won't help, but a really good surgical team can do miracles if they get to him fast enough." She didn't talk about the nasty variables of trauma surgery. Bullets could ricochet off ribs and go in the most unpredictable directions. They could fragment and do damage in widely separated places. Fundamentally, you couldn't diagnose, much less treat, a bullet wound from five seconds of TV tape. So the odds on the Pope's survival were better than even money, but a lot of 5–1 horses had beaten the chalk horse and won the Kentucky Derby.

"Thanks, babe. I'll probably be able to tell you more when I get home. Hug the kids for me, okay?"

"You sound tired," she said.

"I *am* tired, babe. It's been a busy couple of days." And it wasn't going to get any quieter. "Bye for now."

"I love you, Jack," she reminded him.

"I love you, too, babe. Thanks for saying that."

Ryan waited more than an hour for the Zaitzev family. So the offer of a helicopter would have just enabled him to wait here longer—fairly typical of the U.S. military. Ryan sat on a comfortable couch and drifted off to sleep for perhaps half an hour.

The Rabbits arrived by car. A USAF sergeant shook Jack awake and pointed him to the waiting KC-135. It was essentially a windowless Boeing 707, also equipped to refuel other aircraft. The lack of windows didn't help his attitude very much, but orders were orders, and he climbed up the steps and found a plush leather seat just forward of the wing box. The aircraft had hardly lifted off the ground when Oleg fell into the seat beside his own.

"What happened?" Zaitzev demanded.

"We caught Strokov. I got him myself, and he had a gun in his hand," Ryan reported. "But there was another shooter."

"Strokov? You arrested him?"

"Not exactly an arrest, but he decided to come with me to the British Embassy. SIS has him now."

"I hope they kill the *zvoloch,*" Zaitzev snarled.

Ryan didn't reply, wondering if that might actually happen. Did the Brits play that rough? He had committed rather a nasty murder on their soil—hell, within sight of Century House.

"The Pope, will he live?" the Rabbit asked. Ryan was surprised to see his degree of interest. Maybe the guy was a real conscience defector after all.

"I don't know, Oleg. I called my wife—she's a surgeon. She says that it's better than a fifty-fifty chance that he will survive."

"That is something," Zaitzev thought out loud.

"WELL?" Andropov asked.

Colonel Rozhdestvenskiy stood a little more erect. "Comrade Chairman, we know little at this point. Strokov's man took the shot, as you know, and he hit his target in a deadly area. Strokov was unable to eliminate him as planned, for reasons unknown. Our Rome *rezidentura* is working carefully to discover what happened. Colonel Goderenko is taking personal charge. We will know more when Colonel Strokov flies back to Sofia. He is scheduled to be on the regular flight at nineteen hours. So, to this point it appears we have had a partial success."

"There is no such thing as a partial success, Colonel!" Andropov pointed out heatedly.

"Comrade Chairman, I told you weeks ago that this was a possibility. You will recall that. And even if this priest survives, he will not be going back to Poland anytime soon, will he?"

"I suppose not," Yuriy Vladimirovich grumbled.

"And that was the real mission, wasn't it?"

"Da," the Chairman admitted.

"No signals as yet?"

"No, Comrade Chairman. We've had to break in a new watch officer in Communications, and—"

"What is that?"

"Major Zaitzev, Oleg Ivanovich, he and his family died in a hotel fire in Budapest. He had been our communicator for mission six-six-six."

"Why was I not informed of this?"

"Comrade Chairman," Rozhdestvenskiy soothed, "it was fully investigated. The bodies have been returned to Moscow and were duly buried. They all died of smoke inhalation. The autopsy procedures were viewed in person by a Soviet physician."

"You are sure of this, Colonel?"

"I can get the official report to you if you wish," Rozhdestvenskiy said with confidence. "I have read it myself."

Andropov shook it off. "Very well. Keep me informed on whatever comes in. And I want to be notified at once of the condition of this troublesome Pole."

"By your order, Comrade Chairman." Rozhdestvenskiy made his way out while the Chairman went back to other business. Brezhnev's health had taken a definite downturn. Very soon Andropov would have to step away from KGB in order to protect his ascension to the head seat at the table, and that was the main item on his plate at the moment. And, besides, Rozhdestvenskiy was right. This Polish priest would not be a problem for months, even if he survived, and that was sufficient to the moment.

"WELL, ARTHUR?" Ritter asked.

"He's calmed down a little bit. I told him about Operation BEATRIX. I told him that we and the Brits had people right there. He wants to meet the Rabbit we just got out, personally. So, he's still pretty pissed, but at least it's not at us," Moore reported on his arrival back from the White House.

"The Brits have this Strokov guy in custody," Greer let the DCI know. Word had just come in from London. "Would you believe Ryan's the guy who put the bag on him? The Brits have him now at their Rome embassy. Basil's trying to decide what to do with him. Best bet, Strokov ran the operation and enlisted this Turkish thug to do the shooting. The Brits say they caught him with a silenced pistol in his hand. The thinking is that his job was to take the shooter out, like that Mafia hit in New York a while back, to put big-league deniability on the assassination attempt."

"Your boy captured him?" the DCI asked in some surprise.

"He was there with a team of experienced British field spooks, and maybe his Marine training helped," Ritter allowed. "So, James, your fair-haired boy gets another attaboy."

Don't bite your tongue off when you sign the Letter of Commendation, Robert, Greer managed not to say. "Where are they all now?"

"Halfway home, probably. The Air Force is flying them over," Ritter told them. "ETA at Andrews is about eleven-forty, they told me."

THERE *WERE* WINDOWS in the front office, Ryan found out, and the flight crew was friendly enough. He was even able to talk a little about baseball. The Orioles had just one more game to win to finish the Phillies off, he was pleased and surprised to learn. The flight crew didn't even hint at asking why they were driving him back to America. They'd done it too many times and, besides, they never got good answers anyway. Aft, the Rabbit Family was sound asleep, a feat Ryan had not yet managed to accomplish.

"How long?" he asked the pilot.

"Well, that's Labrador there." He pointed. "Call it three hours more, and we'll be feet-dry almost all the way. Why don't you get some sleep, sir?"

"I don't sleep in the air," Jack admitted.

"Don't feel too bad, sir. Neither do we," the copilot told him. And that was good news, on reflection, Jack thought.

SIR BASIL CHARLESTON was having his own meeting with his Chief of Government at the moment. Neither in America nor in the U.K. did reporters write stories about when and why the chiefs of the various intelligence services met with their political masters.

"So, tell me about this Strokov fellow," she ordered.

"Not a very pleasant chap," C replied. "We reckon he was there to kill the actual shooter. He had a suppressed weapon to eliminate the noise. So, it would appear that the idea was to kill His Holiness and leave a dead assassin behind. Dead men still tell no tales, you see, Prime Minister. But perhaps this one will, after all. The Italian police must be chatting with him right now, I would imagine. He is a Turkish national, and I'll wager he had a criminal record, and/or experience in smuggling things into Bulgaria."

"So, it was the Russians who were behind this?" she asked.

"Yes, ma'am. That seems virtually certain. Tom Sharp is talking to Strokov in Rome. We'll see how loyal he is to his masters."

"What will we do with him?" the PM asked. The answer was in the form of another question that she would have to answer. She did.

IT DID NOT occur to Strokov that when Sharp invoked the names of Aleksey Nikolay'ch Rozhdestvenskiy and Ilya Fedorovich Bubovoy, his own fate was sealed. He was merely dumbfounded that the British Secret Intelligence Service had the KGB so thoroughly penetrated. Sharp saw no reason to disabuse him of that notion. Shocked beyond his capacity to react intelligently, Strokov forgot all of his training and started singing. His duet with Sharp lasted two and a half hours, all of it on tape.

RYAN WAS MORE on autopilot than the Boeing was before it touched down at Runway Zero-One Right at Andrews Air Force Base. He'd been on the go for what? Twenty-two hours? Something like that. Something more easily done as a Marine second lieutenant (age twenty-two) than as a married father of two (age *thirty*-two) who'd had a fairly stressful day. He was also feeling his liquor somewhat.

There were two cars waiting at the bottom of the steps—Andrews had yet to install a jetway. He and Zaitzev took the first. Mrs. Rabbit and the Bunny took the second. Two minutes after that, they were on Suitland Parkway, heading into D.C. Ryan drew the task of explaining what they were passing along the way. Unlike his arrival in England, Zaitzev was not under the impression that this might be a *maskirovka.* And the detour past the Capitol Building ended whatever lingering suspicions he might have had. George Lucas on his best day could not have faked this scenery. The cars crossed the Potomac and went north of the George Washington Parkway, finally taking the marked exit to Langley.

"So, this is the home of the Main Enemy," the Rabbit said.

"I just think of it as the place I used to work."

"Used to?"

"Didn't you know? I'm stationed back in England now," Jack told him.

The whole debriefing team was under the canopy by the main entrance. Ryan knew only one of them, Mark Radner, a Russian scholar from Dartmouth who got called down for some special work—one of the people who liked working for CIA, but not full-time. Ryan was now able to understand that. When the car stopped, he got out first and went to James Greer.

"You've had a busy couple of days, my boy."

"Tell me about it, Admiral."

"How was it in Rome?"

"First, tell me about the Pope," Jack shot back.

"He came through surgery okay. He's critical, but we asked Charlie Weathers up at Harvard about that, and he said not to worry. People that age who come through surgery are always classified as being in critical condition—probably just a way to drive the bill up. Unless something unusual crops up, he'll probably be fine. Charlie says they grow good cutters in Rome. His Holiness ought to be home in three to four weeks, Charlie says. They won't rush it with a guy his age."

"Thank God. Sir, when I had that Strokov bastard I thought we'd done it, y'know? Then when I heard the shots—Jesus, what a moment that was, Admiral."

Greer nodded. "I can imagine. But the good guys won this one. Oh, your Orioles took the series from Philly. Game just ended twenty minutes ago. That new shortstop you have, Ripken, looks to me like he's going places."

"Ryan." Judge Moore came over next. "Well done, son." Another handshake.

"Thank you, Director."

"Nice going, Ryan," Ritter said next. "Sure you wouldn't like to try our training course at the Farm?" The handshake was surprisingly cordial. Ritter must have had a drink or two in the office, Jack surmised.

"Sir, right now, I'd be just as happy to go back to teaching history."

"It's more fun to make it, boy. Remember that."

The party moved inside, past the memorial on the right-side wall to the dead officers, many of whose names were still secret, then left to the executive elevator. The Rabbit family went its own way. There were hotel-like accommodations for VIP visitors and back-from-overseas field officers on the sixth floor, and evidently the CIA was bedding them down there. Jack followed the senior executives to the Judge's office.

"How good is our new Rabbit?" Moore asked.

"Well, sure as hell he gave us good information on the Pope, Judge," Ryan answered in considerable surprise. "And the Brits sound pretty happy with what he's told them about that Agent MINISTER. I'm kinda curious who this CASSIUS guy is."

"And NEPTUNE," Greer added. The Navy needed secure communications to survive in the modern world, and James Greer still had blue suits in his closet.

"Any other thoughts?" This was Moore again.

"Has anyone thought about how desperate the Russians are? I mean, sure, the Pope was—I guess he still is—a political threat of some sort to them, but, damn it, this was not a rational operation, was it?" Jack asked. "Looks to me as though they're a lot more desperate than we usually think. We ought to be able to exploit that." The mixture of alcohol and fatigue made it easier than usual for Ryan to speak his mind, and he'd been chewing on this idea for about twelve hours.

"How?" Ritter asked, reminding himself that Ryan was something of a whiz at economics.

"I'll tell you one thing for sure: The Catholic Church is not going to be very happy. Lots of Catholics in Eastern Europe, guys. That is a capability we need to think about using. If we approach the Church intelligently, they might just cooperate with us. The Church is big on forgiveness, sure, but you're supposed to go to confession first."

Moore raised an eyebrow.

"The other thing is, I've been studying their economy. It's very shaky, a lot more than our people think it is, Admiral," Jack said, turning to his immediate boss.

"What do you mean?"

"Sir, the stuff our guys are looking at, it's the official economics reports that come into Moscow, right?"

"We work pretty hard to get it, too," Moore confirmed.

"Director, why do we think it's true?" Ryan asked. "Just because the Politburo gets it? We know they lie to us, and they lie to their own people. What if they lie to themselves? If I were an examiner for the SEC, I think I could put a whole lot of guys in Allenwood Federal Prison. What they say they have doesn't jibe with what we can identify them as actually having. Their economy is teetering, and if that goes bad, even a little bit, the whole shebang comes down."

"How could we exploit that?" Ritter asked. His own blue-team analysis had said something very similar four days earlier, but even Judge Moore didn't know that.

"Where do they get their hard currency—I mean, what do they get it from?"

"Oil." Greer answered the question. The Russians exported as much oil as the Saudis.

"And who controls the world price of oil?"

"OPEC?"

"And who," Ryan went on, "controls OPEC?"

"The Saudis."

"Aren't they our friends?" Jack concluded. "Look at the USSR as a takeover target, like we did at Merrill Lynch. The assets are worth a lot more than the parent corporation, because it's so badly run. This isn't hard stuff to figure out." *Even by a guy exhausted by a long day, five thousand miles of air travel, and a little too much booze,* he didn't add. There were a lot of smart people at CIA, but they thought too much like government workers, and not enough like Americans. "Don't we have *anybody* who thinks outside the box?"

"Bob?" Moore asked.

Ritter was warming to the young analyst by the minute. "Ryan, you ever read Edgar Allan Poe?"

"In high school," Ryan replied in some small confusion.

"How about a story called 'The Masque of the Red Death'?"

"Something about a plague coming in to ruin the party, wasn't it?"

"Get some rest. Before you fly back to London tomorrow, you're going to get briefed in on something."

"Sleep sounds like a plan, gentlemen. Where do I crash for the night?" he asked, letting them know, if they hadn't already guessed, that he was ready to collapse.

"We have a place for you at the Marriott up the road. You're all checked in. There's a car waiting at the entrance for you. Go on, now," Moore told him.

"Maybe he's not so dumb after all," Ritter speculated.

"Robert, it's nice to see that you're strong enough to change," Greer smilingly observed as he reached for Moore's own office bottle of expensive bourbon whiskey. It was time to celebrate.

THE FOLLOWING DAY in *Il Tempo*, a morning newspaper in Rome, was a story about a man found dead in a car of an apparent heart attack. It would be a little time before the body was identified and it was finally determined that he was a Bulgarian tourist who'd evidently come to the end of his life quite unexpectedly. How clear his conscience had been was not apparent from physical examination.